Camileon
Beyond The Veil

A Novel by Shykia Bell

Sometimes taking hold of your dreams means having to let go of all that seems certain. Doing so occasionally brings the realization that between ambition and triumph lay nightmares.

The journey has been long and I couldn't have made it without the tireless support and dedication of my loving husband, Max. He has instilled in me the bravery to share my work with the world while being true to my soul.

Max, thanks for being my beacon and staying beside me through it all.

CONTENTS

ACKNOWLEDGMENTS

Each subsequent page of this novel represents a sacrifice made for the sake of its creation. I, alone, cannot take full credit since it would not have been possible if not for the undying patience of my dear friends and family.

I think it's only fitting that I dedicate this novel, the culmination of nearly a four year struggle, to each of them. I sometimes forget what a challenge it is to cope with the eccentric personality of an author and I truly appreciate your willingness to do your best to understand the process.

I thank each of you for keeping me tethered to reality by giving me the occasional, much-needed break from the intensity of my craft.

More specifically, I'd like to thank:

My parents and family who believed in me, even in times of uncertainty,

Lora Price, for her invaluable friendship and understanding,

Petr Nestratov, for his practical advice and honesty,

LeVar Burton, who with a rainbow, lit the initial spark of my literary journey,

and Brent Spiner, whose talent reignited my passion for writing and whose encouragement reinforced my drive to achieve my dreams.

Chapter 1

Return of the Pariah

Only death could grant her clemency from the torment. At least that's what she figured as she was swept up by the exquisite ambiguity of fear and fury. It carried her with the centrifugal force of a dizzying carousel as she approached the crescendo of her despair. Her attempt to evade oppression only seemed to increase her weight against the cold floor. Constricted by the bondage of radiating pain and a hood of darkness, her body trembled as it pleaded for release only to be denied the mercy it craved.

Useless anger and desperation fogged her mind, fueling her terror-induced disorientation. As she gasped, the salty metallic scent of the thickening air invaded her nostrils, tingling the back of her throat. Despite keeping her eyes squeezed shut as though to preserve her sanity, she could feel it seeping out of her like sweat from her pores. Her anguished voice was all she had left and she used it to unleash an outcry of defiance.

"No! You can't make me!"

Parting her lids cautiously, Camile let the soft glow of her computer monitor guide her to salvation. Her head still propped in her hand, she breathed deeply and basked in the presence of sweet consciousness. Constantly haunted by the recurring nightmare, sleep was often difficult to come by. In fact, it had recently become her newest enemy. Nonetheless, she couldn't resist paying it a brief visit a few hours before her usual bedtime.

The fatigue stemming from her accumulating restless nights was taking its toll. Surprisingly, Akalina made no appearances in any of the nightmares Camile experienced during the few times she managed to sleep. Since the reintegration, Akalina only existed in the memories and distant echoes that resonated in her subconscious mind. Camile didn't like to think of the one who used her own distorted self-image against her, driving her to a suicide that further divided her already shredded soul. She hated the fact she and Akalina were now the same person.

No.

Not quite the same.

Akalina possessed a darkness that swallowed civility wherever she went. Such wickedness isn't easily forgotten, which is why Camile's been living in heavily guarded temporary quarters for nearly two months. She wasn't a prisoner, though at times she felt like one. Camile had been subjected to this period of near-total isolation for her protection and that of the citizens residing in her new environment.

They called it the Transcendent World, a concurrent dimension to the world in which she had spent the last eighteen of her twenty-four years. Based on the information Camile reviewed on her computer, Arvaina— which overlapped a large portion of the United States in the Coexistent World—was one of six continents in the Transcendent dimension. The others were Bauldana, Saulnan, Jypsone, Norcrine and Krohme. From what Camile had read of Arvaina, family life and camaraderie were highly valued. There were few formal holidays since every day in itself was a celebration of life. The Arvainans expressed their gratitude, not necessarily in the form of extravagant parties, but simple acts of appreciation.

There were, however, occasional gatherings to celebrate marital unions, life milestones and to honor the dead. She often wondered about the ceremony of the latter and if she would have received such an honor upon her death. Then she remembered she had already died under rather ominous circumstances. The icy grip of the dark memory sometimes ensnared her attention, but she was always able to hang onto a positive remnant of reality.

For instance, she was to soon travel with her parents to the main section of Caldaq, the compound where she would reside during her training. At present, she dwelled just a few miles away in a hidden branch of the facility, located beneath a large lake. Though she found silent comfort in her current quarters, she felt an ironic nostalgia for the busy city she could never quite fit into. Yet, she had found some sort of stability in the chaotic disorder that once swirled around her.

Prior to recent events, she had become fairly accustomed to the hectic monotony of her former New York residence. Even so, Camile knew that every civilization had its deep dark secrets and learned that Arvaina was no exception. The Arvainan council had ordered her execution just six years after she was born from a forbidden union between Kylie, her Coexistent mother and Zephyr, her Transcendent father—who she knew very little about during her upbringing. Now, in an almost sardonic turn of events, the council needed her help.

Sitting upright in her chair, Camile stretched deeper into her awareness. She knew that the torturous reverie awaited her return, but she planned to evade it by forsaking slumber for the umpteenth time in weeks. Still, she needed to do something to soothe her racing mind and ease the thumping bass, furiously pulsing in her chest. She decided a quick bath would do the trick. It had to be quick. She couldn't risk the chance of relaxation reopening the gateway to her subconscious.

After peeling away layers of cotton, denim and lace, she caught a glimpse of her caramel toned body in the large mirror across the bathroom. Her gaze lingered there despite the fact she often feared to regard her own reflection, afraid of whom or what might look back at her. Aside from her cool gray eyes, Camile could barely recognize herself at times. Her body had undergone changes since her fateful day of self-discovery. Among them were three parallel scars across her right oblique. She would sometimes trace her fingers over them as though to gauge their authenticity. Hers was an averagely feminine body with the typical problem areas most women have, or think they have. She wished her breasts were more proportional to her ample backside, but overall, she made peace with what she saw in the mirror, which hadn't always been the case. Realizing she was admiring her image a little too long, she retreated to the tub.

Camile deeply inhaled the powdery, lavender-infused scent of the warm water enveloping her like a foamy blanket. She soaked her sponge while considering what her parents had told her weeks earlier and figured they were right, she had been reborn and was getting reacquainted with herself. It led her to realize that her physical and spiritual separation from Akalina—her egocentric counterpart—had impeded her emotional stability, leading her to make faulty decisions. With time came clarification, something that had eluded her prior to the reintegration. Still, there was a lingering void that she hoped would eventually heal.

Nevertheless, she now understood why it was necessary to endure so many obstacles in order to facilitate the reintegration. She needed to find her strength, Akalina needed to find humbleness, and Zareah—her former ghost—needed to learn self-belief and determination. In doing so, their energies combined, leaving her with a second chance and the regret of having betrayed life by embracing death too soon.

*   *   *

Camile's parents were an obvious representation of her dual citizenship and diverse ancestry. Kylie, her mother, was a nurturing and protective woman, perhaps overly so. She had sheltered her daughter to such a degree as a child that it fostered her naivety.

Kylie's contemplative hazel eyes were as warm as a summer sunrise partially eclipsed by buttery brown lids. Subtle under eye wrinkles and the off-centered streak of silver in her brunette hair were the only visible indicators of her age. Camile's father, Zephyr, wore his years slightly more generously in his creamy white skin. Even so, his angular face was well-defined and symmetrical and seemed to effortlessly cling to youth despite his mildly graying jet-black hair. Though Camile was just getting to know him, his eyes seemed familiar. They were the same eyes that had stared back at her from the mirror all her life.

As they toured Deltine City, Camile's parents explained that she would meet two of her soon-to-be instructors, Sir Drayden Sebastian and Tabitha Livingstone, later that afternoon. Tabitha, a shaman and spiritual healer, would act as Camile's counselor through the duration of her training. Sir Drayden, Tabitha's overseer, was tasked with appraising Camile's overall progress in all aspects of her instruction.

Camile was informed that her abilities were not dissimilar from those of the average Transcendent resident. Several civilizations within the Transcendent dimension viewed their abilities as a derivative of their spiritual creator. Many individuals were either empaths, telepaths, changelings, or possessed enhanced intuition or hypersensitive hearing. Only a small percentage of the population had multiple abilities. She had read about people with telekinesis in addition to a very select few with coercive powers.

What set Camile apart from the inhabitants of her new environment was the fact she possessed a vast combination of these powers—a very rare anomaly within the Transcendent World. She had the most experience with the latter and several people were tormented as a result. No matter how hard she tried to drive the memories from her mind she couldn't forget how she had somehow convinced several childhood bullies to maim themselves. Nor could she ignore the occasions when she inadvertently drove a woman to suicide and blinded several pedestrians, all with the power of her subconscious thoughts.

Since her reintegration, she found herself unable to use any of her special gifts. She wondered if it was due to her severe exhaustion, from which she was recovering. Curious citizens pierced through her thoughts with sharp uneasy glances. Akalina's lasting effect on them became abundantly clear as Camile skimmed the mosaic of their anguished faces.

Otherwise, they looked like ordinary people. Of course, she was now aware that like her, they were anything but. Nevertheless, their reaction reiterated what she already knew, adjusting to her new atmosphere wasn't going to be easy.

The intermittent dispersal of the bustling crowd revealed congratulatory posters honoring the reinstatements of Arvainan President Atlas Okara and Vice President Clayton Eisner McGrath. As Camile observed the various shops and businesses she was impressed with how some of the architecture in the Transcendent World seemed to be modeled after the Coexistent one, or vice-versa. Her overall impression of her new environment was that it was a hodgepodge of all things organic, agricultural and technological. However, the Caldaq mountain range eclipsing the city was said to be a metropolis in itself. Thanks to her avid studies, Camile remembered the names of its primary peaks; Daebrayk, Quaezar, Dusque and Aqueon, all of which surrounded the main summit, Coronis.

As she and her parents approached the shuttle bay, Camile wondered how the officials would receive her. She knew her parents worked for the government, though the exact nature of their work remained a mystery. Even so, Camile was aware they had no power to prevent the council from ordering her death in the past. For now, she could only hope that history would not repeat itself.

The trio eventually came to an air transport hub where Camile's parents had reserved a small private four-passenger aircraft. Upon arrival, a security officer approached Kylie, informing her of an urgent communiqué. Excusing herself, Kylie departed to take the call in private.

"Well, your mother's conversations are rarely brief, so I guess there'll be plenty of time for you to meet Charles." Zephyr smiled, displaying a charming combination of high cheekbones and deep dimples. Little did he know, his wife wasn't out of earshot.

"I heard that," Kylie replied dryly, glancing over her shoulder as she turned the corner.

En route to the hangar, Zephyr explained that Charles was one of his most trusted engineers and the chief builder of his vessel. There was a soothing, yet gallant quality to his baritone voice that Camile found fascinating. It was the type of voice that could effortlessly tell a story while holding the listener's attention. She bypassed half a dozen of the stately aircraft lining the shuttle bay. She marveled at the exquisite designs and craftsmanship as their metallic skin gleamed in the late morning sun streaming through the entrance. Her father halted upon seeing a man polishing one of the smaller shuttles. Camile admired its sleek circular exterior and mirror-like finish. It almost reminded her of the slick silver buttons on the dark gray uniforms she'd seen some of the officers wearing.

"Not clean enough for you, Sven?" her father greeted the round-faced older man, donning dark shades pushed into his curly ashen hairline. He had the beginnings of a potbelly, which seemed misplaced among his lean and lanky limbs.

"I'm a perfectionist, sir. Besides, I like the feel of it against my hands," Sven replied in a burly voice before tossing the soiled buffing rag into an open toolbox on the ground. Straightening his neon green uniform, he approached, bringing with him a faint smell of sweat, metal and solvents.

"Don't stop on my account. Just don't polish a hole in the hull," Zephyr said jokingly.

"Actually, I was just finishing up, sir," Sven replied as he closed his toolbox and loaded it onto the hover vehicle beside the vessel. The hefty thud was an audible manifestation of its generous weight.

Zephyr introduced his daughter, who accepted Sven's exceedingly firm handshake. Inwardly cringing at the abrasive sensation of his skin, Camile wondered if he thought everything was made of the rigid metal of his trade.

"Pleased to meet you, ma'am." He bowed slightly, momentarily revealing a thinning patch of hair.

"Where's Charles?" Camile's father furrowed his straight thick brows.

"Oh, you just missed him," Sven grunted mid-sentence as he limped into the hover vehicle. Sliding his shades over his eyes and smoothing his disheveled hair, he added: "He's having one of his busy days, but he sends his regards."

"I see. Well, did he work his usual magic?"

"Yep. She streams like lightning across the sky, but that's the last time I ride with that new pilot of yours. The kid's a maniac!"

"Reminds me of someone I know." Zephyr laughed, clapping the mechanic's shoulder. "I'll speak to him."

With a wave, Sven rode deeper into the shuttle bay, disappearing behind one of the larger aircraft.

"Let me introduce you to the crown jewels of our fleet." Camile's father gestured to the rows of shuttles before them as he neared the craft Sven had been polishing.

"Only citizens with special clearance can travel via these ultra high-speed aircraft," he continued as his daughter joined him, watching him inspect the exterior. "Recent events have prompted us to revisit our earlier technology. Regrettably, there have been incidents that have caused a series of plane crashes in the Coexistent World. There are rarely actual collisions between our vehicles and theirs, but sometimes the force generated from our aircraft is so strong it literally knocks them out of the sky."

He mentioned that spontaneous rifts and sudden changes in dimensional borders, otherwise known as *veils* also contributed to such accidents.

6

"This is my *other* baby," he said playfully, briefly smoothing his hand along the hull. "It's a remarkable piece of machinery. Not quite like my old one, though."

"The one you wrecked?" Camile asked, remembering the story her mother had told her years ago about her father getting into a crash in the Sonoran Desert. Until recently, she didn't realize it was a collision of the aerial variety.

"It wasn't out of carelessness, mind you," her father raised his brow. "I accidentally crossed into Coexistent airspace through a spontaneous rift while chasing rebels who had stolen one of our vehicles. By the time I realized what had happened it was already too late. I sustained heavy damage from the stolen ship and I was unable to chase them back into the rift before it closed. Instead, I hit the ground. I knew the crash would arouse the interest of the American government, so I did the best I could to destroy what was left of my ship to preserve the secrecy of our technology. To this day, what became of the rebels and our stolen vessel remains a mystery." His voice and gaze grew distant, as though still pondering what went wrong.

Camile had already learned the rest of the story from her mother. In spite of her father's numerous injuries, he was able to travel to the hospital, nearly thirty miles from the crash site. Kylie, who worked at the facility, had nursed him back to health.

"I was fortunate, really," Zephyr admitted. "I wandered aimlessly until I arrived at the hospital. You'd be surprised at how many people ignored me along the way. They probably figured I was some poor drunk staggering home from a barroom brawl. It was my first visit to the Coexistent World. Up until that point I had only heard stories about it—how cold the people can be at times. I was disappointed to find out how accurate our historians were. Then I met your mother. Such a caring woman, not to mention incredibly beautiful." His smile dazzled in his pale eyes. "At the time, I took a big risk by courting her. Romantic relationships between Coexistent and Transcendent humans had been forbidden ever since the announcement of the prophecy."

Before Camile could ask about the reason for such a restriction, they were joined by her mother. Apparently eager to regain the time lost from their schedule, her parents promptly commenced boarding. Upon entering, she noticed a young man, seated at the controls. He looked no older than seventeen. Zephyr introduced him as Wyatt, their pilot.

"Hey," he greeted casually.

Returning the salutation, she strapped herself into a seat beside her mother as Zephyr took the co-pilot chair. Camile watched curiously as the men operated the controls. The illuminated keys bore Arvainan symbols, similar to those that had appeared on her medallion months earlier.

The panoramic view screen displayed the vessel's air-piercing speed, which contradicted the relative stillness within it. Flashes of tattered leathery wings and strange heads with beaks and horn-like protrusions randomly crossed their path at brief intervals. Fearing a crash was inevitable, Camile gasped, hoping the strangely gigantic birds flying around the ship would disperse. Being the only person to react in response to the sight, she figured it was a normal occurrence. Then it dawned on her. The strange avian beasts had long preceded any bird she had seen.

Pterodactyls? She wondered.

The hand of gravity forced Camile deeper into her seat as Wyatt maneuvered a sharp turn, presumably to steer clear of the flock before them. Her heart leapt into her throat as the shaking ship fell into a steep decline just after the peak of the turn. Her body suddenly felt too light as it pressed upward into her harness. Seeing panic etched on her parents' faces and that of the pilot, she knew something had gone terribly wrong. The skewed horizon confirmed this. It disappeared as the rocky terrain rose like a swelling ocean, prompting her to grip her armrests and brace for impact.

Chapter 2

Intrusion

"Wyatt, pull up!" Zephyr instructed, his face scrunched with concern.

The pilot's eyes grew wide as he feverishly worked the controls. Despite his efforts the shuttle maintained its collision course with the ground. Camile's father acted fast, operating a second set of controls while barking out commands which the pilot immediately followed.

"Almost there, sir!" Wyatt grunted, struggling to bring the ship out of the nosedive.

Camile felt herself lurch forward as they reduced speed. Her safety harness tightened around her body, providing her with a sense of both security and entrapment as it pressed her against her seat. The pressure gradually eased as the horizon returned to its rightful position. Without further incident, the craft slowly descended until its bottom kissed the ground, landing safely.

"Wyatt, give me one good reason why I shouldn't have your license revoked immediately," Camile's father calmly demanded after expelling a deep breath.

"Uh…We're still alive?" Wyatt cringed as though fearful of being punched.

Shaking his head, Zephyr cracked a faint smile. "Next time, try not to get fancy with the steering. I'm already aware of your ability. There's no need to show off."

After a profuse apology, Wyatt helped Camile and her parents disembark from the ship. Camile froze as she was struck with a vision of a hauntingly beautiful dwelling carved into the gigantic mountain. The perimeter was skirted by lush woods and the unmistakable scent of fresh pine needles filled the crisp air. She blinked a few times after gazing at the peak, obscured by misty clouds, but the dream-like image before her remained unchanged, confirming its reality. As they grew closer to the compound's main entrance, she admired its exterior, which resembled polished soapstone. Camile was impressed to know that this was an extension of the place where she'd been holed up for weeks. During that time she had only seen one of the main gathering halls, the view of the countryside from the mountaintop and most of all, her temporary quarters.

She and her parents were less than twenty feet from the entrance when the ground began vibrating slightly beneath her feet. It was an unbroken disruption that led Camile to wonder if it was a sign of an approaching earthquake. As the pattern of sensation changed, she realized the subtle tremors weren't continuous, but were broken by strengthening syncopated thumps from which the vibration rippled. It was the type of rhythm only a powerful animal could beat into the earth. As she turned to her parents something caught her attention. From the corner of her eye she saw something white pouring out from one of the mountain's hidden crevices at ground level. Her peripheral vision was still adjusting, but she could tell it was just a few dozen feet from where she was standing. Now hearing the pulse of the quaking ground—or perhaps her heart—Camile's mounting curiosity pulled her full attention towards the rapidly approaching whiteness. Through the deafening roar, she could barely hear her parents shouting for her to back away.

It was too late.

Camile found herself engulfed in a heavy avalanche. The cottony softness against her front seemed to mock the rough impact her back made with the ground. Gasping, she received puffs of fur filtered air, all the while still blinded and oppressed by the heavy whiteness. Then came the sensation of wet sandpaper across the entire right side of her face.

"What's happening?" was her muffled cry.

Just as quickly as it had happened, she felt the weight being lifted from her body. Gazing upward, she saw two crystal blue orbs embedded into a large mass of fur. Carefully rising to her feet, she took in the image of the most beautiful tiger she'd ever seen. Its gleaming white fur had faint gray stripes, barely noticeable upon first glance. Mildly disgusted with the cooling saliva on her face, she wiped it away with her sleeve. Ensuring their daughter was uninjured, Camile's parents apologized and went on to explain that the tiger, Excelsior, had been her childhood companion.

"You might not remember it now since you were only four at the time, but you're the reason he's still alive today," her mother said before explaining that years ago, during a safari, Camile had spotted Excelsior—then, just a cub—who had gotten separated from his mother. He had been on the brink of death at the time of his discovery.

"After nursing him back to health, we tried to release him into the wild," Zephyr added, his fair cheeks dimpled faintly as he smiled, "but he grew attached to the girl who saved his life. The poor guy was devastated when you left. There wasn't any time for you to say goodbye to him."

"But Akalina was still here, wasn't she? It's not like he could tell the difference. He probably didn't even notice I was gone." Camile cautiously eyed the tiger.

"Don't be so sure about that. How do you think you got that scar on your side?" Zephyr briefly dropped his gaze. Tightening his lips, he met her eyes anew. "You said, yourself, that you didn't have it until you reintegrated with Akalina. You see, Excelsior was forced to attack her one day."

"Why?" Camile gingerly backed away from the tiger while unconsciously touching her right oblique.

"Years ago, she tried to do something unspeakable, something that would have jeopardized your future and the future of both worlds."

The dwelling's heavy door cracked open, making way for an older man approaching them with sure steps. His walk exuded the kind of authoritative pride and confidence that demanded attention, making him seem taller than his apparent six-foot stature. There was something strangely familiar about him. Camile wondered if it was the knowing sparkle in his icy-blue eyes or the silver, feathery hair that he wore in a semi-spiked style, adding a touch of youth to his timeworn face.

"Kylie, it's always a pleasure!" His thin pink lips curled into an easy smile, emphasizing a prominent, nearly aquiline nose. As he embraced Camile's mother his glowing fair skin, moderately weathered with the seasons of his past, contrasted against her brown cheek.

Moving to Camile's father, the man clapped his shoulder.

"Zephyr, you've been a stranger for far too long," he said. "I hope you have a good excuse for missing your last few appointments."

"Sir Drayden, I—" Zephyr awkwardly attempted to explain.

This is Sir Drayden? Camile thought. She had half-expected him to have an exotic accent of sorts, but was surprised to detect a highly articulate vocal inflection reminiscent of an American English professor.

"Nah. You don't have to enlighten me, but Tabitha will *definitely* want an explanation." The knight chortled faintly as he approached Camile, who felt herself shrinking in eyes that seemed capable of prying into the mind and revealing one's innermost thoughts. She couldn't help but wonder if he could read the apprehension that lingered in the back of her mind at that very instant. There seemed to be something ominous upholding his casually dapper appearance, clad in dark denim, a mocha jacket and a blue-gray sweater that enhanced his shimmering orbs. After a brief moment of silence, he offered his hand. Upon taking it, Camile was flooded with a chilling weakness that induced a momentary desire to break away. Yet, she maintained her composure until the feeling passed.

"Camile," he said softly. "You've grown into a lovely young woman." He released her hand, but held her gaze with his electric eyes. An inquisitive expression crossed his features. "You don't remember me, do you?"

Camile shook her head, briefly avoiding eye contact.

"You look a little familiar, but no, I don't."

"Well, I can't blame you. It's been awhile since our last meeting," Sir Drayden replied, briefly smiling at Kylie.

"Camile, you probably remember him as Travis D'Arby, the lawyer I brought to your school to deal with that whole mess about Barry's disappearance," Kylie explained, brushing away a lock of wavy hair a soft breeze had blown into her face.

Barry.

Camile didn't think she'd ever hear his name come up again. He had been the merciless bully who tormented her during her high school years more than nine years ago. In her unwitting retaliation she had somehow made him wander off, but luckily he returned safely. Camile remembered the challenge she faced in convincing her suspicious teacher, Ms. Hawkins, that she had no knowledge of his whereabouts. Evading her bitter reminiscence, Camile's mind gave way to clarity.

"That's it," she acknowledged. Flooded with familiarity, Sir Drayden no longer seemed a distant stranger to her. However, the realization did little to ease her discomfort. This became evident when Excelsior's large head pushed against her, nearly knocking her down in his overzealous display of affection. Camile yelped in horror, feeling embarrassed by what she thought was a slight overreaction.

"Excelsior," Sir Drayden said sternly, gesturing to the den from which the tiger emerged. The massive feline promptly backed down, though releasing a low growl to voice his displeasure. Reluctantly, Excelsior followed the unspoken command after staring at Camile, as though ensuring her continued presence.

"My apologies for Excelsior. He's been awaiting your return for quite some time and seems to have escaped his handlers." Sir Drayden frowned slightly. As though on cue, a man rushed to meet the tiger and lead him the rest of the way, but not before apologizing to the knight.

Sir Drayden chortled almost smugly as he watched the handler lead Excelsior away.

"Come, you must be hungry."

*   *   *

The orange afternoon sun kissed the treetops on the hillside. Their budding leaves held the promise of spring. As Camile toured Caldaq's perimeter with her parents and Sir Drayden she understood why the complex was prime real estate. It overlooked the bustling Deltine metropolis in the distance to the East and the peaceful countryside in the West. Having just finished a hearty early supper less than an hour earlier, Camile felt the weight of her meal slowing her steps. Since her parents seemed engaged in deep discussion with the knight, she lingered behind to watch a flock of swans take flight from the still lake. The water droplets rained down from their wings like golden glitter.

Inhaling the crisp air, she turned her attention to the pink and violet sky. The first stars of the evening were already beginning to emerge, as were a few fireflies studding the grass with their faint glow. Soon, neither would have to compete with the broad glow of daylight and Camile looked forward to witnessing how the luminous insects would mimic the celestial ceiling. Alas, her moment of serenity was suddenly interrupted by thunderous disorder.

Promptly training her gaze over her shoulder she saw approximately a dozen men charging in her direction. She stood slack jawed for a second before going into flight mode, eventually catching up with her parents. She protested when they shielded her with their bodies. Her father drew a device from his holster, pointed it to the advancing group and fired, emitting a pulsing flash of light. It had no effect.

"We need to get out of here," Camile said urgently, concerned for her parents' safety.

"We're not going anywhere. This is our home. I'll be damned if I let these punks drive me from it," Kylie remarked, her tawny hazel eyes ablaze with fierce determination as she and her husband drew retractable batons from their utility belts.

Less than a minute after those fighting words were spoken, Camile's father was caught in a clash with three of the intruders. Their strategy, though well-timed, was poorly executed, which worked to Zephyr's advantage. He quickly immobilized one, then the other before locking in a violent tussle with the third. Camile looked around for something, anything, that she could use to help her father fend off the tower of muscle holding him in a bear hug, but noticed she had problems of her own.

One of the assailants accosted her, nearly seizing her arm, but she promptly struck him square in the face with an open palm. It left him visibly stunned, but otherwise undeterred. His bearded sneer indicated that her action possibly made matters worse for herself. Before Camile could consider her next move, she saw two slender brown hands clap both sides of the brute's head from behind. Clutching his ears, he fell to the ground in a fit of pain, revealing Camile's savior.

"Wow, Mom! That was—"

"No time to celebrate, baby. We're not clear yet."

Following her mother's eyes Camile noticed her father had apparently overpowered the large intruder and was now working on another. Meanwhile, Sir Drayden stepped in and with a single wave of his hand he took down five attackers as their reinforcements approached from the distance. They met the same fate immediately upon their arrival.

My God! What is this guy?

A high-pitched sound cut into her thoughts, a sound she hadn't heard in months—the ringing of a cell phone. Puzzled, she looked around, realizing no one else seemed to hear it. A woman appeared just as Sir Drayden extended his palm to deflect another intruder. She was as translucent as an apparition. Oblivious to the chaos erupting around her, the woman continued about her business, looking both ways as though crossing a street. Unable to reverse his attack, Sir Drayden struck the woman with an invisible current of devastation. She doubled over, clutching her chest as she suffered an apparent asthma or heart attack. Her face contorted in sheer agony as she fell to the ground and faded away. The diminishing sound of the woman's labored breathing was accompanied by the faint wail of what sounded like a horn. Seeing that Camile's parents had the upper hand with the intruders, Sir Drayden vanished into thin air.

What th—?

Camile knew there was no time to stoke her bewilderment by pondering questions she couldn't answer. Returning her attention to her parents, Camile observed her mother unleashing a fury of blows, taking down two additional opponents. Camile was filled with pride as she witnessed her mother's strength yet again. That feeling was replaced with terror as one of the attackers unsheathed a blade, preparing to stab Kylie in the back as she fought with his cohort. Caution be damned, Camile darted in their direction, nearly stumbling over the fallen before colliding with the man in an air expelling crush. Despite the softness of the lush grass, the impact ached her knee and elbow. As they struggled for control of the weapon the man somehow managed to gain the upper hand, bringing the broadside of the cold blade to her throat. Camile's biceps burned with fiery determination as she continued pushing against his knife-wielding hand.

"Just come with us and no one gets hurt," he said, straining against her. His voice was surprisingly benign, but his rancid halitosis threatened to expel her dinner.

A side-eye glance, revealed no less than fifty armor-clad guards swarming in from all directions like ants.

Finally, she thought.

"There's no way you're getting out of here, with or without me," she said defiantly.

As her adversary's expression shifted from cool determination to fiery disappointment she got a better understanding of his underlying desperation. Like a hurricane it spiraled in his eyes with the resentment of failure. Shoving Camile aside he rose to his feet, quickly throwing the knife at Kylie. Crying out to her mother, Camile watched helplessly as the blade traveled toward its target. Kylie turned in time to see the intended instrument of her death slicing through the air toward her chest. Her coppery eyes widened with surprise as she crossed her arms in front of her body.

A lump gathered in Camile's throat as she realized she was about to witness her mother's demise. Instead, she witnessed a miracle. The knife halted, hanging in mid-air before reversing course to hit the thrower in the chest, saving Camile the trouble of killing him as she so desired. He landed beside her in a heap and with a single gasp he was gone. In the end there was only a sliver of pink along the horizon, silhouetting the field, littered with the dead and injured bodies of the opposition. A visibly perplexed Zephyr gave orders to make arrangements for the deceased and to treat and detain the wounded for questioning.

"…and get a team to figure out how the hell so many of them breached security. If I find out anyone on my team dropped the ball, there will be consequences." He concluded his commands as the torches lining the compound activated with a series of whooshes.

Satisfied that her parents were unharmed, Camile asked her mother about the strange appearance of the woman who had been injured in the melee.

"Don't worry. Sir Drayden will handle it," Kylie answered, her eyes sparkling in the light of the orange flames.

"How did you do the thing with the knife?"

"That wasn't me. Must've been your father." Kylie smiled, casting a brief adoring glance at her busy husband.

"Oh, right. For a minute there I almost forgot you're not a Transcendent." Camile acknowledged.

"Neat trick though, huh?" Kylie winked. "In time, I'm sure you'll learn how to do it too. So far you've done just about everything else."

*   *   *

Camile cradled her steamy mug of chamomile tea in her hands, still sore with the memory of the clash. Though the scent of the beverage held the promise of physical comfort, her mind was still wired. She had been out of seclusion for less than a day and people were already on the attack. Try as she might to sip cautiously, the hot liquid bit her lip, prompting her to recoil.

Even the drinks are out to get me.

Her impatient frown softened into a smirk, acknowledging the silliness of the thought. Setting down her mug, Camile admired the view of Deltine from the window-side table. The city lights appeared somewhat frozen against the misty blue-violet backdrop. The rustic design of the tavern, in which she sat in a private room with her parents, was far departed from the urban region in the distance.

"You should be touring your new quarters right now, but we need to discuss what happened out there." Her mother broke the silence. Camile turned to see her breaking off a small bunch of grapes from the crystal platter at the center of the table. Beside the fruit were small pastries and nuts. Whereas Camile passed on the refreshments, her father helped himself to a healthy serving.

Camile's parents theorized that the offenders were members of the rebel group that opposed the Transcendent Council's aid of the Coexistent World. They also explained that a rift suddenly appeared between both realms, which is how the female stranger momentarily crossed over.

"When a person travels through a rift they are usually temporarily cloaked in a cocoon of their previous world's energy, rendering them seemingly invisible," Zephyr said between bites.

Camile also learned that the duration of such cocoons varies from split seconds to hours—or longer. Due to the fluctuations in some cocoons, the traveler may also appear ghostly transparent or fully visible. While she pondered this, Sir Drayden joined them and confirmed what she already knew.

"I couldn't save her. There was nothing left. She already disconnected," he explained as casually as reading a grocery list.

Disconnected? We're talking about a life, not electronics.

Camile frowned, watching as the knight grabbed a handful of filberts from the crystal platter, effortlessly tossing them into his mouth one-by-one.

"That woman's dead because of you," Camile crossed her arms, only then noticing the moderate tear in the side seam of her shirt. It was well coordinated with her now dirty jeans. She returned her arms to her side to conceal the damage. "How can you be so nonchalant?"

She instantly regretted her question once he paused, gripping her with his steely gaze.

Slowly rounding the table, Sir Drayden chewed the remainder of his snack as he eyed her intently. Once beside her, he pulled out a chair. Straddling it, he crossed both his arms atop the back, not once breaking eye contact. His cheek swelled slightly as he appeared to clear the remnants of the filberts with his tongue.

"Life and death are two faces on the coin of existence. Sooner or later, everyone pays their fare," he said through the faintest enigmatic smile. "What happened today was unfortunate, but not unusual. Moping about it is counter-productive and won't bring her back. The fact is, everything aligned perfectly for that woman to make her exit."

"You're saying she was *meant* to die?" Camile grimaced. "How did you come to that conclusion? What made my case so diff—?"

"Camile, don't." Kylie interrupted, shaking her head.

"You've got it all twisted backwards, young lady." Sir Drayden frowned. "Death is supposed to choose us, not the other way around."

"If I understand correctly, the council pretty much chose it for me when I was just a child," Camile's voice cracked slightly as though her throat was trying to suppress the statement.

"It was a consideration that was avoided, unlike your suicide. You have no idea what we went through to bring you back. If you think we made a mistake, let me know right now and I'll reverse your fate myself."

Camile's parents attempted to protest, but fell silent as he raised his hand, keeping his aquatic gaze locked on their daughter.

"Did you just threaten me?" Camile frowned.

The knight's eyes momentarily shifted upward and sideways before reengaging their target.

"I'm merely presenting the alternative. Well, what'll it be?" he asked in a hushed whisper.

Camile hoped he was bluffing, but his hardened expression made her doubt that possibility. She didn't know enough about the knight to dare test him, so she shook her head in response.

"Good," Sir Drayden cracked a wry smile. "Not many people get a second shot at life. Next time, think twice before you take it for granted."

The end of the ominous discussion left Camile wondering what level of protection her parents could offer her. It appeared they were under the weight of the government's influence and she hoped it wouldn't spell certain doom for them all.

Chapter 3

Fractured

Camile always dreaded medical examinations, but knew she couldn't avoid her first checkup since her return to the Transcendent World. Actually, it was her first medical in the dimension as a conscious adult since the reintegration. She was impressed to learn that most Transcendent medicine functioned on a cellular—and in some cases—a molecular level, which provided remarkable specificity in terms of treatment. Even more impressive was the Transcendent's capability to project three dimensional computer images of internal organs—ideal for mapping out the schematics for complex surgical procedures. While walking to her appointment, Camile peeked through the glass window of one of the rooms and saw a surgeon holding the image of a patient's heart in his hands. She found the sight somewhat poetic.

The medical table upon which Camile sat was more comfortable than it appeared. It, like the rest of the furniture in the infirmary, had been designed with sleek, rounded edges—presumably to make the facility look more inviting. Camile surmised it was the same reason for the use of warm beige and cream colors to offset the stark white lights and metallic accents. It made the gleaming silver medical equipment appear less threatening. Nevertheless, she felt anxious as she awaited the results of her physical.

She distracted herself by analyzing the Transcendent anatomical model by the entrance. Shortly before the doctor had excused herself she informed Camile that although Transcendents and Coexistents looked similar in terms of outward appearance, there were marked physiological differences due to their differing environments and evolutionary paths. On average, the Transcendents had a higher bone density, larger lung capacity as well as a pair of small reserve kidneys. Camile had read about this and more, but nothing compared to seeing a representation of it in full scale.

Yet, she knew firsthand that at least some of the Transcendents' physiological advantages sometimes worked against them. She found her high visual and aural sensitivity challenging and nearly maddening at times. Then again, she also considered the possibility that hers was an anomalous reaction due to her mixed background.

"You are very fortunate, Camile," said the mousy doctor upon her return, her large nose pointing downward as she read the results. "The preliminary tests indicate you are still a very healthy hybrid."

"As opposed to what?" Camile furrowed her brow.

The doctor raised her dark saucer-like eyes, resuming eye-contact.

"There have been quite a few Transcendent/Coexistent hybrids that were born after you," she explained. "Many of those who survived developed physical and/or mental defects over time, usually by their mid to late teens."

"Like?"

"Paraplegia, deafness, blindness… Sometimes the conditions are treatable, but our success rate varies."

"Sorry I asked." Camile frowned.

"Don't worry about it. As I said, you appear to be quite healthy. Even those who were born with the challenges I mentioned are able to live their lives to the fullest of their ability." The doctor paused a moment, regarding her patient with mild concern. "We both know the preliminary results of your physical, but I'd like to hear, from you, how you're feeling."

"Still a little dazed by all that's been happening lately. Other than that, I'm fine." Camile cracked a faint smile that quickly sank with the weight of truth.

She had been experiencing occasional migraines and was concerned that it was the result of a bio-neurotransmitter she had been fitted with many years ago. She learned this through her parents, who like many Arvainan residents, also held the technology. She was still vague about the purpose of such devices or how they functioned, yet her parents had promised to reveal that information, as well as the nature of their work with the council, during an upcoming expedition. Even so, she raised her concern to the doctor, who insisted that her headaches were not a result of the device.

"It may be due to the residual effects of your abrupt change in climate," the doctor suggested while typing something on her handheld. "I've prescribed a mild pain reliever. Try it for a few days. If it's insufficient, we'll look into other alternatives."

After filling her prescription Camile was directed to the foyer, where she was said to have a visitor. Upon entering the area she saw no one except the guards who had escorted her to the infirmary.

"I see you pulled yourself together," a cultured voice rang from behind. Her heart flooded with a warmth that could only be triggered by an old acquaintance. Upon turning, she saw a plump cherubic-like woman dressed in green. The copper coils framing her round face blazed in the morning sunlight filtering through the window. Camile recognized the woman as her mother's best friend. Back in the Coexistent World, she had been entrusted with the secret of Camile's true identity and had sworn to protect it, even from Camile herself. She no longer had any hard feelings about the deception since she knew her mother's friend had risked her life in the process.

"Nancy!" Camile eagerly approached, her arms outstretched for a hug.

The redhead flinched, hesitating before joining the embrace. Noticing this, Camile suspected she was still traumatized by the fact Akalina had once attacked her.

"It's good to see you again, Camile." Nancy kissed her cheek. "I'm sorry I couldn't warn you about what was happening. By the time I realized who Akalina really was—"

"Don't worry about it. What's done is done. I'm just glad you're okay." Camile ended the hug, letting her hands linger on the short redhead's shoulders for a few moments. "How are you?"

"Oh, I'm just fine. I was in pretty bad shape for awhile, but I have a way of bouncing back. How 'bout you?"

"I'm alive. That's as good a start as any." Camile forced a chuckle. "The people here would probably disagree, though. Their resentment is as strong as the sky is blue. I'm tempted to ask them what I—" Camile caught herself. "Akalina did, but I'm not sure I really wanna know."

"You'll find out eventually, ready or not. You of all people should know that even the deepest secrets can't stay hidden forever." Nancy winked an emerald eye.

They turned their attention to the foyer's main entrance upon hearing the sharp sound of hard-soled shoes striking the polished floor tiles. Moments later, the knight emerged in black and gray. He greeted both women before focusing on Nancy.

"Nice to see you up and about again," he said.

"Thanks to you, Sir Drayden." Nancy grinned, bowing her head slightly.

Camile didn't feel as at ease. She wanted to sink into the floor to avert the path of his gaze, but found herself submerged in his eyes. His presence

20

was beginning to induce a nauseating discomfort she could neither shake nor comprehend.

"I'll be escorting you to the amphitheater. Your parents are waiting for you there," he announced.

"If it's no trouble, I can take her there, sir," Nancy suggested before regarding Camile with a glance of apparent concern.

Nodding his approval, Sir Drayden made his exit, much to Camile's relief.

"Are you alright?" Nancy asked softly. "I swear you just lost your color."

"I'm okay. He just makes me a little uncomfortable, that's all."

"A *little* uncomfortable?" The redhead arched her brow. "Camile, you looked like you were about to pass out."

"Okay, the man gives me the creeps and then some," she admitted. "I get the feeling something's not right about him."

"Really?" A perplexed expression crossed Nancy's face. "Sir Drayden may seem a little standoffish, but he really is a great man. After all, he's part of the team designated to help you through this whole thing. I see no reason for you to be afraid of him."

"I wish I could feel the same way, but my gut tells me different." Camile exhaled, lamenting her pending increase in contact with the mysterious knight.

*   *   *

The sound of Camile's footsteps deadened as she walked onto the finely patterned carpet. Her parents awaited her at the base of the multiple curved rows of seats, where a large portion of the floor dipped into a circular indentation. Camile inquired about the seemingly faulty construction, to which her father cracked a somber smile as the lights dimmed. The concave section of the floor appeared more vibrant in contrast to the rest of the carpeting, as though a spotlight was shining upon it. Zephyr seemed to hesitate as he regarded Kylie, who took his hand and nodded encouragingly.

"Reveal window," he spoke into the air.

The colors in the concave segment instantly vanished, but the rest of the flooring remained unchanged. Awestricken, Camile gingerly approached the deactivated portion which revealed a dimly lit, barren room below. It was hauntingly familiar as was the single piece of furniture, a type of platform or table, contained within. She could almost hear the distant echoing cries of her memories, pleading to tell their chilling tales.

Her mother's hand touched her shoulder.

"That's—"

"The lab," Camile whispered, her voice as faint as a ghost from the past.

It was still relatively dark as they descended. The little light that entered the room was reflected by the convex mirror in the ceiling, casting an eerie glow upon the table beneath it. Upon closer inspection, Camile likened it to an altar as she slowly rounded it. Each step she took brought her closer to breaching the sealed memory of the evening which had forever changed the course of her life.

By the time she came full circle, stopping in front of her parents, she felt the lingering sense of familiarity getting stronger. Her cheeks tingled with the chill of a sudden breeze that had no identifiable source. The subtle scent of her mother's sweet perfume was now competing with crisp pine. Camile raised her gaze to behold her parents, but her eyes were suddenly wrapped in a pallid sheet of disorientation. At first she said nothing, figuring the flash would dissolve. Then alarm set in as she realized her vision wasn't returning. Squeezing her lids shut, she stumbled into her mother's arms.

Young Camile didn't care much for being carried, but had little choice in the matter. She was just a six-year-old girl and her legs were too short to endure the lengthy journey ahead. Though she knew she should've felt safe in her mother's arms, she was terrified. As they bypassed the final checkpoint, at which Kylie gained the mercy of an empathetic guard, Caldaq's alarms blared into the night. Little Camile's sobs worsened as she remembered the events that triggered them, events that followed her discovery of what the council had in store for her the next day. It seemed a miracle that they were able to avoid the harsh sweeping lights of the helicopters circling above the field.

Upon reaching the edge of the *Forsaken Square*—a massive stretch of dense forest nearly a kilometer away—a panting Kylie took cover behind a large tree and set her daughter down. Little Camile caught a tiny splinter in her palm as she peered anxiously around the trunk to regard the mountainous compound. Still, she kept her eyes fixed, knowing that somewhere in the midst of the emergency lights illuminating Caldaq was her father, who insisted that Kylie flee with their daughter and await his arrival at the rendezvous point. His urgent parting words: "If I'm not there in twenty minutes, leave without me. You know what to do. Follow the direction of the dead log and swim as deep as you can."

Camile had been keeping a close eye on her mother's watch and knew their time was almost up. Each agonizing minute she wondered what would happen to him. He was the orchestrator of the grand diversion that unfolded just minutes earlier. When it started to go wrong, he resorted to brawn, punching out at least one guard in the process.

"I don't want to leave Daddy," she cried, figuring that he'd be killed for his actions.

"Me either, sweetheart." Kylie tenderly cupped her cheek. "I hope it won't come to that."

Despite the calm words, young Camile could feel her mother's fear breaking through her poised façade. It accompanied the apparent doubt lurking behind her wide hazel eyes.

"It won't," a masculine voice grunted.

Zephyr emerged from the ground before them, yet the grass and soil remained undisturbed. The reunited trio indulged in hugs and kisses before venturing deeper into the *Forsaken Square*. Kylie held her daughter securely as they traveled in silence. Eventually, little Camile grew tired and drifted off to sleep on her mother's shoulder to the tune of her parents' footfalls crunching the fallen autumn leaves. A sharp gasp interrupted her slumber a short while later. Upon opening her eyes, Camile saw two dozen or so guards closing in on them beneath the forest canopy, through which the helicopters poured their cold bluish lights. The officers closed in like shadows in the misty night. The sound of her mother's unsteady breathing fed Camile's terror, which escalated when Sir Drayden emerged from the thick barricade of sentinels.

"I know this isn't easy for you, Kylie, but you must give her to me." Sir Drayden outstretched his hands, lowering his voice to a whisper. "Trust me. It'll be better this way."

"Mommy, no!" Camile cried, clutching her mother's arm as tightly as her little fingers would allow.

Following her mother's gaze, Camile noticed her father's intense expression. She'd already seen it once that evening, just before he had attacked the guard. Everyone remained as still and quiet as chess pieces, but the silver-haired knight was about to take the pawn.

"Please, at least allow me a moment to say goodbye to my little girl," Kylie said tremulously, taking a step back.

Camile objected to the surrender, but was hushed by her mother, who slowly searched her pocket. The reason became obvious once Kylie raised her cupped left hand to stroke her daughter's curls. The child felt a firm round object barely brush her cheek. It was cool to the touch.

"It'll be fine, baby," Kylie whispered. "Just close your eyes."

As soon as the frightened child obliged, there was a loud explosion, punctuated by the officers' shouts. An intense flash permeated her sealed lids, revealing the fine veins within them. Then came the jolt. Holding on tight, young Camile's body bobbed around as her mother sprinted into the night. Once the light faded, she cautiously peered over her mother's shoulder. Amidst the lingering smoke was her father, fighting several disoriented guards. The knight was nowhere to be seen, but a group of officers fanned out in pursuit of Camile and her mother, now headed toward a ravine. They were almost in the clear since the rift was located in the water, a dead log ironically pointing to their salvation. All that was left to do was clear another few meters and jump in.

Heavy boots beat the earth behind them like a stampede of wild horses. The sound indicated that Kylie's luxury of a head start was rapidly waning. Camile saw them pouring in from between the dense trees, closing them in from behind, their weapons drawn. Upon feeling her mother halt with a sharp gasp, Camile turned her attention forward and saw Sir Drayden appearing out of thin air, just inches in front of them.

"That was a very foolish move." He frowned, his facial crevices sharpened by the above lighting.

A panting Kylie shuffled backward as the squad surrounded them. The lead officer commanded his team to lower their arms as he raised a baton-like device. He apologized prior to activating it, directing a vivid pulsating light at Kylie's face. The descent was quick and hard as the mother, still cradling her child, met the ground.

Young Camile felt one of the officers grab hold of her waist, pulling her away from Kylie, who fought like hell to resist, but failed to maintain her painfully tight grip on her daughter's arm. The other guards parted, allowing Sir Drayden to pass through. As he approached, his leather duster flowed behind him, rustling the dead leaves in an almost taunting manner. Knowing she would soon face her own mortality, little Camile kicked and screamed, but was no match for the burly officer who passed her to the knight. Once in his clutches, little Camile grew exhausted. Her desire and ability to fight was gone. Kylie grasped at the hem of Sir Drayden's coat and pled desperately for her daughter's return.

"I'm sorry, Kylie," he said softly, turning on his heel to walk away.

Through heavy lids, young Camile saw the broken expression on her mother's face as she remained kneeling on the ground.

"I request the option of core segregation," she cried, her voice saturated with desperation.

Sir Drayden halted his steps.

"Excuse me?" He regarded her anew, his face etched with perplexity. The surrounding officers looked equally baffled.

Kylie's voice grew weaker as she tremulously repeated her request.

"Are you aware of the risk?" Sir Drayden asked.

"It can't be much worse than what the council has already proposed," Kylie bitterly gazed up into his eyes.

"Don't be so sure about that," was Zephyr's ominous response as the guards escorted him before the elder.

He regarded his wife with a shocked expression and said nothing else for several moments. Camile could no longer keep her eyes open or her head from falling onto Sir Drayden's shoulder. Yet, her ears stubbornly clung to her fading consciousness.

"By requesting core segregation you may have just condemned our daughter to a fate far worse than death." She heard her father say, his voice sorrowfully heavy.

Falling deeper, Camile found herself traversing the barriers of time in ways only recollection could permit. Everything around her was white and unbearably bright and it took a few moments to realize she was lying face-up on a table in a stark room. Her eyes now fixed on the circular convex mirror in the ceiling, she saw the image of her tiny frame dressed in a simple white gown. It was only when she attempted to sit upright that she noticed her wrists and ankles were restrained. Wondering where her parents were, she called out for them only to be greeted with silence.

Upon inspecting the rest of her surroundings she saw Sir Drayden near the top of her head and two men—one on each side of her. Like her, they were all clad in white. They stood in silence, their eyes closed as though in prayer. Fear grew into full-blown terror as she writhed in an attempt to break free of the restraints, all the while screaming for the men to let her go. They appeared unfazed as they continued their quiet ceremony.

Young Camile's terror eventually gave way to intense, searing rage. Sir Drayden's eyes opened and went colorless as he stretched his hand over little Camile, letting it hover above her heaving midsection. A warm sensation radiated from the pit of her stomach to her chest. It increased steadily until it felt as though a volcano was erupting inside her. The intensity matched her resistance until she grew still and exhausted, sobbing helpless tears through rampant breathing.

Her mind grew dizzy as she wondered what the men were attempting to do. Looking up into the mirror, she saw something glowing from inside her chest like a spiraling vortex when Sir Drayden moved his hand away. Suddenly her entire body was raided by fiery agony. The light intensified until it violently ripped itself free, pulling a horrific shriek along with it. The object resembled ball lightning as it floated through the air. Young Camile lost consciousness as the burning pain slowly began to subside.

As her eyes popped open, Camile saw her reflection in the above mirror. Seeing her adult form confirmed that the vision was over. Yet, an acidic heat lingered in the pit of her stomach. Realizing she was lying on the very slab on which she had endured the core segregation, she scrambled to her feet. Her parents expressed concern, inquiring about her well-being. Though floored, Camile insisted that she was fine and informed them of her recollection. She then requested that they explain what happened after the painful extraction.

"All procedures are recorded and evaluated," her father explained as they returned to the amphitheater. "I think seeing it for yourself would give you more insight than your mother and I can provide with words alone."

*   *   *

Sir Drayden cautiously watched the entity hover over young Camile's small, unconscious body. He ordered his assistants not to look at it as it may take it as a challenge. However, one of the men couldn't resist his curiosity. A second after he eyed the strange glowing object, it shot across the room, striking him in the chest before it exploded. The force of the blast slammed the men against the wall, knocking one of them out cold. The other managed to feebly mention that Camile's body was rapidly draining of energy. Sir Drayden already seemed to realize the alarming fact and outstretched his hand over the child in an apparent act to replenish her strength.

In spite of the destructive explosion, the violent entity seemed to gain power and suddenly soared towards Camile with apparent aggression. Sir Drayden stepped in its path, outstretching his other hand to prevent its attack. An electrical current streamed out of the entity, passing through his body to Camile and back. It sputtered as it floated to a corner and descended to the ground. As its radiance continued to dim, the object grew in size, morphing into the form of a young girl—an exact physical replica of little Camile. The unclothed copy lay on the ground, shivering in a fetal position. Sir Drayden, who regarded the doppelganger with an expression of grim confusion, removed his cloak and placed it over her body, scooping her into his arms as though she were a newborn baby.

As the view screen retracted into the high ceiling and the lights brightened the theater, Camile's parents allowed her a few moments to digest what she had seen. The silence was followed by an explanation that they had been suspended from their duties as a result of their noncompliance. During that time, they were placed under strict surveillance while the council considered Kylie's request for their daughter's core segregation in lieu of execution.

"I was surprised the council let us take you to Arizona during our final day together," Kylie explained. "You loved it there, so we figured it would be the best place for us to spend our last day as a family. We considered going into exile once we got there, but as I mentioned, the council kept a very close eye on us after our escape attempt."

Though she had been very young at the time, it was a day that was firmly embedded into Camile's memory. She could almost smell the faint aroma of chlorine from the public pool where her father once tried to teach her to swim.

"There was no guarantee the procedure would work or if you'd even survive, only that you'd never be the same." Zephyr's voice seemed as heavy as his eyes. "Neither would we."

"Looking back, I sure wish I did more research on the procedure before I requested it," a glassy-eyed Kylie explained, pausing to bite her lower lip. "But I just couldn't sit there and do nothing while my only child was about to be put to death. I was desperate."

"I understand, Mom." Camile placed her hand on her mother's shoulder. "What I don't get is why the council wanted me dead to begin with."

"The decision to execute you was also made in desperation," Zephyr explained. "There were a series of prophecies that were made pertaining to an imbalance in the *Invisible War* and the endangerment of the *Age of Ascension.*"

The *Age of Ascension* was defined as an era when the Coexistents would discover their true potential while placing higher importance in healing their civilization versus clinging to material excess and an imbalance of prosperity. In doing so, they would abandon superficial conflict and behavior while striving toward global unification. The *Invisible War* was said to be the struggle that precedes choice, a recurring burden which has been present since the dawn of human conflict. Every decision made, whether moral or immoral, contributes toward either the success or failure of the arrival of the *Age of Ascension.*

"The prophecies foretold a string of catastrophic incidents to be initiated by a person who would at worst prevent the *Age of Ascension,* or at least tragically alter the course of its progression," Zephyr continued. "There were terrible accidents, injuries, diseases, agricultural devastation and social unrest, all happening within our society, just as predicted. Eventually, all signs pointed to you."

"In each one of those tragic occurrences you were the only common link," Kylie added. "The council tried every possible solution from counseling, therapy, isolation…but nothing worked."

"Not only did the incidents continue, they worsened." Zephyr's brows raised as his lips sank into a frown. "It was feared that you would taint, if not completely prevent, the *Age of Ascension.* It was that fear that led the council to opt for the most drastic solution. To this day, the council's decision remains one that shames us as a people. Still, it serves as a lesson that as long as there is fear, doubt and shakable faith, there is always a chance for us to relapse to the old ways our ancestors fought to escape."

Chapter 4

Out of Line

Camile lost count of how many times she'd read the same section of text. She sometimes struggled to comprehend certain aspects of Transcendent education, but was told she'd reach her full potential in a matter of time. Still, focus was difficult to come by as she sat in the airy café located on the thirtieth level of Coronis Peak. Actually, the view beyond the picturesque windows played a part in her inability to concentrate on her Arvainan lexicon, as did the hushed conversations and meager clanking of dishes around her as the other patrons enjoyed their breakfasts.

Deciding a break from reading was in order she allowed her eyes to drift to the city skyline just beyond the dense woods, now exploding with the lively colors of a Monet painting. The clean, neutral lines of the café seemed to serve as a frame for the visual masterpiece beyond it. A cool gentle breeze caressed Camile's face and was promptly followed by a kiss from the sun. For a short while she forgot about the guards around the perimeter and the other diners regarding her with curious glances.

"Not slacking off, are you?" a soft voice stole her attention. Camile turned around, but didn't need to do so in order to know it was her mother. Sure enough, she saw both her parents approaching, dozens of eyes trailing behind them. There didn't seem to be a color her mother didn't look good in, but the peach camisole and matching sweater duster really enhanced the golden undertones of her deep skin. Her hazel eyes glowed like amber as her face entered the sunlight. After briefly discussing her progress, they made an announcement.

"Your father's being honored next week." Kylie smiled as she slid into a seat opposite her daughter. "It's not every day someone—"

"Gets older?" Zephyr quipped smoothly as he sat beside her. "I'm grateful for the honor, but I admit I'm not accustomed to such fuss."

Camile noticed her mother's smile grow faint upon hearing his words. Seeing this, Zephyr took her hand and stroked it gently.

Eyeing his daughter, he added, "But you'll still need to pick out something pretty for the festivity."

Kylie instantly volunteered to help her daughter find an outfit. Camile had almost forgotten how enthusiastic her mother was about shopping. It was an interest she shared, depending on her mood. Though she was excited about trying out the Arvainan fashions, Camile also felt apprehensive about the upcoming gathering. She hadn't encountered many of the citizens and the few of which she had made it clear she made them uncomfortable. Camile considered voicing her concerns, but changed her mind when she saw an officer approaching.

"The trespassers aren't who you think they are, but you were close, sir," the officer informed Camile's father. "They're not rebels. They're untagged Coexistents who travelled here illegally."

"How did they get here?" Zephyr furrowed his brow.

"None of them seem to remember, sir. Our best guess is that they were smuggled into this dimension by the rebels under false pretenses. We're still trying to determine the cause of their memory loss."

Zephyr ordered the officer to put a trace on inter-dimensional transfer records for the previous three months.

"Untagged Coexistents?" Camile inquired as the officer exited.

"It's not uncommon for the rebels to carry out suicide missions," her father explained. "In all cases, the rebels are either killed during their assignments or suffer extensive mental damage, making it impossible to extract any information. Now, it appears they're recruiting untagged Coexistents to do their bidding. Hopefully, we'll have better luck getting information from them in the coming days."

Camile's mother explained the rise of a disturbing trend among the rebels—trafficking untagged Coexistents, usually from populous cities like New York, Shanghai and Moscow among many others.

"Why do you need to tag them to begin with?" Camile wondered.

"For their own safety, and because we've been doing some recruiting of our own," Zephyr answered. "You'll find out more as you complete your training. Right now, there's something I think you should see."

*   *   *

There wasn't an empty seat in the meeting hall and the faces of hundreds reflected the tension in the room. All was silent except for the strong voice of a visibly displeased woman. Her dark eyes smoldered like hot coals in contrast to her cool demeanor.

"For years we've been slaves to their cause," she declared, her red lips twisting in apparent revulsion. "Am I the only one who can see the incredible disservice we're doing ourselves? We bend over backwards to help these...these insidious, hypocritical people; all the while knowing that if they had the chance to discover our world they'd rip it from under our feet." She clenched her fist. "We've all seen the historical archives. Coexistent humans are synonymous with gluttony and turmoil. Have we forgotten that we're helping people who are addicted to torment, pain and disaster? Yet they cry and complain when they receive the evil they glorify—just one example of their contradictory behavior. They're opportunistic and with each passing day that we help them they squander our efforts! We have to put an end to this once and for all!"

The room filled with scattered mumbled acquiescence until Kylie signaled for silence.

"Are you suggesting we save one world by defiling the freedoms of another?" Her smooth voice was authoritative, yet calm. "What if the situation was reversed?"

"Theoretical questions solve nothing. We need to deal with the harsh reality." The disgruntled woman frowned. "The only way to do that is to control them before it's too late. What do we reserve for ourselves; several more lifetimes of waiting quietly, hoping they get their shit together? I don't know about the rest of you, but I'm tired of dealing with the backdraft of their emotional diarrhea."

"We all share your concerns. However, I'm disappointed that you would generalize your opinion of the entire Coexistent race." Kylie's hazel orbs appeared to darken as she grimaced. "By helping them we also help ourselves. Yes, they have much to improve on, but at least they're trying, and in that, there's hope."

"Well, a Coexistent *would* say that." The woman snorted disgustedly. Upon doing so, she was promptly removed from her seat by security. "You can take me away, but that won't change my opinion. Unbelievable! After all our society has done for them, we're the ones who are destitute of choice," she shouted over her shoulder as two officers escorted her from the room. Her diminishing voice echoed from the corridor before growing silent.

"Maybe she's right. Maybe we're going about it the wrong way," a middle-aged gentleman said calmly once the disruption died down. "We've been going through the same pattern for centuries and it obviously isn't working. The lives of my ancestors have been wasted in this hopeless mission. Nearly all of them died violent deaths in the process. We need to communicate with the Coexistents in the only language they seem to understand—domination. In each instance where we presented the option of peace versus continued mayhem, they always choose mayhem. Maybe it's time for *their* luxury of choice to come to an end since they keep making the wrong ones."

"Part of evolving is accepting and adapting to change," Kylie lectured. "Those who fail to do so are left behind in the dust of yesterday. The fact is, the Coexistents are evolving and will be capable of standing on their own if only we just support them a little longer. Let's not forget, the Transcendent World has had to go through its own period of trial and error to get to where it is today. Patience is a virtue, but I know it sure as hell isn't easy. As much as we would all love to wake up tomorrow without the burden of worrying about the collapse of either world, the fact is it's not likely to happen. Positive change is among the most powerful forces in the universe, but it doesn't happen overnight. But when it does happen, it'll certainly be worth the wait."

Impressed by her mother's poignant speech Camile's eyes remained on the blank screen moments after the playback ended. Turning her attention to her parents, she noticed their solemn expressions.

"A short while after that meeting we noticed citizens going missing," Zephyr explained. "Turns out, they were forming a council of their own, now known as *the rebels*. They view Coexistents as a hindrance to our own progression. In some ways, it's understandable—the closer we seem to get to leading the Coexistents to a time of peaceful cohabitation with one another, they relapse to their destructive behavior. But, I haven't lost hope. We're getting closer with each attempt. Despite their setbacks, Coexistents have made remarkable progress. They've broken many barriers that at one time seemed impenetrable. Sadly, the rebels don't see it that way. They're so blinded by their own rage and twisted agendas, they fail to realize what they've become."

*   *   *

The days seemed to pass at breakneck speed and before Camile knew it, she was getting ready for the big celebration. She was grateful that her mother was able to walk her through the details of what women traditionally wore at such functions. The Arvainans prided themselves in their ability to maintain dignity in the art of seduction by preserving its main element—mystery. This was reflected in their overall sense of style. Comfortable in their skin, the Arvainans weren't afraid to show it on occasion, though in tasteful glimpses that enticed the imagination to play. Camile had tried on about a dozen dresses, eventually opting for a relatively modest look for her first formal social gathering.

Checking her appearance a final time before leaving her quarters, Camile smoothed the flouncy asymmetrical hem on her white, toga-style dress. She accessorized it with a floral prismatic crystal and ivory choker that matched her earrings. For the evening, her medallion—which she was told to wear at all times—was fashioned into a bracelet. She regarded it for a moment, taking in the tranquil vision of the deep blue stone that seemed to encapsulate a galaxy beneath water. It was this trinket that led her to the world she was now exploring.

No guts, no glory, she thought, adjusting a stray lock of her dark shoulder-skimming waves before entering the enormous banquet hall. Its gilded ivory walls were filled with all the life and jubilation of a carnival. As Camile stepped onto the burgundy carpet she estimated that there were nearly a thousand guests in attendance, enjoying food, drink and conversation amid lively music. She nearly froze at the entrance, wishing her parents had gone into more detail about exactly how many people would be present. Then again, she knew they probably realized she would've refused attendance if they had.

A hush followed her into the room. For a moment, it seemed as though someone hit a pause button on the crowd's merriment. Attempting to distract herself from the stifling crush of attention, Camile busied herself with analyzing the elaborate fashions of the guests. Many of them were wearing medallions similar to her own, though in varying shades. Some were fashioned into leather cuffs, wristlets and bracelets. Others were suspended from necklaces. Most of the sharply dressed men wore theirs in a style similar to pocket watches clipped to their waistbands.

As though on cue, the stark silence was broken by the music of a peculiar band, which included jubilant twins, conjoined at the abdomen, playing a double guitar that had apparently been customized for them. The music roused the crowd to resume their celebration as Camile's mother approached. She was a vision in flowing blue taffeta and silver with her hair smoothed into an elegant updo. Shortly after receiving her mother's warm welcome, Camile inquired about their condition.

"Transcendent technology is advanced, but still has its limitations. In their case," Kylie regarded the musicians with her tawny eyes, "surgical options were much too risky. But as you can see, they've made the most of their situation."

The statement conjured thoughts of Camile's separation from Akalina, thoughts that were broken by several sharp, cracking sounds that echoed throughout the hall. Turning around, Camile noticed a small group of acrobatic men entering the room, lashing whips and twirling staffs in a combative display. Their impeccable almond, cinnamon and chocolate toned bodies were clothed in chest-baring vests and white loose pants, secured with black sashes and matching ankle bands. They moved with easy agility to the thumping beat of drums. Their electrifying performance sparked with danger; one false move would surely result in a devastating injury. Their battle demonstration was poetry in motion set to the entrancing rhythm of their weaponry.

Once the enthralling act concluded, Camile found it slightly easier to breathe, only then realizing that she had been holding her breath for much of the performance. After bowing to Zephyr, the men parted allowing a short, portly pink-skinned man to approach Camile's father.

"I hope you enjoyed the performance, sir." He smiled proudly, gesturing to the men behind him. "These are some of Bauldana's finest champions."

"Yes. They're quite impressive," Zephyr praised, turning his gaze to the glistening performers. "Well done, gentlemen. You've done your country proud."

"And you, sir, have done your parents proud," Ezekiel proclaimed. "They raised a very good man."

Zephyr's smile faded. "They certainly did their best."

"Oh, don't be modest, mister!" Ezekiel's smile broadened. "You had a hand in the efforts that liberated our people from the Dark Days of Bloodlust."

"It was a team effort." Dimples deepening, Zephyr's lips turned upward as he clamped the man's shoulder, guiding him to the refreshment station. "Anyway, wouldn't you rather indulge in a few delicacies rather than talk shop? There'll be plenty of time for that later."

The beverage table was flowing with drinks distributed by cordial attendants. Camile stood in line to receive a serving of wine for the pending toast. Just as the attendant extended the glass to her, Sir Drayden intercepted. He was sharply dressed in a high-collared, white button-down shirt and black suit, giving him a prestigious aristocratic appearance.

"Please, allow me." Taking the glass from the server, he passed it to Camile.

"Thanks." Camile forced a smile as she reluctantly accepted.

"Don't mention it," Sir Drayden replied, gesturing that she take a seat beside her parents. It was a welcome invitation since she was wearing heels for the first time in months and was finding it increasingly challenging to remain steady. A hush swept over the room as the elder took to the head of the room and called for attention.

"Thank you for joining us for this brief celebration of a milestone reached by one of our brothers," Sir Drayden began. "I'm usually a man of few words, so I'll honor that tradition by keeping my sentiments short. When I first met Zephyr, he was a rambunctious, energetic young man in dire need of discipline and direction. But I always had a hunch that beneath his rugged exterior lie a dedicated, driven individual who would accomplish great things." Raising his glass, he turned to Camile's father. Smiling confidently, he said, "Zephyr, thanks for proving I'm always right."

The room momentarily filled with scattered amused laughter as everyone raised their glasses. Sir Drayden punctuated the merriment, declaring, "The measure of a successful life is not how long you live, but how well you live. Live well!"

The sentiment was cheered by the guests to the xylophonic tune of clanking glasses.

Camile overheard some of the attendees commenting on the rich flavor of the libations. However, when she took a sip, she tasted something akin to diluted fruit juice. Confused, she locked eyes with Sir Drayden, who regarded her with a subtle wink and a faint smile as he raised his glass to his lips.

*   *   *

The following morning Camile was scheduled to meet with the knight. He was lying across the dark leather daybed in front of his office window, engrossed in a book as she entered. The sunlight poured through the window casting a halo-like glow upon his hair.

"Catching up on some reading?" Camile asked, attempting to break the ice.

"Translating, actually," Sir Drayden met her gaze, twirling a silver pen in his fingers.

"Where are the originals?"

The elder's eyes crinkled as he cracked a wry smile. Tapping his temple with his pen, he replied, "They're all up here."

The furnishings in Sir Drayden's office were luxurious and seemed like the kind of setup a high-powered executive would enjoy. To the far right of the generous floor-to-ceiling windows was a separate sitting area facing the fireplace.

"We could sit there if you like," he offered. The power and clarity of his voice raided her ears and traveled through her like a mild electric current. Uncomfortable with the enormity of his presence, Camile declined, stating she was content with standing.

"I doubt you'll get any taller, if that's your goal." He chortled, shifting himself into a sitting position. "But since you prefer to stand..." Rising to his feet, he expelled a breath before walking to a window, motioning her to follow.

A glint of light reflected off the silver buckle of the belt encircling his trim waistline, giving life to an otherwise stark black sweater and matching slacks. His eyes seemed to be made of mirror as they appeared to reflect the colors of the sky they were now beholding. The dazzling view of the city and its rooftop gardens did little to quell the imposing discomfort that stemmed from his standing beside her.

His ensuing inquiries were surprisingly casual as he expressed curiosity in her broad interests and hobbies which included history, sketching, reading, poetry and cooking. Camile was equally impressed by his breadth of knowledge in each subject. According to what she had heard about the elder, he was the type who was all-business. She was mildly puzzled by the fact he mainly seemed interested in small talk and wondered if it was some sort of psychological assessment or if he was routinely sizing-up his newest trainee. The latter seemed more likely as the conversation continued.

"What's your impression of this world so far?" he asked, clasping his hands behind his back. "I'd imagine your head must be spinning, given what you've learned in recent months."

"It's something." Camile folded her arms. "Certainly not anything I thought I'd ever see."

"Young lady, you ain't seen nothin' yet." Sir Drayden chortled. "What about your life in the Coexistent World? Do you have any regrets about having to leave?"

"I don't know," Camile said. "Should I?"

"I believe it is I who asked the question first." He raised an eyebrow. "Well?"

"No, sir. Not so far."

"*Not so far.* Hmm. I see," Sir Drayden said almost to himself as though making a mental note of her answer. "How would you describe your upbringing?"

"It wasn't easy growing up without my father, but my mother did the best she could as a single parent."

"Do you hold any resentment?"

"I just said, she—"

"I'm not referring to your mother alone."

"In that case, I guess I'll have to say that even though I'm still working through a few things, I know the situation wasn't my parents' fault. I remember what happened the night of their escape attempt, the night they tried to save me. I also recall how their efforts were tragically interrupted." Camile looked deliberately into the elder's eyes. Her gaze wavered briefly before revisiting his blue orbs. "I was just a little girl. Were you really gonna let the council kill me?"

This time it was Sir Drayden who briefly broke eye contact before giving his response.

"If it's any consolation, the process would've been quite gentle, unlike the core segregation you endured."

I'll take that as a yes.

Camile caught a chill upon realizing she was standing beside the man who, at one time, planned to deliver her to the executioner. She looked forward to her exit, but a question held her back upon dismissal. Sir Drayden had already resumed his previous position on the daybed and continued reviewing his notes. Realizing Camile hadn't left, he paused.

"Something wrong?" he inquired.

"I was just wondering...Did you switch my drink at the party last night?"

"Yes, I did." The knight peered at her over the top of his book. "Maybe you forgot, but you're restricted from consuming alcoholic beverages. We can't risk having your mind steered by the influence of such substances."

"Oh, I see," Camile replied softly. She had, indeed, forgotten that her parents had informed her about the restriction just days after her arrival at Caldaq. "I thought there might've been an exception since it was my father's birthday and all."

"There are no exceptions unless otherwise specified," Sir Drayden said matter-of-factly, returning his eyes to his literature.

"How did you switch it so fast?"

"Easy. You weren't paying attention." The elder peeled his eyes away from his notes to regard her anew. His facial expression hardened a little and seemed to reflect mild impatience. "Will that be all?"

It was clear that he was forcing the conversation to a close. Having no desire to overstay her welcome, Camile didn't resist its end.

The tension lifted as she entered the corridor and saw her father. Curious about his reaction to the subject of his parents the prior evening, Camile decided to question him about it. Her intuition was cautioning her that bad news surrounded the topic in question. Still, she wanted to ask for herself.

"I noticed you didn't seem too happy when that guy mentioned your parents last night. Are they no longer with us?" she asked.

Zephyr's lips tightened as he appeared to consider his response. Finally, he said, "This isn't a good time to talk about this, Camile. I—"

"You have to tell her sometime. You're only delaying the inevitable," the knight interrupted from his doorway.

"Sir Drayden, I understand your concern, but with all due respect, this is a family matter." Zephyr frowned. "I'll tell her when the time is right."

"Alright. If you won't tell her, I will." Expelling a breath, Sir Drayden turned to Camile. "Your grandparents are dead."

Seriously? You just blurt it out point blank like that?

"That was *way* out of line." Zephyr pointed a finger at the elder. The irritation in his voice was evident, yet tame.

"She's bound to find out sooner or later. We'll all be better off if we tell her what she wants to know now and get it out of the way. In case you haven't noticed, she has an uncanny way of figuring things out. Furthermore, we can't afford any distractions on her part, so it's best to clear the air now rather than later." Sir Drayden paused a moment before frowning slightly. "Zephyr, do you need a visit to the EDC? You seem to be losing control of your anger."

Camile could feel the stifling shift in the atmosphere as well. Her father was clearly furious with this man and it seemed to be rubbing off on her. She agreed that Sir Drayden had crossed a major line. He didn't just avoid beating around the bush. He destroyed it.

"No, sir. I'm fine, but I would like to discuss this with you later," Zephyr said firmly. "Now, if you don't mind, I'd like to continue my conversation with my daughter... *Alone.*"

The knight appeared to scrutinize him for a tense moment. Seemingly satisfied, he turned his attention to Camile.

"I'm sorry I had to initiate this conversation," Sir Drayden said. "Your grandparents were decent people. It's a shame you never got to know them." His eyes shifted between father and daughter before returning to his office.

Awkward silence filled the air for several moments after the knight's departure.

"I'm sorry, Dad. That was messed up, the way he—"

"I know, sweetheart. I'll handle it in my own time." Zephyr regarded her with a tight-lipped smile. His somber eyes indicated that he was working to maintain his control. He appeared to be succeeding and Camile hoped it was a hereditary ability. She also hoped she wouldn't tip his emotional balance by inquiring about her grandparents' deaths.

"Hmm." Zephyr chuckled faintly. "I see the ways of the Coexistent World have gotten to you—so focused on death. Wouldn't you rather know how they lived?"

Chapter 5

Faces of the Past

Later that evening, Camile was deep in thought. She hoped the relics of the past would help enrich her relationship with her father. For years she sought to know him, but now that he was finally in her life, she was disappointed by the lingering distance between them. Yet, she understood that it would take longer than a few months to repair an eighteen-year breach in communication. It was a fracture in their relationship she was unsure any amount of time could mend, but she was willing to do her best, especially since her parents were the only family she had. This weighed on Camile's mind as she traveled with the security escorts guiding her to her quarters. A shrill whistle jostled her from her thoughts. As it grew louder she realized it was coming from within the corridor walls. There was an unmistakable Doppler effect as the sound faded rapidly into the distance. Camile noticed marked annoyance etched on the guards' faces.

"Joy-sliders." The tall one palmed his face.

"When will these kids learn that the hatches are for emergencies only?" The short one exhaled.

The sound returned, this time punctuated by squealing laughter.

"Think you can catch this one, Cole?" The short guard smirked.

His partner nodded, walking closer to the wall and thrusting out his palm, but stopped short of hitting the surface. The laughter ceased and was replaced by a thin *uh-oh*. Camile stifled a chuckle as the guard opened a hidden hatch in the stone wall. A young girl peered out, regarding her captors with wide eyes.

"How many?" Cole asked simply as he helped her down. The girl held up three fingers, gesturing that her accomplices had gone ahead of her.

"I'll take her to find the others before reporting this to their parents. You can escort Ms. Leon back to her quarters." Cole ordered, before leading the sullen girl away.

Camile and the officer took no more than ten steps before hearing yet another sound within the walls. The decidedly male voice was equally jubilant as the young girl's had been moments earlier.

Woo-hoo! Down the hatch, baby, the passenger exclaimed.

The guard quickly ran to the wall and performed the same maneuver his partner had done earlier. A teenage boy emerged from the opening and quickly darted past Camile with the officer hot on his trail. Camile soon found herself completely separated from both guards. In her attempt to locate the shorter officer, she submerged deeper into the winding corridors of Coronis Peak. Though the pathways were brightly lit and busy with foot traffic, Camile was intimidated by the unfamiliarity of it all. Had she been in another place and time she would've asked for directions, but nearly everyone around was regarding her with suspicion. They all vanished behind her as she rounded a corner and the sounds of the daily commute faded with them. Traveling further, she heard her father's tension-laced voice emanating from an adjacent corridor.

"Sir Drayden, how could you? It should've been up to me to decide when and how I told my daughter about my parents."

"He's right, Sir Drayden," Kylie added. "What you did was very unfair."

"I don't expect you to understand my reasons for doing what I did today. The sooner you put the past behind you, the sooner we can all help Camile to commit herself to the important work that lies ahead of her," the knight explained.

"And I don't expect *you* to understand the importance of a parent's bond with their children since you don't have any," Zephyr retorted.

"Honey, I know you're upset, but that's a little harsh." Kylie said gingerly.

"His anger's justified," Sir Drayden acknowledged before cautioning, "However, his emotional control is wavering for the second time today. Do you need to visit the EDC, Zephyr?"

"That won't be necessary, sir." Camile's father exhaled, his voice notably lower.

"Good. If there's nothing else you wish to discuss, I'll be on my way. Oh, one last thing, it might be a good idea to show your daughter the archives," Sir Drayden suggested. "Hopefully, that will be enough to sate her desire to know more about her grandparents. It may also help—"

Camile nearly leapt out of her skin when a hand fell heavily on her shoulder, pulling her attention away from the discussion. Whipping around, she saw the relieved expression of the short guard.

"I've been looking all over for you." He expelled a deep breath.

"Likewise." Camile chortled, sharing in his relief.

"For future reference, just stay put and I'll find you," he advised, moping his glistening brow. "This is a very big place. It's not a good idea to go wandering off the way you did."

*   *   *

Though windowless, Caldaq's central library in Coronis Peak was flooded with warm light, enhancing its mahogany and wine colored ambiance. The walls were seemingly constructed by the countless volumes of books, stowed within towering recessed shelves.

A bookworm's dream come true, or an illiterate's nightmare, Camile thought while observing librarians on rolling ladders, retrieving and replacing editions. Detecting the stale scent of archaic parchment in the mildly dusty air, she wondered if Arvaina's most treasured secrets were hidden in the facility.

As Camile and her mother ventured further into the chamber she caught the eyes of a few dozen scholars, who quickly returned their attention to their studies. Even with the small army of guards lining the room, she could still sense their fear. It permeated the air like the stench of toxic waste. They entered one of the archive rooms where her father was awaiting her arrival. It was dim and spartan, except for a corner table inset with a glowing computer screen that reflected in the buttons of his slate gray uniform.

"I guess I'll leave you to your father-daughter chat." Kylie turned to exit.

"You're not staying?" Camile furrowed her brow.

"I've seen these archives dozens of times, but they always make me a little emotional. Your father's parents were the closest thing I had to parents of my own." Kylie sighed. "I know it's been years, but I still miss them. I guess I still have a bit of work to do in letting go. Transcendents make it look deceptively easy." Shaking her head slightly, Camile's mother gently touched her daughter's shoulder before leaving the room.

"Fair warning, I went through a few awkward phases in my youth. Try not to laugh too hard." Zephyr quipped once Camile joined his side.

"We clearly have more in common than our eyes," she said, regarding his gray gaze.

Her father smiled deeply before swiping through the images with a fluid motion of his fingers. Each photo was sequentially projected into life-sized three-dimensional visuals at the room's center.

Awestruck, Camile gawked at her father's childhood images. He was the spitting image of his own father who shared the same striking pale eyes and dark hair. However, the man in the picture was noticeably wiry.

"So, this is grandpa." Camile exhaled, approaching the projection.

Her father nodded, staring at the image for a moment. "His name was Zephyr Leon I, but everyone called him by his middle name, Lysander."

"You look a lot alike, only you're not as skinny." Camile met her father's eyes. "No offense."

"None taken." Zephyr chortled as he joined his daughter's side. "My father was more the spiritual and intellectual type, but don't let his appearance fool you. He was more than capable of kicking some serious ass in his day." He beamed. "I guess you could say it was he, in part, who influenced my decision to work in law enforcement."

"And so you followed in his footsteps."

"Not exactly. Crime prevention is my main interest. My father worked in the judgment and penalty sector."

"Sounds like he was a no nonsense kinda guy," Camile remarked.

"That pretty much sums him up." Her father nodded with quirked brows. "His job was burdensome to say the least, but he always did his best to do what he felt was right."

Camile's eyes fell upon the image of a young petite woman with large dark eyes and pouty lips, curled into a proud smile. Her light-colored glossy locks were perfectly coifed like a 40s-era starlet, framing her face as she knelt behind a young Zephyr, his arms braced in her hands.

"That's my mother, Camelia. Your name was inspired by hers. She always wanted me and my dad to go into medicine with her. Actually, this is a video of me learning to walk," Zephyr explained before prompting the film to play.

Camelia cheered little Zephyr on as he took one wobbly step after the next. After a misstep, the child stumbled into his father's arms.

"That was a close one, little man," Lysander said through jubilant amusement as his son cooed and giggled.

"Nice catch, honey. Looks like we've got a real sprinter on our hands," Camelia said to her husband in a silky full-bodied voice, fit for book or film narration.

The footage continued for several moments, during which Zephyr's parents showered him with praise. This was followed by pictorial chronicles of her father's life. Camile felt as though she were watching him grow before her very eyes. She couldn't help but feel a little bitter about the fact he had missed out on her life. There was something tauntingly backwards about it. At nearly the exact moment the resentment began to chill her mind it was melted away by the warmth she felt when watching the next set of images in which a very pregnant Kylie, was present. Joyful tears stung Camile's eyes as she regarded images of her parents together with her as a newborn.

There were a wide assortment of family photos, including her parent's wedding. The simple floral backdrop complimented what she imagined was a modest, romantic ceremony. Her parents and paternal grandparents stood side by side. Surrounding them were guests including Sir Drayden, a striking raven-haired woman, Nancy and several other people, whom her father described as staff, council members and other government officials. Camile was about to inquire about the dark haired woman when she recognized someone in the wedding party, someone she hadn't seen in nearly a decade.

"Ms. Hawkins?" she asked almost to herself, narrowing her eyes. Ms. Hawkins had been Camile's distrustful high school teacher. In the photo, the woman's diminutive height was all but eclipsed by Sir Drayden, who towered behind her. The crown of her head, spiked with short jet-black hair, barely aligned with his shoulder.

"Excuse me?" Camile's father inquired, prompting her to indicate the youthful looking dark-skinned woman in the photo. "Oh, Jezebel. She was one of your mother's bridesmaids. As I recall she was more than a little miffed that Nancy was picked for matron of honor. I'll never understand these things and I value my sanity way too much to keep trying." He chuckled softly before his expression grew serious. "Jezebel ended up being selected for a more important role. She was assigned as one of your guardians in the Coexistent World. Unfortunately, she failed to meet the council's expectations."

Camile recalled the skeptical manner in which her former high school teacher had addressed her on numerous occasions. She never would have guessed her to be an ally of any sort, particularly since her mother suspected Jezebel was looking for reasons to incriminate her.

"It's strange to hear her first name after all this time." Camile shook her head. "Is she here in the Transcendent World?"

"Yes, but she no longer works for the council."

The slight deviation of Zephyr's eyes alluded Camile to the fact someone was behind her. She followed his line of sight to see Sir Drayden silently approaching. At first she wondered if he had managed to slip into the room with the stealth of a shadow, then she suspected he'd been present all along. The latter seemed more likely since no additional light had breached the room since her mother's departure. Even so, Camile had casually scanned the four walls and corners upon entry and her father was the only man present at the time, or so she thought.

Sir Drayden stopped just a few feet in front of father and daughter. His age seemed more evident in the sparse lighting, which emphasized his under eye bags and the crepey skin around his neck. There appeared to be a sense of understanding between the men, who remained locked in a silent stare. Finally, Zephyr nodded, his expression solemn.

"I suppose you can say your piece since we've somewhat touched on the subject."

Based on her father's statement, Camile knew the knight had somehow asked him a question by way of thought.

Facing Camile, Sir Drayden began, "I understand you're not only curious about the life of your grandparents, but also how they died." He paused briefly to regard Zephyr. "I regret to inform you that I am responsible for their deaths."

Camile quickly toggled her attention between the knight and her father, as though gauging his response. Zephyr pursed his lips, briefly lowering his gaze as Sir Drayden continued.

"I sent them on a mission designed to throw the enemy off our trail. It inevitably cost them their lives. For the sake of national security there's no official record of the assignment or the nature surrounding their passing. However, they believed in the importance of their task so deeply, they bravely chose to sacrifice themselves in order to succeed," Sir Drayden explained, a hint of pride softened his sharp voice. "By helping the Coexistents win the *Invisible War* we'll prove that your grandparents didn't die in vain." He paused a moment, filling the room with deafening silence.

Zephyr's jaw tightened as he regarded Sir Drayden with glassy eyes. Camile couldn't imagine how difficult it was for him to stand face-to-face with the man who was at least partially responsible for his parents' deaths. She knew it must've been a constant reminder that he would never see them again. The thought alone was heartbreaking enough, but then she learned that their end wasn't quick nor easy.

"Since there's nothing further for me to say on the matter, I'll leave you to finish your meeting in private," Sir Drayden said. "Unless, of course, you have any questions."

The tension in Camile's throat obstructed a verbal response. She shook her head, prompting him to exit. The knight's departure alleviated the tension in the room, but the painful consequence of his decision remained in her father's eyes.

"After my parents died, my brothers, sisters and I drifted apart," Zephyr broke the silence.

"I have aunts and uncles?" Camile cracked a smile, her interest piquing further. She found some comfort in learning her family was larger than three people.

"Quite a few." He nodded somberly. "Three aunts, eight uncles."

Camile's mouth fell agape. "From *one* marriage?"

Zephyr nodded anew, chuckling at her stunned reaction. "It wasn't easy being the youngest of twelve children. We rarely keep in touch, anymore. Sadly, it's just not the same as it used to be. It could be worse, though. I guess occasional contact is better than none at all."

So much for a family reunion.

"What happened? Sibling rivalry?"

"Something like that. We had many disagreements. The biggest was over our parents' final arrangements." Expelling a deep breath, Zephyr loosened the cuffs of his jacket. "They were upset about my inheritance. Can't say that I blame them. They thought it was unfair for one person to inherit everything. But, considering the history of things, I think I earned it."

"Are they in here?" Camile gestured to the archive.

Zephyr nodded his head, his nostrils slightly flared. "But if you don't mind, I'd like to show those to you another time."

Having no desire to pick the scab that family drama had left behind, Camile was content with surveying the rest of the preset photos in the archive. In them, everyone seemed overjoyed as though nothing could go wrong. For a little more than an instant Camile found herself wanting to forget everything that had transpired so that she could experience those precious, seemingly carefree moments in the images displayed before her. Sadly, she knew that was an impossibility. Those moments, along with her childhood, were long gone and could never be reclaimed.

Chapter 6

Diplomacy & Defense

The Birquone parliament building, the lead government facility in Arvaina, was located in the northwestern state of Kibara. The building served as a meeting place where various world leaders and dignitaries would congregate. Camile couldn't help but feel a degree of importance to be traveling there with her parents. She also felt as though she were about to partake in the ultimate take-your-daughter-to-work-day.

After using a high-speed railway across several states, they came to a small desert depot where they transferred to a vehicle called the *Sandwinder*. Upon entering the vehicle, the cool air soothed the prickly discomfort the burning sun had caused when it rudely invaded her white cotton tunic and linen pants.

"We should be there in about twenty minutes," her mother announced.

"The Birquone's in the middle of the desert?" Camile raised her brows. "It sure didn't look like this in the archives."

In everything she had seen of the structure in photos and documents, the Birquone was situated in the center of a large city. Yet, endless sand dunes and hazy skies were all that was visible beyond the passenger windows. Disinterested in the monotonous view, Camile sank into her seat and closed her eyes.

"Hey, sleepyhead, you don't want to miss this." Zephyr nudged his daughter moments later, instructing her to return her gaze to the window.

To her amazement, the vehicle was traveling between two raging seas—one of water, the other of sand. The violent currents kicked up billowing clouds of dust, occasionally obscuring their path. Never in her life had she seen sand behave in such an amazing and intimidating manner. Her astonishment climbed when her father directed her attention to the view in the windshield. The vehicle broke through the floating sediments, revealing an enormous pyramid just a few miles ahead of their position. She also saw a few smaller pyramids in the distance. There was a thick haze covering the pinnacle of the larger structure, but Camile was able to make out a faint outline. The top was flat, as though the pointed summit had been severed.

As the vehicle got closer to the foremost pyramid Camile noticed reddish quicksand moving in a massive whirlpool reminiscent of liquid lava. Just beyond the strange phenomenon were the pyramid's base steps, rippling in a distortion generated by the heat emanating from the ground. In a matter of moments, the fiery vortex solidified and cooled, providing a steady surface for the vehicle to venture across.

"Security point," Zephyr explained. "There's a hidden motion sensor device designed to keep out the riffraff."

"Anyone who dares to trespass has to face the heat," Kylie added.

"Who'd be crazy enough to dare?" Camile pressed her head against the passenger window to get a better look at the newly formed ground.

The *Sandwinder* soon came to a stop near the pyramid steps. Everyone but Zephyr exited.

"Where are you going?" Camile asked.

"Somebody has to park this thing," her father answered.

"I can park it, honey. It's no trouble," Kylie offered.

"That's sweet of you, but I'm already in the driver's seat."

"Mmm-hmm, " Kylie hummed in a skeptical tone. "Just like old times. And they say chivalry's dead."

Camile thought she might collapse with relief once she and her mother reached the top of the seemingly endless steps. Her exhaustion was coupled with utter amazement when she saw what awaited them at the pyramid's flat plateau. It was the Birquone, just as she had seen it in photos, media archives and news transmissions. The ivory building, surrounded by trees and manicured lawns, was seven stories tall and appeared to take up the equivalent of approximately four city blocks. The pillars supporting the roof were similar to those of the government buildings Camile had seen in the Coexistent World.

Wiping the sweat from her forehead she looked at the path behind her. Not a big fan of heights, she instantly regretted it. The *Sandwinder's* tracks in the sand far below resembled thin pencil lines. Camile could also see the aquatic and sandy seas on each side of the plain. Distance softened the sound of the crashing waves. A rippling distortion of the air below hinted that the fiery whirlpool at the base of the pyramid had been reactivated. The majestic setting made her feel tiny. It was as intimidating as jumping into the ocean for the first time. Nevertheless, water was something she craved desperately, despite the fact she had nearly emptied her canteen during her second rest stop on the stairs. Feeling a hand touch her shoulder, Camile flinched, fearing she might tumble down the steep structure.

"Sorry I scared you, baby, but you were in a daze," her mother said.

"Guess that teaches me not to stand so close to the edge." Camile chuckled nervously. Although she was still trying to catch her breath, her mother seemed to have already recovered from the strenuous climb. "How can you possibly not be tired?"

"Don't let my looks deceive you. I'm winded, but let's just say this isn't my first time up these stairs." Kylie cracked a half-smile. "We really should get going. There'll be plenty of time for sight-seeing before we head back to Caldaq."

The first thing Camile noticed upon entering the main foyer were the black steps ascending to the next floor. Each step contained reflective particles that shimmered like stars in space. They contrasted against the luminous brilliance of the crystal chandelier above and the white walls, all adorned with paintings.

A young woman named Victoria greeted the duo before engaging Kylie in a few moments of small talk.

"Your Excellency, the Deltine Minister of Defense is awaiting your arrival in the Aster gathering chamber. But, I'd imagine you'd like to freshen up first." Victoria headed for the main staircase.

Great. More stairs, Camile thought, sighing inwardly before inquiring about something Victoria had said.

"Your Excellency?" she whispered to her mother.

"I had to settle. *The Magnificent* was already taken," Kylie joked before explaining that the term referred to her title, *Ambassador-At-Large for Coexistent-Transcendent Relations*. She also mentioned that she reported directly to the *Director of Foreign Affairs*, the third in line for the Arvainan presidency.

"Seriously?" Camile beamed with a mixture of pride and astonishment.

Her mother nodded.

"Wow. You certainly made a name for yourself here."

"It was no easy feat, I assure you. I wasn't exactly well-liked in the beginning. At first, I was called everything but a child of God. It took some time, but the residents got used to the idea of sharing their world with me. The council for the most part embraced me as a member of their society. Never hurts to have friends in high places. After two years of service in the community, I was asked to join the Transcendent effort for peaceful inter-dimensional cohabitation."

"Impressive. So, if you're an ambassador, what does Dad do?"

"He tries very hard to make my job easier, but it works both ways. I should probably let him tell you this, but since he made me walk up all those damn stairs…Do you remember who Victoria said is waiting for us?"

Camile broke her stride upon realizing the Deltine Minister of Defense was none other than her father.

A quick shower washed away the sweaty remnants of her challenging journey up the pyramid, leaving phenomenal memories and a nagging irritation in Camile's thighs. Now wearing a fresh set of clothes, she and her mother headed to the Aster gathering chamber. There, Camile's father sat at a sleek white table with matching seats that gleamed against warm beige floor tiles. There was a shock of royal blue streaming above the seating area, bathed in soft illumination.

"With all the technological advancements in this world, you'd think there'd be a few elevators around here," Camile muttered softly as she sat beside him. Kylie took her place to his left.

"How do you think I got up here so fast?" He winked.

Are you serious? Camile contorted her face in disbelief.

Her father answered her unspoken question. "Sorry. All newcomers take the stairs during their first visit. It's become a sort of tradition, an initiation of sorts."

"Is heat stroke part of the hazing?" Camile asked sarcastically.

"Actually, you got it pretty easy. Your mother didn't find out about the elevator for nearly a full week. I think she dropped about six pounds by the time she did." Zephyr laughed.

"Hmph! More like ten," Kylie corrected.

"Well, of course back then she didn't find it very amusing, but time has a way of strengthening the funny bone."

"I think I broke mine on the stairs," Camile quipped, earning a chuckle from her parents.

The conversation stalled awkwardly for a few moments. Camile knew it was a sign that it was on the verge of a serious turn.

"Remember when your mother and I told you about the bio-neurotransmitters implanted in our brains?" her father asked. Camile nodded, recalling the discussion that took place upon her return to the Transcendent World. These were the very devices that had prevented her parents from informing her of her true identity in the past.

"We have a confession to make," he continued. "We only told you part of the reason why they were implanted to begin with. Truth is, the transmitters are implanted in many Arvainan citizens at birth. Since your mother's a Coexistent, she had hers implanted as an adult when she decided to join our world. There are many reasons for the procedure. The organic devices allow us to monitor several aspects of a citizen's life—their location, occupation, medical and criminal histories—should they choose to break any laws. It also allows citizens to mentally connect and communicate with each other, sort of like cell phones. It enables us to perform many tasks at the speed of thought."

Upon hearing this, Camile couldn't help but think about the possible negative aspects of the program, such as people making errors at such a rapid pace. This would significantly narrow the margin for error while broadening the chance of misfortune. Yet, she said nothing as her father explained of some of the transmitter's features, which included distress signals that operated much in the same way as human instincts. For example, a person may have a sudden urge to contact a loved one. Often, that urge is a response of a distress signal of sorts. Many Transcendents naturally possessed the aforementioned skills, but some benefitted from the technology's aptitude to boost their abilities.

"To ensure that the system isn't abused, the government appointed a special team to oversee the entire program," Zephyr added.

The program was said to have originated in Deltine as a means to evoke peace through enhanced communication, particularly among those referred to as the non-enlightened or non-telepathic. In many cases, the implants were able to 'jumpstart' their innate telepathic abilities. After many years of success, the program was expanded throughout Arvaina. However, the rest of the Transcendent World was slow to adopt the technology and there are regions that still oppose it.

"How do you know the people policing the program aren't abusing it themselves?" Camile asked.

"Like any system there are no guarantees that it's foolproof, but we've implemented a serious review process to ensure that the privacy of our citizens isn't unjustly or unnecessarily compromised."

"So, if everyone's mentally connected, what's to stop them from hearing each other's thoughts?"

"There are several protocols in place to prevent any involuntary sharing of thoughts. It works a lot like a telephone call—one party initiates and the other accepts the call if they want to. Of course, there are exceptions when it comes to the government. We're the only ones who can tap into the external and internal communications of our citizens, but only if it has been deemed absolutely necessary."

"Internal communication?" Camile said almost to herself. "You mean you can actually *hack* into a person's thoughts?"

Her father nodded, briefly pursing his lips. "But it's only done if we suspect illegal plans or activities. Even then, there are still exceptions when it's considered too dangerous."

As Camile tried to digest the information, she came to an alarming realization. "Has anyone been tapping into *my* thoughts?"

"Your transmitter's been deactivated," Kylie answered. "When you reintegrated with Akalina, we couldn't take the chance of you possibly linking up with the other citizens until we were absolutely sure that you were mentally and emotionally stable. You've been doing well, so far, but for now, it's been decided that it's best to keep it dormant. It's as much for your protection as everyone else's."

Camile was relieved at the decision, but it was bittersweet. She knew her mental stability was still under scrutiny and would be for some time to come.

*   *   *

During the tour of the Birquone, Camile learned that there was indeed a city surrounding the facility, but it was located deep underground. Despite its location, the entire area was flooded with artificial sunlight. In addition, the temperature controlled environment was pleasantly cool, a sharp contrast to the sweltering desert climate above. It was explained that a large portion of the city's population was dedicated to protecting its central building at all costs. There wasn't enough time for Camile to explore the city at length as she had done with the parliament building. She wished she could venture deeper into the subterranean town, but was satisfied with having seen some of the numerous meeting rooms and compartments in the Birquone facility.

She and her parents ate lunch at Oasis, a restaurant that had, as her father put it, "…the best damn kebabs this side of Arvaina!"

After taking her first bite, Camile understood his anticipation. The juicy, tender meat was perfectly seasoned with exotic herbs that played a symphony on her tongue. She felt her face contort slightly as one of the accompanying warm tomatoes burst in her mouth with a delicate sweet tartness. The flat bread wasn't bad either. It reminded her of a chewy mildly salted pretzel. The busy activity of the popular eating spot amidst the smoky scent of grilled food was reminiscent of a big city barbecue.

"Hope you're enjoying your meal," Zephyr said between generous bites. "It's the last you're allowed to have until you meet Tabitha."

Camile had nearly forgotten that she was required to fast several hours before her first meeting with the shaman, an event that would take place later that evening. She assumed it was a normal practice that likely had something to do with purifying the body.

"I'll eat slowly." Camile grinned, dipping her next forkful into a cucumber-green condiment she had yet to try.

"Careful, that stuff can melt fillings," her mother cautioned.

Camile had already shoved the food into her mouth halfway into the warning. After a few seconds she was breathing like a pregnant woman in labor while clumsily grasping for her beverage.

*　　*　　*

They chased sunlight during their return trip to Caldaq, but it descended beyond the horizon at least an hour before their arrival. As they crossed the stately main lobby a large-jawed officer approached Camile's father with urgent information regarding the Coexistent intruders. The officer briefly smoothed his immaculately groomed beard that matched his flaxen hair.

"What first, sir, the good news or the bad news?" His voice boomed.

"Just give it to me straight, Prescott." Zephyr briefly massaged his closed lids.

"We traced the transfers to four Transcendents who claimed to have been working with the inter-dimensional cultural exchange program. I'm afraid this might be the most information we'll ever retrieve. They're all dead, sir."

"Dead?" Zephyr frowned, meeting the officer's eyes. Camile noticed her mother was wearing an equally concerned expression.

"Yes, sir. However, the transfers were made through these three ports." Prescott pointed a thick finger to the highlighted areas of a map on a small handheld device. Zephyr took it into his hands and analyzed it.

Leaning in, Kylie frowned at what she saw. "I sure as hell didn't authorize this. I doubt anyone in my department did either, but you can bet I'll be looking into it."

"This certainly smells like the rebels' work." Zephyr exhaled, returning the device to Prescott. "They're getting craftier by the day, but they're bound to slip up some time. When they do, we'll be ready, but we won't sit waiting until it happens. Maximize security at all rift ports. I'll notify our bordering states and suggest they follow suit. All transfer requests will have to be approved by senior officials only. I know it'll create a backlog, but we can't afford to take any chances. Notify me immediately if any of the intruders remember anything about the day they arrived here, even if it's just what they had for breakfast that morning."

"Aye, sir." The guard promptly exited to fulfill his orders.

Camile gazed at her father as he smoothed his salt and pepper hair from his forehead. She still wasn't accustomed to seeing her eyes staring back at her beneath his slightly bushy brows. In spite of the serious conversation he just concluded, he regarded her with an easy smile framed with high cheekbones and shallow dimples. Camile's mother mirrored the expression, as though to reassure her that everything was under control. Yet, she could tell from both her parents' eyes that their minds bore a heavy burden.

Chapter 7

The Lines of Morality

Venturing deep into the east wing of Caldaq's Coronis peak, Camile noticed an increasing number of guards lining both sides of the long, dark gray corridor. They were completely still, their faces emotionless, like toy soldiers clad in crisp dark uniforms. However, Camile knew that at the slightest hint of a threat, they would spring to life in vigorous defense. When she reached the end of the passageway she noticed it was slightly dimmer than her starting point. A young guard approached. Without saying a word he guided her into Tabitha's quarters almost as though he were directing an animal into a cage.

The officer's uniform was unlike that of the other guards and seemed to signify a different rank. Its simple lines emphasized his slender athletic build, which she surmised was wrapped in the same velvety bronze skin as his exotic face. Camile's eyes greedily surveyed his slightly slanted brown orbs, broad rounded nose and the pronounced dimple above his full lips. The hair on his dome wasn't much longer than the fuzz of his five o'clock shadow. His brooding presence made him seem unapproachable, yet also contributed to his mysterious appeal.

Camile was initially unnerved by the indifferent manner in which he treated her, but then figured he'd probably been burned by Akalina's antics. Entering the softly lit room she breathed deeply with anticipation, taking in the sweet aroma of frankincense and sandalwood. The lavender gray chamber was decorated with strange artifacts and tapestries. The rightmost wall housed many shelves that held glass jars containing a variety of liquids, dried herbs and roots. Each jar was clearly labeled with unusual symbols and sat above a large collection of old books—all neatly organized. As she reached out to touch one, she was interrupted by the sound of the guard clearing his throat. Turning her attention to the door, she realized he was keeping a watchful eye on her. Gingerly retreating from the storage unit, Camile called for the shaman. There was no answer, so she crossed into the adjacent room which was separated by nothing more than a few layers of dark gray gossamer curtains.

Upon entering, she immediately noticed the large bed in which an older woman appeared to be sleeping. To Camile's astonishment, she bore a striking resemblance to the woman she had once known as Zareah. She then reminded herself that Zareah had been her own ghost. The recollection summoned an army of goosebumps down her spine. Walking closer to the lavishly draped bed, she called softly to the woman, but she didn't rouse. Growing concerned, Camile called to her a second time, slightly louder. It still had no effect, so she tried gently shaking her and was startled to find she was ice-cold and wasn't breathing. She urgently pressed her fingers against the shaman's neck.

There was no pulse.

"Oh, my God!" Camile exclaimed breathlessly before calling for help.

The guard immediately dashed into the room and began inspecting the elder woman.

"I think she's dead," Camile stammered as the man pried open the shaman's eyelids and looked closely into her pupils. He then checked her pulse.

"Coexistents," he muttered, his moderately deep voice vibrating like a plucked cello string. "She's not dead, she's traveling. She's already on her way back."

Camile furrowed her brow.

"Check her pulse again," he suggested.

Camile held his brown gaze, her apprehension climbing. The man wasn't stunningly handsome, but parts of him were spectacular; like his slightly oversized irises.

"Well, go on," he insisted somewhat impatiently.

Slowly extending her hand, Camile placed her fingers on the woman's stiff neck. She still felt no pulse, only the slight tremble of her own hand. She turned to the guard, who nodded knowingly.

"Wait. Just wait for it…" he instructed.

She followed his instruction and became increasingly uneasy when the situation remained unchanged.

"There's nothing happening. We need to get help for—"

"Wait for it," he whispered. *"Wait for it…"*

As reassuring as his voice should've been, Camile was nearing the verge of panic.

Wait for what? Enough of this. I'm gonna try CP—

A soft gasp escaped her mouth as she felt a gentle swell beneath her fingers. Amazed, she realized the woman indeed had a pulse—albeit a very sporadic one. Camile regarded the man inquiringly.

"This always happens when she travels far. She'll be with you soon," he starkly explained. He stared at Camile with a slight look of distrust before returning to his position at the open doorway.

Bemused, she kept vigil over the resting woman. A few long moments passed before the shaman suddenly wheezed, prompting Camile to stumble backward. She heard a faint chuckle coming from the guard outside.

"Camile, it's so good to see you—and in *one* piece," the woman exclaimed hoarsely. "Sorry I spooked ya."

The woman appeared sluggish as she sat upright. After loudly clearing her throat, she drank a glass of water that had been sitting on her nightstand. Her aged brown skin was becoming more vibrant as she settled into her consciousness. Aside from a few age spots, it was a relatively even in tone for a woman of her season. The wiry gray strands of her salt and pepper hair glowed in contrast to her rich complexion.

"Zareah, I—" Camile stopped herself.

"Zareah?" The shaman furrowed her brow, deepening the wrinkles framing her nearly black orbs. "Ah! Your phantom must've used my appearance while completing the mission. Guess I oughta be flattered. The name's Tabitha. Didn't your folks tell you that before sending you up here?" Her voice, now warm and velvety, cradled words with the ease of a soulful blues singer.

Camile felt silly having forgotten that her parents had indeed mentioned the shaman's name. However, she couldn't get over her striking resemblance and familiar mother-hen personality.

"Yeah, they did. I guess when I realized…" Camile started to explain, but reconsidered. "Never mind. I guess I forgot. Wait a minute. If my parents already knew who you were, how come they didn't catch on that my…ghost looked almost exactly like you?"

"I guess they must've assumed it was really me leading you back here while using an alias. It's a good thing I wasn't physically here at the time. That would've been confusing." Tabitha chuckled before inspecting Camile's medallion.

Apparently satisfied with its condition, the shaman went on to explain that she would serve as Camile's spiritual counselor during the course of her rehabilitation and training. She also suggested that Camile keep a journal in order to help process her thoughts and feelings. Tabitha presented her with a small thick book with beige pages. Its dark brown leather cover was debossed with a small dove on the front and a crow on the back. Running her fingers across the textured exterior, Camile noticed the spine had a small pocket containing a silver pen. She briefly thumbed through the empty pages, all ready for her to fill to her heart's content.

"We have a lot of work ahead of us, child, but we can't accomplish any of it until you learn to center yourself." Tabitha called the lead guard into the room, addressing him as Jeremy. As soon as he entered, she appointed him as Camile's meditation instructor. In addition, she recommended that he teach her basic self-defense in light of the recent attack at the compound.

"I'm sure there's someone else who can—" he attempted to protest.

"Jeremy, it's been ordered that you do it, at least for the meantime. Is there a problem?" Tabitha raised an eyebrow as though daring her subordinate to challenge her.

"No, Your Wisest." Jeremy lowered his head slightly.

"Then I guess we're done here. I'll see you in about a month, Camile. I expect nothing less than your best." The shaman winked before retreating to the adjacent room.

*　　　*　　　*

The Dark Days of Bloodlust. As Camile scrolled through her texts, these words caught her eye, evoking the memory of the night she'd first heard them. According to their location in document, the subject was well beyond her currently assigned studies, but curiosity couldn't wait for the topic to become part of her curriculum. Selecting it, she read an introduction which outlined the global devastation suffered by the Transcendent residents at the hands of bloodthirsty and cannibalistic beings.

Though the people of each continent infused the earth with tears and blood, Bauldana and Jypsone experienced the worst carnage during the ordeal. After many years of suffering, and devastating losses experienced by both the creatures and humans alike, an agreement was reached to end the rampant bloodshed. It is an agreement that has been in place for seventy-five years. Camile made several attempts to access the next page, but the document appeared frozen.

A few moments elapsed before the monitor went blank. Suddenly, a bluish face flooded the screen, eyes rolled into its sockets and a mouth unnaturally contorted in perpetual agony. Startled, Camile pushed away from the desk so quickly she nearly toppled over in her chair. Regaining her composure, she switched on her desk lamp, chiding herself for reading in the dark to begin with. Slowly returning her attention to the image on the screen, she noticed dozens of scratches on the disfigured subject's face and neck. Gender became apparent only after Camile scrolled downward, revealing modest mounds draped in tattered soiled fabric. Gasping, she realized the woman had literally been torn in half and partially disemboweled. Deciding she'd seen enough, Camile promptly closed the document, all the while thinking: *That poor woman! What kind of monster could do all that?*

Then her thoughts circled around something the portly pink man had said at the celebration, that her father had a hand in the agreement that ended the Dark Days of Bloodlust.

How could that be if it all took place so long ago?

Zephyr appeared to consider the question as he chewed a bite of his sandwich. He wiped a few stray crumbs from his mouth before giving his response.

"Transcendent humans have held onto their blessing of longevity. At ninety-seven years old, I can safely say I'm no exception."

"*Ninety-seven?* Stop playing!" Camile's mouth fell agape. Her reaction briefly attracted the other diners in the open air cafeteria.

"I don't kidding." Zephyr laughed, his glossy hair rustling in the gentle breeze. "Transcendents age more slowly than our Coexistent counterparts. A *lot* more slowly. Physically, we age two to three times slower after reaching physical maturity. Up until puberty, Transcendents and Coexistents basically age at the same rate."

"And I thought you looked good to be middle-aged. You'll have to share your secret."

"I don't have to. I already shared my genes." He winked. "Even though you're only half Transcendent, chances are you're just as capable of living a very long and graceful life. That is, if you succeed in your mission. Besides, I *am* middle-aged. Transcendents have an average lifespan of between one hundred-fifty to nearly two hundred years, but it's not unlikely for some to have a lifespan many times that of a centenarian."

Still wrapping her mind around the information, Camile's attention fell on the silver-haired knight entering the room.

"What about Sir Drayden? How old is he?" she asked, watching as he sat among a small group. Though she couldn't decipher his words, his voice conquered the distance between them.

"Honestly, even I'm not exactly sure how old he is." Zephyr chortled. "My guess is he's at least several centuries old."

"That explains why he's so serious all the time." Camile returned her gaze to her father.

"He's seen a lot. Time has a way of hardening people, but don't be fooled. Sir Drayden's just as capable of having fun as anyone else."

Shifting her eyes to the knight, she saw something unusual. A smile lit up his face as he laughed amongst his company. It remained as he resumed the discussion. As his eyes held hers, his smile faded to a subtle smirk.

A thought weighed heavily on her mind as she returned her attention to her barely-touched salad, shuffling it with her fork.

"What about mom? Have you figured out a way to extend her life beyond the typical Coexistent life expectancy?" She asked, fearing she already knew the response.

"I wish I had a positive answer," Zephyr replied solemnly. Lifting his daughter's chin with his hand and cupping her shoulder, he continued, "Everyone has their time. I think it's fair to say she's at peace with the situation. Your mother and I discussed the matter before you were born and even then she vowed to cherish whatever time we were allotted. That's not to say she wasn't initially disappointed that she won't live as long as most of our people."

"That's Mom, for ya." Camile sighed, sinking into her seat. "Ever so graceful."

"But even more grateful," a woman chimed softly. Camile and her father raised their attention to see Kylie, standing beside their table.

Camile's mother tagged along during the trip to her quarters. As they walked, they exchanged occasional glances as though waiting for the other to speak first. Camile didn't want to broach the subject in the presence of the guards escorting them, so she remained silent. Finally, Kylie initiated the conversation.

"There's no need for you to be anxious about my death, sweetheart. I'm not. At least not anymore."

"I was hoping we wouldn't get into this now, but I guess avoiding the subject won't make it go away," Camile said. The very thought of her mother dying someday strung tension around her heart.

"I used to be afraid of the fact that my life on the physical plane would someday come to an end. One day, that all changed." Kylie wrapped an arm around her daughter. "It was the day I realized that with you here, I've eternalized a part of myself. Since then, with the help of your father, Tabitha and others, I learned not to fear death or worry about it. It's such a waste of time and an ironic one at that. By worrying about death—an inevitable occurrence for everyone at some point—people sometimes forget how to live."

Chapter 8

Breaking the Surface

Jeremy Logan was his full name. According to Camile's parents, he was handpicked by Sir Drayden, Tabitha's supervisor, to serve as her meditative instructor. Furthermore, he had honorably withdrawn from the military in his pursuit to explore the healing arts. In exchange for his apprenticeship with the shaman, he provided her with his protective services. Entering the Celestia, one of the compound's many tranquility rooms, Camile instantly adored its unusual atmosphere. Half the room was illuminated with the fiery brilliance of simulated sunlight, the rest was drenched in the cool hue of evening moonlight. The opposing sides of the chamber respectively held images of the large golden star and pale satellite. Not to be overshadowed was the ceiling above, which mimicked the sky, projecting a frozen transition between night and day.

Lowering her eyes, Camile saw Jeremy standing on the brighter side of the room. He was a vision in black and the sun's image appeared to be held in either a setting or rising position behind him. Camile hoped the simulated moon lighting her from behind was just as flattering. Jeremy's firm slender body, clad in a sleeveless t-shirt and matching sweatpants, was like that of a dancer. The outfit was much more relaxed than the stiff uniform he wore the previous evening. Nevertheless, his demeanor towards her remained rigid. His smile seemed forced and obligatory as he approached. Even still, it softened his outward disposition and enhanced his exotic features. After a quick greeting, Jeremy outlined the meditative techniques he planned to teach her. Camile struggled to prevent her eyes from roaming over his athletic physique and tried her best to be subtle about it. She found it strange that though she barely knew the man he was triggering such a response. A sudden spike in his voice prompted her to reel her thoughts out of salacious territory.

"Did you hear me?" he asked, raising an eyebrow.

"Oh. I—uh…Sorry, my mind was somewhere else for a minute."

"Well, keep a leash on it. This is important." He frowned. "In order to gain a higher level of mental and emotional balance, you must first find your center. Now, I'll be teaching you a few simple exercises that will help you do that."

Hmm. You can help me find my center anytime, Camile thought, smiling inwardly before shaking her thoughts to regain her focus. *Stop it,* she chided herself. It wasn't like her to think such brazen thoughts in the presence of company. Then again, she knew she hadn't exactly been herself for quite a while.

Jeremy always provided instruction with the utmost professionalism, but seemed aloof at times as their daily lessons progressed. In spite of this, Camile looked forward to their sessions and grew even more attracted to him as she witnessed his maturity, intellect and wisdom. She wondered if it was Jeremy she was drawn to, or the challenge of possibly pursuing something she couldn't have.

Why am I feeling this way? I've known the guy for less than a month.

As Camile made steady progress, Jeremy began folding exercises like tai chi and yoga into their routine. He consistently stressed the importance of her knowing her mind, body, their abilities and limitations.

Camile was intrigued and even a little envious of how well Jeremy controlled his body. His dexterity and balance were so flawless he could balance himself on one foot while standing on top of a basketball-sized sphere. Not only that, but he could also easily shift from one single-leg pose to the next without breaking his poise. Meanwhile, Camile was so concerned about perfecting her form that it had an adverse effect. Furthermore, she wondered if she looked funny when she was bent over and hoped she wouldn't experience flatulence. As a result of these distractions, her body often shook, wobbled and tumbled over as she attempted some of the more advanced poses. Jeremy took note of Camile's determination.

"I can see how badly you want to succeed, but it's important not to push yourself too hard. Each movement starts from within." He clapped her shoulder. "Remember, it's the mind that drives the body."

Jeremy doubled their sessions during their second week. According to him, Camile was beginning to show significant improvement as a result, something she found encouraging. They frequently practiced while facing each other in the Celestia—she, towards his sun, and he, towards her moon. Eventually, their movements became synchronous and they only seemed separated by gender and a distance of a few feet. However, the harmony was a deceptive contrast to their off-duty interaction.

*   *   *

The fresh scent of the lush grass and caress of the gentle wind was equally as therapeutic as the basic routine Camile was performing. She found that the organic scenery of the meadow worked wonders in easing her tension, which is why she often meditated there in her spare time. Ironically, it wasn't far from where she was nearly kidnapped just weeks earlier. Yet, she was unafraid since the compound was just a stone's throw behind her and security had been stepped up since the attack. Sitting upon a rock, she admired nature's majestic work. It was an unusually warm afternoon and a few harmless feathery clouds flirted around the sun, slowly drifting across the sky. She laughed as she watched Excelsior chasing a blackbird in the distance. The tiger looked confused as his prey flew away. Moments later, he hissed into the open air and bolted past Camile, presumably to return to his den.

"Aw, no one likes a sore loser, Excelsior." She chuckled.

Taking a swig of water from her canteen and returning it to her bag, she decided to take the tiger's lead and head back to the compound. As she stood, something stole her attention. Shielding her eyes from the sun, she saw the earth buckling just beyond where the tiger had been hunting. It expanded like a bubble, but the grassy surface didn't break. Instead, it rolled toward her as though the earth had swallowed something at least fifteen feet in length and about a third as wide. Several others appeared in rows and suddenly Camile found herself in the path of a strange terranean stampede.

Stunned, she wondered what kind of creatures were lurking beneath the lush foliage. They possessed a wicked speed that could outpace even the swiftest sprinters. Still, that didn't stop her from running as she hoped they wouldn't attack once they inevitably reached her. By now, the approaching guards were on high alert, urgently calling for her to run faster. Weapons drawn, they soon surrounded her, attempting to escort her to safety.

Looking back, Camile feared they may have made a one way trip. The mysterious heaps were now merely yards behind them. She could now see their large glowing eyes piercing the rustling blades of grass. Familiar rumbles filled the air and shook the ground, but it wasn't until she saw the glint of metallic teeth that she finally realized what they were up against. As the grass faded, it became clear that these were no living creatures.

"Quick! Step aside," she cried urgently. One guard attempted to protest, so she pulled him perpendicular to their current course until they met something solid, yet invisible. Somehow, she knew their best shot at survival was to lean flat against the surface, side by side. And so, she quickly ordered the others to do just that. Reluctance was written clearly on their faces, but time didn't allow the luxury of argument. Within a matter of seconds they were engulfed by a narrow tunnel, the wind from the passing vehicles roaring in their ears and tugging at their hair and clothes. Camile could now see the tiled wall her back was hugging for dear life. She didn't dare breathe too deeply out of fear she'd compromise the precious space that separated her from certain impact. This changed when she felt herself sink rapidly into the wall. Gasping, she reached out to brace herself only to grab the sleeve of one of the officers, who was also falling. Soon, the exhaust-tainted air grew still. The perilous passageway had vanished, leaving Camile and the officers lying face-up in the grass.

*   *   *

"What you witnessed today was a shift in the veil. I guess the best analogy I can use for it is this." Zephyr placed a glass on the dark wooden table. It contained a dual colored shimmering liquid—the top half a pale yellow-green, the bottom crystal clear.

He had arranged for the demonstration in the shaman's quarters shortly after learning what had occurred in the meadow. A thin smoky stream of invigorating citrus-scented incense swirled around the room, drawing random shapes as Kylie and Tabitha sat opposite from father and daughter.

"Oil and water," Camile's father continued. "Each component remains on its own side of the glass. But if it's agitated enough…" He placed a thin transparent stick into the glass and swirled the contents around, creating a foggy solution, "…the two liquids emulsify. Over time, if left undisturbed, it will return to the way it was before I stirred things up. The same applies to how the Transcendent and Coexistent Worlds are divided. The more the humans on either side of the veil destroy or wreak havoc on themselves or their environment, the more it degrades—much like the way pollution breaks down the Coexistent ozone layer. It creates a condition that allows the two worlds to merge by way of rifts. Each rift causes a destabilization in the veil, a self-healing barrier. But, depending on the size of the rift, it can take many years for a damaged patch to fully restore itself."

"There are smaller rifts that heal themselves much more quickly—sometimes within months, weeks, days or even minutes," Camile's mother added. "But those are very dangerous to travel through since they tend to be extremely unpredictable. Other rifts have been open for centuries and are strictly guarded. The penalty for trespassing is severe."

"The veil is complex. Try as we might to figure out how to accelerate the healing process of the rifts, it won't fix the underlying problem," Tabitha explained. "Before we can repair the rifts in the veil, we have to heal the growing gaps in humanity. We've all seen examples of the malignant rage spreading throughout the Coexistent World. It's destroying the human connection, but the Coexistents possess a powerful arsenal that they must use in order to win the *Invisible War*—patience, love and compassion. If they fail to look beyond their differences and unite to repair what has been damaged, they will be consumed by their hatred. Everyone has their own personal spiritual connection to the universe just as each star has its place in the heavens. Each life has value and definition and should not be taken for granted."

"Though we're trying to restore the balance in the *Invisible War* on a global scale, we must focus on key individuals—those strong enough to create a domino effect of positive actions and rational decisions," Zephyr explained. "You see, every person is a soldier, fighting his or her own battles within the war. Each choice they make results in an energy that goes out into the universe affecting everything it comes into contact with, whether or not that person, or anyone else, realizes it. And like most things in the universe it has a way of coming full circle, which is why it's so important that we sway as many people away from the darkness as possible."

"And I'm the person who has to sway these individuals," Camile acknowledged. "How am I supposed to do that without the full use of my powers?"

"You'll get them back eventually," Kylie said matter-of-factly. "Until then, you'll find that your intuition and unique spirit are equally, if not more powerful, than your special abilities."

*   *   *

Camile felt the cold furnace that once was her heart slowly being reignited and Jeremy unwittingly held the match. However, her growing affection was bittersweet and threatened to cause her more pain than pleasure since the feeling clearly wasn't mutual. Even so, the indifferent manner in which he had treated her just weeks earlier seemed to wane ever so slightly, or so she hoped. Soon, Jeremy began teaching her basic evasive techniques and blocking skills to prime her for her upcoming defense courses. Just when she had started getting acclimated to their lessons, Jeremy was occasionally substituted by Sir Drayden. Camile found it agonizingly difficult to complete her meditative exercises while alone in a room with someone she didn't trust. To her dismay, not only was she unable to avoid Sir Drayden, it seemed he was slowly becoming her shadow.

Compounding her discomfort was her continued taste of the bitter resentment the citizens felt towards Akalina. Most people regarded her with disdainful glances as they went about their daily business. In a strange contrast, witnessing the tightly-knit families throughout the town taunted Camile. They possessed something that had been robbed from her when she was very young. Though saddened by her past, she knew it was well overdue for her to put aside her childhood disappointments. For too long she had suppressed herself in what she now recognized as a childlike mentality, lamenting over things that couldn't be changed. Her current situation demanded focus, commitment and maturity—qualities she was more than willing to contribute since it meant saving lives in the long run. However, she knew it was only human to revisit the lingering echoes of one's youthful despair. She only hoped it wouldn't hinder her quest of moving on.

One day, while killing some time before a meeting with her parents, she caught the eye of a striking young man. His electric blue-green eyes sat below straight dark brows. Framing his face was a full head of thick, silky dark brown hair. Not a strand was out of place. Along with a charming smile on his full succulent lips, he wore a smartly decorated military uniform. Camile wouldn't have been surprised if the well-groomed stranger had the body of an underwear model to match his preternaturally handsome face. Had she seen him wearing civilian's clothes, she would've pegged him for the type of man to capitalize on his looks rather than potentially jeopardize them in battle.

Each day she traveled she would notice something different about her environment whether it was a new item for sale in the shops or an unusual flower in the park she frequented. However, the handsome stranger remained a near-constant, always smiling at her from a distance, never saying a word. A little over a week elapsed before he finally approached. Camile's guards greeted him, addressing him as Commander.

"With your combined training I'm confused why you were assigned the easy task of escorting this lovely woman." He smiled, shaking Camile's hand. "I'm Commander Wilder, but you can call me Brandon."

His was a warm, firm and surprisingly tender handshake. Camile was pleasantly struck by his statement. Her surprise didn't derive entirely from her newly rebuilt self-esteem, but the fact his impression of her was a stark contrast to that of the other citizens. As the handshake ended, she considered the possibility he was just being polite. Refusing to fall victim to the assumption that he knew who she was, Camile introduced herself.

"I've heard about you," the commander said in an almost singsong manner. His mildly husky voice conveyed a mixture of reassurance and mischief.

"That doesn't surprise me. Ordinarily, I'd say *I hope it's all good*, but considering the circumstances…" She let her sentence hang there.

"Well, all good is a bit boring if you ask me. Besides, I try not to judge people based on hearsay alone. Have you been given the full tour, aside from the wildflower garden you like so much?"

"How did you—?" Camile didn't finish the question once she realized he'd been following her routine.

"That didn't come out quite the way I intended." Brandon chuckled softly, showcasing his pearly whites and endearingly crooked incisors. "I just see you by yourself all the time and thought I'd actually speak to you since everyone else around here's been so reserved."

"Did you really volunteer for this, or did you draw the short straw?" Camile smirked playfully.

"I'm here of my own free will. Don't mind everyone else. They'll warm up eventually. In the meantime, will you give me a chance to prove I'm not a complete psycho?"

"Maybe some other time," Camile answered, before realizing he might take it the wrong way. "Not that I think you're crazy or anything." She palmed her forehead. "It's just that I have a few thing to take care of before my first defense class. I'll see you around, though. Nice meeting you, Brandon."

"Likewise, Wildflower." He smiled casually.

Wildflower. Months ago it would have been a name Camile would have disassociated with herself. Back then, she would have likened herself to a lowly weed or a bland fern that goes unnoticed in some shaded corner of a busy room. However, Brandon's comparison of her to a vibrant blossom seemed to suit her recent emergence of an adventurous nature she was unaware even existed until lately. Yet, even before then, time had brought the wisdom that a weed was an unruly flower that dared to thrive in the unlikeliest places.

Still, Camile was taken aback by how quickly he had fitted her with a nickname, but for some strange reason she liked it. Perhaps it was because he was the only one, aside from her parents, to compare her with something sweet in quite some time. It gave her a sense of normalcy and camaraderie. Although the commander had her attention, she would not give her trust so easily. She had been hurt by men, nearly as attractive as this stranger, who used their vanity to put a dent in her confidence. Since then, she made a point to be extra cautious, especially around men who looked as though they spent more time on their appearance than she spent on hers.

Chapter 9

Words of the Wise

The large gymnasium looked even more impressive than what she had read about. It was divided into two sections—the practice area and a rectangular area used for demonstrations and sparring matches. Crossing the hard dark brown floor, a subtle cinnamon-colored sunburst pattern on its dull surface, she noticed the sparring ring to her far left. It was equipped with a light gray mat—designed to absorb the impact of fallen contenders—recessed into the floor. It was surrounded by a black ascending fifteen-tiered platform, which served as spectator seating.

Camile halted her steps to admire the color transition of the main walls as they went from white to a muted blue by way of lighting. The two steel-gray entryways were inset with clear glass that promptly frosted upon closing, signaling the pending start of the session. Floor to ceiling lighting encased in etched black shades complimented the ambiance, as did the nine red vertical tapestries embroidered with Arvainan symbols, hanging from the walls. Camile had learned enough of the flowing language to decipher all of them, which read: *Hope, Strength, Dedication, Peace, Protection, Unity, Faith, Home* and *Life.* Then she noticed a tenth banner, a horizontal one, hanging at the front of the room above where the instructor was to stand. It appeared to be a phrase, but the only words Camile could decipher were *heart* and *mind.*

As she completed a pivotal turn her eyes fell upon the familiar face of a recent acquaintance—Brandon, the handsome commander she had met in the town square. He stood before her, his welcoming smile reflecting through his eyes.

"So, we meet again," he said. His hair was un-parted and tousled, a more casual style than he had worn it when she had first seen him. "Who says lightning doesn't strike twice?"

Camile was momentarily distracted by the difference in his attire. Rather than the polished uniform he wore earlier, he now sported a similar outfit to what Jeremy had worn during their sessions. Commander Wilder's dark t-shirt failed to conceal the chiseled muscles of his upper body.

"Um…You're not following me, are you?" Camile half joked, trying not to smile too broadly in her attempt to mask her mild discomfort.

"Well, I was here first. So, maybe you're the one who's following me. Don't worry, I won't take out a restraining order against you," he quipped, extending his hand. "I just came over to make sure you're finding everything okay."

"How can I not?" She chuckled, eyeing her security escorts by the door. "I'm not allowed to go anywhere alone. At least not for the time being."

Camile shook the commander's hand, once again enjoying his strong grip and the comforting smoothness of his skin. His lingering grasp surprised her, as did his unwavering eye contact. As she suspected, some of the female students were staring at them wearing brief expressions of envy. Her cheeks warmed slightly, not wanting to be the center of attention. Shifting her gaze to the horizontal crimson banner hanging in front of the room, Camile inquired about the inscription as she reclaimed her hand. In doing so, she was reminded how cool the room was.

"It says: *Follow your heart, but allow your mind to refine your path,*" Commander Wilder explained.

"Wise words. I like it," Camile acknowledged.

"It was written by a wise woman. Well, I guess that's enough small talk, class is about to begin."

Camile noticed the instructor still hadn't arrived. "Speaking of which, is the teacher always this late?"

"Give him a break. The class is only a few minutes behind schedule, but he's not late." The commander smiled. "Welcome to my class."

As he took his place in front of the room Camile wondered if she had said anything during their conversation that she should regret. Even in the midst of her thinking, her eyes scoped his sculpted back, taut buttocks and toned thighs shrouded in black relaxed-fitting pants.

Ouch!

When he announced her as the *new student,* Camile found herself more nervous than she had been on her first day of college. Her ears were met with a brief applause before the class began. After taking several moments to guide the students through a brief meditation and warm up, Commander Wilder divided the group into pairs. There were an uneven number of students, so Camile sat on the sidelines. She didn't mind since she had no desire to participate out of fear of getting injured. Nor did she want to be the focus of anyone's attention. Unfortunately for her, she wasn't about to get out of it so easily since the commander teamed up with her for the exercises.

Camile thought her initial nervousness was for naught until the commander said, "I understand you've been learning some basic evasive techniques from Jeremy. Let's see what you've got."

Without warning, he took a swing at her, but she quickly ducked out of the path of his initial blow. She successfully blocked his swift strikes and kicks, feeling the air of each missed hit. Panting, Camile attempted to land several jabs and punches, but Commander Wilder was spry, blocking every one as he continued his pursuit. Camile knew she wasn't in any real danger, but she was suddenly filled with alarm as she tried to run away, tripping in the process. She landed face-down on her hands and could feel him closing in from behind. Before she could calculate her next move, she felt him grab hold of her left ankle. Camile braced herself on her hands, using her instructor's grasp for support as she threw her right leg back, kicking him hard in the shoulder. Losing his grip, he stumbled backward. Upon seeing the result of her overreaction, Camile voiced her regret.

She rose to her feet. Commander Wilder did the same.

"Don't apologize. That was very impressive. Let's see what else you got." He breathed, his eyes aglow with excitement as he lunged for her again.

Once again Camile found herself attempting to put distance between them, but it seemed like they were being drawn together by a magnetic force. She finally managed to push him away before extending her leg to kick his side. She was taken by surprise when the commander caught it, sliding it around his hip as he pulled her body close to his. Camile was forced to grab hold of his muscular shoulders as she tried to regain her balance. Her face grew warm as they remained locked in a tango-like pose for a few seconds. A roguish expression crossed his face as he maintained eye contact, apparently savoring his victorious maneuver. Disarmed with distraction, Camile failed to think of any counter moves as he leaned his face closer.

"Gotcha," he whispered before maneuvering himself to pull her standing leg from beneath her with one of his own.

She landed on her back with the commander kneeling over her.

"Not bad, but you can do better. And you will, with my help," he said, helping her to her feet.

*   *   *

The gentle waves of the lake rippled tranquilly beneath the crescent moon. As the wind slipped through tree branches, they, too, joined the calm dance. Before long, nature's subtle performance concluded. The wind retreated and the water became as still as a sheet of ice, reflecting the deep sky and wispy clouds. Still, the sweet scent of the fresh grass invaded Camile's nostrils. Inhaling deeply, she admired the scene, thinking to herself how romantic it was. She noticed a few couples strolling along the lakeside, taking advantage of the picturesque view and mild weather. Camile nearly got lost in the moment and found her head leaning towards Jeremy's shoulder, but immediately straightened her posture. Reeling her thoughts back to reality, she reminded herself that she wasn't on a romantic excursion. Nor was she sitting beside someone who shared mutual feelings of admiration.

As the two awaited Tabitha's arrival, Camile decided to break the awkward silence between them. She did this by bringing up the subject of her defense training. Jeremy praised Commander Wilder's skills, informing Camile that he was one of the best combat instructors in Arvaina. The commander had been temporarily placed on modified military duty so that he could teach her, and select others, the art of physical self-defense. Still, whenever he wasn't teaching, the commander assisted the council in formulating strategies to suppress the growing rebellion. Jeremy also mentioned that at one time he was also eligible to teach the class, and that he had declined since it didn't appeal to him.

"So, you're a lover, not a fighter," Camile replied, instantly regretting it.

Ugh! Did I just say that? That's as corny as it gets.

"It has nothing to do with love, but everything to do with avoiding conflict," Jeremy stoically responded.

Though admiring his pursuit of peace, Camile disagreed with his statement. She knew conflict sometimes led to the awareness of love's presence. She had seen cases where conflict had been unavoidable in order to fight for its preservation. As she internally debated his comment, she concluded that sometimes conflict had everything to do with love. This led her to wonder if Jeremy even knew what it was or what it really meant. Then again, she was still searching for the answers herself. In that moment, she hoped they could get past the frostiness of their relationship so they could possibly discover it together some day. Camile knew it wouldn't be easy. Jeremy's temperament was restrictive and overly protective, classic symptoms of someone who had suffered heartache, a violation of trust, or

70

both. It was something she understood all too well. Returning her attention to the lake, she noticed a small light in the distance. It was slowly but steadily approaching.

"I think I see the boat," she stated.

"What boat? I never said she'd be on a boat," Jeremy replied.

Confused, Camile took a second glance and realized the object was definitely not a vessel of any kind. As the diminishing light grew nearer, a backlit figure appeared to be walking across the smooth surface of the lake. Camile's jaw slackened, releasing a gasp of amazement as she saw the water ripple gently beneath the person's feet.

"There she is." Jeremy smiled, bringing himself to stand.

"She's walking on water? I must be seeing things," Camile said in a near whisper, rising to her feet.

"Actually, you're only seeing *some* things. That's why to you, it seems like she's walking on water."

"What do you mean?"

"You only see part of what's happening. You don't see beyond the veil. For awhile, I couldn't either. Now, I can see more than I could ever imagine. Sometimes, it's confusing—being able to see life this way. It makes it hard to tell what's in this world and what isn't," Jeremy explained, never removing his attention from the approaching female elder.

For a brief moment, Camile saw bitterness in his eyes which seemed to reflect a remnant of his troubled past, but it quickly faded. In that short instance of seeing his guard come down, she realized her attraction towards him was beginning to deepen beyond curious intrigue and physical infatuation. She had gotten a brief glimpse of his heart and liked what she saw.

Jeremy lagged behind Camile and the shaman as they returned to the compound. Looking over her shoulder, Camile gave him a compassionate smile as they ascended the short staircase at one of Caldaq's westside entrances. She caught his attention, but not in the way she had hoped. She tripped on a step and fell onto her hands and knees. Feeling the heat of embarrassment, she quickly stood up and brushed herself off all the while internally cursing her large feet. The shaman added to Camile's humiliation by drawing further attention to her clumsiness, asking if she was alright. Downplaying the mishap, Camile laughed it off as best she could.

Without further incident they reached Tabitha's quarters, where Camile's progress was assessed shortly thereafter. For the most part, the shaman seemed pleased, but noted distraction as one of her primary weaknesses. She used Camile's recent stumble to help illustrate this fact. Tabitha then broached a topic Camile had been anxious to learn more about—the reversal of her suicide.

"Since no one in the Coexistent World knew of your death, we were able to return your spirit to the critical point of your fateful decision in order to convince you to change your mind," she explained. "That was the only thing that could've saved you,"

"But couldn't Sir Drayden—?"

"My child, everyone has their limits, even my boss. But I must admit that if it wasn't for him, you wouldn't have gotten your second chance."

"He probably regrets his decision. He's doesn't seem very fond of me."

"I wouldn't say that. Yes, Sir Drayden can be stubborn and downright abrasive, but he means well." Tabitha sighed. "It's taken me years to finally realize that. It's hard to see since he has a tendency to run hot and cold."

"I get your point, but I can't help but take his abruptness personally sometimes."

"Well, Akalina's part of you now and—" The shaman's sinking facial expression indicated that she hadn't intended to make the statement aloud.

"Right." Camile exhaled deeply. "What'd she do to him?"

"I'm not sure if it's my place to tell you this." Tabitha's lips nearly vanished in her tight frown. Craning her head, she briefly peered beyond the curtains to ensure their privacy. Resuming eye contact, she whispered, "She took something from him and I'm afraid he's still not over it."

"What did she steal?"

Tabitha opened her mouth to answer, but appeared to think better of it. An uneasy smile crossed her burnt sienna colored features, slightly emphasizing the creases around her face.

"Camile, there are some places you just shouldn't dig," she said, gently patting Camile's hand. Squeezing it firmly, she added, "Trust me, it's for your own good. Forget I ever said anything, okay?"

Camile nodded, thinking, *'It's for your own good.' I've heard that before!*

The conversation was severed by Sir Drayden's sudden arrival, flooding the room with an awkward silence.

"Your counselor and I have something to discuss," he announced starkly, his piercing eyes locked on the shaman. "If you'll excuse us a moment."

With a nod, Camile left for the corridor, all the while hoping her inquisitiveness hadn't caused any problems. For nearly a half-hour she slowly paced a small section of the hall. She locked eyes with Jeremy a few times, though no words were exchanged. Sir Drayden emerged from the room and with a subtle cock of his head, gestured for her to resume her session with the shaman. Upon doing so, Camile noticed something different about Tabitha's eyes. They were glassy and her attitude seemed somewhat diminished.

"Did I get you in trouble? With Sir Drayden, I mean," Camile inquired.

"Oh." Tabitha sighed. "When it comes to my boss, we're all in trouble."

Camile could tell by the sudden shift in Tabitha's demeanor that she didn't want to revisit the subject. She believed Sir Drayden had likely caught wind of the conversation and forbade her from discussing the subject any further. Tabitha ended their session much earlier than usual, reinforcing Camile's assumption.

Chapter 10

The Thirst

Interested in whether or not additional details were uncovered regarding the recent intrusion at Caldaq, Camile arranged to speak with her father. Due to his hectic work schedule, she had to settle for a brief meeting with him on one of the many scenic overlooks located throughout the mountain. This particular one provided a generous view of the thriving city of Deltine. Standing just a few feet away from her was a serious looking sentinel staring intently at the cityscape. Camile wondered if he was on break or was simply enjoying the marvelous view on the council's time. It wasn't until he paced from one side of the overlook to the other that she noticed the large cannon mounted into the floor.

"A sentry post?" she inquired once her father joined her. "I thought Arvaina was peaceful."

"It is, for the most part, but we must take into account that not everyone shares our endeavor for living peacefully. For that, we must be ready to act accordingly," Zephyr explained. "Now, to answer your question about the intruders, we haven't been able to extract any information from them. It looks doubtful we ever will. Their minds were chemically altered in such a way that they were unable to store any new memories. In every case, the last thing they remember was going to sleep in the Coexistent World. None of them have any recollection of the attack on Caldaq."

"But someone had to order them to try and kidnap me. How is it they remembered to do that, but nothing else?"

"Very observant," Zephyr praised. "We believe one of the intruders served as the leader for the group. We think, perhaps, that person was the only one sent into the mission with full memory and awareness. Out of all the intruders who were recovered at the scene only one of them had an undamaged brain. We believe he was the leader."

"Let me guess, he's not talking, right?"

"No, he's not. Then again, being dead impairs a person's verbal skills." Zephyr frowned. "The offender died from a time-released poison he took prior to the attack. One way or the other he was prepared to die during his mission, no matter what the outcome."

"Sir, there's something I need to tell you about that," an urgent voice grabbed their attention. It was Prescott, the lead officer who had been investigating the intruders.

Zephyr nodded in acknowledgement, prompting the officer to proceed.

"I'm sorry to interrupt, sir. Further examination of the intruders has led us to the discovery of new evidence pertaining to the drug that was used in their deaths." He paused to swallow. "It was Utopium."

"Utopium?" Zephyr briefly regarded his daughter. Returning his attention to Prescott, he said, "There must be a mistake. Utopium is restricted for use by authorized medical personnel only. Has any facility reported missing or stolen supplies within the past few months?"

"No, sir. But I don't believe the Utopium used came from any of Deltine's authorized facilities. I already have someone looking into the national medical database to check for any inconsistencies. There was an unusual anomaly in the doses taken by the intruders. Unfortunately for them, they ingested a tainted batch. Instead of experiencing the euphoric rush of the drug shutting down their brain, I believe they witnessed something other than their personal heaven. By the looks on their faces, they experienced the opposite."

A grave expression crossed Zephyr's face as he dismissed the officer. After a few moments he explained that Utopium was a substance used to treat severe cases of depression not treatable by meditation and counseling alone. The substance stimulates the pleasure center of the brain. When overdosed, the user enters a coma-like state and eventually the body and mind disconnect completely, resulting in death. It was considered a peaceful way to die, which is why it was the preferred method of execution in Arvaina. Camile caught a chill upon thinking she, at one time, had faced such a fate.

"The use of Utopium is illegal outside of a medical setting," Zephyr continued. "Still, there are people who defiantly attempt to produce, use and transport it, often resulting in the distribution of defective batches which have the opposite effect, propelling the user into an endless nightmare. This drug is unofficially named Delirium."

The arrival of Sir Drayden caused a second interruption in their conversation. He cast a knowing glance at Camile's father, who excused himself to join the silver-haired elder. The two men said nothing as they looked at one another. Yet, the subtle shifts in their facial expressions indicated that they were communicating on a level beyond spoken language. Neither party seemed particularly happy as both appeared concerned by the time the silent conversation was over. Zephyr rejoined Camile as the knight walked away.

"What was that all about?" she inquired.

"If he wanted you to know, he would have spoken to me aloud."

Camile found her father's response unnerving and wondered if the conversation had been about her.

Although Camile knew of the Transcendents' ability to communicate telepathically, it was the first time she had ever witnessed the practice. She became increasingly aware of how often they were doing it in her presence and it made her uncomfortable. She eventually fell victim to the paranoia of thinking people were telepathically talking about her all the time. She was able to tame her egocentric thinking through meditation. Yet, there was an inherent loneliness in the fact that the other citizens were connected and that she was out of the loop. Knowing nothing could be done about it, she tried to ignore it as best she could, but it would prove difficult in the coming weeks.

*   *   *

Camile's father arranged for her to visit one of the world's largest energy farms, located in Terriguana, a northwestern state in Arvaina. He thought it would be a good idea for her to learn about the Transcendent dimension's energy sources. The vast allotment of land stretched out for many miles with gargantuan trees and lush greenery that receded into rugged desert terrain far in the distance. Hordes of massive creatures, many of them towering above seventy feet in height, roamed the land. Razor sharp teeth and curved talons protruded from wrinkled leathery hides in shades of green, gray and brown. Camile had seen these creatures upon her arrival to the Transcendent World during the semi-annual migration.

The purpose of the migration was to re-settle the land and allow time for crops to recuperate in the creatures' semi-annual habitats. In addition, the event provides the wildlife with abundant exercise and a change of scenery. Specific groups of Transcendent citizens split their time between urban and rural environments to assist in the migrations.

The sauruses traveled in flawless synchronization in accordance to their respective species. Herding each of the groups was a team of no less than ten farmers. One farmer of each squad served as the lead conductor. Camile's main concern about safety was answered shortly after the director of the facility introduced himself to the visitors, which mainly consisted of young students.

Though the animals appeared to roam freely, there were devices known as *invisible fences* erected throughout the farm. This security measure was established not only to protect the staff, but certain species of animals from each other. It was explained that the barriers were part of a computerized system designed to condition the creatures into remaining within their spacious, designated boundaries. If an animal were to get too close to the invisible border, they would receive an electric shock. According to the director, this was facilitated through bio-transmitters, which had been implanted in the creatures. An uneasy feeling washed over Camile as she realized how similar the device seemed to what Transcendent humans were given.

The director prided himself and his diligent employees with the fact that the sprawling ranch had been in operation for nearly forty years without a single incident. It was also mentioned that the animals were generally well behaved and that very few dared attempt to get close to the invisible border.

"Has the system ever gone down?" a young girl inquired.

"Not once. Knock on wood." The director beamed, tapping his knuckles against his forehead.

"What happens if it does?" Camile asked. An awkward pause followed as all eyes darted in her direction.

"If it does," the director finally answered, "which is highly unlikely, we have a series of backup systems and very tight emergency protocols in place to restore the primary system."

He segued into an explanation of how the animals were very well cared for and respected as they are farmed for energy.

"Like many cities, the farm is loaded with nanotechnology. Each footstep these sauruses take produces energy, which is then converted to electricity." The director held up an object the size of a playing card. "That electricity is then transferred into power cells such as this and stored so we can transport them to businesses and facilities throughout the Transcendent World. Each power cell stores enough electricity to power over fourteen thousand homes for approximately 1.8 years. This is one of our older technologies and is used as a supplement to the thermonuclear, solar, wind and hydropower energy produced throughout our dimension today."

The director introduced Adrian, a barrel-shaped man with sticklike arms, one of which held a shovel.

"Hello," he greeted. "One of our rovers was sent in to collect a stool sample from number one eighty-seven, a saurus we believe to be pregnant. Unfortunately, it didn't make the trip back as planned. If you look carefully, you can see it tipped over behind that boulder." Adrian pointed to a section of the pen very close to where a marker indicated the invisible fence. Sure enough, Camile saw a small wheeled robotic machine on its side, propped against the large rock. The copious fecal sample had spilled out of the collection bucket atop the rover.

"Since it's well within the safe zone, I'll be retrieving it manually," Adrian explained. "Then my colleagues and I will finally be able to monitor the efficiency of her digestive system."

And I thought I had some shitty jobs in my day, Camile thought, amusedly.

Without further delay, Adrian approached the pen. He looked tiny compared to the massive creatures roaming within. He slowly approached the device while keeping a close eye on the seemingly oblivious thick-skinned giants. Number one eighty-seven was busy feasting on a large slab of raw meat, but took a moment to cast a curious glance at the worker before returning to her meal. The creature's yellow-orange eyes were like miniature suns ablaze behind leathery lids. Finally, Adrian reached the overturned rover and flipped it right-side up before using his shovel to scoop the large pile of ejected contents back into the collection bucket. Camile overheard two people speaking, but when she looked around she couldn't see anyone's lips moving in sync with the words. That's when she realized the voices were coming from inside her head, but they were male.

Is that her? asked the first voice.

Yeah, that's her, alright. Some nerve of them sending her here, the second answered.

They should at least put her on a leash. Better yet, they should lock her in with the other animals, the first voice contemptuously replied.

Camile looked at the two guards traveling with her, but their facial expressions didn't match the snide tone of the comments. Making a quick visual surveillance, Camile's gaze locked on two young men, smirking suspiciously while avoiding eye contact. It was enough to irritate her, but she figured they were entitled to their opinions no matter how much she resented them.

A thunderous roar ripped through the air accompanied by frantic screams. Startled, Camile returned her attention to the large pen and saw one of the sauruses chomping down on Adrian's thigh, shaking him like a ragdoll. He unsheathed a retractable baton and proceeded to strike the mad beast, but it only seemed to make matters worse. A lanky dark-haired man leapt to action and attempted to coax the creature away. Clad in a black suit and charcoal vest that contrasted against his pasty white skin, he seemed better dressed for a business meeting than a day at the farm.

"Stop fighting him and relax. You're only agitating him even further," he exclaimed in an accent Camile couldn't immediately recognize.

"Transcendent or not, it's kinda hard to stay calm when something's about to chew off your nut sack. I'm just sayin'…" said a mocha-skinned man with dreadlocks.

"Joval, you're not helping," the thin man chided.

Just as Adrian followed the well-dressed man's advice, the saurus released him and retreated to a corner in its pen. However, it seemed far from calm as it huffed through its nostrils, repeatedly sliding a foot on the ground. It appeared to be gearing up for another round as Adrian was pulled away to safety, leaving a trail of blood on the ground like a paint stroke on a canvas. His left leg was badly mauled and nearly severed at mid-thigh. Staff members promptly began directing visitors away from the scene of the accident, all the while assuring everyone that Adrian would be alright.

Everyone moved along in a bizarrely calm and orderly fashion even though the animal still appeared agitated. Its eyes locked with Camile's as it bolted forward, hitting the invisible fence. Jerking violently, it stalled before breaking through and charging in her direction. The limping beast traveled fairly quickly in spite of the damage the fence had caused. It wasn't until Camile noticed the fleeing visitors that she followed suit, becoming separated from her guards in the process.

She ran alongside the other visitors as fast as her feet could take her, but her speed was outmatched by the wild saurus rapidly closing in. The ground trembled violently beneath her as the saurus grew nearer, its raspy breath growing louder. A collective gasp rippled through the air as most of the citizens halted their exodus. Camile didn't dare slow her pace as she looked over her shoulder. The creature was on the heels of a woman lagging a few feet behind her. Before she could witness the inevitable carnage with her eyes, she felt something grip her wrist like a vice as she was pulled away.

An unearthly shriek filled the air as Camile tumbled to the ground. It was immediately followed by the sickening cacophony of cracking bone and squishing flesh. Ignoring her mind's plea not to witness the aftermath, Camile turned around. She was stunned to see that in the short time that had transpired, she had somehow traveled over a thousand miles from *Terriguana*. She knew this since she was now approximately fifty miles away from Caldaq. Camile estimated her distance by assessing the mountain's appearance. The majestic structure now seemed like a boulder on the horizon.

Her view was eclipsed by a woman standing over her, offering a hand to help her up. Though slightly disoriented due to the hectic activity, Camile came to realize that she had somehow passed through a rift. Upon accepting the stranger's assistance Camile cringed at the clamminess of her palms. The comely woman introduced herself as Makeda. Her smile flaunted her high cheekbones, drenched in skin as rich and smooth as dark chocolate. Its surreal dewy texture glowed in the sunlight.

"You lucky that thing didn't kill you, girl," Makeda said. Hers was a rich voice with a mild accent similar to a southern drawl. "What brings you way out here? Not many folks come 'round here no more."

As Camile explained the recent chain of events, the woman stared into her eyes, as though entranced.

"Something wrong?" Camile asked, concerned the woman may have been another one of Akalina's victims.

"Not a thing. My mind just wandered off for a minute. Say, you the defense minister's daughter, ain't you?"

Camile considered the possibility that her father had garnered enemies through his career, but decided Makeda seemed harmless enough. Nodding, she said, "Yeah. Do you know him?"

"Our paths crossed a few times, but that was many years ago. Wouldn't say I know him, though." Makeda smiled. Glancing around the area with apparent apprehension, she added, "We better get moving. That thing might come through and I ain't fixin' to stick around to become its supper. My place ain't far from here. You can take a load off there until your folks find you."

After a fifteen-minute hike they came to a small cabin nestled in the outskirts of dense woods. Camile coughed as she was hit with an unexpected stench of vinegar immediately upon entering. An apologetic Makeda was a cordial hostess and motioned her to sit in the cozy living room. Once again, Camile found herself fascinated by the woman's skin. It almost seemed as though Makeda had no pores at all and appeared bluish in the soft lighting. Her dark waist-length plaits complimented her face and emphasized her hourglass figure. Makeda prepared a tray of assorted meats, crackers and cheeses, but the last thing Camile wanted was to eat anything.

"It looks good, but I'll have to take a rain check," she declined politely. "I really should be heading back to Caldaq. If you could give me directions, I'll—"

"Oh, don't be ridiculous, girl. You need sustenance! And don't tell me you're watching your weight either. Real men like it when a woman has a little something for them to hold onto, yeah? Gotta keep yourself nice and ripe," she insisted with a wink and a ridiculously white smile.

As Makeda poured beverages, Camile noticed vertical scars along the backs of her arms. It looked as though someone had tried to split them open from her shoulders to her elbows. She couldn't stop her mouth from falling agape at the sight. The woman took notice and quickly threw on a shawl that had been draped over one of the chairs.

"Scars from my homeland. Some people find them hard to look at," she explained abashedly, before gulping her drink. It had a lovely shade of pale rose. "Well, drink up."

"No, thanks. I'm not thirsty," Camile replied, her voice nasal since she was trying to avoid breathing through her nose.

Again, Makeda apologized about the smell, explaining it was caused by a clumsy accident while she was catering marinated meat for a large gathering to be held later that evening.

"I've been trying to get rid of it all afternoon." She sighed, gesturing toward her cleaning supplies beside the kitchen entrance. "Guess I failed miserably." The woman laughed, revealing a sizeable lump on her tongue.

Camile cracked a strained smile, trying her best not to stare at the deformity. On the contrary, she thought the place smelled as though it had been washed with the pungent marinade.

Makeda laughed. "You ain't gotta lie. Don't worry, my feelings don't hurt easy."

Feeling she had fulfilled any and all obligation of kindness, Camile reiterated her desire to return home.

"I don't mean to be rude, but I really need to contact my parents. They're probably wondering what happened to me."

"I doubt it." Makeda tapped the base of her own unadorned neck with her index finger. "They'll track your medallion and will find you before you know it. In the meantime, at least have a little sip and tell me if it's too sweet. I have a heavy hand with the sugar sometimes. At least that's what my husband says."

The woman handed her the glass containing the pink concoction. Raising it to her nose, Camile took a cautious whiff. A fresh, fruity aroma flirted with her senses, inciting her thirst and inducing mouthwatering anticipation. She lowered the frosty glass to take a sip. Before it touched her lips, it flew violently from her grasp. Makeda shrieked as she was covered in a slimy dark maroon substance, a few drops of which splattered onto Camile's hand. The woman wiped the syrupy mess from her scowl etched face.

Camile raised her hand to analyze the strange substance. Once again, she was struck by the intense smell of vinegar, prompting her to gag. It was clearly different than the beverage she'd intended to drink and was about as appetizing as regurgitated bile. Camile tried to make sense of how the drink suddenly changed in color, smell and consistency. She was also baffled as to how it managed to soar out of her hand. Camile received a partial answer when she glanced over her left shoulder and saw the shaman standing in the doorway, her open palm extended in front of her.

"Makeda, what do you think you're doing?" the shaman demanded sternly, an incensed expression etched deeply on her face.

Makeda licked her fingers with her pasty tongue.

"Hi, Tabby. Long time no see. I was just offering the girl a drink," Makeda finally replied with a sly smile. "I guess I must've poured her something from the wrong bottle."

Grimacing, Camile alternated her gaze between Makeda and the shaman.

"You tried to poison me?" she asked crossly, taking a step forward, but Tabitha tightly seized her arm. Smirking, Makeda shrugged her shoulders. The nonchalant action prompted Tabitha to approach the unaffected woman, whose body mysteriously levitated off the polished wooden floor. The shaman waved her hand, sending her into a wall. Makeda crashed down to the floor face-down in a rumpled heap. Slowly, she raised her head, peeking through the braids that had spilled over her face like a mop. She laughed as Tabitha approached with a vial filled with white powder. She taunted the shaman, daring her to kill her.

"Go on. Quench me. What you waitin' for?" She slowly sat on her heels while flipping the hair away from her face, revealing a toothy smile over which she ran her tongue.

Tabitha relented at the last minute, returning the small bottle to her pocket.

"Change of heart, Tabby?" Makeda smirked. "I guess you know what would happen if you killed me right now."

"The same thing that would've happened if Camile drank that filth you gave her. Because of that, your immunity is about to expire." Tabitha frowned, gazing down into the woman's dark eyes for a long moment. It was the first time Camile had seen the shaman's normally placid face filled with such burning contempt.

Tabitha nudged Camile out of the cabin, all the while, keeping her icy gaze trained on a smirking Makeda, still kneeling on the floor. As Camile and her counselor made a hasty exit, Makeda's cackle followed them, carrying the words: *Give my regards to the silver hawk.*

"What'd she want to kill me for?" Camile asked as they walked away from the cabin.

"She didn't want to kill you. Quite the contrary, she wanted to adopt you." Tabitha halted her steps, facing her charge head-on. "She's a devourer, Camile."

"Come again?"

"A devourer. In the Coexistent World she would most likely be called a vampire or a cannibal."

"Are you serious?"

"Very. Devourers can be vile creatures. They proved that during the Dark Days of Bloodlust. Makeda was just about to violate one of the most important conditions of the treaty. She was trying to get you to drink her blood so she could convert you. Camile, what did you think was in that glass, fruit punch? What on earth were you thinking when you tried to drink it?" Tabitha scolded.

"Hey, it didn't look or smell *anything* like that at first," Camile explained. "I thought it was pink lemonade or something. Didn't you make it change to blood when you made it fly out my hand?"

"I did nothing more than push it away from you before it was too late. It never looked like pink lemonade or pink anything for that matter. Camile, there was clearly blood in that glass and you nearly drank it...willingly, I might add."

Camile came to the chilling realization that her vision and judgment had been severely impaired. She knew she needed to be extra cautious to prevent similar incidents from happening in the future. Her life depended on it.

*   *   *

Once they reached the main courtyard of Coronis Peak, Tabitha left Camile with her parents and Sir Drayden. They awaited her at a table set with a light lunch, but after her recent experience Camile didn't have much of an appetite. After allowing her to settle, the trio explained that the devourers' were conductors of the Dark Days of Bloodlust, an era when both dimensions suffered centuries of bloodshed at the hands of the devourers. The situation had spawned decay to such a degree that it threatened to drive humanity into extinction. Eventually, Arvaina formed an alliance with the most affected regions and developed Quenching Powder, a devastating weapon which significantly leveled the playing field between the humans and the devourers. Though effective in killing the devourers, the substance is toxic to humans if exposed to prolonged contact. Knowing the devourers were once human, a truce was declared and leaders of both parties signed a treaty that protected the residents of both worlds from being hunted and slaughtered like cattle.

"In exchange for peace, we promised to help them find a way to reverse their condition," Sir Drayden continued. "However, our terms demanded that they go on a restricted diet since humans were no longer on the menu. So, we rationed our livestock in order to satisfy their lust for flesh and blood."

"Of course they complained the substitute wasn't nearly as satisfying as humans," Kylie added, "One of the other conditions of the treaty is that they are not allowed to reproduce or to induct any new members into their family. I'm disappointed that Makeda tried to violate that clause."

"Evidently our animal sacrifices are no longer enough to appease the devourers," Zephyr remarked.

"I agree. I think it's time for us to sever their food supply," Kylie suggested.

"Bad idea." The knight shook his head. "If we do that, they'll simply get their meals elsewhere—in the form of our citizens, no doubt."

"Sir Drayden's right," Camile's father agreed. "We should uphold our end of the treaty until we have tangible evidence the devourers are no longer honoring the agreement. We don't want to hastily initiate an all out war based on the act of a delusional individual. Hopefully, the rest of the devourers will continue to honor the agreement. If not, drastic action will be taken. We've made it abundantly clear that there would be a hefty price for noncompliance. For their sake, I hope they remember that."

Camile was curious about the fact she had seen the female devourer walking in broad daylight.

"Aren't they supposed to die when the sun hits them?" she asked.

"Not all devourers are photosensitive to such an extreme," her father replied. "Some carry a mutation, allowing them to walk in daylight. That doesn't stop them from disarming people by perpetuating the widespread belief that they can only come out at night."

By the time the meeting was dismissed Camile's mind was spinning. Sir Drayden promptly exited, leaving her with her parents. Based on their expressions, she knew they were about to break some significant news.

"Camile, there will be a meeting tonight to discuss the incident at the farm. I think it's important that you attend, but I must warn you, members of the general public will be there too," Zephyr announced.

"This should be interesting." Camile sighed, sinking deeper into her chair.

"Don't be discouraged. They have every right to be upset with Akalina, but they have to get to know who you are. You shouldn't have to live in the shadow of what was done prior to your arrival here. I know what happened today doesn't exactly help matters, but we'll get through it together. It won't be easy or immediate, but I think tonight will present the beginning of a quest for mutual understanding between you and the citizens."

"In order for me to understand them I have to know what Akalina did to them."

"That's exactly what we hope will happen tonight; for the citizens to explain their side of things. By the same token, we also hope you'll get to explain yours," Kylie said.

"It's gonna be a long night, isn't it?" Camile rose to her feet and rotated her head to relax her neck.

"Don't worry," her mother smiled softly. "It'll be fine."

"How can you be sure about that? They already wanted to kill me once and that was when I was just a kid."

"Things are different now," Zephyr said solemnly, "You've been given a chance to prove them wrong."

"No pressure," Camile muttered to herself.

Reaching for her jacket, she flinched when she saw a splash of deep maroon on her right hand. Repulsed, she urgently wiped it on her pant leg.

"You okay?" her mother asked.

"Yeah. I don't think it's my blood. It's probably from the glass that devourer gave me," Camile answered.

"What blood?" Her father frowned.

Camile looked down at her pants then her hands and was bemused to see that they were clean. Once again the focus of concerned stares, she tried her best to laugh it off.

"Guess I'm still a little freaked about the whole devourer thing. I'll be fine." She chuckled in an attempt to mask her somber demeanor. She managed to erect a poised facade, but beneath the surface she feared that her encounter with the devourer had instilled vampiric cravings in her.

Chapter 11

Sins of the Past

A hush swept the room as Magistrate Judge Skye Sui entered. Though apparently average in height, her confident demeanor added to her stature. Her porcelain skin was a radiant contrast against her long pin-straight hair, worn parted to one side and pulled back into a low ponytail. Like a black silky curtain, a side-swept bang draped just above her brow and nestled behind her right ear. The style emphasized her angled almond-shaped eyes, set beneath delicately arched eyebrows.

Prior to the meeting, Camile had learned from her parents that Magistrate Sui was a highly respected official who has held her position for nearly two decades. She co-authored legislative documents that have aided the council in pressing forward in their endeavors to pursue peaceful dimensional co-habitation. These governmental measures also paved the way for significant advancements within the Transcendent security programs—including the tracking, monitoring and recruiting of Coexistent humans for certain key roles in the *Invisible War*—the fight to protect the *Age of Ascension*. Camile also learned about the magistrate's widely known unwavering loyalty, which became evident to the council after the discovery of an underground rebellion—of which her own husband had been a member. Taking his actions as a direct insult to everything she stood for, she personally brought his treachery to the council's attention. As a result, he was court-martialed and sentenced to serve time in a prison known as Agora.

Magistrate Sui took to the bench like an eagle landing at its well-established post. Taking her seat, and a moment to glance at the standing attendees, she granted them permission to sit. Camile knew the hour of reckoning was at hand, but took relief in the fact that although the citizens appeared visibly upset, none were wielding weapons. That fact was probably due to the security checkpoint at the court entrance.

One by one the citizens recounted their tales of horror, taking Camile on a tour of their hellish experiences with Akalina. Some stories highlighted the mischievous nature prevalent in most average children, but others detailed a more sinister series of events. The worst of Akalina's misdeeds led to serious accidents that resulted in terrible injuries and, in some cases, deaths of Transcendent residents. However, she was always a third-party participant in the crimes and never found to be directly responsible for the deaths. Therefore, she avoided the most severe punishments, much to the chagrin of the community.

"It's happening again," one resident exclaimed. "That animal went berserk and nearly killed my sister because of her. How many more people have to suffer before you realize she's a walking plague?"

"Don't they usually bring torches and pitchforks to meetings like this, or is that a little too old-school for them?" Camile muttered under her breath, forgetting that some of the citizens shared her gift of sensitive hearing.

"You see? She still has the same blatant lack of respect," another man pointed out.

"Camile, I know this isn't easy, but your sarcasm isn't helping," Kylie whispered.

Zephyr addressed the crowd, "I understand why you're all upset, but there's no way to prove Camile caused the incident at the farm today. The events that took place today appear to be an unlucky coincidence."

"Coincidence my ass," an older man vehemently exclaimed.

"Nathan, you'll mind your manners when addressing the council," Magistrate Sui ordered sternly. "You know what happens to people who let their emotions overrule their better judgment." She shot him a knowing glance, magnifying the impact of her statement.

"I apologize, Your Honor." Nathan's voice softened, but his wrinkled face remained etched with displeasure as he briefly lowered his clouded gaze. "But surely you must notice that since she has returned, so has the emotional instability of our people. The last time this happened our world came to the brink of war for the first time in over sixty years."

It was explained that several people—after having contact with young Camile—became hostile and traveled throughout the world sparking social unrest. Conflicts quickly arose and threatened to erupt into utter chaos. It was one of the signs that Camile was the dark prophecy incarnate. It was said that the embodiment of the dark prophecy would trigger a significant loss of crops. This, too, had also occurred after young Camile came into contact with vegetation during a visit to one of the produce farms.

Soon, it was time for Camile to address the citizens. She conveyed her sorrow for what had happened during her childhood. However, she also voiced her belief that she would prove her ability to redeem herself in their eyes. Camile expressed her concerns for the futures of both worlds and highlighted the hopes and dreams she held for humanity on both sides of the veil. She didn't expect the citizens to take her word as gospel, so it was no surprise that her statement was met with skepticism.

The gathering lasted no more than two hours, but to Camile it felt like she'd been there for days. By the time it was over, little progress had been made with the citizens. In fact, several of them implored the magistrate to have Camile banished. To her relief, the requests were promptly denied.

*   *   *

The magistrate judge summoned Camile for a private meeting in her chambers. For the first time since the start of the town gathering, Camile saw the judge's eyes up close. They were like the reflection of a hazy desert horizon; blue-gray at the top, medium brown on the bottom. Her enigmatic eyes were intensified with dark eyeliner and full, black lashes. There was something oddly familiar about them and her overall preternatural appearance, but Camile couldn't determine the reason why that was so.

"They're never gonna get over this, are they? Your Honor, how can I convince them that I'm different than Akalina?" Camile asked.

"You can call me Skye outside of court." The judge smiled, making her way over to the refreshment counter recessed into the wall beside her desk. Her voice was clear with a dulcet tone, but had an air of no-nonsense. With her dainty, well-manicured hands, she placed a few ice-cubes in a short square glass, filling it with an amber-colored drink. Based on the small amount, nearly an eighth of the glass, Camile guessed it was some kind of brandy or the like. "Would you like one?" Skye offered, extending the glass. Camile couldn't stop staring into her dual-colored gaze, which somehow distracted her from giving a prompt response.

"Oh...No, thank you," she answered, nearly adding that she wasn't allowed, but didn't, figuring it would make her seem juvenile.

"Very good. I see you're following Sir Drayden's guidelines to the letter." Skye cracked a half-smile as she raised an eyebrow. She took a sip from the glass before setting it on the counter.

Oh, crap! She was testing me? Camile thought, trying not to think of the possible consequences she could have faced had she accepted the offer.

Leaning against the front of her desk, Skye continued, "As you just heard, our people have quite a lot to get over, but try not to worry about it so much. Whether or not they get over the past is their problem, the council's and the EDC's to sort out. You have enough of your own to contend with and you have to focus on getting back to where you belong. In case you haven't noticed, you have a big job ahead of you and it won't be easy. Your parents probably mentioned this already, but you are who you are whether you know yourself or not." She smiled gently, slightly narrowing her slanted eyes. "The same holds true despite what everyone else thinks or expects you to be."

*   *   *

That night, Camile fell into a lengthy and uneventful sleep. Upon waking the following day, she figured she had been too exhausted to dream. Her parents came by her quarters to see how she recovered from the town meeting. Though physically renewed, Camile was still carrying a weight of guilt on her shoulders. She couldn't stop thinking about not only Akalina's misdeeds, but her own. Her mind lingered on the people she had unintentionally made to suffer during her time in the Coexistent World. It led her to wonder just how much of Akalina's defiance she had retained. Camile's parents, particularly her mother, sensed that her disappointment extended far beyond recent events. After some coaxing, Camile expressed her concerns, earning a hug from her mother.

"Remember those people you blinded in the subway?" Kylie asked.

"How can I forget?" Camile sighed, crossing her arms in front of her.

"What if I said you really didn't blind them after all?"

Not knowing what her mother was getting at, Camile sat up at attention.

"You convinced them to physically blind themselves," her father explained. "I've been following their progress ever since the incident. You'll be happy to know that most of them have regained their eyesight."

"What about the rest of them?" Camile asked.

"There's a chance they'll regain their vision as well, but it's not guaranteed. Oddly enough, it doesn't depend on their eyes. They're still living in the instance of blindness you showed them. According to their medical reports, there's no physical reason why they all shouldn't have their eyesight back. The problem lies in their thinking. They've programmed themselves into believing that they'll never see again. As long as they keep that mentality, chances are they won't."

Camile sat in stunned silence. Relief swept over her for a fleeting moment before she remembered yet another group of people who had suffered as a result of her intense emotions. It was an occasion where her lack of control had cost people their lives.

"What about those people at Arizona General Hospital? You mean to tell me I convinced them to make themselves die?"

Camile's parents regarded one another, exchanging glances of uneasiness.

"No one died in Arizona, at least not as a result of you."

"But I read in the newspapers—"

"Those stories were planted as a cover so their families would have some closure regarding their disappearance," Camile's mother explained. "You did launch an attack on them and there were severe injuries, but everyone survived."

"Our attempts to block their memories were unsuccessful," Zephyr added. "We couldn't have them exposing our world to any unauthorized citizens in the Coexistent dimension, so we found it easier to integrate them into our society. Thankfully, they were willing to join our society after their ordeal. It was one of your mother's better ideas which made the council realize just how dedicated she was to solidifying Coexistent-Transcendent relations. It led her to attain her current position."

"What about their families? They'll go on for the rest of their lives, heartbroken, believing their loved ones are dead. That doesn't seem right." Camile grimaced.

"We agree with you on that, but it was the best solution at the time."

Her parents went on to explain their belief that no lives were lost during the attack due to the fact Camile and Akalina had not yet been separated. According to them, although Akalina had been struggling to establish dominance, it was Camile who had restrained her from fulfilling her murderous desire.

*　　*　　*

The afternoon was still in its infancy. The sunbeam pouring in from a small break in the curtain confirmed this. Yet, as she lay in the shaman's quarters Camile could feel herself slipping. Her eyes grew heavy, dimming her view of the room around her until all went black. She tried to resist the feeling of freefalling, but Tabitha instructed her not to. Camile eventually allowed herself to descend out of consciousness and submerge into a brief state of nothingness. The void was soon filled with the soft sound of Tabitha's voice emanating from the darkness.

"Camile, are you okay?" she asked.

"Yeah, I think so. I can't see anything. Where are you?"

"Just a few steps ahead. Walk towards me, but do it very slowly."

Camile progressed slowly forward until the shaman finally came into view.

"What is this place?" Camile asked as she attempted to take another step, but was quickly pulled back.

"No! Don't go any further," Tabitha ordered.

"Why? There's nothing out there."

There was a slight pause. The shaman expelled a shallow breath before responding.

"Apparently you're not ready to see what's out there. Not yet, anyway. We'll try this another time when you're not so resistant. Come on, follow me. We're going back."

Through slowly parting lids she saw the gradually sharpening image of Jeremy gazing down at her, his face just inches away from hers. The breath from his nostrils swept across her skin like a cinnamon-laced autumn breeze.

"Looks like someone's finally back from their detour," he announced before moving away. Camile detected a hint of bitterness in his voice.

Wearing a concerned expression, the shaman urgently approached.

"Camile, where did you go? Why didn't you follow me like I asked you to?" The line between her brows deepened.

"I thought I *was* following you," Camile answered but knew something had gone seriously awry since the moonlight was streaming into the room—an indication that her trip had been dramatically extended. Still, she felt as though no more than an hour had passed.

"So did I, but when I returned you were still under." Tabitha's frown deepened. "You've been traveling for close to six hours. Where did you go?"

Traveling was something Camile had only just learned from the shaman. However, the word used in this context referred to the traveling of one's soul beyond the physical body. This phenomenon most often occurs during slumber or daydreaming. Camile was baffled since the last thing she remembered was trailing Tabitha out of the strange, dark space.

Chapter 12

Nocturnal Shadow

Camile and Sir Drayden usually met in his office or the Celestia, but would sometimes convene in less formal sections of the compound like the conservatory or the main courtyard. Judging by the tone of their most recent meeting, the shaman apparently told him about her wandering off during their travels the day prior.

"When you're not at home within your own mind, you lay out a welcome mat for others to take up residence," Sir Drayden said, his voice infused with caution and disappointment. "It's up to you to guard your turf."

He presented her with a series of tests to challenge her physical and mental skills holistically. An aggressive teacher, Sir Drayden pushed her to the limit, presenting her with a series of theoretical moral dilemmas and trick questions. For that reason, and the general discomfort she felt around him, she dreaded their sessions. The conclusion of each of their meetings was consistent—she was always exhausted, frustrated and grateful it was over. Upon returning from one such session, she rapidly descended into a spiraling free fall, slipping away from reality as soon as her head hit the pillow.

Camile cautiously entered the desolate room, calling to see if anyone was there, only to have her own voice echo back at her. A small table emerged in the center of the chamber along with two chairs—one on each side. The table held a large crystal pitcher of ice water and two matching glasses. Tantalizing candies and pastries were piled high on a gleaming silver platter. The sweet scent of the delicacies filled the air as the area flooded with light, revealing sea foam green walls with gilded molding. The regal setting, complete with crystal light fixtures and mirror, resembled a scaled down version of a swanky ballroom. Camile wasn't sure what to make of the setting as she approached the arrangement.

"Hey, don't start without me." A female voice broke the calm. It sounded so familiar, almost like a recording of her own voice. Yet, there was something coldly calculating about it, something that filled Camile with both dismay and anger. She turned cautiously until she saw her face wearing a mask of mischief.

Akalina? She thought as her doppelganger winked.

Though her parents and advisors had tried their best to prepare her for the event of possibly encountering Akalina in her dreams, the experience still took her by surprise.

"What the hell are you doing here?" Camile demanded.

"Not exactly the warm welcome I expected," Akalina cringed. "I could ask you the same question, you know. After all, you're in *my* territory now. I see you're growing your hair out. Didn't you like what I did with it?"

"It wasn't me," Camile couldn't mask the bitterness in her voice. Though she accepted the fact she had to merge with her nemesis, it wasn't something she enjoyed. In fact, it unnerved Camile that although Akalina chose to wear her sleek hair at chin-length, their resemblance was uncanny. She also noticed that the color was much darker than it had been on the night of their merging. Instead of sporting her usual coppery mane, Akalina's now matched Camile's dark auburn locks.

"Looks like you finally filled out. But why are you keeping the girls covered up? Lord knows you waited long enough for them to finally sprout."

I don't have to listen to this, Camile thought, rolling her eyes before straining them shut in a failed attempt to awaken.

"Oh, but you do. You see, you have no choice, so you might as well just take a seat and get comfortable 'cause you're gonna be here for awhile," Akalina smugly suggested, casually plopping into a chair, placing her boot-clad foot on the table. The boot had a slick metallic buckle with a matching stiletto heel that looked like it could double as a weapon. Everything about Akalina—from her curve-hugging jumpsuit, to her dark, smoky eye makeup and mischievous smirk—conveyed the presence of danger.

"I don't feel like sitting down. Why should I listen to you anyway?" Camile protested, analyzing her surroundings. There was no exit in sight. She repeated her attempt to awaken, but with no success. Akalina chortled, gesturing at the floor with a wave of her hand. Camile shrieked as searing agony ripped into the soles of her feet, prompting her to stumble into the chair.

"Now, see, that wasn't so hard, was it?" Akalina smiled with a bizarre calmness. A groan was the only response Camile could manage as she snatched the pitcher of ice water and poured it over her feet. To her dismay, it provided little relief.

"I went out of my way to arrange this nice meeting and you make such a mess." Akalina shook her head in disappointment. She placed her hand on the empty pitcher, instantly refilling it with ice water. The frosty pitcher taunted Camile as it seemed to intensify the burning sensation ravaging the soles of her feet. Akalina blew a quick puff of air towards them. Much to Camile's relief, the pain instantly ceased.

"There you go, forcing me into the dramatics. I just want to talk."

"What's there to talk about?" Camile glared.

"Well, how's the 'rents? They're probably so thrilled that their *perfect* Camile is okay. You probably feel like you're so special, so loved, so wanted." Akalina's false smile fell into a deep scowl. "Well, don't get used to it. It won't last. Never does."

"You don't know what you're talking about." Camile considered rising to her feet, but instead folded her arms.

"Oh, and I suppose you do? You think Mom always wanted you? How typically naïve of you." Akalina snickered. "Well, I guess she didn't want to hurt your delicate feelings. I guess she didn't have the heart to tell you that you were this close to being eliminated before you were even born." Akalina snorted, snapping her fingers in the middle of the statement. "Honestly, I think the only reason she fought the council's decision to execute us was to nullify her guilt. Little does she know, that single act of charity will never undo the fact she wanted to abort her own child."

Camile took a moment to reflect on Akalina's statement. The speculation was unsettling, but it was speculation, nonetheless.

"How typical of you to slander someone who's not here to defend herself. You just proved that you're just a bitter, jealous liar," Camile said in as dismissive a tone as possible, but she could feel the seeds of doubt being planted in her mind.

"Hmm, you're getting to know yourself pretty well. But I guess I can understand why you'd feel bad about the whole thing. If it makes you feel any better, I was in the same boat. Well, in this case, womb. If someone hadn't convinced Mom to change her mind, neither of us would have ever been born. Who would've thought Mom could even *think* of making such a decision? And to think you thought you knew her so well."

"You're just trying to turn me against her, but it won't work. You're using your lies as a smokescreen to hide your own insecurities. And you call *me* pathetic."

"Hey, don't talk to me like that! I'm *trying* to be cool here and I suggest you do the same," Akalina retorted before filling the crystal glasses with ice water. She took a swig of one and sighed with satisfaction. "Nothin' like a cold drink to beat the heat."

With her words came a sudden intense rise in room temperature. As sweat trickled from Camile's pores, she fanned her collar in a failed attempt to get relief. However, Akalina seemed unbothered by the sudden climate change as she took another sip from her frosty glass.

"Looks like you're burning up, girl. You better drink something before you faint." Her lips curled into a seemingly amused smile.

Camile's breathing grew increasingly labored as the heat began to take its toll. Nevertheless, she wanted nothing to do with Akalina and refused the suspicious offer.

"Let me out of here," she demanded instead.

A sneering Akalina suddenly appeared directly in front of her, small tart in hand.

"Okay, well at least have some dessert before you go!"

She shoved the tart into her mouth so hard, it knocked out two of her front teeth. The pastry was extremely bitter and seemed to instantly dry Camile's mouth. Overwhelmed by her sudden inability to swallow, Camile gagged violently to expel the contents. She made a desperate grab for the glass of ice water and spilled nearly half of it on her chest as she chugged it down. She was tormented when the bitter salty taste in her mouth intensified as the cool viscosity thickened in her throat. Camile retched at the slimy change in texture. Looking at the glass, she saw the unmistakable sight of residual coagulated blood, which also drenched her shirt.

"Cheers!" Akalina raised her glass, wearing a bloody smile as she licked her lips. Her wide-eyed expression was that of a lunatic and Camile felt like she was staring into the mirror of her own insanity.

She was determined to escape the nightmare or at the very least force the disturbing image from her mind. Camile squeezed her eyes shut so tightly they ached. Upon reopening them she was relieved to find herself in the snug safety of her bed. However, there was still a lingering salty taste in her mouth. Tearing out of bed, she rushed to the bathroom mirror. Her relief climbed when she saw that her teeth were still intact, although her tongue had been grazed. It was just a superficial wound that would heal in a matter of days, but Akalina's rumor threatened to leave a much deeper scar. Worst yet, Camile considered the possibility she was being honest for a change.

Even if it's true, Mom wouldn't consider such a thing lightly. There had to be a good reason for it and clearly she didn't go through with it. Camile figured.

She spoke with her parents about the encounter that evening, but kept Akalina's rumor to herself due to the painful subject matter. She figured if she were to ever broach the subject, she would do so privately with her mother. Her parents figured the dark nature of the dream was merely her subconscious illustrating her struggle to reclaim dominance over her psyche. However, they warned her to avoid engaging Akalina in confrontational behavior. Camile knew it was a request that would be easier said than done.

Chapter 13

Heightened Temptation

"Maybe I should avoid sleep altogether," Camile joked after telling the shaman about her previous night's dream, as suggested by her parents. There seemed to be safety in the morning daylight, making the subject a little easier to discuss. Rather than meeting in Tabitha's quarters, as usual, the shaman made arrangements for a lakeside gathering.

"That's the last thing you should do," Tabitha answered seriously. "Sleep is very important. More than you realize."

"I was only kidding," Camile admitted.

"For your sake, I hope so." Tabitha sighed, taking a moment to wave at a few passersby. "Our dreams provide a space where we can disconnect from the restrictive binds of the physical world and reconnect with each other. It's the closest thing to freedom our souls experience before we shed our bodies for good. It gives our souls a chance to recharge, to cleanse itself of the tainted energy we absorb in our consciousness. But doing so means having to let go of our need to have complete control, or rather the illusion of it." Tabitha winked a dark eye.

As the shaman continued, Camile's eyes began to wander and her mind wasn't far behind as it drifted away from the conversation. Her gaze fell upon the magnificent sight of Jeremy's svelte, chiseled form glistening in the sun. As he emerged from the lake, water trickled down his body like golden beads, tracing his lean, velvety butterscotch shrouded muscles in skin. She summed up his appearance in a single word.

Damn!

Camile found herself imagining what it would be like to feel his arms around her, his powerful hands caressing her. She thought about how delightful it would be to feel and taste his full, tender lips. Watching the shimmering water droplets travel along his toned pectorals and abs, she imagined her fingers, then her kisses, traveling along the same path. Soon her tantalizing thoughts capsized her awareness, flooding her mind with the fabricated sensation of his body pressed against her own. The salacious fantasy nearly left her breathless as she tried to stop herself from thinking about caressing his fuzzy, perfectly shaped head and running her nails down his back while he...

"I see I lost your attention. What are you think—?" Tabitha asked, jolting Camile out of her mental excursion. Brows raised, the shaman chuckled while fanning herself. "Oh, my! Maybe we should take a break so you can cool off."

"Huh? Oh! Your Wisest, I was just—"

"No need to explain. I was young once too, you know." She winked. "There's nothing wrong with fantasizing every once in awhile as long as you keep a solid tether on reality."

Gently patting her shoulder, the shaman chortled anew before walking away. However, Camile wasn't amused. In fact, she was outright embarrassed.

Where the hell did that come from? She wondered of her distraction.

She didn't realize she was staring at Jeremy again until their eyes locked. He paused drying his head once he realized he was being watched. Camile gave him a sheepish smile, which he seemed to disregard as he gathered his things and walked away. She wondered if he had any clue about what she'd just been thinking. She was also curious as to why she would fantasize about someone who clearly disliked her, perhaps even loathed her. Camile pondered this while pacing. Her memory was soon refreshed by the image of Jeremy's immaculate bronze physique, dripping with water. She was once again filled with the ravenous desire to explore his body with more than just her eyes. For a moment, she considered diving into the lake to tame her thoughts but figured she'd only boil it with the heat of her craving. As she made an about-face she was met with a cool blue gaze that doused her steamy fantasy as effectively as ice water.

"Whoa!" Camile flinched, chuckling nervously as she palmed her chest. "You scared the living daylights out of me."

"Have a moment?" Sir Drayden motioned her to sit.

"Yeah. Sure." Camile returned to the chair in which she had been sitting earlier. Sir Drayden remained standing despite the vacancy of the shaman's seat. The sounds of singing birds and the placid lapping lake filled what would have otherwise been an awkward moment of silence.

"Truth is, you would've heard me coming had you been paying attention," the knight finally said. "What's got your mind so preoccupied?"

Camile's cheeks grew warm at the memory of her mental excursion. Having to look up at the male elder only made her feel more uncomfortable.

"Nothing. Just stuff," she fibbed, briefly averting eye contact.

"I see." Sir Drayden smiled faintly, gazing into the distance. His large nose seemed more pronounced by his profile. "Would that...*stuff* happen to include Jeremy?"

Camile's heart fell into her stomach and her face grew ablaze as she wondered if he had also read her erotic thoughts. Nevertheless, she decided to try and play it off.

"I'm not sure what you mean by that, sir," she replied, trying to sound as innocent as possible. No easy feat, considering where her mind had just been.

"I've seen the way you look at him," he clarified. "Jeremy's a good man and I can understand your attraction," he then turned to meet her eyes, "but I feel it's my responsibility to tell you that now isn't the time to indulge in your sexual desires. I suggest you focus on the task at hand instead of the fire in your loins."

Camile felt as though she'd been slapped.

Oh, no he didn't!

Just as Sir Drayden turned to walk away, something surprised her even further—the words coming from her mouth.

"And I suggest you mind your own business," she retorted, her voice low with resentment.

Sir Drayden halted his steps and doubled back until he was standing toe-to-toe with her. The sight of his face looming above her carried an eerie familiarity that twisted her insides.

Why couldn't I just keep my damn mouth shut?

"Young lady, in case you haven't noticed, you *are* my business," he said, his voice tinged with irritation. "You're as much my responsibility as you are to your parents and I won't have any of you screwing up what little balance is left here. If my being in your business makes you uncomfortable, that's just too damn bad. Everyone's had to sacrifice something for the cause. I guess this'll have to be yours. Learn to deal with it."

*   *   *

Immediately following her inflammatory exchange with Sir Drayden, Camile sought out her father, eventually finding him in his office. He had several meetings lined up with top government officials including the Arvainan Minister of Defense—the supervisor of all state defense ministers—but made time to speak with his daughter between appointments. As she sat across from his glass desk she admired the view outside his picture window. Dark clouds were beginning to dominate the azure sky as they rolled over the hillside town towards the compound. A storm was brewing and she hoped it wasn't a sign of things to come. Suddenly, lightning struck in the form of belated rationality.

This is childish. Sure, Sir Drayden makes me uncomfortable, but is that reason enough to go running to daddy?

Camile apologized to her father for wasting his time, noting that the topic she had come to discuss was of no grave importance.

"Hey, you can't fool me." Zephyr knowingly raised his full brows. "Your mother gets that same look whenever something's under her skin." He deactivated the computer console he'd been working on.

Camile caught a brief glimpse and deduced the image on the screen was a map or a blueprint. She then noticed the image that replaced it, a photo she had taken with her mother not long after her college graduation.

"Go on, spill." Her father interlaced his fingers on the desk and leaned slightly forward.

"It's Sir Drayden." Camile admitted. "There's something about him I don't trust. This might sound a little bold, but is there someone who can replace him?"

"Slow down a minute, sweetheart. Did something happen?" Zephyr narrowed his pale eyes under furrowed brows.

"I think he's taking advantage of the system and tapping into my thoughts."

"What makes you say that?"

"Because he…" Camile paused to think. She didn't want to reveal the embarrassing fact that she'd been fantasizing about Jeremy. Instead, she said, "He knows too much."

"Certainly seems that way, doesn't it?" Zephyr smiled softly, resting his folded arms on the table. "He's one of the most intuitive people I've ever come across. Took me awhile to get used to the way he flaunts his intuition, though I admit I still find it imposing at times." He paused to scratch his neck. "As often as I disagree with Sir Drayden, I have to admit he's gotten me out of some sticky situations. He's the best there is and I'd trust him with my life if I had to, but I can understand your caution. How can you trust him? After all, you're still learning to trust yourself. Give it time. You'll become more comfortable around him, eventually."

Camile had her doubts, but let the conversation end there.

*   *   *

The rooftop solarium, located in the west wing of Aqueon Peak, was an optimal location for swimming, a skill Camile never got to master as a child. As the morning surrendered to early afternoon, gleaming sunrays filtered through the retractable glass roof, providing intervals of warmth as she walked along the poolside. She figured the length had to be at least one hundred meters and hoped Jeremy didn't expect an Olympic performance during her first time back in the water. Then she remembered that she had mentioned that she was a mediocre swimmer at best, which is why he volunteered to help her in the first place. According to Jeremy, improving her swim technique would increase her focus and agility.

Settling into an empty lounge chair at the shallow end of the pool, Camile draped the towel behind her and awaited Jeremy's arrival. Only then did she realize she'd been hugging it a little too tightly, a fact indicated by the subtle texture now ingrained in her arm. No doubt, a direct result of her self-conscious attitude regarding swimwear. She quickly relaxed as she regarded the scene before her. Women of various shapes and sizes wore their swimwear with confidence, whether remarkably toned or as curvy as renaissance muses. While adjusting the straps of her violet one-piece she spotted Jeremy emerging from behind one of the beige columns lining the facility. Seeing his bronze body, clad in black swim trunks, nearly prompted her to revisit the fantasy that had been interrupted just days earlier.

Camile hugged her knees to her chest and gave as casual a wave as she could. She was puzzled to see two hands waving back. That's when she noticed Commander Wilder strolling beside him, wearing burgundy swim trunks and an almost playful smile. Her eyes took an unexpected detour along the well-defined contours of Brandon's muscular form, likely a result of his vigorous combat training. Once her gaze returned to Jeremy, she was ready to plunge into the water. However, it wasn't ambition that motivated her, but the desire to cool off.

Camile initially found it difficult to coordinate her arms and legs to propel herself. She clumsily splashed in an attempt to steady herself when a sudden thought entered her head.

Sink with fear. Float with confidence.

As Brandon churned the adjacent lane, Jeremy guided her to stretch across the surface. She allowed herself to relax, enjoying the sensation of simply floating. With smooth deliberate motions, she propelled herself forward. The pattern of the floor scrolled faster with each stroke, giving her the liberating sensation of flying. Her ears were filled with the muffled sounds of her breathing and intermittent splashes. Suddenly, a figure swooped beneath her from behind and blocked her path, prompting her to stop. Kinetic energy sent her crashing into Jeremy's arms as she nearly sandwiched him against the wall, a wall she would have met head-first had he not intervened.

"Hey, I thought you couldn't swim." He gave a prying look as he released her.

"So did I." Camile looked over her shoulder and saw the distance she had covered. "Guess I underestimated myself."

After drying off, Camile collapsed into her lounge chair as Jeremy and Brandon engaged in friendly competition. The commander's lengthy frame attacked the water with speed and precision, swimming the entire length of the pool and back at lightning speed. Jeremy's less muscular build streamed easily within his lane, taking the second race. The final lap was a tie.

Their swim trunks clung to their drenched bodies as they emerged from the pool. Curiosity weighed on her eyes like an anvil, pulling her gaze downward as her imagination went to work, wondering what secrets were hidden beneath the fabric. Coming out of her trance, she quickly dropped her attention to the floor as she fumbled with her towel. She slowly raised her gaze and saw them drying off, reigniting her desire to cool off in the pool. It was one of the rare times Camile wouldn't have minded having a second set of eyes if it meant drinking in all the magnificence of these two men. Nevertheless, she made do with what she had, training her gaze on Jeremy and occasionally toggling her attention to the commander. To her embarrassment, Brandon met her eyes when he bent over to dry his feet. Smiling amusedly, he winked. She quickly looked away, taking a towel to her damp cornrows, but knew it was too late.

"You can't blame them for feeling defensive after what Akalina did," Jeremy said of the town meeting once the subject arose moments later.

"I don't, Jeremy. It's just not easy for me to deal with, that's all." Camile was growing slightly defensive. She couldn't help but think the man seated to her left was concealing something behind those mysterious brown eyes of his.

"It's not easy for anyone," he replied.

"Jeremy, it's not like you to carry a grudge," said the commander, who sat to her right. "Sounds like you're still upset about—" He stopped suddenly when Jeremy abruptly shook his head.

"Upset about what?" Camile inquired. Suddenly, it seemed obvious. "Jeremy, did Akalina do something to you?"

"My past dealings with Akalina are irrelevant," he answered dismissively.

"Somehow, I doubt that." Camile countered.

"What's that supposed to mean?"

Deep down, Camile wanted to pour out everything that was on her mind, that although Jeremy treated her professionally, it often seemed cold, forced and obligatory. Yet, despite his emotional distance she was still drawn to him and it frustrated her. Instead, she replied, "Why don't you meditate on it? I'm sure it'll come to you eventually."

Camile decided to retreat to her quarters before she could say anything else she would regret. Heading for the locker room, she looked back and caught a glimpse of Jeremy and Commander Wilder, exchanging surprised expressions.

*   *   *

A pair of distinct voices wrangled Camile's attention as she traversed the conservatory. As she cautiously peered around a tree she snagged her finger-combed waves on a hanging branch. While untangling the mess, she noticed a dark-skinned man in a tense discussion with Sir Drayden. Tareeq, as he was called, was about two inches shy of the elder's height, but his muscular body mass more than compensated for the difference. His flat, lifeless eyes were like those of a shark and he used them to pry into the knight.

"The council is prepared to act swiftly should the devourers decide to resume their treacherous path," Sir Drayden cautioned. "I urge you to relay this warning to Makeda. Her little stunt with my apprentice nearly nullified our treaty."

"I'll deliver your message, but I have one for you as well." Tareeq's thick lips formed a smirk beneath his spade-shaped nose. "Everything that's playing out right now is your doing. The only good thing that came out of this situation is the fact it brought me and Makeda together. Me, my wife, and all the other devourers have as much right to procreate and expand as everyone else. We have just as much a right to live freely and we're prepared to do all we can in order to make that happen. We tried to be civil, but the council has continuously treated us unfairly."

The knight shook his head, cracking a condescending half-smile.

"Oh, I can assure you the government's actions are justified. If you defy the treaty, be prepared for an all out war. We will not allow your tribe to overtake and destroy our population. And as for your so-called marriage, it's corrupt." Sir Drayden scoffed. "Makeda manipulated you into a union based on deceit. You'll soon discover how fruitless it really is."

"You're trying to manipulate me into betraying my wife." Tareeq sneered. "I expect nothing less from you. And to think at one time you had my respect. Maybe I had it confused with envy. For so long my potential was overshadowed because of you. How could a man with so much power accomplish so little?"

"I've accomplished more in a day than you could ever hope to achieve in your entire lifetime. I established my legacy before you were born and it will stand long after your time on this earth has expired."

"That's your problem. You're too arrogant to see beyond the scope of your own reality," Tareeq said, a frown contorting his ebony features. "You know what? I hope for a war. I'd love to get my chance to stand toe-to-toe with you in battle and eliminate you once and for all. And as for your legacy, I won't rest until I eradicate every trace of it." The fury in his eyes seemed to glow in contrast to his dark skin.

"Your poor attempt at intimidation amuses me. I'll tell you what." Sir Drayden stepped closer until they were no more than a foot apart. "If you're looking for a showdown, why waste time on ceremony? What stops you from seizing your opportunity right now?" The knight leaned in and sniffed the glowering man. "No matter how long you steep your body in your pungent preservatives, it will never mask the stench of your fear."

After a still moment, Tareeq jerked his fist back as though preparing to strike his adversary. Sir Drayden didn't flinch. Instead, he smirked as though amused.

"You'd like that, wouldn't you?" Tareeq spat. "I'm not stupid. I'm on the council's turf and you have the comfortable cushion of their protection."

"Again, your inexperience overrules your intelligence. What makes you think I require their protection?" Sir Drayden took a step back, smirking as he did. "As much as I'd like to continue this illuminating discussion, I know it's more important that Makeda gets the message immediately. I think if she hears it from you, we'll stand a better chance at rectifying this matter. If we set all our differences aside we can have peace. However, if a face-off is too tempting for you to ignore, you know where to find me. But I warn you, don't engage me unless you're truly ready to meet certain death."

With that, he summoned the guards to escort Tareeq out of the compound. Now standing alone, Sir Drayden's face reflected somber contemplation.

Camile remained curious about Sir Drayden's visitor well into the evening hours. She wasn't surprised at Tareeq's animosity toward the knight as it was becoming increasingly clear that he had very few, if any, friends. Camile's ponderings would have to wait since her slumber would preoccupy her with a guest of her own.

"So, how do you like life in the Transcendent World? It's a lot better than the weak, so-called civilization you're from, isn't it?" Akalina asked, her voice echoing in the empty library.

Camile decided to take the advice she'd been given and avoided saying anything to anger her negative half.

"It's different," she answered as she joined her doppelganger at the table. Once seated, she realized all the books were facing the wrong way out.

"Well, enjoy it while you can. Things have a funny way of changing. It won't take long for you to realize that this place is far from a freakin' fairytale." Akalina glowered. Her voice seemed to carry further at the end of her statement as every book suddenly vanished.

"In the meantime, just do us both a favor; stay away from the old man." Akalina warned, skewering Camile's orbs with her cold gray gaze from across the table. "The tongue lashing he gave you was mild compared to the vile things he's capable of."

Camile revisited her curiosity about Sir Drayden's clear disapproval of her interest in Jeremy. Her internal thought was immediately addressed with amused speculation from Akalina.

"Well, maybe he's jealous." She shrugged. "The dirty old man probably wants you all for himself. It's a bit of a curse; no one can resist this fine piece of ass." Akalina smirked, training her attention to her own backside, admiring it briefly. "Well, I could be wrong. Maybe he wants a piece of Jeremy's ass." She snickered, peeking through the dark locks that tumbled over one eye.

Growing increasingly uncomfortable with the direction of the conversation, Camile quickly changed the subject to address something she'd been curious about since she first met the knight.

"Why are you so scared of him?" she asked.

"Me, scared? Please!" Akalina rolled her eyes, drumming her fingers on the table. "I think you're confusing your feelings for mine, lady. I ain't afraid of a damn thing."

"Oh, really?" Camile arched her brow, briefly shifting her attention to Akalina's fidgeting hand. "That's not what it looks like to me. Admit it, he scares the crap out of you. Why?"

"I said I'm not scared, so drop it." Akalina crossed her arms over her chest. "Look, just…stay away from him or you'll find out for yourself. As much as I despise you, I don't want you to go through the same things I did. More importantly, I don't want to relive them. If you put me in that position, I swear I'll make your life a living hell. So do us both a favor, if you see that bastard, you walk the other way."

The fearful look in Akalina's glassy eyes and the urgency of her voice poured a syrupy chill down Camile's spine. Based on what she knew of Akalina, she was a ruthless person who respected few and feared even fewer. The person standing before her now was quite the contrary—a desperate woman in fear of her own safety. In those brief moments, Akalina seemed to have been stripped of her confident, brazen exterior. Camile could have easily been looking into a mirror.

Suddenly, that reflection shattered as Akalina returned to her robust rant about how unworthy Camile was of her time. With that, she vanished into the dark recesses of her mind like an inky shadow. Emerging in Akalina's place was a small dark-skinned child, who stared at Camile with large brown eyes. He was well groomed and wore a gray shirt, and brown pants. With an awkward tight-lipped smile, he gave a shy wave before fading away. Upon waking, Camile wondered about the boy and his significance to Akalina.

Chapter 14

Undeniable Impulses

Camile felt odd about arranging a meeting with her parents in the early pre-dawn hours, but knew she was just following their request, which was to immediately notify them if Akalina made an appearance. Red-eyed and yawning, they promptly arrived at her quarters. She greeted them at the door, which partially closed behind them, but reopened upon Sir Drayden's arrival.

"What's he doing here?" Camile whispered, sitting beside her mother on the plush sofa.

"We asked him to join us," Kylie answered softly, adjusting her hair bun as the men seated themselves in opposing chairs. "We thought he should be here since he'll play a significant role in your rehabilitation as well as your training."

Camile's father promptly asked about the subject of her conversation with Akalina.

"It was about him." Her voice grew slightly unsteady as she cast a sideway glance at the silver-haired elder who had a booted ankle casually propped on his opposite knee. "It was about Sir Drayden. Akalina gave me the impression that she's not very fond of him."

"Well, that doesn't come as a surprise. Akalina has always had a problem with authority, myself included." Zephyr sighed, stroking the hairy arms that poured from his white t-shirt.

Camile felt deep in her gut that Akalina's hatred for Sir Drayden went far beyond her disrespect for authority. It was something different, something personal. However, she kept that assessment to herself in order to expedite the conclusion of the meeting and her departure from Sir Drayden, whose deep gaze was now inescapable. She had an overwhelming feeling that he knew she was withholding details, so she decided to steer the discussion by divulging the appearance of the young boy. This seemed to pique the interest of everyone in the bright living room as she was asked to describe him. Upon doing so, her parents and Sir Drayden exchanged curious glances.

"What do you think it all means?" Camile asked.

Zephyr pressed a finger to his lips, his eyes narrowed in contemplation. "Since you've merged with Akalina, it's only natural for you to relive some of her memories. Try not to let it distract you."

Camile figured her father was right. She needed to maintain her focus now more than ever. Right now, she was focused on ending the discussion quickly so Sir Drayden could get the hell out of her quarters.

"Was there anything else?" her mother asked.

Camile shook her head, deciding not to mention the rest of Akalina's warning about the man whose eyes were burning into her at that very instant.

"Are you sure?" Sir Drayden asked, his prying gaze locking with hers.

"Yeah," she answered in little more than a whisper.

Camile was conflicted and unsure of what to make of Sir Drayden. It was painfully apparent that he had a lasting beef with Akalina, as did most people, but Camile wasn't sure why or whether or not it now transferred to her.

As the days continued to rise and fall, Camile was frequently visited by the young boy in her dreams. He always smiled and waved coyly during his brief visits. He rarely spoke, but when he did, he'd always ask, *"Do you miss me?"*

Camile wondered if the boy was Akalina's illegitimate son. The theory was dispelled by her parents, who swore that Akalina never had any children. Still, Camile wondered if they were wrong. After all, Akalina had run away as a teen and could have easily had a son and abandoned him during her lengthy absence from the compound. Things like that happened all the time in the Coexistent World.

*   *   *

With each sloshing step, the corridor grew increasingly unfamiliar and appeared to lead Camile someplace other than her quarters. Nearly a quarter of the way across, she realized she'd exited the lift several levels too soon. Her straightened hair, drenched from the morning rain, breached her collar and tickled her chest. She secured her locks into a loose ponytail as she turned to double back, but the distant rolling sound of chords and melodies beckoned her to continue onward. Following the increasing volume of its audible trail, the notes painted an emotional collage filled with bittersweet romantic nostalgia, a sense of loneliness, longing and belonging. Though it wasn't accompanied by words, the music itself was a language all its own and Camile was curious to see the musical linguist at the other end.

Cautiously entering the large room containing the source of the music, Camile saw a man playing a crystal clear grand piano as a woman sat beside him. She soon recognized the pair as her parents. The instrument, and its platinum and pearlized inner workings, gleamed in the spotlight within the otherwise dimly lit concert hall. Camile watched her father's hands glide across the keys as her mother enjoyed the private concert, smiling contentedly. Concluding the melody, he embraced her, gently kissing her mouth. Kylie raked her fingers through his dark, glossy hair, cradling the back of his head as she pulled him in for a deeper kiss.

Camile smiled at the unexpected sight of her parent's romantic exchange. She was happy their love had endured all the storms they had weathered over the years. Not wanting to interrupt the pair, she retreated to her quarters.

She learned of another of her parent's common interests when they met with her later that afternoon. At first, Camile feared they had been aware of her presence during their private concert, but as the conversation progressed, she realized that wasn't the case.

"The skill of dancing is just a small part of the curriculum for etiquette and social interaction," Kylie explained.

Camile just knew it was coming, the revelation that she would have to take a course in dancing. She had no problem with the pending curriculum, but it was the social interaction she dreaded, especially since she could practically smell the citizens' fear and distaste for her. Just as she suspected, her mother broke the news that her father would escort her to her first class.

"Is this really necessary? I mean, aren't there more important things I should be learning?"

"It might seem frivolous to you, but proper etiquette is extremely important in all Transcendent cultures," Zephyr explained. "It's can be the gateway to civility and allegiance. Off we go, then." He hooked his arm into Camile's, practically tugging her away.

Large mirrored walls magnified the wide open space of the studio. The towering instructor smiled as her young students executed waltz-like moves to the cadence of her wooden staff. Her mahogany skin was moderately weathered and exaggerated her wiry frame. The instructor's sunken eyes lit up upon noticing Camile and her father enter the room.

"Oh, you're just in time!" The woman propped her staff against the wall before eagerly reeling Camile into the room. The red talon-like nails sprouting from the instructor's strong icy hands slightly grazed her arm. "The class is a little uneven today," the woman said to Camile's father. Her voice was as raspy as a seasoned smoker. "Would you mind dancing with your daughter for the first set?"

Meanwhile, Camile's eyes strained upward to the towering bun formed by intricate gray braids. She wondered how the woman's delicate looking body supported the weight of her cumbersome mane.

"It's a little short notice, but it'll be my pleasure, Grace." Zephyr replied, much to the instructor's delight.

Grace took a few moments to demonstrate the steps with Zephyr. Camile chuckled inwardly at the awkward height difference when her father said, "I'm afraid twirling is out of the question."

"That would depend on who's asking," Grace smiled almost cockily.

Lifting Zephyr's arm, she led him into a quick spin, apparently catching him off guard.

Camile grew familiar with the routine through observation, but was uncertain of how it would translate into practice. Soon, it was time to take her place before her father and join the rest of the group in dance. Zephyr was easy on his feet and gentle with his turns.

"You know, this brings back memories." His face was aglow with nostalgia. "When you were just two years old, I used to dance with you a little each day. You were pretty good. Then again, you *were* standing on my feet the whole time."

Father and daughter shared a laugh before Camile accidentally stepped on his toes.

"Some things never change." He smiled through a wince.

Once the lesson concluded she went to her parent's quarters to join her mother for lunch while Zephyr returned to his duties. As they finished their meal, Kylie further explained why Transcendents placed such a high value on manners and decorum.

"The provinces in the Transcendent World that strongly incorporate etiquette into their society experience a significantly low divorce rate." Kylie dabbed her lips with a napkin. "It's a vital part of their education, giving citizens the tools they need to form meaningful courtships and relationships rather than empty physical digressions."

"Wow. So people here don't, you know, before marriage?"

"Now, I didn't say that." Kylie's hazel eyes crinkled as she sipped her tea. She lowered the cup, revealing a warm smile. "Transcendents have hormones and desires just like Coexistents do." Her smile deepened as her eyes shifted to the table on which she now leaned an elbow. Twirling a lock of her thick coils, she continued, "Actually, their hormones are a lot more intense, depending on which region they're from." Meeting her daughter's eyes anew, she straightened her posture and cleared her throat. "That's why they work so hard to maintain self-control. If the Transcendents all acted as impulsively as most Coexistents…Well, this world would be a lot more chaotic."

"Intense hormones, huh? Well, that explains—" Camile stopped herself.

"Explains what?" Her mother arched her brow.

Camile reluctantly explained her recent spike in attraction towards some of the men in the area, but she didn't dare specify who they were.

"I was afraid this would happen." Kylie sighed. "As if you didn't have enough to distract you already. What you're going through now is called *Lah'klav*. It's when a Transcendent has an intense desire to mate. During this time, temptation seems ubiquitous to Transcendents and can be maddening if left uncontrolled. Your father and I hoped you wouldn't go through this for another year, but physically, the timing seems accurate, if not overdue."

"So, that's all because of the hormones?"

"Possibly. Your body is adjusting to its new environment, so it's normal."

"Normal?" Camile narrowed her eyes.

Kylie nodded. " Your body is mainly Transcendent. You're bound to have drastic hormonal changes every now and then."

"Great. I'm halfway into my twenties and puberty strikes again," Camile muttered sarcastically.

"Don't worry." Kylie laughed softly, patting her daughter's hand. "You'll be fine as long as you continue your meditation and keep yourself occupied. Just let us know if you think your impulses are going out of control. And don't be surprised if you start attracting suitors."

"I doubt it. Almost everyone here already thinks I'm a walking biohazard." Camile expelled a deep breath, massaging her temples. "Anyway, with all that's going on, I won't exactly have time for dating. It's probably just as well."

"Don't be so sure about that. I used to have the same mentality until I finally learned that there's always time and room for love." Kylie beamed.

*   *   *

Tabitha requested that Camile meet her at the amusement park located in Daebrayk Peak—aptly named since it faced the morning sunrise. The funfair was larger than any Camile had seen in her entire life, or at least the life she remembered. Though located in a mountain, the luminous atmosphere possessed many of the same qualities one would find in an outdoor environment. The clicking of the energetic crowd's heels reverberated against the brick-laid streets and stone sidewalks which lined the outside of souvenir shops and restaurants.

Animated squeals and laughter emanated from the young and young-at-heart, filling the candy-scented air. Festive music complimented the widespread mirth and frivolity. The setting seemed to induce the crowd's tolerance of Camile's presence. Either that or she had somehow gotten used to their reserved reactions. Through the mob, she spotted a pair of female guards looking her up and down. The tough-looking women concentrated their attention on her midsection. Their eyes appeared to be wired with some kind of computer circuitry.

Although Camile had noticed Transcendent humans with varying degrees of unusual orbs, some similar to Magistrate Sui's, she'd never seen anything quite like this. Maybe she simply hadn't paid close enough attention. Suddenly, it dawned on her. The female guards were somehow looking into her body. She was frequently inspected prior to her meetings with the shaman, but this was the first time it had been done without her awareness or permission. Shaking the uneasy feeling as the officers disappeared into the crowd, Camile resumed her admiration of her jubilant surroundings.

Without fully realizing it, she cracked a smile as she took in the lively colors of brightly lit signs and vendors selling balloons and various sweets. Her gaze followed the trail of the vivid display, her mouth gaping in awe as her eyes met some of the larger rides that dominated the park. The twists and turns of the attractions were mind boggling, but paled in comparison to the massive fun wheel. Judging by the long line, it was undoubtedly one of the most popular rides. Having heard more than a few favorable things about the park from her father, Camile was eager to explore it as soon as time would permit, but made a note to avoid the monstrous coasters. She had already stared mortal danger in the face more than once, so she had no desire to tempt fate or taunt gravity.

"I suggest you start off with the smaller ones," a velvety voice chuckled from behind.

Camile turned to see Tabitha, whose eyes dazzled with delight.

"That is, after we're done with our business," the shaman added, leading her to an empty table at a sidewalk cafe. Having fasted for a full day prior to their gathering, Camile's hunger was rebounding. As they approached the restaurant, her hopes and appetite continued to rise only to be dashed by the revelation that she was to maintain her fast until their meeting concluded. What Tabitha said next shifted Camile's attention from her hunger pangs.

"You'll be returning to the Coexistent World soon," the elder announced.

Only upon hearing the shaman chuckle did Camile realize her face was twisted in concern.

"Don't worry, you're not being banished or anything," Tabitha said. "I'll be completing an assignment. Thought it would be a good idea for you to come and observe. Nothing serious. I just have to pick someone up. Jeremy will be coming along, of course." She leaned in slightly, arching a brow. "That won't prove to be a distraction, will it?"

Before Camile could answer, a woman with a boyish figure approached coyly, her arm around a small girl, hanging her head.

"Sorry for interrupting, but I was wondering if you could help my daughter. Her name's Gia," the woman said softly, brushing her waist-length braided ponytail over her shoulder.

Camile noticed silent tears trickling from Gia's eyes. Her resemblance to her mother was uncanny. She appeared no older than preschool age.

"Sure." Tabitha smiled easily, welcoming young Gia into her arms. "Why is this beautiful girl crying, hmm?"

Gia's mother explained that her daughter was mourning the loss of the family's pet dog.

"I take it he died unexpectedly," Tabitha inquired, to which the mother nodded. "Well, in that case, I understand your difficulty in understanding his passing."

Gia shook her head, her two ponytails bouncing like springs.

"I understand what death is, ma'am," she said softly. "I studied it in my lessons already."

"Yes, I'm sure you have," Tabitha nodded. "But, this is your first time dealing with it directly and you're having trouble figuring out what happens beyond the transition."

The girl nodded, wide-eyed with amazement, "How'd you know?"

"It's my job to be insightful." The shaman smiled sweetly. "Besides, I used to feel *exactly* like you're feeling now, when I had my first experience with death; although that was a very long time ago."

She stopped the balloon vendor about to bypass their table and requested two of the items. She was given one yellow and one green, the latter of which she handed to Gia, who immediately thanked her with a brief smile.

"Haven't held one of these in a long time." Tabitha sighed nostalgically, playfully tugging at the string suspended from the floating inflatable. "Do you know what gives it its shape, what holds it up like this?"

"Air, of course!" Gia chuckled at the question which obviously struck her as silly, but then palmed her head. "Well, actually, it's a gaseous compound, but air can inflate a balloon too."

Camile was impressed by Gia's poise and intelligence, yet sympathized with her struggle to accept one of life's most drastic changes.

"Ah, right. But how do you know that?" The shaman regarded the girl knowingly.

"I learned it in school."

"Yes, but how do *you* know it really exists? You can't see it. Yet, you know there's something inside that balloon that you can't see with the naked eye, the same way you can't see the gases in the air around us that allows us to breathe."

I guess I just...*know*." Gia shrugged, to which Tabitha nodded, deepening her warm smile.

A sudden clap erupted through the air as the girl's balloon exploded. Camile noticed that Tabitha glanced at it a split second beforehand. The slightly over-dramatized look on the elder's face confirmed that she had somehow caused the balloon to burst. Gia's frown deepened, but she shed no new tears as Tabitha inquired about the occurrence.

"It popped," Gia answered glumly.

"Yes, but where did the air go? Despite our inability to see the air rejoin that which surrounds us all, we still believe it does, mainly because science has proven it. The same is true of the energy that propels our physical being. When we die, our energy leaves us to rejoin that which surrounds and permeates all things that aid in life's continuation; earth, wind, fire—"

"I think my dog is helping the wind!" Gia said enthusiastically, prompting her mother to caution her not to talk out of turn.

Tabitha raised her hand, signaling that it was okay.

"Oh, why is that?" she asked, the wrinkles around her eyes deepened with her smile.

"Because the wind is fast. So was my dog. That's why we named him Breeze," Gia explained.

"You know, I think you might be right." Tabitha winked, extending her balloon to the child.

Before Gia could get a full grip of the string, a sudden gust of wind swept the area, carrying it along the street. The girl's face lit up as she chased after it, eventually catching it just before it could hover beyond her reach. Thanking the shaman with a wave, Gia skipped away, her balloon bobbing in the air behind her. After expressing her gratitude, the girl's mother jogged to catch up with her daughter.

Chapter 15

Much to Learn

Camile's strong desire to know her father had always been enough to fuel her perseverance in times of difficulty. Now that she finally had the opportunity to learn more about him directly, instinct no longer seemed sufficient. There was an apprehension that accompanied her concerns that her idea of him wouldn't match with reality. In fact, it seemed odd for her to refer to him as *Dad* since he had been absent during much of her life. The fact he was back in the picture didn't ease matters as she had hoped. If anything, it created yet another complication.

Her ability to keep up with her studies was just as difficult. It presented her with challenges that surpassed those she faced in her college career. Conversely, the Transcendents seemed to absorb information with remarkable speed and ease. The common presence of child prodigies was evidence of this fact. Though it fueled her determination, it also evoked uncertainty, envy and concern.

She had been discussing the matter with her parents in Zephyr's office while watching the busy sky, speckled with midday traffic. Her stomach grew mildly queasy at the thought of her first shuttle ride.

"I'm not sure I can keep up with everyone else. My brain is not like theirs," she said.

"Yes, you can," her father encouraged. "You just have to break away from your old way of thinking and awaken your Transcendent brain.

There's no reason why you can't meet and surpass the capabilities of your peers. The potential is all there. You just need the will."

"I do, but these demands are impossible." Camile gestured to the text on her handheld device.

"Clearly you don't. If you did, you would focus on your goal, not the obstacles." Her father gently squeezed her shoulder. "Sweetheart, you need to tackle one thing at a time and find your own way instead of pouring all your attention into what everyone else is doing. You can't see where you're going if you don't look ahead. Don't stress yourself out."

"I guess you're right. I'll stop whining," she said through a half-hearted smile. "How come you're so sure I can learn all this stuff?"

"Because Akalina already did," Camile's mother answered. "Your capacity is the same as hers. It's your choices that set you apart, in a manner of speaking."

Camile saw logic in her mother's statement, but found the comparison between her and Akalina somewhat disturbing.

*   *   *

The next phase in Camile's education included the subject of Transcendent courtship and sexuality. In preparation, she was given a book called the *Leih'klav*, the Transcendent equivalent of the Coexistent World's Kama Sutra. The title of the text had often been misinterpreted as *Meih'klav* and was rumored to be the origin of the Coexistent phrase *make love*. The *Leih'klav* was a compilation of each culture's methods of attaining intimacy through the merging of physical and spiritual energy. In the rarest and most powerful cases, mating could be accomplished even if a couple was physically separated by great distances.

Camile's mother had cautioned her that the course would go into specific detail, not only about the Transcendent human anatomy, but also various techniques of how to thoroughly please one's partner.

In the overview, the *Leih'klav* was described as a tribute to Transcendent love, sexuality and the human body. Similar customs were present in the Coexistent World, but were overshadowed by the glorification of promiscuity. So often Camile had witnessed the growing perversion of the human body and what the Transcendents considered the final act of bonding. Too often this sacred act was devalued, diluted and made to signify something dirty. Instead of it being used to fortify an existing bond, it was often used as a means of emotional disconnection by way of focusing solely on the physical act.

Ashamed, Camile briefly recalled being duped into prematurely venturing into a physical relationship that was based on false promises of something more. She acknowledged her regret, but refused to dwell on the thought a moment longer. She felt she had already lost enough to the deception when it took place a few years earlier.

Sitting alone at a table in the solarium's adjoining atrium, Camile flipped through the *Leih'klav*, using her lexicon to translate some of the more difficult Arvainan words she had yet to master. There was a preface which outlined the importance of reading the supplemental references for the other cultures within the Transcendent World since there were variations in customs. Getting past the introduction, Camile was impressed with the remarkable beauty in which the theory of courtship, intimacy, foreplay and mating were tastefully described. The physical union of Transcendent lovers was considered to be the culmination of what had already been achieved through the compatible joining of their minds and emotions.

Though the *Leih'klav* acknowledged the ability to achieve pleasure solely on a physical level, it was considered to be a far less gratifying level of bonding and a diluted form of total intimacy. Such relationships were described as prematurely plucking the petals of a budding flower, ultimately destroying it in order to experience its scent before it reaches full bloom.

As Camile read about the stages of courtship, she noticed many parallels between it and basic friendship. Though it seemed simple, the book highlighted it as a vital role in determining the compatibility of potential couples. It went on to explain that engaging in challenging tasks and activities was recommended in order to strengthen the bonding process. At the same time, the couple would understand each other's method of thinking and test their ability to accommodate one another's personalities. Camile's eyes lingered on the following passage:

> *The physical stage of bonding is at its most powerful when all other forms of bonding have been achieved. If this has been done, the final petals of the flower have reached full maturity and unfold, leaving no restriction for pleasure, physical or otherwise. Having learned your partner and when to push, pull away or work together in fluid unison; having learned what enthuses and delights their senses, you are prepared to carry all of this knowledge into the sweet cadence of your unity.*

Turning the page, she was shocked to see graphic illustrations of some of the physical techniques. One series of depictions stood out in particular as she figured one would have to master extreme flexibility and contortionism, not to mention synchronization with their partner, in order to safely achieve such positions. The drawings were as artistic as the positions they depicted, but Camile couldn't get over the unexpected surprise. She surmised that the artwork was located in the back of the book so that the student would mentally evolve and mature, grasping the full meaning of the complete text before seeing it in living color. Considering her flustered reaction, Camile knew she hadn't quite reached that stage in her development. She had always been somewhat shy, though not aloof, when it came to the topic of sexuality. Nevertheless, she couldn't pry her eyes from the bizarre entanglement of limbs etched on the page. She tilted her head and angled the book in an attempt to make sense of the arrangement.

"I see you started the course on *Leih'klav.*" A trombone-like voice cut into Camile's thoughts. Flinching slightly, she was immediately filled with the guilt of someone who had gotten caught looking at pornography. Raising her attention, she met the eyes of Joval, the wisecracker she had seen at the farm. They had also crossed paths in the corridors a few times since. Though they had never exchanged more than a simple hello, she knew Joval was an apparent jokester. He'd always contort his face in a child-like manner to earn smiles and laughter. His light-hearted humor was refreshing and made Camile wonder if his name was derived from the word *jovial.*

Joval's wiry frame was a meager height for an average male and was coated in skin the color of sparsely creamed coffee. The tiny blotches across his cheeks were indicative traces of clearing acne. Hoping he hadn't noticed her reaction, Camile put on a relaxed smile.

"Yeah, so?" She abruptly placed the book face-down on the table before taking a swig of water. The cool drink did little to soothe the prickly heat in her cheeks.

"So…" Joval droned, turning the book face-up, "…you're gonna need a partner to help you master all the positions. I hope you're limber."

Camile choked on her water, dribbling some of it down the front of her shirt. Joval barely suppressed his laughter.

"Excuse me?" Camile grimaced.

"I'm just kidding. Didn't think my suggestion would get you all wet," he quipped, handing her a napkin. She all but snatched it from him before hastily wiping the water from her shirt and chin, wishing she could wipe away her embarrassment as well. Instead, it seemed to increase as Commander Wilder approached in full uniform.

"Don't mind Joval," he said. "He's just taking part in an unofficial tradition. Supposedly, it's meant to break the tension and uneasiness of older students taking the course for the first time. It's childish, to say the least, but some traditions die hard," Brandon explained, casting a quick glance at Joval, who ceased laughing as though on cue.

"You gotta admit. I got her good, Commander. I mean, did you see the look on her face?" he chortled.

"Yeah, Joval. I saw." The commander's voice quivered in an apparent attempt to stifle his amusement. "Be that as it may, the *Leih'klav* isn't just a book about sex. Weren't you paying attention in your studies, or did you skip ahead to the good parts?" He smirked.

Seemingly abashed, Joval lowered his head as though hiding his crooked smile. Meeting Camile's eyes anew, he changed the subject.

"You should've seen your face though, Cam. Classic!" Joval chuckled, raking his fingers through the dark, well-groomed dreads skimming his shoulders.

Cam?

Camile realized she had earned yet another nickname she liked.

Joval had the type of personality that made it nearly impossible to stay upset for long. Camile tried to hide her mild amusement, but it broke through in a faint grin as she rolled her eyes. In doing so, she caught a glimpse of Jeremy sitting several feet away wearing a smile that seemed to indicate that he shared in their merriment.

*   *   *

Camile's dreams hosted the appearance of the young boy almost nightly. His smile gradually faded with each visit. Emerging in its place was an expression of sadness that resonated in his voice when he asked for help, finally revealing his name; Isaac.

"Please find me. Don't let them give up on me. I'm ready to go home now," he said before asking, "Do you miss me?"

"Where are you?" Camile asked, unsure of how else to respond to the large-eyed boy.

"I can't remember, but it's dark and cold." Isaac's face scrunched bitterly. "They used to let me out at daytime so I could do my drawings, but not anymore. I think they're mad about the last thing I drew."

"Who? What drawing?"

The strengthening grip of her consciousness reeled Camile away from the dream as Isaac faded before her eyes. She tried to hang on with all her might, but it was useless. Isaac dissipated completely as she awoke, frustrated and without answers, except for the boy's name. She asked her parents if they knew anything about Isaac. They stared at her in an apparent state of astonishment before telling her that there was indeed something she should know about Isaac. However, since she was scheduled to depart for her mission with Tabitha and Jeremy, Camile's parents arranged to meet with her about the subject upon her return.

Chapter 16

Intermediary

A deep breath carried the soapy scent of freesia into her nostrils. Licking her drying lips, she regarded Jeremy standing on the other side of the shaman's bed. His eyes caught the flickering candlelight like obsidian marbles set against his bronze face. Following his intent gaze, Camile's eyes fell upon Tabitha as she peacefully drifted off to sleep. The shaman's salt and pepper hair spilled onto her shoulders in loose waves created by the twists she sometimes wore.

"Might be a while before she makes contact." Jeremy said, spritzing the elder's face with water. "You might want to rest your feet. Could be a long trip."

He gestured for Camile to sit beside him on the cushion-topped trunk at the foot of the bed. Camile obliged, noticing the noose-like silence that gripped the room. Growing uncomfortable, she figured she'd try to break the ice that had formed between them since her mild outburst at the solarium. She began by asking about the duration of his work with the shaman.

"Fifteen years," Jeremy answered simply.

Camile was taken aback by his response since he looked no older than twenty-eight.

"That long?" She briefly rubbed her hands on her knees for no other reason than to give them something to do. "Were you specially selected, or did you have to apply for the job?"

"I was specially selected to apply." Jeremy cracked a short-lived smile. "I was promoted. I actually started out as one of the shaman's assistants. My predecessor was devoted to protecting her. She gave her life in order to succeed in doing so."

"Did you know her very well?"Camile furrowed her brow.

"I guess you could say that." Jeremy's gaze dropped briefly as a nostalgic smile emerged. "She was my mother after all."

"Oh, I'm so sorry." Camile fought the temptation to touch his arm. "It must've been really tough for you to lose her."

Jeremy shook his head. "Not particularly."

Camile's mouth fell agape at the unexpected response and the nonchalant tone in which it was delivered.

"You weren't close?" she inquired, now noticing a warmth to Jeremy's face she'd never before seen.

"Forgive me, I don't think I'm being clear," he said softly. "I loved my mother very much. I still do and always will. Everything I am now I owe to her, but it wasn't tough for me to lose her since she was never mine to lose in the first place. Besides, she's not lost, just transferred."

Camile smiled compassionately, honored that Jeremy was finally beginning to feel comfortable enough to reveal something personal about himself. She opened her mouth to say something supportive, but was interrupted by a sigh from the shaman. Camile tried to hide her disappointment as she and Jeremy checked on Tabitha, who was murmuring incoherently. Suddenly, the shaman sat up and climbed out of bed.

"Follow me," she instructed softly. Her dark eyes seemed to look through, not at, them.

*   *   *

The trio traveled quietly beneath the darkening amber sky for nearly an hour before reaching the heart of Deltine. The city's pulse was gradually increasing with commuters and those looking to enjoy the nightlife. The shaman halted outside of a rather sleepy looking pottery shop tucked in the middle of a main avenue. Traversing the entrance, Camile noticed it seemed as tightly guarded as the Federal Reserve. The security presence led her to wonder if priceless artifacts were stored among the merchandise. Yet, from what she could see, much of the earthenware appeared average at best.

One of the officers nodded to Jeremy and led them to a dingy workroom, where an artist was forming a vase. The chalky scent of clay wafted through the still air as they made their way to the back closet. Camile detected the faint smell of disinfectant as the door was opened. Not even the generous light of the workroom seemed to penetrate the darkness within. The shaman was the first to disappear into the space. With the gentle guidance of Jeremy's hand on her elbow, Camile followed suit. The warm humid air slowly grew colder as the scent of clay was overpowered by the sterile odor of rubbing alcohol. Camile knew what venue awaited them on the other side even before clearing the darkness. The distant mechanical beeping and intercom pages were a giveaway. Sure enough, within moments she was engulfed in harsh florescent lighting and pale walls that seemed standard in hospitals. A lone security guard nodded to the trio in apparent recognition. Looking back, Camile no longer saw the pottery room, but a solid wall with an abstract painting just inches from her face.

She pointed to it. "Did we just—?"

"Sure did." Jeremy cracked a brief smile, but resumed his professional demeanor upon noticing the shaman on the move.

With closed eyes, Tabitha led them through the stairway to an in-patient room two floors up, all the while talking to her contact. The floor was quiet except for a nurse's station that had a radio playing music that seemed overly syncopated for a hospital environment. The nurses were so busy chatting amongst themselves, they failed to notice the three travelers roaming the halls. A sleep talking patient was apparently desperate for the shaman's arrival. He urgently mumbled his location, oblivious to the presence of the visitors in his room.

Tabitha opened her eyes, smiling as she gently touched his shoulder to wake him. The man jumped from his bed and immediately stretched his arms for the shaman. Jeremy quickly intercepted, twisting him into a secure hold.

"Hey, man!" The patient struggled. "What gives? I just wanna thank my savior."

The shaman placed her hand on Jeremy's shoulder, signaling him to stand down. After a brief moment, he released his grip and stepped aside. Even so, he kept his eyes locked on the scruffy man, who wasted no time in wrapping the shaman in his eager embrace.

"Thank God, you're real," he said tearfully. "I knew I wasn't crazy. I just *knew* it!"

"Touch is just an indication of my presence, Blake." Tabitha cupped his cheeks as the two ended the hug. "In your heart of hearts, you knew I was real long before this moment."

Blake bashfully broke eye contact.

"I kept tryin' to warn everybody that time is running out for us, but of course they didn't listen. They *never* listen!" He scowled before giving the shaman the rundown of what occurred as a result of his warnings. Declared mentally unstable, he had been committed. According to Blake, his chance of regaining his freedom came with the price of outwardly denouncing his former claims. For this, he begged the shaman's forgiveness.

"I knew they'd never let me out of there if I kept tellin' them the truth, so I let them all think I realized I was hallucinating because of stress. Then they transferred me here," Blake explained. "It's backwards. I had to lie to get closer to my freedom. I'm sorry I failed y—"

Tabitha raised her hand, gently silencing him.

"You didn't fail anyone," Tabitha hushed softly, cradling his head as though he were a child. "You've proved your worth in your attempt. That was the whole point. In actuality, your mission has yet to begin. You're a messenger, alright. People may not have listened to you this go 'round, but I assure you, when time pulls the trigger of providence your words will resonate. Until then, you have to build your resolve and learn about the cultures we're trying to protect. Everything will be explained when we reach our destination, but I warn you that it's much different than what you're used to."

That's an understatement! Camile thought as she glanced out of the room.

She noticed her favorite candy bar in a vending machine across the hall. There was only one left and she wished she had the money to buy it. In that moment, she realized it had been a very long time since she needed to pay for anything. In Deltine, all her needs were provided for. She watched as a portly orderly approached the machine to order a snack. Camile's heart sank when she saw him order the same candy bar she had been fantasizing about. The item's red wrapper snagged on the mechanism, prompting the employee to fight for the snack, but to no avail. In his surrender, he muttered that he needed to lose weight anyway.

Just as he departed, the treat fell into the receiving bin. Feeling like she'd just hit the jackpot, Camile dashed to retrieve her prize. She wasted no time tearing open the wrapper and devouring the confection. For a brief instant she was struck with a wave of guilt for the unauthorized breaking of her fast, but it quickly dissolved like the sugar hitting her taste buds. Leaning against the wall, she closed her eyes and relished the taste of sweet decadence. It was like pure ecstasy dipped in chocolate.

Upon opening her eyes she spotted a bizarre looking man, leisurely walking into a room two doors down. His immaculate dark clothing harshly contrasted against his sallow skin, gleaming under the bright florescent lights. Intrigued, Camile cautiously tailed him and quietly followed him inside. There was a woman at the bedside of a frail elderly man, hooked up to at least three machines.

The ominous stranger was gaunt and his oddly translucent skin revealed black and blue veins. The purplish region around his sunken eyes indicated a major sleep deficit. As he poised himself beside the bed, the distraught woman seemed oblivious to the fact there were now four people in the room.

"Dad, I know my life didn't exactly turn out the way you expected and I hope that it's not the reason why you're in this condition now. I just wish…" The woman sobbed. "I wish I had more time to make it up to you."

Camile knew firsthand how difficult it was to watch a parent's health deteriorate and understood the helplessness that accompanied such a trial. She wished she could somehow comfort the woman, but knew it was an unlikely possibility. For one, she didn't exist in this stranger's eyes and furthermore, she knew that time, though often tauntingly slow did the best job at healing such agony. She shelved the thought when she saw the sinister looking stranger moving closer to the ailing patient.

"Hey, what are you doing?" Camile asked forcefully, but the strange man ignored her, continuing his advance as he outstretched his large bony hand.

A chill washed over her as she realized that the only way to stop this man was to physically intervene. Hand extended, Camile started toward the stranger. She was just inches from touching his arm when someone abruptly yanked her backwards by her sleeve.

"What do you think you're doing?" Jeremy's eyes were wide with profuse alarm. It was the first time Camile had seen him lose his composure.

"What are *you* doing?" she retorted, pulling her arm away. "That man's up to something shady. We have to stop him!"

Jeremy vehemently disagreed. Calming his voice as he released her, he explained, "We can't. Camile, that's not a man. It's an *Intermediary*. We don't *dare* mess with them. I strongly suggest you don't either."

Before Camile had a chance to ask questions, she saw the Intermediary touch the patient's stomach. A smoky stream poured out of the point of contact, forming a figure of his likeness. It was unclothed and either didn't notice or care as it took its place next to the Intermediary at the bedside. Bemused, Camile noticed that the patient's frail body continued to live as though nothing had happened. Then she saw the thin, wispy thread-like strand, connecting the two. It seemed a sort of umbilical cord floating weightlessly in the air. The spirit stood beside his weeping daughter, regarding her with a gentle smile as she continued to address his unconscious body.

"I know you can't move or speak," she said. "I'm not even sure if you can hear me, but if you could find some way, *any* way, to send me a sign that you forgive me and that you still love me…"

Touching its former body, the spirit caused it to tremor briefly. The daughter stared in bewilderment.

"I love you too, Dad," she whispered tremulously, taking his hand. "I know this is a level of survival you don't want to endure if it means you won't get any better. It's okay. You don't…" She took a deep breath, as though gathering the strength to utter her next words. "You don't have to hold on anymore if you don't want to. You don't have to suffer anymore."

The spirit smiled, planting a gentle kiss on the woman's forehead as the Intermediary stepped forward. In a single motion, it severed the wispy strand at the point closest to the spirit's living counterpart. Almost immediately afterwards, the patient flatlined. The daughter sobbed anew as doctors entered the room to revive her father despite her protests to leave him be. After the attempt failed, they recorded the time of death as the spirit and *Intermediary* vanished.

Astounded, Camile turned to Jeremy. "How did he make his body shake like that?"

"It usually happens when a person tries to reenter a body that's too weak to support their core," he explained. "The body strains to accommodate the energy, but sometimes it's just too much to hold onto. Somehow, I think he knew that and used it as a sign to communicate to his daughter."

"But aren't all ghosts able to communicate with people?"

"Technically, but there are so many complicated factors involved. It's similar to other forms of communication, your message only gets through if your audience is ready and willing to listen." Jeremy scratched his fuzzy head. "Then there are cases where ghosts choose not to interfere with the living world for some reason or another. That doesn't mean that they don't visit occasionally. Each case is different and there are many exceptions, just like in the lands of the physically living."

"Where did the Intermediary take him?" Camile asked, briefly turning her attention to the grieving daughter.

"Where we all go… Eventually." He smiled gently, glancing at the spot where the Intermediary once stood.

*   *   *

A full moon peaked through violet-tinted clouds against a blackened sky, casting a glow over Caldaq. The fragrant balmy air welcomed the trio back with a gentle caress. Shuffling through the corridors leading to Coronis Peak's main dining hall, they were greeted by Camile's mother.

"You're just in time for dinner," she said. "You must be starving by now,"

A knot of guilt swelled in Camile's chest since she knew she had cheated during her fast. However, she tried her best not to let it show on her face.

The packed dining hall was abuzz with patchwork conversation, through which occasional pops of laughter rose to the fore. The main table had just enough remaining seats for Camile, her mother and Jeremy. Tabitha had decided to dine in her quarters. The rest of the overseers were gathered at the long table for the feast, as were a number of government officials Camile had seen in her travels around Caldaq. Her parents sat near the middle, Commander Wilder just to their left in deep conversation with the officers sitting across from him. Sir Drayden sat just a few seats down from Camile, who sat beside Jeremy for the meal. She thought it was the perfect opportunity to speak to him about Akalina on a more personal level since all the other dinner guests were engaged in their own discussions.

"Something tells me you have less than fond memories of Akalina," Camile said. "You two butt heads often?"

"That's putting it mildly," Jeremy replied before sipping his beverage.

"Bad relationship?"

Jeremy grimaced slightly as though wondering about her sanity. "We had no relationship. The only thing Akalina and I had in common was misery."

Damn!

Camile finished off her tri-colored potatoes before inquiring about what had transpired between him and her darker half. Jeremy raised his index finger as he chewed his final piece of gravy-sopped bread.

"Akalina was as cruel as they come. She got off on people's suffering." He said after swallowing, pausing to wipe his face with a napkin. "The worst part was her laugh. It was so…contradictory. That kind of laugh has no place among chaos and pain."

Camile pondered his words while trying to decipher whether his frown stemmed from resentment, sadness or both. She pushed the thought from her mind as dessert was served. Each guest received a small covered dish containing a gold-dusted parfait. The soft scent of vanilla and coconut beckoned her taste buds to further awaken. However, when Camile raised the silver lid, she realized she saw something that sent her heart into her stomach. It was the wrapper of the candy bar she had eaten at the hospital. Raising her gaze, she was mortified to discover all eyes on her.

"Something wrong with your dessert?" Sir Drayden smirked from the far end of the table, eliciting subdued laughter from some of the other guests.

Feeling she was being treated like a child, Camile was resentful. Even so, she opted not to reply. Instead, she quietly excused herself and retreated to her quarters.

Chapter 17

Visionaries

Camile's parents summoned her to their private study later that evening. She braced herself for a lecture about her failure to adhere to her fasting regulations. Much to her relief, the topic never arose. She figured they felt she had already learned her lesson through sheer embarrassment. They did, however, remind her about their pre-scheduled meeting to discuss her dreams about Isaac. Though the appointment had slipped her mind, her interest was firmly rooted.

"In our society, there are people known as intuitive scribes," her father began. "Scribes are most often young children and usually retire once they reach puberty, when their minds can be colored and confused by hormones and outside influences. During their retirement, they usually train to become shamans and spiritual counselors."

"Camile, Isaac is a scribe," Kylie explained. "The rebels kidnapped him nearly two years ago."

"Why?" Brow scrunched, Camile's mouth fell agape. "Do they want ransom?"

Kylie shook her head. "Most likely, they want information they can use against the council. It's difficult to know for sure since he's severed contact with us."

"Maybe that's why he's showing up in my dreams," Camile wondered aloud. "He wants me to find him, personally. Maybe it has something to do with my transmitter being inactive. He might be trying to protect the council as best he can by using a neutral."

"No." Zephyr shook his head, a faint dimple emerging on one cheek. "It's a bad idea for you to get involved any deeper than you already are. As we explained before, we already have a team working to locate and return Isaac. What you need to do is focus on your training."

Feeling an inexplicable connection to Isaac, Camile was reluctant to accede to her father's wishes, but knew she had no choice in the matter. Sighing, she hung her head as she slumped in her chair.

"It just seems a little unfair to Isaac that I'm busy learning about culture while he's in danger," she muttered.

Rising from her seat, Kylie circled the table to stand beside her daughter. "I know it's frustrating, sweetheart, but you're helping us more than you realize," She stroked Camile's straightened locks. "You're providing information that may seem insignificant to you, but is providing valuable insight to the team we have in place."

Camile learned of another scribe, Donovan, who foresaw the prophecy nearly a year prior to her conception. He predicted that a child would be born within a year of his forecast, a child that would hold the key to leading the Coexistent World to the path of healing and rehabilitation. He also foretold the birth of a nemesis who would stop at nothing to prevent this from happening. The scribe repeatedly conveyed that both children in his vision would be conceived by a couple from opposite worlds. Naturally, Transcendent communities were shocked since cross-dimensional breeding was considered taboo during that time, which meant one of two things; either the scribe was false, or at least one resident would break a solemn rule.

Zephyr was one such person who, after meeting Kylie, engaged in a relationship that ultimately resulted in Camile's creation. Months later, Young Donovan had been taken to many expecting mothers in an attempt to locate the two children he had envisioned. When he came across Kylie, he declared her unborn child to be the lighter side of the prophecy, but when asked about the darker side, Donovan could only say that it had not yet been produced.

Camile caught a chill upon deducing that she, herself, had given birth to the dark prophecy with Sir Drayden's help. Silence swept the room as she considered the deepening spiral of her past.

"I'm sorry, sweetheart." Kylie expelled a deep breath, breaking the audible stillness as she held her daughter close.

Looking upward, Camile saw the watery twinkle in her mother's eye.

"You deserved to be treated like a child, not a commodity," Kylie continued. "I wanted you to experience the life of an ordinary kid. So, I protected you as best I could by keeping you in a bubble of innocence. It's just that…" She paused a moment as though searching for the right words. "Well, you had such a beautiful, untainted view of the world and I wanted you to keep it as long as possible. You saw potential and goodness in everything, but one day it all started to change. The world's negativity started to get to you. The fact that I couldn't tell you about your father and your true identity didn't help matters."

"You did what you had to do, Mom." Camile stroked her back. "Don't blame yourself. I don't."

Kylie regarded her daughter with sweetly curled lips before pressing them tightly together. "Akalina was different," she said, her voice tart. "She seemed to thrive on negativity. She was transfixed by it. Everything we tried to do to make her life easier failed because she thought we were either patronizing her or insulting her intelligence."

She went on to explain that Akalina used her cleverness as a weapon to spread her twisted perception of the world while manipulating people and vilifying those who actually cared about her.

"The two of us were separated at the time of her most violent offenses." Camile paused before asking, "Why didn't the council elect to eliminate her if she was such a danger?"

"Because of you." Her father leaned forward, propping his elbows on the desk, tenting his fingers. "We began to notice that whenever Akalina got sick, so did you, and vice-versa. At first, we thought it was just a coincidence, but as time went on, we realized that you both had a strong connection despite your physical separation. Something happened…" He drummed his fingertips together, "…something that made it very clear that although your soul was divided into two entities, if death claimed one, the other would be affected. I think it's only fair to warn you that what you're about to see may disturb you."

His hand hovered above the recessed screen and hung there for a few moments as he held his daughter's gaze. As his finger hit the monitor, his head lowered sorrowfully to the video. In it, a catatonic Akalina sat on a grimy sidewalk, a maniacal grin firmly affixed to her face. Her wide eyes stared into space as she rocked back and forth, drooling on herself. Camile swallowed hard, mentally reassuring herself that she wasn't looking at herself, but at her darker counterpart. Zephyr explained that the video was taken shortly after Akalina was found wandering aimlessly in the streets, years after she had run away from Caldaq.

"What happened?" Camile grimaced.

"This is the result of your suicide before it was reversed. It was documented by one of our high-ranking officials. I know this isn't easy to watch." Her father frowned. Meanwhile, Kylie leaned her back against the table, facing away from the screen.

"Not that I'm not grateful for the second chance or anything, but wouldn't it have been easier to just leave Akalina the way she was, even if it meant me staying dead? I mean, if she stayed in that condition, she wouldn't have been able to cause any more trouble."

"That's a dangerous assumption many people make about the physically restricted." Kylie explained, occasionally turning her pink-tinted gaze upward. It was a tactic Camile, herself, sometimes tried in an attempt to use gravity to thwart falling tears. "Just because a person is limited in one way or another doesn't mean they are incapable of making significant contributions to the world—positive or negative."

"Your mother's right. Take a good look at her face." Zephyr gestured towards the screen. Camile reluctantly obliged. "Look at how calm and peaceful she seems. Beneath the deceptively serene surface lurks the imp of chaos and unbridled madness. Had we allowed her remain in this condition, she could've done far more damage than she could do with you alive."

After deactivating the screen Zephyr moved to a lighter subject, informing Camile that she would soon be learning yet another skill— *Animal Studies and Communication.*

Attempting to mask the apprehension she felt as she recalled the saurus attack that had taken place just weeks earlier, she inquired, "I won't have to work at the farm, will I?"

"No. Not yet anyway." Kylie cracked a smile, taking a seat beside her daughter. "Soon, you'll learn that sometimes animals can be our greatest allies. When all else fails, we often have to rely on them. Unfortunately, some people take this ability for granted, sometimes even using animals to perform spiteful attacks."

"I'm guilty of misusing the ability, but not in the way your mother described." Zephyr pursed his lips, expelling a deep breath through his nose. "When I was restricted from contacting you, I was devastated. As you know, my bio-transmitter—and your mother's—was designed to prevent us from giving you any premature information. I didn't let that stop me from at least trying to give you a little help to find your way back home. I figured out a way to get around the restrictions and I used it to my advantage the night before your reintegration. I only wish I was smart enough to have thought of it years earlier. It could've prevented needless suffering."

Zephyr exchanged a tender glance with Kylie before continuing, "Technically, I didn't contact you that day in the tunnel; not directly, anyway. I enlisted the help of a medium. I mentally transferred my messages for them to pass on to you, like an audio-visual communication device, albeit an organic one."

"The fireflies," Camile said almost to herself, recalling the ghostly image of her father the swarm of insects had projected prior to her reintroduction to the Transcendent World.

"It was a clever idea if I do say so myself." Zephyr smiled.

Curious, Camile pressed for specifics of how he beat the system that night.

"Sorry. Can't say. Besides, when the council found out about what I did and how, I ended up in very hot water. They're determined to prevent it from happening again," Zephyr explained. "I was suspended from duty for a week and was ordered to report to the EDC for evaluation and treatment."

"What is the EDC, anyway?"

"It's a treatment center that's helped the council maintain order for many years," Kylie explained. "After a brief stint there, your father was placed on modified duty for a while."

"Considering the possible consequences, that doesn't sound too bad." Camile figured.

"Oh, it would've been much, much worse had Sir Drayden not stepped in." Zephyr chortled softly. "Remember when I said I'd trust him with my life?"

Chapter 18

Primal Instinct

All work and no play makes Jeremy a dull boy, Camile sometimes thought. That is until time clarified his depth as a man in her eyes. Not only was an he avid reader, he also enjoyed sketching, practicing the violin, and playing a game called *Salvage*. The breadth of his intelligence and wisdom became even more apparent whenever he'd discuss history, philosophy and world events. Camile mostly agreed with his theories regarding the correlation between deteriorating humanity and progressing technology and grew increasingly fascinated with his confident mind and spirit. Somehow, they radiated, enhancing the allure of his otherwise average physical appearance.

His dedicated work ethic ran deep, much like his desire for constant personal growth and an insatiable curiosity for life, something Camile also possessed. Despite learning so much about Jeremy, she still sensed a forced civility in their interaction. She would sometimes try thawing the frosty atmosphere with jokes, but could barely warm his serious disposition.

One day, she finally witnessed a change in Jeremy's demeanor when they met for one of their sessions. Though the simulated sun of the Celestia was behind him, his face lit up as she entered the room. It was a welcome reaction, but Camile wondered what had motivated it. She thought perhaps it was because she was wearing a different workout uniform. Instead of the usual black or white, she opted for powder blue, a color she'd been told accentuated her gray eyes.

"Wow," Jeremy said softly. "You look wonderful!"

Pleasantly surprised, Camile blushed inwardly as she returned his smile.

"Thanks. You don't look too bad yourself, handsome."

Camile was puzzled. She was thinking that exact sentiment, but the words seemed to leave her mouth before she could open it. Furthermore, the voice was slightly heavier than her own. That's when she realized Jeremy's compliment wasn't intended for her. Whipping around, her ponytail hit her cheek as her eyes landed on the graceful form of a mocha-skinned woman. Camile felt her presence diminish as she watched the two engage in a tight hug.

"You should've told me you were coming early," Jeremy said, briefly stroking the woman's shoulder-length cornrows. "When did you get back?"

"Two hours ago," the woman said through plump, wine-colored lips. Winking her dark brown eye, she slid her hands from his shoulders to his chest, cracking a pearly white smile. "I wanted to surprise you."

Unable to stomach any more of the exchange, or the sickening envy churning beneath her poised facade, Camile cleared her throat, prompting Jeremy to commence introductions.

"Justine, this is Camile, my newest student," he said, referring to the woman as his friend.

Camile saw a drastic contrast between how Jeremy behaved around her and this woman. Was Justine the reason for his distant manner? Were the two more than friends? Judging by their locked eyes and lingering embrace, it certainly appeared that there was more to their relationship. Camile subconsciously analyzed Justine. In doing so, she noted that although Justine was attractive, she wasn't strikingly so. Then again, envy had a way of tinting one's perception of beauty. She also noticed that Justine's body wasn't very curvaceous, but was tight enough to bounce a coin off of. Justine proudly displayed that fact by wearing a midriff top that showcased abs to die for. Her fit, slender thighs seemed all but smothered in her tight jeans. Camile spotted a plastic card of sorts trying to escape her pocket. Curious, she tilted her head to read the inscription. Above Justine's likeness, mostly covered by her pocket, was the following:

SATHRI
Secure Acquirement, Tactical Handling &

Before Camile could read the rest, Justine reversed the card and secured it.

"I was about to tell you about that," Camile said, extending her hand. "It's nice to meet you."

"Uh-huh." Justine smirked as she briefly shook it.

"Any chance you can tell me about your last assignment?" Jeremy asked.

"Controlled leak of a few scientific and ecological discoveries," Justine replied, briefly regarding Camile with a suspicious side-glance. "Nothing I can get into specifically. Of course, unless you don't mind me killing you."

"Only if I get to choose the method." Jeremy laughed. "All jokes aside, I can't wait to catch up. What's your schedule like?"

"I'm free for the next half-hour, then I'll be stuck in team meetings all damn day."

Camile got a clear sense of her position on Jeremy's list of priorities when he postponed their session for an hour. As she made her exit, she heard him resume his conversation with Justine. Turning once before traversing into the corridor, she saw the two laughing and sitting closely together.

Peas in a pod, aren't they? So, how come I'm the one feeling green?

Camile felt taunted by the fact she was an outsider to their amusement, especially since she had recently failed to incite the reaction Justine was generating with ease. Humor was a tough aspect of life for Camile to grasp at times, but she understood that in order to make someone laugh, you had to go beyond their defenses and vulnerabilities in order to coax it out. Camile's desire to either climb or break the glacial obstacle between her and Jeremy was conflicted by the fact he was apparently already in a relationship—and a happy one at that.

She soon began dreading her sessions with Jeremy. They had become an awkward reminder of how differently he viewed her versus Justine. After showering and changing into dark jeans and a violet tee, Camile decided to visit the Daebrayk Botanical Garden to regroup. The quiet calm of the midday herbal-scented air slowly soothed the crushing sensation in her chest. Still, her mind lingered on the memory of Jeremy and Justine's mutual adoration. Unable and unwilling to voice her feelings to anyone, Camile turned to her journal, reflecting on one of her previous entries:

> *The warmth of your heart is tauntingly near, but you reserve it as you shut me out in the blizzard of your doubt. Is it because you don't understand the freakish assembly of my soul, a soul that was once broken? In some ways I guess I don't blame you. If I had the opportunity to avoid the vague horizon of my future, I would. But these are the cards I've been dealt and I still don't know all the rules of the game. My burden is heavy and becomes harder to bear each day. I know I have the ability to endure it alone if I really persevere, but I prefer a steady hand to help guide me along the way and maybe even hold me in times of uncertainty.*

Knowing any kind of personal relationship with Jeremy was impossible, she considered destroying the page, but knew it wouldn't silence her yearning heart. She later muffled it with curiosity as she looked up the term

SATHRI, discovering that it was a Transcendent organization responsible for the *Secure Acquirement, Tactical Handling & Release of Intelligence*. The group was designated to obtain, research and manage vital information that could potentially help or hinder civilization on both sides of the veil. Comprised of covert agents and supportive staff, each member was charged with the responsibility of achieving expertise in a variety of fields. Only the very best were selected to become members of the SATHRI, a society that took pride in their inconspicuous nature.

Days later, Camile was concluding a pleasant breakfast in the atrium when her father and Sir Drayden joined her. Amid informing her that her education was being accelerated ahead of schedule, they were interrupted.

"Hello, Camile," greeted a vaguely familiar voice, saturated by what she guessed was a British accent. Training her gaze over her shoulder, she saw a rather intense looking man approaching. His slender body stood around six-foot five and was draped in a duster as black as his smoothed back hair. Camile could see the smoky gray collar of the shirt he was wearing underneath. His smooth pale skin gleamed in contrast, giving him the appearance of a person who might appear in a vintage vampire film.

"Camile, this is—" Sir Drayden attempted to commence introductions once the man joined them.

"Vincent. Vincent Thornton." Bowing slightly as the knight frowned at the interruption, the man smiled broadly as he shook her hand. His palm was surprisingly cool, but his expression possessed a hint of fiery danger. "I was beginning to think they'd never introduce us. It's a pleasure to finally meet you, love."

His nearly chin-length hair was receding at the temples, placing emphasis on his widow's peak and large forehead. She then recognized him as the man who had chided Joval for his remark during the farm incident. His otherwise stark appearance was warmed by his brown eyes and a charming, yet impishly toothy smile that accented his enigmatic presence. As Camile appraised him, she wondered why he was dressed in so many layers on such a mild day.

"Vincent works for the Department of Wildlife and Environmental Conservation," Zephyr explained. "He's a deputy commissioner for the Deltine region. He'll be teaching you Animal Studies and Communication."

"You mean like carrier pigeons?" Camile inquired flippantly, then remembered her discussion with her father just a few nights prior.

"Not quite." Vincent chuckled.

The commissioner wore his enthusiasm in plain view during the lengthy hike through the thick forest. It resonated in his generous stride, making it a challenge for Camile to keep up with the lanky man. They traversed through a botanical corridor of dark bark beneath a lit canopy of leaves of green, red and every shade in between. The fallen foliage sparsely carpeted the path in kaleidoscopic colors. Clearing the darkness, they came to an open field. Caldaq's shadow crept behind them as the afternoon sun slowly dipped beyond the peak.

"Here we are," Vincent announced, eagerly gesturing to the vast area before them. "I bet you can't wait to get started. I know I can't, but it appears we have no choice, given my assistant's tardiness."

Several uneventful moments elapsed before Camile appeased her tired legs by sitting on a nearby tree stump.

"That seat is reserved. I don't suggest you sit there," the commissioner said, not once removing his gaze from the empty space in front of him.

Camile promised to surrender the seat once the commissioner's assistant arrived. However, her words went unaddressed since something caught his attention.

"Ah, here she comes." His deep brown orbs lit up like the orange-tinted sky above. "Gorgeous, isn't she?"

Camile strained her eyes, but all she saw was a vast stretch of lush grass. She brought this to Vincent's attention. He quickly crouched before her, taking her head into his hands. His face was so close their noses nearly made contact. Recoiling, she pressed her palms against his shoulders to widen the space between them.

"What the——?" she attempted to protest.

"Don't be frightened, love. I'm just making a little assessment," he said softly. "Look into my eyes."

Camile met his gaze after a moment's hesitation. The intensity of it held her with the sticky grip of a tar pit.

"That's it." Vincent nodded. "Our eyes may be different in color, but you can see her just as well as I can. Don't let logic restrict your vision. Don't let your eyes deceive your soul, love."

He pulled away, gently releasing her from his grip. As he did, a warm puff of air caressed Camile's left cheek. Turning to see the source, her nose touched that of a massive black bear. It roared loudly, baring dagger-like fangs. An instant jolt shot through her body just before she fell backwards from the tree stump, nearly losing control of her bladder in the process. Her trembling hands flew to her ears, now stinging with the residual sound of the bear's rippling bellow. As it faded, she heard Vincent laughing heartily. Cautiously rising to her feet, Camile glowered at him. She could still smell the lingering, rancid stench of the bear's last meal.

"Not funny!" She folded her arms, her voice low so as not to startle the animal.

"Maybe not from your perspective, but from mine it was hilarious." He grinned toothily, stroking the bear, now perched on the tree stump. "After all, I did tell you the seat was reserved, did I not? In the future, I suggest you heed my advice." He winked. Turning his attention to the bear, he said, "Okay, Buttercup. Lead the way."

Sauruses and tigers and bears, oh my, Camile thought.

Buttercup guided them about a quarter-mile into the field before sitting on her haunches. Vincent said nothing as he stood between student and beast. He placed one of his large hands on Buttercup's neck, sliding the other across the small of Camile's back. She turned her head to face him, mildly contorting her features as she did.

"What are you trying to—?"

"You'll need to face forward, love," he instructed.

Camile hesitated, not knowing what to make of his bizarre request. She opened her mouth to inquire, but her breath caught in the back of her throat. She grimaced, feeling her midsection suddenly growing cold, sending a wave of goose bumps across her skin. Her lungs felt as rigid as ice blocks and she gave in to her impulse to expel the frigid air. Facing forward, she exhaled a deep breath.

Though the weather was warm, she could see her breath leave her body and cling to the air nearly a foot away from her face. The frost expanded before her eyes, revealing a wall she wouldn't have seen otherwise, despite its close proximity. Removing his hand from her back, Vincent extended a slim, lengthy index finger. He tapped the surface, prompting a vertical crevice to emerge as small superficial cracks sprouted outward. During the event, Camile's body temperature returned to normal, rising in contrast to the descending sun.

"Cool, isn't it? Pardon the pun." The commissioner winked. Waving his hand, he prompted the icy wall to part, creating an entryway. "Ladies first," he said, gesturing her to enter. After a moment's hesitation, she obliged. She heard him call for Buttercup to follow.

The grassy field hardened with each step, transforming into dull well-worn pavement as lively figures emerged. What was once a broad orange sky was now red and white tarp. It stretched over cage-dwelling animals and a multitude of excited onlookers, most wearing special passes. Analyzing the crowd, Camile's gut told her that the circus was located in the Coexistent World. There was something about the lax, impatient manner in which the patrons and workers shuffled about that contrasted with the methodical style of the Deltine people.

Camile thought it odd that though the air filled her lungs, it had no taste or smell. She wondered if it was a side effect of the trick the commissioner had performed moments earlier. After seeing one of the giraffes releasing a golden stream, she figured it was probably for the best. Her contemplation was cut short once she heard Vincent order Buttercup back to her cage. Much to Camile's amazement, the bear obeyed, walking through the bars like an apparition to join the rest of her group. Soon, Buttercup became just as solid as the bars containing her. This became obvious when she shook the cage slightly, drawing attention to herself. Spectators voiced their confusion, swearing that the creature hadn't been there before.

"Looks like VIPs get a preshow with their backstage pass," a bald man said to his family, which included a redheaded toddler riding on his shoulders.

Distracted by the occurrence, Camile collided with a patron and promptly apologized.

"Watch where you're going, bitch," the woman snapped before rejoining the crowd.

Damn! No need to get all hostile.

Camile rolled her eyes. Shrugging off the rude statement, she caught up with Vincent.

He explained that some Transcendent residents possessed a strong ability to communicate with animals in both dimensions. Such individuals often collaborated with creatures in order to achieve specific tasks.

Most of the explanation seemed redundant since Camile's father had already outlined this information just days earlier, but she didn't mind hearing it again while walking through the tent. Before long, Camile realized they were tailing the woman who had lashed out at her moments earlier.

"Classy lady," Camile muttered sarcastically upon seeing the commissioner's fleeting scowl.

"Her attitude was rather nasty, wasn't it?" he acknowledged.

"Whatever. I'm used to it by now. It's her problem."

"I guess it's best you couldn't hear what she was thinking, love." Vincent cracked a subtle grin.

"That bad?" Camile arched a brow.

"Yes, darling, but I won't taint your ears with her vile thoughts. Jealousy and self-importance can fuel the most violent, despicable notions in people—particularly the simple-minded ones." He eyed the woman, now among a crowd of spectators watching a small capuchin monkey juggling apples. The brief performance was rewarded with unanimous applause. Regarding his trainer with large glistening eyes, the monkey received approval to distribute souvenirs. In doing so, he nearly tripped one of several props people transporting cream pies, undoubtedly for a clown act.

"You were honorable to take the high road, love," Vincent said softly, hunching over slightly to shorten the distance between his voice and her ear. "Most people would have slapped some manners into her. That's sort of an amusing thought, actually. Even so, I'm a gentleman. I'd never advocate hitting a woman, though she hardly qualifies as such."

He locked eyes with Camile, who suddenly pictured the woman with a face full of frosting.

The commissioner smirked. "Something funny?"

Camile didn't realize she had chuckled.

Before she could answer, she felt a tiny hand tugging her pinky finger. She looked down and saw the adorable face of the black and white monkey. He smiled broadly, offering her a souvenir, a rubber ball with a circus logo. Camile accepted the item, quickly returning her attention to Vincent.

"Don't be rude to the little guy." He chuckled. "Aren't you going to thank him?"

As soon as she made eye contact, the monkey shrieked loudly before climbing onto the woman's chest. Camile was astonished to see the creature acting like a remote control for her resentment as he slapped the woman twice. The trainer went after the agitated primate, who darted off into the crowd, tripping several props people. Pie in hand, one of them awkwardly danced to maintain his balance. He succeeded, after connecting the pastry with the dazed woman's face. Knowing she had foreseen—perhaps even provoked—the event, Camile stood slack jawed as mild anxiety breached her amusement.

"You naughty girl." Vincent shook his head, the unsteadiness of his voice revealing his suppressed mirth.

"I didn't mean to—" Camile stopped mid-sentence. "Hey, you made me do that!"

"Now, how exactly did I manage to make you do it?" He paused after the question to allow Camile to answer, but she couldn't think of one.

"You have nothing to blame but your inability to control your own anger." The commissioner wagged his finger. "As a result, the little fellow not only picked up on it, but absorbed it. Raw emotion is the easiest to communicate, but as you can see, it's also the most dangerous. Consider this your first lesson."

Watching the fuming woman being whisked away, Camile grew concerned at how easily she had lost control. It was the second time an animal had hurt someone seemingly as a result of her emotional negligence.

"No worries." The commissioner winked. "I won't report this incident, unless you enjoy those little town hall meetings."

Chapter 19

The Vas Navelle

Beads of sweat trickled down Camile's face. The few drops she couldn't catch with her hand stung her eye, so she calmed the irritation with a few blinks. Her workout uniform clung to her damp body, but allowed just enough room for stray drops of perspiration to tickle the skin of her back and cleavage. The discomfort proved an inconvenient distraction as she pushed through yet another demanding physical training session.

Her impact with the ground was becoming increasingly rough, so much so that she would sometimes forget she was practicing with one of her classmates. As a result, she would sometimes fight as though her life depended on it. Much to her relief, the match finally came to a close. A brief applause echoed through the room before the class and spectators all dispersed upon dismissal.

"You okay?" Commander Wilder called from the front of the room before sipping from his canteen.

Her breath still escaping in rugged gasps, Camile forced a smile and nodded. With a wave, she signaled that she was fine. On the contrary, her muscles felt like flaming gelatin. After wiping her face with a towel Camile noticed Justine stalking her combat instructor from behind one of the columns in the gym. Before she could say anything, Justine jumped onto his back.

The sound of his fallen canteen echoed throughout the room as she cleared the distance between them, hoping she had enough energy to help him. By the time she reached the sparring pair, Camile realized her assistance wasn't needed. During the brief tussle, Brandon flipped Justine's petite frame over his head. Amazingly, Justine displayed cat-like reflexes, landing on her feet. To Camile's surprise, the two embraced shortly thereafter. Brandon spun her around as he lifted her slightly off the ground.

This chick really gets around, Camile thought.

"You're getting kinda rusty, babe," Justine quipped.

"Don't be so cocky. I knew it was you all along. For such a small woman, your footsteps are as heavy as a saurus'." Brandon teased. "Even so, it's good to see you again."

Justine laughed, playfully poking the commander in the ribs. With a broad smile, he attempted to commence introductions.

"No need for that, Bran Bear." Justine interrupted. "We've already met."

Brandon furrowed his brow.

"We're not kids anymore," he said, keeping his voice low. "How many times do I have to ask you to stop calling me that?"

"Sorry. I guess Kibble's a better fit for you."

"Funny, I thought you already took that title. Or did you eat it?" Brandon said sarcastically, earning another playful poke.

"Do that again and I'll have you charged for assaulting a superior officer." Brandon puffed his chest comically. "Besides, you should know me well enough to tell when I'm kidding. Anyway, it's been too long. So, tell me, how's life in—?" Brandon suddenly went silent, his cheerful expression dissolving into poised seriousness.

It was the first time Camile had seen him react in such a way. She had a hunch that someone was communicating with him telepathically. What he said next confirmed her suspicion.

"Duty calls," he announced, meeting Justine's dark eyes. "Hey, let's meet up for dinner later. I wanna hear all about your trip."

Clapping Camile's shoulder, he commended, "Great match today. Keep up the good work."

After giving Justine a quick hug and a peck on the cheek, Brandon made a swift exit, leaving the two women standing in silence. Justine stared at Camile for a moment, as though sizing her up. Finally, she spoke:

"I saw you clocking him. He's way out of your league, girl, so don't even try."

The blatant comment caught Camile by surprise, but she wasn't about to let it slide.

I oughta clock you, she thought before saying, "That sounds like something a threatened woman would say. Aren't you involved with Jeremy? What do you care whether or not I'm interested in Brandon?"

"You're kidding, right?" Justine winced as though tasting something rancid. "Brandon's my brother!"

Confused, Camile furrowed her brow. Justine and Brandon had absolutely no resemblance whatsoever, something their contrasting skin color emphasized.

"If you must know, his parents adopted me," Justine explained. "But that's beside the point. If you don't want any more drama in your life, don't get any ideas about my brother."

Justine turned to walk away, but faced Camile anew with a parting thought.

"By the way, I'll be his assistant for the foreseeable future." She smirked.

Looking forward to it, Camile thought sarcastically.

*   *   *

The transport hub was bustling with activity as commuters headed to and from their scheduled flights. The otherwise drab ground sparkled with the metallic skin of the gleaming aircraft lining the path to the private hangars. Camile looked forward to spending some time with Jeremy outside the Celestia. He was to personally see to it that she arrived safely at the *Vas Navelle*, or what some referred to as the sacred crater.

Much to Camile's discomfort, Commander Wilder was part of the security convoy ordered to escort them. Now in the presence of the objects of her lopsided dual desire, she found herself unsure of how to react. She wanted to say something to distract herself from the anxiety-fueled tremors in her stomach, but was unable to find the right words. Her apprehension was compounded by her fear of flying. Conversely, the commander was looking forward to the pending flight.

"It's been almost a year since my last pilgrimage to the *Vas Navelle*. I miss the open sky." He rubbed his hands together in anticipation. "I don't know about you, but I can't wait to blaze my jet across it like a comet."

"Brandon, you know we have to observe the temporary speed restriction zones," Jeremy said with a knowing glance.

"Well, while you're *observing* the speed restrictions you can observe my ass slicing the air in front of you," the commander joked. Camile joined the two men in laughter that was truncated by Commissioner Thornton's sudden appearance.

"I'm sorry to delay your trip, Jeremy, but I need your help with something," he announced. "Camile, you can ride with Commander Wilder."

"It's alright. I can wait." She offered.

"I'm sure you can, love, but this is a case where expediency is paramount. Don't want to keep your parents waiting. Jeremy will catch up in time to join you for the return trip. Now, off you go then," the commissioner said in a tone that bordered on condescending.

Upon reaching the commander's shuttle, Camile was impressed even though it wasn't as stately as her father's vessel. Its matte black and silver body was sleekly designed with sharp, intimidating angles. There were two Arvainan symbols engraved on the starboard side of the craft. She found one of them vaguely familiar, but failed to recognize the other.

"What does it mean?" she asked.

"Oh, this?" Brandon traced his fingers over the symbols. "It's the name of my shuttle, the *Night Hound*. Of course it's not really my shuttle. Sure, I'll probably be the only who'll ever pilot it, but this baby was commissioned by the Arvainan government, just as our bodies were commissioned by the stars."

Cracking a soft smile, Camile thought, *Brandon's got a little poetic streak in him, I see.*

Once seated inside the craft, he held her gaze a few moments before breaking the silence.

"If I didn't know any better, I'd say you were trying to avoid me by hiding behind Jeremy." He smiled curiously. "What's up with that?"

"Oh, that's not it," Camile started, all the while wondering if she was really that transparent. "I just thought it might be best to stick with the original itinerary."

"I get it. You're nervous." He laughed. "There's nothing to be afraid of. Well, other than the fact your life's in my hands."

Camile regarded him with mild concern before anxiously fastening her harness.

"Hey, don't worry." He tapped her hand, giving it a tender squeeze before resuming his preflight check. "Like I said, there's nothing to be afraid of. Besides, my hands are very capable. I've noticed you've been a little distant these past few days. Have I done something to make you uncomfortable?"

Camile wondered whether or not she should mention her tense exchange with Justine. She decided against it since she didn't want to drive a rift between the siblings. Instead, she answered, "No. Everything's fine."

"Right." Commander Wilder pursed his full lips as he read the controls and entered a few commands. Meeting her eyes with his penetrative aquamarine gaze, he cracked a boyish smile. "Care to try the truth now?"

"What?"

"Your eyes betray your lips."

"Sorry." Camile hung her head, briefly eyeing her twiddling fingers before resuming eye contact. "I just don't feel like talking about it."

"See? That wasn't so hard. That's all you had to say from the jump." Brandon propped his elbow on the edge of the control panel, resting his temple against his fist. "I know I'm your instructor, but I also consider myself your friend. I hope that's not too bold."

Camile shook her head.

Cupping her shoulder with his free hand, Brandon continued, "Listen, whatever's going on, don't let it get you so tense that you can't enjoy yourself. It's okay to relax and let go every once in a while." Sitting upright in his seat, he secured his safety harness. "Speaking of which, we better get moving."

As it turned out, the commander lived up to his last name. He was an even wilder pilot than Wyatt. He indulged himself, maneuvering the craft into hairpin turns, barrel rolls and loops. Struck by a sudden thirst for adventure that overshadowed her fear, Camile was powerless to protest. Even so, her screams filled the cabin during the intervals where the shift of gravity reiterated her lack of control. Her frantic heart rushed adrenaline-laced blood through her body, prompting her to breathe rapidly. Flooded by an intense concoction of emotions, Camile felt more alive than she had in a long time.

When they arrived at their destination, Camile had mild difficulty regaining her stability. On shaky legs, she exited the shuttle and stumbled onto a vast wasteland. Commander Wilder followed with a broad smile, as though proud of himself. Though partially upset with the commander, she admitted to herself that it was indeed an exhilarating experience.

The blazing sun commanded the afternoon sky, beating down on them as they walked towards Camile's parents. Stray clouds granted transitory moments of relief surpassed only by the promise of shade provided by the taupe tent pitched a few yards away. Once they settled beneath the soothing refuge of the makeshift shelter, Camile noticed what appeared to be an excavation site nearly half a mile away. It soon became evident that it was the reason for her trip. Her parents began to explain the nature of the adornment hanging from her neck.

"Our medallions are created from these." Zephyr held up a dull stone with shimmering flecks.

"Looks like an ordinary rock, but I know looks can be deceiving." Camile acknowledged.

"You're right." Her father winked. "These aren't just any rocks. Does the name Chicxulub mean anything to you?"

"The crater in the Yucatan?"

Nodding, Zephyr set the stone on a folding table surrounded by five chairs. "We're standing on the Transcendent side of the Chicxulub crater. The crater is said to have originated in the Coexistent dimension millions of years ago when a massive meteor collided with Earth. We believe that's the event that created the originating rift between the two dimensions. Our early ancestors found these rocks to possess special properties that enhanced their natural abilities."

"Many people have had the misconception that these rocks are the primary source of our abilities. They're just tools that make it easier for us to control our powers," Commander Wilder added, helping himself to a bottled water from the cooler. Grabbing a second, Brandon handed it to Camile, who joined him and her parents at the table.

"Since the discovery, these rocks have been carefully mined and distributed in raw form to Transcendent citizens during their first pilgrimage here," Zephyr continued. "A limited number of stones get processed and made into medallions. Shaman sages are assigned the task of determining who gets such special pieces. Almost everyone who has ever received such medallions has had business with the council, some on the wrong side of the law."

"As you know by now, not everyone was on board with the idea of inter-dimensional peace." Kylie dabbed her forehead with a towel.

Drinking the ice-cold water, Camile released a satisfied sigh as the liquid chill washed over her midsection. She then raised a question that had been on her mind for quite some time.

"If so many people have these medallions, why did Akalina try to take mine specifically? What makes it so special?"

"Medallions are usually created for children no younger than two years of age. Yours was created before you were born," her father answered. "The shaman who created your talisman was overwhelmed with the impulse to produce it. She had a premonition that the person who would receive it would play a vital role in the *Invisible War*. The day you were born, the talisman seemed drawn to you like a magnet. It was then that she knew it was destined for you."

"The shaman, was it Tabitha?" Camile asked.

Zephyr shook his head. "No. Her predecessor."

Chapter 20

Hazy Boundaries

Camile observed several surveillance missions as time elapsed. The subjects were being studied for a variety of reasons; some for potential recruitment, others for their own protection from possible attacks from Transcendent rebels. Select members of Coexistent governments collaborated with the Arvainan and Transcendent councils in pinpointing potential targets of malicious intent. Camile's latest assignment was to accompany Tabitha to a busy Los Angeles office building where she would anonymously evaluate one of her recruits.

She spotted a young man in the busy maze of cubicles, slumped in a chair. Dropping his head backward, he slowly palmed his face. A deep sigh indicated his exhaustion and taxed patience. Not long ago, Camile had been in a similar position, working a dead-end job with little to show for it other than under eye bags and a vacant social life. She was amazed at how much she had changed since then. The things that had once caused her stress and anxiety now seemed comically trivial. She now knew there were more important things at stake other than who came in first in the corporate rat race.

"Can't we do something about this?" she asked the shaman. "By the looks of things he's gonna snap any minute."

"No," Tabitha answered. "He's exactly where he needs to be right now. His presence here is very important."

"How so?"

"He's a buffer. He helps to maintain an emotional balance here," Tabitha replied, describing a buffer as an absorber and neutralizer of negative energy. The duration of the neutralization process depended on the magnitude of negativity.

"Hang in there, man," Camile said almost to herself, knowing the disgruntled worker couldn't see or hear her.

"Oh, don't worry about him." The shaman chuckled. "He's a lot stronger than he appears and trust me, he's in for one heck of a reward once he's served his purpose here."

"Heaven?"

"Not exactly. At least not yet. He's been hoping for a big career change and a chance to pursue his dream of owning his own restaurant. Although the dream has faded, he's kept it alive for ten years. Little does he know, in the near future he'll run into a great change in his fortune." Tabitha winked.

*   *   *

Unpolished puzzle pieces continued to fall with the passage of time, forming a disturbing jigsaw of Akalina's past. Though the fragmented memories left gaps as vacuous as black holes, they were gradually revealing Sir Drayden's unhealthy relationship with Camile's darker half.

Camile could taste the sharp, nauseating fear that crept through young Akalina's veins as her small body crashed into the wall. Within moments, the child's defiant laughter transmuted to rugged gasps of horror as Sir Drayden approached. Pinned high against the hard surface, young Akalina struggled to free herself from the knight's unrelenting grip. It slowly constricted her as his callous blue eyes burned into hers.

Her body suddenly felt too small for her lungs to properly expand. She forced out a desperate cry for her father, but her delicate voice didn't carry far. Sir Drayden scorned her distress call and finally released her, letting her fall painfully to the floor. Her rampant breathing threatened to morph into full-blown sobs as she watched the knight approach the guards.

"Remove her from my sight before I kill her," he ordered. One hand on his hip, he pointed at the officers. "And you're to mention none of what you've witnessed to anyone. That includes the minister and ambassador."

Those words chased Camile into her consciousness as she gasped for air like a fish out of water. She wondered how a simple thing like laughter could inspire such brutal treatment, especially of a child. Were the flashbacks an authentic glimpse into repressed memories, or simply the wild digressions of her subconscious? Unable to find an answer, Camile took solace in her journal:

> *What separates dreams from memories when both are equally vivid? According to my latest vision, Sir Drayden did something so awful to Akalina that she's tried to block it out. Her residual fear is infecting my soul and I think the only cure is to seek the truth, but where do I begin? Some say ignorance is bliss, but I think it's something people tell themselves to cope with living a lie. Sometimes I wonder if I should just leave it alone, but how can I pretend everything's okay and entrust Sir Drayden, especially if he's capable of such violent behavior?*

*   *   *

After making steady strides in her physical defense skills, Camile graduated to weapons training. She didn't take to it as quickly, so Commander Wilder suggested occasional private lessons in order to give her more personalized instruction. Naturally, Justine—who watched her like a hawk during each session—wasn't pleased with the idea. The extra practice paid off and Camile began to catch up with the rest of her classmates. Even so, the commander saw room for further improvement.

Camile trailed the class dispersing from the gym when the commander summoned her.

"You're improving your technique, but your form still needs a little work." He handed her a weapon, a retractable baton. "Let's fix that, shall we? Assume your attack stance."

As Camile followed the command, she noticed Justine lingering by the exit before making her exit, visibly disappointed.

"You're a little hunched." The commander wrangled her attention, slowly positioning himself behind her. "Here, let me show you." His words melted in her ear as he adjusted her posture slightly. His strong hands lingered at her waist before moving to her shoulders.

"There, that's better," he commended. "Your form looks perfect from where I'm standing."

Feeling the warmth of his eyes grazing her backside, Camile grew mildly self-conscious. She took a deep breath, hoping that doing so would calm her nerves. It didn't help much. Her hands became unstable as she overcorrected her grip on the weapon. Commander Wilder gently seized her wrist, pulling her slightly closer to him. The tremble in her hand seemed to radiate through her entire body once she felt the strong contour of his abs and chest brush against her back. His gentle touch and the salty sweet scent of his skin sent an effervescent chill down her body, inconveniently awakening the silken erogenous patches beneath her shirt. She hoped the fabric was good at keeping secrets.

This can't be happening, she thought, wondering why her body was suddenly calling for the commander when her mind and spirit longed for Jeremy.

"You're shaking." The commander craned his neck to meet her gaze, his features wearing a curious expression. "Are you nervous?"

"No. Just tired from today's lesson, I guess," she answered, slightly out of breath.

"You can rest when we're done here. I suggest you conserve your strength in the future so you can keep up." Cracking a slight smile, he took her weapon. Camile swore she saw a seductive twinkle in his eye.

Commander Wilder deactivated the baton, analyzing it as he walked around to face her head on.

"I remember this model." He smiled deepened while inspecting the piece. "If you're not careful, you can end up with some pretty messed up hand cramps." He extended his hand to return the weapon, but before Camile could take it, he pulled it back slightly.

"Hold it gently, yet firmly," he instructed. "It should feel like an extension of your own body. Relax. Don't fight against it, embrace it. Know when to take control and know when to let it work for you and you'll find your goal easier to reach."

With a skillful twirl of the baton Brandon finally allowed her to take it. Apparently pleased, his smile broadened. "See, Wildflower, isn't that so much better?"

Is he still talking about the weapon? If not, man, this guy is slick with the double entendres!

Camile then considered the possibility that she had taken his words out of context. That, and the fact her hormones were apparently running amok. In any case she knew one thing was certain, she needed to test the cold shower theory.

*   *   *

Eclipsed in the shadow of the rest of the mountain, Dusque Peak received the least amount of sunlight of all the Caldaq summits. It seemed only natural that it housed Arvaina's foremost planetarium in addition to various facilities, including the Black Garden, a conservatory dedicated to the study and preservation of rare plants and nocturnal creatures. Camile had heard of the peak's spectacular view of the night sky, something she'd rather been exploring as opposed to doing yard work under Sir Drayden's annoyingly close supervision.

Kneeling in the dirt, Camile unearthed fifteen plants called *Ganli* to the sound of the chirping crickets and hooting owls lurking in the darkness of the lantern-lined forest. She was tasked with aerating the soil and infusing it with fertilizer prior to replanting. Once out of the ground, the thorny roots snaked around the dark violet blossom to protect it, giving off the appearance of a volley ball-sized tumbleweed. It was explained that the flower was most often used by shaman healers to create elixirs with potent hallucinogenic effects. Such elixirs were used for spiritual travels and the highest levels of therapeutic meditation. The key to a thriving *Ganli* plant was to carefully bury the roots deep into the ground to ensure a steady foundation. This meant carefully unraveling them. As Camile did this, Sir Drayden circled around her like a vulture. Casting distrusting side glances at the knight, she nicked herself several times and could no longer contain her frustration.

"This is bullshit," she muttered under her breath.

"You're wrong," was Sir Drayden's casual response. "It's not bullshit. It's saurus dung."

Camile was initially puzzled by his statement, then realized he was referring to the fertilizer with which she was planting the *Ganli*. She protested the fact that she had to touch it with her bare hands. However, the elder insisted she continue. And so, she established a cautious, steady rhythm by the time she reached the eighth plant. Just then, a roaring sneeze ripped through the air. As Camile jumped, she nicked herself yet again.

Jeez! The man could give Excelsior and Buttercup a run for their money.

"Do you mind?" she fumed, suspecting he had purposely distracted her.

"You and you alone are responsible for your concentration. Keep planting…and mind your temper."

"I should get this looked at," Camile said of her wound. "It's—"

"You'll live. Keep planting," Sir Drayden said matter-of-factly.

Why is he punishing me like this? Camile thought, hoping it wasn't a prelude to whatever trauma he had apparently inflicted on Akalina.

Grunting to herself, Camile angrily snatched the next plant. As a result of her carelessness, she received several pricks to her palms. She dropped it, swearing under her breath. When she went to retrieve it, she noticed the plant rapidly withering as it died. Confused, she regarded her supervisor. With a grim expression, he broke the strained silence.

"This exercise is to not only test your patience and focus, but to reintroduce you to the earth. You'll need to learn how to sense its energy as it senses yours. The earth is a living organism that communicates in its own way. That's also why it's important to pay attention to the animals since they are in ways mediums, communicating what humans are too distracted to understand."

Sir Drayden's eyes shifted slightly. Following his stare, Camile noticed Excelsior lying several feet behind her.

"Their vision is pure in that their main focus is genuine survival," the knight continued. "Not so with average people, who seek to conquer, divide and destroy." Sinking into a squat, he tapped the dead plant with his finger, reducing it to mulch. "I've been meaning to ask, how did your first meeting go with Commissioner Thornton?"

Recalling the incident that had taken place at the circus, Camile swallowed hard before responding that it had gone well.

"Nothing out of the ordinary took place?" he pressed.

Camile chuckled awkwardly. "With all due respect, sir, nothing in my life has been ordinary for a very long time."

"So, nothing notable occurred or came up in conversation? I'll be meeting with him later today and I want to be sure we're both on the same page."

Counting on the commissioner's promise not to disclose the incident, Camile responded, "Not that I can recall, sir."

Sir Drayden held her gaze a moment, then gestured to the unplanted *Ganli*. Upon his unspoken request, Camile continued the task and eventually reestablished her rhythm. By the time the last *Ganli* was firmly in the ground, she received at least another two lacerations due to his distractions, though none as deep as the first. Camile's father was a welcome sight as he entered the garden. Sir Drayden made his exit shortly thereafter.

As her father continued his approach, two large insects made their way up Camile's legs. Although she had seen the arachnids on several occasions since her reintegration, she still found their appearance jarring. Something still seemed menacing about their furry bodies and plentiful appendages. Yet, she was well aware of their healing capabilities and therefore allowed two small ones to crawl onto her injured hands. She recognized their attributes; a silvery stinger, two bundles of glistening eyes, and a double set of legs—one growing out of the other. The creatures currently working their medicinal magic were about the size of her hand. They were delicate in using their stingers to inject the medicine that healed her flesh and eased her pain. Within minutes, she was good as new and the peculiar insects went on their way.

"I think Sir Drayden should definitely consider sensitivity training." Camile exhaled, massaging her hands. "I kept getting cut because of him."

"Actually, it wasn't him," her father said. "It was you. You're in control of your mind and body. Your reaction to his sneeze was just that, your reaction."

Camile furrowed her brow. "How did you know he sneezed? You just got here."

"Sir Drayden has trained many people over the years and I've seen him use certain techniques. You should be proud of yourself. You managed to do a lot better than most people have during their first encounters with the *Ganli*." Zephyr then gestured to an arachnid that had settled on top of a nearby signpost to cleanse its legs. "Ever wonder about these guys?" he asked.

Not waiting for a response he coaxed the creature down, petting it as it settled on his forearm. Taking it into his hand, he held the arachnid upside down and stroked its belly. As the legs splayed out, he drew a short knife from his utility belt. Almost instantly, dozens more arachnids sprang out from the trees and bushes, surrounding Camile and her father. They hissed menacingly, stingers raised, as they closed in. The leader was twice as large as the rest and brazenly approached Zephyr's feet.

"Dad, put the knife down." Camile suggested, cautiously stepping closer to him.

Kneeling slowly, Zephyr addressed the creature. "This one is ours," he said gently, presenting the spider in his hand. "See?"

After apparently inspecting the contents of Zephyr's hand, the arachnid leader retreated into the surrounding foliage with its group. Standing, he resumed his demonstration, slicing the furry creature down the middle. Camile cringed, bracing herself for a pain-filled shriek, but the sound never met her ears. Instead, her eyes were graced by intricate mechanical workings within the spider's frame.

There were no less than three flexible chambers, all containing liquids of varying colors and consistencies. In addition, there were several conduits leading from each chamber, merging into two separate tubes that tapered off into the fangs. Another thin conduit flowed into the silvery tail. Equally as impressive was the circuitry that fed into the bundles of lenses forming the creature's eyes, a facade for a sophisticated visual recording device. Zephyr explained that as lively and realistic as the arachnid seemed, it was actually one of the Arvaina's most impressive technologies.

"These are Tarconian Spiders, named after their inventor, Professor Thaddeus A. Tarconian," he explained. "The professor formulated Tarconian Extract, a very powerful healing serum. He synthesized the serum after thoroughly studying the healing properties of the Diwata, tree dwelling changelings located throughout this dimension. The Diwata primarily live in trees and are relatively peaceful, but as you've just seen, they're highly defensive if someone endangers their environment or one of their kind."

Immediately upon setting the open spider on the ground, another raced forward and worked to close the seam.

"At one time they were hunted to the brink of extinction until the professor found a way to replicate their blood in a serum," he continued. "The Diwata have a remarkable ability to change their appearance, much like some of our residents. Once the serum was perfected, Professor Tarconian integrated it into the form of these spiders. They look remarkably similar to one of the Diwata's preferred forms. Many can't tell the difference between the real ones and these guys. In addition to *Tarconian Extract*, the spiders also carry a sedative and a numbing agent since they're designed to perform non-critical surgery."

Camile watched as both creatures scurried into the bushes. "Do they treat *everything?*"

"No. But, if a person has a condition beyond their ability to treat it, the spiders are programmed to immediately notify the nearest medical professional. Also, there are certain, more personal, medical services we feel should be left to those who can provide a more human touch."

Camile was relieved. She found the thought of possibly having a robotic spider as a gynecologist unnerving to say the very least. Her father went on to explain that one of the Transcendent World's most valuable medical advances was the harvesting of human organs. In many cases, this technology enabled humans to replace limbs and essential body parts that had been lost due to disease or accidents. Yet, the technology was used as a means to improve the quality of life, not necessarily to cheat death.

During her time in the Coexistent World, Camile had read speculative articles which predicted such advancements, but not for many years into the future. Once again, she found herself amazed at the advancements of the Transcendent people. Even so, she was concerned about the ratio between science and ethics.

Chapter 21

Chronicles

Camile found an easy friend in Joval. He had a willing ear and managed to lighten even the most serious conversations. One day, during a trip to the Caldaq Museum, Joval invited Camile to a theatrical production to take place early that evening.

"I wish I could, but I have an appointment with Sir Drayden," Camile said as they traversed the external stone corridor. "I doubt I can get out of it."

"Wait a minute...*The* Sir Drayden Sebastian?" Halting his steps, Joval turned to stand toe-to-toe with Camile, who nodded.

"Oh, man," he exclaimed, raking a hand through his shoulder-length dreads. "You're lucky to be training under his fine instruction."

"How so?" Camile asked, occasionally glancing at passersby.

Joval stood slack-jawed. "*How so? How so?* Sir Drayden don't train just anybody. Come to think of it, he don't really train *anyone* at all these days. To my knowledge, you're the first one he's taken on in years. He's very selective, not to mention he's the grand high master of badassness. You must be pretty damn special for him to want to train you. I guess it's obvious because of the whole prophecy thing and all, but *man*, I'm jealous!" He chuckled.

Don't be. He's more like the grand high bully of Deltine, as far as I can tell, Camile thought, chortling at both the term *badassness* and Joval's unbridled enthusiasm. He struck her as the type who was fanatical about his idols—undoubtedly memorizing their entire careers, collecting anything he could find that was remotely associated with them. Camile recalled reading several instances of such obsessive behavior in the Coexistent World, where fans would pay top dollar for things as trivial as a snotty tissue of their favorite celebrity.

"Well, not for nothing, I get the feeling he has a pretty hefty obligation to undo the mess that was made when Akalina and I were separated." Camile fingered her medallion before jamming her hands in her denim jacket pockets. "Hey, if you admire him so much, why don't *you* train with him?"

"It's not for lack of trying. The council said I was much too eager. Go figure." Joval shrugged.

Smirking, Camile briefly raised an eyebrow. "I can see how they'd think that. I'm just hoping Sir Drayden gets off my back soon. He's really getting on my nerves. Not to mention, the man gives me a serious case of the creeps and then some," Camile muttered before noticing the stunned wide-eyed expression on her friend's face.

"Sorry, Joval." She chortled. "I almost forgot how much you like *Mr. Badass.*"

As soon as the words escaped her mouth, she immediately regretted them. The twinge in her shoulders told her that Sir Drayden's eyes were burning into her back. Reluctantly turning her head, her eyes confirmed her fear as they met the serious face of the subject of their discussion.

Shit!

She and Joval promptly continued their journey. To Camile's dismay, Sir Drayden was walking alongside them, apparently also headed to the museum. He carried on as though he hadn't heard her remarks, but Camile knew otherwise. Meanwhile, Joval grinned stupidly, nearly walking into a wall as he admired his idol.

"Uh…Good d-day, Sir D-Drayden, s-sir," he stuttered.

Bemused, Camile regarded her unusually nervous friend as he continued.

"I was w-w-wonderin' 'bout…If I could ask you—"

"Maybe some other time, Mr. Hall," the knight said coolly.

Joval's jaw dropped. "Some other time's perfect, sir! I don't got plans or nothin'."

Ordinarily, Camile would've laughed, but silent tension was building with each step as she wondered if the knight was upset with her.

"Sir, about what I said back there—" she began.

"I don't require your admiration. Only your obedience," Sir Drayden interrupted.

Camile inwardly cringed at the word *obedience*. It made her feel as though she had no choice but to follow his every command like an animal. However, she knew better than to contest the statement since the last thing she wanted was to anger the man who intimidated her most.

*   *   *

The museum contained the nostalgic quality of many Camile had visited in the Coexistent World. The entrance hall was adorned with carefully preserved textiles and artifacts that served as a promising preview of the collection to be seen. The warm colors and polished furnishings added to the prestigious atmosphere while establishing a subconscious boundary which communicated the message: *feel free to observe and enjoy, but do not dare touch!*

And observe is exactly what Camile did as Joval showed her various primitive carvings, etchings and other artwork. The renderings, as most artwork did, told a story. The depictions indicated times of darkness and bloodshed, broken by peaceful respites that varied in frequency as they progressed into the more modern periods of the gallery. Her gaze traveled meters ahead, meeting a blank wall that had yet to be filled. As much art as her eyes had just ingested, Camile had barely made a dent in the vast collection to be explored.

"I think we've given you two enough time to play." Camile's father smiled, approaching with Kylie and Sir Drayden. "I don't want you to forget the main reason why you're here."

Indeed, it had nearly slipped Camile's mind that Joval had been sent to accompany her to the museum, where her knowledge of Transcendent history would be further enriched. Joval, was staring at Sir Drayden with an almost comical look of admiration and nearly missed Zephyr's order of dismissal. Camile laughed quietly to herself as he exited, flashing a thumbs-up and a smile. His playful personality was reminiscent of one of her closest friends, Rhonda, whom she had lost when she was a teenager. In remembrance, her smile faded as she returned her attention to the trio standing before her.

Traveling through a labyrinth of snaking corridors, they toured through segments dedicated to the Transcendent efforts for world preservation. There were also sections devoted to the history of medical, technological and scientific advancements. Camile spotted an astronaut uniform mounted on a wall. Beside it was a plaque commemorating the first successful Transcendent launch into orbit.

"There's a space program here?" she asked.

"Numerous ones." Zephyr's dimples deepened, framing a proud grin. "Coexistents aren't the only ones with a thirst for exploration, you know."

"So, is there life on Mars after all?" Camile half-joked.

"There's life teeming throughout the entire solar system," Zephyr replied. "Transcendents have known this to be true for years. To most Coexistents, the planets appear to be deserted wastelands, but the contrary is true. If one planet contains multiple realms of existence, can you *imagine* the possibilities of what exists on the others? Once Coexistents really acknowledge and make an attempt to harmonize with each other, the likelihood of them actually seeing and experiencing these life forms will increase significantly."

Considering this, Camile was reminded that her life was very small in comparison to the complex universe. Of all the life that existed, hers was like a grain of sand on a vast island and yet, according to her parents and the council, it was worth so much. In many ways, it increased the weight on her shoulders to not ruin the chance she'd been given.

As they continued through subsequent galleries Camile's feet began to ache, but she pressed on. The discomfort dulled with the arousal of her interest when they reached a large room dedicated to ancient musical instruments. Each implement, whether string, percussion or wind seemed to possess a life all its own. One device in particular caught her attention and wouldn't let go. It was an odd wooden pipe of some kind, proudly displaying its age and the fact it was well-used. Camile looked for information about the object, but there was none. Only a tiny plaque that read: *Promise and Payment.*

"It serves as a reminder of what many have gone through and may possibly go through again if we take our freedoms for granted," Camile's mother explained.

"It's very unusual. Is it one of a kind?"

"More like one in a very exclusive collection," Sir Drayden answered. It was only then that Camile noticed the neighboring flutes and horns, all ridden with age, but relatively well preserved in individual, spacious display cases.

"Do they still work? What do they sound like?" Camile wondered aloud.

"I'm not sure, but most of these are best left unheard." Her mother smiled glumly.

Chapter 22

The Phantom World

Camile reflected on a statement her shaman counselor made awhile back, that if it wasn't for Sir Drayden, she wouldn't have been given a second chance to live. After mulling it over for days, a question arose. She presented it during their next meeting.

"How did Sir Drayden know I was dead?" Unconsciously drumming the pad of her index finger on the table, Camile glanced out of the window. The sun was trying to peek through the overcast sky, nearly as gray as the gossamer curtains shielding the entrance to the shaman's private quarters.

"I was wondering when you'd ask. Took longer than I thought." Tabitha exhaled as she finished grinding herbs with a mortar and pestle. She scooped the contents into two shimmering mesh cloths, fashioning them into sachets before tending to a glass kettle of steaming water sitting on a hot plate. While preparing two cups with the herbal packets, she gave her response.

"One day he was conducting business in the *Terra Mori*, also known as the Phantom World, or land of the dead. He came across your ghost wandering among the lost souls. To say he was disappointed was an understatement. After all he went through to convince the council to consider core segregation in lieu of execution, on your mother's behalf, you went and killed yourself anyway." She sighed, stirring the concoctions. "He thought it was best not to mention a word about your suicide to your parents until he tried to bring you back first. Of course, I disagreed, but as you probably know by now, that did nothing to change his mind." Tabitha paused a moment, placing a steaming mug in front of Camile. "I think we should try it again, my child."

"Try what?" Camile's eyes narrowed.

"The same thing I tried to show you before." Tabitha sat across from her, scooting her seat closer. "That is before you decided to take that little detour. I'm hoping this time will be more successful. If so, it'll clarify a few things on the matter."

"I'm still struggling with the knowledge of my sui—" Camile paused. "Reversed suicide. If you can make me understand it all, I'm game. Maybe it'll help me prevent the same mistake from happening again."

Jeremy peered from behind the curtain, shooting her a glance as though questioning her rationality.

"Not that I've been thinking about it. I'm certainly not!" she added urgently, acknowledging the morbid tone of her statement.

"Understanding is something you'll have to reach own your own." A somber expression crossed the shaman's tan features. "I can't *make* you understand anything. I can only show you what was done to bring you out of a bad situation."

Camile nodded, cradling the hot mug as the marshmallow-scented steam rose to her nose.

The shaman expelled a deep breath, meeting her eyes.

"Alright, but I warn you that this may not be easy for you. Like last time, it might not even work." She gestured to Camile's mug, instructing her to drink the contents.

"What's in it?"

"Secret recipe. It's meant to relax and open your mind while easing the transition."

Camile sipped the beverage and gagged almost immediately.

"Ugh! I can see why the recipe is still secret." She grimaced at the sharp bitter taste, removing a bit of pulp from her mouth. It was a familiar shade of violet.

"Complaining won't make it taste any better, so drink up," Tabitha ordered before chugging her own beverage. "I must warn you, though, you'll feel pretty strange."

After downing the rest of her drink, Camile leaned back in her plush reclining seat as the shaman instructed. Looking into the shaman's dark eyes, the hue flickered between brown and blue. The appearance against her deep colored skin and graying hair seemed cartoonish. Camile's chuckle incited the shaman to narrow her crinkled gaze. It was a reaction that prompted her calm amusement to grow to hysterical laughter. Yet, Camile didn't understand what it was she found so funny.

"I figured you'd be a laugher." The shaman sighed, her eyes now flashing in every color of the rainbow. Vibrant hues streamed from her gaze, painting objects and walls in a wacky array of color combinations.

"Whoa! I must be trippin'. What's in that stuff?" Camile laughed uncontrollably while attempting to stand. The shaman suggested she remain seated. From that moment on, Camile couldn't understand anything else the elder was saying. Every word sounded like gibberish. Suddenly, she felt her body falling away, or rather something within her being hoisted as the room circled around her.

Her body lurched as she grabbed hold of the chair in an attempt to catch her balance. Tabitha urged her not to resist. After a moment's hesitation, Camile allowed her body, and the world, to fall away as she and the shaman drifted into the shadowy abyss of the unknown.

*   *   *

Just as with the previous attempt, Camile floated like an aimless bubble in the dark until she felt the shaman grasp her arm. Only this time, she saw something she hadn't noticed before. In the far distance was a tiny blast of light occurring at varying intervals. From Camile's vantage point it seemed no larger than a standard sized light bulb, but there was something terrifyingly intimidating about it. Other images slowly emerged like a developing snapshot. Finally seeing the whole picture, she shuddered, grasping the shaman's hand tightly when she realized they weren't alone.

"Do you want to go back?" Tabitha asked, her eyes filled with urgency and concern.

Astounded beyond words, Camile could only shake her head as she released the shaman from her grip. She knew that stopping meant possibly never working up the nerve to try again. Determined to push through the fearful chill in her heart, she returned her attention to the inhabitants of the space.

Their structures were seemingly composed of the same smoky substance as the apparition she had seen at the hospital. Each spirit appeared to be self-illuminating—some more than others. Men, women, children and animals were all traveling in a massive multi-tiered circle. There appeared to be as many of them as there were stars in the vast universe. Each human spirit was devoid of clothing, though some retained the appearance of their former bodies whereas others had taken on more obscure forms.

"What is this place?" Camile asked breathlessly.

"You already know." Tabitha smiled somberly.

Camile clenched the shaman's sleeve as they floated upward. Soon, they were hovering above the crowd of slowly circulating phantoms. She noticed that the tiny light was continuously shifting along the outer perimeter of the massive circle of traveling phantoms. It rapidly increased in size and brightness as it grew nearer, its visual blasts more intense. Some of the phantoms closest to the light shrank back as if to protect their flesh, forgetting that it no longer existed. Thousands of *Intermediaries* frequently appeared with new spirits, which they poured into the large circle before vanishing, no doubt to collect others.

As Camile continued to observe, she recalled a statement Jeremy made at the hospital.

Where we all go, his voice resonated in her head.

She saw another light equally as large and as powerful as the bright one shifting around the circle, but it seemed like a glowing void. Camile was puzzled as to how something so dark could actually glow. Then a name she had heard earlier returned to the fore of her recollection.

"*Terra Mori.* Is this is where we all go…after we die?" Camile asked quietly.

The shaman nodded. "For awhile anyway. Some stay longer than others until they decide to move on. Sometimes it's decided for them."

"Move on? You mean there's more to this?"

"Camile, there's always more. *Much more.* Watch." Tabitha indicated the scene below.

The Intermediaries continued to come and go silently, but there were other, less reserved, beings among the ghosts. They serenely hovered over the circling crowd, commenting on their actions.

"Who are they?" Camile asked.

"High-level Intermediaries," the shaman answered after following her gaze. "They're among the toughest guardians of the Phantom World."

Camile noticed another brilliant blast of light, this time even larger, an indication of its increasing proximity. It seemed to bear all the intensity of an atomic explosion. Gasping, she shielded her eyes and braced herself for thundering noise and scorching heat, but there was only peaceful silence. She could make out the faint shapes of a group of ghosts entering the light as it faded, but a portion of them appeared to have been rejected before it grew dim.

"Nope. Still not ready yet!" One of the guardians laughed as he addressed them from high above. His voice was aged, raspy and nasal. "Timothy, you have to let her go. She can't come with you now. Diane, you have to accept that you did your best. The rest is up to them! Oh, and you, Gerald, you need to let go of that resentment of yours. It won't fix what's already been done." Wagging a finger, he said, "As for the rest of you, you're trying to gain admission to where you don't belong."

The guardian barely finished his sentence when another blast of light appeared to nearly engulf some of the ghosts along the edge of the massive circle. Most of them pushed away from it as they cried out fearfully. One ghost could be heard above the others as he screamed, moving as far away from the light as he could. A small puppy scurried through the air and hovered just a few feet above the man.

"No! It's gonna burn," the man cried. "I don't wanna—"

"Die?" the pup asked gruffly, wagging its stubby tail. "I got news for ya, pal—your body's long gone! The only thing holding you back now is yourself."

Turning her attention to the shaman, Camile's face contorted with bewilderment. "Flying talking puppies?"

"That's no puppy. Guardians don't have a fixed appearance," the shaman explained. "They can appear to be different things to different people. Apparently, that man has a soft side for animals."

Camile looked around and saw the other guardians shifting their appearances. A little boy stole her attention. He seemed confused and afraid as he wandered with the other spirits. The light opened up once more and he took a few steps toward it, but hesitated before entering. As he stared at the gigantic opening, the puppy-shaped guardian, still floating, ran over to him. Camile expected the guardian to maintain its benign form, but was surprised to see its soft fur give way to dark iridescent scales. It stretched into an amphibious tower with a powerful tail, broad shimmering wings and fiery eyes. She figured the boy would react in terror to the imposing dragon. Instead, his eyes lit up with amazement.

"Why did you stop?" the guardian asked.

"I - I don't know." The boy looked up into its large eyes, his smile fading. "I'm tired and I really want to go in…but I can't find my mommy."

"Byron, there are still some things your mother has to do before she's able to come here. She'll join you once she successfully completes her journey."

A pained expression crossed the boy's face. "Maybe I can go back. Don't I still have stuff to do, too?"

"No, Byron." The dragon shook its head. "Your work is already done."

The boy's frown deepened. "Will it take long for my mommy to get here?"

"Byron, you'll see that by the time she gets here, it will seem that very little time has passed. Time is *very* different in this place. Even though she's not ready to come here yet, there are ways you can see her again before her time comes."

Apparently thinking a moment, Byron smiled. He then took a step toward the light, but it quickly faded away.

"No! I—I was finally ready!" He wept.

"Are you still ready?" the dragon guardian asked softly to which Byron nodded tearfully.

Suddenly, the boy levitated until he was high above the crowd. The guardian swooped underneath Byron, seating him on its back. Another blast of light opened up in the far distance. The dragon flew toward it at full speed with Byron clinging to the hair on its back. Camile strained her eyes as she watched the dragon and a laughing Byron vanish into the light before it disappeared.

Tears of bittersweet amazement pooling in her eyes, Camile observed the phantoms rejoining formation to await the next cycle of lights. Some eagerly entered the bright light while others slowly, but boldly, entered the dark light. Then there were those who were seemingly sucked into the latter. Camile noticed another interesting occurrence, as most of the ghosts continuously traveled in a circle, some seemed to vanish.

"Where do they go when they disappear like that?" Camile asked.

"I guess the easiest way I can describe it is that when a phantom isn't ready to go beyond this point, or if they really haven't completely let go of the physical world, they go to a place that's between the Phantom World and the physical world...until they're ready. It's most often referred to as the Shadow World."

"You mean like my ghost? But she appeared to be *in* the physical world. How could a ghost do that?"

"Such a simple question. I wish I had a simple answer," The shaman tapped her shoulder. "As you know, all dimensions are separated by what we call veils. Think of each veil as a multi-layered divider between worlds. Each layer acts as a boundary for each of the senses of the beings on either side of it. Based on our experience, it's a principle that's applied to all worlds. When people see ghosts—or other beings—in the physical world, it means that either the visual barrier of the veil has been altered or that the person who sees the ghost has the ability to see beyond what has been rooted into our existence for many centuries."

"And what's that?"

"Doubt, fear of the unknown...Just about everything that prevents a person from being able to see beyond what logic dictates and what others believe."

Camile considered the statement. "So, if a person is able to make full contact with a ghost, it means that they can go beyond the veils, even if they haven't been altered?"

"It's extremely rare for that to happen since the veils would generally have to be altered in order for such an occurrence to take place."

"But it's been done?" Camile said in more of a statement than a question.

164

"Yes, but it requires extraordinary focus and belief. Especially for the Coexistent World that currently thrives on what can be seen and touched, which is the exact opposite of how sublime contact works." Tabitha raised her finger. "You must fully believe *before* you can see and touch what's beyond the veil."

Camile did a double-take upon seeing her own naked phantom walking in formation with the others. It bore an expression of disconnection and utter confusion and appeared trapped in its final state of discontent. A portrait of perpetual despair, the phantom repeated slashing motions along its arms, all the while staring vacantly into nothingness. Ashamed, Camile turned her gaze away from her wandering ghost and stroked her arms. She caught sight of a guardian accompanying the silver-haired knight.

Biting her lip, she watched as Sir Drayden urgently communicated with the guardian, but couldn't understand the words being exchanged. The knight shook his head, wearing a grim expression as the two traveled through a light created by the guardian.

During their absence, the shaman explained that Sir Drayden had gone to meet with one of the sub-councils of the Phantom World to negotiate the release of Camile's soul. Tabitha went on to elaborate that like life and death, revival and birth were all governed by strict rules. Strict, but not inflexible.

Sir Drayden reemerged alone, his face slightly more relaxed, but still heavy with apparent determination. As he walked through the massive herd of ghosts, some reached out to touch him, expressing desperate pleas through tormented moans. Despite all this, none were able to make physical contact and were repelled by an unseen force as he passed each of them. Camile's phantom jerked to a halt when Sir Drayden seized her arm and turned her to face him. Watching this, Camile felt disconcerted about the fact the knight had seen her naked in both, body and spirit. The corners of his mouth upturned, barely forming a tight, solemn smile as he searched the empty eyes of the ghost standing before him. They both vanished shortly afterward.

"Sorry, Your Wisest. Time's up." Jeremy's voice chimed like a tower bell.

Her vision slowly sharpening, Camile witnessed him bringing the female elder a glass of water.

"Sir Drayden made a deal for your return." A weary expression weighed heavily in the shaman's eyes. "Exactly what that deal is, I'm not at liberty to explain."

Chapter 23

Growing Suspicions

Sitting up slowly from a slouched position, Camile inquired about what happened after her apparition had vanished with the knight. Jeremy stepped forward before the shaman could answer.

"Her Wisest must rest," he said. "You can continue your questions another time."

Camile was disappointed, but understood Jeremy's concerns. Tabitha's fatigue was clearly visible. Perched on the edge of her seat, she prepared to stand, but the shaman seized her hand.

"Wait, child. There's something I want to give you." Tabitha blinked sleepily, motioning Jeremy to retrieve a small box from the closet. "It's the yellow one in the back," she added.

Following the shaman's instructions, Jeremy opened the large storage area.

"Which shelf is it on?" he called, his back still turned as he searched for the item. Camile's eyes roamed over his backside, but quickly returned to Tabitha's face before the elder noticed her visual detour. There was a remorseful expression etched on the shaman's features as she extended her hand in Jeremy's direction. It was an expression that resonated in her voice as she whispered, "I'm sorry."

Faster than Camile could blink, the shaman made a pushing motion that rippled through the air, sending Jeremy deep into the storage space. With two quick sweeping motions, the shaman closed the doors and barricaded it with her heavy work table. As the wooden legs screeched against the floor, a few jars were sent tumbling to the edge, but somehow righted themselves.

"You just— Why?" At a loss for words, Camile pointed to the shaman's handiwork.

Hearing Jeremy's fervent protests as he tried to break free, Tabitha bit her lip.

"We don't have much time." She exhaled deeply.

Eyes narrowed, Camile shook her head. "Time for what?"

The shaman held her by the shoulders. "You want to know how we reversed your suicide, don't you?" Her confident voice contradicted her uncertain expression and uneasy gaze.

Camile nodded, trying to ignore the strong premonition that something impermissible was about to take place. Leaning back in her seat as the elder instructed, she closed her eyes.

"There's a chance the *Ganli* brew is still in effect, so I'll avoid giving you another dose," the shaman said.

Ganli? Camile frowned, remembering the brew the elder had prepared earlier.

I knew that stuff looked familiar.

"Think of only the absence of light behind your eyelids. When your mind is completely empty only then will you see the path to my memory."

After several moments, Camile saw a distant tunnel with a sliver of light across the top. It resembled a partial lunar eclipse.

"I think I see it," she said, tightening her eyelids.

"Don't force it. Go into it slowly," Tabitha instructed, her voice growing progressively faint. "Embrace it. Embrace me."

After crossing the blinding threshold, Camile found herself standing beside Sir Drayden in Tabitha's quarters. He seemed a few inches taller than usual. Camile's initial reaction to gasp and recoil was physically denied. Even stranger was the fact that her intimidation of him drastically diminished within an instant. If anything, she felt a high degree of respect and admiration for him. Addressing him involuntarily, she realized the voice escaping her mouth was not her own. It was heavier and belonged to a much older woman.

"Do you have it?" she asked, unflinchingly holding Sir Drayden's blue gaze.

Patting his left breast jacket pocket, he answered, "I'm always prepared, Tabitha."

His response, and her sideway glance at a mirror, confirmed that not only was Camile a passenger in the shaman's memory, but her body as well.

"I sure hope this works. I really don't want to have to break the news to her parents that their daughter is dead despite all their efforts to save her."

Tabitha expelled a tremulous breath. Pacing, she occasionally glanced at her bed—on which Camile's phantom sat, naively entranced by the crackling flames of the hearth across the room.

The phantom, draped in a simple white gown, appeared frozen in place despite the warm flames on which it was fixated. Like a newborn child it appeared blank and confused, yet curious about its surroundings. Mild fear and intimidation were prevalent in its eyes as they were bombarded by things they couldn't understand. The shaman halted her steps upon feeling the knight seize her elbow.

Meeting her gaze, he said, "We've done all we can. The rest is up to Camile, her phantom and Akalina." He shifted his gaze to the phantom as he continued. "It's time. Bring her out of it."

Waving her hand in front of the phantom, the shaman brought it into awareness. She and Sir Drayden explained the situation to the spirit, stating that she was to go on an important mission to save herself. The journey entailed choosing a disguise so that her living counterpart wouldn't become alarmed.

"Under no circumstances are you to reveal your true identity to anyone," Sir Drayden sternly instructed. "You can select any one appearance of your choosing, *except* that of your former self or anyone she knew directly in the Coexistent World. Once you receive the signal, you are to lead both halves to the designated area."

In a flash, all three parties were on a fire escape. Camile couldn't get over how strange it felt to be standing in Tabitha's body in the memory. It was incredibly surreal to see everything through the shaman's eyes, yet it also seemed normal. Everything from the sound of the New York City police sirens to the vague salty, metallic scented air was so crisp. Regarding the knight briefly, she felt a wave of sadness that intensified when she saw her former self from the outside of her old Brooklyn apartment. Watching her depressed former self, the scene was all too familiar. Excess drinking, profuse sobbing and a knife on the table. It was the blade that, with a quick slash, abruptly ended her life as she knew it, leaving behind a gushing river of consequence.

I was a damn fool, Camile thought shamefully.

Standing between Sir Drayden and Tabitha, Camile's phantom regarded the scene with diminishing confusion as the harsh reality began to set in. Sir Drayden removed a small orb from his pocket, looking upon the ghost with an expression of uncertainty that rarely crossed his otherwise confident face.

"Moment of truth," he said before smashing the object into the phantom's chest with his palm.

An explosion of light filled Camile's eyes, triggering a brief, but violent headache. When it faded, she found herself sitting across from the shaman, whose face was heavy with concern. It wasn't until Camile heard Sir Drayden's voice booming around her that she realized they were back in the Transcendent World, in real time, and no longer alone.

"I can't believe you would go behind my back and do something so irresponsible! You just violated a direct order—*no unsupervised contact*," the knight chided the shaman. "Do you realize how badly things could've turned out had your little experiment gone wrong? I don't have the time nor the luxury to train someone else to replace you right now, so I expect you to exercise extreme caution at all times!" Although Sir Drayden wasn't shouting, he didn't need to. His scathing anger was as glaringly clear as the red in his face.

Still disoriented by the mental link and sudden disconnection, Camile breathed deeply while trying to regain her bearings. She noticed that the table was now in its rightful place and the closet was open. Jeremy was nowhere to be seen.

"Just because you're my superior doesn't give you the right to treat me like this," the shaman replied coolly, reaching for the pitcher on the table.

"A hypocritical statement, given what you just did, don't you think?" The male elder gestured to the closet before yanking the glass jug from her hands.

Well, that's spiteful of him! Camile thought as she watched him disappear into the kitchen. She heard sloshing water and ice hitting the metal sink as he dumped the contents. The sound repeated itself, this time against glass.

"With all due respect, Sir Drayden, you used to steamroll Hyacinth the same way even though she was your wife," Tabitha said gingerly once he returned with a fresh pitcher of water, from which he had poured a serving into a goblet. "That's why she defied you, to prove she could be right every once in awhile." Meeting his gaze, she took the glass and continued, "And you know how dreadfully that ended. It's high time someone told you this. I guess that person has to be me. Your opinion isn't the only one that counts around here."

Sir Drayden turned his head away slightly, momentarily closing his eyes as though he'd been slapped. Knowing no good could come of this, Camile didn't want to stick around for the fireworks, but figured if she remained still she'd steer clear of flaming embers. Seeing the knight's eyes burning into Tabitha, she thought, *Oh, boy. Here we go!*

Assessing the expression on her counselor's face, Camile guessed she was sharing the same sentiment.

"How *dare* you bring her into this?" Sir Drayden placed the pitcher on the table rather loudly, causing Camile to flinch. "You're one of the last people I would have expected to play that card. For future reference, if you have an issue, you're to speak with me privately…and leave my personal life out of it." His scowl deepened as he pointed at Tabitha. "There's a reason why I objected to your request for unsupervised mental connection with Camile. Needless to say I am highly disappointed in your disobedience. I respect your difference of opinion, but this kind of insubordination will *not* be tolerated. If anything like this happens again, I will personally audit all of your services and you won't be able to make so much as a cough drop without my approval. Am I understood?"

"Yes, sir. I understand perfectly," Tabitha answered, a hint of resentment in her voice.

"Sir, it's not her fault. She was just—" Camile attempted to explain the situation, but stopped when the shaman raised her hand, never wavering her bitter gaze from her displeased superior.

"You don't have to defend me, my child. I'm a big girl. I can take care of myself," Tabitha abruptly replied before asking her to leave, possibly to spare herself the embarrassment of getting further reprimanded in the presence of company.

$$* \qquad * \qquad *$$

"Some things never change." Camile's mother shook her head upon hearing the news of what had transpired between Sir Drayden and the shaman. The silver streak in her hair shimmered against the rest of her deeply waved dark auburn locks, barely skimming her shoulders.

Noticing the expression of bitter disappointment on her mother's caramel face, Camile inquired, "Something like this happened before?"

Kylie hesitated. Expelling a deep breath, she answered, "Not quite like this."

She turned her hazel gaze to her brushes, gathering them from the easel and washing them in the water bucket on the ground. Camile eyed her mother's finished piece, a painterly rendition of Caldaq and the surrounding forest reflected in the lake. Comparing it with the scenery before them, she noticed a few minor inaccuracies, but was nonetheless impressed with her mother's work. Turning to her own canvas, Camile grew envious of its blankness, wishing her mind could be as clear.

"She's defied direct orders in the past." Kylie tapped her wet brushes against the rim of the bucket before blotting them in a towel. "As a result, I partially blamed her for getting this whole thing started. I thought if it wasn't for her, you'd still be living a relatively normal life in the Coexistent World, away from all this."

"I don't get it." Camile frowned.

Gazing into her daughter's eyes, Kylie said, "Tabitha's the one who planted your necklace and the picture of you and your father, knowing that you'd find it. She knew it would trigger a series of events that would lead you back here."

Sitting in the grass, she draped her arms across bent knees. Camile followed suit.

Kylie continued, "Once the necklace was in your possession, there was no turning back. And of course, I couldn't tell you a damn thing because I was fitted with mental handcuffs." She huffed, softening her expression. "I'm not mad at her anymore, just the situation. I guess blaming Tabitha gave me some company in a responsibility that I thought was mainly my own. Now, I know there's no sense in blaming anyone."

"Why'd she do it?" Camile stroked her lower lip with her thumb.

"I'm not sure. I guess she also felt you had the right to know about your heritage, only she had the guts to actually do something to make that possible. I try not to waste time wondering about how things should've or could've been. I've come to accept things for what they are. We just have to make the most of it."

"I'm not sure Sir Drayden will be as forgiving. He was livid when she dragged Hyacinth into the discussion." Leaning back on her hands, Camile enjoyed the dewy lushness of the grass as she briefly described the context in which the topic had been raised. The revelation earned her a surprised stare from her mother.

"I had no clue he was married," Camile continued. "Did his wife leave him because of his domineering ways?"

"I don't know much about Sir Drayden's marriage. Even if I did, it wouldn't be my place to tell. He's a very private man." Kylie raised her brow anew. "Tabitha will be walking on thin ice for awhile for broaching the subject like that."

*   *   *

The elusive details of Akalina's dealings with Sir Drayden continued to taunt Camile in darkening nightmares. The skewed memories were gradually sharpening, etching an increasingly disturbing portrait as more gaps began to fill. Camile couldn't ignore, or draw conclusions from, the recollection of Sir Drayden manhandling young Akalina and threatening to kill her. Even more disturbing was the fact that she could actually feel the anger, helplessness and despair experienced by her more brazen counterpart during those occasions. Worst of all was the sound of little Akalina begging Sir Drayden to stop whatever it was he was doing only to hear his response: *It only hurts because you're fighting me.*

The last memory contained no images. Camile assumed it was because little Akalina was either blindfolded or squeezing her eyes shut. Feeling sick to her stomach, Camile decided to immediately alert her parents about her recent experience. This time, she urgently requested that they not include Sir Drayden in the meeting.

"I think I know why I don't trust him," she began shortly after entering their quarters. "I think he did something to Akalina. I don't know exactly what, but it had to be pretty bad."

"Is this something you saw in a dream?" Camile's father furrowed his brow, stroking Kylie's shoulder once she joined him on the sofa.

Camile nodded. "Sort of. I didn't exactly *see* what was happening to her, but she was obviously suffering because of him."

"This is a very serious accusation, Camile. Are you sure this wasn't just a bad dream?" Her mother's face scrunched in deep concern.

"I have more than enough experience with nightmares. This was different. It felt too...*real,*" Camile explained.

Upon being asked if there were any witnesses in the bizarre flashback, she described the guards who were present.

"Alright. We'll have this investigated, but keep in mind you're still getting acclimated to this new part of yourself," her father stated. "It's only natural for your mind to play tricks on you."

"*Tricks?* Dad, I don't think these are tricks. They're memories. They just have to be."

"If they are indeed memories, they're incomplete. You said so, yourself, that there are pieces missing. It might be in your best interest to leave Akalina's past behind you, at least in the meantime."

Camile cocked her head, furrowing her brow as she considered her father's words.

"You know what Sir Drayden did to her, don't you?" she said in nearly a whisper, to which Zephyr reacted with a confused expression.

"Does the transmitter in your head prevent you from telling me what happened? I don't see your head twitching or anything," Camile said a bit more forcefully than she'd intended.

"Honey, I know you're upset, but that doesn't give you the right to speak to your father like that," her mother interrupted. "If he knew something was going on that would have placed either you or Akalina in jeopardy, I would have been among the first to know about it."

"Sorry for lashing out, but something's not right. I can feel it." Camile turned to her father. Taking his hand, she said, "Please, Dad, don't feel like you need to protect me from the truth this time. Whatever it is I can handle it, even though I know I'm not gonna like it."

Before Zephyr could fully address her concerns, the discussion was interrupted by an incoming communiqué:

"Minister, Your Excellency, my apologies for the interruption, but there has been a new rash of coordinated uprisings in the Coexistent World," the intercom voice announced. *"President Okara has called for an urgent meeting with the Joint Council. Your attendance is imperative."*

"On our way," Zephyr announced, ending the transmission before turning to his daughter. "We'll have to finish this later. In the meantime, try to stay rational."

"Don't worry, sweetheart. We'll sort this all out when we get back. I promise." Kylie kissed her cheek, an action repeated by Zephyr.

How convenient!

Camile watched her parents leave with the security entourage that had arrived for them.

Seeing no other option, Camile relied on her neutral companion. Though nothing more than an abundant series of pages bound in old leather, her journal usually did wonders in helping her collect her thoughts and gain at least some degree of clarity. This time around, she found herself even more unsettled upon skimming through the words she had written:

> *Before my return to this world, my parents lied to me in an effort to protect me. This time, I get the feeling my father's lying to protect someone else. I'm convinced the nightmares I've been having are actually Akalina's memories. As a result, I've inherited the terror she felt for Sir Drayden. The dreams are always incomplete, which makes me wonder, what was so horrible that she felt the need to block it out? I'm trying my best not to let my mind run away with me, but all the clues are adding up to a disturbing equation. I think Akalina was his target, but for what I don't know. Now, I think there's a chance he has me in his sights. Maybe he's afraid of what I'll remember from Akalina's childhood. Maybe that's why he's so obsessive about monitoring my every move.*

Chapter 24

The Brink of Malice

The Celestia was slightly darker than usual. The simulated night that was Camile's half of the room was slowly stretching past the midway point. Jeremy attributed it to negative thoughts distracting her mind. This became evident when Sir Drayden made an unannounced entrance. Simultaneously, the nocturnal presence quickly swallowed most of the artificial daylight, leaving Jeremy standing in the remainder of it, just enough to cast a faint glow on his body. Camile and Sir Drayden, however, stood in the darkness, their frames made visible by the soft touch of the artificial moon.

"Follow me," Sir Drayden ordered.

"We're not scheduled to meet today," Camile replied, reluctant to go anywhere with him.

"We are now," he replied plainly, saying nothing further as he left the room, clearly expecting her to accede to his command.

Camile was grateful that Jeremy was tailing them quietly, no doubt to satisfy his own curiosity. Nevertheless, she felt a wave of apprehension when she realized Sir Drayden was leading her to the gym. It wasn't until they approached the sparring ring that he broke his silence.

"You don't like me. It's obvious. I don't particularly care, but you should get it out of your system," he said plainly.

"What?" Bemused, Camile narrowed her eyes.

"I'm giving you a chance to release all the pent-up hatred that's been blinding you and polluting your ability to focus." The knight beckoned her forward with a wave of his hand. "Come on, fight me."

It came as no surprise to Camile that he was well aware of her disliking of him. In fact, she had been wearing her resentment like scalded flesh. Nevertheless, she wasn't prepared to do battle with him.

"Sir, I don't think that's a good idea," Jeremy cautioned.

"Jeremy's right." Camile massaged her throbbing temples. "Besides, I'm getting a headache."

"Don't worry. I'll go easy on you." Sir Drayden cracked a half-smile, motioning everyone else to leave. Jeremy lingered with a concerned expression before following suit.

The gym, now empty, filled with deafening silence.

"Why'd you send them out?" Camile inquired.

"You'll need to focus," Sir Drayden approached slowly, throwing one of the two long practice sparring batons he retrieved from the wall.

Alright, old man. You might intimidate me, but I don't have to show it. You wanna tussle? Let's do this! Camile thought as she caught it.

The two slowly circled one another like prowling animals looking for the opportune moment to strike. The knight twirled his weapon with the fluid ease of a veteran drum major. Camile had a strong feeling he wanted her to make the first move. Against her better judgment, she went for it, swinging her weapon at him. His parry was so swift and forceful she barely recovered in time to leap over his baton as it approached her knees. As soon as she landed he swung at her again, striking the back of her legs, knocking her feet from beneath her. The stinging in her calves was nearly surpassed by the ache in her back as she met the floor.

Apparently celebrating his successful hit, Sir Drayden twirled his weapon before hurling it into the air and catching it. Camile huffed, jerking herself to her feet to reengaged the knight. She unleashed a rapid succession of blows as they shuffled around the arena. Each strike hit nothing but air, depleting her energy. Just when it seemed like she was on the losing end of the match, she managed to knock his weapon from his hand. She had only a few seconds to enjoy her accomplishment.

"Let's level the playing field, shall we?" Sir Drayden waved his hand, sending Camile's weapon flying across the room so hard, a piece of the wooden baton broke off when it hit the wall.

After a moment's hesitation, Camile lunged at him with a series of kicks and punches—all of which he successfully blocked. Conversely, the knight was able to repeatedly shove her off course, exacerbating her aching head. By now, each breath carried the heat of exhaustion, burning her throat and chest. Her body was crying out for surrender, but her pride roared a battle cry, demanding she land at least one blow.

Staggering forward, she launched her fist at the elder. Sir Drayden, however, used her own momentum against her, sending her to the floor. The hard landing left her dazed for a few moments. Her bruised body was a patchwork of agony, accessorizing her throbbing crown. Shakily supporting her body on her knees and forearms, she stared at the wooden floor while catching her breath. Her messy locks were damp with sweat and formed a curtain through which she saw Sir Drayden's leather shoes approaching. She had nothing left and she knew it. Yet, the words she heard next would halt her surrender.

It only hurts because you're fighting me, Sir Drayden's voice tauntingly repeated like a broken record, yet his smirking lips weren't moving.

Camile found herself losing her fight with two opponents; the first was Sir Drayden, the second was her anger. Determined to win at least one of the battles, she rolled across the ground to retrieve her broken weapon. Feeling the warmth of his shadow behind her, she whipped around quickly, thrusting the weapon into Sir Drayden's chest. Her ferocity escaped in a fiery yell. The elder gasped, his face contorting with surprise. Sliding off the weapon, he stumbled to the ground, staring up into nothingness as his blue eyes faded. Still holding the instrument of his death in her hands, Camile froze in shock.

Oh, God! What did I just do? Staring at the jagged tip, coated in deep red, she immediately wondered if she had intentionally killed him, or if it was an act of desperation. Her memory failed her ability to reason, giving way to panic.

Dropping the weapon, she ran to the exit. It wouldn't open. She pounded on the door, praying someone would let her out. She didn't want to be sealed in a room with a dead body. The very thought of it terrified her as she was introduced to her first bout of severe claustrophobia. She was halfway to the next exit when something caught her attention, Sir Drayden's body was gone. Eyes widening, her breathing grew shallow as she glanced around the room. He was nowhere in sight. A heavy hand clamped down on her shoulder, prompting her to scream.

"Hey, you okay? What happened?" Jeremy asked. He had a look on his face similar to the expression he wore when he stopped her from touching the *Intermediary.*

Camile was baffled to see that she was still seated in the Celestia with Sir Drayden standing beside her. Other than the three of them, the room was empty. Raising her hands to palm her face, she flinched upon seeing blood on them. In a blink of an eye, it vanished.

"I—I don't know," she stuttered, unable to keep her eyes off the knight she had just murdered in her apparent daydream.

"Oh, I think you do," Sir Drayden whispered, casually running a hand over his chest. "Camile, the truth won't break my heart, but it might break yours."

It suddenly occurred to her that Sir Drayden had just given her some sort of mental test, which she clearly failed.

"Wh—? How dare you do that to me? Don't *ever* mess with my head like that again!" she fumed as she scrambled to her feet. The sparse sunlight that had been clinging to the room had completely disappeared. All that was left was the subtle illumination of the simulated moon.

"If anyone should be disappointed, it's me," Sir Drayden said, the dim light emphasizing his dark smirk and facial lines.

"After all," he continued, "had it been a real match, you would've tried to kill me. This just proves we have a lot of work to do. In the meantime, I suggest you keep your temper in check."

*　　*　　*

Engrossed by the disturbing incident, Camile began questioning her mental freedom. She found it hard to pinpoint how and why the knight was able to breach it by inducing the hallucination. Her futile attempt to figure it out made her headache explode into a full-blown migraine. She moved to her outside terrace, hoping the fresh air would do her some good. Washing down her medicine with water, she sat in a chair to await relief. She turned her attention to the guard towers adjacent to her terrace and watched the silhouettes of the pacing sentinels.

As she set her glass on the small table, an avalanche of light smothered her vision as a piercing ringing skewered her ears. Had she not been sitting she probably would have fallen over the terrace railing. This phenomenon had happened to her a few times in the past, so she didn't panic. Based on her experience, Camile knew she would regain her vision once the worst of her migraine subsided. Just as soon as she reminded herself of that fact, her headache was gone. As her vision returned, she found herself not on her terrace, but in one of the private studies in the library, sitting across from her father.

"Akalina, if you work with us instead of against us, it'll make things a whole lot easier," Zephyr said softly.

"For who, Dad? You? Why should we keep helping them anyway?" Akalina asked, her voice dripping with a combination of teen angst and indifference. "They only take what we give them and twist it around to hurt each other. Who's to say that our help won't make things even worse?"

"It's within our power to at least try. The Coexistents are our neighbors. Wouldn't you want their help if the roles were reversed?"

Rolling her eyes, Akalina sank back in her chair and sucked her teeth.

"You're kidding, right?" She laughed bitterly. "Do you honestly believe they'd help us? What's so important about the Coexistent World anyway? What do you have over there to protect?"

An uneasy look crossed Zephyr's face as he briefly avoided his daughter's cold stare.

"Civility, order, hope...what's left of it. We're trying to protect all the things that ensure the continuation of humanity. It's just the right thing to do." Leaning forward, he crossed his arms on the table and met her gaze. "Contrary to popular belief, what happens there affects us a great deal. We can't just turn a blind eye to what's happening in the Coexistent World."

"Why not? They do it to each other all the time." She shrugged, propping her feet on the table. "Based on the information I've seen about that world, they prostituted their civility a long time ago and threw their hope in as a bonus. They're ignorant, stubborn, ungrateful and cruel. So, in a way, by not helping them we'll be teaching them a lesson, won't we? Cruelty is a philosophy they live by, it's only fair that their demise follows suit."

Zephyr leaned back in his chair, mouth agape. "Don't you realize that just sitting idly by has led to catastrophe again and again? Do you know that countless lives could've been saved if more people got involved and actually gave a damn? What's the matter with you? How can you be so cruel?"

"How can *I* be so cruel? I don't believe this! You're defending a group of selfish, incompetent strangers and you yell at me, your own daughter! Where the *hell* were you when *I* needed your help seven years ago, in spite of how many times I begged you for it? You just stood by and let those things happen to me, hoping I'd somehow forget." Akalina closed her burning eyes for a moment to hold back the tears as she chortled. "Now, who's the one with the screwed up priorities, Dad? I'm not nearly as naïve as you think I am. I know more than you could *possibly* imagine. Maybe, if you realized that, you'd treat me with a little more respect and put me first for once."

Akalina rose from her seat, purposefully kicking over a glass of juice that had been set down in front of her. The contents spilled across the table as the glass rolled toward the edge, on the way to an inevitable crash. Zephyr called after her as she stormed away. Shooting a furious glance over her shoulder, Akalina exited.

The sound of shattering glass jolted Camile back to her reality. Startled, she sat up in her chair, noticing the source of the noise. Scattered in a puddle at her feet were the fragments of her water goblet.

Chapter 25

Playing with Fire

The following morning Camile leaned against the ledge of the overlook facing the lake, hoping to catch a glimpse of Jeremy. She figured if she was lucky, he'd be out for an early swim and perhaps she'd be able to at least indulge her eyes in what her body couldn't have. It wasn't until she adjusted her hooded sweater that she remembered how chilly it was—far too brisk for swimming. Summer at Caldaq took some getting used to, scorching hot days capped with late autumn-like temperatures before sunrise and after sunset.

Maybe it's for the best, she figured.

Feeling coherent enough to write, she inscribed another entry in her journal. In it, she poured out her feelings about her previous night's experiences. She decided to begin by recounting the incident she had during her mental battle with the enigmatic knight:

> *Sir Drayden finally went too far with his head games, but I think he got the message after I surprised him yesterday. Hell, I surprised myself! I'm just glad it wasn't for real or else I'd be back on death row. On the other hand, he shouldn't be toying with my mind the way he has. I considered telling my parents about it, but I'm not sure what good it'll do since it probably won't change anything. He's abusing his power and it sucks that people are either too blind, powerless or afraid to do anything about it.*

Hopefully, I won't have to deal with him as much, if at all once my training's done. If not, I'm afraid that I might do what I did in my imagination for real. I'm starting to feel angry more often and I seem to be developing an unhealthy fixation on figuring out what happened to Akalina. I wish I could drop it, but I can't ignore this crushing sense of danger that comes with being uninformed. The more pity I feel for her, the more upset I seem to be getting at everyone else. Maybe that's why I...

"You up for company?" a voice startled Camile out of her thoughts. She quickly closed the book and slipped it into the large pocket of her sweater. When she looked up, she saw Nancy standing there.

"Oh! Hi, Nancy."

"Whoa! You're wound up pretty tight there." Nancy chuckled, her green eyes dazzling. "How's it going?"

"It's going." Camile sighed.

"Uh-oh. Rough day, huh?"

"Rough day preceded by over two rough decades. I'll deal with it, though. It's just a lot to get used to, that's all. The Transcendent World, I mean." Camile tried her best to downplay her anxiety.

The sun climbed higher, generously pouring its warm rays upon them. Feeling her skin tingle with the threat of perspiration, Camile removed her sweater and hung it on the ledge.

"You'll get used to it here. If I can, anyone can." Nancy winked, nudging her with her elbow.

"I never asked, how did you find out about this world?"

"By being nosy." The bubbly redhead laughed. "Not in the way you'd think, though. When your mother was younger, she was very sweet, but a bit naive. Kinda like you. No offense."

Nancy raised an eyebrow as she continued, "She was always getting into the wrong types of relationships, so when she became interested in your father, I paid a little extra attention to him. At first I was a little annoyed since he appeared to have a squeaky clean personality, but then I saw the body scans. Woo, boy! Now *that* was very strange. Well, at least to Coexistents like me, your mother and some of the doctors. Your father fed them some cockamamie story about growing up next to a power plant. They actually bought it!" Nancy laughed anew.

"Thing is, people were really interested in studying your father. We knew something was unusual when the CIA showed up at the hospital. But he was so taken with your mother that he eventually told her the truth. The feeling was mutual, because she ended up helping him escape. Of course my crazy ass went along with the plan. Lucky us, your father promised that he would protect us in return—and he did."

Nancy went on to explain that Zephyr had sent a team to the hospital to alter the memories of those who met him. As a precaution, Nancy and Kylie's memories of the escape and knowledge of his true origins were also altered, but were restored years later. Hearing about the great lengths her father went through to protect them offered Camile some much-needed reassurance amidst her moments of doubt.

Just then, Camile was summoned to meet with her father in the main atrium. When she reached the location she figured the open atmosphere was an appropriate setting for clearing the air. However, she was informed that her mother would be tied up at the Birquone facility for at least another day. Camile would have to await her return so both her parents could help her uncover the source of her distrust of Sir Drayden.

When the discussion was over, Camile decided to use her spare moments to complete her journal entry. Reaching into her pocket, her heart skipped a beat. The journal was gone. She frantically searched the other pocket but to no avail. Realizing she may have dropped it during her conversation with Nancy, she raced back to the overlook to search for it. It was nowhere to be found. Looking over the ledge she saw Magistrate Sui speaking with Vincent, who looked up and waved casually before rejoining the discussion.

Where did it go?

Camile worried that her parents, Jeremy—or worse, the knight—would get a hold of it. Especially since she'd been using it to vent about him to no end.

*   *   *

Relinquishing her search, Camile decided to take a swim in the solarium to calm her nerves. It wasn't until a guard approached that she remembered her session with Tabitha was rapidly impending. Even so, she still had time for a few more laps. Satisfied with her promise to end her aquatic workout momentarily, the guard left her in privacy. Her solitude was short lived. She spotted Jeremy traversing the solarium, heading toward the adjacent wing of the compound.

"Hey, Jeremy! Come on in. The water's great," she called, surprised at her laxness.

Jeremy broke his stride, apparently considering the invitation, but changed his mind after looking around.

"The water's always great," he said plainly.

"You afraid someone will catch you having fun for a change?" Camile followed his gaze over her shoulder. "There's no one here but us. I know you're still on-duty, but a quick dip won't kill anyone. Just one race. What do you say?"

"Thanks, but I really should go. Enjoy your swim," Jeremy swiftly walked away almost as though she had frightened him off.

Your loss, she thought, watching him leave. *Mine, too.*

Camile swam a slow, lazy lap before floating serenely on her back, gazing through the clear roof and at the passing clouds in the late-morning sky. Without fully realizing it, she began humming a languid tune. Suddenly, she was gripped by a strange feeling she was being watched. Roaming the solarium with her eyes, she saw no one at first. A few moments after resuming her melody, she saw Sir Drayden watching her from the opposite end of the pool. Drifting nearer, she noticed he was wearing a subtle smile that faded once their eyes locked.

Camile suspected he was the reason for Jeremy's abrupt departure. For the life of her she couldn't figure out how come she hadn't noticed him before. He wasn't exactly easy to miss. Aggravated to be the object of Sir Drayden's attention, yet again, Camile decided she'd get to the bottom of his seemingly obsessive interest in her. However, her method in attempting to do so would surprise even her. Slowly emerging from the water, she approached him.

"See something you like?" She smirked bitterly.

Oh, God! was all she could think as she tried her best to get her mind to slam the breaks on the inevitable train wreck.

"Excuse me?" Sir Drayden grimaced, his voice had more than a tinge of confusion before taking the usual authoritative tone. "You're going to be late for your lesson with the shaman. Dry off and get dressed."

Camile snickered, her voice growing progressively bitter and unstable.

"I doubt you came here just to tell me that. You have a bad habit of spying on me and I doubt that's part of my training."

"It's all in your head." The knight cracked a condescending smile.

"Last time we met, *you* were all in my head. I don't appreciate it." Camile trembled, whether from fear-tinged anger or the cool air against her wet skin, she didn't know.

"You know, you have a colorful imagination." An inquisitive expression crossed Sir Drayden's face as he folded his arms across his chest.

"Go on, mock me all you want," Camile smirked, taking a step closer. Tilting her head upward, she stubbornly held his gaze despite how badly she wished to evade it. "Can't be any worse than what you did to Akalina. Messing with her mind wasn't enough for you, was it?"

Narrowing his eyes, the knight pursed his lips, curling them into a smirk.

"Like I said, you have a colorful imagination. Quite fascinating, actually."

"Really? I wonder, what else about me you find fascinating? Is it the mystery about how different or alike I am to Akalina?"

Reaching to touch his face, her hand met an invisible barrier. It generated a sensation similar to a shock one might get from static electricity.

"Why so shy? Am I a little too old for your taste?" tears stung her eyes, but refused to let him see them fall.

What the hell am I doing?

She internally prayed that he wouldn't give in to her advances, especially since she had no plans to follow through. She knew she was playing a very dangerous game. Nevertheless, she found herself unable to avert her collision course with certain disaster. Sir Drayden's reddening face betrayed his otherwise poised demeanor. It was evident that her antics were having an effect on him, though it wasn't immediately clear what it was.

"I'm cancelling your session with the shaman. After you're done getting dressed, you'll be escorted to the EDC for immediate emotional detoxification." Sir Drayden frowned, attempting to walk away. His dismissive response aggravated Camile even further.

"One more thing." She stepped in front of him. "What, exactly, did Akalina take from you?"

No! Don't provoke the man. Just walk away! She could practically hear her voice screaming in her head.

"Was it your pride?" she continued, her tone a calm contrast to her thoughts. "Maybe it's something else. Maybe Akalina insulted your manhood when she tried to reject you. Are you that pathetic that you couldn't find a woman your own age? Oh, right...You had one and she left you."

"That's enough!" Sir Drayden hissed, his eyes flaming with an anger that usually preceded a slap. He appeared to take a moment to compose himself with a deep breath. Camile realized she had gone too far.

"You have no idea who you're dealing with, young lady," he said, his tone ominous and foreboding. "The guard will be here soon. Make yourself decent." He started to walk away, but faced her anew, adding, "I don't know what you think you're trying to pull, but one day you'll deeply regret this."

As Camile watched him exit, she felt a chill in her heart as she contemplated how badly the situation could end for her. This lingered in her mind for a moment or two before her thoughts were truncated by the abrupt sensation of soft fabric engulfing her face. Although the object itself was plush, the impact was hard enough to cause undeniable discomfort. As the item fell into her hands, she recognized it as her towel. Looking up, she saw the shaman wearing a scornful expression.

"Get dressed, *now!*" Tabitha ordered.

"Your Wisest, I—" Camile's voice shook as she tried to explain herself, but before she could say she had no clue of what had just occurred, she was cut off.

"Save it, child. I saw *exactly* what you were trying to do and frankly, I'm disgusted! You should be ashamed of yourself." The shaman frowned.

*　　　*　　　*

Two things became obvious to Camile. The first, she was to discover first-hand what the EDC was. Secondly, she would surely face the wrath of her parents in response to her recent unpredictable behavior. Much to her surprise, the guard led her to her father's office instead of the EDC as ordered. Upon her arrival, it became clear Zephyr had been the one who intercepted Sir Drayden's command.

"I heard about what happened in the solarium." Zephyr frowned, his face reddening slightly. "What in the world did you think you'd accomplish by coming on to Sir Drayden like that?"

"I wish I knew. I don't know what came over me. I only wanted to get to the truth. I had no intention of actually...*sleeping* with that monster." She grimaced.

Zephyr's jaw slackened. "What are you talking about? Sir Drayden is one of our most respected and trusted council members."

"Well, the council hasn't always had the best judgment now, has it?" Camile muttered.

Palming his face, her father ran his hands through his hairline, revealing a frown. "Where's this all coming from?"

"I told you something shady went down between him and Akalina. I've been reliving memories of him mistreating her as a kid. What could possibly justify a grown man treating a child like a ragdoll and mocking her cries for help? From what I can tell you're protecting him. No wonder Akalina turned out the way she did." The words poured out of her mouth like scalding water through a sieve.

"Camile, there's still a lot you don't understand."

"Then make me understand it rather than keeping me in the dark." Camile rubbed her upper arms. "Are you afraid to lose your privileged status? Is that why you keep defending him?"

"No. That's not how it is at all." Zephyr's lips formed a tight line.

"Then what is it, Dad? Something's not right and I don't feel safe around him. Why does everyone keep ignoring that?"

"We're not ignoring anything. In fact, we spoke with each of the officers you said were present in your flashback. Neither of them have reported anything negative about Sir Drayden. Nor have any of them witnessed any maltreatment of Akalina by his hand. On top of all that, I know Sir Drayden very well. I know him better than I know…" Zephyr let the sentence hang and let his head fall with it. Clearly, he hadn't intended to utter the statement aloud.

Eyes briefly closed, Camile finished her father's sentence. "You know him better than you know me,"

Nodding, he sighed. "To prove how seriously I take your accusations, I'll file a petition with the council to make arrangements for you to begin therapy. Hopefully, it'll help you to sort out hallucinations from reality so we can unblock your memory and get to the bottom of what may have happened between Sir Drayden and Akalina. I hope it'll reveal that this whole thing is just a misunderstanding. Please be patient, the petition process can take a week or two."

"Why so long? Everything else in this world gets done with the utmost expedience."

"Camile, the therapy is a delicate procedure, one that requires much planning and care. Rushing it could bring terrible consequences. These are all things the board must consider before giving their approval."

Lowering her head, Camile sighed. "Okay. I'll try to be patient, but make sure he stays away from me."

"Sorry, sweetheart, but we can't do that. It's an awkward situation, but Sir Drayden's an integral part of your training. If it makes you more comfortable, we can have your sessions evaluated in the meantime."

"What choice do I have?" Camile grunted.

Before her dismissal, Zephyr said something that struck her heart with the heavy weight of guilt.

"Sweetheart," he said, "you've obviously lost faith in me and your mother, but we still believe you can get yourself back on track, emotionally. That's why I opted to give you a chance to do so on your own through a course of intense meditation in lieu of a visit to the EDC. Jeremy's waiting for you as we speak."

Camile practically bumped into Jeremy upon exiting her father's office. His golden features wore an expression of puzzlement and disapproval.

"How did you manage to get into trouble so fast?" he asked, his dark eyes searching hers.

"I take it you heard about what happened."

"Sure did," Jeremy answered plainly.

"Well, I know it sounds crazy, but—"

"No need to explain. If you want to make a complete fool of yourself, that's your business."

"Hey, I'm no fool." Camile crossed her arms. "For someone who preaches neutrality, you seem to do a lot of judging."

"Meet me in the Celestia in one hour," Jeremy instructed before walking away.

Add one more to Team Drayden. Camile sighed.

Her desire to retreat to her quarters to nurse her wounded pride was delayed as Joval approached. He had overheard the end of Camile's tense conversation with Jeremy. Forsaking her desire to avoid further embarrassment, she relented to her desperate need to convince someone to see the situation from her perspective. Unfortunately for Camile, her friend wasn't willing to oblige.

"You *what?*" Joval nearly choked on his fruit as they entered the lift. "Why the hell'd you try to do that for?"

"Honestly, I don't know." Camile tightened her bun, still damp from her swim. "I guess I just wanted to find some sort of proof that he abused Akalina as a child."

Joval frowned. "Do you hear yourself? You ain't makin' no sense, Cam. Let's say he took the bait you were dangling in front of him—"

"Joval, please. I don't wanna go there." Cringing, Camile held up her hand, not wanting to consider the alternative to what had actually happened.

"But you already did. Sir Drayden was the one with enough self-control not to. But if he jumped at the opportunity, how would that prove anything other than the fact he has the same impulses as any other healthy Transcendent man?"

Until that moment, she hadn't considered that possibility. Joval's statement sent a bitter jolt of reality into her mind. It spawned the possible scenario of the knight conquering her body in an arena other than battle. Covering her mouth, she suppressed the urge to gag as she realized the gravity of her mistake.

"I don't know, okay? Can we please get off the subject? And for the record, I know you're a huge admirer of his, but I don't appreciate you judging me."

Camile knew she was only redirecting the anger she felt towards herself and her current situation. Her attempt to wrangle her thoughts away from the memory of her lapse of control had failed, resulting in a queasy sensation in the pit of her stomach.

"Hey, I'm not judging." Joval raised both hands, one bearing a half-eaten fruit. "I just know that's not something you would do. It's beneath you, Cam. I know you're better than that."

Yeah, I thought so too.

Chapter 26
The Agreement

After two days of isolation and intense meditation the realization of just how drastic and embarrassing her actions were had completely set in. Camile could only attribute her momentary loss of control to the paralyzing fear that stemmed from her warped rationalization. Though reluctant to do so, she knew she owed apologies to several people, including her parents. However, she needed to build her courage a little further, so she took a walk in the open field where Vincent had introduced her to Buttercup. It was peaceful, empty and provided an ideal background for her to soothe her thoughts.

She was thankful her mother wasn't due to return until that evening, so she had some time to practice what she would say, at least in her head. The clouds in the sky weren't as arid as they appeared as they released a soft drizzle. With closed eyes, she faced skyward, enjoying the fresh sweet scent of the grass as the rain caressed her cheeks. She took a quick breath through her nostrils as she wiped the droplets away. Then for no reason at all, she began sobbing, her voice becoming unusually small.

"Akalina, are you crying?" her father asked.

Her back still turned to him, young Akalina hastily wiped the stray tears from her face and swung her legs as she leaned in her chair.

"No. Why would I be crying? I'm not a baby. I'm almost 9-years-old, you know." She snickered faintly.

Zephyr knelt before his daughter and looked into her eyes.

"It's okay to cry. You've certainly earned the right." He frowned. "I know what Sir Drayden did to you at the memorial today. It wasn't right."

"Why can't you just keep him away from me? He hates me and he keeps hurting me!"

"Akalina, we've been through this before. I—"

"But I'm your daughter! You're supposed to do everything you can to protect me, no matter what," young Akalina shouted before lowering her voice. "Maybe you just hate me too."

"I don't hate you," Zephyr murmured, placing an arm around his daughter's shoulders. "Listen, I'll speak to him about this. Hopefully, we can come to a resolution."

He instructed young Akalina to remain in her room, but she snuck behind him as he made his way toward the knight's quarters. Before reaching the halfway mark, he bumped into the elder between two adjoining corridors. Little Akalina carefully peered from behind a corner and witnessed the two men talking.

"You helped me a lot over the years and I'm forever indebted to you, but I can't allow this to continue. Drayden, this is a difficult decision for me to make, but I need you to relocate until we can sort everything out," Zephyr suggested.

"I'm sure a conclusion can be reached without my departure, Minister." Sir Drayden smiled confidently.

"I don't think so. With you here, you'll constantly be in Akalina's presence. Things will continue to get out of hand. That's why you have to leave, because if—" Zephyr paused a moment. "If you keep harassing my daughter, I'll have you brought up on formal charges."

The knight frowned, pressing a finger to his lips in apparent contemplation. "I see. I take it you're trying to back out of our agreement."

"It would appear so. I should never have agreed to something so barbaric in the first place." Nose flaring, Zephyr clenched his jaw. "I was misguided and went against my better judgment. Be that as it may, I'm still as guilty as you are by allowing this to go on for as long as it has."

"Must I remind you, you're much too invested in this to back out now. So, don't even try," Sir Drayden cautioned, his expression serious. "This discussion is over. I expect you to have her brought to me at the usual time."

Saying nothing further, Sir Drayden walked away as Zephyr slumped his shoulders in resignation. Young Akalina gasped quietly before running away from the corridor as fast as she could.

Now saturated with rain and the memory of her father's treachery, Camile was revolted. The very thought of her own father allowing Sir Drayden to use and harm Akalina was enough to make her stomach turn.

Reaching an unprecedented level of rage, Camile feared she was losing control again. She felt like she was becoming a passenger in her own consciousness.

Breathe, she thought to herself as she attempted to meditate. It wasn't working. She couldn't rid her mind of the infestation running through it.

Her attempt at calming herself before visiting her father proved impossible. She wasn't even aware if anything she had seen was actually true, but she was determined to find out. Entering his office, she greeted him as cordially as she could in her current state of bewilderment. Her relaxed facade was shaky and her father saw through it, asking if she was okay. Avoiding the inquiry with a quick nod, Camile began dropping a trail of small questions about Akalina's childhood. In his responses, her father revealed that Akalina always had a fondness for sweets. Additionally, he mentioned her ability to coerce other children to lie, steal and engage in truant behavior.

"At first, she was just the average precocious child. Then, her pranks and tricks took a darker turn." Her father frowned.

"I see. So, did she start acting out before or after Sir Drayden started harassing her?" Camile asked casually.

"Bef—" Zephyr caught himself as he locked eyes with his daughter.

Camile gasped quietly, surprised at both the confirmation and how easy it was to obtain.

"What makes you think—?" he tried to ask.

"I don't think. I remember," Camile interrupted. "He couldn't even leave her alone at the memorial, could he? I can't believe you! How could you sell out your own daughter?"

"What are you talking about?" Zephyr scrunched his face in apparent confusion.

"You know damn well what I'm talking about! You were selling Akalina out to Sir Drayden the whole time! *That's* why you wanted me to put her past behind me, isn't it?"

"No, it's not. I wanted you to put it behind you because I knew it would disrupt your progress. Akalina led a complicated life. It's not what you think."

"What else am I supposed to think? According to these memories, you practically handed her over on a silver platter. It's torture to relive these things and I'm exhausted! I need to know what happened to Akalina or else I'll lose what's left of my mind." Camile briefly clenched her hair. "If you care about me as much as you say you do, you'd tell me what happened."

"I can't. At least not yet. Your mother will be back in town this evening. I think it's only fair to wait until she returns before I say what I must." Zephyr frowned. "There are things I want to be sure she hears directly from me."

Camile wanted to push further and demand that he tell her everything right then and there, but feared such an action would land her in the EDC. She still wasn't exactly sure what it was. For all she knew, it could've been a receptacle for those who questioned authority. Reluctantly, Camile agreed to be patient. She trusted her mother more than anyone and figured she would help see things through once she returned. Based on Zephyr's reaction, Camile figured her mother was oblivious to whatever had gone down with his arrangement with Sir Drayden.

Her father accompanied her down the corridor, all the while trying to reassure her that everything would work out for the best. He bade her goodbye as he rounded a bend. A few seconds later Camile froze upon hearing the voice of the silver-haired elder emanating from where her father had ventured. Filled with an eerie sense of déjà vu, she crept closer to the sound of the discussion between the two men, carefully keeping herself tucked behind the wall.

"Why did you interfere with my order to have her sent to the EDC?" Sir Drayden inquired, his voice stern.

"I wanted to try a less drastic approach for once. So far, it appears to be working." Zephyr answered.

"Even so, her curiosity can still prove damaging. Now, if we eliminate the source of the problem—"

"Please, let me try to handle this on my own. I've been absent nearly her entire life. This is my chance to make things right and be the father I should've been...for her and Akalina."

"By telling her what happened? That's a bad idea and you know it. Need I remind you of the damage it will do us both if she remembers?"

The knight's question was met with silence.

"Right," he continued. "I'll give you some time to think it over, but I think you already know what needs to be done. In the meantime, I suggest you keep quiet."

If that's not a conspiracy, I don't know what is, Camile thought as she slinked away quietly so as not to be spotted by either man. She knew she would surely be sent to the EDC if they discovered she had overheard their discussion.

Chapter 27

Kiss of Chaos

Camile found it strange to see Jeremy guarding her door in place of the two officers who usually held that duty.

With narrowed eyes, she asked. "Is this your way of making sure I don't get into any more trouble?"

"Your usual sentinels will return soon," Jeremy responded. The smile on his face seemed out of place.

Nodding, Camile exhaled a deep breath. She was still shaking slightly from her angry confrontation with her father and her subsequent eavesdropping of his conversation with Sir Drayden, which confirmed their dark arrangement.

"You look tense. Are you okay?" he inquired.

"No, but I really don't want to talk about it." Camile retreated to her quarters, took a quick shower and slipped into her pajamas.

Stepping onto her terrace, she wondered how she could successfully feign ignorance until her mother's return. Her anger was driven by the fear that she was at the mercy of two untrustworthy men in the meantime. Training her gaze upward, she realized the sentinel towers adjacent to her terrace were empty for the first time since her arrival at the compound. Concerned, she threw on a robe and approached Jeremy, still stationed outside her quarters. She alerted him of the situation.

"You sure?" He frowned.

Camile led him to the balcony and pointed to the adjacent veranda which was still empty.

"There's usually at least one guard stationed at the towers," she said. "I'm not complaining, because I like my privacy, but there's something big going on tonight, isn't there?"

"I can't get into specifics, but there's a major briefing taking place right now for select military personnel," Jeremy explained, his dark eyes briefly meeting her gaze before returning his attention to the sentinel towers. "Even so, there should be someone— See, there they are." He pointed at the structures.

Camile saw the guards' silhouettes against the cool light of the station.

"Oh, my mistake." She forced a smile.

Returning to her quarters, Camile sat at the foot of her bed. Placing her head in her hands, she looked at the floor. Jeremy's shiny boots partially entered her line of sight.

"Can I show you something?" he asked.

"Depends on what it is," Camile answered, meeting his eyes.

"You'll have to come with me to see. You need to get away from this place for awhile. If we're quick, we can be there and back before the other guards return."

Camile thought this was a refreshing change for Jeremy. Still, considering all that had just happened, Camile had a brief moment of apprehension as she wondered if he was about to lead her to the EDC. However, she realized if she was to be taken to the facility, Sir Drayden or her father would make it their best interest to escort her personally. Since Jeremy insisted there was no time for her to get changed, Camile swapped her robe for her long wool coat and followed him outside. He swiped one of her silky scarves as they exited.

"You'll need to wear this." He held up the length of fabric once they entered the corridor.

"That's sweet, but I think this'll be enough to keep me warm." Camile tugged her collar. "Besides, you said we're coming right back, right?"

Jeremy circled around her and whispered into her ear from behind, "It's not for your neck."

She shuddered softly at the touch of his warm breath against her skin.

"To fully appreciate the beauty of what you're about to see, I suggest travelling there in darkness." He said, placing the fabric over her eyes. "Don't worry. The mystery's part of the appeal."

Camile's heart fluttered with nervous anticipation as she felt his strong hand on the small of her back. It remained there as they traveled through the corridors and along several turns. She knew they had exited the compound when the chill of the night air breached her collar. Dirt and gravel transitioned into grass beneath her feet as Jeremy continued to guide her cautiously over minor obstacles.

There were a few occasions during the trip when he instructed her to remain still and quiet, leading her to further wonder about the safety of their destination. She reassured herself that it wasn't like Jeremy to take unnecessary risks and that she was in good hands. An audible tapestry of chirps, hoots and howls filled the air around her as he finally removed the blindfold. They were standing beneath a thick wooded canopy that obscured the sky like an umbrella. A subtle, yet unearthly, blue-green tint danced beyond the darkness.

Regarding her with a playful smile he signaled her to follow him.

"So does this mean you forgive me for—?"

"Shh…" He held a finger to his lips. A broad smile crossed his golden features. "You had your reasons for what you did. Let's leave it in the past, okay?"

"That might be hard, considering what I found out today. Looks like I was right about—"

Jeremy hushed her anew as he gestured for her to keep moving.

"Whatever it is, better be worth it. My feet are *killin'* me!" Camile half-joked. Had she known more about the trip, she would've worn shoes with better shock absorption.

"Oh, it's worth it alright." Jeremy smirked.

Camile was taken aback by his sudden mischievous tone, which was matched by the expression on his face. After a few moments they cleared the last remaining trees they came to a large patch of lawn surrounded by the dense forest. A few stray rocks littered the grassy ground.

"Okay, look up," Jeremy instructed.

Camile's eyes were met by a spectacular display of light as she gazed into the night sky. Colorful electric ribbons lit up the heavens, already sparkling with celestial diamonds. It was like a painting framed with bountiful branches.

"*Beautiful!*" she said in little more than a whisper.

"You got that right," Jeremy replied.

Returning her attention to Earth, she saw him smiling warmly, hand extended. Upon taking it, he guided her to sit on one of two large stones positioned in close proximity. As he sat beside her, she was sandwiched between the warmth of his body and the caress of the cool night air. Camile inwardly chided herself for reading too much into the way he was looking at her and how closely he was sitting. She tried to ignore the fresh citrus and amber scent of his cologne and the aphrodisiatic effect it was having on her. In an attempt to distract herself from her attraction, she started a conversation about the brilliant light show above.

"How often does this happen?" She turned her gaze skyward.

"Almost every night," Jeremy answered, his sultry voice melting in her ears. "What you see is the result of a permanent and very powerful electromagnetic distortion. As a result, it's virtually impossible for any electronic device to function properly in this area. That's why they call this area the *Forsaken Square*. It's forbidden to those who don't have special clearance to be here, but that doesn't stop people from coming here to find out if the legends are true."

"Wait a minute. We're here illegally? I appreciate you wanting to show me this, but we should head back now before you get me in trouble."

Camile slowly rose from her seat, but Jeremy gently seized her arm.

"Too late." He smirked, pulling her onto his lap. "You're already in trouble."

Camile was taken by surprise, but made no attempt to break away. If anything, she enjoyed the sensation of his muscular thighs supporting her bottom. Shrouded in the strength of his warm embrace, she felt a surreal sense of familiarity and profound belonging. She felt so at home, everything she had been worrying about and obsessing over seemed to melt away, leaving only her desire for that moment to last. And if that moment happened to be her last, she would have been content, having finally banished loneliness.

This has to be love. What else can be this invigorating, this confusing...this scary?

Her blissful carelessness was briefly interrupted by a sudden thought.

"What about Justine?" She wondered aloud.

"Don't worry about her. She's not a factor in my romantic life, but that doesn't keep her from meddling in it. She means well, but it's intrusive to say the least. Enough about her." Jeremy stroked her deeply waved hair. His eyes sparkled like obsidian, accentuating his alluring smile. "I want tonight to be all about us."

The night hues emphasized his smooth skin and masculine features. For awhile neither said a word to each other. Their eye contact and body language communicated in a way that defied verbal speech. Camile placed her slender hands on his shoulders, gazing deeply into his eyes. Jeremy gently cradled her face in his large hands, gliding his thumb across her lips before moving closer. It had been so long since the last time her lips had joined another pair and she found they were all but desperate for company.

Finally! Camile thought, meeting him halfway, pressing her lips against his, slowly pulling their bodies tighter together. His lips had the perfect balance of salty and sweet and were as delicious as kettle corn. It was an effective distraction from her latest unsettling nightmare, or rather a disconcerting thorn in Akalina's tangled past.

"I've been waiting for this moment for a *very* long time," he murmured, kissing her along her jaw line and down her neck. "It's been torture restraining myself. I can't do it anymore. I can't deny my feelings for you."

Pushing him away gently, Camile smiled, gazing seductively into his shimmering orbs. "That makes two of us, baby."

Jeremy attempted to kiss her again, but she placed her index finger on his lips. After all the time he'd made her wait, she decided she'd return the favor—at least for a few moments.

"I'm curious, what kind of legends are there about this place?" she smiled, letting her eyes float up to the animated sky above.

"Well," Jeremy sighed with a note of mild impatience. "It's been said that anyone who visits this area receives an elevated sense of their internal life force, the energy that transcends the physical. It's also been rumored that the electromagnetic energy here dramatically enhances stamina, agility…libido…" He smirked, softly stroking the side of her neck with the back of his hand.

"Is it true?" she met his eyes anew.

"Depends on who you talk to. It's widely debated. Some say it's fact, others disagree. There's only one way for us to find out for sure." Jeremy raised an eyebrow.

"I'd say it's fact. I've never seen you this way." Camile chuckled softly.

"Disappointed?" He winced.

Shaking her head, she replied, "Hell, no."

Joining in another passionate kiss, the two hungrily caressed one another. Unfastening her coat with his nimble fingers, Jeremy returned his attention to the sweet spot on her neck. He teased it with his tongue before tenderly grazing it with his teeth. The heat emanating from his body compensated for the cold air piercing her open coat and she craved more of it. Moaning softly, Camile found it increasingly difficult to break free of his spell and the enchantment of the *Forsaken Square*.

Swept up in dizzying desire, the bed of plush grass seemed to creep up behind her. Despite the incredible effect he was having on her body, something didn't seem right as he laid alongside her. Camile's mind and body were in a turbulent battle and the latter seemed to be winning as she continued to kiss Jeremy, her tongue mingling with his. The smoky painting in the sky above served as yet another distraction for her willpower. It wasn't until she felt him trying to undo her pajama top that she found power to resist.

Though Camile craved him so much her heart ached, she realized she wasn't ready. Knowing that she was a bit emotional, she didn't want to make such a big move out of haste. In addition, though she had left her virginity in the Coexistent World, Camile found herself filled with feelings of anxiety and uncertainty. She was unsure of her ability to please a Transcendent male. Furthermore, she was apprehensive about what the experience would be like. Gently pushing at his chest she met his gaze. The wondrous dark eyes she'd been reveling in earlier were now an electric shade of blue-green. After a moment of near-drunken disorientation, she realized the person she'd just been making out with wasn't Jeremy.

"Oh, my G—! Brandon? What are you doing?" she recoiled, accidentally tapping her head against the ground.

"Tonight, I'll do whatever you want me to do to you, baby," he murmured, eagerly continuing his tender ministrations.

Camile protested, pushing him away—harder this time. Pausing a moment, Brandon regarded her with a perplexed expression.

"Akalina, are you teasing me?" He smiled playfully, quirking his brow.

"*Akalina?*" her face twisted in shock. "No. I'm Camile, remember?"

Sitting upright, she hastily fastened her coat.

"No. Bring her back," he demanded, taking her by the shoulders. "Don't you dare take her from me again!"

Disturbed by his sudden volatile behavior, Camile broke free and immediately scrambled to her feet.

"Brandon, what's wrong with you? Are you drunk?" she asked forcefully, but decided not to wait for an answer. "Look, I think you should stay away from me until you come back to your senses. Apparently, I'm already breaking rules just by being here and I've got enough problems as it is. I sure as hell don't need any more."

She turned to walk away, but Brandon seized her arm, quickly knocking her legs from under her.

"Oh, no, you don't." He scowled, joining her on the ground and climbing on top of her. "I'll *make* you bring her back."

"No! Get off me!" Camile roared, struggling beneath him. However, her cries seemed to fall on deaf ears.

"Akalina, come back to me, baby," he whispered into her ear, ignoring her demands. "You're really in control and you know it. I'll make you remember how good it feels to be wild and free, not repressed by this tame woman."

Camile slapped him, scratching his face in the process. She was shocked to see that it had very little effect on him. Brandon was a complete contrast to his usual, relaxed self. He caught hold of her wrists, pinning them over her head with one of his large hands. In her heart and mind Camile knew her body could fight harder—she'd gotten out of tighter holds during some of their defense classes. She wondered what was holding her back. To her horror, she realized she had stopped struggling altogether and even ceased screaming, though she was still doing so in her mind.

I won't let this happen. This isn't right.

She was bemused upon hearing her sentiment escape Brandon's lips as he, too, halted the struggle, but retained his hold on her. The quiet anger stemming from her apparent helplessness rattled her heart like a wild beast in a cage. Breaking her momentary lapse of surrender, Camile resumed her attempt to break free.

"I can't...This isn't right," Brandon said a second time. With tightly closed eyes, he shook his head.

"Damn right it's not." Camile panted, demanding release.

She felt his grip ease significantly as he slowly freed her wrists. She used the opportunity to shove him away as far as she could after striking him once more for good measure.

Suddenly, Brandon was tackled to the ground by a third party. It happened so quickly, Camile didn't see who it was at first. Rising to her feet, she realized it was Jeremy. His surprise attack appeared to spark the return of Brandon's abnormal rage. The ferocity of the fight was so intense Camile feared the two might kill each other. At first, the fight appeared evenly matched, but Brandon was showing signs of gaining the upper hand. Camile's concern abruptly shifted as she tried to figure out some way to prevent Jeremy from losing his life. She called for Brandon to stop as she carefully approached the sparring men, but Jeremy vehemently demanded that she stay back. As the men continued to tussle, Jeremy tried to talk Brandon down. It seemed to be working although they remained locked in the dying clash.

"What's going on here? Stop this immediately," a familiar voice ordered sharply. Based on the accent, Camile assumed it was Vincent. As she turned around she received visual confirmation of her hunch. He was standing just a few feet away wearing a bewildered expression. A pair of guards joined his side. The fight came to a halt and both men stood tall as they faced their superior. Glaring at Jeremy, Brandon said, "You should know that butting in other people's affairs is hazardous to your health."

"Is that a threat, Commander Wilder?" Jeremy asked, visibly unfazed.

"Just clarifying the boundaries." Brandon smirked, taking a step toward Jeremy.

"That's enough, Commander! Back down!" Vincent ordered sternly, pushing him back with his hand. "You're obviously not yourself this evening. I'll personally escort you to the EDC. Until further notice, you are relieved of your duties. Jeremy, the same goes for you after you escort Camile back to the compound."

The darkness in Brandon's electric aquamarine eyes appeared to lift as he surveyed his surroundings. His face was etched with confusion when he looked at Camile as though for the first time.

"Hey. What happened to you?" he asked of her disheveled appearance. His eyes narrowing in apparent concern as he tried to approach her.

"You happened!" Camile fumed, backpedaling to maintain their distance. "If you know what's good for you, you'll stay away from me."

"What are you talking about?" Brandon's mouth fell agape. "Oh, no. Don't tell me I—"

"No. You were stopped before you could go through with it," Jeremy interrupted, wiping the blood his own mouth.

"Did I do that?" Brandon grimaced, referring to Jeremy's bruising cheek.

"Unfortunately, yes." Jeremy frowned.

"I'm so sorry," Brandon apologized shakily, shifting his gaze to Camile. An agonized expression washed over his face. "I'm not that kind of man. Please believe me."

Camile said nothing as she broke eye contact, but not before she saw the apparent lament in his eyes.

"Yeah, I know," Jeremy replied. "Hopefully, we'll figure out what got into you."

Camile's mind raced during the trek back to the compound.

Why did I stop fighting? Why couldn't I move? Damn it, I even stopped screaming.

Still reeling, she stormed the path of the dimly lit forest and was startled by the touch of Jeremy's hand on her arm.

"Don't touch me!" She pulled away. Calming her voice, she said, "I can find my way back."

"Really? Then how come you're going the wrong way?" Jeremy arched his brow.

Camile said nothing. Instead, she muttered under her breath as she made an about-face. She didn't understand why she was so upset with Jeremy. If anything, she figured she should have been grateful that he came to her defense. Immediately upon exiting the *Forsaken Square*, *Tarconian Spiders* repaired their minor injuries en route.

Chapter 28

Agitation

Camile promptly retreated to her quarters to get cleaned up. It seemed as though it would take a force of nature to drive the memory of the kiss from her spinning mind. Before long, the recollection of her bizarre interlude had taken over and she felt as though she was back in that sweet, blissful moment before it had soured. Only this time, she was well aware it hadn't been with Jeremy. What greatly disturbed her was the fact she didn't care. Acidic thoughts of the events following the romantic exchange washed away her conflicted amorous reminiscence.

What's happening to me?

While climbing into bed, her mind revisited every twisted occurrence she had endured that day and she soon found herself utterly fatigued. As she shut her eyes, they burned with misty bewilderment as she wondered when her mother would return. The vortex of her subconscious pulled her under so rapidly she nearly missed the line between it and reality.

She desperately tried to move, but felt the oppressing weight of something or someone pinning her to the ground. Her erratic breathing filled the silence. Fiery anger gave way to frigid terror as her strength gradually slipped away.

"No! You can't make me." She sobbed, her voice cracking with agony.

Emerging from the darkness was Sir Drayden's face looking down at her.

"Oh, is that right?" His thin lips curled into a subtle smile.

Quivering, she looked into his taunting, aquatic gaze, taunting in that the cool shade contrasted with the white-hot agony coursing through her body. Getting reacquainted with her sense of smell, she detected the stench of fresh blood she knew was her own. Then came the tide of blackness, through which a loud cry echoed all around her. All eventually faded and she found herself meeting Sir Drayden's eyes anew. She felt him pulling her limp body toward him as he knelt beside her.

"No! Don't touch me! Leave me alone," she cried hysterically. "You got what you wanted from me!"

Bolting upright, Camile was relieved that she was still in the sanctuary of her blankets. Judging by Akalina's moderately mature voice in the flashback, she knew she was no younger than her late teens at the time. It took Camile a moment to realize that she was trembling with fear and residual agony. She now had a better idea of why Akalina feared Sir Drayden so much. In addition, she now had a clearer picture of the dark history between the two, which apparently spanned over a decade. Even more disturbing was the fact that the memory was triggered by Brandon's halted attempt to violate her. Her thoughts were rudely interrupted by a stinging slap across her face. When Camile looked up she was beside herself, literally.

Her face twisted in an astonished frown, she asked, "Akalina? But how——?"

She was pulled from her bed by the hair and thrown onto the floor before she could finish the question.

"You stupid idiot," Akalina spat. "Oh, you just *had* to go there! I drew a line and you crossed it. Bad move."

Camile knew she needed to act quickly. Scrambling to her feet, she planted kick to Akalina's abdomen, sending her flying into the nightstand. The fight was on as Akalina lunged with a fury of swings. Camile awkwardly ducked out of the way of the blows, straining a muscle in her back as she did. She saw her chance, Akalina had left herself wide open for a strike. Wasting no time, Camile swung hard, catching her face with her fist. She followed up by tucking one of her legs behind her doppelganger, slamming her to the floor. Straddling Akalina, Camile pulled her fist back to strike again when something caught her off guard, a hit to the eye. The impact and sharp pain knocked Camile backward and she immediately felt powerful hands pinning her to the floor. Looking up out of one eye, clamping the other shut due to pain, she was dumbfounded to see Jeremy above her.

"Jeremy, you got the wrong person. We need to go after her before she gets away," she exclaimed, struggling in his grip.

"Before who gets away?" He scrunched his brow.

"Akalina! She was right here. Didn't you see me fighting her?"

"Oh, I saw you fighting alright." Jeremy sneered, wiping the small stream of blood trickling from his nose.

"Wh—?" Realizing she had hallucinated her struggle with Akalina, Camile didn't bother completing the question.

She and Jeremy both bore physical evidence of their brief, but violent tussle. Apparently, they had caused enough of a ruckus to rouse the attention of Kylie, Excelsior and a few guards.

"Mom, I'm so glad you're back," Camile exclaimed, joining Kylie's side. "I really need to talk to you."

"What was all that noise?" her mother inquired. The startled expression on her golden brown face intensified. "And what happened to your eye?"

"I guess you can say there was a misunderstanding, Your Excellency," Jeremy explained, tilting his head upward, still nursing his injured nose. "I came up here to check on her, as the minister ordered. I saw that Camile had fallen out of bed and went to help her, but apparently she felt the need to challenge me to an impromptu sparring match."

"Wait, you two were fighting?" Kylie's jaw dropped.

"Actually, *she* was fighting, I was forced to defend myself. It's obvious she's still unstable. Something needs to be done about it before someone gets hurt or worse." Jeremy frowned.

"Jeremy, I understand your concern, but rest assured the situation will be handled in the manner Sir Drayden, Zephyr and I see fit. You're starting to lose your cool. Pull yourself together," Kylie advised.

"Tell that to Ms. Jekyll and Hyde over here," he muttered. Realizing he'd overstepped his bounds, he quickly apologized to Kylie, who immediately called a meeting in order to get to the bottom of what happened that evening.

*　　　*　　　*

Camile and Jeremy were escorted from the infirmary to the small meeting chamber where Camile's parents and Sir Drayden awaited their arrival.

"Camile, how did you end up in the *Forsaken Square* tonight?" her mother inquired as they took their seats. "It's restricted for a reason."

"I don't know. I guess I must've been sleepwalking or something," Camile fibbed. She didn't want to get into the embarrassing details— especially with Jeremy sitting in the room.

"Well, apparently Jeremy's not the first person you fought tonight. Are you sure you're okay?" her father asked.

Camile whipped around to face Jeremy.

"You *told* them?" she said in more of a statement than a question.

"I didn't have to. All medical procedures are immediately reported to base," he explained.

"Are you serious? You're telling me that spider— Whatever..." Camile rolled her eyes before turning to her parents. "I was a little clumsy, that's all." She shrugged, averting her gaze.

"Camile, tell us what really happened out there tonight. Don't lie to us," her father commanded.

"*Don't lie to you?* I don't have to tell you everything if I don't want to, not that you'd listen. It runs in the family, doesn't it, the inability to tell the truth?" Camile chuckled. "Besides, I'm a grown woman. Don't you think it's a little late to try to raise me after all these years, *Dad?*"

"Camile!" Kylie said sharply. "You may be a grown woman, but so help me, if you don't change your tone right now...What happened that's got you all worked up?"

Camile wanted nothing more than to inform her mother of her most recent memories of Sir Drayden's maltreatment of Akalina, and her father's apparent support of it. Before she could broach the subject, Vincent sauntered into the room and took a seat beside Jeremy.

"It appears Commander Wilder wasn't quite himself this evening," he announced.

"Commander Wi—? Can someone please tell me what the hell's going on?" Kylie asked, a perplexed expression crossing her face.

"He attacked Camile. He tried to force her into an act of the *Leih'klav,*" Jeremy explained.

"*What?*" Camile's parents asked in unison before inquiring about their daughter's wellbeing.

Hanging her head, she picked at her nails. "I'm fine. He stopped himself. Can we move on, now?"

"The commander has been admitted to the EDC for evaluation," Vincent announced. "So far he seems to have returned to normal. He's very remorseful. I think his sudden uncharacteristic behavior may have resulted from some sort of...agitation," he shifted his eyes to meet Camile's.

"*Agitation?*" Jeremy grimaced as though tasting something sour. The expression increased the exotic slant of his dark brown eyes.

"I'm curious, Vincent. What were *you* doing in the *Forsaken Square* tonight?" Sir Drayden asked, not bothering to conceal his suspicion.

"They don't call me the *Eyes of the Forests* for nothing," Vincent bragged. "I noticed the light of a lantern and decided to investigate. It's a good thing I did or we'd likely be investigating a homicide. Isn't that right, Jeremy?"

"I only attacked to subdue him—not to kill him, sir." Jeremy grimaced.

"Be that as it may, you were still involved in a violent attack and should be evaluated as well," Vincent shifted his intense gaze to Zephyr. "We're not playing favorites, are we, Minister?"

"No, we're not." Eyes closed, Camile's father pinched the bridge of his nose. "Jeremy will be evaluated as soon as we're done here."

"Excellent." Vincent smiled toothily.

The whole time Sir Drayden said nothing while staring at Camile from across the table. It disturbed her beyond measure and she found herself growing increasingly resentful at his unwanted attention. Her boiling irritation reached a point where it finally overflowed.

"Stop looking at me, you sick bastard," she yelled, launching from her seat.

"Camile, calm down! What the hell's gotten into you?" Kylie implored, concern written on her face.

"I just need to be alone! I need to wrap my head around things," she replied, bolting for the exit.

Sir Drayden headed her off and blocked her escape. Camile immediately backed away.

"You, stay away from me!" she demanded, her voice trembling. "I don't know what the hell you did to Akalina, but I'll be *damned* if I let you do it to me! Let me out of here! I just need to be alone!"

"I know." Sir Drayden frowned, waving a hand in front of her face.

Camile stumbled backward as the room went black. She never felt her body hit the ground.

*   *   *

The Zen-like ambience resembled something similar to what one might see in a travel catalog. The only source of lighting in the room, a pale blue illumination, was emitted by a large, frosted decorative glass panel etched with foliage similar to cherry blossom branches. It was a refreshing sight to awaken to. As her lethargy lifted, Camile admired the calming view of the gentle water streaming down the floor-to-ceiling glass wall. A variety of rocks lined portions of its base, sparkling like gems in the misty water. As she sat upright, the room gradually flooded with normal lighting while a harp and flute arrangement played softly in the background. Before she had a chance to contemplate her location and the possible reasons for her being there, the glass wall split in two, gently sliding apart as her mother entered.

"Hi, sweetheart." She smiled softly. "How are you feeling?"

"Fine, I guess." Yawning, Camile palmed her forehead. "What happened?"

"You were emotionally overwhelmed after the incident in the *Forsaken Forest*. Sir Drayden put you under before you could cause yourself further emotional damage. In other words, you were about to snap." A forlorn expression crossed Kylie's face as she shook her head. "I see he acted not a moment too soon."

Camile suddenly felt an urgency to inform her mother about something the knight had done.

"Mom, Sir Drayden —!"

"Shh. Try not to excite yourself. You can't afford to have another breakdown. You need to get well."

"But I really have to talk to you about him! He..." She squinted, failing to recall the urgent message she wanted to convey.

"What is it, honey?" Kylie furrowed her brow and touched her daughter's shoulder.

Frowning, Camile shook her head. The most notable things she remembered about the elder was his harsh suggestion that she focus on her training, and the fact that she killed him in an imaginary battle. Not wanting to divulge the specifics about either incident, she answered, "He's rude to me, sometimes."

"Don't take it personal. He's pretty strict when it comes to his work. Maybe your father and I can convince him to cut you a little slack, at least for the time being."

"How long have I been out?" Camile asked, swinging her legs around to dangle off the bed.

"Almost a day."

"A whole day? Man, guess I was really wiped out."

Camile couldn't recall dreaming and was happy for it. In fact, the last thing she could remember was returning to the compound after her incident with Brandon. Everything after that was a blank.

Her mother explained that the facility they were in was an EDC—an emotional decontamination center. She further clarified that when a Transcendent exhibits strong signs of irrational thinking due to an emotional imbalance, they must be immediately admitted for treatment.

"You make it sound like a disease," Camile remarked.

"Well, in many ways it is. After all, a disease impairs a person's ability to function. What happened to you last night was no different."

"So what, people in this world aren't allowed to lose their temper? Is this some kind of emotionally deprived society?"

Closing her eyes, Kylie briefly chuckled. "That's what I thought when I first got here, but no. Transcendents strive for emotional balance. It's a daily, life-long commitment. To deprive a person of their emotions is just another form of enslavement. Doing that denies them the essence of their humanity. This facility is designed to help people protect and control their emotional centers—their compasses. Those who have failed to do so were easily misguided and eventually lost."

"I don't know what kind of treatment that was, but, I feel better already." Camile smiled as she rose to her feet, only to be blocked by her mother.

"Honey, your treatment didn't start yet. Your rest was just preparation for what's to come," Kylie informed.

Chapter 29

Givers & Takers

The EDC seemed far less menacing than she had imagined. The interiors were open and warm with fireplaces in most of the common rooms. Then again, she knew she was currently residing in one segment of many within the therapeutic Aqueon Peak facility. During her second evening there, Camile was scheduled to meet a counselor atop the facility's west tower. Stepping onto the circular moonlit observation deck, she spotted a young woman leaning on the guardrail, gazing at the starry sky. Ivory was the shade of both her smooth skin and cottony upswept hair. Upon first glance, the white clothing she wore made it seem as though she was nude.

The woman faced Camile once she reached her side. She had sparkling eyes of pink quartz and a radiant quality that reflected her name, Lumera Blanch, a native of the Coexistent World. Peering over the railing, Camile's eyes met the source of the roaring crush that filled the air. A series of white, frothy cascades crashed into a plunge pool far below. The sight caught her by surprise since the facility, though expansive, was just three stories high. Jerking back, she heard the woman chuckle.

"That was my first reaction, too." Lumera's exaggeratedly plump lips formed a smile.

The two admired the beauty of the clear evening before delving into Lumera's history. All her life, she knew there was something different about her, not just physically. She realized people seemed drawn to her, but for all the wrong reasons. People would gather and flock to her, usually to ridicule and chide her about her appearance, but there was something else taking place, something that nearly cost Lumera her life.

"One day, I was on my way to school when a pack of bullies began harassing me," Lumera explained. "I was used to it since it was a daily event, but something was different that day. I decided to ignore them by walking away. It pissed them off. I felt myself getting weak, like the energy was being sucked out of me. So I ran, but somewhere along the way I fainted. Woke up three days later, in the hospital. The doctors said it was dehydration, but now I know what really happened."

"What's that?" Camile bit her lip.

"In life, there are givers and takers. I'm a giver. Based on what I've heard, so are you, Camile."

"What is it that we give?"

"Energy. Positive energy, to be exact. At first, we might give it away willingly to help others. Then they take more and more until there's not much left for ourselves." Lumera paused a moment to moisten her lips. "When that happens, we end up in places like institutions, hospitals, psychiatrist offices… Sure, those treatments might work for the short term, but eventually we have to go back and face reality. My bullies were draining me of my positive energy and I responded by running away. That made them realize they were succeeding. It also angered them because they were in danger of losing their fix."

"Fix?" Camile's eyes narrowed. "You mean this positive energy's like a drug?"

Lumera shook her head. "It's more potent than that. Drugs are a poor imitation. When I ran that day, I felt the bullies panicking. Not only did they nearly drain me of my energy, but they overloaded me with theirs. I was poisoned by their negativity, the kind that makes you forget why life is worth living. That's what landed me in the hospital. That was ten years ago and since then, I've learned to control what I let in and what I allow out. Kind of like a diet for the soul." She chuckled.

"You're not telling me this story just to break the ice, are you?" Camile smiled softly.

"Nope." Brows raised, Lumera cocked her head. "This topic was always on the agenda for you to learn, but recent events have forced us to speed up the process. Had you not been charged with the tasks you have been, it wouldn't be as dire a situation, but a lot of people will suffer if you don't learn to safeguard your inner self. Camile, once people know they can get positive energy from you, blocking access won't be enough to deter them. You have to strategically maneuver around these people. They won't give up easily. Believe me, I know it all too well." Lumera's pink orbs lowered to her wringing hands. "When someone is given such pure, positive energy that's suddenly taken away, they'll go to drastic measures to get it back. When they realize the energy is no longer at their disposal, they'll sometimes attempt to destroy the source."

Lumera's pearlescent nails shimmered in the moonlight as she shakily raised her hands to the high collar of her tunic. Expelling a deep breath, she lowered it, revealing a long slash across her throat. Camile suppressed a gasp by covering her mouth, all the while trying not to stare. She thought it was such a shame that an otherwise flawlessly beautiful woman had been tainted by such a wound. It was like looking at an immaculate blanket of snow that had been tarnished with animal waste.

"Did your bullies do that?" She grimaced.

"No." Lumera raised the fabric, concealing her scar anew. "My ex-husband did. I married young, not knowing what I was getting into. At first he seemed charming enough, but things changed. He treated me badly and I was in a constant state of depression. He kept me that way by saying I was ugly and that no one else would want to be with me. Over time, I actually began to believe him, but a person can only take so much.

"One day, I had enough and decided to call it quits. As I packed my things, I felt my dignity coming back. It was strange, like seeing a long lost friend again. That's when I knew I was doing the right thing. My husband, on the other hand, rather saw me dead than free. You see, for all those years he'd been taking my positive energy, replacing it with his negative. With me gone, he wouldn't have had anywhere to direct it. Not only that, he wouldn't have my positive energy to feed off of anymore."

Camile nodded. "So, are you...a ghost?"

"Quite the contrary. I'm more alive now than I've ever been." Lumera smiled broadly. "The Transcendents rescued me and nursed me back to health. If not for them, I would have died. Apparently, they had been looking for me for some time. They had a job for me to do. As for my ex-husband, he's paying for his crimes. Sadly, I was just one of many in his path of destruction."

"What about your family? Do they know you're here?" Camile wondered.

Lowering her gaze, Lumera shook her head.

"Only my sister, Monica," she answered before explaining that the council had sworn her to keep her whereabouts a total secret, even from her distraught family. However, she couldn't bear the thought of them suffering. So, she let Monica know that she was okay. Sadly, when Monica attempted to pass the message along to the family, they figured she had lost her grip on reality. She was eventually declared insane and institutionalized.

"That was three years ago." Lumera sighed.

"Can't the council get her out?"

"The council thinks it's best she remain there. Apparently, she has her own job to do, though no one truly knows exactly what it is. The shamans and scribes can be annoyingly vague, but are rarely wrong."

"What job were you picked for?" Camile scratched her temple. "Maybe your sister was picked for something similar."

"Defense." Lumera chuckled. "Ironic isn't it? Someone like me, who was nearly killed, being selected to teach others how to defend themselves. Quite a mind job, huh? Apparently it was my true calling in life. I've trained up quite a few impressive students, including my prized pupil, Estrella."

Over the course of the following two days, Camile learned that Lumera specialized in teaching people how to protect themselves against negative invading energy. In addition, she also taught her students how to control their release of positive energy. On the second afternoon, Camile awaited her arrival at the facility's main entrance. Lumera's pallid appearance in the bright sun was nearly blinding as she approached.

"It's a perfect day for a picnic, don't you think? The Courtyard of Serenity is lovely this time of year." Grimacing, Lumera said, "Oh, I forgot to leave these in my room." She extended her hand, which held two handball-sized objects—one blue, one yellow. "I'm too lazy to go back there now. Would you mind holding them for me 'til we get to the courtyard?"

It sounded more like a request than a question.

Camile wondered why Lumera didn't carry the objects for herself, but then noticed the picnic basket in her other hand. As they traveled, Camile carried the small balls carefully, noticing that with each step they became progressively heavier. What had started off as featherweight objects now seemed as cumbersome as bowling balls. Oddly enough, the weight also seemed to add uncomfortable pressure to her right leg. Upon reaching the courtyard, they came to an empty table, on which Lumera instructed Camile to place the objects. Camile eagerly dropped them down, surprised at the feeble sound they made upon impact.

"What the hell are those things?" she asked through an exasperated breath.

"Go on, open them." Lumera cocked her head. "I know you're curious."

The last thing Camile wanted to do was touch them again, but her curiosity got the best of her. Upon further inspection she noticed that each orb had a thin crevice around the middle. Applying slight pressure, it popped open and a small parchment slipped out. Camile unfolded it and read the single word imprinted on it, *anguish*. The second orb contained a note that read *sadness*.

Shaking her head, Camile narrowed her eyes before regarding Lumera, who said:

"The whole time, you were carrying anguish and sadness—all because I convinced you to. That's exactly how it is with humans and emotions. They can carry other people's feelings without even realizing it." She winked, shifting her pink gaze downward. "Check your right pocket."

A wave of apprehension washed over Camile as she obliged. Her hand made contact with yet another capsule. She inspected the smooth red surface before opening it. Inside was a note on which the word *anger* was inscribed. She wondered how the item had been slipped onto her person without her knowledge.

"You see, I didn't even have to ask you to carry that one. This was just a practice exercise, but I could burden you with any emotion I choose, so can anyone else—that is unless you properly guard and protect yourself. The best way to do that is to know yourself first. Once you do that, you'll have a better sense of what to do when the ball's in your court, so to speak."

Lumera went on to explain that Camile's empathy and sensitivity would serve as a benefit to both, the Coexistent and Transcendent Worlds. However, it would require Camile to make herself more like a buffer, absorbing negative energy like a sponge, then filtering it out before releasing it in either a positive or neutral manner. To Camile, the prospect sounded as difficult as processing a cesspool for drinking water with no more than a household sieve.

*　　　*　　　*

Camile knew Commander Wilder was also being treated at the EDC, but was nonetheless surprised to bump into him at the entrance later that afternoon. He requested to speak with her, but she quietly refused, attempting to bypass him. Stepping in her path, he prevented her evasion, but was careful not to lay a hand on her as he extended his palms as though at gunpoint. Even so, Camile backpedaled, ensuring her protection with distance.

"Please, just hear me out," the commander implored, a mild tinge of urgency in his voice, "Let me apologize. I owe you at least that much."

Camile glanced around to make sure they weren't completely isolated.

"Brandon…" She started to object, but changed her mind. Sighing, she said, "Okay, but make it quick."

As they sat on the steps, the commander took a deep breath as though summoning the strength to make eye contact.

"What I did was immoral, out of character and unbecoming of an officer," he began. "I was trusted to help you build your defense skills and I ended up not only betraying my vow, but hurting you in the process. I'm still trying to figure out how I allowed my emotions to disrupt my self-control. Look, I never meant to hurt you. I truly hope you believe that. And I hope you'll find it in your heart to forgive me, but I understand if you can't bring yourself to do it."

"You done?" Camile exhaled, swaying her feet. Forgiveness wasn't something she wanted to give out on a whim. She somehow felt doing so would be a sign of justification of the incident or weakness in her character. However, that didn't mean she didn't empathize with him to an extent. She, too, had inexplicably acted on impulse. Her illogical behavior had thrown her into the sickening tides of consequence. Still, the fact they had both acted in error didn't excuse the situation.

"Not exactly," Commander Wilder answered. "I have a confession to make. You probably figured it out already, but Akalina and I were involved. It wasn't a conventional relationship, but it was good while it lasted. But I guess all good things must come to an end."

"And you blame me for taking her away during the reintegration?" Camile frowned, remembering his scathing words.

"I did, at first." He hung his head as though recalling the same comment. "But I was just kidding myself. I know it wasn't your fault." Meeting Camile's eyes anew, he continued, "In truth, I lost her awhile before the reintegration. She broke it off with me, said she didn't want to be tied down. That night in the forest rekindled old feelings I thought were dead. I swore I was with her again. So kissing her seemed natural. Well, I guess it was you I was kissing after all. When you kissed me back it..." Brandon let the sentence hang as he expelled an amorous sigh. "It was incredible. I thought that the woman I loved had finally returned to me."

"But I'm not her." Camile narrowed her eyes. "You do realize that, don't you?"

"Yeah, I know." He exhaled sharply, briefly turning his gaze skyward as he rubbed his neck. "It's so damn cruel. I don't have anything against you, really. It's just that you look so much like her. God, you even smell like her. So sweet...intoxicating..." Brandon chortled softly before dropping his head into his palms. His voice grew heavy and tremulous. "What did I do to deserve this?"

"Are you okay?" Instinctively placing a hand on his shoulder, Camile lowered her head in an attempt to meet his gaze. He recoiled, rising from his seat. She was startled by the sudden reaction.

"Please, don't do that." He shuddered softly, pulling away. "I'm sorry. I guess I wasn't as ready for this as I thought. I just figured you deserved to know the truth, even though it'll never justify my actions."

Camile watched him traverse the entrance, fascinated at the incredible difference a few minutes had made. Just moments ago, she borderline loathed the man who tried to attack her. Now, upon hearing his story, she was actually beginning to pity him a little. Based on his explanation of his failed relationship, he was just as unlucky in love as she was.

Chapter 30

Sparks of Clarity

Aside from Lumera, Camile had very few visitors in the coming days. Her parents briefly visited and reiterated the reason for her isolation. Like her albino counselor had already mentioned, she needed to spend a significant time alone in order to re-center herself without outside distraction or influence. Though she understood the reasons given, a small part of her viewed her involuntary recess as an adult time-out. Yet, her solitude afforded her the opportunity to learn more about the EDC and its housing summit, Aqueon Peak.

The EDC—*Emotional Decontamination Center*—was considered a vital part of Caldaq's wellness division. The facility, situated atop Aqueon Peak, stood at eight stories, though only three were visible above ground. The subterranean levels housed a shamanic temple and training center for former scribes and other visionaries. Aqueon Peak was among the most enchanting of Caldaq. Like silvery ribbons, the water of Aqueon Falls flowed strategically throughout the property, generating power before emptying into Coronis Lake—otherwise known as the *Lake of Renewal.*

A week into her stay, Camile received an unexpected visit from Magistrate Sui. The magistrate wore her hair in long flowing waves that further emphasized her exotic bi-colored eyes.

"I've spoken with Commander Wilder," she stated, admiring the wall fountain in Camile's room. "Apparently, he believes you were both involved in a mutual romantic exchange just moments prior to the incident. Does his recollection of the events accurately correlate to how you remember them?"

"Kind of. You see, I thought Bran—" Camile caught herself. "Commander Wilder was someone else at the time. I really didn't mean to lead him on or anything."

"Unfortunately, that's exactly what seems to have happened." The magistrate cracked a somber smile, presumably to ease the tension caused by the subject. "Apparently, you sent him some pretty intense vibes that escalated the situation, whether intentional or not."

Feeling a bout of guilt, Camile realized she had, indeed, sent Brandon very passionate signals, though she thought he was someone else. She knew it would be unfair to shoulder the full burden of what had taken place, yet she couldn't help but notice her contribution to the disturbing events. Be that as it may, Camile felt the magistrate was implying she had somehow provoked the situation.

Does this woman think I asked for this? she wondered, searching for the words with which she would try to defend herself. Before she could say anything, Magistrate Sui said something that almost led Camile to suspect her mind had been read.

"Don't misunderstand me, I'm not placing responsibility solely on you," the magistrate calmly explained. "Commander Wilder should be held accountable for his part in the incident. With his level of training, he should have been able to regain his composure long enough to walk away. Nevertheless, his remorse seems sincere. I guess that will be something the council will have to measure in time. You see, when such events as these occur, as rare as they are, the council gives the apprentice the option of receiving an alternate instructor. This case is unusual in that both you and Commander Wilder had a mutual misunderstanding that led to an intense loss of control." Magistrate Sui took a moment to pause as her face grimaced slightly. "Just out of curiosity, who did you think he was that night?"

"If possible, I'd like to keep that information private, Your Honor." Camile profusely hoped she wouldn't be forced to divulge the name she was desperately trying to keep secret.

The magistrate nodded her understanding before stressing the importance of Camile's adaptability.

"I must be frank with you, Camile. You've suffered a major setback, one that can severely hinder our efforts to help the Coexistents win the *Invisible War*. You're going to have to decide whether to run from a challenge or meet it head on," she stated, further gripping Camile's attention with her eyes. "It seems that although it will be a difficult task for the commander to reassume his position as your instructor—once he's rehabilitated and completes his probation—he's willing to put the situation behind him for the sake of your advancement, but it depends on you. Are you willing to do the same?"

"I honestly don't know. I realize time is of the essence, but it seems a bit soon for me to decide that right now."

"At the present time, you're not obligated to do so, but you'll have to make a decision before you're released from the EDC. Preparations will have to be made in case you decide otherwise."

Camile didn't want Brandon to lose his job, but she didn't want to take the chance of history repeating itself either.

"Why don't you test it out?" the magistrate suggested after a weighty pause. "Spend a little time with him while you both complete your rehabilitation and see how you feel about it. If you feel uncomfortable with him, even in the secure confines of this facility, then your choice will be obvious."

*   *   *

After much contemplation, Camile decided to take Magistrate Sui's advice. She saw it as an opportunity to find out more about Brandon's relationship with Akalina. However, before venturing into that potentially dangerous matter, she played it safe by talking about average topics. In doing so, she learned more about his playful, generous sense of humor, his interests in astronomy, cross-dimensional cartography, and his impressively diverse athleticism. In addition, he enjoyed speaking several languages and even indulged Camile by saying a few foreign words upon request. Camile deduced he had said something particularly naughty since he refused to translate what had rolled off his tongue like warm honey.

The more she got to know Brandon, she realized there was a depth to him that seemed to mask a painful past, much like Jeremy—perhaps even more efficiently since it didn't seem as obvious. Camile found herself becoming vaguely afraid. It wasn't due to the fear that she and Brandon might lose control again, but the fact she was beginning to connect with him on an emotional level. Physical infatuation was easy to dismiss for what it was—a combination of idealistic desires mixed with hormonal impulses and superficial attraction. However, what Camile was currently experiencing had crossed that threshold much more rapidly than she could have ever anticipated. She couldn't understand it. Nor was she willing to trust it right away. After all, she was still recovering from a traumatic ordeal, which made it all the more unsettling and confusing.

Several days and conversations later, Camile finally felt it was safe to ask the question she had been withholding. As she approached Brandon's table in the cafeteria she noticed her mother rising from the seat across from him.

"I'm so glad we had this talk, Commander." Kylie placed her hand on his shoulder. "You'll keep my words in mind, won't you?"

"Yes, Your Excellency. And again, I'm honored you agreed to speak with me," Brandon replied.

After briefly greeting her daughter, Kylie exited, leaving the two alone to begin their lunch.

"What was that all about?" Camile asked, allowing her eyes to trail her mother out of the room before meeting Brandon's gaze.

"I figured I owed your parents an apology for what happened. I'm surprised your mother agreed to meet me, but I think your father prefers to deal with me once I'm out of here."

"But what was that whole thing about keeping her words in mind?"

Brandon swallowed hard, scratching the back of his head.

"Oh, that." He laughed in a seemingly nervous manner. "Your mother promised to…personally confiscate my manhood should I repeat my mistake. I'm paraphrasing. Her language was a little more colorful. Let's just say the procedure she described isn't exactly clinical."

Ouch! Camile thought before saying, "You can't blame her for being upset."

"I don't," Brandon concurred before requesting a change in subject.

"If you don't mind me asking, how serious were things between you and Akalina?" Camile inquired.

"Serious enough. We were together for almost a year." Lowering his gaze, Brandon leaned back in his seat and rubbed his nails together.

"So, did the two of you, uh…" Her cheeks tingled as she tried to ask the question as delicately as possible.

"Make love?" He quirked his brows, shifting his aquamarine gaze upward to meet her eyes. His full lips curved upward. "A gentleman doesn't kiss and tell, but being that our past now involves you I think it's safe for me to give you a straight answer. Yes, Akalina and I were sexually involved. I'm surprised you didn't inherit any memories through the reintegration." His smoldering eyes bore deeply into Camile's as though trying to conjure up one of Akalina's repressed memories.

Shifting in her seat, Camile looked away, knowing that Brandon had seen Akalina in various states of undress and that it likely made it easier for him to imagine her in the same manner. Curiosity flooded her mind with personal questions her discretion wouldn't allow her to ask.

"That wasn't all there was to our relationship, though. There really was significance behind it," Brandon continued. His playful expression faded, becoming slightly forlorn. "At least there was on my part."

"So, you were the only person she really got along with back then, huh?"

"I was one of the few people patient enough to put up with her. As you probably know by now, Akalina was always a bit of a smart-ass, always causing somebody some kind of grief. Even as a kid she had a fresh mouth. I'll never forget the trouble she used to give her teachers. I remember one occasion in particular. When asked to describe hormones in a biology class, Akalina said: *It's what a slut does when she's having a good time.*" Brandon chortled when Camile's jaw dropped.

"She really said that?" she asked, already knowing the answer.

Brandon nodded. "She was a handful. You'd figure she'd fail all her courses with that kind of attitude, but it turns out she was paying closer attention to her studies than anyone realized. *Especially* the *Leih'klav*, as it turned out," He scrunched his face, apparently recalling the nights of scintillating passion he shared with her negative half. Knowing he was talking from experience, she was growing uncomfortable with the direction the discussion was taking. Then she reminded herself that it was she who steered it that way.

"You know, she had the sweetest little strawberry-shaped birthmark. I'm curious. Did it transfer over along with her scars?" Brandon asked before immediately retracting his query, palming his face in the process. "Sorry. That was inappropriate. You don't have to answer the question—unless you want to."

Camile immediately declined. She wouldn't have divulged the details even if she had an answer. The truth of the matter was that she had no clue whether or not she was currently bearing the birthmark. As far as she could recall, she had never seen it, even when showering. However, she had always been self-conscious about her body and tried to avoid over-analyzing it. Redirecting the conversation, Camile asked why Akalina had broken up with him.

"I guess I was too much for her to handle," Brandon quipped. Camile figured he was using his humor as a defense mechanism in order to guard his feelings, but the facade gave way as he presented his response. "I'm still trying to figure it out, to be honest. I think maybe she was just afraid to get close to anyone. A lot of people let her down, but I never did. I guess she didn't want to give me a chance to do it. Akalina hated living in fear and the possibility of losing control. I think that hatred was embedded into her psychosis. She was satisfied with having a physical relationship—don't get me wrong, so was I—but it was incomplete. I wanted more. You know…settle down, maybe start a family, someday. Guess that wasn't her thing."

"It's tough to love someone who doesn't feel the same way." Camile's mind wandered a moment, thinking of her unreciprocated feelings toward Jeremy. "Couldn't have been easy for you."

"Sure wasn't." Brandon pressed his lips together.

The conversation made Camile realize that his feelings were genuine and that he truly felt an attraction to Akalina on more than just a physical level. However, Camile was worried that he, in some way, still saw her as a mere container for her darker half.

*   *   *

I bet Brandon would get a real kick out of this, Camile thought later that night, carefully inspecting her nude body with the aid of the wall mirror and a small handheld mirror so she could view her back. She slowly pivoted her body from one side to the next like people do when trying on clothing. Her skin was nearly flawless. Aside from the scars on her abdomen and a subtle blotch on her inner elbow, there wasn't a mark to be seen anywhere. Camile chuckled softly, feeling rather foolish as she placed the small mirror on the counter. Brandon had obviously been pulling her chain. Either that, or Akalina's birthmark didn't transfer in the reintegration. As Camile grabbed her robe, the mirror slipped and fell onto the floor. To her amazement, it didn't break, but instead spun a few times before landing face-up between her feet. Sighing with mild impatience, she squatted slightly and reached for it. That's when she realized Brandon hadn't been fibbing after all. Gasping softly, she quickly grabbed the mirror and chided herself for not ignoring her curiosity. Though Brandon already admitted having an intimate relationship with her darker half, Camile couldn't resist the disconcerted feeling coming over her.

*   *   *

Upon her release from the EDC Camile felt ready to take on anything that awaited her. It was an invigoration that mounted upon seeing Jeremy again. His casual attire indicated that he was off duty. The medium blue v-neck cardigan complimented his golden skin and dark brown eyes. His hair was freshly cut, with little more than peach fuzz blanketing his round head.

Camile wanted to run her hands over it to feel the texture, but kept desire in its place.

Not much was said during the shuttle ride between Aqueon Peak and Coronis. The railcar threaded in and out of Caldaq's exterior, providing occasional views that made the awkward silence less abrasive.

Camile arrived at her father's office just as Sir Drayden was leaving. She overheard him telling her father, "Don't feel bad about this. It's all for the best."

As the knight made his exit, he regarded Camile with a nod and a smile which she returned.

I hope that's a good sign, she thought, figuring her recent breakdown had sent a message that he should stop pushing her so hard.

"I didn't want to discuss this until your release, but I understand Magistrate Sui has spoken with you regarding Commander Wilder's statement about the incident," her father announced.

"Yes." Camile exhaled, settling into a chair. "Now, I guess you have questions for me too."

"I sure do." He paused, briefly training his eyes on a small computer device lying before him on the glass table. "According to her—and this report—the liability of the incident was fifty-fifty. In other words, your affections were mutual, at least in the beginning of the rendezvous. Is this true?"

"Do we really have to discuss this now?" Camile massaged her temple.

"I'm afraid we have no choice. This is very important. Depending on your statement, Commander Wilder can still lose his job and face serious charges, none of which would equal the extent of my wrath." Zephyr frowned.

"Yeah, it's true. We shared a mutual kiss, but I thought he was someone else," Camile answered reluctantly.

"Who?" her father furrowed his brow.

Camile nearly blurted out Jeremy's name, but considered the awkward consequences. She didn't want Jeremy to have the satisfaction of knowing she had feelings for him that weren't mutual, so she fibbed. "I thought he was my ex-boyfriend, from the Coexistent World. Guess I got caught up."

"Well, that explains a lot, but it's unsettling to know you're still having hallucinations."

"Hopefully, they'll stop after the treatment I just went through. I really am feeling a lot better." Camile regarded her father with a smile, which faded slightly before asking: "Did you know about Commander Wilder's relationship with Akalina?"

"Not until recently. Had I known about it, I certainly wouldn't have chosen him as one of your instructors." Zephyr's jaw tightened. "I send the man on a mission and he ends up sleeping on the job—with my daughter, no less."

Camile narrowed her eyes. "What kind of mission was it?"

"I can't discuss that."

"More classified information, huh?"

Zephyr nodded. "I realize you've decided to keep him as your combat instructor. There's still time to rethink your decision."

"I don't think that's necessary. Brandon and I have made amends. I just think this whole incident was a horrible misunderstanding all around. I thought he was someone else and vice-versa. I guess in our loneliness we found each other in some bizarre way," Camile explained.

Her father regarded her inquisitively as though asking: *Are you sure?*

"Don't worry, Dad. If he so much as breathes the wrong way I'll put in a transfer request immediately," Camile reassured.

"If he slips up again, he might not be alive for the transfer," Zephyr remarked.

Chapter 31

Earning Trust

Camile melted into her routines as though her schedule had never been disrupted. Enthused to be back on track, Camile pushed herself to excel and to make up for the time she had lost during her recuperation. Jeremy and Brandon both cautioned her to pace herself so as to avoid burnout. Though unexpected, Brandon and Camile were slowly beginning to develop a blossoming friendship she had hoped to cultivate with Jeremy, whose vulnerability seemed to be heavily guarded either by his stubborn machismo or complex apprehension.

Camile would often wonder if their thoughts crossed paths. She figured if they did, she and Jeremy would be united on some level if only for a brief, fleeting moment. Such pondering led her to feel less alone on some levels and even more lonesome on others. In her moment of self-pity, she remembered the likely primary factor of Jeremy's distance when Brandon—carrying a medium sized case—entered the room with his adoptive sister.

Justine! Camile thought, realizing she had totally forgotten about Jeremy's girlfriend. Like Camile, Justine was sporting a single braid and a high collared, short-sleeved shirt. It was an unsettling coincidence, especially since she was wearing a noticeable scowl that Camile knew was meant for her. This suspicion was confirmed when Justine approached her side and whispered: "Didn't take long for you to screw things up. I'll be damned if I

221

let you ruin everything my brother's worked for. I strongly suggest you keep your distance from now on."

"The situation has already been settled. If you disagree, I suggest you take it up with your brother and the council," Camile said coolly.

"Hey, no time for girl talk. It's time to get started," Brandon called from a short distance, regarding his sister with a knowing glance. He waved for the women to join him.

Curiously eyeing the box he was crouching next to, Camile wondered if he had any clue of what she and Justine were discussing. Brandon opened the container, revealing a metallic volleyball-sized spherical cluster of orbs the size of golf balls. Each of the small orbs was covered in raised bumps. He explained that the four of them were about to participate in an exercise designed to test and sharpen each player's instincts and reactions while encouraging teamwork. Just as she opened her mouth to inquire about who would be joining them, Jeremy entered the room. Justine distributed special gloves as well as the mandatory protective padding and headwear. As Camile suited up, her enthusiasm declined as she imagined how painful it would feel to get pelted by the dangerous looking object.

The game, as Brandon described it, was called *Salvage*. The ball, called a *Meteor*, would purposefully aim to collide with the floor and /or walls. The goal of the players was to prevent that from happening since the impact would cause an event called a *break*, when the ball would split apart into *meteorites* and attack the players. Victory is achieved when each player has blocked the ball an equal number of times—in essence, purposefully achieving a stalemate between all players. The amount of blocks required depended on the difficulty level of the game. Such a feat would require impeccable communication and cooperation. As though that wasn't difficult enough, the *Meteor* is programmed to learn and adapt to each player's moves. In addition, it was designed to break apart at an unspecified point in the game, at which time all players would have to deflect the small orbs with their gloved hands, protected knees, elbows or feet.

Jeremy warned Camile that she might feel weird at the start of the game. Sure enough, as soon as Brandon ordered the computer to begin the first sequence, she immediately felt lightheaded. Jeremy was quick to lend her his arm to stabilize her while inquiring about her condition.

"I'm good." She said as she steadied herself.

It was then explained that the program operated on magnetic propulsion which would drive the ball all around the room based on physical responses. Camile noticed Brandon manipulating the ball back and forth between one gloved hand and the other. It didn't touch his hands. Instead, it hovered just centimeters above them.

Without further adieu, the game began once the ball was tossed into the air. At first, it traveled in slow motion, but soon accelerated to a furious pace. Each player was assigned a specific quadrant to defend. Camile successfully blocked the ball from making contact with the floor at least twice. Upon doing so, she felt an unusual vibration travel through her palm and up her arm. The strange sensation caused her to stand in place.

"Keep going!" Justine ordered. "You can't afford to stand still!"

The *Meteor* was now moving so fast, it seemed like a streaming glittering trail of silver as it shot across the gymnasium. It was a stellar optical illusion that made the sphere resemble its namesake. As it traveled between two quadrants, Justine and Jeremy both leapt to block it at the same time. Colliding with one another, the two fell onto the floor, Justine's body landing on top of Jeremy's. Camile was so distracted by their accident and the slight amusement written on their faces, she didn't realize the cluster had also crashed to the ground and had broken formation. Nearly half of the small projectiles were heading in her direction at an alarming speed.

"Camile, look out," Brandon shouted, expertly swatting the ones attacking him. In doing so, they began to rejoin formation, hovering in place as though awaiting the others. "Camile, look out!"

Camile broke into a run, scaling the bleachers when the floor ended. Knowing she couldn't outrun the broken cluster forever, she instinctively deflected many of the flying orbs. Even so, one struck her ankle. Losing her balance, she tumbled from the top row of bleachers all the way down to the sparring mat. Rolling onto her back, she got a clear view of the remaining orbs rebounding. Shielding her head, Camile prepared herself for the inevitable pelting she was about to endure. Much to her pleasant surprise Jeremy leapt to action and deflected them all.

"Are you okay?" he asked, kneeling beside her.

"I feel beat up from the feet up, but I think I'll live," Camile quipped. Her ankle was throbbing with agony, but she didn't want to look like a wimp in front of present company—especially tough-as-nails Justine. For a split-second, she could have sworn she saw the flicker of a smile on the outer corners of Jeremy's lips. Had he found her response amusing?

"I'm pretty sure the infirmary will patch me up in no time." Camile smiled shakily, nearly biting her lip to offset the pain. Figuring the quicker she received medical attention, the better, Camile rose to her feet only to topple anew. For the second time that afternoon Jeremy caught her in his arms before setting her gently on the floor, kneeling before her. He then took her injured foot into his hand, resting it on his thigh.

He slowly rolled down her sock and winced at the darkening bruise on her swelling left ankle. Meeting her eyes anew, he said, "This pretty bad, but you're handling the pain very well. I'm impressed."

Brandon, now sitting beside her, placed a hand on her shoulder. "I'll take you to the infirmary right away before the pain really kicks in."

Oh, if you guys only knew! Camile thought, fighting to maintain her poised facade, but inside she was shouting as though to drown out the pain. It wasn't working.

"No. I'll do it since you have to finish your cross-dimensional cartography research. Don't forget our meeting about the upcoming mission," Jeremy said to Brandon while easily scooping Camile into his arms.

As Jeremy carried her out of the room Camile saw an expression of marked jealousy burning on Justine's face.

*   *   *

"Half the battle is to establish at least some degree of trust," Vincent lectured. "Without it, the animal won't approach you even if you're holding something it wants. In order to earn that trust you must communicate on the same level as your target."

"Are you saying I have to bark?" Camile chuckled half-heartedly.

The two stood at the edge of the woods on the northwestern side of the compound. Sitting beside Vincent's tall frame—clad in a long-sleeved charcoal gray top, black vest and matching pants—was a large black dog with brown highlights. The sheen of its coat made it easy to see the well-defined muscles beneath it. Its black eyes were like an abyss of nothingness, sandwiched between pointed ears and a long snout. The top of the dog's head was aligned to where Camile guessed Vincent's navel was.

"No." He chortled almost condescendingly before continuing his lecture. "You need to communicate on the level of need and desire. Strip away the complicated intricacies of verbal human language and operate on the fundamental levels of communication through energy. Clear your mind of all that clouds it until all that's left is the basic command. But that's not all. You must visualize the successful luring of the creature."

Camile took a moment to focus and suddenly she could almost feel herself petting the black dog she'd been trying to command for days. To her exhilarated surprise, the animal slowly approached her and sat at her feet. She smiled in silence as her dark-haired instructor nodded with approval, waving the dog back to his side.

"Yes, very good, but you mustn't get cocky. You still have much to learn. Even so, I must admit, you've just taken an important step." Vincent slowly walked around her as he continued speaking. "Today, you've come one step closer to embracing your pure animal instinct. It's difficult for most people to venture beyond the fortress of complex communication they've spent years constructing around themselves. It's difficult for them to surrender to what it is they truly desire—and forsake their comfort zone in order to pursue it. Which brings me to the question…" He halted his steps in front of Camile, his eyes burrowing into hers. "Why don't you give Commander Wilder a chance? He's clearly interested in you, which is more than I can say about Jeremy."

Camile was thrown completely off guard by the question and she wondered how he knew so much. By now, the dog was snoring softly while curled up at Vincent's feet. In the back of her mind, she wondered how it was possible for something so intimidating to look so adorable.

"Why does this concern you?" Camile stacked her arms across her chest.

"I'm a competitive man and it's important that my pupils strive for perfection. I can see you're not as happy as you could be. The more content you are with yourself and your life, the better you'll perform—and, the better I'll look as your instructor. Of course, the latter is just an added bonus." He winked.

"With all due respect, sir, I'm perfectly capable of handling the situation without your help."

"Ah, in other words, you have no intention in giving up your worthless pursuit of Jeremy. How romantic. Incredibly stupid, but romantic."

"Excuse me?" Camile frowned in annoyance.

"You have a perfectly suitable man pining for you, yet you decide to go after the one who views you as little more than a pesky obligation."

"Brandon confused me with Akalina. Anyway, did you forget what he tried to do to me? He—"

"Wasn't himself." Vincent interrupted. "Commander Wilder was in an unfortunate state of confusion, but apparently you were projecting some of your attraction for him as well. Now he sees the truth with crystal clarity. He now knows who you are and apparently has true feelings for you, from what I can tell. Akalina may be his past, but you can be his future."

"I may have forgiven him for what happened, but I can't forget and I'm certainly not prepared to start that kind of relationship with him on a whim." Camile grimaced. "Wait. Why am I even explaining myself? With all due respect, you're single, aren't you? Why aren't you—?

"I'm flattered, love." Vincent chortled condescendingly. He smirked, brushing a stray lock of Camile's hair from her forehead. "But I think you and I should maintain a professional relationship. At least for the time being."

"What? No." She pulled back slightly, much to Vincent's amusement. "I mean, why aren't you worrying about your own love life?"

"There's no need for you to bring my romantic situation into this, love. I'm not the one with the problem, here. You see, I have the luxury of time on my side whereas you…Well, let's just say if you hope to give your mum and dad a little grandbaby in the future, you'd best get yourself a suitable mate before you dry out. After all, you're part Coexistent, you might not have the blessing of having the extended fertility of a fully Transcendent female."

"You did *not* have to go there, but that's beside the point. I missed the part where any of this is your business," Camile retorted. "Seriously, does anyone understand the concept of privacy around here?"

"Sorry. Point taken. Just thought I'd give you a little food for thought, that's all. Didn't mean to hit a nerve." Vincent smiled before concluding the lesson. "You've done a good job today. Next time, we'll work with something bigger. Not to worry, I'm not talking about Buttercup."

Camile noticed the shaman approaching them. She was approximately twenty feet away when the dog suddenly roused. After unleashing a loud bark, he charged at the shaman, his tail wagging slightly. An expression of sheer surprise crossed Vincent's face as he raised his hand in preparation to call off his dog.

"No," Tabitha shouted, her face contorting in horror. She promptly extended her right hand in front of her, causing the dog to whine. It flipped through the air before landing on its side, motionless.

"What the hell did you do that for? He wasn't going to attack you! I was about to call him back!" Vincent exclaimed as he rushed to look over his four-legged friend. He nuzzled the canine's head while stroking his dark fur. "Come on...Wake up, my treasure," he whispered tenderly.

"I'm sorry. I guess I panicked," the shaman admitted.

"Panicked?" Vincent grimaced bitterly. "Your Wisest, I'll have you know that this is a very old dog. Surely, he's no match for someone of your stature."

"Again, I offer my sincerest apologies, Commissioner Thornton. I assure you, your dog will be just fine," the shaman said. As though on cue, the dog moaned softly while gently opening his eyes.

"You see, he's coming to as we speak," she added hurriedly. "Camile, let's go. It's time for our session."

Camile had never seen the shaman so shaken. Nor had she ever seen her walk as fast as she was as they headed back to Caldaq. Limping slightly due to her healing ankle, Camile found herself lagging a good two to three steps behind her counselor.

Camile's mind lingered on her conversation with Vincent. It prompted her to contemplate her romantic future. In some ways he had opened her eyes to her denial and the difficult choice she knew she would have to make. Should she pursue Jeremy, who appeared disinterested in her, or should she spare herself the possible humiliation and take a chance by giving in to Brandon's advances? Camile mentally compared the two. Both were attractive, extremely intelligent and ambitious. However, the incident with Brandon had tainted her attraction towards him. Not only that, but she'd originally pegged him as a potential cad with a wild streak—not exactly the type of man a woman would take home to her parents.

Still, there seemed to be much more beneath his flirtatious exterior, which he seemed to use to guard his deeper feelings. Jeremy, on the other hand, had a more docile personality and seemed more likely to hold a steady relationship. Once again, Camile reminded herself that he was already in one with Justine, a complication she couldn't get around. It wasn't in her nature to step between a couple, but Camile hoped that somehow the cards would eventually stack in her favor.

In either case, Camile didn't want to end up in the same heartbreaking position she repeatedly found herself in during her relationships in the Coexistent World. To her, Jeremy and Brandon were like water and fire. Though attracted and drawn to both men, Camile was afraid of drowning in the depths of Jeremy's ambiguity or burning in the heat of Brandon's intensity. She found herself wishing she could extract portions of each of them and construct the ultimate mate, but chided herself, knowing from experience that being divided is one of the worst things that could happen to a person.

On the way to the Celestia for her session with Jeremy, Camile saw him speaking with the commander in the atrium. Figuring she and Jeremy could walk to the meditation room together, she approached. The two men greeted her, invited her to sit, but politely excused themselves as they wrapped up their discussion.

"Are you sure you don't want me to present our plan to the minister?" Jeremy asked Brandon.

"There's no need for concern. The defense minister is fair and will be judging our plan for what it is, not who's proposing it," Commander Wilder answered. "Besides, I'm determined to rectify my standing with him after what happened." He frowned subtly, meeting Camile's eyes. Cracking a gentle smile, he looked away. "Camile may have saved my job, but it's up to me to ensure that I keep it. Not to mention I have a lot to prove if I want to make captain someday."

"I'm sure you'll manage. You've come this far." Jeremy smiled. It was a rare event to behold, which was shameful since it was a fine addition to his face. His rich brown eyes glistened beneath his otherwise intense brows. After a short moment, he resumed his usual studious demeanor. Camile was amazed at how well he and Brandon were getting along just a few weeks after they were viciously fighting each other.

"I'm hoping this will help me get ever further." Brandon tapped the side of the computer screen with his fingers. "The mission plan is nearly flawless."

"Nearly?" Jeremy raised one of his full eyebrows.

"There's been an unexpected development. Within the last two hours, an unstable rift popped up right in the middle of our planned route in the Coexistent dimension." Brandon used his finger to indicate a point on the onscreen map. "But there's a steady rift here. We can use it to cross over. According to my calculations, this is now the best way to make our approach." He drew a path. "There's just one inconvenience, once we reach the other side, we'll have to travel the rest of the way on foot—unless we're lucky enough to come across an alternative method of transportation."

"Sounds like a plan to me. Nice catch," Jeremy commended.

"Just curious; what kind of mission will you be going on?" Camile inquired.

"We're not at liberty to discuss it at this time, but I think your father will explain it to you once final planning and preparation is complete." Jeremy replied.

"You didn't hear it from me, but I think there's a good chance you'll be joining us," Commander Wilder added.

Chapter 32

Strengthening Bonds

Camile was excited about the prospect of going on another mission. She hoped she would be able to actually contribute something the next time around. However, she hadn't heard any further details since speaking with Brandon and Jeremy in the atrium. She decided to exercise patience and give her father some time to approach her about the mission when he saw fit.

After another taxing game of *Salvage*, Camile all but collapsed into a sitting position on the gymnasium floor. Jeremy made a quick exit as soon as the game concluded, leaving Camile with Brandon and Justine. Camile blotted the sweat from her face and neck, enjoying the cool sensation of the towel. Though the game objective hadn't been achieved, Camile internally celebrated a personal victory in that she had averted injury. Brandon excused himself before turning his attention to Justine, who turned her back as she packed the cluster into the case. Suddenly, she whipped around to meet his gaze. Based on the expression on her face, she was none too pleased.

"What? You're kicking me out?" She smirked in apparent disbelief.

"Justine, I initiated telepathic communication for a reason." Brandon whispered, his face reflecting mild embarrassment.

"I'm sorry, but I'm not giving her anymore time to sink her toxic claws into you. I don't trust her and I'm not ashamed to say it aloud."

Feeling uncomfortable seeing the two debate, Camile reluctantly offered to leave. She decided it was best to remove herself from the situation before tensions worsened. Having just gotten back on track with her training, she didn't want to jeopardize her progress by remaining in an environment that could potentially trigger another emotional outburst. Before she could make her exit, Brandon asked her to wait.

"Justine, you're being irrational." He frowned. "You may be my sister, but as an officer I'll have to report you to the EDC if this continues."

"You're pulling rank on me and threatening to have me sent to the very place you were in because of her?" Justine grimaced before taking a deep breath. "Okay. I'll leave, but you haven't heard the end of this, brother." With that, she made her exit, after which time Brandon apologized for her behavior.

"Sometimes she takes her role of big sister a little too far even though she only has a few months on me. I think she still sees me as an innocent young boy. Little does she know, I left my youthful innocence behind a long time ago."

"Reminds me of my mom." Camile laughed. "There's such a thing as over-protecting, but I know she meant well. I think Justine does too, in her own way. Growing up with such a tenacious sister must've been interesting to say the least. Did you ever feel the need to compete for attention from your parents?"

"What do you mean?" Brandon asked. A look of confusion crossed his features.

"Well, when Justine was adopted it must've—"

"No. You got it confused. Justine wasn't adopted. I was."

"*You?* But she said—"

"Remind me to throttle her later." Brandon's mildly amused smile turned somber. "She thinks she's trying to protect my privacy. That chapter of my life wasn't exactly the model for an ideal childhood. My parents were killed when I was very young and I was eventually adopted by Justine's."

"I'm so sorry to hear that. How did it happen?"

"If you don't mind, I'd rather not get into that right now."

"Still too painful to deal with, huh?"

"Nah. I'm used to it by now. I just think you have a full enough plate as it is. Besides, a little mystery is just added incentive for you to get to know me better." He cracked a smile which soon faded. "There's something I've been meaning to talk to you about, but until now, I didn't know how I should go about it. It's about what happened that night in the woods."

"I thought we settled this." Camile sighed, not wanting to revisit the topic.

"So did I, until recently. One of the most important things I ever learned is that the *Leih'klav* and the *Bol'krah* should never be crossed. That's one of the most sacred principles of the *Leih'klav* practice."

Seeing the perplexed expression on Camile's face, Brandon paused to explain that the *Bol'krah* was the book of war.

"Unfortunately, that doesn't stop people from getting them mixed up," he continued. "I never thought I'd fall into that same pattern. Mutual consent is among the highest values of the *Leih'klav's* moral doctrine and I desecrated it all for the sake of clinging to the dissolving memories of days that no longer exist. As a result, a lot of damage has been done."

Camile understood and shared his regret regarding the situation, but she knew that dwelling on the past would do nothing to mend the emotional wounds they had both sustained. His disappointment in himself was so strong she felt constricted by his disgrace. She sought to alleviate it by shedding light on the fact he attempted to use the little self-control he had to halt what could've been a tragic event.

"I'm not gonna pull punches. What you tried to do was messed up, but you didn't go through with it. You stopped, even before Jeremy showed up."

"The fact the physical act wasn't completed doesn't nullify the consequences. My past and present collided and I allowed you to get trapped in the middle. I just found out you suffered a breakdown because of it."

"Is that what this is about? I admit, it was a bad night, but you're not the one who caused my breakdown."

"Then who did?" Brandon frowned.

Camile's mind hung on the question and she found herself unable to answer.

*　　*　　*

Had she been in the Coexistent World, the old woman may have been dismissed as a second-rate fortuneteller; the kind who conducted their business somewhere between a nail salon and a pizza shop. Yet, this woman's success rate at matchmaking was indisputable according to many of Deltine's couples. Camile felt slightly embarrassed about going to such extremes to attempt sorting out the matters of her heart, but in her mind she had few other options. She was aware that her full focus and attention needed to be reserved for her education and her upcoming mission, which remained a mystery. In addition, she wanted to know whether or not she was wasting her time even considering a union with either Jeremy or

Brandon. Using her hope for answers and guidance to propel her forward, she entered the humble quarters of the woman, known as the matchmaker.

After a few long moments, she shuffled in slowly. Her awkward movements prompted her to stumble in spite of her small, cautious steps. Camile immediately rushed over to help, but the woman vehemently refused.

"I may be a tad wobbly, but I can make it across the room. You here for *my* help, ain't you?" She cackled.

Camile nodded, slightly abashed.

"Well, if you're here for a quick fix or one of them so-called magic love potions, you can just keep walkin'." The woman narrowed her cloudy eyes.

"I'm just here for advice...guidance. They call you *the matchmaker*, don't they?"

"Shoot, I know what they call me!" The woman rasped, giving a dismissive wave of her hand as she collapsed into a chair. "I ain't no matchmaker. I just show people the path to their true love. Whether or not they take it or not is entirely up to them. But I think you already made your choice long before you met me. What you're lookin' for is someone to validate your decision by tellin' you what you wanna hear. You come here to waste my time, girl?"

"I've come for clarity." Camile answered, knowing the woman's assessment was accurate.

She also knew she wasn't the first to resort to such measures. After all, many people relied on various rituals in hopes of offsetting the responsibility that comes with the power of choice. Still, hers was a decision far too important to chance on a flip of the coin or rock, paper, scissors. That's where the matchmaker came in.

"Right." The old woman sighed. "Have a seat. Let's get started."

Camile sat in the chair across from the woman and asked her name.

"Hmph. Out of all the years I've been doing this, do you know you're the second to ask me my real name?" A subtle smile hinted at the warmth beneath her weathered appearance. "It's Amoura."

Camile couldn't help but notice that the name was remarkably close to *Amore*, the Italian word for love in the Coexistent World. She asked Amoura how long had she been in the business of match-making.

"Too long, perhaps." She chortled, raking her hand through her stringy cotton candy-like hair. "Former scribes have limited job options after retirement, but I guess them's the breaks."

"You were a scribe?" Camile smiled with amazement. "What's it like? Do you know anything about a scribe named Isaac? He's missing and I've been having dreams about him."

Amoura's lips nearly vanished as her eyes darted around.

"Forget I said anything. Let's get down to business." Amoura said quickly, tightly grasping Camile's hands as she closed her eyes. Her face scrunched as though trying to focus. "Who are your interests? Don't tell me their names. Just think about them. See them in your mind."

"How do you know there's more than one?" Camile asked.

"You just told me." Amoura winked. "Besides, I'm the expert, remember?"

Camile closed her eyes and immediately saw Jeremy, then Brandon. A sudden gasp prompted her to reopen her eyes. When she did, she noticed Amoura staring at her with her mouth agape.

"What's wrong? Do you know them?"

"No," Amoura said almost breathlessly. "In the many decades I've been doing this, this has only happened once. It seems like…history is repeating itself."

"What, are they both wrong for me?" Camile asked. In contradiction to her heart, her mind half-hoped this was the case. At least then, love will be one less complication in her life. However, her frown deepened once she realized how empty her life would be without it.

"Quite the opposite. You can have a successful relationship with either one. Your soul is equally compatible with both these men."

"Hey, that's not so bad. It's a win-win."

"Not so fast. Even though you can have a decent relationship with either man, one of them holds a strong possibility of distracting you from what you need to do. As a result, things will go very wrong for a lot of people if you end up with him."

Figures there'd be some fine print, Camile thought before asking. "And I bet you can't tell me who it is, can you?"

Amoura shook her head.

"Figures," Camile muttered before asking a question she hoped she wouldn't regret. "You said this happened to someone before. To whom, Akalina?"

"I keep my clients confidential. If they want to sing my praises, that's their business. But I can assure you, it wasn't Akalina."

"Can you at least tell me how things turned out for the couple?"

The woman lowered her head a moment before meeting Camile's gaze anew with watery eyes. "Tragically," she answered.

*   *   *

Jeremy's eyes sparkled as his fingers danced gracefully across the screen. His studious expression bore the unmistakable fire of passion and contentment. Given what he was doing, Camile wasn't surprised by his enthusiasm. Cross-dimensional cartography was something he had a great zeal for, perhaps even more than Brandon had expressed. However, she was pleasantly stunned that Jeremy agreed to show her what he, and a select few, have had the privilege to work on. She had expressed her interest in the subject from the day it arose during her discussion with Brandon while at the EDC.

Her anticipation had grown with every step as she and Jeremy made their way to the cartography drafting facility, located in the upper portion of Caldaq's Dusque peak. Somehow, it felt as though he was about to reveal a secret that no one else knew. Then she replaced her quixotic fantasy with the fact that scores of people had already seen what she was about to observe.

Jeremy described cross-dimensional cartography as a system of measuring and cross-tabulating information of various topographic regions and translating that information to layered maps. Keying in a computer command, Jeremy cloaked the room in near-total darkness. The illumination emanating from the flat table screen bathed them in an ethereal shade of blue. For a moment, Camile felt herself submerge into Jeremy's deep gaze.

"You ready?" His relaxed face contrasted with his eyes, which were as vibrant as the screen before them.

"Whenever you are," Camile answered.

"I'll make this as simple as I can," he said, keying in another command.

The walls of the circular room were flooded with the panoramic image of the Transcendent World map. The continents and provinces were all outlined in sky blue against a black background. Only a few labels were present throughout the map to indicate continents and large bodies of water. States and provinces were left blank. Camile wondered if Jeremy had simplified the map because he underestimated her intelligence.

"Now, this might look a little confusing at first, but it's fascinating, nonetheless." He hit a key on the computer, prompting a second map to overlap the first. Like the foremost layer, it was in wireframe view. However, it was outlined and labeled in bright green. Camile realized Jeremy wasn't underestimating her map reading abilities. The vision before her was indeed perplexing despite the simplified appearance.

"This is what the Transcendent and Coexistent dimensions look like in conjunction with one another." A broad smile crossed his face as he marveled at the dual topographical depiction.

"This is amazing!" Camile exclaimed, walking along the massive wall screen. "I can see why you spend so much time studying this."

"It's a requirement. Cartography requires a great deal of focus, skill and painstaking attention to detail. This is doubly so for cross-dimensional cartography. I won't even go into how complicated other forms of cartography can get." Jeremy chuckled faintly, scratching the back of his neck.

Camile couldn't believe how relaxed and open he was being with her. It was the most personable he had been since they first met. She decided not to question it and instead decided to milk the moments for all they were worth.

"Sounds like a rigorous job. I get the feeling only the elite are selected for such a delicate responsibility," Camile stated. "This sounds like the type of occupation where mistakes can be devastating."

"Because it is. In this line of work, mistakes can be catastrophic." Jeremy's face suddenly grew serious. Turning to face Camile, he crossed his arms and leaned his back against the table. "Billions of people throughout both worlds rely on our work, whether they realize it or not. The demands are high, but the rewards are great. I get a sense of fulfillment in knowing that I'm contributing something valuable to not only this world, but the Coexistent one."

"Does it ever bother you that you work anonymously, that no one will ever know that you're among the gifted people working to map the foundation of the world they're living on?"

She apparently caught Jeremy off guard with the one question he hadn't considered until that very moment.

"It used to." Tapping his bicep with his fingertips, his lips slightly upturned. "But I've since come to realize that their recognition isn't needed for my validation. Nor is it a deciding factor in how well I use my abilities. When it comes down to it, those responsibilities are my own."

"Well said." Camile joined his side, cautiously leaning back against the table. "Most people go their entire lives without coming to that conclusion. I'm striving not to be one of them."

"You won't be."

"What makes you so sure of that?" Camile smiled.

"Because you have it in you. I've seen it. That's why I believe in you," Jeremy's eyes locked with hers before returning to the map. After biting his lip, he said, "That's why we all do. I think you're just too stubborn to see it for yourself sometimes. Reminds me of how I used to be. The thirst to connect with others, to distract yourself from what's going on inside…It can blind you, but only if you let it."

Camile didn't have to pry any further in order to understand that he was now talking more about himself. She got the sense that he wanted to reach out, but didn't know how, or had simply forgotten. She also wondered if or when she should extend herself to him. The situation was still complicated by Justine, who was still clearly in the picture. She figured she could still attempt to form a bond with him as a friend. Then again, deep down, she questioned if simple friendship would be enough.

"Looks like it's our time now, Camile," Jeremy's voice suddenly broke through her thoughts. His eyes were now burrowing into hers in such a way Camile wondered if he had heard her inner ramblings.

"Uh...Our time?" She scrunched her brow.

"Excuse me." Grimacing slightly, he palmed his forehead. "For a moment there, I forgot you don't have telepathic abilities. I just received a notification from your father. It's time to meet with him about the mission we discussed a few days ago."

Camile was both excited and anxious to learn more about the mission, but her amazed curiosity remained on the maps.

"You can map rifts too, can't you?" she asked, recalling the discussion between Jeremy and Brandon. "Can you show me an overview of how it's done before we go to the briefing?"

"There's no time." Jeremy swiftly returned to his usual stolid demeanor almost as quickly as he shut off the display.

Chapter 33

Consequence

Camile couldn't see the portal they used to cross into the Coexistent World, but was struck with a crushing shortness of breath during the transition. She caught a chill upon reaching the other side and was mildly disoriented.

"That's a normal reaction." Jeremy said in response to her expressed concern. "In the future, you might want to hold your breath as you cross over. It might help."

Due to a last minute change of plans, Jeremy had replaced Brandon, who had been ordered on an important surveillance assignment in the Transcendent continent of Bauldana. She was grateful for the modification, figuring it would make it easier for her to sort out her bottled up emotional conflict. She was also happy that Joval was chosen to tag along with them.

This was Camile's first time in the city of Chicago. Though she knew this was not a leisurely visit, she still hoped to catch a glimpse of some of the famed landscapes. This was not to be since she and her group were deep in the inner city and only had a brief window to complete their task. The mission was considered low-risk since all that was required was to observe a potential recruit, record the findings and return to base. A sudden wind gust rustled loose plastic bags and sent bottles and aluminum cans tumbling haphazardly towards a locked metal fence at the end of the alley.

"We're only half-in, so be careful," Jeremy cautioned, turning to face the dirty brick wall in front of them.

"What do you mean, *half-in?*" Camile inquired.

"It means we can do this." Joval smiled before walking through the wall like an apparition. It was a phenomenon Camile had witnessed on the night of her reintegration, but she still found it fascinating.

"Why did they choose him for this? The man has heart, but lacks patience." Jeremy expelled a deep breath. He shook his head before explaining, "Physically, we're only halfway inside this dimension. That's why we can walk through certain walls and objects on this plane of existence. In this condition, objects can harmlessly pass through us as well." He briefly glanced at the oblivious passersby. "So far, the Coexistents don't seem to be aware of our presence. Even if they were, they would probably take us for ghosts or hallucinations."

Camile nodded, thinking how cool it was. On the other hand, she realized it was equally chilling since not so noble people were using this ability to their advantage against the Coexistents. Passing through the same wall Joval had traversed, they entered a lobby. The glass in the entrance door was cracked and the foyer was lightly littered with snack wrappers and supermarket circulars, some partially singed. Camile suspected the culprits sat among the small group of foul-mouthed children congregating in the area unattended.

They were in a heated screaming match, vulgarly declaring that the others perform a variety of lewd acts Camile, herself, hadn't learned about until she was nearly twice their age. The degrading comments were clearly meant as insults and not as serious requests, at least that's what Camile hoped. Another child vociferously accused some of the others of having venereal diseases. Their brazen display of their early knowledge was not only disturbing, but revolting. Camile assessed that the kids were no older than eight years old, yet possessed a type of blatant brashness they could only have learned from irresponsible adults or provocative entertainment.

Disgusting! Camile thought. *Instead of learning their ABC's they're learning about STD's.*

She felt compelled to talk some sense into them. Judging by the disappointed expression on Joval's face, he seemed to share the sentiment. Before either of them could say or do anything, Jeremy spoke.

"I know what you're thinking. Don't," he warned. "They're not part of our assignment."

Camile noticed one of the boys drinking something out of a soda bottle, but instead of the dark cola advertised on the packaging, it contained a clear liquid. As she bypassed him, she could smell the distinct scent of liquor. She figured there would be no harm in preventing the boy from drinking it, though his actions indicated that he had already ingested a copious amount. As Joval and Jeremy walked ahead, Camile made her move.

Just as the boy held the bottle to his lips, Camile knocked it from his grip, unintentionally spilling the contents all over his clothes. The other children laughed while teasing him about needing a baby bottle. He shouted expletives in response, all the while looking for the cause of the mishap.

Jeremy whipped around, his face wearing a scowl.

"The mission objective is to observe, not interfere, unless otherwise instructed," he chided. "Do I even want to know why you felt so compelled to break protocol?"

"I've got a nagging conscience. I couldn't just stand by and let him drink that stuff," Camile explained. "Anyway, it's not like they can see us or anything."

"That's not the point. When a boundary has been set you need to respect it. I see you still have a lot to learn." Jeremy furrowed his brow. "If the council hears of this, there'll be hell to pay."

"I'm sorry I broke protocol, but in this case I don't see that there was any real harm done. I mean, no one got hurt, right?"

"Let's make sure we keep it that way." Jeremy frowned.

After they entered the selected residence, Jeremy evidently had a change of heart. He instructed Joval to escort Camile back into the corridor. According to Jeremy, he felt there was a risk Camile would emotionally contaminate the subject and sway their natural reaction. Upset, but not overly so, Camile stated that she could see herself out. Making an about face, she proceeded to walk through the wall through which she entered.

At least that was the plan.

She crashed with a thud, nearly knocking down items on a nearby shelf. The fact that she had just proven Jeremy's point left her feeling thoroughly abashed. If there was an upside to her embarrassment, it was the fact that it detracted from her physical pain. After explaining to Camile that she had missed her mark by a few feet, Joval guided her safely out of the apartment.

The narrow corridor smelled of oatmeal raisin cookies emanating from one of the apartments. The sweet scent lingered with the sounds of obnoxious arguing and conflict-thirsty cheers blaring from someone's television set.

Good old-fashioned dysfunctional entertainment.

Camile was amazed the trend was still in full swing. It spoke of the hair trigger irrationality that currently plagued the world. Joval busied himself by grooming his shimmering dreadlocks, twirling them between his bony fingers.

"Hey, don't mind Jeremy," he said, leaning against the wall. "He takes his job seriously, but he's no stranger to breaking rules."

"Thanks, but somehow I doubt that." Camile inspected her nails, thinking they could benefit from a trim and polish.

"You don't have to take my word for it. Just ask him about the time he, my brother and Commander Wilder got busted for catching hang time on Dead Man's Crest."

No way, she thought as her eyes darted upward to meet her friend's smug face.

Dead Man's Crest was one of Caldaq's most awkward rock faces. Protruding from the top of Quaezar Peak, it attracted many daredevils who sought to climb to the outmost point, many without the aid of safety equipment. The sport itself wasn't illegal, though government officials were barred from partaking in the challenge.

"Brandon I can understand, but Jeremy?" Camile scrunched her face. "Are you sure?"

"Absolutely." Joval nodded. "He wasn't always so reserved. Used to be a lot more fun, actually. As for Commander Wilder, he has the second place record for the most successful climbs."

"Who came in first?" Camile flinched upon hearing the familiar slam of a trash compactor door.

"Your old man." Joval winked. "It was before our time, but I'm told he caught a lot a heat for it."

While Camile's brows flirted with her hairline, Joval's eyes lit up upon seeing a burly man waiting for the elevator.

"Hey, wanna see something cool?" He clapped Camile's arm. Before she could answer, he tugged her down the hall until they were standing right beside the large man. They were so close, Camile could see the pores in his medium-tan skin and the shave bumps along his jaw line.

Ignoring Camile, shaking head in protest, Joval extended his hand, palm facing upward. Slowly, he slipped it through the center of the man's chest like a cloud.

"Don't worry. We're on different planes of existence, remember? Dude can't feel a thing," Joval explained. "But if you really focus..." Closing his eyes, he made quick, subtle movements with his hand, still up to the wrist in the subject's chest.

The man began hiccupping to Joval's rhythm. It seemed like Joval was using him as a puppet of physical disorder. Camile was impressed, but nonetheless disturbed as she wondered if any of her previous bodily reactions had been the result of outside manipulation. Gently removing his hand from the man's midsection, Joval used a finger to tickle the inside of his throat, causing him to cough.

"Cool, huh?" Joval chuckled before catching a case of the hiccups himself. A look of horror washed across his face as he met Camile's eyes. She backed away slowly as a tall shadowy figure emerged behind Joval with a hand deep in his back.

"Not so cool anymore, is it, Joval?" a familiar voice asked with perfect articulation.

As the florescent light caught the surface of the emerging figure, Camile stopped breathing for a few moments. She knew Joval was in serious trouble. There, before her very eyes, with his hand lodged in her friend's back was Sir Drayden.

"Drayd—! I mean, Mr. Sir Drayden Sebastian, sir! I was just—" Joval panicked, searching for an explanation.

"Learning that you never know who's watching you." Sir Drayden interrupted, his voice slow and soft with an air of foreboding danger.

*   *   *

Just as Camile had expected, her parents and senior instructors scolded her for her impulsive behavior and lack of self-control. Though unhappy with the outcome of her actions, she knew she had brought it on herself. Even so, she was more concerned about Joval. However, he seemed to be his usual cheerful self in spite of the fact he had been reprimanded for misusing the veil.

Nearly a week had elapsed and she was beginning to think the whole thing had blown over. Then she received evidence of the contrary. She was studying in her quarters when Sir Drayden paid her an unexpected visit. He looked more serious than usual, something she didn't think was possible.

"Come with me," he ordered, immediately leaving the room without waiting for a response.

By the time she exited her quarters the knight was already nearly halfway down the corridor. Once she caught up to him she could no longer hold her curiosity.

"Is there a problem, sir?" she asked.

"You'll find out soon enough," Sir Drayden answered gruffly.

As they entered the small meeting hall Camile saw her parents and the shaman seated at a table. All were wearing grim expressions.

"Word of the day is *consequence*. You do know what consequence means, don't you?" Sir Drayden asked.

"Of course, I do." Confused, Camile frowned as she took her seat. She didn't like where the conversation was headed.

"Well, I'm here to tell you that consequence doesn't wait for you to open the door, it kicks it in before you can look through the peephole."

Sir Drayden pushed an 8 x 10-inch film across the table. It landed in front of Camile with remarkable precision. Flipping it over, she was appalled to see the brutal image of a face covered in purplish bruises. The dark eyes were swollen shut above a nose and mouth, caked with dried blood.

"Why are you showing me this?" she asked, rediscovering her voice.

"Remember that kid you stopped from drinking a few days ago?" Sir Drayden asked.

"No," Camile whispered, not out of failure to recollect, but in disbelief that the battered victim in the photo was the same person. "What happened to him?"

"His father was so upset to find his son drenched in alcohol, he beat the kid within an inch of his life. *That's* what happened." Sir Drayden frowned.

"Oh, my God," Camile gasped softly. "I was only trying to help. I just…" Camile's voice trailed off as she painfully refrained from crying. She received an aching throat for her trouble.

"We know you didn't mean for this to happen, but in the future, please stick to the guidelines that you've been given," Zephyr said softly. "Deviating from our orders can result in more incidents like this or worse."

Guilt-ridden, Camile felt like she was creating a bigger mess for everyone, especially her parents. She never imagined she'd ever find herself longing for her old jobs in the Coexistent World. What at one time had seemed so complex now seemed trivial and simple. The stress she endured at her previous jobs paled in comparison to what she was now experiencing. At least in those positions mistakes would at most cost money and time. In her current position, mistakes could ultimately cost people their lives.

"I—" Camile struggled to find words to make everything better, but there were none. The most she could say was, "I won't let it happen again."

Feeling the need for solitary contemplation, she excused herself. Before she made her exit, her father had a few parting words.

"Compassion is one of your biggest strengths, but it's important that you take heed to the fact that it can also be used against you," he cautioned, gently pulling her into a hug. "You have to learn to determine how to use it and at what frequency."

"It's important that you learn this for your own protection. Many people have been tricked, their own compassion used to entrap, enslave and defeat them," her mother added as she joined the embrace.

"That's how we lost Duncan." The shaman sighed.

"Duncan?" Camile inquired, gently pulling away to meet her mother's eyes.

"Duncan was an officer with the Deltine Task Force," Kylie explained. "He went missing after he openly set out to bring one of the rebels to justice on his own. We believe the rebels kidnapped him in retaliation for his efforts. Duncan strongly suspected that the rebel in question was responsible for Isaac's abduction. He got too close to the case and found himself consumed by it."

"It's such a shame. He was one of our best men." Zephyr frowned. "Now, nearly three years after his disappearance, we still haven't been able to locate him."

"Do you think the rebels killed him?" Camile asked.

"I'm almost certain of it," her father solemnly replied. "The trail he once left in the living world has long since gone cold."

"Maybe you can track him down in the Phantom World and find out what happened. There might be a chance he can still give you a strategic advantage against the rebels," Camile suggested.

Her father cracked a soft smile while her mother raised her eyebrows. Both seemed equally impressed.

"Innovative thinking," Zephyr stated. "That'll be a valuable addition to our joint efforts. However, it's not possible to do as you've suggested. The amount of time it will take to comb through the Phantom World would be staggering since we don't have nearly enough manpower to do so. We could barely carry out the widespread searches we've attempted in the past in the living world. Besides, only a very rare, select few are able to perform such a task." He and Sir Drayden exchanged knowing glances.

"It was a lucky coincidence that we found your lost soul, wandering the Phantom World," Sir Drayden explained, to which Tabitha nodded. "Searching that realm for someone, specifically, would be like searching this world and the other many times over."

"Maybe his medallion can be tracked to determine his location," Camile replied.

"It was the first thing we tried. No luck." Zephyr expelled a breath. "That's part of the reason I feel it's doubtful that he's still alive. In addition, his transmitter is no longer registering on our sensors. Hasn't been for quite some time. There's a remote possibility that he may have defied the odds, but that remains to be seen."

"I'm sorry." Camile lowered her gaze in mild abashment. "I can't even get myself to function properly on these missions and here I am telling you how to do your jobs. I guess in some twisted way I'm trying to redeem myself by fixing something after the mistake I just made."

"Try not to dwell on it," her mother suggested. "This is not the first mistake you've made, and I'm sure it won't be the last, but always remember that we believe in you. So, believe in yourself too."

As the evening darkness gently fell upon the compound, Camile found herself taking solace in writing. This time she used a temporary journal while hoping the old one would somehow turn up:

I'm trying my best to develop into the person I need to be, but in spite of my best efforts I keep failing. Everyone tells me not to get discouraged, but it's easier said than done, especially when there are so many innocent people suffering the consequences of the wicked.

The children are the worst off. So many of them come to know heartache, pain and misery before they see the light of joy. For so many of them, that light is just the faint glimmer of hope that someday their pain will go away, that someday their tiny voices will finally be heard and no longer lost in the screaming chaos around them.

There's so much pressure in knowing that if I keep failing, people will die and many others will be lost—dying internally, as Dad put it. Sometimes, the thought of possibly having their blood on my hands is too much to take. I know that nothing sturdy comes out of a rushed tempering process, but I can't help but feel impatient. I guess the key is to take one step at a time, because if I look at how far I have to go, I'll be too afraid to move.

Chapter 34

Lost & Found

"Let's hope your counselor doesn't come by and attack any of my prized mounts," Vincent said sourly, brushing the lustrous platinum mane of a stately beige horse before fitting it with a saddle.

Camile turned her face away from his line of vision to steal a yawn. Her previous night's disappointment left her sleep deprived and lethargic. The early dawn mist did nothing to rouse her alertness. The thin fog lazily drifted across the grassy plain and poured into the woods like diluted milk.

"Horseback riding? Why, exactly, do I need to learn this?" Camile asked, carefully stroking the horse's velvety muzzle.

"Come on, Camile." Vincent smiled with a slight roll of his brown eyes. "Must I remind you that Transcendent citizens stress the importance of backup plans? We must become masters at improvisation. Therefore, it is imperative to know how to use multiple forms of transportation in case one or the other fails. Modern technology is a remarkable representation of our abilities, but like all humans, it's not without its flaws. Besides, staying connected with nature keeps us connected to who we are beneath all the politics."

Vincent went on to instruct Camile on how to mount the horse, named Monticello. After doing so, he explained that Camile's designated steed sometimes exhibited feisty behavior, but also had a loyalty that was beyond compare, qualities that reminded Camile of herself. Out of all the horses in the two dozen stables scattered throughout the compound, Monticello was among the fastest and strongest. In addition, the steed was no stranger to battle as he had ridden into combat several times. Monticello's flawless appearance contradicted this fact since he didn't have a scar on him.

"It's very important to know your animal and his limits before climbing into the saddle, much like a lover should know their partner before climbing into bed," Vincent continued. "Like people, animals have bad days and changeable moods. Monticello is no different. Pushing him beyond his limits can be deadly for you both. Of course, there are exceptions. For example, in a life or death situation you wouldn't have time to coax your animal companion into submission. Then, and only then, will you have to dominate it if the occasion calls for it. At all other times, however, you are to treat him with respect and dignity. He'll do the same in return."

Gently patting Monticello's wither, he nodded to Camile. "Okay, go on."

Camile regarded her instructor with a quirked brow.

"Well, are you expecting him to climb on *your* back?" Vincent quipped, a note of condescendence in his voice.

Smoothing her hand over the steed's face and mane, she approached the deep brown saddle. A sudden grunt from Monticello prompted her to recoil.

"Nah-uh." Vincent waved his finger. "You mustn't display your fear so readily. Always make your approach with confidence."

After taking a moment to regroup, Camile finally mounted the horse, taking the reins into her hands as Vincent went over the basics of maneuverability. It felt odd, yet somewhat satisfying that she was now looking down at the vertically blessed Vincent, who smiled as she successfully lapped around the track at a slow pace. Eventually, she worked her way up to a leisurely trot. Once she rejoined Vincent he congratulated her on a job well done, slapping one of Monticello's hindquarters.

The spirited animal reared, nearly throwing Camile off the saddle. Crying out, she gripped the reins for dear life as the horse sped off, galloping wildly around the track. The white wooden fence was rapidly approaching and Monticello showed no signs of slowing down. Soon, they were airborne as the horse cleared the fence and dashed into the woods. The scream that had been imprisoned in Camile's throat freed itself. The band that had been securing her hair had fallen out and her locks were now whipping in the air as she ducked random twigs and branches.

It seemed like an eternity had passed before she finally saw that they were approaching a similar fence to the one they jumped earlier. Monticello soared over it, landing back in the vicinity of where the wild ride began. Finally, he slowed to a trot then a slow walk before coming to a full stop at Vincent's side. Breathless, Camile quickly dismounted, nearly falling to the ground in the process. Her butt, back and thighs were sore and her energy was mildly taxed.

The ride probably wouldn't have taken as much out of her had she gotten adequate rest the night before. However, she couldn't deny the fact that there was a certain exhilaration to the whole experience. Though tired, she couldn't ignore the jolt of adrenaline that injected her with life. She understood that there was something liberating about being driven by an external living force, chasing the wind and catching it in her hair.

"Next time, can you warn me first?" She grimaced, unconsciously rubbing her tender posterior.

"You did very well." Vincent chuckled. "The first time's always the toughest, but it's also the most exciting. I didn't want to cheat you out of the experience. Besides, I wouldn't have done that if I wasn't certain you had a decent grip on the reins. You're just as brave as your father." He gave her a pat on the back before leading Monticello to his stall.

Camile followed. "I'll take that as a compliment."

"As well you should. If I ever had a son, I'd imagined he'd be like your father," Vincent said, feeding the steed a few sugar cubes from a woven sack. "But, you and I have a lot in common, as well."

"Somehow, I'm not so sure about that." Camile exhaled, stretching her muscles.

"Really? What about Sir Drayden? I know you hate the man. I can't say that I'm very fond of him, myself. Don't get me wrong, I respect him as a colleague. His dedication to his work is admirable. However, his lack of interpersonal skills can be a real pisser." Vincent finished feeding Monticello his treats and turned his full attention to Camile.

"I can't say I disagree with you there, but to say that I hate him is a little extreme." Camile used her fingers to detangle her hair. "Sure, I have some reservations about him, but he seems to have that effect on a lot of people. He's been easier to deal with since my stint in the EDC."

"Come on, Camile. There's no need to be coy about the subject. It's okay to admit you don't exactly have love for the man. He's burned you, that's something we both have in common. What separates us is the fact that you're in a position to do something about it. So, spill it, love." Vincent smirked, pulling a dark rectangular object from his inside jacket pocket. "Confession is good for the soul, but I guess I don't have to tell you that."

It took Camile's mind a few seconds to register why the item looked so familiar.

"My journal!" She seized it from his hands. It finally dawned on her how he had come to know so much about her conflicting feelings for Jeremy and Brandon. Contrary to her earlier suspicions, he hadn't been reading her mind, but her personal chronicles.

"What are you doing with it?" she asked in almost a whisper.

"Returning it," he answered coolly, stroking his dark hair. "Oh, don't give me that look. I didn't know it was yours until after I read some of the juicy contents, but only some of them. The sultriness of some of your entries was rather fascinating. I guess what they say is true, it's the quiet ones you have to watch out for." Vincent winked knowingly. "Anyway, now there's no need for you to go on pretending nothing happened."

"I'm not pretending anything. I don't know what you're talking about," Camile insisted.

"Now, that's interesting." Narrowing his eyes, Vincent cupped his chin. "In that case, this should prove to be an illuminating read for you."

*   *   *

Still drenched from the early evening rain, the tree leaves sparkled like gems in the soft glow of the moonlight and the lamps lining the compound. Camile had been staring at the blue-green tinted foliage much longer than she normally did. This wasn't due to fascination, but because she was afraid to open her own journal. After indulging her eyes a few moments longer, she somehow mustered up the strength to do so.

Skimming the entries, she focused on finding the ones in which Sir Drayden was mentioned. At first, the words seemed foreign, as though someone else had written them. However, with each passage the words sparked a chain reaction of unfolding memories. Stark recollection swept Camile's mind with the force of a hurricane, shattering her tranquil obliviousness. Within minutes, the events seemed as fresh as though they were all happening at that very moment. Every dream and flashback she had experienced about Sir Drayden prior to her visit to the EDC were now excavated. Camile found herself wondering what had caused her to repress them to begin with. None of the possibilities seemed good.

Unsure of what she was dealing with, she held off on informing her parents about her uncovered repressed memories. However, she needed to find out exactly what was going on. Had her memory been altered and did her father have anything to do with it? If so, why? These were the main questions preventing Camile from immediately approaching her parents about the situation.

It didn't take much effort for Camile to keep herself busy due to her regular training and counseling sessions. She struggled to uphold her ignorant facade, especially during her sessions with Sir Drayden. His piercing eyes seemed to cut through to the core of her soul. She wondered if he knew about her renewed awareness of what he had done. The pressure was overwhelming, but she refused to crack. She was determined to remember every unpleasant detail in order to uncover substantial evidence to bring about his downfall, knowing the likelihood her father would join him in the tumble.

Conversely, Camile's individual sessions with Jeremy and Brandon provided her mind with the relief of distraction, albeit for a short while. In some odd way, these meetings gave her a sense of normalcy. She wanted to confide in them about her suspicions and concerns, but opted to err on the side of caution since she knew both men were loyal to the council.

Nevertheless, Camile found it difficult not to ponder her bizarre dilemma. She wondered if her mother was aware that her father had made some sort of unscrupulous arrangement with Sir Drayden. She also wondered who was behind the cover up, which encompassed the obvious tampering of her memories. The more Camile weighed the facts of these recent events, the more her heart became laminated with distrust. She hoped she would find additional clues in dreams or flashbacks, but she was ironically met with the peaceful sleep she'd been craving since the onset of her nightmares.

*   *   *

After much thought on the matter, Camile decided not to make a move on filing any official complaints against Sir Drayden, at least not until she had substantial evidence to support her suspicions. The last thing she wanted was to compound her problems by going to the council with a fallible case, lose and suffer the consequence of reprisal.

Vincent failed to conceal his disappointment when Camile informed him of her decision. She explained that it wasn't an easy choice for her to make. In fact, it left a sizeable fragment of frustration that she had to process and control.

"Come on, love. Stop making excuses and do what you can to stop him from hurting anyone else," Vincent urged.

"Like what?" Camile threw her hands to her sides, unintentionally startling the horse he'd been tending to. "He works for the council, Vincent. I mean, let's be real. I don't have any proof of whatever he did to Akalina. No one will believe me based on a few of my memories, no matter how disturbing they are. It'll be dismissed as my word against his and you know it."

"But you can *make* them understand he's causing you stress, thus hindering your training. At the very least he'll be reassigned while the matter's investigated." Vincent placed his hands on her shoulders, hunching over to look into her eyes. "You're the one who can send a message to Sir

Drayden once and for all, that no one is so tall as to overlook the face of justice."

Camile found it comical that a man taller than the silver-haired knight was talking about height. Behind her sparse amusement lurked curiosity.

Why is Vincent so eager to see Sir Drayden brought up on charges?

"Alright, spill it," she requested.

"I beg your pardon?" Vincent stood up straight, clasping his hands behind his back.

Camile squinted against the sun that had broken through the clouds. "You already know why I don't like him, but what'd he do to you that's got you so riled up?"

"I have my reasons." Vincent paused. "They're personal. Let's leave it at that, shall we?"

"Wait, you read my journal, now you want me to respect *your* privacy?" Camile folded her arms. "Sorry. I don't think so,"

"Fair enough." The corners of his mouth quivered. "I lost a family member because of him. Someone very dear to me."

His gaze grew distant as he fingered the blood red talisman clipped to his waistband. It was framed in gold and suspended from a matching chain, smartly coordinating with his dark outfit. "That person would still be alive today if it wasn't for his negligence," he said in almost a whisper.

"Who—?"

"Don't ask for details, love. You'll get none from me," Vincent abruptly interrupted, meeting her gaze.

Camile decided against pushing the matter. Vincent's expression had grown darker than she had ever seen. It was a darkness that resonated in his voice.

Chapter 35

The Accusation

Life had taught Camile, long ago, that the fabled white knight was just an exaggeration of a person, just as flawed as any other. Though heroic, he still had his imperfections, the proverbial chinks in his armor. In spite of all she knew, she still hoped the fantasy of such an ideal person would miraculously come into being to help break the chains of her dire situation, to burst through the door and rescue her from her frigid chamber of loneliness. This was a distraction she used to obscure the fact that she could feel a cool weight beginning to shroud her. It was the sensation of her emotions beginning to harden, encasing her in an armor of her own. All she needed to do now was find a way to bear the extra weight and battle through the uncertainty of her predicament.

The subsequent days seeped from the calendar as slowly as molasses, but were far from sweet. Camile was determined to spend nearly every waking moment digging through her texts, opening herself to anything she thought might stir up more of Akalina's memories. Camile needed to piece together the nonsensical puzzle that had been scattered around her. History and repetition seemed to go together as well as gasoline and fire, and Camile was determined to avoid the explosive results. She impressed herself with how well she hid her inner chaos beneath the cordial facade she had created.

One morning she was unexpectedly called to the magistrate's courtroom and considered the possibility that maybe her facade wasn't as convincing as she thought. Upon entering the magistrate's chambers Camile was shocked to see not only her parents, but also Vincent, Sir Drayden, Magistrate Sui and several members of the Deltine Council. Noticing the grim expressions on all their faces, her heart sank.

It was obvious to her that Vincent had made the unilateral decision to present her accusations to the council. She traversed the aisle, approaching the two oblong tables facing the judge and the council members. To one side was Vincent, to the other were Camile's parents, standing beside Sir Drayden. Camile found the arrangement disheartening as she wondered if her mother was siding with the knight. Her discouragement climbed when her mother seized her arm and whispered, "Camile, what the hell did you do?"

"Me?" Camile grimaced. Before she could fully address her mother's inquiry, the magistrate ordered her to sit beside Vincent.

Magistrate Sui announced that they were all gathered to participate in a preliminary hearing that would determine if Sir Drayden should be charged with a criminal offense. She then proceeded to read excerpts from Camile's journal, exposing some of the fear she had hoped to keep private. Avoiding eye contact with her parents and Sir Drayden, Camile could only imagine their facial expressions.

"Ms. Leon, is it true that you wrote these passages in your journal?" Magistrate Sui asked.

"Yes, I did, Your Honor, but—" Camile attempted to elaborate, but the magistrate was already on to the next question.

"And do you genuinely believe that Sir Drayden, your primary instructor, has mistreated Akalina?"

"Yes."

"Do you believe he is capable of mistreating you as well? Do you feel endangered in his presence?"

Camile was reluctant to continue her testimony due to fear of retribution. The noose-like tension surrounding the room was making it increasingly difficult to breathe. She now understood why crime victims sometimes dropped their cases in an attempt to dispel their problems.

"I don't know," she answered tremulously.

"I'm afraid that answer isn't acceptable, Ms. Leon. Yes or no, do you feel you're in danger around Sir Drayden?"

"Yes, but—" Camile felt a nagging sting in her eyes. Though she hadn't shed any tears, she felt angered and ashamed at the fact she was failing to uphold her calm facade. She couldn't understand it. She was just moments away of possibly being liberated from Sir Drayden's seemingly obsessive attention, and yet, she was feeling a twinge of guilt.

"Magistrate, it won't be long before we prove this claim is nothing more than a *baseless* defamatory accusation," Sir Drayden interrupted, a venomous intonation shrouding his steady voice. "Until then, I believe it's imperative that I continue supervising Ms. Leon's training. She has already proven she's not ready to hold her weight during missions, including basic surveillance assignments."

"With all due respect, Sir Drayden." Magistrate Sui cracked a condescending smile. "I know you're a valued member of our society and that you have done much to assist the council, but today you're a guest in my courtroom and it's up to me to determine the best course of action."

The magistrate's words brought a faint smirk to Vincent's face as a quick puff of air exited his nostrils. Several council members exchanged glances of uncertainty before resuming their somewhat stolid expressions.

"Now that we've cleared that up…Sir Drayden, given the serious nature of this complaint, I'm afraid we have no choice but to place you under suspension pending further investigation of this matter," Magistrate Sui said. Camile noticed the knight whispering into her mother's ear as the Magistrate continued. "As for your temporary replacement, I will appoint—"

"Magistrate, I apologize for the interruption." Camile's mother shot up from her seat, an urgent expression on her face. "But under the circumstances, I would like to request Captain Kwan Kepner to serve as Sir Drayden's replacement."

"Captain Kepner?" The magistrate furrowed her brow, searching through her computer. "That's odd." She frowned. "I thought he retired years ago."

A pregnant pause filled the room as the magistrate's eyes shifted from one side of the chamber to the other. Finally, she voiced her decision.

"Sir Drayden, please make the necessary arrangements to forward your notes to Captain Kepner." She exhaled, massaging her closed eyes.

"Yes, Magistrate." Sir Drayden acknowledged, his voice a mere shadow of its usual confident tone.

With widening eyes, Vincent rose from his seat. "Your Honor, I believe since I already have an established rapport with Ms. Leon, I would be the best candidate to replace Sir Drayden in the interim."

"You make an interesting point, Commissioner Thornton. However, my ruling still stands. The primary focus of Ms. Leon's education isn't fraternization or friendship and the council unanimously agrees that Captain Kepner's credentials are more than adequate for the task."

Nodding his comprehension, Vincent bit his lower lip.

Sir Drayden was escorted out by at least a dozen guards. Camile knew he could easily take them down within seconds, yet he didn't. She could feel his eyes burning into her and couldn't bear to look at him directly as he slunk out of the room. The only person who seemed happy was Vincent, who placed a hand on her shoulder.

"You've done the right thing by confessing the truth, love. He shouldn't get away with his offenses," he whispered.

Camile pulled away and looked him in the eye.

"I didn't have a choice, Vincent. You violated my privacy not once, but twice. This should've been my decision to make, not yours. This isn't about me at all, is it? You have some kind of personal vendetta against Sir Drayden and you're using me, aren't you? I might not like him, but I despise being used even more," Camile fumed. "You forced me into this. I should march over to the magistrate right now and recant my statement."

Despite the fiery confidence behind her words, Camile knew the intent wasn't there. She knew she had just been freed from the oppressing presence of Sir Drayden and couldn't bear to relinquish that liberty. Vincent apparently knew this since he seemed visibly unfazed by her threat.

"You're not feeling sorry for him, are you?" Vincent asked. "If so, you're even more naive than I gave you credit for. You're right about one thing, love, this isn't about you. It's about all the lives that will be jeopardized if you fail to get your shit together and learn what you must. You've been falling behind because of this whole situation and someone had to set the events in motion to get it sorted out. The fact my arrogant colleague just got his arse handed to him is merely an added bonus. If accusing me of using you is your way of expressing your gratitude, you're welcome." Vincent punctuated his remark with an expression of disbelief and a soft shake of his head.

*　　　*　　　*

Captain Kepner was a hefty dark-skinned man with a bald head and a well-groomed goatee. Despite his burly appearance, he had a gentle, friendly demeanor. Camile likened him to an oversized teddy bear. However, he was strict and strong-willed when it came to studies, but he balanced his discipline with patience. Kwan, as he preferred Camile to address him, tested her on everything from meditation, combat, self-control and how she incorporated her acquired skills into her everyday life. He ascertained the latter by watching her interact in situations when she wasn't aware of his presence. At first, she found it intrusive, but over a short period of time, Camile began to see him as the big brother she never had.

"So, what was the deal with Sir Drayden? He get on your nerves or something?" Kwan stroked his strong jaw as they admired the view from Caldaq's Twin Peak Bridge, which threaded between Daebrayk and

Dusque. His was a hearty voice and his smile emphasized the slight narrowness of his eyes.

"It's complicated." Camile rubbed her fingers on the gritty stone ledge.

"Hey." The captain's deep eyes appeared chocolaty in the sunlight. "I know we're not really supposed to talk about it, but I've been curious for awhile and just have to ask. What'd he do to warrant a suspension and an investigation?"

Camile hesitated before briefly explaining her suspicions about the knight.

"Oh, man. That's pretty messed up," Kwan remarked gruffly, briefly shifting his gaze to the horizon. "Sir Drayden may be a lot of things, but he doesn't strike me as the type to do crazy stuff like that. You sure it all really happened?"

"That's the thing, the memories are all jumbled up, but they can only add up to one thing." Camile cringed. "Turns my stomach to even think about it."

"I'm not choosing sides or anything, but maybe there's more to the equation." The captain scratched his head. "You'll never know exactly what happened until you see all the memories. Do you think you already have?"

"Probably not, or else I wouldn't be so confused, or would I?"

"Girl, I don't envy you one bit. So young and so much to deal with." Kwan shook his head. "I'm sure you'll get everything straightened out in time. Until then, use it as an opportunity to use the skills you learned to make it through this. Just don't expect me to go easy on you. You still have a lot to learn in a short amount of time. Okay, break's over. Let's get back to work," he said, patting her on the back.

Chapter 36

The Keepsake

On her way to Caldaq's main entrance, Camile saw Joval struggling to get Excelsior into his den. Though exhausted due to Kwan's grueling mental and physical tests, Camile offered assistance.

"Is this part of your punishment for misusing the veil?" she asked, slowly beckoning the white tiger to follow her into the dwelling, recessed into the side of the main entrance. In the back of her mind, she was impressed with how well the structure was hidden, like a secret weapon. Her amazement grew once she saw the interior of Excelsior's den for the first time.

The first thing she noticed was a basin inset into the ground. It was the size of a small swimming pool, just large enough for the tiger to settle in for a comfortable bath, something Joval explained he had been trying to accomplish. Other accommodations included oversized animal bedding, a simple water fountain for Excelsior to drink from, and a few toys to keep him entertained. Together, he and Camile managed to achieve the impossible. During this time, Joval answered her question. He, indeed, had been given the responsibility of grooming the tiger as a result of his reckless behavior.

"Could've been a lot worse." He grinned. "This is mild compared to what insubordinates used to receive."

"Considering the fact I was on death row as a kid, I believe you. Was that the punishment other insubordinates faced?"

"No. Nothing that serious." Joval laughed, before apologizing for his misplaced amusement. "Depending on the offense, a person could face prison time, or worse, banishment. At least a prisoner has a better chance of repaying their debt to society and returning to rejoin it. With banishment, there's no chance a person can come back. At least that's how most of Arvaina operates. Now, the death penalty is still in effect, but only if it has been proven without a doubt that an offender has killed without just cause."

"That's some no-tolerance policy," Camile remarked.

"Yeah, but it's kept people in line for as long as I can remember."

The two continued their discussion for awhile, touching on the subject of freedom versus order. Like many philosophers and intellectuals before them, Camile and Joval found themselves running the conversation in circles, unable to escape the fact that the answer often shifts based on the perspective of the beholder. Apparently, Excelsior grew tired of the endless discussion and he bolted out of the den.

"Aw, man! He's still wet! We can't let him get into the compound like that. The senior officers will have a fit." Joval scrambled to his feet to give chase. Camile followed after him. Upon exiting, they saw no sign of the tiger.

"Now, how does an eight-hundred-pound tiger just disappear like that?" Camile asked.

"How do you know how much he weighs?" Joval quirked his brow.

Camile frowned, equally confused. To her knowledge, she never heard about the tiger's weight, but was nonetheless certain her estimate was accurate.

"I don't know. The number just came into my head." She shrugged.

Racing through the compound, they dashed down several corridors before seeing the tiger's tail whip around a corner. Joval went down hard after skidding in a puddle. He motioned for Camile to continue.

She finally caught up to Excelsior on one of the middle floors after she followed him into an office. She tried her best to use the skills Vincent had taught her in luring animals, but something on one of the bookshelves stole her attention. There was something very familiar about the rich, deep woods of the furniture and the lavish drapes and carpet that accented the space. Despite the inviting atmosphere, there was a hovering shadow of prohibition that told her she didn't belong there. It was accompanied by an overwhelming sense of déjà vu. Nevertheless, she approached a skewed book on the shelf.

The book wasn't what caught her eye, it was something behind it, a slender wooden box with a gold latch. Upon opening the mahogany colored container she saw a small stack of photographs. The first one Camile saw showed a slightly younger Sir Drayden—his hair, parted to his right and neatly brushed, was more salt and pepper than gray. His arm was wrapped around the woman standing closely beside him. It was the same blue-eyed raven haired beauty Camile had seen in her parent's wedding archives. The couple both wore simple matching gold rings on their left ring-fingers.

This must be Hyacinth.

The couple appeared to be a chronologically mismatched pair. It was obvious that Sir Drayden was the winter in their May-December relationship since Hyacinth looked about half his age. Even so, they seemed happy and very much in love. Flipping the photo over, Camile noticed an inscription in a language far departed from English or Arvainan. Suddenly, the picture was snatched from her grasp along with the box.

"Do you always snoop through other people's belongings?" Sir Drayden returned the picture to its rightful place, sealing the container with an audible snap. He appeared visibly tired, but nonetheless alert and irritated.

"No. I—I was just…Well, the book was sticking out of the shelf—"

"And this jumped over it and into your hands, no doubt." The elder sneered, raising an eyebrow. "Don't worry. I don't jump to conclusions like *some* people. I won't have you charged with trespassing and attempted theft."

Camile sighed. She knew there was no point in arguing.

"What are you doing here? Not trying to plant evidence, are you?" Sir Drayden pried.

"No." Camile explained what had happened with Excelsior, but when she turned to face the tiger, there was only a puddle of water in his place.

"Well, he's no longer here. Now, if you don't mind—" The knight stopped as Captain Kepner entered the room.

"Camile, what are you doing here?" Captain Kepner's face was the picture of bafflement.

"She was just leaving." Sir Drayden frowned, settling in his chair. "Please, escort her out of here before she accuses me of anything else unsavory."

Once they exited, Captain Kepner gently took hold of Camile's arm, wasting no time in quizzing her.

"Do you really think it's a good idea to be hanging around a man you want investigated?" he asked.

"I didn't go there on purpose," Camile replied, explaining that Excelsior had led her there. She caught a chill, feeling that she had somehow repeated a series of events.

"You okay?" The captain asked, releasing her arm.

"Yeah, I'm fine. I don't know why I feel so guilty. I know he hurt Akalina, but..." Camile shook her head. "I guess it just feels weird to know he hates me too now."

"Well, I don't deal with him much, but from what I know of Sir Drayden I get the impression he doesn't waste his energy on hate. When you hate someone it does you more harm than the other person, so what's the point?"

"Sounds like what my mother used to tell me back when I was a teenager." Camile smiled.

"The ambassador is a wise woman," the captain acknowledged, looking over his shoulder. "We shouldn't linger here too long. Let's get out of here. I'm sure the knight will be back and forth, wrapping up his business."

At that moment, Camile noticed something strange. Halting her steps, she turned her attention to the entrance to Sir Drayden's office.

"Hold on a second. Where are the guards?" she asked.

"Sir Drayden hasn't been arrested, just ordered to cease contact with you until this matter is investigated. Besides, the guards are no match for him anyway," Kwan explained, guiding her down the corridor.

Chapter 37

Shaken to the Core

Gazing at her reflection in the oval wall mirror, the gray orbs staring back at her seemed unfamiliar. They were hers and yet they weren't. They conveyed a demeanor of menace and conceit. A plump, shady smile revealed what Camile had begun to suspect, this brief moment of late adolescent self-adoration wasn't happening in real time. She was wrapped up in another of Akalina's memories via a dream, in which she was meeting Jezebel in an isolated portion of a restaurant. The two were discussing the topic of deception on the part of her parents.

"Akalina, the ambassador isn't just a family friend like she claims to be," Jezebel said softly before pausing a moment. "I hate to be the one to tell you this, but I think you deserve to know the truth. She's your mother."

"My mother?" Akalina chortled, thinking it was a joke. However, upon seeing the solemn expression on Jezebel's face, she figured otherwise. Her faint amusement instantly transmuted to angry disbelief.

"*What?* Why would they lie to me all these years?" Akalina demanded, keeping her voice low so as not to draw unwanted attention from the other patrons.

Camile awoke to the touch of a hand nudging her shoulder. According to the guard, she had overslept and was in danger of running late for her prearranged meeting with her mother. Thanks to her latest dream, Camile found herself trying to suppress anger that was clearly targeted at her.

According to Kylie, Camile would be tested on her ability to maintain her center of control. Not knowing why she was doing it at that moment, Camile decided to reveal her latest dream to her mother as they waited outside the small meeting room.

"I know who spilled the beans about you to Akalina," she announced. "It was Jezebel."

"Deep down, I always suspected it, but hoped it wouldn't be true." Kylie pressed her lips together. "Believe it or not, Jezebel and I used to be very good friends, or so I thought. She turned out to be extremely manipulative, not to mention a remarkable liar."

"Why do you think she went out of the way to undermine you?"

"Because of you." Kylie expelled a breath. "Remember the incident in the lab?"

Camile nodded.

"The technician that got hurt was Jezebel's husband," her mother continued. "He never recovered from the accident. As you could probably imagine she was devastated and didn't take it well. Ever since then I've had a strong suspicion that she was involved in turning Akalina against me and your father. I also suspected that she was trying to set you up at every turn during your years in the Coexistent World. The incident with Barry was the last straw. That's why I decided to call Sir Drayden to investigate her at your high school."

"I always wondered what she had against me. I guess now I know."

As they entered the room, Camile saw a conference table and several chairs. All the paintings were covered with white sheets. Her mother instructed her to sit at one end of the table before she opened a door at the far end of the chamber. A young girl entered.

"Camile, I'd like you to meet Estrella." Kylie guided the girl to a seat opposite Camile. The name sounded familiar. Lumera had spoken of the young girl, but Camile also recognized the moniker from a basic foreign language course she had taken in high school. She was aware that, in the Coexistent World, the word, pronounced *es-tray-ah*, was the Spanish name for *star*. Rising to her feet, Camile made a motion to approach, but Kylie held up a hand, prompting her to stop in her tracks.

"Something wrong?" Camile asked.

"No. Just stay on your side of the table," Kylie instructed.

Camile did as she was told and regarded Estrella from afar. She appeared to be no older than twelve and seemed painfully shy. A silky curtain of jet black hair fell just past her shoulders, long bangs shielding her eyes.

"Nice to meet you, Estrella," Camile greeted, but the girl said nothing, concentrating her gaze at the table.

261

Camile surmised that the young girl was even more shy and socially awkward than she had ever been. Kylie leaned over, whispering into the girl's ear.

"Estrella, it's okay. Go ahead." Camile heard her say.

Slowly, and with apparent reluctance, Estrella raised her gaze to meet Camile's inquisitive stare. The girl's eyes were the fieriest shade of amber she had ever seen. Camile put on a friendly smile and attempted to say something reassuring, but realized something was wrong.

"What's happening? Why is she staring at me like that?" Camile shifted her weight in her seat.

Estrella's expression was stark, her eyes transfixed.

"You feel it, don't you, Camile? You feel what she's doing," Kylie replied.

"Yeah, make her stop."

"I can't. Only she or you can do that."

Nauseating dizziness seeped into Camile's senses, sapping her strength and giving way to a migraine that skewered her right eye and temple. She loudly demanded Estrella to stop whatever she was doing, but the request fell on deaf ears. Camile's head throbbed synchronously with her syncopating heartbeat as the pressure escalated. She became overwhelmed, first with panic and fear, then finally an uncontrollable burst of anger.

"I said stop, you little brat," she bellowed, standing so quickly, her chair fell back with a violent thud.

With a shriek, Estrella lost consciousness. Her body spilled onto the floor like overcooked spaghetti. Kylie urgently rushed to aid the motionless girl. Camile's seething anger gradually reduced to simmering relief. However, when she realized the girl still wasn't moving, guilt, worry and sorrow began to weave themselves into the tapestry of her emotions. Fearing she had somehow killed Estrella, Camile inquired about her condition.

"I think she'll be okay, but you have to leave the room now," her mother urgently requested as she tended to the unconscious girl.

Camile left the room feeling terribly about what had transpired. In addition, she was struck with the selfish thought of the possible punishment she could face for her outburst.

After several minutes, Camile's mother called her back. Upon reentry, she noticed Estrella was gone. Before she could ask any questions, her mother spoke.

"Camile, it seems that you are already capable of protecting your inner energy, but that's another ability you'll need to learn how to control."

"What, that girl was damaging my energy?"

"No. She was siphoning it from you."

"Is that why it bothered me when she stared at me like that?"

"Her staring only bothered you because it was a physical manifestation of what she was doing," Kylie explained. "Had she not been siphoning your energy, chances are you wouldn't have reacted so aggressively. Estrella isn't the only person that's capable of doing something like that. There are many others, some of whom live in the Coexistent World. Surely you've noticed the aggression some people show when they can't stand to have someone staring at them. However, most of the time it's not only staring that's taking place, their energy is being drained without their knowledge or permission. They often feel that something's happening to them and they become afraid, then eventually very angry. As a result, violent actions sometimes follow."

"What are these people and why do they drain other people's energy?"

Kylie described such people as devourers who hadn't physically evolved. Instead of feeding on a person's blood, they feed on their energy in order to compensate for what they lack.

"Some aren't even aware that they're doing it or that they even have the ability," she went on. "But others abuse it and cause all sorts of problems. We've seen many cases where a person's energy was so badly depleted, only the core was left. It usually takes a long time, but eventually they recover, if they choose to."

"Sounds a lot like depression." Camile pressed her fingers to her lips.

"That's one of the results of such abuse."

"Wait a minute. You said the devourers are physically evolved." Camile grimaced. "In what way? The devourer I saw in the woods looked like an ordinary woman."

"Unfortunately, you'll find that out in time. I'm afraid I can't find sufficient words to describe their evolved forms, but know this, when the time comes for them to feed, they look unlike any human," Camile's mother explained in an eerie whisper. "Don't worry. I'll make sure you receive text and photos on the subject, but I warn you, what you'll read and see will be graphic."

Camile swallowed hard, looking forward to a change in subject. She facilitated this by inquiring about the core. She had an inkling as to what it meant, but wanted to be sure.

"It's the foundation that continually generates a person's internal energy," her mother explained. "The core is a constant fixture in a person and it remains there until they die—even if the body itself appears to live on for awhile. Like everything else, different people have different names for the core—*soul* and *spirit* being the most popular ones."

"If there are certain people who are able to extract energy from others, aren't they capable of taking a person's core?"

"No." Kylie shook her head. "That's a common misconception. They can only draw off the energy the core provides. Despite its name, inner energy can branch outward just beyond the physical body and can even affect others if they're not strong enough to resist it. Contrary to popular belief, no mortal has the ability to steal the core of another. Every person only has enough physical strength to support one core for as long as their body lives, no matter how long or short a time that may be. Eventually, the body falters when it can no longer accommodate it. Though, there have been cases when more than one core has been housed in a single body. At times, it's an unintentional, involuntary phenomenon for the host, but in most of those cases, it usually accelerates the aging process, leading to shorter lives. Even more frightening, a dual or multi-core body runs a higher risk of suffering from intense confusion and insanity."

"Sounds a lot like possession to me," Camile remarked.

"That's how the Coexistent World recognizes it." Kylie nodded. "Many people are able to detect a person's mood just by being near them. That's often a result of coming into contact with a person's radiating inner energy. Although she's very young, Estrella is a master at all these things. You're actually the first person to defeat her."

"It looks like the Transcendents are trying to create a science to analyze the human soul."

"I used to think the same thing when I first got here." Tabitha said, entering the room as softly as a summer breeze. "I soon came to realize that they're trying to *understand* the human soul, but not necessarily with science." Her cheeks rose, crinkling her eyes. "You see, science is a practice based on physical properties, things that are visibly tangible or explainable. Many scientists have made countless attempts to disprove the theory of the soul since they have failed to find a way to see or explain its mysterious existence. They are simply not equipped to do so.

"This is not a down-putting of their intelligence, just an acknowledgement that they are not ready to figure it out. Personally, I think it was never meant for them to figure out. After all, wouldn't life be so incredibly dull if we had all the answers from the beginning? What would be the point of reading a book or seeing a movie if you already knew the ending? What would be the point in living if everything was laid out for us? People are always searching for the ultimate meaning of life. They expect the definition to be overly complex and convoluted when it's right there in front of them from the day they're born. Life just is. We live for the experience."

Chapter 38

The Choice

Camile sat on the sofa in her parents' living room, praying her father wouldn't enter. After all that had gone on, she wasn't sure she could face him. Having a hunch that her mother would broach the topic of why she had been avoiding him, Camile figured she'd divert the conversation before Kylie got the chance to start it. She did this by inquiring about why she had lost her powers.

"You didn't lose them," her mother answered from the kitchen among the business-like clanking of glassware. "After the reversal of your death an anchor was put in place. It's temporary, but it'll restrict your powers until you enter the advanced levels of your training." Kylie entered the living room with two glasses of water, handing one to Camile as she continued, sitting as she did. "What you demonstrated with Estrella today was only a brief burst of your full potential."

"I don't even know how I did it. I guess I just got mad, that's all." Camile drummed her fingers on her knee.

"No, that's not all," her mother replied. "Not only did you stop her from siphoning your energy, you channeled your negative power and hit her with a concentrated blast. At the same time, you reclaimed the energy she stole from you—as well as some of hers. That's what knocked her out."

"I did all that?" Camile asked, "How do you know? Did you see the transference?"

Kylie shook her head. "I was instructed about these things from Tabitha."

"Oh, right." Camile took a generous gulp of water. "Does that ever bother you? You know, to be so different from the Transcendents? Have you ever felt inferior to them?"

"Inferior?" Her mother laughed. "No, but there were times when I wished that I could do the things they could. That is until I realized that I could fulfill my life's purpose just as I am." Kylie stroked her daughter's head. "As for you, you've already proven your ability to use your power. Now it's time to learn to control it. In order to do that, you'll have to control your mind, your thoughts…"

"How can I control my thoughts when Akalina—"

"Is a *part* of you. Remember, your negative half is not its own entity. Fighting against it only gives it more power over you." Kylie said urgently, tenderly squeezing Camile's shoulder. "You have to make both sides of yourself work together to achieve whatever goal you have in mind. Camile, *everyone* struggles with the positive and negative aspects of their personality. Don't you see? The procedure only gave your negative side physical form. You were already divided before you went into the procedure. Everyone's emotionally divided to some degree or another."

Camile nodded her comprehension, taking a moment to contemplate whether or not she wanted to ask the questions that had been on her mind for months. Knowing she might receive unwelcome answers, she decided to go for it.

"I know this whole situation hasn't been easy for you either." Briefly lowering her gaze from Kylie's honey tinted orbs, she asked, "Do you ever regret not going through with the alternative to bringing me into this world?"

Kylie looked as though someone had punched her in the stomach.

"Who told you about that?" she whispered through quivering lips.

Camile's heart grew heavy. She knew that if the statement was mere speculation her mother would have automatically become defensive. The contrary confirmed Akalina's disturbing declaration about the fact her mother had considered an abortion.

"At this point, I don't think it matters," Camile answered gently. "I know you wouldn't consider such a thing lightly, but did you not want me, even before all this started?"

Shaking her head, Kylie hugged herself and said nothing at first as her eyes watered.

"It's not what you think. I was scared." Her voice cracked.

"Scared of me? Did someone tell you that you were carrying the devil's baby or something?" Camile inquired, trying her best not to sound harsh being that her mother was visibly upset.

"No. I was scared I was going to die." Kylie sniffed as the first tear raced down her caramel cheek. "I was told that there was a severe complication and if I didn't end the pregnancy, it would result in both our deaths. I went to several specialists in Deltine and other cities throughout the Transcendent World, but the diagnosis was the same. I thought it had something to do with your father being from a different dimension." Taking her daughter's hands, she continued, "Baby, you're right. It wasn't something I considered lightly since both of our lives were on the line."

Kylie explained that in her desperation, she had secretly sought an opinion outside of the Transcendent World, which was strictly forbidden at the time.

"It was a risky decision, but given the alternative, it was the lesser of the two evils." She bit her trembling lip. "As it turned out, everything was fine. It was a perfectly normal pregnancy—until you started blending in with my energy during the last trimester." Kylie chuckled through her tears, dabbing them with her fingers.

"I don't get it." Camile scrunched her face. "How could so many specialists in the Transcendent World be wrong? I thought the technology here was more advanced."

"It is." Kylie's voice spiked, but calmed after a deep breath. "Not a damn thing was ever wrong with the pregnancy or the technology here. Turns out the Rebels orchestrated a plan to make me think there was something wrong." Her eyes stared into the distance, her nose flaring. "They *wanted* me to abort the pregnancy since they feared you were the culmination of the prophecy that predicted their downfall. But I wasn't ready to give up so easily. I'm glad I didn't."

Kylie tearfully regarded her daughter, who returned the sentiment. The two embraced before the conversation steered to Camile's less emotional inquiries.

"Why didn't the council have this anchor thing put on me in the first place instead of voting to have me killed?"

"Because it wasn't a viable option until after you took your own life." Kylie adjusted her tan blouse collar. "The anchor was part of a package deal in your redemption."

"Feels like I'm under house arrest, only I can't see the ankle bracelet." Sinking in her seat, Camile swayed her feet. "What does the anchor look like? Where's it located?"

"I understand your curiosity, but for your own safety I can't give you that information." Kylie sipped from her glass, meeting her daughter's eyes over the rim. "Do you plan on avoiding your father for the rest of your life?"

The dreaded question had finally arisen. Camile took a deep breath before responding.

"Shouldn't be too hard since I lived most of my life without him to begin with." Camile walked to the window overlooking the Lake of Renewal, remembering the section of compound beneath the water where her current saga all began. She felt her mother's warm presence drawing closer from behind.

"Look, baby, I want to get to the bottom of all this as much as you do, but this isn't the way to go about it. You're only making things worse for yourself," Kylie said, touching Camile's shoulder.

"Actually, Dad's the one who worsened the situation, letting Drayden knock me out before sending me to have my memory tampered with," Camile turned to meet her mother's eyes. "If that's not avoiding the truth, I don't know what is."

Their conversation was interrupted by an urgent video communiqué from Magistrate Sui. Kylie accepted the call upon returning to the living room and activating the large screen on the wall. Judging by the serious expression on the magistrate's face, Camile knew she wasn't calling with good news.

"I regret I must inform you that I am no longer in control of your case. It's been handed over to the Supreme Magistrate Judge of the Arvainan High Court. Someone from their camp will be in touch with you soon. Sir Drayden has already left for Kibara." Her blue and brown bi-colored eyes appeared glazed over.

"It turns out, Sir Drayden's the Chief Advisor of the Transcendent *Council*," the magistrate informed, going on to explain that the elder's promotion had been kept top secret from even her. She suspected the reason was due to the fact the knight had been tapped to covertly audit the operations of the Deltine Council and report any suspicious activity.

"The matter is beyond Deltine's jurisdiction," she continued. "So, the High Court will be launching an internal investigation to evaluate his conduct and overall work ethic."

"*Chief Advisor?*" Camile's mouth went agape. "Well, easy for him, he'll just advise them to drop the whole thing!"

Kylie and the Magistrate did their best to assure Camile that the council's investigation would be thorough, but it did little to settle her uneasiness.

Chapter 39

Unsuspecting Prey

Once again, Camile found herself back in the heart of a bustling Coexistent metropolis, this time traveling with the shaman and Jeremy, who kept close guard of his superior. Their assignment was to make contact with one of the Arvainan Council's newest recruits and bring him to Caldaq, where he would lend his extensive skills in science and medicine. According to the shaman, he would serve as the ideal candidate to help her perfect a serum she'd been working on for years, a serum she suspected would be needed sooner than she hoped. Jeremy tracked the target to a subway, not far from their point of entry to the Coexistent realm. Along the way they passed a disheveled man with wrinkled oversized clothes. He gave Camile a wink and an overly wide gap-toothed smile as she and her travel companions ducked into the subway.

A bloodcurdling scream shattered the monotonous drone of the afternoon rush hour. She was suddenly reminded of the day she blinded a half dozen people during a subway ride shortly after the discovery of her necklace. Her flashback was interrupted when she noticed the reason for the outburst. A middle-aged man had collapsed to the ground, clutching his chest. Even more startling was what was hovering over him—*a devourer*. Just as Camile's parents had cautioned, it didn't look anything like the one she had previously seen. Even though she had researched them, she still wasn't prepared for what her eyes were showing her.

The devourer was missing the lower portion of its body from the chest down. Its clammy gray skin ended in a jagged hem at its midsection. Camile nearly gagged when she saw the gory sight of its lower lungs and spinal cord, trailing out from the torso like a semi-rigid snake, dripping with a foul-smelling solution. The creature's arms pinned the man to the floor as it fed on him. However, it didn't do this by the use of fangs, as many tales often depict. Instead, it used a long, sharp, proboscis-like tongue to suck the victim's blood directly from his heart.

"Someone call 911! My husband's having a heart attack," a woman cried as she knelt beside him.

None of the Coexistent commuters were able to see the creature, greedily extracting the victim's vital fluids. Dazed and in pain, the man continued clutching his chest. Still, it didn't disrupt the devourer's feeding. His hands passed through the tongue of his attacker like it wasn't even there. Camile turned to address the shaman, but saw that she had already leapt into action. Tabitha approached the devourer with a vial of what looked like finely grained salt. After pouring the substance in her hand, she blew it directly onto the creature.

A shrill roar ripped from the devourer's throat as it was slowly vaporized. The deafening scream filled the air, but only Camile, Jeremy and the shaman seemed to hear it. Camile watched in disgust as the skin dissolved off the creature, exposing the rest of its moldy internal organs. When it was finally over, all that remained of the devourer was the foul stench of burnt, decayed flesh.

"Phew! Smells like something died down here," one pedestrian remarked to her friend as they walked along the platform.

"Whoever smelt it, dealt it." The other woman quipped.

The exchange caught Camile's attention as she watched the pair walk into the distance. Based on her analysis, no one else in the station was experiencing the sickening odor bombarding her senses, except for the young woman who had just passed by. In the aftermath of the excitement, one of the only sounds echoing through the station was the devastated wailing of the victim's wife. Camile didn't need to look in order to know the man hadn't survived the attack.

"The mission's over. We must return to Caldaq immediately." The shaman frowned, wiping her hand on her sleeve.

Camile inquired about the recruit.

"That was him," Jeremy answered, visibly sharing in his boss' disappointment.

A sudden, slow rush of spectators gathered around to view the dead body. None of the commuters made physical contact with Camile, but seemed to generate a counter magnetic force, separating her from Tabitha and Jeremy, pushing her out into the street.

270

For the second time that afternoon Camile found herself watching the old man pacing a short section of the sidewalk. This time, she was close enough to see the weathered details of his cinnamon-colored skin. Long gray dreadlocks framed his sallow face, emphasizing his dark, cataract clouded eyes. His sinewy body was clothed in torn, dirty jeans, a gray hooded sweatshirt, and a long overcoat, several sizes too big.

"Oh, yeah! Me ready for ya, mon! Me ready!" He staggered awkwardly, raising a clenched fist to the sky. "I old, but me got plenty fight lef'."

A few young teenagers mocked the awkward man as they walked by.

"You wan' mess wit' me, bois?" he yelled.

Startled, the teens scurried away.

Man, you should sit down before you fall down, Camile thought.

Suddenly, the man turned to her with a broad smile.

"Hey, baby! How ya doin'?" he greeted.

Camile wondered how he could see her, but then remembered what she'd learned so far, that people in altered states of mind are sometimes able to see beyond the veil. The trick was sorting them out from the crazies. Looking away from the peculiar old man, she continued to wait for her companions, who had yet to emerge.

"It's too early!" a woman screamed. "I can't have this baby now! I'm barely seven months,"

Camile's mouth fell agape upon seeing a pregnant woman slide to the ground, breathing heavily while gripping her belly. A few strangers came to her aid and tried to calm her.

This can't be happening, Camile thought as she regarded the scene in full.

It became very clear that premature childbirth was the least of the expectant mother's problems. There was a devourer gripping the pregnant woman's belly as it pierced the surface with its slithering tongue. Though the woman's stomach indicated no sign of the penetration, her eyes and mouth widened in a silent scream. She managed a faint whimper, using her feeble voice to plead for help.

"We're gonna help you, mommy. Just try to relax," one man said before urgently instructing his friend to use his cell phone to call for an ambulance.

Camile felt a looming shadow approaching her from behind. Looking over her shoulder her eyes met a sight of certain doom. Dozens of devourers were tearing through the otherwise calm misty sky, racing toward the oblivious crowd. Camile knew the spectators only had a few minutes at most to clear the area. Knowing the crowd couldn't see her, she attempted to scare them into fleeing. She facilitated her attempt by randomly shoving people. Unfortunately, it had the opposite effect and scattered arguments broke out as people accused each other of hitting. Remembering the pregnant woman, Camile was determined to save her. She brushed past a few people before shouting at the devourer in an attempt to shift its attention.

When the creature ignored her, Camile held out her necklace, prompting the creature to stop feasting. Her plan had worked as a brief beam of light emanated from the medallion. However, she failed to contemplate what she would do next. She backpedaled, trying to avoid becoming the devourer's next meal when it suddenly exploded in a cloud of dust. Camile's nostrils were instantly filled with the familiar stench of burnt flesh and scorched vinegar.

Her relief was put on hold when she realized the mother-to-be had fainted from the ordeal. Medical technicians and several police officers arrived at the scene and struggled to get the situation under control. Camile was concerned about the woman and her baby, but had larger issues to contend with. Raising her gaze to the darkening sky, the situation seemed impossible. Tabitha and Jeremy were nowhere in sight and Camile knew her training wasn't advanced enough to deal with such a large opposition. The flock of devourers, now a little over a block away, was rapidly closing in. Only hints of light seeped through the cracks of their tightening formation. Seemingly oblivious to what was coming up behind him, the untidy man laughed wildly, rummaging through a trash can.

Yanking an archaic looking cane from the receptacle, he thrust it into the air. The wind picked up considerably as drizzle fell from the sky. Whipping around to face the devourers, he clasped the cane with both hands, bringing it down hard to the ground. At the moment of impact, a bright streak of lightning struck the pavement just a few feet in front of him. The crowd reacted to the sudden electrical occurrence with gasps and exclamations as a gale-force gust simultaneously rushed throughout the street. The roaring wind was momentarily swallowed by the loud crackle of ground shaking thunder. As the wind subsided, Camile could hear the residual screams of the ill-fated devourers.

Once her eyes adjusted, she noticed the thick fog in the place where the creatures had been. She barely caught a glimpse of the old man again as he bundled himself up. Placing the hood of his sweatshirt over his head, he wobbled into the thinning fog, winking at her as the mist engulfed him. It rapidly vanished, apparently taking him with it.

During the return trip to Caldaq, the shaman put Camile's concerns about the pregnant woman and her child to rest.

"They'll be fine," Tabitha reassured. "But, the baby will have a heart murmur that will most likely be permanent. It's not at all uncommon. Survivors of devourer attacks sometimes suffer from ailments that mirror the symptoms of anemia, lupus, cancer, heart conditions, asthma... The list goes on and on." She sighed. "It's tricky to differentiate the actual disease from the adverse reactions of a devourer attack, but it's not impossible if you know what you're looking for."

The shaman changed the subject to the matter of her supervisor's investigation.

"Is there a particular reason why you didn't speak to me about your concerns regarding Sir Drayden?"

"I tried, but as I recall, you were upset with me at the time." Camile cringed inwardly, remembering her foolish behavior in the solarium. "Not long after that, I ended up in the EDC. Then, when Vincent returned my journal, I realized that he was the only one being up front with me. That is until he went behind my back and reported everything against my wishes."

"Vincent was out of bounds to do what he did. I already warned him that he has no clue what he's meddling in." Tabitha frowned.

"Do you?" Camile arched her brow.

"What I know is that Sir Drayden would never prey on an innocent child." The shaman's voice was strong, yet her confident expression seemed to waver.

"I'm not so sure about that. I get the feeling that no one, including Sir Drayden, ever thought Akalina was innocent, child or not," Camile replied. "If that's the case, I think he saw her as fair game."

Upon their arrival, Camile, the shaman and Jeremy were called to an urgent meeting to discuss their unsuccessful attempt to secure their recruit. Gathered in one of the larger meeting halls were Camile's parents, Vincent, Magistrate Sui, Commander Wilder, as well as several council members. Arvainan military personnel and Sir Drayden were present via streaming video. Camile wasn't in love with the idea of him being included in the meeting, but then figured if the High Council had approved his presence, there must've been a valid reason. Besides, he was hundreds of miles away from her and wasn't in violation of the magistrate's orders.

"It's becoming increasingly evident that the rebels are stepping up their attacks in the Coexistent World," Zephyr began as Camile, Jeremy and the shaman took their seats. "As if that weren't bad enough, our latest suspicions have been justified. They've apparently enlisted the help of the devourers. I think it's safe to say we can consider our treaty with them officially terminated."

The statement was met with a few hushed sighs and concerned glances.

"This is all we need," one of the elder council members moaned, palming his forehead.

"It would have been foolish of us to think the devourers wouldn't jump at the first tempting offer they could sink their slithering tongues into," Kylie added.

"Unfortunately, it also seems Duncan isn't the helpless captive he's appeared to be all this time," Magistrate Sui pursed her lips. "Duncan has always expressed his disapproval of his mother's betrayal and was adamant in his stance to have her brought to justice. It seems his efforts were part of an elaborate act. In fact, based on new evidence, we have reason to believe he's assumed command of the rebels, taking over for his mother. His apparent kidnapping was just a ruse to throw us off. Sadly, it has worked very well. Duncan has proven to be a formidable challenge. He is every bit as ruthless and deceitful as his mother was, so we'll need to act carefully, yet swiftly in order to bring him to justice."

"The rebel he challenged was his own mother?" Camile narrowed her eyes. "Who was she?"

Zephyr nodded as he tapped a button, prompting Duncan's photo to appear on one of the blank screens. The facial features on the man's smooth, dark face looked strikingly familiar, especially the deep eyes.

"Can you think of no one with similar traits?" He asked.

"Jezebel?" she whispered, her voice saturated with astonishment. "What about Isaac? Was his kidnapping a fake too?"

"I'm afraid not. Unfortunately, his abduction was very real," her father replied glumly.

"In addition to breaking his vow to uphold the law, we believe Duncan assisted Isaac's kidnapping and staged his own in order to cover his tracks." Magistrate Sui tented her fingers. "Any suggestions of how we should go about locating this deceptive delinquent?"

"Maybe the best course of action is to smoke him out," Sir Drayden suggested. "If we apply enough pressure, our enemies will reveal themselves."

"Or dig themselves even further underground." Vincent chortled. "Sir Drayden, I see you haven't changed much. You always had more balls than brains."

"I see you still haven't gotten over the fact you were shortchanged in both departments, Commissioner Thornton." Sir Drayden smirked.

Ooh, that's gotta sting, Camile thought, trying her best not to laugh at the bitter exchange between the two men.

Camile watched as Vincent's smug expression faded. For a fleeting moment, he looked as though he wanted to throttle the silver-haired knight, but quickly calmed his demeanor. His pride clearly lacked the intricate fortification possessed by Sir Drayden, who seemed unfazed as the insults rolled off his back. It appeared to allow him to preserve his strength and wit so he could deliver a few zingers of his own.

Most of the attendees were divided between Sir Drayden's suggestion and Vincent's more passive approach. Surprisingly, after much debate, the knight appeared to have a change of heart and recanted his earlier proposal. By the conclusion of the meeting, it was decided that the council's options were frustratingly limited and there was little choice other than to wait for the opportune time to act.

Chapter 40

Injustice

Soon, the recruiting process was stepped up and Camile found herself traveling to more places in the span of few months than she thought she'd ever visit in a lifetime. However, she was always meant to observe, not actively participate in the missions and was always under the watchful eye of chaperones. She sometimes grew restless, feeling more than capable of pulling her weight, but maintained her patience. Nevertheless, she enjoyed traveling the various countries and cities in the Coexistent World.

Authorized Transcendents had the privilege of using the stable portals to travel to various areas between dimensions. This enabled them to travel to more places in a fraction of the time it would take by using traditional transportation. Though Camile spent no more than a few days in each location, it was an amazing experience for her. The Coexistent World was unfolding before her very eyes in ways that both impressed and frightened her.

At the end of the tour, Camile was to accompany her father and Jeremy to collect the final recruit of the trip. It was just after midnight when they crossed a quiet, dusty intersection in a small desert town. In case they were to be spotted, Camile wore a long, cotton gown and a matching head covering. Both men wore tunics and loose-fitting pants, not at all dissimilar to what some Arvainan males wore on occasion. The silence of the dark early morning was broken by a panicked wail. The source soon became clear when a woman in beige veils dashed out from behind a building, nearly bumping into Zephyr. Staring at him with frantic, imploring eyes, she begged for help.

"My brother." The woman sobbed, now clinging to Camile. "He's going to kill me! Please, help me!"

The woman explained that she was targeted for an honor killing since she refused to go through an arranged marriage in order to be with her true love.

"It is a love that led him to his death," she cried. "Now, my family wants me dead in order to restore their honor. As much as I would prefer to spend eternity with him in the afterlife, I know I must remain alive. I cannot allow this evil to prevail over something that should have been beautiful."

A man was screaming for someone in the distance. His voice was growing nearer. The woman's resolve gave way to emotional hysteria as she implored Camile's father to hide her.

"Hiding you will solve nothing," he replied.

"Dad, we can't just leave her here to die." Camile protested.

The voice of the doomed woman's pursuer was growing even closer. In contrast, Zephyr's distant gaze seemed misplaced among the urgency around them.

"Listen." He finally said to the woman, prying her away from Camile. "Your best chance of survival is to go there."

He pointed to an rusty pickup truck, nearly two-hundred meters away.

"You want her to drive? You don't even know if the keys are in there. We don't know if the thing even works," Camile exclaimed quietly.

"There's no time for debate," he said to Camile before turning to the young woman, shoving her gently, yet firmly. "You have to run there. *Now!*"

The woman's sobs intensified as she reluctantly ran towards the truck. Much to Camile's dismay, the woman's brother spotted her escape attempt and quickly pursued. Even more horrifying was the fact he had an angry mob with him, throwing stones at the woman while shouting sullying insults. She made it inside the truck, but it didn't budge. The crowd was rapidly closing in to seal the woman's fate. Yet, her fate was not carried out by their hands, but the volatile explosion that lit the vehicle ablaze with a bang.

Blinding flames erupted into the air as the crowd recoiled. After processing the unexpected event, they began to cheer and dance, taking victory in the woman's demise. Horrified and disgusted, Camile couldn't believe the scene playing out before her very eyes. She was devastated to know the woman lived her final moments in fear and loneliness. Filled with a combination of sadness and outrage, tears stung Camile's eyes as she turned to face her father.

"You sent that woman to her death." The words barely escaped her mouth at first before growing steadier. "She died alone because we neglected her!"

Her father said nothing, turning his gaze away from his daughter, toward the fire. His expression seemed more analytical than remorseful.

The morning sunlight broadened the dreadful reality of what had occurred just hours earlier. Though the vicious revelers had dispersed shortly before dawn, the metallic frame remained. It lay among smoky debris, a contorted reminder of what once was a vehicle. As she walked by, Camile was grateful she couldn't see the woman's incinerated remains. She was filled with resentment upon hearing the news that the recruit they had come for had been collected just prior to their arrival since his life was in grave danger. It made her feel like the mission accomplished nothing but sowing another bad memory into her mind as she considered the life that had been lost.

Is a non-recruit not worth saving? she wondered.

Jeremy was designated to escort her back to the compound while her father attended a meeting to address the last minute change in plans. Eager to settle in her own bed and tuck herself away from the brutality, at least for a brief while, Camile matched his zealous stride. They were just a few feet away from the small jeep they were to use to reach their designated rift. Suddenly, the air warped in front of them. They immediately halted their steps, but it was already too late.

Upon emerging on the other side of the spontaneous rift, Camile and Jeremy were confronted by the sound of rapid gunfire. They had both walked into the middle of a brutal battle between opposing military forces. Jeremy pushed Camile to the ground, landing on top of her next to a pair of soldiers behind a sandbank. Completely unaware of their company, the militia men continued exchanging blazing gunfire.

"Aren't we half-in? The bullets can't hurt me, can they?" Camile shouted to compete with the deafening volley.

"These can!" Jeremy swept his eyes across the area as though reading one of his maps, "We're a lot further than halfway in. The devastation here has severely damaged the veil. That's why we were able to travel through it. There's not much left of it to protect us. It's only temporary as long as the fighting doesn't get any worse."

"We need to go back!" Camile attempted to sit up, but Jeremy pushed her shoulders back to the ground.

"Unless you can outrun a bullet, I suggest you stay down," he ordered as he continued to hold her in place. "We're no good to the council if we're dead."

Lying beneath Jeremy, she nearly lost herself in his smoldering eyes. They seemed to convey a wisdom far beyond their youthful appearance. For a fleeting moment, they also seemed to reveal an underlying amorous desire that mirrored her own. Camile inwardly chided herself. Now was certainly not the time to wonder about the complexities of Jeremy's feelings toward her, but she couldn't help but realize how his eyes reflected an internal conflict. Maybe she was afraid of dying out there on the field, emotionally alone. Maybe she needed something to cling to during what could possibly be her final moments of physical existence. Jeremy gingerly rolled off of her, but remained close.

One of the nearest soldiers suffered a devastating gunshot to the neck. Bleeding profusely, he convulsed on the rocky ground. Camile witnessed the life rapidly draining from his body. Though the doomed soldier faced her direction, his eyes looked through her. The light in his eyes was dimming as he grimaced. Yet, in his final moments he reacted as though he could see her. Through his pain, he managed a shaky smile, narrowing his eyes in apparent recognition.

"Angel?" he murmured, stretching out his shaky hand in an attempt to touch her face. His arm dropped to the ground before he could do so.

Camile glanced at Jeremy before looking into the soldier's eyes anew. It was like peering through the windows of a house that should have been occupied, but wasn't. The full devastation of the situation set in. For the first time, she realized they were surrounded by dozens of corpses that had been torn apart by bullets and shrapnel. The sickening stench of blood and gunpowder filled the air so strongly, it left a salty, metallic taste in her mouth. Paralyzed with the fear that accompanied the overwhelming sight of gruesome death Camile wanted to scream, but no sound escaped her open mouth. Instead, her body quivered as she came close to hyperventilating.

Jeremy was eventually able to bring her back to her senses, reminding her to center her thoughts rather than to fall victim to her adrenaline. After what seemed like an eternity, the boisterous volley stopped. As Camile lay in a sticky pool of someone else's blood, she heard the wails of the dying soldiers and wounded survivors left behind. She clamped her eyes shut, flinching slightly upon feeling Jeremy signal her to rise. It took several moments of convincing before she felt confident it was safe to do so.

There was a bizarre calm in the midst of the aftermath of destruction. Through watery eyes she saw dozens of Intermediaries traveling among the shattered corpses, extracting the souls of the departed for transport. She watched the smoky spirits rise from the cadavers in various forms like butterflies emerging from their lifeless cocoons. It was like visual poetry that conveyed a message that no matter how battered or broken the body may become, the soul remains resilient. There was something strangely beautiful about it, but Camile felt guilty about finding beauty in such a somber landscape. Tears tickled her cheeks as she regarded the scene in awe, her mouth silently agape.

"You see it too, don't you?" Jeremy hugged her. Camile nodded quietly, taking solace in his strong arms, wishing their first embrace hadn't been the result of such an atrocity.

When he pulled away, she noticed the dead soldier's blood on her hands. Some of it had smeared onto Jeremy's white shirt and screamed in contrast. The sight of it caught her eyes and refused to let go. She seemed hypnotized and felt as though the sight would trigger a repressed memory, but it failed to arise. She figured whatever was hidden away in that part of her mind couldn't be good. Its association with blood made that abundantly obvious.

*   *   *

As much as Camile's body longed to rest in her bed when she finally returned to Caldaq, she found herself unable to sleep for the second evening in a row. Her mind was too preoccupied with conflicting emotions pertaining to the turbulent events that had taken place that morning and the evening prior. Oddly enough, she didn't feel burdened by her restless night as she watched the dusk being chased away by the morning sunrise, slowly caressing the mountainside. The serene display held a sense of promise. Yet, as she watched it, knowing that so many were no longer alive to witness such beautiful events, Camile couldn't disregard the sorrow resonating in her heart. As a tribute, she decided she would appreciate the moment for them. Little did she know, the radiant daybreak would soon be obscured by ironic clouds of revelation.

Entering Magistrate Sui's chambers, she saw her parents sitting across from the judge.

"What's he doing here?" she asked, referring to her father. She wasn't in the mood to face him just yet.

"I called both your parents here," the magistrate explained. "I received an update on your case from the Arvainan High Court. Apparently, the supreme magistrate has found no grounds on which to charge Sir Drayden with any crime due to lack of evidence. Therefore, he will resume his position in guiding your training."

"I don't believe this." Camile sighed, leaning her head back. Chortling in disbelief, she returned her attention to the magistrate. "This is exactly why I didn't wanna say anything in the first place," she paused as she recalled the onlookers present in some of Akalina's memories. Camile could think of three people, other than the guards, who witnessed Sir Drayden's harsh treatment of her darker half.

"What if there were witnesses?" she asked.

"There was never any mention about witnesses," Magistrate Sui leaned forward. "Give me their names and I'll summon them for inquisition."

Camile regarded her parents, two of the three witnesses to whom she was referring. However, something prevented her from revealing that fact. She wondered why she cared to protect the very people defending the man who assaulted their daughter. Shaking the thought, Camile revealed the name of the third witness—Jezebel.

"Unfortunately, Ms. Hawkins isn't eligible to testify due to extraneous circumstances." The magistrate frowned, expelling a breath. "I'm sorry, Camile. I've done all I can, but my hands are tied. I'm just as disappointed as you are."

"A little trip to the EDC should clear that up," Camile muttered.

The judge's frown deepened.

"Given the circumstances, I'll let that slide," she said. "We can file an appeal to—"

"No. I'm not gonna drag this out any further," Camile calmly interjected. The bitterness in her voice was crystal clear. "This world has proven to be just as corrupt and hypocritical as the Coexistent one. The only difference is that this world is wrapped in prettier packaging."

Wasting no time after the meeting, Camile searched for Vincent and found him sitting in a shaded corner of the atrium. With his left ankle propped on his knee, he sipped a steaming beverage while reading from his handheld. His lips curled downward as he sat up at attention, setting his mug on the table.

"I take it you got the news?" Camile placed her hands on her hips.

Tilting his head towards the screen, he widened his eyes. "Just."

"You do realize that this is your fault, don't you?"

"Don't get upset with me, love." Vincent narrowed his eyes. As he stood up, Camile craned her head upward to meet his elevated face.

"In case your memory eludes you, none of this would have happened if you minded your journal more carefully." He said. "If not for my persistence, Sir Drayden would have gotten the message that he can do whatever he damn well pleases."

"Evidently, that's *exactly* the case," Camile fumed. "All you managed to accomplish is to make things worse. Now, he'll—" She stopped upon seeing the man in question strutting towards them, his smile ever so defiant as he joined them.

"Are you done, Commissioner?" Sir Drayden's confidence seemed to overshadow Vincent.

"Yes, I believe I am." The commissioner's shoulders slumped as he left the knight alone with his student in awkward silence. Camile's throat mimicked the tension in the room as she locked eyes with him.

"I hope you're ready to resume our usual schedule." Sir Drayden clasped his hands together. "I'll be reviewing everything you've learned during my absence. I suggest you rest up during the next two days you have off. For now, you can bid Captain Kepner farewell. He's waiting at the main entrance."

"What? Kwan's leaving?" Though Camile hadn't known the captain very long, she was highly disappointed that he wouldn't permanently replace Sir Drayden.

"There's no need for him to remain since I've been rightfully vindicated." Sir Drayden tilted his head slightly upward. "Besides, the man has other business to attend to. Because of his babysitting stint, he's fallen behind on his work."

Sir Drayden escorted her to the main courtyard where the captain stood with his luggage at his feet. Camile rapidly approached him. After thanking him for his time, patience and support, she requested a hug, which surprised even her. Then she came to the understanding that in the short time she had been under the captain's instruction she had found some peace. Now, that she was on the verge of losing it, she wanted to hold onto it for as long as she could.

"I'm not sure that's such a good—" The captain's sentence was cut short as Camile threw her arms around his large, muscular frame. She understood that Kwan valued the importance of professionalism. She also realized that his caution had probably derived from the fact she had suspected his colleague of abuse. After an awkward moment, his strong arms encircled her, patting her back. She closed her eyes as he cradled her head against his chest with one of his massive hands.

"I'm gonna miss you," she whispered tremulously.

"Why? I'm only leaving physically." Kwan's voice boomed in his chest. "My heart, mind and thoughts will still be here. Besides, you have a lot of people here who care about you a heck of a lot."

Camile opened her eyes, meeting Sir Drayden's chilling gaze. His expression denoted his mild impatience. She knew he wouldn't approve of such an affectionate display, but she didn't care.

"You'll be just fine, lady." Captain Kepner ended the embrace, clapping her shoulder. "You're learning from all the best. As for all the confusion, I'm sure things'll work themselves out eventually. Just hang in there and find your faith. You've already proven you're a tough soldier."

Sir Drayden and the captain said nothing as they bowed slightly to one another. Without so much as a handshake, the captain left Sir Drayden to resume his role in Camile's education. As she watched him walk away, that all too familiar tightness in her throat returned. Succeeding in restraining her somber emotion from flooding from her eyes, she forced a smile as she waved goodbye.

Disgusted by what she saw as blatant injustice, Camile considered fleeing the compound, but where was she to go? She knew the council would eventually track her down, especially since her abilities were limited. In addition, she was still unclear of whether or not her mother was aware of the cover up. Camile was tempted to protest by making Sir Drayden's job as difficult as possible, but realized doing so would likely earn her a return trip to the EDC. Her memory was valuable to her and she didn't want it to be tampered with again, so she gave her full, though reluctant, cooperation.

Apparently, Camile wasn't the only one displeased at the result of the investigation. She had overheard a portion of a heated discussion between the magistrate and Vincent as they bypassed her in the corridor one afternoon. Magistrate Sui was upset that the commissioner had, in her words, *used the courtroom to wage revenge.*

"In the future, I would appreciate it if you presented *all* the facts and not use my courtroom as a battleground for your personal feuds," the magistrate said. "Because of that whole mess, I'm facing a possible inquisition. I spent my entire life getting where I am and my job is tough enough without the internal government breathing down my neck."

"I apologize, Magistrate. I just thought that—"

"No, commissioner. I don't think you did. If you thought about the possible repercussions beforehand, you would have known I would have been put in an awkward position."

Chapter 41

Sinister Pact

When sleep finally came, it fell over Camile like a lush down comforter in the dead of winter. She floated peacefully into unconsciousness, welcoming her overdue rest. At first, she journeyed through nonsensical dreams reminiscent of her naive childhood. However, it would prove to be a buffer for the emergence of one of Akalina's darkest memories yet.

Little Akalina tiptoed into the shaman's quarters, hoping to maintain her discrete presence. Her goal, listen to a conversation taking place between Hyacinth and Kylie.

"I understand your concerns, Ambassador, but you should know that the council has changed." Hyacinth swept her cascading black hair behind her shoulder. "When the signs begin to arise, they will be impossible to ignore. The medallion will confirm it. I felt her energy when I created it." She squinted as she shook her head. "I'm afraid it's inevitable."

"I don't want the signs to come," Kylie said through an exasperated breath. "You don't understand. My whole life, I've only come to know the meaning of family several years ago with the birth of my daughter. That's something I'm not prepared to lose. I've already come close to losing it once."

The shaman sighed, gently placing her hand on Kylie's shoulder. "Ambassador, I'm afraid neither of us has any say in the matter, but I assure you—"

The conversation came to a halt when Hyacinth spotted little Akalina, hiding behind a wall.

"Young lady, you need to remember that you are still a child!" Hyacinth scolded, sweeping away the glossy locks that had tumbled over her pale blue eyes as she craned her neck. Her voice was as soft and as lively as her appearance. However, her tone held the subtle strength that commanded attention, much like her husband, Sir Drayden. Her smooth porcelain skin seemed to glow against her lustrous mane.

"You have a ways to go before you inherit the privilege of joining such discussions." Hyacinth laughed in a manner young Akalina found patronizing.

Akalina stormed off, intentionally stomping loudly to disturb the quiet. As she turned a corner, she bumped into Jezebel in the main corridor.

"My, my! Who lit a fire under *your* butt?" Jezebel asked.

Akalina only looked in the direction of Hyacinth's quarters and exhaled her displeasure.

"Ah!" Jezebel sang through a chuckle. "Good to know I'm not the only one who can't stand that woman. She's always on my back about something. Know what I mean?"

Little Akalina pouted, "I wish she would just leave me alone."

Jezebel's small eyes lit up beneath a slightly raised brow. She glanced around then tugged Akalina's arm, guiding her to her quarters. Once they entered, she addressed the angry child anew.

"So, you want to be rid of the miserable woman, huh?" Jezebel smiled broadly, her bright white teeth sharply contrasting against her dark skin. "What if I said you could make that happen?"

"How?"

"Can you think of more than one way to do it?"

"You want to kill her?" Akalina responded. It was more a statement than a question.

Jezebel said nothing as she crossed the room and opened the top drawer of her vanity. She removed a tiny bottle that had been hidden in a side compartment. When she returned, she placed the bottle in Akalina's hand.

"No, Akalina. I don't want to kill her." Jezebel smirked. "I want *you* to kill her."

There was no doubt in Akalina's mind that the bottle she was holding contained poison. At first, the notion of her being the vehicle of someone's death intimidated her, but that fear was rapidly transmuted to a sense of impending power as Jezebel continued to speak.

"I know you're curious to see what it's like to witness death and to be directly responsible for it. It's a temptation few can ignore. I already know what it's like to take a life." Raking a hand through her short black hair, Jezebel licked her lips as though savoring the aftertaste of her victories. "I know the power and respect that comes with it. The need for revenge burns so vigorously in your heart, it alone could scald your enemies. That's why I think it's fitting that you be the one to do it—take Hyacinth's life. In the end, she'll not only be rid of, but will be taken down to a level where she'll realize her greatest opponent was the same child she repeatedly underestimated."

*   *   *

Young Akalina walked as casually as she could to Hyacinth's quarters. As usual, passersby stared cautiously at her. Some even dared to whisper amongst themselves and roll their eyes at her. She wanted to lash out, but she knew time was too critical to indulge herself. Jezebel had spent weeks coaching her on every aspect of the plan in order to ensure no snags would be made. When Akalina arrived at the entrance she prepared to be searched. She assumed a spread-eagle stance as a young female guard walked around her, thoroughly scanning her through digital contact lenses. She passed the test and was granted entry.

All she could think of was visiting the bathroom to clear her stomach. She wasn't nervous; however, she didn't enjoy the fact that the most effective way of carrying the poison was to swallow it. Knowing it would be suspicious to head straight for the bathroom, she assisted Hyacinth with a few mundane tasks before their therapy session. Soon, Akalina knew it was time to make her move.

As Hyacinth prepared a pot of water for the tea they typically drank before each session, Akalina took her bathroom break. After waiting a few moments she ran the sink water and paused a moment before sticking her fingers in her mouth to force regurgitation. There was one tiny pellet she needed to remove from her system. When, it didn't come up right away she feared the casing had already degraded, releasing the poison into her small body. She was relieved when the pale golden pellet fell into the sink on her second try. She caught it before it could slip into the drain.

After exiting the bathroom, she intercepted Hyacinth's path to the cupboard.

"I can make the tea this time," she offered.

Narrowing her eyes a moment, the raven-haired shaman relaxed her expression and nodded. "Yes. I guess you can." She sighed.

As Hyacinth took her place at the table, Akalina retrieved two cups, one of which had a chipped handle and the image of a crow flying alongside a dove. It was Hyacinth's favorite mug and the only one of its kind in the cupboard. Akalina had learned that assassins sometimes kept trophies of their victims and figured she'd take the mug once the job was done. She occasionally looked over her shoulder as she hastily broke the liquid-filled pellet, surreptitiously lacing the cup with poison. The toxin was odorless and said to be tasteless, though she wasn't willing to test that theory for herself.

As Jezebel had previously instructed, she pricked her finger and squeezed a few drops of blood into the cup after filling it with steaming water. Then she submerged the sachet, containing tea herbs, into each cup. Bringing the beverages to the table, Akalina was on edge. She watched intently as Hyacinth raised the tainted mug to her lips. A guard entered the room, shattering the silence as he announced Sir Drayden's arrival at the compound. Akalina nearly jumped out of her skin as she briefly turned to face the officer.

"Well, *he's* a bit early. I'll meet him in the courtyard for lunch after I—" Hyacinth grimaced as she sometimes did when communicating telepathically. Shaking her head, she said, "Never mind. Apparently, he prefers to meet me here." Her delicate lips turned slightly upward.

"Yes, ma'am," the guard acknowledged before exiting.

Hyacinth set down her tea and began pouring over her notes.

"Akalina, I'm afraid we'll have to continue our session some other time," she stated, casually securing the top half of her hair with jeweled hair sticks, never peeling her eyes away from her documents.

Young Akalina knew her time was running out. She needed to get Hyacinth to drink the poison before Sir Drayden arrived. She figured she would still be able to get the job done and leave before he got there.

"I guess that's okay," Akalina said in the saddest voice she could muster, her eyes fixed on the cup. "Can you try the tea before I leave though? I think I made it just how you like it. I hope I got it right. It would be nice to know I can do at least one thing right, even if it's just making tea." She sighed.

She tried her best to look natural as Hyacinth sipped the beverage.

"Well, it's not quite how I prefer it, but it's very close. I'm sure you'll learn to—" Hyacinth gasped almost inaudibly.

The cup slipped from her hands, shattering on the polished floor. Hyacinth soon followed, clutching her chest. As she fell, she concentrated her wide-eyed watery gaze on her young assassin, her mouth contorted. There was no convulsing or screaming as Akalina had expected and hoped for, only an exasperated exhalation of the shaman's final breath as she lay motionless. Young Akalina frowned, not because of remorse for what she had done, but because it happened so quickly she felt cheated out of the experience.

The guards quickly rushed into the room and were alarmed at the sight of their mistress lying dead on the floor. After inspecting her, the female guard grabbed Akalina's arm.

"What have you done?" The woman demanded as Sir Drayden entered the room.

Visibly perplexed, Sir Drayden surveyed the scene, picking up a large piece of the shattered mug to analyze it. He touched it to his tongue before staring at Akalina with a fury that seemed supernatural. The child said nothing while watching him, crouched next to his wife, trying in vain to revive her. Meanwhile, the guard repeated her question again and again.

"I was just helping her travel." Akalina giggled, shrugging her shoulders.

With eyes of blue flame Sir Drayden glared at Akalina, who stumbled backward as he rapidly approached. Infuriated, he waved his arm, sending her flying across the room until she met the wall hard with her back, knocking the wind out of her. The impact was so violent she swore she felt her brain shake. She remained pinned high against the wall as he continued his approach.

"I am going to rip that little smirk off your face, young lady!" Sir Drayden scowled.

Akalina felt her chest tighten, prompting her to gasp for air as she regarded him with wide eyes. She had read accounts of boa constrictor attacks and thought this must be what it felt like to be a victim of one. However, her constrictor was standing just a few feet away from her in the form of a very powerful and furious widower. She looked at the guards, hoping one of them would interfere, but they only exchanged apprehensive glances with each other. Realizing she was on her own and in serious trouble, her panic broke through the surface in the form of tremulous sobs.

"D—daddy!" She gasped in her attempt to call for help as she wriggled in a vain attempt to escape.

"Do you honestly think your father will save you after what you just did? I should make you pay for this right now. I'm sure he'll understand my desire for swift justice." He hissed, raising his other hand to exact some form of punishment.

Preparing herself, Akalina squeezed her eyes shut. After a moment, Sir Drayden appeared to change his mind and sent her falling to the floor with a loud thud. Akalina landed unnaturally on her arm. The intense pain led her to believe it might've been broken. Her ability to move it convinced her otherwise. Yet, her vision had gotten slightly blurry. Looking upward, she saw a fuzzy vision of something among the pile of books the shaman had set on a chair earlier. She was too far across the room to see it clearly and she dared not cross the knight to take a better look. Instead, she remained on the ground as her vision sharpened.

Turning to the guards, Sir Drayden ordered, "Get her out of my sight before I kill her! Then think of a good reason why you should keep your own lives."

The anxious officers helped a coughing Akalina to stand before escorting her out. Her eyes locked with Sir Drayden's for a few intense moments. He returned his attention to his dead wife, stroking her hair as he cradled her limp body in his arms.

*　　*　　*

Camile was beginning to realize that Akalina wasn't Sir Drayden's helpless victim. In fact, it was now abundantly clear that she had provoked his aggression. She now understood the reason behind her mandatory fasting routine. It was likely put into place to protect the shaman due to the devastating event that had just flooded Camile's recollection. Once she recovered from the initial shock, she discussed the matter with her parents.

"You had enough of Akalina's consequences to face," her father explained. "We didn't want to add to the burden by revealing her connection to Hyacinth's death. When you started remembering Akalina's bitter past with Sir Drayden, we were faced with a choice—either tell you that your other half murdered his wife, or let you believe Akalina was his victim until you could see the truth for yourself."

Camile found herself unable to ascertain the righteousness of her parents' decision. It was a murky situation in which the grayness obscured the defining contrasts of morality. She wondered how a young child could have killed such a powerful woman. Then she remembered how Jezebel stressed the importance of the inclusion of Akalina's blood in the poison. Camile deduced that the drops of blood significantly increased its toxicity.

She understood that Akalina had been duped into doing Jezebel's dirty work by being made to believe that she was the only one who could successfully execute Hyacinth. As a result, Akalina had become ensnared in the thorny vines of murder that sprouted from the deceptive seeds Jezebel had planted into her mind.

"If you knew all this, why didn't you spare Sir Drayden from the council's inquisition?" Camile cradled her cheek with her palm.

"Because it was his decision. He thought you would have a more difficult time accepting Akalina's role in murder than the possibility that she was abused."

Silence filled the room as Camile weighed her newly found knowledge.

"I'm sorry I doubted you, Dad." She bit her lip. "I guess I still have a lot to learn about you."

"Everyone's got some learning to do, including me. So does Commissioner Thornton, for that matter. Magistrate Sui is not pleased that he used her courtroom to add fuel to an already volatile situation. Can't say I was happy about it either since it cast me in suspicion as well."

"I don't understand why Vincent did what he did behind my back. Especially since he sees you as the son he never had."

The statement earned a bemused expression from her father, who placed a hand on her shoulder.

"Where'd you get that idea?" he asked.

"Straight from the horse's mouth," Camile explained.

Zephyr's befuddled expression melted into that of mild displeasure.

"With all due respect, I buried my father a long time ago. Vincent is a highly accomplished man, but he doesn't exactly fit the bill to fill his shoes."

Chapter 42

Unexpected Mercy

Camile got the feeling she would soon be allowed to actively participate in upcoming assignments since she was fitted for a utility belt to wear during expeditions. It included a torchlight, knife and a multi-purpose weapon called a *Styngrae*. Through the use of non-verbal commands, the *Styngrae* could transform into a variety of weapons including a circular boomerang-type device, a lasso or a whip, which had the capability of splitting into multiple strands with nodules resembling floating pearls. The only portion of the weapon that remained consistent throughout the transformations was the handle, about a third shorter than a relay baton, but with the same girth.

Since Camile's neurotransmitter had been deactivated long ago, she was given instruction on how to manually operate the weapon. She had been training for nearly two weeks with a practice model, but today was the first time she would get to operate the real thing. Holding the inactive device in her hand, Camile was amazed at how little it weighed. Her sparring match with Justine was swift and intense. Camile repeatedly and unsuccessfully attempted to strike her with the multi-strand weapon.

Each time, it appeared to break against something invisible in front of Justine's fist, which she threw out in front of herself. Justine then activated her lasso to trap Camile. Thrown off guard, Camile ducked out of the way just in time before attempting to take cover behind an arena column. She managed to take approximately two steps before a fiery ring of pain coiled around her upper body. Her arms pressed tightly against her sides as she fell onto the floor like a freshly lumbered tree. Rolling onto her back she looked up at her opponent, who was using the lasso to subdue her. Suddenly, it began to pulsate, delivering rhythmic electric shocks. Camile instantly learned how the *Styngrae* got its name. An agonized grunt filtered through her gritted teeth as she kicked at Justine's leg.

"That's enough, Justine," Commander Wilder said.

Justine deactivated the weapon, freeing Camile of her electrifying bondage. Stunned, she lay on the floor for a few moments to catch her breath, wondering if she had sustained any permanent damage.

"What the hell did she do that for?" Camile demanded as she sat up, accepting the commander's hand to help her rise to her feet.

"It's standard procedure," he explained. "To accept the responsibility of using such a weapon, the user must understand what it feels like. These weapons must be handled with respect and should only be used when absolutely necessary."

"Damn! It hurts all over." Camile shook her arms, attempting to relieve the sting, now slowly subsiding.

"If you'd like, I could kiss it and make it all better," Brandon whispered.

The unexpected statement made Camile forget about her soreness for a moment. Furthermore, the subtle warmth of the commander's breath against her ear was coaxing her temptation. His comment was meant for her ears only, but had also reached an unintended pair.

"Last I checked, that wasn't listed in your job description," Justine said pointedly.

"And last I remembered, you're still my subordinate. Which reminds me; I thought I specifically ordered you not to use your transmitter to activate the weapon features. It's considered an unfair advantage since Camile can't do that yet," Commander Wilder replied strictly, glaring at his sister as though daring her to challenge his authority again. "I believe you owe Camile an apology."

Justine reluctantly apologized before walking away.

Coincidentally, Camile saw the very man she wanted to speak to immediately following her weapons training session. She was on her way to her quarters when she intercepted her father in one of the main halls.

"This anchor thing stinks. Where is it and how do I get rid of it?" Camile demanded. "It's slowing me down."

"It's not time yet. It'll happen soon, but first, there's more for you to learn," her father answered.

"If getting fried to a crisp is gonna be a factor in my education, then by all means let me be ignorant."

"Let me guess, you figured out what happens when you get on the wrong side of the *Styngrae*. If you're anything like me, you'll learn evasive techniques real fast. Let's just say the initial sting I sustained greatly motivated me to become proficient in that area of my defense training." Her father chortled.

"It's not funny. Those shocks hurt like hell," Camile replied. Though serious, she cracked a slight smile as she considered her father's last comment.

"Hell's a lot worse, trust me," Sir Drayden said as he joined them with Kylie at his side. Turning to Zephyr, the elder stated, "Now that certain facts have been revealed, I believe it's time to show your daughter how my mercy spared her life."

*　　*　　*

"Why don't we just execute the darker half?" a cotton-haired woman asked. Her pursed lips emphasized the dry wrinkles surrounding them.

The red-orange sun poured into the council hall, flooding half of it with blazing natural light. In addition to twelve members of the Deltine council, Sir Drayden, Commissioner Thornton, Magistrate Sui and Jezebel Hawkins were also present in the chamber.

"Because we can't," Sir Drayden answered promptly. "Although the two halves are physically separated, they're still linked. If we kill one, the other will become incapacitated."

"I see," Jezebel replied softly, slightly sinking back in her seat. She put a finger to her lips and trained her squinting eyes out the window.

"Must I remind all of you that the prospect of execution is what led us to this predicament in the first place?" asked Zephyr.

"Actually, it was the Ambassador's request that got us into this. Had the council's original decision remained unchallenged, we would not be having this discussion and Hyacinth would still be alive." Vincent frowned.

"And my daughter would be dead." Kylie glared.

Zephyr took her hand and attempted to meet her eyes, but they were fixed ahead.

"Commissioner, you're sadly mistaken if you believe I somehow evaded suffering in this whole ordeal." She continued shakily, her jaw tense. "My husband and I are paying the price for my decision and so are my daughters. Do me a favor, when you have a child and willingly offer them up for execution, feel free to judge me all you want, but until then, why don't you shove it."

293

"All the same, I guess you could say that I am partially responsible for this given the fact the core segregation went awry," Sir Drayden replied. His facial expression appeared numb at first, but grew heavy as the sun ducked behind a thick cloud. "Be that as it may, it's a tad too late to speculate what could've been. Pointing fingers at each other will get us nowhere, so let's end it right now."

"If we can't eliminate her, we should at least imprison her for the things she's done. To do otherwise is letting her get away with murder!" one of the members exclaimed. "At least let Sir Drayden have a say in the matter since he's lost the most to Akalina."

The decision was unanimous and all eyes turned to Sir Drayden. As he rose from his seat, a pregnant pause filled the room until he finally broke the silence.

"Before I announce my decision I would like to start off with some equally important news. After weeks of careful consideration, I have finally completed the difficult task of selecting Hyacinth's successor. My selection may come as a surprise to some of you. This person isn't as experienced as Hyacinth was and is in the beginning of her career, despite her age. However, she has great potential and I am confident that after she trains under my close supervision, she will continue Hyacinth's work with the utmost care and respect. Without further delay, I hereby announce Tabitha Livingstone as the acting lead shaman of Caldaq. She'll be joining us in a few weeks once she has wrapped up her affairs in Bauldana."

A hush swept through the room as everyone awaited his decision on Akalina's fate.

"As far as Akalina's concerned," Sir Drayden continued, "I think she should be placed under residential arrest. She is not to leave the compound without direct approval from either myself or the Arvainan High Council, and is to be strictly guarded at all times. I've decided against traditional imprisonment out of concern for the psychological effects it might have on Camile, an innocent party who had no part in this tragic event," he proclaimed. "If the day ever comes for reintegration, I want the positive half to be as strong as possible. She will need every ounce of it in order to hold her own."

The room was speckled with shocked reactions, but no one challenged his decision until he requested that Akalina's mind be tapped for information regarding the assassination. Zephyr argued that the procedure would likely cause worse psychological trauma to both halves than incarceration. The council agreed.

When the video ended, Camile turned her attention to her parents, her mouth slightly agape with awe. She was grateful that Sir Drayden had left the room once the video had started. Her guilt was a heavy enough burden to bear without his presence.

"For the most part, the arrangements worked out okay," Kylie explained. "That is until Akalina found a way to escape. She clearly had help from the inside."

"It was Jezebel," Camile said, finally mentioning her flashbacks. "She's the one who put Akalina up to murdering Hyacinth in the first place."

"We gathered that." Kylie sighed. "Too bad we found out about her treachery when it was already too late."

"So, she's gonna be forced out of retirement to pay for her crimes?" Camile asked.

Her parents said nothing as they exchanged knowing glances.

*   *   *

At first, Camile wondered about Justine's absence, but decided it was a welcome change that she should enjoy, not analyze. She could tell Commander Wilder was struggling to slow himself down so she could acclimate to manually operating the weapon. Nevertheless, she still found herself pushing her body to the extreme in order to keep up with him. Still, that didn't deter her motivation to avoid receiving a second shock of the *Styngrae*.

Prior to the session, the commander explained how Justine had managed to avoid being struck by the weapon during their last sparring match. As it turned out, Transcendent humans, with training, could tap into their core energy and expand a portion of it beyond their physical bodies, using it as a shield. This was referred to as *Propulsion* or *Core Projection*. Such a technique was extremely difficult to master and required the utmost knowledge of one's self and limitations. Should a person attempt the technique without such knowledge, they would likely suffer emotional or psychological damage and in rare cases, even death.

Brandon voiced his confidence that Camile would someday be able to utilize the *Styngrae* to the fullest extent while reaching her maximum potential. However, he cautioned her to be patient and make the most of the skills she already had.

Before long, the session concluded and the weapons were stowed. Like a curtain, Brandon's professional demeanor parted, allowing his desire to shine through his glistening aquamarine gaze. His expression was one that took Camile back to that night in the *Forsaken Square*. Though her mind remembered how entrancing their moment had been before the subsequent confusion, her body longed for a reminder of its own. Yet, despite all this, her mind kept going back to Jeremy and the slow progress they were making in getting to know one another. It was something she wanted to preserve, not jeopardize.

Oh, boy. Time to go, she thought, expelling a deep breath.

She turned to make her exit before realizing she had left her water canteen on the bleachers. Making an about face to retrieve it, she was startled when she bumped into Brandon, who had it in his hand to return it to her. The two stood frozen for a long moment, loosely in each other's arms. The warmth between them grew and Camile could feel a slight tremble, not knowing if it was coming from her body or his. Their eyes locked and in that instant, it seemed their thoughts were linked as well. Neither looked away as the canteen fell to the floor, shattering the silence for a brief moment. Camile found herself reluctantly fighting the magnetic force narrowing the gap between their bodies. Apparently, Brandon could feel her feeble resistance.

"Please, Wildflower," he whispered, stroking her neck with the back of his hand before slowly tilting her face up towards his. "Don't torment me like this. I know we share mutual feelings. What's the harm in sealing it with a kiss?" Their lips were just inches apart and she could feel the sweet, welcoming warmth of his breath against her face. However, something prevented her from following through in achieving her desire. Perhaps it was the memory of the consequences that stemmed from their first kiss. Knowing she needed to do something, anything, to rescue them both from temptation, Camile resorted to a technique Brandon had shown her earlier. Strategically placing a leg behind his own, she sent him to the floor. Visibly stunned, he regarded her with a bemused, yet amazed expression.

"Constant vigilance. Remember?" She smiled, offering her hand to help him up. He accepted it, but as she tugged he didn't budge. In an instant she found her body tumbling on top of his.

"Apparently, you still have much to learn." A barely noticeable grin crossed his lips.

Again, there was that smoldering look in his eye that threatened to set her ablaze. For the second time, the space between their faces was dangerously narrowing. Camile didn't want history to repeat itself. She was clearly having as much of an effect on Brandon as he was on her and she didn't want either of them to end up in the EDC again.

"I think I better go now." She turned her face away, prompting Brandon to gently release her.

Complicating matters even further was the fact that she had genuine feelings for him as well as Jeremy, who she noticed at the entrance as she got to her feet. Based on his facial expression, she knew he had witnessed the near kiss. A jolt of adrenaline-fueled guilt coursed through her body as though she had just been caught doing something wrong.

Damn it! Why am I so hung up on Jeremy? He's clearly not interested in me. If he is, he has a hell of a way of showing it. Then there's Justine. What's keeping me from giving Brandon a chance?

As Camile approached the exit, she wondered if she was holding a grudge against the commander because of the incident in the *Forsaken Square*. Then she remembered his prior involvement with Akalina, a fact that further tainted him in her eyes. She left the two men, figuring they needed to discuss plans for their upcoming assignments, but was surprised when Jeremy followed her into the corridor.

"May I have a word?" he asked, his voice unusually strained.

"Sure. What's up?" Camile tried to sound as casual as possible.

Jeremy tugged at his collar while shifting his dark eyes from one end of the corridor to the other. They briefly sank to the floor as he said, "I don't know how else to say this, so I'll just say it straight out." Locking eyes with her, he continued, "I advise you not to get too close to Brandon."

"Why? Is something wrong?" Camile wrinkled her brow.

"It could create complications."

Yeah. It's called jealousy. Stinks, doesn't it? Camile smiled to herself, deciding to use Jeremy's possible envy to her advantage. She figured that just maybe it would make him open his eyes and view her as a woman—not just another one of his obligations.

"We have no issues spending time with each other. I don't see a problem."

"That may be the case, but that doesn't mean you should throw caution to the wind." The corners of Jeremy's mouth sank downward and his eyes seemed as though they were searching for something.

"I thought this was all settled." Camile leaned against the wall as a group of gym students shuffled by. "He finished his treatment at the EDC and thoroughly apologized for what he did. Besides, the fault in that incident was fifty-fifty."

"Exactly my point. Professionally, you and Brandon work well together, but personally, you both appear to be a volatile combination." Jeremy expelled a deep breath, pursing his lips as he appeared to consider his next words. "Look, I mean well. I'm only looking out for both of you."

"I appreciate that, but I can look out for myself, Thanks. Besides, shouldn't you be focusing your attention on Justine?" Camile quirked her brow.

Jeremy grimaced. "She's irrelevant to this discussion since she isn't one of my students." After a brief pause, he said, "If you insist on continuing to see Brandon on a personal level, I plan to be present during your gatherings."

"Are you serious?" Camile chuckled in disbelief. "What next, you'll assist us in exploring the *Leih'klav* if the relationship happens to progress that far?"

She inwardly chided herself for saying the words aloud.

Jeremy cleared his throat. "That was uncalled for. I'm concerned for your safety and Brandon's. A loss of either one of you at such a crucial stage would be devastating to the council."

"Are you sure there's not more to it than that? If there's another reason for your concerns just come out and say it," Camile said softly, her voice laced with hopeful anticipation.

"Excuse me?" Jeremy's facial expression indicated clear bafflement at her implication.

"Forget it." Camile sighed before gently saying, "Please, just stay out of my personal business and I promise I'll do everything in my power to maintain my emotional control."

With that, she retreated for some much needed meditation.

Chapter 43

Extracting the Truth

Sitting in one of the private tranquility rooms, Camile shut her eyes. The sound of the small fountain gently trickled into her ears, reminding her to make her thoughts as fluid and free as the water. Behind the stark darkness of her eyelids, she visualized the faint sparkles of a stream pouring from a spout. The broadening illumination revealed a large stone tub, recessed into the ground. Camile looked into the drum of water and saw the rippling reflection of her 9-year old self. Only it wasn't herself, but young Akalina. She turned, coming face-to-face with the white tiger.

"Go on. Get in, Excelsior. I don't have all day, you know," she impatiently commanded while picking up a large brush.

The tiger sniffed the water and grunted before bolting out of his den. Akalina immediately went after him.

"Get back here, you stinking coward," She bellowed, running out of breath as a result of the chase.

She followed the tiger up several winding ramps and snaking corridors and eventually traversed an entryway. She froze when she realized she had been led into Sir Drayden's quarters. There he was, petting the tiger's head before it settled on the floor by the crackling fireplace.

"I've been expecting you, Akalina," he announced. "I think it's time we had a little talk. Come. Join me for a snack."

"I can't. I—I have to give Excelsior his bath," she panted, backpedaling a few steps, patting her thigh to summon the tiger. "Excelsior, c'mon, boy."

"Don't worry. I have no intention of hurting you despite what you've done. I know it wasn't *entirely* your fault. I just want to clear the air by asking you a few questions," he coaxed, gesturing to a chair. "Sit. This shouldn't take very long."

Akalina regarded him apprehensively before reluctantly sitting at the table. The knight hummed as he plated small cakes and poured a steaming beverage that smelled of chocolate and vanilla. Wanting nothing he had to offer, Akalina immediately refused the dish and mug he slid before her. Yet, her mounting hunger betrayed her pride as her body demanded replenishment of the energy she had expended during her lengthy sprint. Unable to resist the temptation any longer, she all but dove in face-first, eating one confection after the other. Occasionally, she came up for air and a swig of her hot beverage.

"I see you haven't lost your sweet tooth." Sipping from his mug, Sir Drayden casually relaxed in his chair. "Go on. Have your fill."

Noticing his shadowy leer, Akalina paused her gluttonous feast. A sudden wave of extreme disorientation filled her with alarm.

She dropped the cake she'd been eating.

This is his revenge. He's poisoning me! How could I be so stupid?

Akalina made a desperate move to use her fingers in an attempt to expel what she had just ingested. Sir Drayden promptly countered the move by using his invisible grip to restrain her, pinning her arms to the armrests of her chair.

"Nah-uh-uh. I won't allow you to waste perfectly good food." He smirked. "I said not to worry. I don't plan to hurt you. I just need some information. Since you're such a good liar, I've decided a little synthetic persuasion is in order."

She flinched when the door slammed shut, reinforcing her confinement. He positioned his chair directly across from her, adjusting her seat so that she was facing him head on. In her futile attempt to free herself, Akalina repeated her need to bathe Excelsior.

"It can wait," Sir Drayden countered dismissively. "In the meantime, just relax and open your mind."

Her entire body was virtually fused to her chair, yet the room appeared to spin around her. Nearly paralyzed, the most she could do was clench the armrests with her small hands. She was determined not to wear her fear on her sleeve, but her plan quickly failed when she heard Sir Drayden's voice again, even though his lips weren't moving.

You need to tell me who gave you the idea to kill Hyacinth. His voice poured into her mind like hot tar, rippling slowly and repeatedly.

"How did you—?" was all Akalina could tremulously utter before she realized the knight was getting inside her head.

Akalina shuddered as she mentally began to back track everything she did from that very moment. It seemed like Sir Drayden, now holding her head in his large hands, had hit a rewind button in her brain, prompting her to freefall backwards through time. The pace was blaringly fast at first, but slowed as she fought back as hard as she could. She knew exactly what he was after and she tried her best to lock away those precious memories.

Her success in slowing the rate of her mental retrace came at a price. She now had an excruciating headache which felt like Sir Drayden was splitting her head open from the inside out. He'd occasionally throw her off guard by telepathically asking her frivolous questions before continuing to dig for the information he wanted. This ordeal made it nearly impossible for Akalina to think creatively enough to construct any new lies. In addition, her recent mischief and misdeeds had been uncorked and were spilling out for Sir Drayden to see. He was readily soaking it all in like a sponge.

"Ah, I see someone's been a very busy girl," he crooned, his eyes never blinking, all the while fixated on hers.

"No!" she cried. She hated feeling so powerless and defenseless. Whether her memories were good or bad they were hers and he was taking her secrets away. The headache intensified and tears escaped her eyes as she finally voiced her extreme discomfort. "Stop! You're hurting me!" she choked out in barely a whisper.

"It only hurts because you're fighting me. Don't. Just let go," he instructed calmly.

Fearing she'd lose her mind to Sir Drayden completely, Akalina attempted to cry out. All she could manage was a brief yelp before he silenced her.

"Shh," he hushed. "The more you relax, the sooner it'll all be over."

She could feel him continuing to peel away the layers of her memories, prying deeper inside her mind despite her spirited attempt to resist him. He was almost there. Her mind had finally traveled back to the day Hyacinth had chided her, the same day Jezebel instructed her to kill the female elder. Akalina's only defense was to black out Jezebel's image in her memory so it wouldn't be revealed to Sir Drayden. It was working, but she knew she couldn't keep it up forever. Her defenses were slowly seeping away like the tears from her eyes and mucus from her nose.

You need to tell me who gave you the idea to kill Hyacinth, his voice repeated anew as it began to change, transmuting to her own.

I...I need to...tell you who gave me the idea to kill Hyacinth, young Akalina thought as her mental barrier continued to crumble.

She realized Sir Drayden was right, the harder she fought, the more it hurt. Her desire for relief had finally betrayed the promise she made to herself that she'd keep Jezebel's involvement a secret.

"It was..." Her voice stalled. Her resilience was still hanging on, though by a fraying thread. The knight seemed determine to shake it loose even if it meant physically shaking her.

"Go on," he demanded, jerking her slightly. "Who was it?"

"It was..." Akalina pried her eyes away from the blue inferno before her and trained it on the figure that had suddenly emerged over his shoulder. "Daddy..." she cried feebly as she hoped her father would end her torment.

From the corner of her eye she noticed Sir Drayden's face contorting in puzzlement.

"Sir Drayden, what the hell are you doing?" Zephyr asked, his voice reflecting his livid facial expression.

With a jolt, Akalina gasped sharply as Sir Drayden suddenly released her. It was like coming up for air after being trapped under water for what seemed like an eternity. For a brief moment, her mind felt completely weightless as though gravity no longer existed. Then without thinking, she quickly seized her opportunity, breaking free and leaping out of her chair before the elder could reestablish the connection. She stumbled due to the disruption of her equilibrium.

"I *hate* you," she shouted at Sir Drayden through violent sobs before stumbling past her father and bolting out of the room. Wiping her face, she saw that the mucus trickling from her nose ran red.

*   *   *

Akalina stood beside her father, clutching his arm as though for dear life. Kylie stood behind her and placed a hand on her shoulder. The traumatized girl wondered why she had to be present during the heated discussion. Ordinarily, she would have been eager to listen in on the conversation of her elders, but she wanted nothing more than solitude and distance from Sir Drayden, especially after what had happened in the previous hour. Her mind temporarily escaped the moment as she heard the sound of the pouring rain in the courtyard, just outside. Random flashes of lightning provided the room with extra illumination at brief intervals, outlining the silhouettes of the officers, standing just beyond the closed translucent doors. It added to the trapped feeling that overwhelmed little Akalina. As the storm moved closer, the wind speed increased, the sound of it partially drowning out the rumbling thunder rolling in from the distance.

"Sir Drayden, I understand the gravity of the situation full and well, but there's a reason I objected to your request of mind-breaching!" Nostrils flaring, Zephyr pointed at the knight. "She's *my* daughter and it should be up to me to decide how to get the information we need."

"Well, clearly you haven't been doing a very good job," the knight replied pointedly. "She may have resorted to murder, but despite her claims, I know she didn't act alone. Someone convinced her to kill Hyacinth and I intend to find out who it is."

"I understand your position on this, Sir Drayden, but she's just a child!" Kylie's hazel orbs were ablaze with anger. "What you did was brutal. Torture is ineffective. There must be other ways to get your information."

"Ambassador, I know what I'm about to say will sound insensitive, but Akalina forfeited her childhood the moment she acted in cold blood, slipping that poison to Hyacinth. She was a willing participant and to this day she has yet to express remorse of any kind, other than the regret of getting caught. Zephyr, can you honestly say you would've acted differently had you been in my place?" Sir Drayden shot a quick side glance to Akalina, who cringed in response as he continued. "She's proven herself to be a very skillful liar. The only way to get the information I need is to extract it—unfortunately, by force if necessary. I don't like it any more than you do, but if there's another party involved in Hyacinth's death we need to capture the mastermind before they strike again. More lives will be lost if we fail to do so. As Defense Minister, you of all people should understand that we need to safeguard the lives of our council members as well as our residents and Coexistent neighbors."

At an apparent loss for words, Zephyr's gaze dropped to the floor as he expelled an almost defeated sounding breath. He turned to Akalina and kneeled before her, taking her face into his hands.

"Akalina, please…just tell us everything you know. You're hiding something. I can feel it. We all can," he implored, his voice strained. The drab look of his normally radiant eyes was indicative of the weight of his thoughts—thoughts, Akalina figured, that centered around saving his own skin.

"You're taking his side, aren't you? Thanks for defending me, Dad," Akalina spat, pushing his hands away. "I already told you everything. If you don't believe me, that's your problem! You should be ashamed. The ambassador seems to be more on my side than you are and she's not even family!"

As she stormed out of the chamber she heard the ambassador call for her return. Ignoring her, Akalina returned to her room as quickly as she could.

Only a few moments had elapsed before the distraught girl heard someone enter behind her. Much to Akalina's relief, it wasn't the knight, ambassador or her father, but Jezebel.

"Akalina, is there a reason you didn't come to class this after—? Hey, what's wrong?" she asked, her dark face etched with concern.

"Everything's wrong! Just go away!"

"Maybe I can help."

"You're joking, right? Nobody can help me, not even my own father." Akalina chuckled bitterly before resuming her somber demeanor. "What will it take for him to stand up for me? I can't believe he didn't do anything after Drayden—"

Akalina felt herself becoming frightened at the very memory of the experience. Even at that very moment she felt as though she wasn't alone in her mind. The sensation shook her to the core and she hated the lack of control that resulted from it.

"I don't want to talk about it!" Her small voice cracked as she attempted to wave Jezebel away.

"You're in no condition to be by yourself right now. Look at you, you're falling apart! What happened to you?"

Akalina reluctantly explained the situation through angry tears. She hated crying. Even worse, she hated doing it in front of others. In her opinion, it was a sign of weakness and imperfection—two things she refused to associate with herself.

"Oh, my goodness!" Jezebel hugged Akalina, before looking into her eyes, still holding her shoulders. "I know he's a vicious man, but I had no idea he was capable of doing something like that to you. I'm so sorry I put you in this position. At the same time, I must say I'm very proud of you. You were strong enough not to rat me out. Loyalty like that is hard to come by these days."

"I hate him. I want him to pay for what he did to me. Let's kill him too. I'll do it, myself," Akalina suggested.

"Well, *you're* ambitious. You'll find it to be a valuable trait sooner than you think." Jezebel smirked. "Unfortunately, there's nothing we can do. He's much too powerful. Anyone who tries to kill Sir Drayden now would be a fool—and a dead one at that. I'm not sure what it is, but there's more to that man than meets the eye. I've seen countless squads fall by his hand. Maybe someday he'll get what's coming to him, but until then, I wouldn't suggest going against him."

"That's not good enough! I don't want to spend another day around him. I don't want him to get another chance to mess with my head. My own father refuses to protect me. He's all talk, no action. Maybe that ambassador woman can help. She seems to have the hots for him and I think she's using me to get closer to him. Maybe if I start being nicer to her, she can convince him to do something about Sir Drayden."

Jezebel briefly hung her head, shaking it before returning her gaze to Akalina.

"I'm sorry to have to tell you this, Akalina, but I think you're giving the ambassador too much credit. She's been lying to you along with everyone else. For awhile, they even had me in on it, but I realized how wrong it was. I can't get into details now, but believe me, they're playing you for a fool. Akalina, you're a very special girl and people are jealous of you. That's why so many of them shun and avoid you. They feel insignificant compared to you and know they can never measure up to the great woman you're destined to become. Look, I can get you out of here, but it won't be overnight. It's going to be very hard, so I have to be careful about this or else it won't work. I could lose everything—even my life. I wish I could tell you everything now, but it'll only jeopardize your chance at freedom. All I ask is for your trust and patience. This might take months if not years. In the meantime, I'll do all I can to protect you from Sir Drayden."

"*Years?* No! I might not last that long!"

"Shh," Jezebel hushed. "Yes, you will. You're strong and you know it. I'm here for you, okay? I'm your friend. Always remember that."

After a brief hug, Jezebel left the room only to return fifteen minutes later with an urgent expression on her face. It was enough to alarm young Akalina.

"Damn it!" Jezebel leaned against the door. Her dark eyes darted from side to side as she raked her fingers through her short spiky hair.

"What's the matter?" Akalina asked.

"He's coming! I heard the bastard telling your father he's coming here to take another crack at your brain. Quick, take these!" Jezebel whispered urgently as she handed Akalina two small pills.

"Now, you want me to kill myself?"

"Don't insult me. You know you're much too important. He's too strong for you. He'll crack your brain open like an egg and then we'll both be exposed. We can't afford that. There's no time to explain. Hurry! Take them now!"

Jezebel instructed little Akalina to open her mouth before bursting the pellets open, allowing the bitter-tasting serum to drip onto her tongue. Akalina gagged at the taste.

"I know it tastes rancid, but they'll work faster this way. At least I hope so."

Once Sir Drayden entered the room Akalina grasped Jezebel's hand and held it tightly as though by reflex.

"Jezebel. Strange seeing you here," Sir Drayden's eyes narrowed curiously as he approached his shivering target.

"She seemed upset, so I decided to stay with her," she explained before asking: "Is she in some kind of trouble?"

The knight ignored the question and dismissed Jezebel as he stopped just inches in front of Akalina, who dug her nails into her mentor's hand.

"She's terrified! What's going on here?" Jezebel inquired.

"That's none of your concern. I gave you a direct order and I expect you to follow it." Sir Drayden waved Jezebel away before addressing Akalina. "Young lady, this doesn't have to be difficult. Please...just give me the information I'm looking for and I'll be on my way."

Zephyr and Kylie rushed into the room and tried their best to calm her and talk the elder out of his decision, but to no avail. During the commotion, Jezebel slipped out of the room.

Be strong, she mouthed to her young protégé, who fell into a violent seizure, forcing Sir Drayden to immediately disengage from her mind. Amid the chaos Akalina could hear Kylie pleading with the knight to stop, voicing her concern that the girl would be killed in the process. Fading into the darkness, Akalina worried the ambassador's fears were about to come true.

The recent wave of recollection left Camile filled with a complex mélange of understanding and disdain. Though she understood Sir Drayden's motive to acquire the name of the mastermind behind Hyacinth's death, she found his method highly disconcerting. Akalina's intimidation of him was shrouded in fear and hatred. Though it faded with the dissipation of the reverie, the sensation lingered with Camile and would likely remain for some time to come.

Figuring it would do no good to reveal her latest recollection to her parents, Camile decided to keep it to herself. She didn't want to take the chance of them sending her back to the EDC for another treatment to alter her memory. Though Akalina's thawing memories were uncomfortable to relive, it was bringing Camile a better understanding of exactly what happened prior to her arrival in the Transcendent World.

Chapter 44

Rituals of Heartache
& Renewal

It was her second time in Chicago and this time, though it still wasn't a leisurely visit, she was able to see the famed landscape from the cafe window. Camile felt tempted to order one of the hot steamy mochas she had seen a few of the patrons enjoying. However, she knew that her fast was still in effect. She wouldn't be able to eat or drink anything until after she and the shaman parted ways later that afternoon. Though Tabitha and Jeremy were simply following up with one of their successes, the shaman was adamant that Camile tag along.

"I think there's a lot you can learn from Michelle's story," the shaman said earnestly.

Camile wasn't told a great deal about Michelle, only that she was a dedicated individual who didn't surrender to darkness or accept defeat. Jeremy and Tabitha had been counseling the woman for months.

A woman entered the shop, bypassing the busy ordering counter as she made her way toward their table. She appeared to be in her early to mid-thirties and was wearing a neatly pressed suit. Her green eyes and olive skin were complimentary, but culminated in plain looks at best. What she lacked in attractiveness, she made up for in height. Michelle greeted Tabitha with a warm hug, bending slightly at the knees to accommodate the shaman's height as best she could. Jeremy and Camile received kind handshakes.

For awhile, Michelle reviewed her emotional progress with Tabitha, stating that time hadn't necessarily made things easier, but enabled her to build enough strength to endure. Not fully aware of Michelle's background, Camile was puzzled, but knew she would soon gain clarity.

"Looks like someone's out of the loop," Michelle remarked, eyeing Camile before shifting her gaze to Tabitha. "You didn't tell your associate about my case."

Tabitha shook her head. "I was hoping she could hear it straight from you, if you don't mind, of course."

Michelle nodded her acquiescence, returning her attention to Camile.

"Do you have any children?" she asked.

"Not yet. Maybe someday," Camile responded, thinking: *If I ever get my life in order.*

"Well, if and when you do, don't take for granted how precious they are. That's the biggest mistake I ever made. It cost me everything," Michelle said, tears welling in her eyes. "It cost me my only son."

"What happened?" Camile asked cautiously.

"I didn't pay close enough attention to him. I thought I was doing a good job as a provider, but I didn't realize I was paying more attention to my career. He kept asking me if he could swim in the pool, but I decided to send just one more email since my work was backed up. It was nothing unusual since I always ended up taking my work home. I never dreamed my boy would have gone into the pool on his own." Michelle sighed, wiping the tears that escaped her eyes. "I can't believe how stupid I was."

She went on to explain that just months after losing her son, she was laid off from her job due to budgeting issues. She bitterly noted the irony of the whole thing.

"Since then," she continued, "I dedicated my life to helping others learn from my mistakes—to get parents to really pay attention to their children. I figured if I helped at least one other family, Byron's death wouldn't have been in vain. Before I knew it, I created a foundation in his name. This organization has allowed me to do for other children what I wish I had done for Byron—be there for them," Michelle rummaged through her purse and pulled out a pamphlet, handing it to Camile. "It's doing so well that we recently expanded our services to help abused and neglected children. Matter of fact, my colleague is supposed to meet me here with one of our kids to help out with a presentation."

As she skimmed the material, Camile's mind hung on the name Michelle mentioned moments earlier.

Byron?

The name sounded strikingly familiar. It wasn't until she saw the image on the back of the brochure that it finally sank in.

The boy in the photo, wearing a dragon adorned t-shirt, was the same little boy she had seen in the Phantom World via Tabitha's memory. Camile felt her jaw slacken, but she quickly adjusted her expression before Michelle could see her reaction. She very well couldn't tell the mourning woman that she had seen her son riding a dragon somewhere in the great beyond. Doing such a thing would only rip open the emotional wound of Michelle's grieving heart. Looking at Tabitha's reaction, Camile was reassured she had just made the right decision.

"Oh, look who's early!" Michelle rose from her seat. With her arms outstretched, she squatted to greet the boy running toward her. In his enthusiasm he bumped into a customer, whose coffee became a caffeinated grenade. Luckily, the floor and a few pant legs were its only casualties. The woman traveling with the child offered an immediate apology that was not well received by the caffeine deprived patron.

Camile's warm amusement transformed when she saw the boy's face, tattooed with faint scars that looked all too familiar. The last time she looked upon his face it was through a photograph shown to her by a disappointed Sir Drayden. All at once, she recalled the repercussions this boy had suffered as a result of her violation of protocol.

"Oh, my G—" she said in barely a whisper. "It's him."

The shaman nodded.

"You see," she began. "The initial result of your decision was unfavorable, but it started a chain reaction that brought Andre to the best place he can possibly be. It linked him with Michelle. As a result, they are both healing and changing in ways that otherwise may have never happened."

"Andre? That's his name?" Camile asked, watching Michelle and the boy releasing their crushing embrace as they did some catching up.

The shaman nodded anew, explaining that Michelle's organization quickly took on Andre's case and worked with him to reverse his delinquent behavior. In turn, Andre's grades improved dramatically. Additionally, through Michelle's organization, he's been reaching out to other children by telling his story in hopes of preventing them from following his footsteps. Apparently, Andre had been secretly suffering abuse for years, but it was never exposed until after he finally ended up in the hospital.

"Strangely enough, your mistake probably saved his life," the shaman added.

"I understand why you brought me here, Your Wisest, but I wish you had given me a little more preparation for all this," Camile said tremulously, fighting back tears of relief.

"What do you think I've been doing all these months, blowing smoke?"

*   *   *

Though she had seen them in passing, this was the first time Camile had seen a ceremonial gazebo up-close. Palpheons, as they were called, were color-coded structures used for marking important occasions such as birth, union, and departure. The respective main colors of these stone structures were green, beige and light blue, the shade of the palpheon in front of which Camile was now standing. The accents of the base, columns and roof trimming beautifully coordinated with the main hue.

A chill caressed Camile's body as she took in the sight of the intricately carved gazebo. Assuming the cool breeze was the culprit, she fastened her long coat. The guards reminded Camile about her schedule, but she insisted on admiring the palpheon for just a few moments longer. She hesitated before entering since she was well aware that it had been used for departure ceremonies, better known as funerals in the Coexistent World. Her heart skipped a beat when she noticed someone lying inside of the palpheon. As her curiosity overrode her mild apprehension, Camile ascended the short steps, getting a better look. She was shocked at who she saw.

Hyacinth's body, draped in a white gown, lay on a matching funeral bed accented with orchids and tiger lilies of the same color. Her hands were interlaced on top of her stomach and held a bouquet of purplish-blue hyacinth flowers. Her black hair cascaded into soft, elbow-length ringlets framing her face, which bore the serene expression of perpetual slumber. Sir Drayden entered the palpheon through the entrance opposite of the one Camile had entered. Like his deceased wife, he was clad in all white, a color Camile had rarely seen him wear. It brought out the subtle pink tones of his skin, sometimes washed out by his usual dark attire. For the first time since walking up the steps, she noticed the large space was packed with people who had come to pay their respects, including major members of various Transcendent governments. They had all seemed to emerge like apparitions from the shadows. The mood was somber, though none of the gatherers shed any tears.

Sir Drayden used one of the many candles to light three incense sticks before placing them in a small silver holder. Though it was still daytime, the flames in the votives shone brightly since the palpheon was blanketed by a deep shadow cast by the mountain. Facing the observers, he knelt before his deceased wife in silence and bowed his head for several moments as though in prayer. Once he rose to his feet, he addressed the gatherers as the sweet scent of jasmine filled the late afternoon air.

"Fellow citizens, friends and colleagues; Today we are gathered to pay homage to Hyacinth, my loving wife and an esteemed member of the community," Sir Drayden announced softly. "Though the manner of her departure from the physical world was tragic, we should not allow that fact to mar her legacy or her place in our hearts and memories. Instead, we should—" Stopping his sentence short, his frown deepened after seeing Akalina sitting beside her parents in the back row. He excused himself before exiting.

Akalina and her parents met with Sir Drayden privately behind the ceremonial structure. It was apparent that he had telepathically summoned them to join him. Based on his irritated expression, it wasn't a pleasant invitation.

"What is she doing here?" he hissed.

Before anyone could answer, Vincent swaggered over. "Normally, I don't agree with Sir Drayden, but this time he's right. She shouldn't even be alive, much less attending the memorial ceremony of the woman she murdered in cold blood." He glowered, his displeasure seemed to intensify his accent.

"We knew you'd probably be upset about her being here, so we decided to sit in the back," Kylie explained. "Look, Akalina may have made a huge mistake, but she shouldn't be exempt from paying her respects."

"*Respects?* I doubt she knows the meaning of the word." Sir Drayden sneered. His voice denoted a faint twinge of amusement as he glared at little Akalina.

"That might've been a poor choice of words, but what the Ambassador means is that Akalina should face the reality of what she's done, that her choice has had a domino effect on all who knew your wife," Zephyr explained.

As Sir Drayden appeared to consider the request Vincent regarded him with an expression of disbelief.

"Alright." Sir Drayden huffed. "She can stay, but she's to sit up front and witness the result of her offense."

Vincent said nothing, but the look on his face was more than enough to express his disapproval.

The ceremony proceeded soon after. As per Sir Drayden's request, young Akalina sat up front with her parents. At the close of the ritual, the gatherers were each given a flower to place upon the funeral bed. Kylie and Zephyr were among the first group, as was Akalina. When it was her turn to place her flower she froze. It seemed as though she was looking at Hyacinth's dead body for the first time.

Strange, Akalina thought. *She looks like she's sleeping, but her skin looks so…gray.*

"You're holding up the line," Sir Drayden whispered firmly. "Place your offering and move on."

Tilting her head upward, young Akalina briefly met his heart-stopping stare before returning her gaze to Hyacinth's body. She couldn't get over how empty Hyacinth seemed and found herself wondering what a dead body felt like, but decided against satisfying her interest. Extending her small hand, she dropped the orchid onto the funeral bed. However, before she could move away, her hand suddenly lurched forward and touched Hyacinth's arm. The movement wasn't voluntary and she surmised that Sir Drayden had somehow manipulated her with his unseen force. Based on what she heard next, she knew her assumption was correct.

So, you wanna touch her, huh? Here's your chance to get up close and personal with death. Sir Drayden's voice echoed inside her head as she struggled to let go of Hyacinth's arm.

Stricken with terror, Akalina's breathing became shallow. Her hand was sandwiched between the lifeless body and a powerful force holding it in place. The sensation of Hyacinth's arm was ice-cold and rigid—as though her body was morphing into stone.

You feel that? Sir Drayden's contemptuous voice filled her head. *If you continue to act up, you'll end up like this a lot sooner than you think. Long after your icy body has been broken down and consumed by the earth, you will indeed suffer!*

"No!" Akalina shouted, startling the other guests. She stumbled backward as her hand was finally released.

As soon as she regained her balance, she bolted out of the ceremonial chamber, clearing her path by shoving anyone in her way. Feeling someone grab her from behind, she screamed, demanding they let her go.

"Why are you running? What's got you so spooked?" asked one of the officers, donning a confused expression. The faces of the other guards mirrored the sentiment.

Camile was now several paces away from the palpheon, which was completely empty. It appeared she had literally run out of Akalina's memory.

*   *   *

For the second time that day Camile found herself standing in front of a palpheon. This time, it was beige in color. Joining her were her parents and Amoura, whose lithe body was camouflaged in blue and white robes. Confused, Camile inquired about the purpose of the small gathering.

"You're about to witness an important ceremony." Her father smiled before looking over her shoulder.

Following his gaze, Camile saw a man approaching them, walking with the aid of a cane. He wore loose beige pants, a white tunic and a brown cloak-like coat. The outfit was accessorized with a brown neckband. Though he wore a bittersweet smile, the bruises on his deeply-tanned face marked the chapters of a tragic past. He regarded Camile and her parents with a polite, humble greeting. Based on her father's interaction with the man, named Omar, it was evident the two have had prior dealings.

"I do not know of this surprise you speak of, but surely I am not worthy of it." Omar spoke with a heavy tongue. "If anyone should be presenting gifts, it is I. But like many other areas of my life, once again, I have failed."

Zephyr opened his mouth to respond, but was interrupted as a voice called out from a slight distance.

"Omar? Is that really you?" The voice came from a young woman in veils. She had been escorted to the area by a petite female officer. Camile squinted as though it would help her mind process where she had seen the woman before.

"Yasmeen? Either my weary eyes are deceiving me or I am truly in heaven!" Omar breathlessly exclaimed as the woman ran to him.

Camile recognized Yasmeen as the same woman she had seen killed in the truck explosion during one of her expeditions. Her gut tightened at the memory of the cruel revelers who celebrated the tragic event. However, her eyes now showed her the image of a vibrant young woman whose face bore only a few superficial scars as a souvenir of her adventure. As Camile watched Omar limp as fast as he could to meet Yasmeen halfway, her expression slackened in awe as she tried to make sense of it all.

"See? We did save her, and she was never alone," Zephyr whispered to his daughter. "You see, we fulfilled our mission that night in the desert town. It was to recruit Omar." He explained, making sure the couple was out of earshot. "Yasmeen was…Well, unexpected. We didn't know about her connection to Omar until the night she ran into us. Lucky she did, too. Anyway, we needed to improvise and find a way to bring her to our world without the chance of any of her Coexistent foes following her here or exposing our existence. So, by witnessing her death, it provided them, and her, with closure. My only regret is that justice eluded Omar and Yasmeen in their homeland, but everything has its time."

"Why didn't you just tell me this from the beginning?" Camile asked in a whisper.

"Because, you have to be taught to extend your belief beyond what you can see. In this case, beyond death and into what's everlasting. Love."

Without further delay, Amoura announced that if the newly reunited couple had no objection, she would bless and endorse their union with matrimony. In essence, she offered to grant them a right that was deprived of them in the Coexistent World. The couple enthusiastically agreed and neither wanted to wait a moment longer to fulfill the culmination of their perilous quest for the right to love without limitations.

"Love that exists in its truest form can defy many things," Amoura began, her twinkling eyes framed with cracked leathery lids. "It's sometimes the most elusive form of energy that ensures the continuation of life itself. Those whom are unable to attain it sometimes try to eclipse love's light with the shadow of hatred. Both of you have witnessed this first hand. So I'm sure you already know that when something so precious comes along, it must be embraced, cherished and defended, not taken for granted. To love so passionately, so purely is the closest thing to blessed immortality. In times like these, we need to preserve such love more than ever," Amoura said solemnly, her gaze and voice both saturated with the wisdom only time and experience could bring. "Do you both agree to the solemn vow of undertaking such a responsibility? In the name of love itself, do you commit yourself to its preservation throughout your lives and beyond?"

"I have done it once already and I would gladly do it again," Omar said, still clinging to Yasmeen, who agreed with the sentiment.

"A simple *yes* would've sufficed, but you've done me one better." Amoura chuckled almost to herself before having the couple repeat the following passage to one another:

> *In honor of you, my chosen one, I vow to willingly use my love to fortify you when you can no longer do so for yourself, knowing that all shall return. It is my promise to be your song should you lose your cadence, your compass should you lose direction, and your peace should you lose tranquility. Let us freely rejoice as we extend our love throughout not only this day, but all the days of our lives.*

During the recital of the vows, Camile noticed her parents mouthing them as well. In some ways, it seemed as though they were renewing their marital promises at that very moment.

"Remember what led you here, but don't allow it to rule your new life together," Kylie advised the blissful couple at the close of the ceremony.

In the span of an afternoon Camile had witnessed the division of one couple and the union of another. Though the ceremonies were polar opposites in nearly every way, both contained a sincere sweetness that Camile found extraordinary.

Chapter 45

Bad Medicine

Young Akalina turned her gaze up to meet the knight's face as they traversed the corridor. She inquired about where he was taking her, but he either didn't hear or simply ignored her question. With each step her body grew colder, but still didn't compare to Sir Drayden's frigid expression. Yet his calculating eyes seemed to burn a path before them as his steamy breath escaped his large pointed nose. Crossing the doorway and entering the darkened room with the knight behind her, little Akalina trembled sharply, hugging her body as a bitter chill breached the pores of her clothes and bit into her flesh.

By the time they moved into the center of the chamber she could make out about a dozen tables around them, each with various masses on top of them. She ceased moving once the room's illumination increased, flooding her eyes with a gruesome reality. She spun around to evade the sight only to crash into Sir Drayden's midsection, in which she buried her face. Her voice muffled there as she pleaded with him to let her leave. Though her vision was now eclipsed by the darkness of his wool sweater, the image of the horribly dehydrated corpses was burned into her memory. One in particular stood out. The cadaver closest to the front. It was Hyacinth, her body noticeably duller than it had been at the memorial.

Akalina jumped when the knight's large hands gripped her shoulders, gently turning her to face forward.

"If you're old enough to commit murder, you're old enough to witness this," he whispered, his voice chillingly tender. "Is there anything you wish to confess before we begin?"

Still shivering, she shook her head, her fists clenched tightly, her nails digging into her palms.

"Guess I better make this quick," Sir Drayden said flatly. "Can't have them thawing out or you getting hypothermia."

The knight crossed the room and retrieved a bowl of water sitting beside a strange tabletop instrument of horizontally stacked spinning glass bowls of graduating sizes. Dipping his hands, he cocked his head, gesturing her to watch the gaunt corpses as he played. Xylophonic notes vibrated through the air with a delicate soprano-like sweetness. The melody reverberated throughout the chamber inciting the cadavers to a tremor. Akalina wondered if they were somehow awakening, but the passing of a split-second quashed the thought. Accompanying the knight's solo performance was a sound akin to granulated sugar pouring on tin foil. Each corpse steadily disintegrated until all that remained were tables covered in their powdered remains. Akalina's rugged breathing only allowed her a brief whimper, but her eyes offered a more generous aperture to convey her screams.

Camile often wondered about Sir Drayden's torturous attempts to coerce Akalina to reveal her accomplice. Her contemplation culminated in a single question:

"Why didn't he convince the council to probe her mind?" she asked her father. "You mentioned earlier that they have the ability to hack into people's thoughts and memories."

Zephyr, who prepared himself a beverage, raised his brow, pausing to regard his daughter.

"What makes you think Sir Drayden didn't go that route first?" Expelling a breath, he resumed his preparations. "The council quickly rejected his request, despite what was at stake."

Leaning against his office desk, he sipped from the glass and set it aside before meeting his daughter's eyes. He continued, "Forcefully tapping into one's mind and dreams is considered to be one of the most potentially damaging violations of humanity. The council feared that you would somehow be compromised during the procedure. It was a risk they couldn't take. It was a risk *I* couldn't take. You see, it was my vote that swayed the council's decision against Sir Drayden's proposal. So, you can imagine my frustration when he went behind my back and started doing it anyway."

"Why didn't you report him?"

"I couldn't. I was bound by a rather large obligation. If it wasn't for Sir Drayden, neither you nor Akalina would have had any chances of survival. Not to mention the fact he saved my own life on more than one occasion.

So, I found myself in the uncomfortable position of aiding and abetting his behavior while begging Akalina to come forward with the truth." Zephyr sighed. "Sadly, she inherited my stubbornness."

He walked to the window as he rerouted the discussion back to the council's ability to tap into the dreams and thoughts of targeted humans.

"It seems desperate times call for desperate measures. In all the years I've served as Defense Minister, this is the first time I've witnessed a unanimous willingness of the council to utilize this technology. It's sporadically put into practice with our mediums, who have the natural ability to gain entry into one's dreams and thoughts. In a few days you'll be meeting Raine. She's one of our finest."

Camile's father went on to explain the delicate nature of deciphering the complex thoughts and abstract dreams of the human mind. The process was undoubtedly tricky and required finesse, which is why the government had spent many years investing time and resources into the endeavor.

"Magistrate Sui fully backs the project and is confident it will support the council's efforts in aiding the Coexistent World during its plight. Personally, I'm not sure the program's entirely ready for prime time. While it may be well beyond the experimental phase, I'd prefer a little extra time to see if there are any remaining kinks to be worked out. But, the way things are going, we may be left with few options other than to launch the full-scale program ahead of schedule." Zephyr frowned, shifting his gaze from the window to his daughter. "Unharnessed freedom leads to complete chaos. So, naturally, everything operates on a system of laws—in this world, the Coexistent one, and even the realms that exist beyond the physical plane. Once again we're faced with the challenge of sacrificing, or limiting, some freedoms for the sake of others by extending these laws."

*   *   *

The shaman scrunched her face, her aged brown eyes peering from behind large goggles. She concentrated her attention on a three-inch square piece of material, stretched taut across a simple tabletop contraption. Her salt and pepper hair was piled atop her head in a loose bun, a few unruly tendrils hanging from her temples and nape. As Camile leaned in to take a closer look at the odd material, she could see the distinct fine cross-hatching of lines and the stippling of pores most commonly found in human skin. Tabitha cautioned her to stand back. Camile, who had arrived at the shaman's quarters for their usual session, was intrigued to see her mentor working intently at the makeshift lab table.

With a gloved hand, the shaman applied a small drop of a pasty concoction to the membrane, smoothing it on gently like a lotion. After a few uneventful moments, she smiled, making a motion to remove her goggles. She halted her action upon seeing the faint stream of smoke, rising from the patch of skin as its color gradually darkened from tan to black. Almost as soon as the shaman had risen from her seat, the patch burst into flames that quickly extinguished on their own. What had once been a smooth piece of flesh now resembled a burnt strip of bacon. Visibly disappointed, Tabitha slid back into the chair, expelling an exasperated sigh as she removed her goggles, letting them crash to the table.

"I get the feeling that didn't exactly go as planned," Camile said, fanning the foul-smelling smoke that encircled her face.

"No, Camile. It didn't." The shaman massaged the bridge of her nose.

She explained that she had been working on a topical devourer repellent and was testing it on human skin.

"After all the years I've put into this project, I've made significant progress," she continued. "But, obviously, it's nowhere near ready to be used on humans, Transcendent or otherwise."

"Where do you get the skin, from? Corpses?"

"No. Dead flesh is no good for this experiment. Living tissue is needed for these trials for the most accurate reaction. We receive the samples from Transcendent humans who have donated a small portion of their stock."

"Stock?" Camile inquired, not entirely sure she was prepared for the answer.

"In some parts of the Transcendent World, societies partake in an organ harvesting program. It's optional, but those who enroll have replacement parts engineered in labs and stored in the event they may need them in the future. In other cases, the organs are donated. I'm not too keen on the program, which thankfully is extremely limited, but I find myself in a position where I have to choose the lesser of the two evils to help solve a greater problem."

Tabitha explained that just days prior to her recent experiment there had been an attack on a convoy that had been transporting organs to medical facilities. Though the devourers spared the lives of the transport crew, they had stolen an entire batch of organs.

"That's part of the reason why I'm working so hard to make a repellent. I want the devourers to know their take-out comes with a hefty price tag."

Judging by the sour expression on the shaman's face, she apparently had a score to settle.

*   *   *

As time progressed, the memories began to come faster. Camile was getting what she wanted, a deeper understanding of Akalina's past. The memories were steadily unraveling like a thread in her subconscious mind.

"The ambassador is my mother?" Akalina asked, her voice laced with adolescent angst. "They've been lying to me all this time?"

"There's more." Jezebel frowned, lowering her onyx orbs. "You have a sister, a twin sister. Her name's Camile. She was taken into the other dimension when she was about six years old."

"I don't believe this. Why would they hide something like this from me?" Akalina fumed, briefly catching her silhouette in the living room window. Her father wasn't due back for at least another hour, which was probably just as well, given her climbing rage.

"Because they think you're unworthy. The ambassador was too ashamed to admit you were her daughter. You were too imperfect, too challenging, but Camile... Oh, how she loved Camile!" Jezebel laughed, her eyes floating upward. "*Everyone* loved Camile. While you spent the past ten years trying to figure out where your mother really was, she was raising and cherishing your sister in the other dimension, showering her with the love you could've had, *should've* had. The two of you were separated since they feared you would taint your sister with your so-called imperfect ways." Arms folded, Jezebel shook her head. "I hated lying to you almost as much as I hated the injustice that was being done. While you all but screamed for attention, your sister was getting everything she wanted, practically on a silver platter. As a parent, I honestly can't understand how a mother can disown her own child."

"Why did I have to go sixteen years without knowing who my mother is? Why didn't you tell me this sooner?" Akalina hissed.

Tears stung her eyes, but she refused to let them fall. She didn't want to waste precious tears on people she felt didn't give a damn about her.

"Because at the time there was nothing I could do about it. Things were what they were, but now..." Jezebel's words trailed into a sigh.

"Now what?"

"You're in danger." Jezebel's frown deepened as she sandwiched her protégé's hand in hers. "Your sister is set to return here to claim an inheritance that's rightfully yours. Once she gets here, there'll be no room for you. Chances are you'll be banished...or killed."

"The hell I will," Akalina exclaimed, pulling away. Clenching and unclenching her fists, she began to pace as she declared, "I've been through enough as it is. I'm not gonna let that spoiled bitch come here and ruin what's left of my screwed up life. Not without a fight. I'll kill her first!" She punched her palm.

"That's my girl." Jezebel cupped Akalina's cheeks with her cocoa skinned hands. Looking up into her eyes, her smile flickered as she said, "I always knew you were a fighter, a natural born fighter. In some ways you're like the daughter I never had."

Her protégé nodded simply. Her mind was focused.

"Where can I find this Camile character?"

"I'll tell you when the time is right. She'll be at her most vulnerable when she starts receiving the signal."

Akalina's eyes narrowed. "What signal?"

"The one that'll lead her here. We're not exactly sure when or how it'll happen, but it will. For years we doubted it since she appeared to be devoid of power, unlike you. Then one day, quite recently, she started exhibiting signs that proved the contrary. Of course, your powers are far greater. Anyway, we're trying to figure out exactly how and when she'll receive the signal. Once we do that, we'll be better equipped to make our move."

"So, we just sit here and wait in the meantime?" Akalina wrinkled her nose.

A sly smirk spread across her mentor's face.

"Not exactly." Jezebel's dark eyes twinkled. "You're about to go on a very dangerous mission. It'll be the greatest test of your allegiance."

As Camile awoke, she found herself empathizing with Akalina even more. It was becoming increasingly clear that Jezebel had worked tirelessly to corrupt her mind, but for what reason? She wondered what mission Jezebel had in mind for Akalina. Then she realized the memory had occurred several years earlier and that the mission had likely already taken place. Rather than approach her parents with incomplete information, she decided to bide her time and wait to see if the answer would be revealed in subsequent dreams. Not knowing the outcome, Camile was already certain of one thing, it couldn't be good.

*   *   *

In preparation for her next expedition, Camile was informed of security protocols designed to uphold the veil dividing the Transcendent and Coexistent dimensions. Such a feat was facilitated by way of invisible fences at fixed rifts, keyed in to biological transmitters which were implanted in Coexistent humans by specially selected operatives. The process of the implantation was known as *tagging*.

The combined result of the technology was said to act as a repellent, causing the Coexistents to experience temporary discomfort, thus deterring entry into the adjacent world. Such effects include severe headache, extreme panic attacks, disorientation, nausea, fainting and other temporary ailments designed to get them to either reverse or halt their course, hopefully long enough for the rift to close. As for the Coexistent citizens recruited by the Transcendent World, their bio-neurotransmitters are programmed to counteract the effect. The fences also use the same technology to double as a barrier to prevent unauthorized Transcendents from trespassing into the Coexistent World.

"The fences only solve part of the problem," Camile's father explained as he settled into his chair. "Once we globalize this technology it'll be easier to prevent people from crossing through the rifts that spontaneously appear between our worlds."

"What about the Coexistents currently coming into this dimension? Do you catch them and erase their memories?"

"Memories can be blocked or altered, but can't be completely erased without causing permanent brain damage to one extent or another. Doing such a thing violates not only the Arvainan constitution, but that of many governments within the Transcendent World. Arvaina banned the practice around the same time it was decided to eliminate the eligibility of children for the death penalty." Camile's father dropped his gray gaze, momentarily massaging his temple. "Unfortunately, both practices are still observed in several countries in our world, but we're working hard to change that. Ironically enough, the Coexistents' skepticism actually proves beneficial in maintaining the secrecy of our dimension from non-recruits and non-potentials. The few individuals who've tried to expose our world to others were usually dismissed and ignored. It's very rare for people to believe them, but in any case we don't take chances. We modify their memories and tag them to prevent reentry, much like we did with Barry, your troublesome high school classmate."

"I get the feeling these people aren't exactly volunteering to be tagged." Camile scratched her temple. "Don't you think that's intrusive? Don't you think those people have a right to know the truth about what's happening?"

"I admit our methods aren't conventional. Then again, neither is our problem. Unfortunately, this is the only option we have to ensure their safety as well as ours." Zephyr tented his fingers. "That's the only reason why select members of their governments have agreed to it, with strict regulations of course. You see, many of their people have fallen prey to devourers, rebels and our wildlife—among other things—after wandering into this world. To answer your other question, if we were to openly introduce our society to theirs at this time there would be a widespread panic. As I've seen all too often, panic inspires tragic actions. Someday the Coexistents will earn the right to discover our world, but first, they must prove that they can work harmoniously within the limits of their own dimension. The council wants this more than anything, because we'll need their help to stabilize the world as a whole."

"Makes more sense now that you explain it. What does the tagging procedure involve?"

"A bio-neurotransmitter is implanted at the base of the subject's skull via an injection. We're working on a less invasive method in which the transmitter could be ingested through food or drink and would be programmed to navigate itself to the implantation site in the body. There will be another round of teams deployed to the Coexistent dimension for routine tagging missions tonight. I'll assign you to join one of the squads, but since this is your first go 'round you are only to observe, unless your assistance is specifically requested." Zephyr raised an eyebrow as though cautioning her.

*   *   *

There were over fifty-thousand Coexistent residents scheduled for tagging that evening and approximately two-thousand teams assigned to the task. The teams assembled in Caldaq's main hall an hour prior to the mission. Camile stood with the squad she was set to accompany, which included Justine, Commander Wilder and a short full-figured woman named Raine, though some called her *Raindrop*. She wore her black hair in short spiky layers with a few blue-violet streaks. It complimented her deep brown skin and brought out her astonishing violet eyes, heavily rimmed with black liner. Her daring appearance properly accessorized her outgoing personality.

So, this is who Dad was talking about, Camile internally acknowledged.

The room grew quiet as Zephyr traversed one of the two sets of stairs located on either side of the platform, which stood one level above the ground floor. It was partially supported by columns and also housed a large organ consisting of illuminated crystal pipes. Colorful glass window panels allowed light to stream across the decorative arched ceiling, supplementing the light generated by the hanging chandeliers lining both sides of the hall. Although nearly every square inch of the floor was occupied with people, Camile was able to see hints of an intricate pattern etched into it.

Taking center stage, Zephyr made a brief announcement highlighting the importance of the operation. In closing, he said, "You have your assignments. Please try your best not to do anything that will force us to alter the memories of any of your subjects. We have a large enough workload as it is."

The squad, led by Commander Wilder, was assigned to tag only five subjects since it was Camile's first time going on such a mission. The first four went off without a hitch. During each of the separate procedures Raine merely made small talk with Camile as they both observed Justine and Brandon tagging the subjects. It wasn't until they arrived at the fifth location, a duplex apartment in an upscale metro area, that Raine's specialty was revealed. She was to pull the fifth target, a chronic insomniac, away from her consciousness. As they stood in the dark living room a low growl rippled through the air, indicating they weren't alone. Crouched beneath the coffee table was a dog. The subtle moonlight filtering through the tree lined window illuminated its menacing teeth and reflective marble eyes. Camile hoped she wasn't suffering an ill-timed bout of overconfidence, but thought she could calm the animal.

"Mind if I try?" she whispered to the commander.

"Sure. Careful, though," he advised.

"I will." Camile chuckled uneasily.

Operating solely on instinct, she lowered herself slowly until she was kneeling on the plush carpet. She could hear the excited throbbing of her pulse accompanying the dog's rippling snarl. Knowing animals had the peculiar and intimidating gift of detecting the smell of fear, Camile pushed her anxiety aside.

Remember, bravery is not the absence of fear, but the ability to persevere despite its presence.

Her breathing ever so controlled, she focused her thoughts on the soothing sensation of the floor beneath her in hopes she could find some common ground with the canine. She remained optimistic in this regard, but wished she had access to treats to appease him with in case her attempt went sour. As the thought entered her mind, she felt her appetite stirring up. Visions of cookies and crackers circled the back of her mind, but she knew her cravings would have to wait. No longer baring its teeth, the dog reduced his semi-continuous snarl to a series of hushed whines.

That's it, Camile thought, unconsciously licking her lips. *We're not here to hurt you or your master.*

Something changed in the creature's marble-like orbs. They widened with a voracity that was confirmed by its salivating jaws. Panting wildly, the dog pounced toward Camile, who instinctively shut her eyes, willing herself not to make any sudden moves. Her breathing quickened to the point she matched the dog's heavy panting. They seemed to be on the same respiratory rhythm for an instant and she wondered if her reaction stemmed from fear, or something else. She could feel the canine drawing dangerously nearer as the reverberation of his impact intensified with each step. Yet, her knees remained planted firmly on the floor. A sudden rush of air hit her body as the creature darted by, lashing her with his tail in the process. Now behind her, his huffs faded along with the patter of canine paws across the uncarpeted corridor leading into the kitchen. Opening her eyes and training her gaze upward, she saw Brandon extending his hand to her, is face aglow with pride. Raine seemed equally amazed.

"Well, done. I'm impressed," Brandon praised, helping Camile to her feet. "I see Vincent's schooled you well. He'd be proud."

"Thanks. It was strange."

"The first fully successful connection with a non-human is always weird," Brandon explained. "How did it feel?"

"I don't know. Almost like an out of body experience. But the main thing that stood out is that I suddenly felt so—"

She was interrupted by a scratchy sound akin to a box of cereal as something landed on her foot. As Camile and her comrades turned their attention downward, they saw the dog sitting before her expectantly, tail wagging wildly. In front of it, still partially propped against Camile's foot, was a box of dog treats, dented with a single bite mark.

"Hungry." She grimaced, not sure if she instilled her hunger in the dog, or vice-versa.

It was time for Raine to make her connection. She prepared herself by lying on the plush carpet on the floor.

"She's upstairs in the bedroom. I don't know what she's doing, but she's not sleeping. Her restlessness is starting to rub off on me," she said.

"Would it help if I brought you some warm milk and read you a bedtime story?" Commander Wilder quipped.

"Hmph! I got your bedtime story." Raine smiled sarcastically, holding up her fist. This incited all to a cautious chuckle.

"You sure she's alone up there?" Justine raised an eyebrow, "Would be pretty awkward to walk in on something."

"Justine, you're talking like a rookie. I would expect that from her, not you," Raine said, shifting her glance to Camile and back. "But yeah, she's alone. I don't sense anyone with her. No one alive, anyway."

"Yeah, sure. Just make sure our catch stays asleep."

"Whatever makes your job easier." Raine yawned.

Within minutes she was out cold. The canine curled up beside her and followed suit.

Once upstairs, Justine peeked through a wall and gave the all clear, indicating that the subject had fallen asleep. Camile and Brandon followed her into the dim bedroom. The soft illumination from the moon shone through the window, highlighting everything with a soft glow. Camile watched as the silhouettes of her two comrades crept slowly toward their sleeping target, who was still clutching a book she had been reading. There was something sinister-looking about their stealthy approach. Like they had done in their four prior operations that evening, Justine gently turned the subject's head to face away from the commander. She held it in place while he prepared to inject the bio-transmitter at the base of her skull, just inside the hairline. Prior to the injection, he used a scanner to ensure optimum placement of the device. Suddenly, the subject attempted to adjust her position.

"She's waking up. We have to abort," Justine whispered.

"Shh. I'm almost there. Besides, chances are she won't be able to see us anyway," Brandon said.

Just then, the woman opened her eyes and screamed. Justine quickly covered the woman's mouth with a gloved hand, muffling her cries.

"That doesn't hurt as much as you think, and it won't work, so stop it!" Justine grimaced before turning her attention to the commander. "So much for her not seeing us. Can you *please* hurry up?"

"I can't. She's moving too much. I'll paralyze her."

The woman thrashed around violently to fight off whom she undoubtedly thought to be her attackers. She elbowed Justine's ribs so hard, she fell backwards. Screaming wildly, the woman swung her book, catching the side of Brandon's head as he tried to restrain her.

"Hold her down!" Justine instructed as she scrambled to her feet. Without fully understanding what she was doing or why, Camile leapt onto the bed and knelt astride the woman's legs, tightly squeezing them with her thighs to prevent her from kicking. The woman flung the book, hitting Camile's forehead. Though her ears were ringing slightly in accompaniment to her now dazed disposition, Camile continued to maintain her hold on the subject. Physically, she was still in the moment, but she felt her mind drifting away.

The woman beneath her began to change. Her alabaster skin caramelized to the shade of butter pecan as her hair spiraled into a mess of auburn curls. She was no longer lying on a bed of quilted blankets, but that of the changing autumn leaves. The deep night faded into daylight as Camile analyzed the curly haired woman, groaning while clutching her side. Surrounding her were dozens of men and women who did nothing as they watched her writhe in agony.

"What's taking the spiders so long?" The wounded woman grimaced.

"They don't come out here." Jezebel stepped out from the circle of spectators. "Don't you remember that, Stacy? This is forsaken territory. No need to worry. You have us." She smiled, her voice slowly caressing each word with a sinister sweetness. "We're your family now."

She nodded to one of the other rebels, a tall, wiry man with skin as dark as night. He stepped forward and handed her a vial containing vibrant liquid, the color of fiery lava. Jezebel passed the small bottle to Akalina.

"Here, you'll treat her injuries." Jezebel smirked.

"Is that what I think it is? You can't use that! It's illegal!" Stacy protested, her eyes wide with panic. She attempted to scramble to her feet, only to be restrained by two rebels upon Jezebel's command, a simple snap of her fingers.

During the struggle Akalina thought she heard footsteps approaching. Upon inspection, she only saw the branches of a large bush waving gently in the breeze. Jezebel's voice recaptured her attention as she addressed the wounded woman.

"You're right about one thing, Stacy." Jezebel crouched her petite body beside the frightened woman. "That's *exactly* what you think it is and it is illegal, but the rebels no longer answer to authority. This is an important lesson. You must learn what happens when you let your guard down. I'm disappointed in your carelessness. Your mistake could've cost us all. Still, I give you credit for one thing, you didn't let them catch you. Know this; if that ever happens, you'll be worthless to us even if you are released. If you ever get caught by the enemy, you'd better not come looking for us afterwards, because one way or the other it will result in your death. It's nothing personal, Stacy. This is what's ensured our survival for years. We're free and we'd like to keep it that way. Unfortunately, freedom doesn't come cheap. Now, it's time for you to pay for yours," Jezebel lectured, smoothing the sobbing woman's hair before placing an object in her mouth. "Bite down on this. It'll help with the pain."

Akalina was curious about the hysterical reaction the woman had upon seeing the vibrant liquid. Looking into Stacy's pleading eyes, she felt no pity. Anxious to see the serum in action, she rolled up her shirt, revealing a bloody mess. Akalina knelt on the ground astride the woman's legs, tightly squeezing them with her thighs to prevent her from kicking.

"Lady, I've heard about this stuff and what it does. Sucks to be you." Akalina smirked before pouring the vibrant serum onto the deep wound.

Stacy unleashed a muffled throat-shredding scream as she convulsed violently. After a few long moments she abruptly lost consciousness. All went quiet, except for a soft, amused chortle from Akalina.

"She'll live." She shrugged. Her amusement faded upon seeing a visibly disappointed Tabitha standing among the group.

Akalina alerted them to the intruder, but was regarded with confused expressions. It was then that she realized Tabitha was either travelling within the Shadow World, the world that lies between the Phantom World and the land of the living, or was somehow telepathically communicating with her.

"I warn you that if you don't turn your life around, things will turn out very badly for you," Tabitha cautioned.

"Is that a threat?" Akalina laughed.

"That's life. One day, this'll all come back to bite you in the ass."

"I've already been bitten. This is me, biting back." Akalina sneered.

"Are you done yet?" Justine asked impatiently.

"Yeah. Got her," Brandon exclaimed softly.

Camile was no longer in Akalina's recollection torturing a woman in a forest, but back with her teammates. As they wrapped things up, she noticed their subject was peacefully asleep. Joining Justine's side, Camile attempted to digest what she had just witnessed.

"Looks like Raine finally decided to do her job." Brandon exhaled, moping his brow.

"And not a moment too soon. That lady's got one hell of a bite!" Justine removed her leather glove, revealing a nasty looking mark. Though bruised, the skin wasn't broken. Using her other hand, she clapped Camile's shoulder. "Good job, girl. Looks like you've done this before," she commended.

Camile thought it odd to receive a compliment from her. However, her mind was too preoccupied to fully appreciate it.

Chapter 46

Eyeing the Target

Caldaq's main entrance hall was relatively empty with the exception of the dozens of officers on guard duty. Upon seeing Commander Wilder, they nodded respectfully as he entered with his small squad. Camile, still pondering her latest flashback, was operating on autopilot during the walk to her father's office, where the team would give their full report. She listened as Brandon and Justine discussed the technical difficulties experienced with their last assignment. Both were concerned that the woman would remember the events that transpired that night, thus warranting the council to order a memory alteration to remedy the problem. Raine did her best to reassure them otherwise.

"Don't worry. She didn't see you, guys. She just freaked out when she felt your presence, but I worked my magic as usual. I convinced her the whole thing was just a bad dream. *Damn,* I'm good!" Raine proclaimed as they turned a corner, bumping into Zephyr, who didn't look pleased.

"You could be better," he said. "The subject slipped from your grip, didn't she?"

"Well, that hasn't really happened to me before. I'll try not to let it happen again, sir."

"I know. That's why you're going to start refresher training with the shaman. You need to be on top of your game at all times. We're coming to a critical stage in our bid to win the *Invisible War* and we can't afford a slip up like this in the future. It can very well cost you and your teammates their lives."

"Understood, sir," Raine acknowledged, biting her lower lip.

"Wait, I don't think it was Raine's fault. Something was different tonight, but it wasn't her. It must've been Camile," said Justine.

"Me?" Camile grimaced.

"We've done these types of missions hundreds of times. Tonight, the only thing that changed in our routine was you."

*   *   *

The excitement of the evening weighed heavily on Camile's mind. As she lay in bed, her lethargy continued to pull her downward. It was as though a hole had formed beneath her body, causing her to sink into the mattress, through the floor and into a steep pit of darkness until finally, she found herself standing in Akalina's body for the second time that evening. She stood with Jezebel at the edge of the field overlooking the city. The Caldaq range was a towering backdrop beneath the amber sky.

"Tabitha stands in the way of getting this whole situation with your sister under control," Jezebel stated, squinting her eyes against the sun. "As long as she remains in her current position, it'll increase the chances of Camile replacing you in this world and inheriting everything that should be yours—including your powers. The powers she has now actually belonged to you. Why do you think you can't remember certain parts of your childhood? They tampered with them—and with good reason. They figured since your sister was more obedient to authority, she was better suited to have your powers. Camile had none before they tried to transfer yours to her. Luckily for you, their plan didn't work. Otherwise, they would have gotten rid of you. To make matters worse, the pathetic girl doesn't even realize she has them. I'm sure she will someday, though. When that happens, you have to be ready to reclaim what's yours and take your rightful place in this world. Eliminating Tabitha is our best chance of that happening. Apparently, she's the one who'll help Camile gain your inheritance. She's her bridge to this world and we have to destroy it."

"How will I go about doing that? I can't do it the same way I killed Hyacinth. Hell, I doubt I'll have a moment alone with Tabitha. They've been keeping an annoyingly close eye on basically everything I do. I'm amazed I was able to get away from them today." Akalina grunted, briefly glancing over her shoulder to make sure she wasn't being watched.

"You're right. We can't use a seven year old trick even if it was successful the first go 'round." Jezebel sighed. "We'll have to launch an attack on the compound. It's brazen, but it's the only way. There'll be a diversion while you do what you must with Tabitha. The rebels and I have been going over the details for months. I didn't want to tell you anything until we had a solid plan. Tabitha's most vulnerable when her spirit is traveling. It should be pretty easy to sever the connection to her body while she's under."

"What about Sir Drayden and all the guards?"

"We have it all figured out. We'll choose a day when he's scheduled to meet with the council at the Birquone all the way in *Kibara*. And don't worry about the guards. You'll have plenty of backup to take care of them for you." Jezebel smiled.

"Sir Drayden and Tabitha are always at each other's throats about something. Maybe if we're lucky, they'll kill each other and we won't have to do this."

Jezebel laughed briefly.

"We can only hope. I doubt we'll get off that easily though." She raised an eyebrow. "Hey, you're not afraid of a challenge, are you?"

Akalina shook her head.

"Good. So, I guess it's official."

Camile's confusion mounted, as did her mixed emotions. So much so, she actually hesitated before informing her parents of her latest recollection. If not for the fact Tabitha's life was possibly in danger, Camile wasn't sure if she'd tell them at all. Her parents expressed concern, but said very little in the matter. They informed her that everything would be taken care of and that the shaman was well-protected. Once again, Camile was struck with the overwhelming impression that they knew something she didn't.

*   *   *

To supplement her physical defense training and her growing knowledge of the *Styngrae*, Camile was introduced to a variety of other weapons, including that of the non-lethal variety. The latter included a light-emitting stopping device called the *Dysarrae*. It closely resembled a flashlight and was designed to not only blind a subject temporarily, but to induce nausea and unconsciousness. Depending on the power setting, the *Dysarrae* had the capability of stopping as few as one person or as many as a small crowd. Commander Wilder explained that it was necessary for Transcendent military officials to become well-versed in not only the weapons of their world, but the other as well. He led Camile deeper into the immaculate weapons range located deep beneath the base of Caldaq's

Dusque peak. Getting there from the central peak required a fifteen minute trip via the compound's rapid railway system and a long ride down a lift.

The range was packed with officers and military personnel. Some were performing weapons maintenance while others practiced their targeting skills with various weapons. The area was predominantly medium gray with metallic accents and the layout was reminiscent of a bowling alley. There were counters at the head of each lane with protective barriers on either side. One lane was assigned per person, but since Camile was just starting out, she shared with Commander Wilder at the far end of the facility.

"It's rare, but sometimes our technology fails in the Coexistent realm," Brandon explained, "To this day, our scientists have been working to determine exactly why that occurs. Until that happens, we believe the best way to increase our adaptability is to learn the ways of Coexistent weapons in case we ever have to fall back on them. You might find these to be more your speed than the *Styngrae.*"

He pushed a button on the panel, prompting a concealed storage compartment to slide open. Inside, were over two dozen types of handguns. Camile unconsciously took a step back as Brandon continued to speak, "The craftsmanship of our neighbor's weapons are quite impressive, but I still prefer the silent, agile qualities of the *Styngrae.*"

Camile had never held a gun before, but had witnessed its deadly capabilities more times than she cared to admit. In addition, she had found herself at the wrong end of one at least twice in her life. Brandon selected a handgun from the collection and handled it expertly. After thoroughly explaining the proper way to hold and operate the weapon, he inserted a preloaded magazine into the bottom of the handgrip, resulting in a sharp click, causing Camile to flinch. Pulling back the slide at the top of the weapon and releasing it with an even louder clank, Brandon explained that the action had loaded the first bullet into the firing chamber. He then directed her to step back before he opened fire on the target hanging at the end of the lane.

Metal shell casings ejected from the firearm, flying through the air and raining on the ground producing a wind chime-like sound. Brandon's protected eyes reflected the brief flashes being emitted from the gun's barrel. His face bore the expression of calm intensity as he emptied ten rounds into the target. The accuracy of his marksmanship became increasingly evident as the target was retracted to their counter. The area representing the human heart was completely riddled with bullet holes.

After installing a new target, Brandon handed Camile the preloaded weapon. She hesitated before taking the cold steel into her hands, which took a few seconds to steady themselves and support the weight of the weapon. Her breath deepened with the quickening of her pulse, stemming from the understanding of the potentially deadly power in her grasp.

Enshrouded in her intimidation was a twinge of excitement as she eyed her target and anticipated her first shot. Brandon's smooth voice steadied her nerves, instructing her to remain calm while reassuring her safety.

"Your posture's excellent. Now, lock your arms and line up your shot like I showed you earlier," he instructed. Camile followed his directions to the letter. "Very nice. See? You're a natural. Fire when ready."

After taking a few moments to mentally prepare herself, Camile gently squeezed the trigger. The air was instantly filled with a vociferous blast as the gun fired. The recoil of the weapon jolted her hand upward, slightly straining her wrist. There was a sudden vibration traveling through her arm and upper body like thunder. The sensation was repeated with each shot until she was out of ammunition. Brandon cautioned her not to move her hand in anticipation of the recoil and stated it would help improve her aim. He retracted the target with the push of a button. As it approached, she saw that she had struck it in the neck and chest. She was instantly hit with the brief image of the dying soldier who had reached out for her in the desert. The vision dissipated just as quickly as it had emerged. She knew that no matter how often she meditated or how much distance she put between her heart and the reality of what had occurred, nothing short of a visit to the EDC would remove the vision from her mind.

"Hey, you're not traveling on me, are you?" Brandon waved a hand in front of Camile's eyes.

Camile apologized for her momentary lapse of attention before explaining what had caused it. Noticing she no longer needed to raise her voice, she realized that everyone had stopped firing their weapons. A ceasefire had been called so that lane maintenance could be conducted.

After checking the gun to make sure it was empty, Brandon returned it to the compartment in the wall. He casually swept his hand across the surface of the table, brushing the stray shell casings onto the floor. They rolled into a groove and onto the conveyor system carrying the shells to a recycling area. Brandon placed his fingers under Camile's chin, gently guiding her gaze to meet his earnest eyes. Their usual blue-green hue appeared steely gray amidst the tones of the weapons range.

"Listen," he said softly, "nothing can prepare a soldier, or anyone for that matter, for the atrocities that take place on the battlefield. I've seen things that go beyond most people's wildest nightmares, but when I come home I put it aside. At least I try to. I've learned to take comfort in the fact I'm doing all I can to make things better rather than discourage myself for the things I can't fix. Sometimes we have to separate what we do from who we are or else, we'll lose sight of ourselves."

Brandon paused briefly to greet a passing plain clothes officer, clapping him on the shoulder as he walked by.

Folding his arms, he continued, "I've heard Coexistent recruits accuse our people of being desensitized, but that's not the case. Our sensitivity is the essence of our humanity and a precious reminder of how delicate it is. Something that valuable, that powerful, should be protected. If you expose it so readily for the wrong person, they'll try to strip it away from you and use it tear you apart in the process. I've seen it happen to the best of people. Still, dwelling on painful events does nothing to change the past, but contrary to what some people think, we don't ignore what we feel. Instead, we channel all our sadness, anger and hate that comes from tragedy and focus on making damn sure it never happens again."

Brandon's statement prompted Camile to realize that although she had come a long way in controlling her emotions, she still had much work to do in order to gain full control of them.

Chapter 47

Tested

Over time, Deltine officials noticed residents falling off the grid. Simultaneously, several recruits had also fallen beyond detection in the Coexistent World. Camile's father called a meeting to discuss the situation with military personnel and asked that Camile join them. As she took her place at the table, she saw a few familiar faces. Her mother, Sir Drayden, Commander Wilder and Jeremy were among them. After explaining the specifics of the situation, Zephyr turned to his daughter. What he said next would surprise her.

"Camile, how do you suggest we approach this problem?"

Knowing all eyes were on her, Camile thought hard and cleared her throat before giving her response.

"I think we should triangulate the location of missing Transcendents based on their last known coordinates. We should also conduct a thorough inspection for any rifts in the veil within those locations. If any are found, security teams should be assigned to the areas in order to prevent any further trespassing. Depending on how important or dangerous these people are, a bulletin should sent to neighboring states notifying their local governments to be on alert."

"Very good. I see you've been paying close attention. I think I need to keep an eye on my job." Her father beamed, turning his attention to the officers before delegating assignments.

Once the meeting was dismissed, Camile's parents informed her that she'd be working on a special assignment with Jeremy.

"It's routine, but potentially very dangerous given the circumstances," said Zephyr.

"What does it involve?" Jeremy asked.

"One of our potential Coexistent recruits has vanished from our tracking system. Her name's Jade Crawford and she's in the running to participate in one of our most important operations."

"And which operation is that?"

"For now, that information is classified, but trust me, you'll know about it soon enough," Kylie answered.

"Your mission is to find Jade and if she's stable, return her to the compound," Zephyr explained. "In the event she's beyond recovery..." His eyes shifted to Jeremy. "Well, you'll have to make a judgment call."

Before Camile could inquire as to what his last statement meant, the private meeting was adjourned.

*   *   *

The room was in total disarray; a clear sign of a struggle. Camile found the silence unsettling, knowing how deceptive it could be. They entered the sunny kitchen, where they saw a woman sprawled face down on the floor, a knife clutched loosely in her hand. After kicking it away, Jeremy cautiously analyzed the woman before declaring her to be alive, although critically injured. Upon getting a look at her face, slightly obscured by dark, wavy hair, Camile knew it was Jade. Justine, who was ordered to accompany Camile and Jeremy on the mission, returned from inspecting the other rooms and gave the all clear.

"It looks like whoever beat us here is long gone," she announced.

"They did quite a number on her," Jeremy informed.

"I'll say. She's a hot mess." Justine frowned.

"What now?" asked Camile.

"She comes with us. It's not safe to leave her here in this condition. Whoever's responsible for this might come back to finish the job," Jeremy explained, positioning himself to lift the battered woman, but suddenly paused. "You're right. She should be scanned."

Since no one in the room had said anything, Camile deduced he was responding to a telepathic suggestion from Justine, who approached an unconscious Jade and scanned her with a small, remote-control sized device. It had a tiny screen which displayed a view of the woman's bones and veins. Justine invited Camile to come closer to get a better view as she explained how to operate the gadget. As the device was passed over Jade's right shoulder, Camile noticed a tiny object, the size of a small nail head.

"What's that?" she asked.

"That's just one of our tracers," Justine explained in a singsong manner. "Maybe we could find a clue why it suddenly went back online the day before our mission."

She continued moving the device along, but stopped at Jade's right hand, spotting something between the base knuckles.

"What the—? There's a second tracer here and it sure as hell ain't one of ours." Justine's lips tightened.

"Do you think that's what's causing the interference? Could it be the reason why people are dropping off the grid?" Camile inquired.

"It's too early to determine." Justine shrugged, turning her attention to Jeremy. "You think the rebels are the ones who beat us here?"

"That's certainly a possibility, but I can think of at least one other group capable of something like this. One thing's for sure, this wasn't a random incident. Change in plans." Jeremy knelt beside the woman and removed a small pouch from his utility belt. It was less than an inch in length on each side and contained thin strips. Any other time, Camile would have guessed was a breath freshener, but she knew otherwise as she watched Jeremy part the woman's lips with his fingers. He was about to poison her.

Was this the judgment call Dad was talking about?

Appalled, Camile attempted to halt the process.

"No, wait. I think we should stick with the original plan. We might be able to learn something from her."

"She's a liability we can't afford. Chances are she'll die anyway," Justine replied. "At least this way it'll be quick and painless."

"If she dies, it should be on her terms, not ours," Camile said sternly.

"Okay. Just remember this is a matter of cross-world security." Jeremy returned the items to his pocket before lifting the woman into his arms. The shocked expression on Justine's face was immeasurable.

"Yeah, and if something goes wrong, it's your ass. That's for damn sure." She sneered.

And that's supposed to scare me? Whatever, Camile thought.

*   *   *

Jade was immediately taken to Caldaq's central infirmary where she was treated for serious injuries. Camile, Jeremy and Justine watched the surgery from a booth above the operating room as the patient was stabilized. Finally, the surgeons focused their attention on Jade's hand, where the mysterious tracer was located. According to the doctors, the device was heat sensitive and programmed to emit an alert upon removal since it required constant contact with Jade's DNA. After cautious consideration, the surgeons decided to carefully insert a small inflatable capsule into the patient's hand and fill it with some of her blood before guiding the tiny device inside. Finally, they were able to extract the capsule, containing the tracer, and placed it in a small bath of water designed to mimic Jade's body temperature.

"You've taken a great risk by bringing someone with an unknown tracer into our facility," Zephyr stated as he entered the observation booth. His disappointment was abundantly obvious. "Whose idea was this?"

"Hers," Jeremy and Justine said in unison, indicating Camile.

"Jeremy, you had the authority to overrule. Why didn't you?"

"Because in that moment, I agreed with her, sir. In hindsight, I can't fully understand why I failed to request a team to remove the device offsite, prior to bringing the subject here," Jeremy replied, his face mildly contorted with confusion. "Minister, I think I should be relieved of duty. My judgment was impaired and until I can figure out why it happened, I believe I'm a liability to the team."

"Jeremy, I can't afford to lose one of my best men right now. Your request is denied. Nevertheless, we will get to the bottom of this," Zephyr said before dismissing Jeremy and Justine. Once they left, he turned to his daughter.

"Camile, I think I know what happened today."

"You think I had something to do with swaying Jeremy's decision, don't you?"

Zephyr nodded, his expression grim. "I was hoping I wouldn't have to make this request, but I have no other choice than to have the weight of your anchor increased.

"Where is this anchor, anyway?"

"You know I can't tell you that, sweetheart."

"I know it's restricting me from using my powers, but how am I supposed to learn how to control them if I can't use them? Don't you think this method of control is counterproductive?"

"It's necessary for the time being. Before you can be trained to control your powers you need to be more stable than you are. You're almost there. Just be a little more patient. Your mother and I believe in you, so do a lot of other people, whether or not they come out and admit it. You just need to believe in yourself." He paused a moment, cracking a proud smile. "There's something you should know. You passed another test."

"What test?"

"It was Jeremy's job to test you today. You fought to preserve Jade's life when he suggested ending it. He had no intention of killing her, but wanted to see if you possessed the strength to object to such a suggestion, even if it meant standing up to authority. But somewhere along the line you managed to color his judgment, which is why we have to strengthen your anchor."

Camile's father suggested that she return to her quarters for a nap. Naturally, she didn't feel much like sleeping, so she decided to do some sketching, something she hadn't done in a long time. Before her pencil could touch the paper, Camile felt a sudden sense of panic. It almost seemed as though the ground had fallen from beneath her. She wasn't in any physical pain, but she felt like her soul was about to be ripped from her body. If Camile had to explain the sensation, she would have described it as being dangerously close to death. The most terrifying thing of all was the fact she couldn't see or fight it. Much to her relief, the uncomfortable sensation had eased, but lingered faintly. Carefully making her way to her bed, Camile suspected her father had suggested rest since he knew she would experience the episode. She knew the tiring experience was due to an adjustment in the mysterious anchor.

*   *   *

Jade's recovery had come quicker than anticipated and she began to rouse just days after her surgery. Camile stood with her father at the woman's bedside. When Jade opened her eyes, Camile had a hunch of what inspired her namesake. Jade's eyes were pale green and complimented her sun-kissed skin, softening the appearance of her otherwise sharp facial features. After going through the inevitable questions, *Where am I?* and *Why am I here?*, Jade gently rolled onto her side. She propped her head on her hand, regarding Camile's father with a smile and gluttonous eyes.

"That's an interesting getup you're wearing. So, handsome, what agency do you work for? FBI, CIA, NSA…?" She smirked.

"Jade, you were in pretty bad shape when we found you. We need to find the people responsible, but we need your help," Zephyr stated, ignoring the question.

"Hmm…Is that so?" she said in a singsong manner, gliding her fingers across the neckline of her infirmary garb. "What are you gonna do for me in return?"

Rolling her eyes, Camile decided to end Jade's miserable attempt at seduction.

"We saved your life. That already makes it a square deal, don't you think?" Camile deadpanned.

Based on the expression on Jade's face, the reminder interrupted her fantasy like a needle scratching a music record.

"Not that I'm not grateful or anything, but I was hoping for something a little more...fun." Jade winked at Zephyr.

"Not interested," Zephyr said flatly. "What I am interested in is finding out who attacked you."

"You're no fun. Oh, well...There's plenty of fish in the sea, honey." Jade snorted before noticing Jeremy enter the room. "Ooh, and I see me a keeper."

"Lady, this isn't a night club, so spare yourself the humiliation and start talking," Camile said forcefully, hoping it would finally prompt Jade to cooperate.

"Ouch!" Jade grimaced, feigning offense. "Looks like someone got up on the wrong side of the bed this morning. From what I gather, it must've been empty."

Though mildly irritated, Camile decided against responding to the snarky remark.

"Do you remember anything about what happened to you or who attacked you?" Jeremy asked.

"No, sugar. I can't remember a damn thing. One thing's for sure, I'd certainly remember a sexy man like you." Jade giggled, flirtatiously biting her lower lip. "I'd rather talk about you. You got a girlfriend, baby?"

Jeremy appeared to think for a moment before giving his response.

"Maybe we can discuss that later." He smiled, "but now it's important that you help us to the best of your ability."

Discuss it later? Camile thought. *I sure hope he's only trying to appease her. Oh, who am I kidding? He's with Justine, so it's not my problem.*

"Try to focus and remember exactly what your attacker looked like," Jeremy continued.

Jade closed her eyes for a few moments, exhaling a deep breath.

"Sorry, baby. I got nothin'," she said, transfixing her gaze on Jeremy, clearly undressing him with her eyes. "It's not for the lack of trying. If there's anyone who could make a girl talk, I'm sure it would be you. Maybe if you take me back to the scene of the crime it'll jog my memory. We could make a date out of it."

That was all Camile could stomach.

"Well, it'll have to be chaperoned, 'cause we're coming too," she said.

"You're overstepping a bit, sweetheart, but nonetheless it's a good idea," Zephyr whispered, a faint smile indicated his mild amusement.

"Looks like I'll be the fifth wheel on this one," Sir Drayden announced casually as he entered.

For the first time Camile wasn't the central focus of Sir Drayden's attention. It was clear he saw something in Jade he didn't trust. Based on the expression on Jade's face, the feeling was mutual.

*   *   *

Once back at her residence, Jade explained everything she did on the day of her attack. Sir Drayden and Jeremy followed closely on her heels while Camile and her father traveled behind them. Jade's demeanor took a gradual shift as she began remembering sounds and smells from the day in question. However, she recalled seeing no one. Immediately upon entering her kitchen, she gasped, clutching her chest as she stepped into the spot where she was discovered.

"Oh, God," she exclaimed softly.

"What did you remember?" Jeremy asked.

"I'm not sure. It's just...*weird.*"

"Try to relax," Camile instructed.

"I need a minute. I gotta use the bathroom. Please, excuse me." Jade zipped out of the kitchen. Sir Drayden and Jeremy were quick on her tail. Camile and her father followed shortly after. She heard Jade shouting in protest as they entered the hallway.

"You gotta be kidding me! I said give me a minute. Can't a woman pee in peace?"

Camile saw the furious woman waving her hands around as she continued to give Jeremy and Sir Drayden—both of whom were standing in the bathroom doorway—a piece of her mind. "I promised to cooperate with you. The least you can do is give me a little privacy."

"Fine, I see how this makes you uncomfortable. Camile, take our place," Sir Drayden replied.

"Is this really necessary?" Camile quirked her brow.

"Okay, fine! I can't hold it forever. Just know that I'm gonna sue your asses off," Jade snapped.

Sir Drayden and Jeremy stepped aside to let Camile through, but at the last minute, Jade shoved her out and locked the door.

"Sorry guys, but this is a private matter," she said from the other side of the door.

They soon heard the sound of liquid streaming into the toilet and regarded one another with semi-amused glances.

"See? You guys are lucky she didn't go on your shoes." Camile laughed softly. "What do you think she saw? Do you think she remembers her attackers?"

Jeremy shrugged. "I'm not sure, but she seemed—"

"Shh," Sir Drayden hushed. "Hear that?"

"Yeah, she's like a racehorse," Camile quipped before hearing a dull thud.

"No, she's not. She definitely remembered something. She just doesn't want to share it with us," he frowned before kicking the door in.

"What are you doing? She's—" Camile paused when she looked in the bathroom.

Jade was gone.

The sound they'd been hearing wasn't that of her relieving herself, but a strategically placed bottle of mouthwash that had fallen into the toilet. Jeremy snatched open the shower curtain, revealing an open window.

"She's good," Camile acknowledged.

By the time they arrived at street-level, Jade was nowhere to be seen. However, since she was still fitted with a tracking device, Jeremy was able to pinpoint her location. Jade was on a city bus nearly a block away. Camile attempted to break into a run, but her father stopped her.

"Wait," he instructed before facing Sir Drayden, who sighed with marked annoyance.

"I hope you know how hard it is for me to get these things," he said, pulling something small from his pocket.

Camile didn't get a good look at the object before he hurled it towards the bus. There was a streak of light that resembled a small shooting star. To her surprise, it struck the bus and momentarily surrounded it with what appeared to be a ball of rippling water. Once the distortion disappeared, the bus had slowed significantly.

"Now we can run. This stuff doesn't last long," Zephyr said.

They ran, catching up to the bus with little effort. When they boarded, they were met with a chaotic scene playing out in slow motion. Passengers were regarding Jade with disdainful glances, their mouths contorted as their shouts filled the air like a slow dense fog. However, she seemed to be enjoying the madness.

"Brace yourself. Things are about to catch up."

As soon as Zephyr finished his statement, the scene played out in real time, accelerating the disruptive racket.

"How did she manage to cause so much trouble in such a short time?" Camile asked.

"Easy," Jeremy answered, his lids heavy.

The energy on the bus went from gray to black in a matter of moments as behavior grew increasingly uncivilized. Jade was amused and continued laughing wildly at the situation, egging people on.

Sir Drayden walked to the front of the bus, looked out the front window, then returned to Camile, Zephyr and Jeremy.

"Hold on," he said simply before vanishing into thin air.

Camile opened her mouth to say something, but was promptly interrupted by her father.

"Don't ask. Just do it."

Just as they braced themselves on poles for stability, there was a sound of a car crash up ahead. The bus driver slammed on the breaks, prompting people to fly around like ragdolls. When it was over, Camile witnessed injuries sustained by most of the passengers, but nothing too severe. Sir Drayden reemerged as Jeremy retrieved Jade, who was pinned beneath a heavyset woman.

"What's her condition?" he asked.

"A couple of fractured ribs, but she'll live." Jeremy gingerly positioned a grimacing Jade away from the rest of the passengers, most of whom were nursing each other's injuries.

Sir Drayden knelt beside Jade and looked deeply into her eyes. After a moment of apparent transfixion, he frowned as he touched her shoulder.

"Not for long," he replied. "I'm not gonna lie to you Jade, this will hurt a lot if you resist. Just remember, the pain is temporary."

"Wait, you can't just—" Camile protested.

"Let him do it," Jade cried. "I don't wanna die, but I have a feeling it's supposed to be this way. I don't know what's happening to me."

"I do. That's why I have to do this," Sir Drayden stated. "Are you ready?"

Jade's breath quickened as tears streamed down her face.

"Not really. I'm scared as hell. Do I get at least get a last request?" she asked.

"What is it?"

"Him." Jade glanced at Jeremy. "I want him to kiss me. Actually, I want him to do a lot more than just kiss me, but something tells me that's not gonna happen."

Jeremy cautiously approached Jade and knelt beside her, opposite Sir Drayden. Camile could already feel the jealousy bubbling inside her even though she knew he was already spoken for.

"I can't kiss you, but I'll hold your hand," Jeremy said.

Jade sighed in mild disappointment. "Well, that answers my question. You *do* have a girlfriend, don't you? Whoever she is, tell her I said she's one lucky bitch," she smiled, extending her hand to take Jeremy's. Sir Drayden didn't wait for her to fulfill her final wish as he placed his hand over Jade's chest before her hand made contact with Jeremy's. She whimpered in agony before she fell silent.

"Just when I thought you couldn't get anymore cold-hearted," Camile said in disbelief. "I didn't like her, but a promise is a promise."

"Young lady, first of all, I didn't promise her anything. Second of all, she was corrupted and had to be dealt with." His eyes shifted to Jeremy. "And you of all people should know better than to try indulging a person's desire for physical contact during their passing."

Still stricken with disbelief, Camile exited the bus to get some air. As she surveyed the scene of the accident, she saw flames shooting from beneath the hood of one of the smashed cars. To her horror, it still held occupants—an unconscious driver and a crying toddler. At that moment she could feel her father and Sir Drayden approaching from behind.

"There are people in there!" Camile made a motion to come to their aid, but was stopped by Sir Drayden, who stepped in front of her.

"It's not your place," he said calmly.

"Excuse me? Look, you can put me on punishment later, but you're not gonna stop me from going over there," she snapped.

Camile made a motion to walk, but felt as though both her feet were super-glued to the pavement. Startled, she looked to her father.

"Tell him to let me go," she demanded.

"I'm afraid I can't do that, sweetheart. Sir Drayden has a point." Zephyr turned his eyes to the fiery scene. "They have to do it."

Camile stopped struggling when she saw people uniting in a joint effort to rescue the people trapped in the blazing car. She witnessed people—some of whom had been arguing just moments earlier—working in harmony, forsaking their differences for the sake of saving a life. After several minutes, the flames were under control and the victims were freed from the wreckage. Though the fire had been extinguished, Camile witnessed a flickering flame amidst the charred wreckage and smoldering rubber. It was hope. Sir Drayden returned to the bus, leaving Camile alone with her father.

"Unfortunately, Jade got jaded, but she wasn't beyond salvation," Zephyr explained. "She'll be fine."

The statement struck Camile as odd since she had just witnessed the woman die.

"What? But Sir Drayden—"

"Did what he felt was necessary after he saw what we all missed. No one bothered to investigate whether or not our tracer was affected by the one implanted by Jade's attackers. Apparently, ours was corrupted and triggered chemical reactions in her body, prompting her to act out. Since we're too far from the facility to safely extract and replace the tracer, Sir Drayden decided to take a drastic, yet proactive approach."

"By killing her?"

Zephyr nodded. "By doing that, the tracer automatically deactivated thus eliminating the problem. She's already been revived, but has been sedated until we return to Caldaq. She's been through a lot these past few days and needs all the rest she can get."

I know the feeling, Camile thought before asking, "If he only needed to reboot Jade, why did he cause the accident?"

"He did it to jolt those people back to humanity. Unfortunately, they're often at their best during times of crisis. This is no exception."

"They can also be at their worst," Camile muttered.

"You have no idea, but you'll see for yourself soon enough," Sir Drayden replied, a haunting certainty in his voice.

*   *   *

A meditative recharge was just what Camile needed after such a chaotic day. Sitting across from Jeremy in the Celestia, she found herself unable to relax completely. She couldn't help wondering if he would've eventually indulged Jade's desire for a kiss had Sir Drayden not intervened. At the close of the session, Camile approached Jeremy as casually as she could.

"How's Jade?" she asked.

"She's recovering well. Can't remember much, though. In her case, that's a good thing. It'll give her a better chance at making a fresh start. It's just a shame we'll probably never know who attacked her. The important thing is she's okay and will be ready to go to Saulnan for her training."

"Well, it's a good thing Justine wasn't there to see Jade flirting with you like that," Camile said half-jokingly.

"Why's that?" Jeremy furrowed his brow.

"She's your girlfriend, for starters." She laughed, joining him in the simulated sunlight. "I think she'd be a little jealous about something like that."

"Justine's a secure woman who doesn't allow such trivial things to bother her. She's not my girlfriend, though. Where'd you get that idea?"

"My own stupid assumption, I guess," Camile answered, keeping her demeanor as poised as possible. On the inside, she was all but doing back flips.

The artificial moon faded as the room suddenly flooded with daylight. Jeremy grimaced, turning his gaze upward.

"That's unusual," he said before resuming the discussion. "Anyway, we used to be a couple, but it didn't work out. Thankfully, we're comfortable enough to remain close friends."

I sure hope it's not a friends-with-benefits type of relationship, Camile thought to herself.

Chapter 48

Strange Alliance

"Damn it!" Camile recoiled.

She had been petting the commissioner's dog when it suddenly bit her arm, grazing her skin.

"Let me see it," Vincent reached for her arm, but she refused. "Oh, come on." He gently seized it and rolled up the torn sleeve. "It's not that bad. The skin's barely broken."

"Thanks to my quick reflexes." Camile eyed the large dog.

"Don't do that. You're challenging him," Vincent said urgently, prompting Camile to look away.

"What's the point to all this again? I like animals, but the feeling clearly isn't mutual."

"You disappoint me, Camile. All this time I'd figure you'd have gotten it by now." He smiled faintly. "Animals often serve as our compass to the world's changes. They help keep us connected to nature. Furthermore, in times where humans fail, animals can be our greatest allies. Their actions, no matter how trivial it may seem to the uninitiated, can help generate a drastic shift in human behavior. Animals see past false fronts and facades and into the depths of intent. They are not as easily fooled or disheartened as humans. Nor are they intentionally vicious when unthreatened or undisturbed."

Vincent doused Camile's arm with water from her canteen. "Animals may kill, but they usually only do so to maintain their survival. What makes humans different is that they dress up their malicious acts with their twisted agendas and present it as their quest for survival when in fact it's nothing more than a bid for power, greed or revenge."

Vincent retrieved a container from his pocket. It resembled lip balm. He uncapped it and glided it across the scrape on Camile's forearm.

"There," he said. "That should take care of the sting."

Camile found herself entranced by the sight of the fading scratch and the shimmering solution that was healing it. Stricken with a frightening sense of déjà vu, she shuddered, instinctively wrapping her arms around herself.

"Is something wrong?" asked Vincent, his face slightly scrunched with an inquisitive expression.

"No. I'm fine," Camile replied, knowing that wasn't entirely true/

Feeling the need to do something constructive with her pent-up energy, Camile decided to go horseback riding after their session since doing so always seemed to make her feel liberated. Monticello trotted around the track for two leisurely laps. Camile found her mind wandering as her tension lifted. She wondered why she hadn't figured out the nature of Jeremy's relationship with Justine on her own. It led Camile to contemplate potential ways to strengthen her own bond with him. She hoped Jade wouldn't prove to be an obstacle in her endeavor, but remembered she was set to leave for Saulnan. Suddenly, Monticello grunted loudly and bucked twice before breaking into a full gallop in the opposite direction of the trail, clearing the entrance to the track and pushing past three guards who unsuccessfully tried to stop him.

This can't be happening again, Camile thought as she hung on for dear life.

"Camile, what are you doing? You're going the wrong way," Vincent yelled as she bolted past him.

"I can't get him to stop," she called over her shoulder, seeing Vincent dash over to one of the stallions and mount it. When she returned her attention forward, she saw the familiar rippling distortion in the air, several feet away. For a moment, Camile considered jumping off the steed, but she knew she would sustain serious injury and possibly get trampled by the animal. Pulling the reins as hard as she could, she sternly ordered the horse to stop. Monticello finally heeded her command, coming to a sudden halt just inches from the rift. Unprepared for the sudden stop, Camile was thrown forward and into the aperture. Luckily, she landed in a soft pile of mossy grass, but the impact still left her with a sore back and aching head.

After slowly rising to her feet, Camile made an about face to exit the rift she had just entered. In doing so, she nearly bumped into a woman, but was able to stop in time. Just when she was about to apologize, she realized it was Makeda—the devourer whose blood she nearly drank during a moment of confusion. Makeda wasn't alone, there were three men with her, each digging a shallow grave, presumably their own. Impatient, Makeda ordered them to dig faster.

"I ain't got all day. Put your spines into it!" She laughed. Suddenly, her jubilation halted and her deep dark eyes met the path of Camile's stunned gaze. The men also looked in her direction, puzzled.

With her breath caught in her throat, Camile backed away slowly, as though retreating from a pack of voracious dogs. To her surprise, Makeda turned away and continued barking orders to the men.

They can't see me, Camile thought, trying to remain as still and quiet as possible while watching them, wondering why the men weren't putting up a fight to escape their inevitable burial. Noticing that they each had biceps nearly half the size of her own waist, she figured they were more than capable of overpowering the female devourer. Analyzing them a bit further, Camile assumed two of them were brothers. They each possessed similar eyes and large spade-shaped noses on their ebony faces. Even their athletic body types were similar, though one was a few inches shorter than the other. The third male was slightly lighter with a deep mocha complexion and his build was just as muscular as his male comrades. His strong features were set off by his lifeless black eyes. Camile immediately recognized him as Tareeq, the man she had seen in a verbal dispute with Sir Drayden.

Once the men were done digging, they stood at the foot of their respective graves. Camile noticed a fourth grave off to the side. Makeda was standing at the edge of it, her back towards the opening. Camile then began to wonder if she was about to witness a group suicide, but the next words she heard quickly disproved that theory.

"Time to go hunting!" Makeda declared before gyrating her statuesque body, slowly winding it like a belly dancer.

Makeda's midriff top provided a generous view of her smooth ebony abdomen, on which an uneven horizontal indentation formed just above her navel, stretching out across her torso. Groaning through clenched teeth, Makeda shifted the upper portion of her body, which now resembled that of a doll that had been twisted at the waist. The elongated wounds on the back of her arms split open as crepe-like flesh began to scroll outward, forming translucent wings. After the wings flapped a few times, the lower and upper halves of the body separated as the latter portion rose into the air. Her lower extremities fell into the grave with a slosh.

The other devourers followed suit, performing their own grotesque transformations. Camile had read about the devourers' need to detach their lower halves and preserve them in brine. It was the only way they could fly long distances on their delicate wings. Still, their cringe-worthy appearance left Camile unable to suppress her gasp.

She would soon regret it.

Her presence no longer a secret, the devourers quickly advanced in her direction. The speed of her stride was easily outmatched by her flying pursuers, who located her with their sensitive hearing. One of the devourers threw a light dusting of soil in her direction, revealing her exact position.

"Don't kill her! Remember, we have to keep her alive so we can turn her," Makeda urgently instructed.

The two identical males tackled Camile to the ground, knocking the wind out of her. Makeda hovered above, brutally attempting to pry her mouth open. Camile fought as much as she could, but after Tareeq held her nose, she eventually relented, giving in to her need to breathe. He leaned in as though preparing to kiss her, but Makeda stopped him.

"Nah, baby. Let me do it," she smirked, giving him a deep passionate kiss on the lips. Makeda brought her face close to Camile's, opening her mouth.

Seeing the thick, slimy saliva seeping down the devourer's long, tapered tongue, Camile became nauseated and intensified her futile attempt at escape. She tried to bite down on the clammy fingers holding her mouth open, but it was useless. The attempt left her with an acidic taste in her mouth as she unintentionally sampled the flavor of the devourer's digits. Her jaw ached so badly it felt as though it would become dislodged. All that was left for her to do was scream in hopes someone would hear her cries and rescue her before the creatures could strip away her humanity.

"Don't worry. In just a few moments, you'll be thanking us for this," one of the male creatures hissed, his tongue whipping around her ear.

"Of course she will. She's the one who asked for this." Tareeq sneered.

Camile heard an object whizzing through the air, rapidly approaching from the distance. Just when it came into view above her and the creatures it exploded, releasing a fine white powdery substance. The noise distracted the creature holding Camile's head, allowing her to turn just in time to avoid receiving a mouthful of Makeda's saliva, which splattered across her cheek. As the powder rained down, the three males painfully deteriorated. Makeda somehow managed to escape the fatal downpour after hastily rejoining her lower body. Briefly regarding the scene where the males had met their end, she let out a mournful wail before fleeing subsequent shots of the deadly ammunition. When it was all over, Camile furiously wiped the slime off her face while standing to see her savior.

"That was a little too close for comfort," her father remarked, approaching with an unusual looking weapon in his hand. Camile deduced it was a grenade launcher of some kind. Overwhelmed and relieved, she threw her arms around him.

"You're telling me?" she asked, her voice shaky due to the adrenaline pumping through her body. "I'm sure glad you got here when you did." She took a deep breath as the gravity of the situation set in. "I was about to become one of them."

*   *   *

The minor scratches and bruises Camile had sustained in her tussle with the devourers were healed upon her return to the compound. Though the test for devourer infection took about an hour, to her, it seemed like years. However, she considered it well worth the wait since the results turned out to be negative. Assisting the doctor was Nancy, whose red-headed, cherubic appearance soothed Camile's weary eyes.

"Looks like you're all set to go." Nancy's bright smile dissolved into a frown upon noticing her distant gaze. "Am I boring you? You seem preoccupied."

"It's just something one of the devourers said." Camile frowned. "He said...I *asked* for the attack, but that makes no sense whatsoever. I didn't ask for anything. I never said a word to them. I was too busy fighting for my life."

"You're right. That doesn't make sense. Maybe it was just one of their tactics to get inside your head."

"I think it might be working."

"Did you tell your parents about this?"

Camile shook her head. "Not yet. I didn't want to worry them, but I think I have no choice considering the circumstances. I have a feeling it might be important."

"Now's a good a time as any. They're waiting for you in the briefing room."

While traveling the corridors, Camile felt a migraine coming on. Just when she considered returning to the medical facility, the pain rapidly dissipated. Upon entering the meeting hall she saw her father, seated at the head of the long table. Her mother was sitting to his right. Camile also noticed two large men casually entering from the opposite side of the room. One of them bore an uncanny resemblance to one of the male devourers she had fought during her recent encounter. However, he appeared to be at least two decades older. For a split second Camile wondered if the reason they'd gotten past all the security was to renegotiate the treaty or apologize for what had transpired just over an hour earlier. Her question was quickly answered when they used swift, brute force to knock her parents unconscious. Stricken with instant shock and anger, Camile attempted to run to her parents' aid, but was intercepted and grabbed by the larger of the two devourers.

"Don't you dare move a muscle, little lady," he commanded, pulling Camile into a tight chokehold. She instantly felt the pressure build in her head as her circulation was restricted. "You don't have any of them fancy weapons now, do you, my dear? Come with me, and my brother won't kill your folks."

Smelling the stench of death on his breath, Camile nearly retched.

"I'm not gonna leave them here to be infected. I won't let them join your pathetic family!" she hissed.

"Pathetic, huh?" He smirked, sharply turning her head so she could see her parents. "Look at them. *They're* the pathetic ones—can't even protect their own daughter. Thanks to your old man, my boy is dead. That's why you're coming with me. I think it'll be a fair exchange. My only problem is figuring out exactly what to do with you."

The all too familiar sense of fleeting consciousness engulfed Camile with a vice-like grip as the devourer tightened his hold, severing her air supply.

When she finally came to, she had no clue of how long she had been unconscious. Nor did she know where she was. The only things that were obvious to her was the fact she was cold, tied to a banister of some kind and surrounded by angry devourers. The slightest move of her head resulted in a dull pain in her neck, reminding her that she had been choked out. The barren room was meagerly lit and silent except for a faint humming sound in the background. As her eyes adjusted, Camile saw the two devourers who had taken her captive. With them were several others, all with eager expressions. She masked her terror by demanding to know the whereabouts of her parents. The large devourer added to the chill of the environment with an icy laugh as he knelt to face her head-on.

"You're in no position to give orders." He laughed, revealing his crooked, blood-stained teeth. "Rest assured, your parents are fine...for now. If you want to keep it that way, you'd better cooperate with us. Just answer a few questions, but answer them carefully—they will help us decide whether or not you become one of us...or one of them." His voice lowered significantly as he gestured to a pile of dismembered carcasses in the distance. At that point, Camile also saw the source of the faint buzzing sound, a cloud of flies feasting on decaying flesh. A sudden gag interrupted her gasp as he continued, "As you can see, we've had a good hunt tonight, but I think we can make room for dessert."

The lead devourer's statement incited faint jubilation from his followers, all of whom instantly began taking dibs on Camile's internal organs. Panicking, she wriggled as best she could in an attempt to break free of her restraints. The act only seemed to intensify their hold on her, making it even more difficult to breathe.

"Stop it!" he demanded. "Struggling is useless. Now, tell me why you've changed your mind about joining us."

"What are you talking about?" Camile grimaced.

"I'm asking the questions. I suggest you answer them."

"I—I don't know what you're talking about. I never asked to—"

"Ah. So you're saying my son was a liar, huh?"

"Yeah," Camile answered before quickly shaking her head. "I mean no."

"Well, which is it?"

"I don't know."

"Okay. Here's an easier question, one that will prove whether or not you're an imposter; which of the devourers did you make your arrangement with? Give me the name and I'll make you one of us. I already know who he is, so make sure you give me the right answer."

"I can't remember. I think his name began with a 'V' or something."

The devourer exhaled a deep breath and rolled his head as though to loosen the muscles in his neck.

"I see this is going nowhere." He sighed before opening his mouth to reveal his pale tongue splitting down the middle. Out of it, a second proboscis-like tongue sprouted out, whipping around between random words as he continued to speak, his speech slightly hindered by his transformation.

"At least this night won't be a total waste. I'll get my snack and my revenge all in one neat, convenient package."

He reached for Camile's collar to undo her shirt, no doubt to get a clear shot at her thumping heart.

"Vlad!" she cried out. "That's the devourer's name. We made the arrangement awhile ago, but I can't remember when. Now you can turn me. You don't have to kill me. Please, turn me now before it's too late!"

"I'll do nothing of the sort until you tell me your name."

"You already know my name. It's..." Camile's mind drew a blank for a few moments. "My name is...Camile. Why did I almost forget that?"

"Jeremy, take her back to her parents."

Camile was flabbergasted as the devourer in front of her began to change before her very eyes. His deep colored skin drastically lightened to a creamy peach tone and his black eyes faded to a shade of aquatic blue. His dark cropped curly hair sprouted and relaxed into a semi-spiked style in gleaming silver. Camile nearly hyperventilated when the devourer ultimately morphed into Sir Drayden's form. All the other devourers vanished except for one, which transformed into Jeremy. It was a sight that left her questioning reality.

"No! This isn't happening. Why can't you just stay out of my head?" Camile moaned. It wasn't until she brought her hands to her face that she realized she was no longer bound to the pole. In fact, she never was. Upon inspecting her surroundings, she realized she had never left the infirmary. Furthermore, she was still sitting on the examination table.

"Why do you keep doing this to me?" she cried wearily.

"I had no choice," Sir Drayden said in a near whisper, his expression somber. "It was the only way I could find out the truth and confirm my suspicion."

"And what's that?" she asked through clenched teeth. She felt the tears burning her eyes. Resisting the desire to cry, it achingly lodged in her throat.

"Akalina made a deal with the devourers sometime prior to your reintegration." Sir Drayden's frown deepened.

Chapter 49

Indemnity

"A deal? Why?" A concerned expression dominated Kylie's face. "If they turn her, she'll only become one of them. What did Akalina expect to accomplish from that?"

It was a question that apparently plagued everyone sitting at the round table in the briefing room. Sir Drayden, the only person standing, regarded the shaman and Camile's parents with a heavy gaze as he answered.

"My best guess is that Akalina saw it as a way out," he explained. "If Camile were to be turned by the devourers she'd be highly susceptible to her negative impulses, possibly giving in to them. If that happens, Akalina would have a clear path to regain complete control of her body and actions."

"And, chances are, Camile would be lost forever." The shaman's face seemed heavy with concern.

"Obviously that's a chance we can't afford to take," Zephyr stated before turning his attention to Sir Drayden. "She was there today— Makeda. I'm aware you've had dealings with her tribe in the past. Is there any chance you can convince her to spare my daughter?"

"It's unlikely since you killed one of her family members today. If she's anything like the person I knew back then, she'll be hell-bent on getting revenge, no matter what the cost. Nevertheless, I'll try my best to contact her and press upon the importance that her tribe stay out of the council's path and more importantly, away from Camile."

"Wait, you can't trust her. She's been out to turn me into one of those monsters since the day she tried to feed me blood," Camile stated, the very thought turning her stomach. "For all we know this whole thing could be a setup. Besides, who knows if Akalina was banking on the possibility you'll attempt negotiation?"

"We don't, but we have to take decisive action," her father replied. "We have to focus on what is instead of *what if*. All the same, the need for caution is clearly indicated no matter how we ultimately decide to proceed."

*   *   *

The fact that Akalina apparently had a backup plan put into place prior to the reintegration unnerved Camile greatly. Although she had been ordered to rest, doing so proved an impossible task for her anxious mind. She found herself trying to figure out Akalina's thought process in hopes it would help reveal the grand scheme of her plan. Yet at the same time, Camile feared doing so could possibly open a door for her return. Nevertheless, she knew that Akalina's plans could possibly affect lives other than her own and felt compelled to expose the endeavors of her dark half. Camile stood before the mirror in her room and stared into her own eyes. Despite the clarity of their color, she found herself trying to break through the gray haze obscuring the remnants of Akalina's misdeeds.

"What did you do?" she wondered aloud. "What exactly were you up to, Akalina?"

After a few uneventful moments of straining to remember something, anything that would help her uncover at least one more piece to the puzzle, Camile paused. She realized that by struggling she was actually pushing herself away from what she wanted to know. In order to get what she wanted she had to do the opposite of what she normally would. Taking a deep breath, she released the tension in her mind, giving in to the relaxation that flowed through her body like a stream. In a blink of an eye, everything around her seemed to liquefy as the border between past and present began to dissolve. Camile's reflection gradually vanished and was replaced with Jezebel's petite frame.

Akalina looked at her mentor, pacing slowly back and forth as she spoke.

"We have to protect our plans," Jezebel said. "Once again, they're at risk of being exposed."

"Wait. I thought we already handled this. Are you saying Hyacinth was killed for nothing?" asked Stacy, who brushed her shoulder-length ringlets away from her tan face. Her vibrant, unfazed demeanor led Camile to believe this discussion had taken place prior to her torturous healing at Akalina's hands.

"Hey, idiot, use your brain for once." Akalina sneered. "It's gonna be an ongoing fight to keep our plans safe."

"Right," Jezebel confirmed. "Tabitha isn't nearly as cunning as her predecessor, but we have to eliminate her regardless. The same goes for anyone who works closest to Sir Drayden. The scribe mentioned that his right hand must be eliminated in order to safely assure the secrecy of our plans."

"But what if he's left-handed?" Stacy scrunched her face.

"It was a figure of speech. Akalina's right, you really are an idiot," Jezebel spat before dismissing the woman. She then regarded her apprentice with a grim expression. "You know, there's always a chance of something not going according to plan. If for some reason you get caught, it's critical that you protect the safety of the rebels. The council has proven ways of loosening the lips of even the most hardened criminals. In order to prevent that from happening, everyone involved in the mission will be provided with an escape in the form of a pill. It'll be quick and painless compared to what's in store for anyone who gets caught."

"I've already proven that I'm tougher than most people."

"Yes, you have, but in the worst case scenario that won't be enough."

"Don't worry. I'm not afraid of dying if it means preventing Camile from getting everything I earned, but I don't think that will be necessary. I have a little insurance."

"What are you talking about?" Jezebel furrowed her brow as she halted her pace.

"I made an arrangement." Akalina beamed. "If I happen to get caught and if I'm lost in this supposed 'reintegration', one of the devourers will convert me. I'd rather be one of them than under that bitch's control. Plus, I think it'll increase my chances of coming back to finish my work to reclaim what's mine."

"*I* don't even dare attempt to communicate with them directly. How did you manage to do that without getting caught?" Jezebel's eyes nearly matched the diameter of her open mouth.

"My little secret." Akalina smirked.

"That was very foolish of you to have done that without informing me first."

"I thought I'd surprise you. You're the one who always told me I should be more proactive, remember?"

"What stopped them from turning you right then and there?"

"Didn't you know?" Akalina asked, overdramatically feigning surprise. "They want Tabitha dead as much as we do."

*   *   *

Unnerved by the latest revelation, Camile spent her days looking over her shoulder—not knowing who was a rogue or a devourer just waiting to dig into her. However, she managed to avoid allowing her fearful caution to paralyze her. One of the few people she felt comfortable around was Nancy, whom she met for lunch a few days after her latest incident with Sir Drayden, which she discussed at length.

"I hate it when he messes with my head like that. It always makes it hard for me to make heads or tails of anything. Was the whole checkup even real? Did I even see you that day?" she asked.

"Yeah, of course, you did," Nancy answered, avoiding eye contact. It was enough to rouse Camile's suspicion.

"You didn't have anything to do with it, did you?"

"Okay, I confess. I told him about your concerns right after you left to meet with your parents." Smiling faintly, Nancy finally met her gaze. "He intercepted you before you could leave the infirmary. He knew the best way to unlock the truth from your mind was to get to you before you could clam up and dismiss your own concerns. I hope you're not mad at me. I know how you feel about him, but I truly believed he could help. I guess I was right."

Camile's disappointment and mild irritation took a backseat to her curiosity as she noticed something. Nancy's behavior was predictable when it came to Sir Drayden. She would smile excessively, her face would flush with color and she appeared slightly flustered whenever she spoke about him.

"Oh, my gosh," Camile exclaimed in an almost songlike manner. "You're in love with him, aren't you?" she asked softly as though to avoid publicizing a terrible secret.

Nancy's face nearly turned as red as her hair, confirming her suspicion. Camile was filled with a mixture of disbelief and confusion.

"But why?" Camile grimaced.

"I've always had a thing for older men, but Sir Drayden helped me out of some rough spots, not to mention he saved my life. In addition to that he's smart, witty, powerful, secure, incredibly sexy—" Nancy gushed, her eyes seemed entranced by the very thought of him.

"I think I heard enough," Camile interrupted through a deep breath, feeling uncomfortable about the references Nancy was making.

"Hey, you asked." Nancy shrugged.

"Did you tell him how you feel?"

"Yeah, and I regret it."

"Why? Did he turn you down?"

Nancy nodded. "Said there was no place in his life for a romantic relationship with me."

"Well, that's putting it delicately," Camile remarked sarcastically.

"To be honest, I think that's as delicate as a man like Sir Drayden can get," Nancy said through an empty chortle. "I think the real issue he had was our age difference. He said I was too young for him. On top of everything else, I don't think he ever got over losing his wife."

"Looks like we're both unlucky when it comes to love, huh?" Camile sighed softly.

"Something tells me you'll be a lot luckier than me. After all, you're much younger, so you still have time. As for this old girl, I'm apt to grab whatever I can get at this point." Nancy laughed, but it did nothing to conceal the heartbreaking loneliness in her eyes.

"Don't be like that. There's gotta be someone out there for both of us. They just need a map and maybe one of those shuttles, 'cause they're taking too damn long," Camile quipped. Nancy voiced her amusement through a subtle laugh.

"You certainly got your father's sense of humor." She smiled.

Camile thought about what Nancy said earlier about being rejected by Sir Drayden and something struck her as odd.

"Wait a minute. Hyacinth wasn't too far from your age, was she? How could he say you're too young for him?"

"Let's just say Hyacinth looked damn good for her age. Then again, so does Sir Drayden," Nancy blushed anew.

Oh, boy, Camile thought. *Poor Nancy's got it bad for the guy,*

"What about you? Got your eye on someone in particular?"

"I guess you could say that, but he barely knows I'm alive. Story of my life." Camile forced a halfhearted chuckle.

"I see you don't want to name names, but I think your odds of getting his attention will improve over the next few days. According to your blood workup, your hormone and pheromone levels are going off the charts. It's normal—for a Transcendent female, anyway. It should regulate by the end of the week, but until then, you'll have a physiological advantage in attracting the opposite sex. There's no guarantee, though."

"There never is, but uncertainty is something I've had plenty of practice with. I should be able to handle it like a pro," Camile replied, hoping her words would inspire her ability to do so.

Chapter 50

Contagious Vibes

In the days that followed, Sir Drayden's noticeable absence and unceremonious return culminated in his failure to locate Makeda or any of her followers. Disappointed, he and the rest of the council agreed that Camile's defense training should be upgraded to include evasive ambush tactics and, eventually, devourer slaying—something she would have to learn in a hands-on setting. During the meeting in which her new curriculum had been laid out, Camile expressed her concern of being in the presence of any devourer, given Akalina's apparent deal with them. The magistrate mentioned that although the council has a preference of avoiding confrontation, doing so in this case could prove more damaging since it would allow the problem to fester.

Reflecting on the meeting, Camile wondered how soon she would have to face the creatures again. Her thoughts were interrupted by the twinge in her back, warning her that she was no longer alone. Whipping around, she saw Excelsior watching her from a distance. Camile was unnerved, not knowing how long the massive tiger had been there or why he seemed so interested in her. Not wanting to turn her back to him, she decided to head back to the privacy of her quarters. Before she could take a step, she was suddenly taken down to the ground. After a brief struggle, she managed to flip herself onto her back to battle her attacker face-to-face.

"Jeremy?" She grimaced, looking up into his chocolaty almond-shaped eyes set in skin as creamy as peanut butter. His five o'clock shadow balanced his fuzzy dome, giving him a more rugged appearance than she was used to. There was no denying that he looked delicious in his off-duty attire; denim jeans, deep blue cardigan and black jacket.

"You're still unprepared," he said simply as he continued to remain on all fours, hovered over her. He seemed to go out of his way to take care not to make any contact with her body that might be considered inappropriate.

"I thought Brandon was supposed to be teaching me how to handle an ambush," she wondered aloud.

"Then I guess you failed your first lesson. The first thing you must learn is that you shouldn't assume anything. Open your mind to the possibility that anything can happen." Jeremy smiled subtly, the dimple above his lip accentuating his adorably flat nose.

"Anything?" Camile sat up as Jeremy sat back on his heels. "You mean like this?" She poked him in the ribs and was surprised to hear him cry out in jubilation. A faint chuckle escaped his throat as he gently pushed her away. Camile felt as though she had just struck gold.

"Oh, I think I found your weakness," she sang slowly, rebounding for another poke at his midsection.

Jeremy continued to resist and before long they were rolling around in the field trying to tickle one another. Camile succeeded in landing a couple more jabs and was rewarded with his laughter. For her, it was like an audible drug. She relished the sound with the satisfaction that she had caused it. Camile was caught off guard by Jeremy's sudden retaliation and before she knew it, her laughter was mingling with his.

Their voices formed a duet of feral amusement. She tried to shield herself from his agile fingers, but it was useless. Soon, her mirth grew to the brink of agony. She turned her narrowing gaze to the blue sky, surrendering to her child-like delight as joyful tears pooled in the outer corners of her eyes. Jeremy abruptly stopped and stared at her. His light-hearted demeanor fell like a heavy boulder as his smile briefly transformed into a bitter scowl. She could feel the strain of resentment lurking behind Jeremy's normally composed demeanor as he rose to his feet. Recovering from her hysterics, Camile could only bring herself to sit up slowly as she watched him.

"What's the matter?" she asked.

"I just thought…" His voice trailed off as he broke eye contact for a moment. "I think we should keep our relationship strictly professional from now on."

With that, he left after confirming their session for the following day. Camile wondered what had happened to set him off. Then it dawned on her as she recalled something he mentioned months earlier.

My laugh. It must've reminded him of Akalina!

*   *   *

Sitting beside the calm lake, Camile watched as tents were set up on the other side. The beige cloth was aglow with the setting of the orange sun, bursting through the blotchy purple clouds in the late afternoon sky. She wondered how the fabric would hold up to the chilly air of the approaching autumn night that seemed to bring with it a preview of winter. Based on what Camile had heard of the nomadic visitors, they were from a small city called Fyelaun, located in the southern region of Jypsone. They were known as the Fehlahni and traveled the Transcendent World, sharing their gift of song and dance with many nations. It was the same reason that had brought them to Deltine, to perform for the Caldaq council and invited guests during the upcoming festival.

A raft pulled up to the lake bank, several feet away from where Camile was sitting. Boarding it was a small group of glamorous looking women, wearing flowing hooded cloaks and glittering gold headpieces. One of the women stopped upon seeing Camile, who gave the group a welcoming smile. Stepping away from the rest of her flock, the bronzed woman approached, introducing herself as Reena. Her glossy raven mane seemed too perfect to be natural. Every wavy strand was immaculately coifed and caught the light like a mirror. Her eyebrows were straight and full, accentuating her luminous black eyes, the whites contrasting with her deeply tanned reddish skin.

"You're Camile Leon, aren't you?" she asked, her modestly plump lips curled into a smile beneath her long narrow nose.

"How did you know?" Camile inquired, surprised that the woman actually seemed happy to meet her.

"Your eyes. They're just like your father's. Not many people have eyes like steel that reflect a heart as warm and true as the sun."

"That's poetic. I'll take that as a compliment."

"I can't take credit for such verbal ingenuity. I'm better suited to speaking through my art rather than words." She grinned. "As for the phrase, we've heard it from people who have seen you personally, well before you were divided. You were very young, but you had quite an impact on people, which led to the phrase being circulated throughout my tribe and many others across the world. I know many people are intimidated by your presence, but it truly is an honor to meet you. We're about to return to camp to practice our routine. If it's not an imposition, I would be doubly honored to have you as our guest to preview our performance."

"Sure. But I think it's only fair to warn you that I'm obliged to bring a few guests of my own." Camile indicated the three guards watching her from a few feet away.

Once the raft reached the other side of the lake, the sun surrendered the heavens as the day was swallowed by the early evening. The darkness of the sky made for an intense contrast with the trees, reflecting the warm yellow-orange illumination of the Fehlahni's campgrounds. It seemed as though the tribe had captured a small piece of daylight and harbored it at their camp.

The main tent was much larger than it had appeared when viewed from the opposite side of the lake. The rich burgundy and gold velvet interior greatly contrasted with the light-colored fabric on the outside. The versatile interior and exterior walls could either be tied into a swag or rolled up and tucked into one of the many valances along the top of the structure. Lush pillows provided comfortable seating in abundance which, along with draped tables, coordinated with the rest of the decor. As Reena showed Camile around their makeshift home, several tribe members trailed them at a respectable distance. Though they didn't utter a word, their ankle and wrist jewelry jingled softly, eliminating their anonymity. With a simple nod from Reena, they dispersed, respecting their leader's unspoken request for privacy.

Reena disappeared into one of the adjourning compartments and returned with a medium-sized box. It was wrapped in golden iridescent material similar to taffeta and adorned with a sprig of small dried flowers.

"I was hoping to present this to you after the banquet, but as they say in your adopted world, *there's no time like the present,*" she said, handing the gift to Camile.

Surprised, Camile paused a moment before taking the package and helping herself to a seat so she could open it in comfort. She was unaware of the council's policy on accepting gifts, but was nonetheless curious. Upon opening it, her nose was immediately greeted with the warm scent of musky vanilla. Camile thought it odd that a box the size of a garment container was being used to deliver a fragrance set of perfume and lotion. It wasn't until she removed one of the bottles from the box that she noticed the bejeweled fabric lying beneath a clear divider. After setting the partition aside, Camile carefully removed the first part of an outfit, realizing it was a costume, much like the ones she had seen the Fehlahni women wearing. The two-piece outfit included a jeweled midriff-baring top and a matching skirt with a high slit. As she held the skirt against herself, Camile noticed it appeared at least two sizes too small.

This won't fit over my thigh let alone my hips! she thought before saying, "Thanks for the kind gesture, but I don't think I can accept this."

"Is it not to your liking?" Reena asked, a concerned frown crossing her face.

"Oh, that's not it. It's gorgeous. There's just no way this is gonna fit me." Camile flashed a smile to make Reena feel more at ease.

Laughing, Reena pressed a hidden clasp on one side of the jeweled waistband causing it to expand. "It's adjustable. See?"

Reena urged Camile to try on the outfit to ensure it was a perfect fit. She did this in one of the compartments designated for wardrobe. Camile found herself feeling differently once she had slipped into her new gift. It almost felt as though she was playing dress-up, something she often did as a young girl.

"It's perfect," Reena exclaimed proudly. "Why don't you dance with us. You're already dressed for the part."

Camile politely declined, informing Reena that she didn't know their routine.

"You don't have to. Just follow our lead. Oh, come on! It'll be fun. Besides, do you know how many people have asked us for private lessons? You will likely be the first and the last we'll grant one to."

Camile knew the tent was of ample size, however, she doubted it would sufficiently accommodate the nearly three dozen dancers in the group. Reena quickly quelled the concerns, mentioning the practice performance would be held outdoors.

"What? But it's freezing out there," was Camile's final excuse not to participate.

"Only at first, but once you start dancing, you'll forget all about it. It's part dance, part meditation. All discomfort will disappear when you let your soul become one with the music."

"I'm worried about my body becoming one with hypothermia," Camile said to herself as she followed Reena out of the tent. Immediately upon exiting, her body tensed in reaction to the cool air.

"Jeez, Louise!" She shivered. The women responded with amused laughter.

The group grew silent as they took their places. The sound of the singing crickets echoed through the air as though to incite the flute players to join in. Mingling with the high pitched melodies were the thumping of drums. Folding into the soothing music, at brief intervals, were the smooth vocals of several of the women. Camile didn't understand a word they were singing, but the harmony transcended the boundaries of language and spoke to her soul. As they began to dance, Camile remained still and quietly observed. After seeing the pattern of their routine, Camile half-heartedly repeated them, her body rigid from the cold and her self-consciousness.

The group of women formed a circle around her. The pulsating beat of the drums was nearly synchronous to her heart and radiated throughout her body. She gently rocked to it as the women cheered, fueling her flowing movements. The cool night air dissipated as her temperature steadily climbed along with their tempo. Allowing the rhythm of the music and syncopation of the drums to dictate her movements, Camile felt herself gradually escaping her inhibition. She gyrated to it, swaying her hips in time while getting reacquainted with her sensual femininity.

"That's it. Dance with your heart and soul!" Reena beamed. "Celebrate your body and the life flowing through it! Revel in your womanhood! The more you give yourself to the music, the better the chance of your partner being drawn to you."

Camile felt liberated as she repeated the rhythmic spins of the other dancers. Halfway through her third rotation Reena stopped her by gently taking hold of her arm.

"As I suspected, your power of persuasion only enhances your gift of seduction." She smiled before training her eyes on something over Camile's left shoulder. Upon following Reena's gaze, Camile saw Jeremy, several paces away, staring at her. His face donned an expression she could only compare to befuddlement with a hint of intrigue. He had apparently broken the guards free of the captivation of the exotic performance, still taking place. The officers stood tall and tight lipped as Jeremy gave them orders that Camile couldn't decipher over the excitement. After bowing in acknowledgement, the two guards separated to carry out their commands. One traveled to the lake bank to halt the departing raft and the other spoke with one of the tribe's sentinels. Camile wondered about the subject of the discussion, but figured her attention was better suited elsewhere and returned it to the object of her affection.

"I'm afraid the fun's over. It's time to return to the compound. Reginald is retrieving your clothes," Jeremy said once he reached her side, his soulful eyes taking a round trip along her body as he bit his lower lip.

Camile's heart fluttered as an unusual feeling swept over her, a combination of freedom and confidence. She felt as though she could proclaim her love for him at that very instant, but couldn't find the words. Instead, she translated the sentiment into her dance, wondering if he'd be able to decipher it.

"You expect me to get changed out here? I may be wearing less than usual, but I still have my modesty, you know." Camile laughed softly, pirouetting around him. She could see a slight frown crossing his face, perhaps indicating mild impatience. "Oh, come on, Jeremy! I'm having the most fun I've had in awhile. Let's stick around for a few more minutes."

"Sorry. No can do." Jeremy turned in place to maintain visual contact with her.

She stopped in front of him. "Why not? Afraid you'll have fun too, for a change? Maybe you're not as graceful in dance as you are in meditation?" she teased, earning a meager smile.

"If that wasn't absurdly untrue I'd almost be insulted." He removed his long wool overcoat.

"Besides, neither my grace nor dancing abilities are up for scrutiny tonight." Jeremy continued faintly, draping it over Camile's shoulders as though she were a child. She shuddered inwardly upon feeling his residual warmth in the fabric that carried his scent. It was the next best thing to being nestled in his arms.

At that moment she realized there was an opportunity available that might not come around again for quite some time, if at all. It was the chance for her to get him to see her not as an apprentice, a warrior heiress or a walking complication, but as a woman.

"Oh, yeah? Says who?" She smirked playfully.

Not waiting for his response, Camile pulled him into the prime dancing space. The coat dropped heavily to her ankles once she stopped backpedaling. Jeremy knelt down to retrieve it, but with a smooth glide of her long leg she kicked it aside. The slit in her skirt momentarily revealed a flash of thigh, as she extended her left hand towards Jeremy.

"Care to enlighten me?" she asked tenderly.

The orange glow of the flickering lanterns intensified the golden tone of Jeremy's face. A seemingly unwilling participant, he initially resisted, but eventually relented to the seductive sway of her body and joined her in the rhythm. Camile enjoyed the sensation of his hand on her bare waist, his muscular frame close to hers as they gyrated to the beat. Their bodies were dangerously close, separated only by his uniform and her delicate costume. Any doubt about Jeremy's attraction towards her melted away as he held her even closer against him. Meeting his gaze, Camile was nearly hypnotized by his deep brown eyes. In fact, she could feel her mind drifting, wondering what he was thinking in that instant.

The narrow space between their faces was filled with magnetic energy, pulling them even closer. His eyes were apparently marking the target for his lips as he cradled her head in his hands. Closing her eyes, she prepared herself for the sweet union of their mouths. Instead, she felt his grip slacken as he pulled away. Reopening her eyes as she was reunited with the evening chill, she watched helplessly as he walked away. Oblivious, the women continued to parade around, dancing and singing their hearts out. Jolted out of her rhythmic fantasy, Camile wondered about the reason for Jeremy's abrupt departure. Then she saw Sir Drayden staring at her from the distance. It incited an annoying embarrassment similar to what one might feel after being caught dancing like no one was looking—only to realize they were, in fact, being watched.

Chapter 51

Interrogation

Lying in bed, Camile tried her best to forget about her glacial trip back to Caldaq under Sir Drayden's watchful escort. Instead, she reflected on her passionate dance with Jeremy. She smiled to herself upon realizing that they shared a mutual attraction—no matter how hard he had been trying to fight it. Filled with a sense of hope, she welcomed sleep, hoping to fall into his arms and relive their encounter in her dreams. However, as she reached the precipice of her consciousness, an uncomfortable twinge in her veins hinted that she was about to plummet into the clutches of something far less pleasant.

The still deepness of the night served as the perfect backdrop for the incursion. Just as Jezebel had indicated, it was almost too easy to bypass security. This led Akalina to suspect that more people were involved in the plot than she had been informed about. Even with the comfort of numbers behind her, there was a knotted sensation in the pit of her stomach telling her something wasn't quite right. Dismissing her intuitive apprehension as nervousness, a weak emotion, Akalina decided to press on after slipping into the outfit of a fallen female officer. It was an act her comrades followed as they pushed deeper into the compound attacking everyone in their path.

All the while, it took much effort for Akalina to ignore the recurring eerie sensation that it was all going much too smoothly. Almost as soon as the thought had entered her mind, Jeremy and Sir Drayden arrived at the scene and joined the guards in defending the wing. They had apparently been summoned by one or more distressed officers. As they clashed in battle with their adversaries, the duo managed to carefully step around the bodies strewn in the corridors. The rebel intruders, however, were far less courteous as they kicked the corpses and the wounded out of their path or simply walked on them.

Excelsior had also apparently been summoned to the scene, possibly upon hearing the devastating screams of the victims. The massive tiger proved extremely agile and virtually impossible to defeat. He seemed focused on wounding the intruders, not killing them. Though most of the invaders had fallen, Akalina and seven other rebels managed to hang on as they continued their rampage, heading for their target, the shaman's chambers. Sir Drayden instructed Jeremy to head them off and join his mother in guarding the shaman while he attempted to fend off the rebels.

Eight against one was an imbalanced face-off, but Sir Drayden was more than a match for them. Akalina was well aware of this fact and was shocked by his presence. After watching him take down his adversaries with brute force, she cursed under her breath, realizing she and her battle comrade were among the few remaining in the raid. The others rushed to battle Sir Drayden and fend off the incoming guards. Akalina hoped the strategy would provide enough of a distraction for her and her cohort to move forward.

"Oh, somebody *really* screwed up," she hissed in a voice filled with anger and a hint of fear. "What the hell is he doing here?"

Regaining her composure, Akalina attempted to reassure herself that she had an advantage over him, albeit a small one—he had not yet seen her. However, that advantage was rapidly diminishing and was nearly lost when he faced her direction. Gasping softly, she hastily recoiled behind a column and hoped she hadn't lost the element of surprise. She devised a plan, instructing her partner that they would strategically battle their way around the knight, avoiding him at all costs by using specific corridors that would lead them away from his path. The plan worked and they bypassed him unnoticed, but their numbers continued to dwindle.

For the first time, Akalina realized that with so many of the rebels falling behind her, she'd have no one to help battle her way out of the compound. Just then, as she turned the corner, she bumped into a man whose face was completely obscured by a helmet that coordinated with his armored uniform. Akalina recognized it as a uniform worn mostly by some of higher-ranking officials of the Caldaq Task Force. The officer urgently warned her that she was heading into a trap.

"Jezebel lied to you. This whole thing was a setup," the man urgently suggested, taking Akalina by the arm. His voice was distorted by his helmet. "You need to leave, now, while you still have a chance."

"What? You tell me this *now?*" She sharply pulled away from his grasp. "It's a little late for that, don't you think?"

"I only just found out about what she's really up to. She doesn't care whether you live or die, only what she stands to gain from all this. This is just a calculated step in a grander agenda you don't know about."

Akalina sensed he was telling the truth, but felt compelled to complete her mission. In her mind, there was no other way out of her sticky predicament.

"It's too late to turn back. There's too much invested in this as it is. Nearly all our people are already dead or soon will be!" Akalina granted herself a moment to compose herself. "What Jezebel said about Tabitha being Camile's bridge is true, isn't it?"

She gasped slightly upon hearing Sir Drayden's voice echoing from a distance. Even though he wasn't in visual range, he was still way too close for comfort.

"If she crosses into this world, there's a good chance I'll die later even if I happen to survive tonight, right?" she asked hurriedly, anxious to increase the distance between her and the approaching elder.

The man expelled a deep breath. It in itself was his reluctant confirmation. "It's not definite—"

"And if I surrender now..." Akalina whipped her head around as three rebels flew into view at the end of the corridor. Their bodies crashed into the wall before landing with sickening thuds. More determined than ever, she returned her attention to the officer.

"Well, that's a chance I'm not willing to take. If I'm gonna die, you better damn well believe I'm gonna die fighting! If you don't wanna get taken down with me, I suggest you keep your distance," Akalina hissed before running down the long corridor leading to the shaman's quarters. She ignored the man's plea for her to reverse course as her rebel cohorts followed.

*   *   *

Akalina and her allies fought back to back, feeding off each other's energy as they took down the guards in their way. Finally, they reached the outside of Tabitha's chambers when Jeremy and his mother joined the battle. Her prize was so close. She could see into the shaman's quarters, but Jeremy and his mother were guarding it. Akalina was running on empty and dropped to one knee. Her breathing was labored and felt as though she was trying to do so under water. As she raised her head she saw the source of her sudden exhaustion. Sir Drayden was standing several feet away from her with his palm outstretched in front of him.

His blue eyes appeared shaded with intent as he siphoned her energy. However, she saw a source of replenishment—Jeremy's mother. Akalina mustered her remaining strength to fling herself across the floor to get as close to the woman as possible. Figuring a seven foot distance was the closest proximity she could achieve, Akalina drained all she could from Jeremy's mother, causing her to stagger against a wall for support. As soon as Akalina received the sudden boost of rejuvenation, she immediately ducked behind a column to stay out of Sir Drayden's line of vision.

She could hear another wave of guards approaching. Their boots pounded the floor like a stampede of wild bulls. She knew her time was quickly running out, but she had yet one more advantage. Jeremy's mother had been left wide open for a deadly attack from Akalina's last remaining associate. Akalina's jubilation echoed throughout the corridor, grabbing Jeremy's attention. The laughter was an anomalous accompaniment to the heart wrenching sound of his mother's death. It was enough to distract him for a few moments, but that was all the time Akalina needed to dash across the hall and disable him, leaving him unconscious on the floor. She considered killing him, but instead decided to reserve her time and strength for the completion of her task. Catching her breath, she smirked as she anticipated victory. The triumphant feeling was premature. Her final ally, had been dropped by Sir Drayden in an overwhelming exchange of blows. Being the last of the group, Akalina was left to her own devices.

Knowing she had to make her move immediately, Akalina swiftly entered the shaman's quarters. She was engulfed by a loud roar. The ground quaked beneath her feet as something approached from behind. Before she could completely turn around, a sharp pain sliced through the right side of her abdomen. She shrieked, twisting off-balance, falling to the floor with a loud thump. Dizzy and exhausted from the taxing battle and loss of blood, she attempted to get up to resume her fight. However, two things restricted her—Excelsior's massive paw on her chest, and Sir Drayden once again siphoning her energy as he approached.

Akalina could barely breathe and reached a point where she could no longer scream. Silent tears trickled from her eyes and the scent of her own blood sickened her. Sir Drayden waved the tiger away before crouching beside her body, which had been reduced to a quivering, rumpled mess of pain. He dismissed the guards and approaching spiders before they could enter the room to heal Akalina's wounds. Seeing this, she whimpered quietly.

"Tsk-tsk, Akalina." Sir Drayden sighed forlornly, briefly shaking his head. "See what you get when you deal with the rebels?"

"You d—don't...understand," Akalina stuttered faintly, seething with anger. "You're t—too simple minded!"

"Really? Is that so?" Sir Drayden smirked subtly. "Well, maybe you can enlighten me. What are the rebels planning and why, exactly, were you attempting to murder Tabitha?"

Akalina forced out a brief chuckle. It morphed into a cough as she winced in pain, her breathing still labored.

"You m—must be senile, old man." She glared.

"Akalina, there's no need for you to suffer." Sir Drayden smoothed her disheveled hair. "I can help you heal quickly and painlessly. Just tell me what the rebels are up to and this will all be over. What do they hope to gain in the event of Tabitha's death?"

"I'll tell you. After you go to hell!" Akalina sneered.

"Been there, done that. Since you insist, we'll do this your way, Akalina." The knight glowered, casually walking over to one of the shaman's medicinal shelves. He strategically began removing a few vials. "You know, years ago when you murdered my wife I wanted you to pay for what you did. I wanted you to pay dearly. You know what stopped me? You were only a child, susceptible to the mental conditioning of the rebels. Sure, you took the blame all on your own, but I always knew they were behind it. Only a coward would use a child in order to further their own agenda. Hyacinth was a good woman. She deserved a better way to pass than the way she did and you helped the rebels to steal that away from her. Now, I can no longer blame them entirely for your behavior. You're old enough to make your own decisions and still you've decided to cross my path, yet again. A lot has changed since your first offense. You can no longer hide behind the excuse of your naive childhood curiosity. Oh, no. Not this time."

Akalina used Sir Drayden's lecture as an opportunity to attempt escape while his back was turned. It was useless. Her limbs were dead weight, as though they had all fallen asleep. Furthermore, she could barely lift her head from the ground. Upon returning, Sir Drayden knelt beside her, meeting her eyes with his prying gaze as he continued.

"Now, you're old enough to pay the price for your misdeeds. I think this is an opportune time to educate you on healing serums," he said.

Akalina burst into a painful fit of laughter as she mocked him, but the fear beneath the surface was growing. Ignoring her taunts, Sir Drayden held up a vial containing a silvery liquid.

"This, my dear, is *Tarconian Extract*. It's widely revered for its remarkable healing abilities. It dramatically accelerates a human's regenerative rate. One drop can painlessly heal a small wound in a matter of minutes. It's so effective that the treated area looks as if no damage had ever occurred. Unfortunately, there's not nearly enough here to treat the extent of your injuries. You see, I find myself preoccupied in wondering why you and the rebels tried to kill my apprentice tonight and I can't seem to remember where she keeps the rest of her supply." He frowned theatrically, taking a half-hearted glance around the room.

It was obvious to Akalina that he did in fact know where the rest was. He was simply using it as a bargaining tactic.

"Now—" Sir Drayden stopped talking when he noticed Akalina losing consciousness. With a wave of his hand, he supplied her with just enough energy to keep her awake.

"No. You can't sleep now. The lesson's just beginning," he whispered, gently tapping her cheek.

As Akalina wept with quiet exhaustion, Sir Drayden set down the vial before raising another—containing a clear liquid.

"This is *Reogolene*. It's a decent healing agent, but it's not as effective as *Tarconian Extract*. Unfortunately, it's quite painful and takes much longer to work. Those who've received this treatment compare it to the sensation of their insides roasting slowly over an open flame. I'd hate to administer this to you, but seeing as there's no other way of—"

"Shut up and...leave me alone!" Akalina choked out.

"Alright. Have it your way." Sir Drayden sighed as he opened the vial and poured the contents over her gaping wounds.

A horrifying sensation tore through her flesh, causing her to cry bloody murder as she quivered violently. Her muscles tensed as she tried to resist the intense pain. Sir Drayden allowed her to writhe for a few seconds before applying another solution to her wounds, calming the effect of the first elixir. Akalina lay motionless while catching her breath, relieved that the burning pain was beginning to subside. However, there was lingering discomfort that continued to singe her beyond physical levels. Unable to resist her curiosity, she lifted her head slightly to inspect her injuries. Much to her disgust, her sight met the image of four gaping wounds under a massive amount of deep red blood. As her torso rapidly expanded and contracted in time to her breathing, she caught a brief repulsive glimpse of the meat beneath the open wounds. Regretting what she had just seen, she dropped her head back to the floor.

"The soothing serum I just applied is called *Sivegian Ice Water*." Sir Drayden explained casually. "I guess you can see how it got its name. Ironically, it doesn't contain much water at all. Alright, my dear, *now* are you ready to cooperate?"

Akalina cried hostile tears, shaking her head violently, much to Sir Drayden's dismay.

"No! You...can't make me!" She sobbed, her voice cracking with agony.

"Oh, is that right?" His lips upturned a moment before falling into a scowl. "Damn it, Akalina! Don't force me to do this. You don't have to go through this for them. Tell me who's leading you. I already know whoever organized this was also behind Hyacinth's assassination. So tell me, who gave you the order to kill Tabitha?"

"Maybe it was *you*...you sadistic bastard," she spat through angry sobs, her voice growing even fainter. "I'll never tell you! So you might as well just kill me! But you can't, can you? I know I'm too important for you to just throw away. You have no choice but to let me live."

Akalina strained to lift her head to inspect her torso anew and was relieved to see her wounds were almost completely healed. Nevertheless, she was still disturbed to see the pool of blood she was lying in. This time, the sight sent her drifting into a state of welcomed unconsciousness. Yet, Sir Drayden still wouldn't grant her the luxury of sleep.

Trembling, she regarded her silver-haired captor with a shakily defiant sneer. She was determined not to allow him to break her and knew she had the upper hand. She somehow knew he had no choice but to release her, or so she thought. Her eyes widened in horror as Sir Drayden revealed yet another vial. The menacing, fiery red and orange liquid in the container glowed like hot lava. The somber expression on Sir Drayden's face sent shivers down her spine. The thunder in her chest echoed in her ears as she desperately struggled to regain control of her body, but to no avail.

"Ah! You know about this one, don't you?" he crooned. Seeing she was too terrified to answer, he filled the brief silence. "This is commonly referred to as Serpent's Flame, one of the most vile, forbidden substances known to this world. However, a very select few are allowed to keep it in stock, but there are those who manage to get their hands on it illegally." He regarded Akalina with a prying look, as though he somehow knew she had used it before. "I'm sure you don't want to experience how this works first hand. Now, I'll give you one last chance to answer my question. I won't ask you again."

Filled with unshakeable terror, Akalina failed to respond. She hoped desperately that he was bluffing, but knew otherwise. She could only shake her head as she braced herself for the next wave of torment he had in store for her. A delusional fantasy crept into her mind that perhaps, somehow, the shaman—asleep in her bed just a few feet away—would come to her aid. As Sir Drayden applied the substance, she was submerged in a cruel darkness, allowing her to focus on nothing but the agony she was experiencing.

After a few seconds, an earsplitting screech filled the air. The sound was comparable to the noise a fatally wounded animal would make. To her surprise, the sound was coming from her own mouth. The burning pain ravaging Akalina's midsection made it feel as though Excelsior was repeatedly ripping into her flesh with fiery claws. The agony coursed throughout her entire body and her blood pressure increased to such a degree she feared her head would explode. The combination of mental and physical torment proved too much for Akalina's stubbornness. She just wanted it to be over. Even if it meant death.

Finally, Akalina shrieked her confession through intense sobs. It seemed as though someone else was making the confession for her.

"It was Jezebel," she screamed until her voice failed her as the pain gradually intensified.

Now that he finally had his answer, Sir Drayden quickly uncapped a larger bottle of *Sivegian Ice Water* and urgently doused it over Akalina's screaming wounds. While she struggled to catch her breath, her vision slowly returned, albeit blurry. She witnessed Sir Drayden retrieving something from one of the medicinal shelves before returning to her side. He repositioned her trembling body and began dressing the wound, which was inflamed and tender, but already healing. Akalina tried her best to fight, but once again, her limbs proved useless. She was feeble and disoriented from her ordeal.

"No! Don't touch me! Leave me alone! You got what you wanted from me!" She sobbed tremulously once she regained some control of her voice. Her exhaustion was surpassed only by the intense fear and hatred she felt for the man who had just broken her.

"Shh...It's all over," Sir Drayden gently hushed. There seemed to be a twinkle in his crystal blue eyes, but the emotion they reflected wasn't as clear. "It's a shame you had to go through this. It could've been avoided if you just told me what I needed to know from the beginning. Your wounds will heal, but let the scars remind you of what happens when you side with the rebels. I hope you've learned a very valuable lesson from all this, Akalina. I hope for your sake you really have, because if you ever try to cross me again," he paused a moment to lean closer, his lips nearly touching her ear, and whispered, "I won't be so lenient next time."

Sir Drayden cleansed and dressed her injuries with a tenderness that was a taunting contrast to the earlier punishment he unleashed.

"Rest. You'll regain most of your strength by morning." He gently stroked her tousled hair in a single pass, finally granting her the mercy of sleep. Akalina whimpered as she drifted out of consciousness, involuntarily sinking into his arms.

Camile awoke to find herself trembling and sobbing while clutching her scarred side. The physical presence of the pain had faded, but the mental anguish wouldn't relent as easily. She got the impression that although Akalina's physical torment lasted for a night, pain was an ongoing feature of her life, sometimes self-inflicted in some manner or another. Camile was finding it increasingly burdensome to shoulder the weight of the tortured half of her soul.

Chapter 52

Clarity & Corruption

The rays of truth were finally shining through the clouds of uncertainty, illuminating the facts behind Sir Drayden's dark connection with Akalina. She felt guilty and remorseful about the inaccurate accusations she had made against the knight. Yet, she still feared him greatly as a result of the latest revelation. She was so fearful, in fact, her clumsiness increased when in his presence. To alleviate this, she figured she'd apologize for her error in basically mislabeling him a pedophile. In doing so, she hoped it would make him disassociate her from Akalina's past misdeeds.

While descending from the height of her fear and anger, the weight of her shame increased. It tugged at the pit of her stomach, reiterating the need to own up to her blatant misunderstanding. Walking to Sir Drayden's quarters, the heaviness continued to bear down with every step until she finally reached his door. Suddenly, there was a shift in her demeanor that cautioned her against announcing her presence. The thought of expressing her regret no longer seemed appealing. Though the intensity of her emotions wasn't as vivid as it had been during the memory of Akalina's torturous healing, it continued to haunt her. Not only did it hinder her ability to seek forgiveness, but to give it as well.

Turning on her heel, she froze as she came face to face with Jeremy. She now viewed him through different eyes. Knowing that Akalina had caused and enjoyed his mother's death, she felt an awkward understanding of his stark attitude towards her. Furthermore, she experienced an empathetic sorrow as she imagined how tough it must've been for him to help who he felt was the same person who brought about his mother's demise. Quickly lowering her gaze, she silently bypassed him.

*   *   *

It was unusually easy to break away from his sudden grasp. Nevertheless, she allowed him to get within striking distance. Camile didn't do this for thrills, but the satisfaction of being able to launch a defense—something she felt powerless to do in her nightmares or within the confines of Akalina's murky memories. However, even though she managed to thwart the commander's mock attacks and bring him down to the ground at least once, she felt no satisfaction. It seemed too easy, almost like he was purposefully allowing her to defeat him, despite the fact the point of the exercise was for her to learn evasive tactics.

"You going easy on me today?" Camile panted.

"Not a chance. I'm just getting warmed up." Commander Wilder breathed, raking his lush hair away from his sweat-beaded forehead. "I was distracted, that's all."

"By what? There's no one here but us." Camile's eyes shifted to the officers guarding the gym entrance, supervising the match. "And them."

The commander shrugged, his lips curving into a barely detectable smile.

As they continued sparring he encouraged her to try to keep him at a distance as they blocked each other's blows. He managed to knock her to the floor a few times, nearly sapping her will to continue. Somehow, she found the strength to recover quickly each time. He seemed to be toying with her, much like a cat would play with its prey. Refusing to fall again, Camile went against the purpose of the exercise by lunging at him.

Subconsciously, she figured taking control of the situation would give her the empowerment she lacked when she relived Akalina's memories. As soon as the move was made Camile realized her mistake, she had launched an attack based on blinding emotion rather than strategic analysis. Seeing the opportunity, Commander Wilder seized her arm, using her own momentum to rotate her body until she was facing away from him. Pulling her sharply, he brought the intense match to a standstill as he used his strong arms to pin hers to her sides.

"What's that you're wearing? Smells amazing." His voice droned in her ear, his arms tightening around her, pressing her back firmly against his midsection.

"Probably my sweat," Camile quipped in her unsuccessful attempt to break the tension. In fact, she was sure he could feel her racing pulse. She had forgotten she had applied the lotion the Fehlahni had given her. As she turned her head towards her shoulder, her memory was refreshed upon catching a whiff of the vanilla-based musk, now seasoned with her salty perspiration.

"There's no need to dance around such a simple question," the commander murmured. "Speaking of which, your moves are impressive. Very graceful."

Camile was unable to avoid the expression of her surprise.

Oh, no. Don't tell me he saw me, she thought as she slowly pulled away from his slackened grip in order to resume eye contact.

"Oh, yes. I saw you the other night," Commander Wilder sang as though reading her mind. "I hope the Fehlahni were kind enough to let you keep the costume. It really becomes you."

She could feel his eyes traveling the length of her body.

"You were there? I didn't see you." Camile felt slightly humiliated that he had witnessed her dance with the tribe. She folded her arms as though it would prevent him from visually undressing her.

"I'd be impressed if you did. From the look of things, you were caught up in the moment. My squad and I were returning from an assignment and decided to take the path along the village lakeside. There was a small devourer problem that needed to be dealt with. Small, but ugly. Needless to say, the vision of you winding around in that gorgeous outfit was a thing of beauty after the day I had. It's a shame I couldn't stick around long enough to watch you finish your performance. I bet it was a lot more interesting than the debriefing I had to attend. Maybe next time you won't have to dance alone. It would be an honor and a pleasure to join you in harmony rather than battle."

Though flattered, Camile felt a slight mixture of relief and guilt when she realized he hadn't seen Jeremy join her.

"There was another issue with the devourers?" she inquired. "They don't quit, do they?"

"I see what you're doing." The commander chortled. "You're deflecting. Honestly, I'd much rather talk about your dancing, but I see you're not up for it. How about a little wager? One match. If you win, I'll drop the subject and tell you all about my expedition with the devourers."

"And if I lose? Not that I plan on it."

"If you lose...not only will you tell me about your adventure, you'll give me a demonstration of what you learned from the Fehlahni." The commander smiled.

"That seems like an uneven bet to me."

"Fine. You can forget about the explanation and jump straight to the demonstration," he quipped.

"Nice try, but I don't think it's such a good idea." Camile smirked.

"While you're thinking about it, why don't we multitask?"

Commander Wilder lunged at Camile, who quickly averted his grasp. Assuming a defensive stance, she shuffled backward, increasing the distance between them. There was a pause as both partners calculated and anticipated the other's move. Then with a jolt, they engaged once again, each strike and block evenly matched until he knocked Camile's weight from under her. Her back met the floor with a crash. For a moment, she saw nothing but the ceiling as time seemed to slow. The floor beneath her no longer seemed as firm and the lights of the room had dimmed. In fact, the room itself had shrunk to about a tenth of its original size. Someone approached her side but it wasn't the commander.

"You're healing well." Jezebel smiled. "It's good to see you, but it wasn't a good idea to request to see me so soon. It might trigger suspicion."

"I know it's risky, but this couldn't wait." Akalina winced as she sat up in bed. "There's something I need to ask you. Did you know Sir Drayden was gonna be at the compound the night of the raid?"

"Of course not," Jezebel exclaimed, her voice hushed. "I'm surprised you'd even ask me such a thing! Where is this coming from?"

"Well, some of us were wondering how such a huge oversight was made."

"It was more like a very unfortunate happenstance." Jezebel's irritation came through in her voice as she observed Akalina with prying eyes. "*He* put this in your head, didn't he? I know he still sides with the council despite his so-called allegiance. He's got a lot of nerve trying to turn my own people against me. I wouldn't be surprised if *he's* the one who tipped Sir Drayden off. Guess we have no choice but to eliminate him."

"No. We can use him and gain a strategic advantage."

"How exactly do you plan to do that?"

"Let's just say I have something he wants. Maybe he'd be willing to make some sort of arrangement."

"Figures." Jezebel rolled her eyes. "He works so hard to maintain a poised, professional demeanor, but I've seen the way he looks at you. You may very well be the one to draw the fiery beast out of that cold, stolid man. Go on, use your womanly wiles to charm him and get as much information you can about the council's strategy against the rebels. But after that, I want him *dead.* At least you'll have a little fun before you get rid of him, lucky girl."

An ominous smile crossed Jezebel's dark brown features as her eyes sparkled with an apparent thirst for death. The expression faded into a look of curiosity.

"I have a question of my own." Jezebel furrowed her brow slightly. "You're even a tougher cookie than I pegged you for. I can't fathom how you managed to go through all of that pain without confessing what Sir Drayden wanted to hear. Are you sure you didn't tell him anything?"

"Yeah, I'm sure. If I did, don't you think you would've been apprehended by now?" Akalina replied confidently, but beneath the surface lurked a twinge of ambiguity that could only accommodate a lie.

She tried to stand up, but couldn't due to the oppression of a powerful force. The bed hardened, causing discomfort in her back and shoulders. Jezebel's form had been replaced by a mass of broad muscle, holding her down. Camile immediately began to struggle. Burning through the haze of confusion was the commander's face looking down at her. She found herself lost in the moment of panic as she briefly relived their incident in the woods. Stricken with helplessness, she cried out for him to release her.

"Hey. What's wrong?" Brandon asked, instantly loosening his grip, but maintaining a light hold as though to console her.

It was as though a light had suddenly gone off in her head, illuminating the fact that she had briefly lost sense of time and reality. Taking a deep breath and forcing out a nervous laugh, she tried to assure Brandon that she was fine. By then, the guards had rushed over to investigate the matter, but Camile assured them there was no cause for alarm. Satisfied, they returned to their post at the entrance.

"Are you sure I didn't do something to make you uncomfortable?" Brandon asked, helping Camile to her feet. "I shouldn't have tackled you like that. I didn't know it would…" His voice trailed off as he hung his head for a moment. "I'm sorry."

"No. It's not your fault, really. You were just doing your job. My mind just got discombobulated for a minute there. I hit the floor pretty good." Camile cracked a smile, mostly to make Brandon feel at ease.

"I guess we can settle up some other time, but for now you should get yourself checked out." He returned the expression, but it couldn't erase the remorseful concern Camile saw in his eyes.

By the time Camile had received confirmation that she hadn't sustained any serious injuries, she convinced herself to make her best attempt to avoid getting too close to Brandon. It wasn't due to not trusting him, but the fact she didn't trust herself around him. In addition, she didn't want to jeopardize the belated blossoming of her connection with Jeremy. It seemed like a relatively simple decision in theory, but somehow she knew it would prove difficult to put into practice.

In the meantime, she found herself wondering who the mystery man was in the discussion between Akalina and Jezebel. In her mind it could either be Jeremy or Brandon, however, the former seemed to fit Jezebel's description to a tee.

Had Jeremy been entirely honest about his history with Akalina? Had there been an underlying attraction and did he surrender to it? Was his mother's death the result of a bitter end to a volatile relationship? Camile also considered the possibility Akalina and Jezebel were talking about a different man, altogether. Camile decided the best course of action was to wait it out, hoping another memory would unfold and reveal the solution to the puzzle.

*   *   *

It was the first time she would see Jeremy at length since their encounter at the Fehlahni camp. She had been anticipating their next meeting for hours. Prior to their session that afternoon, Camile devoted extra time to be sure she looked her best. She didn't go as far as applying elaborate makeup or coifing her hair in a formal style since she knew she'd be meditating and working out. Besides, she didn't want to send the message she was trying too hard. Instead, she opted for a braided ponytail, darkened lashes and a sheer tinted lip moisturizer. Poised outside the entrance of the Celestia, she did a last minute check of her workout attire to ensure everything still flattered her figure. She accessorized her look with her best smile as she entered the room. It quickly faded when she saw who was standing in Jeremy's place.

"Good afternoon, Sir Drayden," Camile greeted as cordially as she could. "Is Jeremy running late?"

"Jeremy has other engagements."

"For how long?"

"As long as it takes." The knight clasped his hands behind his back.

Camile felt as though her heart had dropped into her stomach. It was bad enough she had to face him during his appraisal of her overall progress, but to have him as a substitute for Jeremy was almost unbearable for a multitude of reasons.

"If you don't mind, I'd like to get started." Sir Drayden gestured for her to sit in her usual spot. It was only then she realized she had slipped into a stunned daze, wondering what had gone wrong that day.

Throughout each exercise Camile felt her mind lingering on the evening of the raid led by Akalina. She couldn't get her mind off of what Sir Drayden had done to her. The very thought of it caused her to tremble, making her physically and emotionally unsteady. It was something her substitute instructor reprimanded her for at the close of the session, which wasn't easy to take given the situation she was in.

In the following two days Camile saw Jeremy in passing. His reserved, yet easygoing mood changed slightly upon seeing her and suddenly he was in a hurry to get someplace. It made it impossible to approach him about the subject of Sir Drayden replacing him as her meditative guide, something she sincerely hoped was a temporary arrangement. Jeremy's increasing distance was threatening to bring their relationship back to square one and she got the feeling it was exactly what Sir Drayden wanted after witnessing their dance at the Fehlahni camp.

Chapter 53

Heart of the Matter

The Fehlahni's spectacular performance came to a close, earning a clamoring applause from the crowd. Every seat in the indoor amphitheater was filled with eager spectators as the festival continued. After various performers from around the globe took the stage to showcase their talents, Caldaq residents and council members followed suit by sharing a few of their own. Among them were Camile's father and Sir Drayden, who collaborated in a storytelling segment. Though it was entertaining for most, it seemed to be geared towards the audience's youngest members, who stared in wide-eyed amazement as they watched the theatrical reenactment taking place behind the narrators.

The tale encompassed the devastation of a land under siege by a gigantic carnivorous beast with an insatiable appetite for human flesh. It took the bravery of a few men of a neighboring village, which had been unthreatened, to attempt to slay the creature. Their valiant efforts resulted in the creature's death, but it claimed the brave men's lives during its final moments.

When the story was completed, there was a brief intermission before the concluding performance. Camile, who was seated beside her parents in the first row, overheard children discussing the story.

"If they refused to fight the beast, they would've been spared," said one girl, seated at the end of the row with her friends.

"Ah, but what of the quality of such a life that permits neglect on the grandest level of all?" Sir Drayden asked as he stood before them. Softening his face with a faint smile. "There are consequences to every decision that we make, even when that decision is to do nothing. Chances are, had the soldiers decided against the quest, the adjoining village would have been wiped clean. And what happens when a hungry creature runs out of food in one area?"

"They search for more somewhere else," a boy answered.

"Right. So you see, although there was a single village under attack, much more was at stake. If everyone acted in cowardice, they would have basically surrendered to their predicament."

"It's kind of like what we're learning in school, about what's happening now between our world and the Coexistent World," the boy stated.

"Right, again." Sir Drayden winked.

Camile found herself intrigued by the polar opposites of his gentleness with the children versus what she had seen through the windows of Akalina's memories.

"But it's not the same," a young teen interjected. "The Coexistent World isn't at war with monsters. They're at war with themselves. So, in a sense, they are their own monster, destroying each other and the world around them. Does that mean it's our job to slay them before they figure out a way to harm our people?"

The audience members seated nearest to the teen reacted in surprise.

"You raise an interesting question." Sir Drayden raised his eyes to meet the young man's gaze in the third row. The elder's expression was noticeably more serious than it had been when he addressed the children.

"I'm glad you brought it up," he continued. "I don't think I need to name the specific group who views the situation in that manner. However, it's a skewed outlook of reality. In the case of our Coexistent neighbors, their monster lies within their way of thinking. The victim is their hope, something that is being destroyed by their overwhelming focus on negativity."

"Their capacity for love greatly outweighs their apparent thirst for destruction," Zephyr added, briefly shifting his gaze to Camile and her mother. "It's our job, not to slay them, but to remind them of that fact. It's their choice to decide whether or not they want to make a positive change or to continue on their path of negativity."

The girl wrinkled her nose. "Why do they need our help to make such an easy choice?"

Sir Drayden cracked a somber half-smile as though appreciating the girl's sweet naivety.

"Unfortunately, it's not an easy decision for everyone," he said. "That's why we need people like you to hold on to the fundamental fact that the decision to preserve life should never be difficult." His smile faded as he regarded the young teen. "On the other hand, you'll find that with age comes the understanding that even the most basic decisions can branch into an entanglement of complications."

*   *   *

From the doorway, Jeremy's quarters appeared orderly, but lived in. Camile couldn't see very far into the space since he was blocking most of the entrance with his robe-clad body. Based on the balmy look of his skin and the extra shimmer of his very short, black hair, she figured he had just come from the shower. It was a theory supported by the light, airy scent rising from his skin.

"I don't think it's a good idea for you to be here at this hour."

"What do you mean? It's barely sunset." Mildly amused, Camile chortled. Then a thought crossed her mind.

Maybe he's not alone.

She decided to pry gently to make a clearer determination of that possibility.

"I'm not interrupting anything am I?"

"Yes, and no. I was about to work on some schematics for a meeting, but I guess I can spare a minute or two before I get started."

Jeremy cleared the doorway, allowing her to enter. She immediately noticed the quiet reading corner with a tall, slender bookshelf. It was opposite from his computer workstation. Sliding floor to ceiling partitions separated the more private areas of his quarters while adding simple accents to the living space. She could see the neck of a violin peeking out from behind one of the black and white dividers.

"Were you at the festival? I didn't see you." Camile asked, attempting to thaw the frosty atmosphere between them.

"No. There will be other festivals. I'm sure my absence didn't cause people to enjoy themselves any less."

"Well, because of your absence during meditation my sessions are certainly not what they used to be."

"So, the true reason for your visit arises." Jeremy raised his brow, curling his lips into a subtle smile. "The sentiment is appreciated. Nevertheless, if you don't understand by now that your ability to synchronize your body and mind depends solely on you, then I've failed you as your instructor."

"I guess you have a point," Camile said, appeasing him in order to get closer to the question she wanted answered. "Old habits die hard. When I get accustomed to a certain routine I tend to stick with it. So, why do you think Sir Drayden made the decision to switch things up, and how long do you think it'll last?"

"It was a joint decision, not that it should matter. We both felt it was the right time to shift my responsibilities, but the duration of this adjustment has yet to be discussed."

"Really? In that case it sounds like you're avoiding me. Is this all because of what happened the other night?"

"If I didn't know any better I'd say you were delusional. Have you been skipping your meditation exercises?"

"No, I haven't. But you've clearly skipped your good judgment by deciding to switch gears before the course was even finished. There's a deeper reason beneath all this and you're too stubborn to just let it out so we can move on."

"You're overanalyzing the situation," Jeremy said plainly.

"I don't think so, Jeremy. Look, I know it's hard for you to get past what happened with your mother, no matter how strong you make yourself out to be. No amount of meditation can erase the pain of losing someone you love."

Jeremy's expression changed from apparent indifference to astonishment. Camile had blindsided him, as well as herself, with a topic she didn't plan to bring up. Knowing it was too late to backpedal, she continued.

"Yes, I finally know why you keep pushing me away. Deep in your heart you know you're furious about the way your mom died and I can't blame you, but I want you to know that I'm not the person who's responsible for her death. I'm *not* Akalina. She may be a part of me, but..." Camile paused. Exhaling deeply, she continued, "...but she does *not* define who I am. I'm my own person. Why can't you see that?" she said in an attempt to not only convince Jeremy, but also herself. "That's the main thing standing in our way."

"What do you mean *standing in our way?*" Jeremy's eyes narrowed.

Smirking, Camile exhaled a puff of air through her nostrils in mild amusement, seeing the perfect opportunity to turn the phrase he said earlier. "If you don't understand by now that I'm attracted to you, then I've failed as a woman."

"You're talking out of your head. I think you should stop," Jeremy said flatly, but his stern facade was wavering.

"If you want me to stay emotionally balanced, I suggest you let me get this off my chest."

Crossing his arms, Jeremy turned away and sighed.

His reaction was an unusual deviation from his reserved personality. Camile had clearly struck a nerve and for the first time she was seeing Jeremy's raw emotions emerging like an image on a developing photograph.

"I know you're still upset about what happened years ago, but I can't change that." Camile's voice grew calmer, but the words didn't come easy. It was like stripping off the outer layers of her soul and casting her true self into the wind of uncertainty.

"Hell, I didn't even know it happened until recently," she exclaimed, fighting back tears. "I know you don't share my feelings and I don't expect you to. As much as it'll hurt, I'm willing to spend every day around you knowing we'll never be more than colleagues. I wish things could be different, but I understand why they can't." She averted her gaze, her voice trailing into a faint chortle of mild embarrassment that tapered into an exasperated sigh. "I know it'll be hard as hell, but I'd rather be your friend than to be nothing to you at all."

The floor blurred as she continued, "I know that declaring my feelings to you right now leaves me wide open for embarrassment. I'll probably regret this tomorrow, but I just needed to tell you the truth. I needed to do it to set myself free. I'm sorry if that inconveniences you." She turned on her heel to leave his quarters, but something held her back; it was Jeremy's grasp.

"Wait," he said softly. "You're right. I've been treating you unfairly and I've been a hypocrite to my own teachings. I apologize. Please, sit. There's something I need to get off my chest too."

When the two sat on the sofa Jeremy surprised her by taking her hand and regarding her with glassy eyes.

"I've been fighting my feelings for you for too long, but it's not just because of what Akalina did." He stroked her hand with his thumb. "I know you're not her. I know you're trying hard to sort out the sins you've inherited and I admire you for that, Camile. I admire you for that very much. You had my attention long before today even though I didn't show it. I *couldn't* show it and I probably shouldn't...I wish it didn't have to be so complicated." He sighed, lowering his gaze.

"It doesn't have to be." Camile sandwiched his hand in hers. "If we clear the air now we can move forward."

"I wish it was that simple. For one thing, I'm your instructor."

"I thought Sir Drayden replaced you. At least for the time being." Camile arched an eyebrow.

"Right. Almost forgot about that." A boyish smile crossed his golden face.

"A Transcendent with a faulty memory? Someone alert the EDC," Camile quipped, earning a laugh. His jubilant voice was something to hear, like holiday bells during the winter season.

"Maybe someone should, because I must be out of my mind to ask you this…" Jeremy paused as they locked eyes. "May I kiss you?"

A few seconds elapsed before Camile realized she had stopped breathing. Speechless, she nodded. She felt his warm hand slip slowly from her grasp, making its way up her arm and nestling beneath her chin. Marking his target with his deep brown orbs, he moved closer until finally his lips met hers. They were even softer than she'd imagined. She enjoyed his delightful scent and the firm touch of his gentle hands as they caressed her face. Camile it felt as though she had entered a warm refuge after years of wandering in an arctic wasteland. The kiss held the promise of soothing her blistered heart, which had long suffered the frostbite of rejection.

Chapter 54

Split-Progression

In spite of her high energy stemming from her breakthrough with Jeremy, Camile managed to get some sleep. Her dreams were empty and for hours she floated in an abyss of blissful nothingness. When she opened her eyes the following morning, she knew she hadn't fully awakened when she saw Isaac standing at her bedside.

"Did you forget about me?" he asked.

In truth, Camile had been so preoccupied that he had indeed been obscured by her hectic thoughts. However, she wasn't prepared to reveal that to the little boy.

"No. I was actually beginning to think *you* forgot about *me.*" She smiled faintly as she sat upright.

"That'll never happen. I need you," Isaac said with imploring eyes.

"So help me find you. Tell me where you are. That's all you have to do, sweetheart," Camile urged, realizing she sounded strikingly like her mother in that moment.

"I'm closer than you think. You'll find me where there's writing on the wall."

"Come on, Isaac!" Camile expelled an frustrated sigh. "You keep speaking in riddles. You've gotta give me more than that. I need something I can work with, here!" Camile implored. "Are you speaking in codes because of the rebels?"

Saying nothing further, Isaac vanished into the shadows as Camile awoke. Hoping her parents would somehow be able to help her put the pieces together, she informed them of the young scribe's latest clues regarding his location. Unfortunately, Camile's parents were just as stumped as she was.

Isaac ceased appearing in Camile's dreams in the succeeding nights and she immediately began to worry. Not only that, she realized how much she was growing to miss the strange comfort of his presence. All she had left to cling to were the memories of their previous encounters. However, the strong urge to find him still remained. She felt it pulling her with the gravitational force of a planet. No longer able to hold her tongue about the situation, she confronted her parents about the sudden end of his communication.

"His subconscious contact may be limited since he probably hasn't slept in some time," her mother explained. "The rebels sometimes use forced insomnia as a tactic in order to confuse their captives and sever their telepathic communication."

"We need to find him before it's too late," Camile urged. "Why is everyone ignoring the clues he's been giving me?"

"We haven't ignored them, but right now we have to worry about higher priorities."

Camile wrinkled her nose. "*Higher priorities?* There's a kid out there in the hands of the rebels. He needs our help! Who knows what they're doing to him right now. We have to save him." She paused a moment before wondering aloud. "You don't believe me, do you? You think I'm hallucinating about my contact with him."

"No. That's not it at all," Zephyr replied. "Camile, I understand your urgency in wanting to rescue him, but even with the limited information he's given you, locating Isaac will be a daunting task. We can't afford to be irrational, nor can we expend all of our resources. Our best bet is to determine the rebels' next move and act accordingly. Besides, for all we know the rebels could be using Isaac to lure us into a trap. Even so, you should be reassured of the fact we are doing all we can to investigate the matter. We haven't given up on finding him."

"I don't doubt you. It's just so frustrating to hear his pleas for help and not be able to do anything about it."

"We share your frustration. Believe me when I say that." Zephyr's lips tightened as he exhaled through his nose.

Knowing there was nothing else she could do, Camile decided to trust in him and his experience to bring Isaac back safely. She hoped it would happen sooner rather than later, knowing Isaac's life, as well as her peace of mind, depended on it.

*   *   *

Standing in the desolate amusement park, Camile came to the chilling realization that without people, the joy that would have otherwise filled the space would never exist. Without the presence and laughter of the patrons, the place had an eerily lifeless calm. It almost felt as though she was standing in death's playground. As she cautiously walked further away from the rift, she came across a large carousel. The soft moonlight traced the silhouettes and vague details of the carved horses, giving them an ethereal appearance. Without the luxury of daylight, they seemed like skewered lifeless animals that had been left in a sadistic public display. In the distance were shadowlike buildings, their windows aglow in random patterns. That, and the sparse traffic, reassured Camile that life was still, indeed, present. Once her father crossed into the Coexistent realm with Sir Drayden, he brought with him disquieting news.

"I've been summoned to return to Caldaq for an urgent meeting with the council." He announced. "You and Sir Drayden will have to go on without me."

Camile felt uneasy about traveling alone with a bitter man who seemingly had a penchant for torture. In addition, the dull strain of guilt over her misunderstanding of him hadn't waned.

"Please, Dad. Not him," Camile whispered as softly as she could, but got the overwhelming feeling Sir Drayden could still hear her. "Can't you—?"

"Camile, there's no time for debate," her father interrupted. "I'll see you back at the compound," he said before disappearing into the rift, which sealed behind him.

Camile traveled beside Sir Drayden in silence as they walked through the urban streets. As they progressed, she noticed they had come to a rather dodgy part of town and concluded that was why the street population was light. Growing increasingly uneasy, she broke the silence to inquire about the directions, asking if they were lost.

"No. Quite the contrary. We're here." Sir Drayden cracked a half-smile, halting his stride in front of an abandoned structure. Gesturing to the building, he motioned for her to enter. Camile regarded the structure with wide-eyed apprehension. The graffiti-ridden plywood haphazardly covering the broken windows was an indication it had been condemned. Judging by the broken rusty chain on the metal door, the building had new— undoubtedly shady—occupants, neighbored by two homeless men sleeping outside beside their shopping carts. Camile gagged on a sickening scent of booze, cigarette smoke and urine, wafting through the air.

"Are you serious? This can't possibly be—" She stopped talking when she saw the seriousness etched on Sir Drayden's face.

Reluctantly entering the building, Camile was on high alert as she took one cautious step after another. Suddenly, a loud bang echoed throughout the foyer. She whipped around to see that Sir Drayden had shut the door behind them. It was at that moment she prayed for better lighting. When she turned to resume her course she bumped into a large man. He was as tall as Vincent—if not taller—and he was at least three hundred-eighty pounds. As if his towering frame wasn't intimidating enough, half his face donned an intricate tattoo, barely visible due to the dim lighting and his dark complexion. The man wore a distressed leather jacket that emphasized his large, muscular build.

Expelling thick cigarette smoke from his nose and mouth, the man glared at her. To make matters worse, he had company—lots of company. There were about twelve other men, some with beer bottles in hand as they emerged from the shadows. The acoustics of the foyer echoed the menacing sound of their low chortles as they continued to move increasingly nearer. Within a matter of moments Camile and Sir Drayden were completely surrounded.

"You know what? I bet we have the wrong address." Camile chuckled nervously, turning to the knight. Eyes widening, she whispered, "Quick! Do something! You can take them!"

Her heart sank when Sir Drayden joined the men in laughter, bowing to them slightly in salutation. After reciprocating the greeting, the men returned their attention to Camile, who thought:

Great! I'm all alone in a deserted building with a group of creepy-ass men! This cannot end well!

The men parted, creating a path for her to walk further into the building. Camile felt a nudge on her back, presumably from Sir Drayden, forcing her to continue onward. She nearly collapsed with relief when she reached one of the empty rundown apartments and saw the shaman waiting for her inside.

"Your Wisest!" She exhaled a deep sigh of relief before turning to Sir Drayden. "Why didn't you just tell me she was here? You and those guys scared the crap out of me."

The shaman smiled before waving the men out the room. Sir Drayden, however, remained. Nevertheless, the environmental tension slackened. The dusty room was empty except for two facing wooden chairs and a tattered, black trash bag, which served as a makeshift curtain. The plastic flapped in the gentle breeze coming through the window. Tabitha instructed Camile to sit while taking her place in the opposite chair.

"Who are those guys?" Camile inquired.

"That will be explained after the demonstration. We're already running behind schedule," Sir Drayden replied as he positioned himself in a corner of the room, away from Camile and her counselor.

Camile noticed a small brown leather sack in Tabitha's hand.

"What's that?" She inquired.

"A surprise." The shaman's lips parted, revealing perfect white teeth gleaming in contrast to her mocha skin. "But first, close your eyes and focus on your breathing."

Camile hesitated a moment, but did as instructed.

"Slow, controlled breaths," the shaman continued. "Focus on nothing but your senses—the smell of the air, the sensation of it against your skin, the taste in your mouth, the sound of my voice, the darkness of your eyelids…"

As Camile focused on all those things she began to relax. She felt herself sinking as the hard chair beneath her became soft and malleable. The stale air suddenly became somewhat fresh and salty. The slight chill of it had transmuted to intense warmth. Without invitation, she opened her eyes. Startled, she leapt to her feet, inspecting her surroundings. She and the shaman were no longer in the desolate room, but a vast desert. Tabitha chuckled to herself before reaching into her leather sack, pulling out two golden apples. She tossed one to Camile.

"I brought us a little something to snack on," the shaman stated. "But there's something I want you to do before you eat it. We don't have very long."

She instructed Camile to experience the apple with each of her individual senses. Not sure of what the elder woman was getting at, Camile obliged by feeling, seeing, tasting and smelling the apple. She tapped it with her index finger to hear the sound it made. When she was done, she returned her attention to Tabitha, who smiled knowingly, taking a quick bite of her own apple, savoring its flavor.

"Try it again on my mark." The elder woman glanced around the empty desert before retuning her gaze to her young student. "*Now. Quickly!*"

Camile sniffed the apple. The sweet aroma that had been there just seconds earlier had mysteriously vanished. Puzzled, she went on to tap it, but heard no sound. Taking another bite, she experienced no flavor whatsoever. Suddenly, the apple slipped through her hand like an apparition. When she tried to retrieve it from the sand she found it impossible to grasp as her hands passed through it. Bewildered, she regarded the shaman before returning her attention to the apple. It was nowhere to be seen. The only trace of it was the diminishing dent that remained in the sand dune. All sound was beginning to falter as the whistling wind grew more intense.

"Do you understand, my child?" Tabitha raised her voice slightly to compete with the howling wind. "The veils are shifting! You might not be able to see them, but they're there—most of the time, anyway." She smiled.

Camile shielded her eyes against the hot, prickly sand being carried on the wind, brushing against her face as her hair whipped around wildly. She caught a brief whiff of the salty air before the scent faded away. Soon, the blowing sand no longer stung her face and the sensation of the wind itself had dissipated, though she could still see it reshaping the sand dunes. The shaman simply stood there, smiling softly as she regarded Camile with squinted eyes. She said something, but Camile couldn't hear her voice. In fact, she couldn't hear anything at all. Her vision was her only remaining sense, but she knew it would soon be gone.

Here it comes, Tabitha appeared to say. A second later Camile found herself completely submerged in darkness. All of her senses seemed to have abandoned her, suspending her in a state of nothingness.

Is this what death is like? she wondered, but figured she couldn't possibly be dead because she was still thinking.

Maybe Rene Descartes was right, 'I think, therefore I am.'

Shortly after the thought entered her mind, her ears were greeted by the steady, yet excited rhythm of her heartbeat. The blackness peeled away as her senses gradually returned. Lying on the dirty floor, she saw the shaman looking down at her. Astonished, Camile realized they were once again in the tiny rundown room in the old abandoned building. Beside her was her partially eaten apple.

The shaman explained that the phenomenon they had just experienced was called a split-progression. A split-progression was an instance where a veil's layers would suddenly divide as the position of the phenomenon gradually travelled.

"Over the years, split-progressions were monitored by select members of the Transcendent World," she continued, helping Camile to her feet. "A pattern was eventually established to predict such occurrences by mapping their projected paths. However, there are sometimes spontaneous changes that cannot be predicted."

Speechless, Camile shook her head in amazement while dusting herself off.

Sir Drayden's voice sliced through the silence.

"To answer your earlier question, the men you met when you arrived are nomadic guardians designated to monitor and protect the split-progression on this particular path," he said, stepping out from the shadowy corner. "It has been their job for many centuries. They disguise themselves as drunkards, thugs and misfits to deter and prevent unauthorized people from crossing these portals."

Amazed, Camile realized how well the guardians' disguises had worked as far as inciting intimidation.

*   *   *

Sir Drayden seemed less than pleased to run into Commissioner Thornton as they exited the building. The commissioner smirked, setting down a metal crate he'd been carrying. Peering out of a small slot were two large orange eyes. Keeping her distance, Camile craned her neck to get a better look. She jumped as a shrill bellow escaped the now rattling container.

"He's still miffed, I'm afraid." The commissioner laughed, explaining that the mysterious creature had escaped from Krohme.

Excusing himself, he pulled Sir Drayden aside and whispered something Camile couldn't make out.

"Who?" The knight's lips tightened as his gaze grew cold.

"I thought it would be obvious. You must be a busier man than I pegged you for." Vincent's grin broadened as he leaned in, whispering anew. The knight's jaw clenched, nostrils flaring.

"Since you have other obligations, I'll be happy to escort Camile back to Caldaq." Vincent offered.

"That won't be necessary. She's coming with me." Sir Drayden answered abruptly. "Besides, you have obligations of your own."

"Very well. Sorry your bargain wasn't more successful, but at least you'll show her what happens to people who renege on their agreements." The commissioner chortled.

"You know what the biggest difference is between us, Vincent, other than your obvious need to overcompensate? Although I do my work, and do it efficiently, I don't always have the luxury of enjoying it." Sir Drayden glared before walking off. As though pulled by a magnetic force, Camile followed.

Chapter 55

Claiming Innocence

Camile and Sir Drayden entered the residence, which seemed typical of a young single parent. It was reasonably tidy, except for a few toys and books strewn here and there. Sitting back in the recliner, the woman popped a few tablets into her mouth, downing them with a glass of some kind of spirit. Her face appeared heavily abused by the hands of time. Closing her eyes, she released a long sigh as whatever she had ingested began taking effect.

She recoiled upon reopening her lids and screamed unintelligibly, falling on her backside in her attempt to run away. Scrambling to her feet, she staggered into the adjoining room. When Camile entered she saw the sobbing woman huddled in a corner, clutching a small child. The vision of the cowering woman caused Camile to recollect how her own mother had fought to prevent her from being taken by Sir Drayden as a child.

"We can't do this. It's wrong." Camile protested, stepping in the knight's path, blocking his approach. In turn, she was now directly in the trail of his icy purposeful gaze.

"You're in no position to make that determination. I'm bound by my duty to remove the child. A lesson must be learned. Step aside."

"What can you possibly teach him in death that he can't learn in life?" Camile asked, hoping to stall for time as she figured out a way to protect the child from Sir Drayden, but had no ideas.

"What makes you think the lesson is for him?" He grimaced. With a casual wave of his hand, he forced her out of the way with unseen propulsion.

Falling onto the child's bed, she watched helplessly as the knight loomed over the woman like a towering shadow of inevitable doom. Still weeping, she shielded her son as best she could. The child whimpered, training his large watery eyes on the leather duster clad man staring down at him.

"Mommy!" He cried tremulously, his small fingers digging into her arm.

"Shh. Don't be frightened, little man. I'm not going to hurt you," Sir Drayden hushed, sweeping a hand over the boy's head, lulling him into a deep sleep. "You'll be just fine."

Camile shudder inside as she wondered why the action seemed so familiar. Her mental voyage was cut short upon realizing they had company. An intermediary had slipped into the room. Undetected by the mother, it knelt beside her, touching the sleeping boy's stomach. As Camile had witnessed several times before, the life energy streamed out of the body and was carried away by the intermediary. Afterward, she noticed the boy had stopped breathing. His body slumped lifelessly in his mother's arms, the color draining from his serene face.

"No!" The woman wailed, making repeated failed attempts to rouse her son as the knight walked away; Camile reluctantly joined his side. Frantically trailing behind him, the mother pleaded to trade places with her son. She gasped sharply and recoiled as he suddenly turned on his heel, pointing a finger at her like a sword.

"There are no easy outs for the dishonorable! There are people who go their entire lives wishing for the chance you've been given and you squandered it," Sir Drayden said forcefully, his voice heavy with resentment.

Camile could no longer contain her sorrow as silent tears burned tracks down her face.

"Do yourself a favor. Next time you make a promise, you *keep it!*" Sir Drayden chided the woman. Lowering his arm, he frowned at Camile. "Save your tears. Trust me, she doesn't deserve them. Sometimes, a second chance is all you get, if even that." The urgency of his voice spiked, matching his intense stare. "Don't waste yours like she did."

Camile later learned that the woman had broken a solemn vow to turn her destructive life around for the sake of her son—who was dying of an inoperable illness at the time. Her plea had been considered and she was granted the opportunity to care for her child, forsaking her life of partying, drugs and alcoholism. Unfortunately, her brief bout of sobriety eventually came to a crashing end and her addictions rebounded, replacing her son as her top priority.

*   *   *

Somewhere in the distance a lone wolf was howling, perhaps separated from its pack. It led Camile to recall the flawed mother and doomed child, rekindling her disapproval of how Sir Drayden had handled the situation. She wondered if he was bitter at the world due to the loss of his wife and sought to share his grief by destroying other people's bonds. Rubbing her arms to offset the chilly air permeating her pink sweatshirt, she moved from the terrace to her quarters. She heard other wolves joining the first in a chorus of howls as she crossed the threshold.

At least one family has a happy ending tonight.

Jeremy was a welcome sight when he arrived at her door moments later. The two sat awhile and discussed her feelings, but Camile held back. She was feeling more emotional than she was letting on, but didn't want him to think she couldn't handle it. Even so, he seemed to detect the gravity of her mood and suggested a brief meditation session to help ease her mind.

They sat in facing chairs and Jeremy coached her to concentrate on her mental relaxation. Thoughts of the day's unsettling events slowly drifted to the back of her mind until all she was aware of was herself sitting across from her partner. Her eyes closed, she could still see his face in her mind as her focus shifted to his lips, remembering what they felt like. The warm pressure against her mouth seemed so real. Parting her lids, she saw that Jeremy was leaning forward, kissing her tenderly. She returned his amorous gesture as they rose slowly to their feet, coming together in a passionate embrace. Retiring to the sofa, the two continued their tender ministrations, their soulful hands cautiously exploring one another over obstructive fabric.

Camile's temperature climbed as Jeremy gently brushed the entryway of her mouth with his tongue. Parting her lips further, she invited it inside as he reclined, pulling her on top of him. The pressure of her body against his masculine frame increased her arousal. She could feel the fiery pent-up desire radiating from his body. It pulsed with each heartbeat as he gently stroked her back. Burying his face into the crook of her neck, he took in her scent. Camile shuddered, feeling the electric warmth of his fingers as they ended their journey to the small of her back, where her undershirt had escaped her waistband. Instinctively, she nuzzled against his fuzzy head, caressing his firm biceps. Jeremy expelled a tremulous moan, heating her skin.

"I know we don't want to, but we have to stop," Jeremy said softly. The tone of his voice struck a chord of arousal in Camile's mind, sending cruel signals to her throbbing femininity which she knew she'd have to ignore. The intoxicating combination of anticipation and anxiety all but consumed her. Knowing her body's craving had already gotten her into trouble once before, she reluctantly began peeling herself away. Jeremy stopped her, encircling his arm around her waist.

"I'm sorry," he said. "This is just going a little fast. I don't think it's a good idea to consummate our relationship just yet. When the time comes, I want us to be ready not only physically, but also spiritually and mentally. Something like that is special and shouldn't be rushed. I hope you understand."

Looking into his eyes, Camile nodded, trying not to let her face reveal her body's disappointment.

"Yeah, I understand," she said shakily. "I just hope I'll be able to control myself as easily as you do."

Jeremy's chest tremored with a soft chortle. "Trust me; it sure as hell ain't easy, but it's the right thing to do."

Lying in his warm embrace, she sank deeper into relaxation. It was as comfortable as a soothing blanket, shielding her against the harsh elements. It ached her to know they would have to part for the evening.

"If you don't mind, I'd like to stay like this a little longer," she said.

"If I didn't know any better, I'd say you got your telepathy back." A subtle smile emerged as he kissed her forehead, tightening his embrace. "I'm not ready to let go just yet, either."

Nestling against his chest, Camile breathed deeply, relishing the wondrous moment, wishing she could make it last.

*   *   *

Awakening in his arms, Camile realized she and Jeremy were bathed in sunlight, streaming from the window. She had no idea of how long she had been asleep, but knew it was the best she had gotten in quite some time. Looking upward into Jeremy's slumbering face, she realized that they had fallen asleep in each other's arms, remaining there through the night. Maybe their hunger for a connection had finally gotten the best of them, throwing them together just short of physical intimacy. Perhaps their unexpected slumber was to do with emotional exhaustion upon realizing they had finally found what they were both seeking—understanding and growing trust.

Camile wasn't sorry about having slept the night away in his arms. Looking at Jeremy, who suddenly roused, she wasn't sure if he felt the same way. After regaining his sense of location, he appeared to ponder the potential consequences they could face for their night together. Inspecting his timepiece, his face had hardened into that brooding expression she knew so well. Catching a glimpse of the time, Camile understood why. He was late for his shift.

"We're gonna catch hell for this, aren't we?" Camile sleepily murmured into Jeremy's warm chest as he stroked her tousled waves.

"There's a strong possibility." He sighed. Camile enjoyed the sound of his voice vibrating in his chest.

"What's the worst that can happen?" she asked, not fully wanting to hear an answer.

"To you? Not much."

"But you?" She met his eyes.

"That's complicated." Jeremy gently nudged her aside as he sat up on the sofa, running his hands over his head. Sitting beside him, Camile massaged his cotton-shrouded shoulders, kissing one of them.

"How so?"

"I violated my agreement." He frowned, turning his body slightly to face her. "When I was signed on as your meditative coach I specifically had to agree to a set of conditions; one of them was for me to keep our relationship professional. Given the sensitive nature of your unique and highly valued persuasive abilities, it's been feared that if you were to—" Jeremy expelled a breath, letting the sentence hang there. Seeing Camile's encouraging nod, he continued, "There's a possibility that intimacy can interfere with your abilities."

"Are you serious? Were you specifically asked not to sleep with me?"

"It wasn't put in such a crude manner." Jeremy frowned.

"Probably not, but essentially I was fitted with a chastity belt in the form of some sort of contract I wasn't even aware of. Besides, we didn't actually do anything last night, so I guess it's working."

"Even though we didn't make love, we came close. That's enough to cross the line and it's mostly my fault." Jeremy rose to his feet, smoothing his rumpled clothes. "I'm sorry, but this can't happen again."

"But nothing happened!" Camile laughed in disbelief as she stood before him. "Come on, Jeremy. Why should we deprive ourselves of a chance at happiness and love? It's not fair to let the council rule your personal life, even if I am the defense minister's daughter."

"I understand where you're coming from, but that doesn't change the fact that I have guidelines to follow."

"Newsflash: You already broke them by getting as close to me as you did," Camile said. "Anyway, you're technically not instructing me anymore since Sir Drayden reassigned you. Doesn't that nullify your agreement?"

Jeremy went silent for a few moments, apparently considering Camile's statement.

"My reassignment was meant to be a temporary arrangement; no doubt to prevent this from happening."

"As far as I know, chances of changing the past are slim. Why not make the most of the present? When I'm done with my training, chances are I'll be headed into some life-threatening situations. I don't have a third strike, so I want to make the most of the life I do have and I want love to be part of it." She took his hand. "I want you to be part of it, Jeremy."

He sighed, pulling her into a tight hug. "You realize this won't be easy, don't you?"

"I expect nothing less." Camile leaned her forehead against his.

From that night on, the two progressed their romantic relationship. Since they were testing the waters of their changing bond, which they knew was highly unlikely to be accepted, they thought it best to keep it secret. Deep down, Camile wanted to proudly declare to the world that her heart had finally captured the once elusive joy, now fluttering within it. Nevertheless, she joined Jeremy's cadence as they carefully choreographed their relationship, safeguarding it from prying eyes. It made Camile feel as though she was having an affair with a married man, only in this case, the man happened to be married to his duty.

Though she felt it was unjust, having to hide their relationship, Camile also found it somewhat exhilarating. There was something alluring about getting closer to sampling the forbidden fruit of their passion, while at the same time building a bond with the man she loved. The danger of their secret relationship being exposed made the thrill all the sweeter. She and Jeremy had something that belonged solely to them, tucked safely away from controlling overseers. There was a sense of empowerment that their love was prevailing against the odds. Still, she couldn't help but wonder how long they could keep up the charade.

Filled with jubilant contentment, Camile found new motivation to succeed in her endeavors. As a result of her inspiration, she was able to accomplish almost everything with ease. She felt as though her soul had been inoculated against doubt and despair. She wasn't the only one to take notice of her newfound attitude. After one of her sessions with Sir Drayden, Camile found her mood to be the subject of his analysis.

"Good job, today. You seem more at ease than usual. Should this be attributed to a change in your routine?" Sir Drayden inquired.

"I guess I'm just having a good day, that's all." Camile flashed a quick smile, wanting to exit the room before he could see through her deceptive response. "Am I dismissed?"

The silence was deafening as the knight seemed to continue his appraisal of her demeanor. Finally, he nodded, allowing her to go on her way.

Camile wondered if he was onto her. Thoughts circled her head as she was hit with a brief wave of fear of what might happen if he found out about her and Jeremy. Finding the strength to put it in the back of her mind, she decided not to waste any time worrying about it.

Chapter 56

The Visitor

Shortly after her session Camile was informed that her parents wanted to see her. The officers escorted her through a series of unfamiliar passageways, leading her to a room with a heavy iron door, left ajar. She traversed the entryway, noticing antique-looking adornments and fixtures. Her parents greeted her before announcing the reason for their impromptu meeting.

"Camile, I think it's long overdue for you to meet Charles, the engineer who helped build my ship," Zephyr announced. "We figured he'd be the best person to provide you with the information you're about to learn. We've held back certain things because we knew it would be easier for you to grasp once you hear his story."

Camile's eye drifted to an unusual chair located beside her seat; it resembled a gel filled stress ball. She surmised it was for the man in question. While awaiting the arrival of their guest, Zephyr inquired about the progress she was making in all aspects of her training. She responded by mentioning that she was getting the hang of using the weaponry she was currently studying. Additionally, she mentioned that the shaman was helping her to control the intensity of her moods.

"How are things with Sir Drayden?" Zephyr inquired. "I'm aware he's taken over for Jeremy."

Camile tried not to blush at the sound of his name.

"It takes some getting used to, but I'm taking it all in stride." She wrung her hands in her lap.

"So I've heard." Zephyr cracked an encouraging smile. "For once, Sir Drayden's had nothing but praise for your progress. That's reassuring given the decision we'll have to make soon, but more about that later. Charles is here."

A cloaked, hooded figure slowly approached the oval table where Camile and her parents were seated. Her mouth fell agape as the person pulled his hood back with long bony fingers. As the fabric was pulled away, it revealed a clammy, sallow face with dark saucer-like eyes; the most prominent of his facial features. He resembled what Camile could only describe as:

"*An alien?* They really exist?" she whispered to her father.

Her mind was suddenly careening through vague thoughts of speculative propaganda of paranormal activity, perpetrated by numerous Coexistent media agencies over the years. She had always thought the documentation was an exaggerated presentation of random facts, but never imagined she'd witness how accurate some of the reports really were.

"Alien?" Charles snorted bitterly, his voice thin and dry. "*Alien* is a state of mind, sweetheart."

So, this is Charles, Camile thought. *Who'd have thought that such an unusual creature would have such a simple name?*

Without warning he removed his loose-fitting cloak, revealing his lithe body. Camile only caught a glimpse of his bare flesh before turning away in astonishment. However, she didn't avert her eyes in time to avoid seeing the details of his vein-laced physique.

Charles apologized hesitantly before neatly covering the seat with his cloak, carefully settling into the chair. "I thought you knew. I probably should've warned you first."

"No. We should've," Zephyr palmed his forehead, turning to his daughter. "Charles and his people have a very delicate skin condition. He's been cordial enough to wear clothes when conducting public business. Your mother and I are aware of how painful it is for him to do this, so we allow him a respite when he meets with us."

"Well, not all of my people are as accommodating as I." Charles chortled. "Not that I blame them. Wearing clothing is quite literally a pain in the ass...and everywhere else. I mostly do it as a test to see if I could get used to them. So far, I haven't."

Camile felt herself teetering between averting her gaze completely or keeping her eyes fixed on him. Knowing both options would be considered rude, Camile kept her gaze on her hands, taking brief, occasional glances at him instead. Curiosity got the best of her, making it impossible for her eyes to resist wandering to the lower region of his fragile looking frame. Her eyes widened when she realized he had no visible genitalia.

That definitely has to put a damper on his sex life, she thought, surprised such a thing had crossed her mind.

"I understand this must be disturbing for you; to see someone like me up close, said the frail looking man. "Would it make it easier if I put my robe back on?"

Though his offer was polite, Camile could tell he dreaded the prospect of getting dressed. She couldn't imagine not being able to tolerate something as soft as clothing. Then she remembered the time she'd gotten a mild case of sunburn as a teenager. Having a low threshold for pain herself, she sympathized.

"It's fine," she answered. "You can stay as you are."

Charles' eyes closed briefly in apparent relief as he thanked her.

"Still, I can't say that I blame you for being a bit intimidated," he said. "Others like me have given my race a bad name. As a result, we've been demonized throughout the Coexistent and Transcendent Worlds."

Camile's eyes narrowed. "You're referring all the stories about alien abductions, aren't you?"

Charles snorted bitterly. "Yes. But I loathe the term *alien*. We prefer to call ourselves *Talis*. It sounds a little more dignifying to our race."

"Which planet are you from?"

"Planet? My dear, you're not even close."

"Then where *are* you from; another dimension other than the two I already know of?"

"As they say in the Coexistent World…*Bingo!*" Charles exclaimed with a smile that seemed somewhat strained on his thin lips. "When the Coexistents first witnessed the appearance of what they believed to be alien aircraft, they concentrated their attention deep into space. It never occurred to them to evaluate their own planet to locate the origin of our advanced society."

Floored, Camile toggled her attention between Charles and her parents.

"How many other dimensions are there?" Camile asked herself, unaware he had heard her.

"No one really knows, but it's refreshing to know we aren't alone. Ironically, it's also quite unsettling," Charles replied somberly.

"Does everyone in your—?" Camile stopped herself. "Oh, never mind. It's too rude to ask."

"No, go ahead. Not much offends me anymore. My race has done most of that for themselves."

"Does everyone in your dimension…*look* like you?"

Charles nodded, his large black eyes watering. "We didn't always look this way. For the longest time we actually looked more like you. You see,

Camile, although people call us *alien* and we call ourselves *Talis*, there's no denying who we really are; *human*."

Camile's jaw dropped as she felt a similar shock to what she experienced when she discovered the true identities of Akalina and Zareah.

"What happened? Who did this to you?" she inquired, her face contorted.

"We did it to ourselves," Charles answered solemnly. "We were so wrapped up in improving the quality of technology, we eventually overlooked the quality of our lives as well as our environment. We became so obsessed with technological advancements and focused our attention so far into the future that we didn't pay attention to what was happening right in front of us. We overlooked the damage that was being done to our environment—and to our very bodies. The transformation was gradual. By the time we realized what was happening it was already too late. The damage had already been done and had reached a point of irreversibility.

"The environmental conditions had become unlivable for many species in our world. Hundreds of our wildlife suddenly began to mysteriously fall dead in disturbing numbers. Many species became extinct in a matter of decades. Air pollutants acted as a curtain, blocking our most cherished star from shining down upon us. In fact, the sun disappeared for so long that many forgot what it looked like and when it finally returned, we wished to God it hadn't. Many of my people were permanently blinded and their skin badly scorched." Charles briefly lowered his attention to his hands. Shaking his head, he continued:

"Everything had drastically changed, from the air quality to our way of life. *So many* people suffered and died. Most of them gladly embraced their deaths in the end. Ironically, our overzealous attempts to improve our lives nearly wiped out our entire race. The survivors began to physically evolve in order to withstand the conditions of our new environment."

Charles went on to describe what had caused the emaciated appearance of his people. It was due to the fact their bodies lost the ability to absorb nutrients as efficiently as they once did. He also explained that the discoloration and sensitivity of their skin was a condition brought on by air pollutants in addition to their intolerance to sunlight. As a result, Charles' people suffered chronic pain and a heightened, agonizing response to pressure.

"Nevertheless," he continued, "we lowered our standard of living and adapted to the degraded conditions of our world. Then one day, an opening was discovered; an opening that led us here, to the Transcendent World and eventually into the Coexistent World. When my people first crossed between dimensions many years ago, most of them died as soon as they passed through the veil. The air was so fresh it was a shock to their systems.

Many others became violently ill and had to slowly acclimate themselves to the new environment.

"When we noticed that there was another entire race of humans in the Transcendent World, we regained a new sense of hope. We rejoiced at the chance of restoring what we destroyed. My people were anxious about approaching the humans directly, so we...*abducted* them." Charles sighed, hanging his head before resuming eye contact. "The reason for this is not nearly as malicious as it sounds. We analyzed them for research purposes. We tracked them over time and monitored their biological progression as well as their adaptation to the changes in their own environment. Our goal was to figure out exactly where our genetic code had been rewritten. It took many years for us to figure it out, but when we did, the next logical step was to attempt to re-sequence and repair our own genetic structure by copying the DNA from humans in the Transcendent and Coexistent World*s*."

"Those experiments didn't work, did they?" Camile deduced.

"As you can clearly see, they did not," Charles replied bitterly, gesturing to his appearance. "It's unnatural to have to grow your offspring in labs. We have no choice since we've lost the ability to reproduce by traditional breeding. It's equally unnatural to not have the ability to engage in physical intimacy with our loved ones. Well, I guess you came to that conclusion on your own."

Camile felt slightly embarrassed. It was painfully obvious that Charles had caught her gawking at his vacant crotch earlier. Yet, she understood what it was like to endure unquenched desire.

"Unfortunately, we noticed the Coexistents were having volatile reactions to our experiments." Charles explained. " The Transcendents, who were more physically resilient, offered to assist us in our endeavor under the condition we leave the Coexistents be. In return for their alliance, we granted them the gift of some of our technological advancements, which they handled more responsibly than we did."

According to Charles, not everyone was satisfied with the accord. Some of his people wanted more and were dissatisfied with the rate of their progress. They eventually defied the agreement and proceeded to continue abducting, and experimenting on, humans without the approval of our government; often for devious purposes."

*   *   *

Silence fell over the room as Camile reflected on what she had just learned. Still in awe, she had no immediate questions, so her father resumed the discussion.

"As you've already been informed, the Coexistents are fighting the *Invisible War*." Zephyr's deep gray eyes reflected the ominous subject matter. "No doubt you've seen the malignant rage spreading throughout the Coexistent World. It's destroying the human connection. The more they isolate themselves from each other, the more they're disarmed from what they're up against. Every negative decision they make accumulates and contributes to their potential demise. The current state of their world is making it evident that they are running out of time."

"They ignore the damage they're doing to each other and to their environment," Kylie added. "Even worse, their compassion is rapidly diminishing. It's ironic; the more advanced they become in the fields of technology, business and communication, the more detached they become from their awareness of their spiritual connection. That's exactly what happened to Charles and his people." She turned her amber gaze in his direction. "He recognizes the signs so clearly."

Camile noticed Charles' head nodding with a slight bend of his fragile-looking neck. He wore a somber expression as he regarded her with what she could only guess were sad eyes.

"He wants to salvage the Coexistents because they, along with us, may hold their last chance to correcting the damage they've done to themselves." Zephyr held his wife's hand. "This is not to say the Coexistents are mindless of the challenges before them. We are aware of the fact they are trying their best to reestablish their connection with one another, but the adversity they're facing is far too great for them to shoulder on their own."

Turning his attention to his daughter, his expression turned grim. "Charles knows that in a matter of years, the Coexistents will lose their chance to reduce the damage being done to their world and each other. Of course we, the Transcendents, are equally passionate about helping them win this phase of the war. In order for them to do that, they have to reconnect with each other and realize that in spite of their differences, they face the same challenges and battles. They need to realize that they are similar where it counts. This isn't as easy as it sounds. Quite the contrary. It's a daily struggle. Getting people to care is often a stupendous challenge in itself. Most are inclined to shut themselves off to disconnect from the devastation going on around them. It's a defense mechanism, but in the process, they only blind themselves and live in a world of ignorance. Caring can be exhausting, but it's necessary to keep humanity alive and connected. Of course there is such a thing as caring too much, allowing things to bombard your heart. However, there is a balance that can be achieved. Everything must be seen in rational perspective."

"And I have to do all that?" Camile raised an eyebrow.

"We never said your job would be easy, but hopefully, you'll manage once your anchor is lifted," her mother responded. "You'll be relieved to know that it'll be happening soon, provided your next few missions go smoothly. Ideally, we'd like to hold off on lifting it awhile longer, but in light of the situation we're facing, it appears time is of the essence."

"That's certainly a refreshing prospect to look forward to," Camile stated, feeling all the more motivated to do her best on her upcoming assignments. "There's something I'm not clear on; when will the next phase of the *Invisible War* begin?"

Zephyr's somber expression spoke volumes, as did his next words: "It will begin if we fail. So, let's hope like hell it never arrives."

*   *   *

Camile was mildly disgusted by the idea of having to clean up the Coexistent's messes as they were mostly unaware of her existence. There was a familiar tightness in her chest, no doubt connected like a taut cord to her envious thoughts. Her contemplation circled the apparent obliviousness displayed by the inhabitants of the world she once called home. Yes, these people, too, had their problems—many of them self-imposed—but even so, they were able to carry on with a petty disposition that seemed to mock her plight. Even with meditation, Camile felt imprisoned by her emotions and sometimes found herself wishing to be rid of them.

At times, she longed for the ability to ignore them as skillfully as some of the Coexistent residents she and her group were sent to observe. Why was she one of the few chosen to experience the full depth of her emotions to such a degree that it brought her to the precipice of her sanity? In time, her self-pity evolved to acceptance, giving way to her determination to make the most of the situation. After all, there had to be some kind of advantage she'd be able to gain from her burdensome gift, or so she wished.

Since the attack on Jade, the council initiated security efforts, including sentinels, to guard potential recruits. Similarly, Camile was sent to witness how recruits were initially selected. In a world filled with billions of people, she knew the task was a difficult one. This is something with which Raine concurred before explaining that the first phase of finding a suitable potential began with assessing various people's behavior. Patience, courtesy, respect and general intelligence were among the highest of the basic values sought in each individual. If the person passed the initial evaluation, they were slotted for more in-depth assessment before contact was made. Up until that point, the subject remained oblivious to the fact they were being thoroughly studied.

"Sometimes, searching for the right one is like trying to find air under water. So, we watch, evaluate and wait, and wait…and wait…" Raine sighed exhaustedly as they sat on the park bench. The purplish tint of her hair intensified in the light of the setting sun.

"There's dishonesty and perversion everywhere you look. For example…" She pointed to a stocky businessman with a slick receding hairline. "Mr. Baldy there has been double dipping in the corporate business account for years. You don't even want to know how many lives he screwed up. Can't wait 'til this prick gets what's comin' to him. He's been embezzling money and splitting it with his assistant. A small payment for some of her…*unofficial services*." Raine air quoted the words with her fingers. "I wonder if her husband minds. Probably not since he's been busy with transgressions of his own. I don't know why some Coexistents get married in the first place. Apparently people confuse *I do* with *I do you and you and you.*"

"Seriously, if some of these people spent as much time using their heads as they do giving it, they wouldn't be in such a jam." Justine yawned. "This is the monotonous part—sitting, watching, waiting…"

Camile understood their frustration. She, too, saw the Caligula-like sadism blazing through many parts of the Coexistent World. Some allowed their flames to burn brazenly while others concealed theirs beneath a blanket of false propriety, but like smoke, their actions contaminated society whether or not the fire had spread. Still, she felt compelled to defend her former world of residence and did so by stating that all Coexistents shouldn't be based on the misdeeds of a few unscrupulous people. She also presented her mother as living proof of the existence of their generous, compassionate nature. Like a diamond, it remained obscured in the soot of their resentment, which had formed due to years of crushed hope and shattered dreams.

Chapter 57

Jealousy

As previously arranged, Camile arrived at the Coronis Pier to meet Jeremy, but he was nowhere in sight. It wasn't like him to be late. He had informed her of a surprise he wanted to show her. Though highly curious as to what it was, she patiently awaited his arrival. Watching the water shimmering in the afternoon sun, she found her mind drifting to the recent knowledge she had acquired. She never imagined how deeply complicated the Transcendent/Coexistent situation truly was. It presented an air of uncertainty that she couldn't shake. The full extent of her quest was drawing nearer and it only fed her anxiety.

Will I be ready for this? she wondered before internally answering her own question.

I sure as hell better be. My failure will sign a lot of death certificates.

"Finally managed to get rid of your hidden shadow, I see," a male voice broke her ominous contemplation.

It was Brandon.

Camile had been so preoccupied she didn't notice him standing several feet away, skipping stones across the mirror-like water. His lush dark hair slightly brushed over the upturned collar of his black wool jacket.

What's that supposed to mean? Camile wondered as she approached him.

"I guess I can't blame the man," Brandon continued, his eyes a near-perfect color match with his faded jeans. "If you were mine I'd be on you like a second skin. So, you and Jeremy, huh? Have to admit I never saw that one coming." He smiled bitterly, breaking his sparkling gaze to cast another stone into the water.

He knows? How did he find out? Camile thought, trying to figure out if either she or Jeremy had made an error in their attempt at anonymity.

"Brandon, please...Don't do this," she implored as she reached his side, making sure to keep a respectable distance.

"Don't do what?" He frowned. "Point out your lapse in judgment? I'm not sure what rationalization you used to make your decision, but your outlook was obviously skewed. You and I are better suited for each other and you know it. Jeremy's a very good friend of mine, but even I must admit he has baggage you don't need. I know you can feel it."

Camile cocked her head. "Everyone has baggage these days, including me. Besides, I get the feeling you're not exactly packing light yourself."

"I only pack heavy where it counts," Brandon quipped, his plump lips forming an impish smirk as he met her eyes.

Camile figured the saucy remark was his attempt at deflecting the validity of her statement. However, his naughty expression didn't have its usual fire and quickly faded, reflecting the tenderness in his voice.

"Please," he continued, "I'm just asking you to consider all the factors involved here. Don't rush into something you know you'll regret later. *Follow your heart, but allow your mind to refine your path,* remember?"

Though she was happy with Jeremy, Camile cared about Brandon and didn't enjoy seeing his obvious disappointment. She was desperate to find a way to be with Jeremy without losing Brandon's friendship. However, she knew the odds of that were slim for two reasons—the fact that there was thickening tension between them, and that Brandon was a very proud man, driven by the allure of winning. The choice of sacrificing one relationship for the other seemed as difficult as having to choose between food or water.

"I'm sorry, Brandon, but—"

"If you thought you made the right decision, you wouldn't be sorry."

Camile exhaled. "Look, I don't regret my decision. I just feel bad you got hurt in the process."

"So much for your mind refining your path." Brandon sighed with apparent disbelief. "My ego is slightly bruised, but I'll learn to deal with it," he said in a patronizing tone she wasn't used to, at least not from him.

"You seem pretty attached to the choice you've made. That usually happens when you've taken a step towards commitment." A lengthy pause filled the space between them before he asked a question Camile wasn't prepared for.

"Did you sleep with him?"

"With all due respect, I don't believe that's any of your concern." Camile unconsciously folded her arms across her chest.

Frowning anew, Brandon briefly shut his eyes before casting another stone into the water. Camile noticed that he threw it harder than the previous ones. Realizing she had unwittingly struck a defensive pose, she lowered her arms, but knew it was already too late.

Brandon's nostrils flared as he clenched his jaw. Though Camile didn't like the fact he was upset, she couldn't help but notice how well he wore his anger.

"We didn't explore the *Leih'klav*, if that's what you're getting at," she answered, not knowing why she felt the need to explain herself.

His face relaxed slightly as he exhaled. To Camile, it sounded like a sigh of relief.

"I'm curious. Why'd you choose him over me?"

"Brandon, I'm not gonna stand here and—"

"Here's what I think," he interrupted, turning his body to face her straight-on. The afternoon light made his eyes appear bluer than usual. For a brief instance, they held an intensity that bore a disturbing likeness to Sir Drayden's. "I think you chose the safety of being someone you're not over the danger of being yourself."

"Wh—? No. It's just..." Camile's voice trailed off. In her mind she knew he was right. Deep down, she felt choosing him would be a direct admission that she and Akalina weren't as different as she hoped. Of course, she couldn't come out and make Brandon aware of her reasoning. It would only strengthen his argument that they were a compatible pair.

"Look, you're my friend and I don't want to jeopardize that." She buried her hands in her pockets, wriggling her fingers. "Friendships don't exactly come easy for me and I value ours. I just couldn't risk losing that by complicating things more than they already are."

"Oh, don't feed me that bullshit, Wildflower. You don't believe that any more than I do." He a deep breath, briefly turning his attention skyward. "You're afraid of me, aren't you?"

Camile openly denied it, all the while thinking: *I'm afraid of us.*

"Okay. If it's not that; did you make your choice based on the fact we're not color coordinated?"

"That's ridiculous!" Camile's eyes widened. "I can't believe you'd insult me by thinking something like that. Besides, have you taken a look at my parents? My ethnicity isn't exactly monochromatic, you know."

"You're right; I'm reaching." He held up his hands. "That wasn't fair of me. For that, I apologize, but I think it's only fitting for me to warn you that this isn't over. I'll find a way to get you back."

"Get me back?" Camile slowly shook her head, eyes narrowed. "You never had me, Brandon."

"Keep telling yourself that, but we both know the truth. There will come a time when you'll no longer be able to deny it. I just hope that time comes before it's too late. Now, if you'll excuse me, I have business to attend to." He paused a moment, briefly training his gaze over her shoulder. "It's probably just as well. He's looking for you. I'd wish you a good time on your date, but I'm not usually very good at lying."

Sure enough when Camile turned around Jeremy was approaching the area. As she watched Brandon walk away she knew it would take something special to lift her spirits.

*   *   *

The temperature dropped as the sun slowly descended towards the horizon, setting the sky ablaze with orange and yellow. The color intensified the hue of the woods, which were beginning to reveal their autumn tints. Camile and Jeremy enjoyed an early supper at one of the taverns located at one of the higher levels of the Dusque peak of the Caldaq range. Camile voiced her concerns over the fact that Brandon was now aware of their relationship. Jeremy attempted to put her at ease, but it did little to extinguish her smoldering apprehension. When Jeremy suddenly rose from his seat Camile had a fleeting moment when she wondered if he was about to propose. She figured it was a silly thought since they hadn't been together very long; not to mention their relationship was against all odds. In fact, whenever they were out together in public, they were careful not to sit too closely or make physical contact in a manner that would be perceived as romantic.

Camile often had a difficult time adhering to the restriction and caught herself reaching for his hand on occasion only for him to remind her to uphold their secrecy. Those occasions were somewhat embarrassing for her, yet they also prompted her to wonder if she was more emotionally invested into the relationship than Jeremy. Guiding her out of the restaurant, he mentioned they would soon be joined by someone who would help make the excursion possible. However, he also noted the person was running inconveniently behind schedule.

"You have an accomplice in this? What, are you breaking rules now?" Camile laughed, but Jeremy maintained his serious demeanor.

"It wouldn't be the first time, but don't remind me." He shut his eyes for a moment as though calculating the possible repercussions if they were to get caught.

Camile saw Brandon approaching the tavern entrance and quickly averted her gaze. She figured if she didn't look his way it would spare her from the crushing sensation of awkwardness. When she heard his footsteps come to a stop just inches from where she and Jeremy were standing, she knew she wouldn't be so fortunate.

"You're late," Jeremy stated. "Was there a problem?"

"I ran into some untimely delays on my way here. I would've notified you," Brandon's eyes burned into Camile's, "but it would have been rude to interrupt your meal. Anyway, there's not much time left. If we head out now, we can still catch it."

Camile inquired as to what Brandon was referring, but Jeremy insisted it was a surprise. As Brandon led the way through a hidden tunnel, located a few levels above the tavern, she grew increasingly uneasy. Just prior to her romantic excursion with Jeremy, Brandon clearly voiced his displeasure about the fact they were together. Now, he was assisting them on their date. In Camile's mind, the situation completely redefined the word *awkward*.

Jeremy finally explained that they were headed to a scenic overlook, located at one of the higher plateaus above the restaurant. For safety reasons, the area was restricted to most. Brandon was among the few who had access. He pulled some strings and figured out a way for the two to enjoy the landscape. Camile was puzzled; his behavior didn't add up.

Once they reached the end of the long, unfinished tunnel, Brandon disappeared into what looked like a dark cave after instructing Camile and Jeremy to conceal themselves behind a rocky wall adjacent to the cavern. Prior to entering, he stated that he would inspect the portal and return shortly. Camile used the opportunity to voice her discomfort to Jeremy.

"I don't think this is such a good idea. Maybe we should do this some other time," she whispered.

"What's wrong?" Jeremy furrowed his brow.

Are you for real? Camile thought before responding, "Don't you think it'll be a little...*awkward*, him seeing us together like this? Especially since you had a prior relationship with his sister, not to mention the fact I remind him of you-know-who."

"I understand your apprehension, but Brandon is one of my most trusted colleagues and one of my best friends despite my history with Justine. I have full confidence that he has gotten past the situation and is fully aware that you aren't Akalina. He views you as you are, Camile." Jeremy smiled, stroking her hair.

I know. That's part of the problem, Camile thought, watching Brandon emerge from the cave with a fellow officer, thanking him for filling in.

"Being that you declined to have him replaced as your instructor and have since become friends with him, I thought you figured just as much," Jeremy added, retrieving her full attention.

"Yeah, well...I just wish you would've discussed this with me before telling him about us," she whispered.

"If I did that, then this wouldn't have been much of a surprise, would it?" He gave Camile a prying look. "Hey. Is there something I should know about?"

"No, I guess I'm just anxious about this whole thing. I never had to hide a relationship before." Camile sighed, knowing that revealing her last conversation with Brandon would do no good. "Did you at least...*ask* him if he was okay with this?"

"Actually, he—"

"He didn't have to," Brandon interrupted as he rejoined them. "You're all clear, but I doubt you'll have long." His eyes locked on Camile as she and Jeremy entered the portal, leaving him to stand guard. Somehow his statement seemed to carry a dual connotation.

The further Camile and Jeremy entered the aperture, the brighter it became until they found themselves on a cliff facing the sunset. Camile was astonished to see they were located on one of the smaller mountain ranges across from Caldaq. It boggled her mind to know that in just a few steps, she had traveled hundreds of miles. She was so stunned, in fact, she didn't immediately realize she had followed Jeremy to the very edge of the cliff. When this awareness kicked in, she leapt backward, pulling him with one hand and clutching her thumping chest with the other.

"Oh, God! Are you trying to get us killed?"

"Far from it." Jeremy smiled calmly as he offered his hand. "Trust me."

Camile briefly closed her eyes as she hoped she wouldn't regret giving him her trust. Together, they slowly approached the precipice of the cliff. She could feel gravity beckoning her eyes downward to the scarily distant ground and she hoped it wouldn't have the same success with her body. Jeremy stepped off first. With a deep breath, Camile followed and was instantly filled with kaleidoscopic emotion. Relief, liberation and electric exhilaration flowed through her body as she realized she had not fallen. Shifting her gaze to her feet, her heart rate elevated upon seeing nothing between them and the ground, far below. Each step the pair took triggered a subtle, but noticeable distortion. The air below rippled beneath their feet like water as the distant terrain faded and soon they were walking on air, both literally and figuratively.

Looking at Jeremy's smile, she could feel his adoration as his warm hand firmly engulfed hers. He halted his steps, prompting Camile to do the same, returning her eyes to the strange phenomenon at her feet. Fish-like shadows were darting beneath them in random patterns, slipping in and out of view like staggering figments of her imagination.

"Confusing, isn't it?" Jeremy asked. "So beautiful, yet scary and confusing all at once. There's no telling if we're really up or down. Everything seems to be here, nowhere and everywhere. It's the quintessential contradiction. Nothing about it seems to make any sense, but it's so amazing you don't need to understand the complexity of it, just admire its remarkable beauty. I wanted to show you this because whenever I think of this place, I think of you, Camile. You're so complicated and it confuses the hell out of me, but there's no escaping how I feel about you. I've tried."

Camile found herself without sufficient words to express the amorous joy incited by Jeremy's sentiment. Instead of attempting to assemble a collection of spontaneous fumbled words, Camile made use of her lips by applying them to his. It was an act he readily reciprocated. His warm embrace gave her a sense of security. That, coupled with the sensation of floating on air, filled her with a feeling of invincibility.

"Time's up," a voice boomed, ripping them from their kiss.

The two turned to see Brandon, standing in front of an approaching navy-blue curtain of star-studded night. The sun was nearly completely set behind the embracing couple as Brandon beckoned them to the rift. As they approached, Camile could see the brief return of his clenched jaw and flared nostrils before he quickly neutralized his outward demeanor.

"You were spotted," he announced. "Jeremy, since it's almost time for your return to the shaman, I'll take Camile back to her quarters."

Not wanting another awkward discussion with Brandon, Camile offered to travel solo. Jeremy rejected the idea.

"It'll only look more suspicious if you go back to the compound unescorted. You should go with Brandon. I'd take you myself, but there's no time for me to make it there and back before my shift. I'll see you in the morning," he said before muttering, "I knew this little adventure was probably ill-timed, but I'm glad I got to show you this."

He leaned in for a kiss, but Camile turned her face so it would land on her cheek. The action came as a reflex, but she wasn't sure why. Perhaps it was the nagging guilt she felt due to the fact Brandon had already witnessed them kissing once. Returning to the port entrance, Jeremy smiled to Camile as she departed with the commander.

*   *   *

During the trip back to Caldaq's central peak, Camile noticed how unusually calm Brandon seemed for someone whose career was on the line for assisting in trespassing. He walked at a leisurely pace while giving her the silent treatment, keeping his eyes fixed on the path before them. Camile was determined not to be the first one to speak, but the silence was unbearable. Her need to ascertain his wellbeing outweighed her stubbornness. However, she didn't ask him about his mood. Instead, she inquired about who had spotted them.

"That's not important," he answered blankly, not once breaking his gaze from the road ahead.

"Not important?" She frowned. "Don't tell me you're withholding information because of what happened back there."

"Okay, I won't."

The dismissive tone in his voice was getting under her skin and she had a feeling that's exactly what he wanted. Reclaiming her stubbornness, she refused to lose her cool. Camile took advantage of the renewed silence as an opportunity to reevaluate the past fifteen minutes. Something seriously didn't add up.

If we were spotted, the council would've sent about a dozen guards to escort me back, not to mention Sir Drayden would be all over my tail, she thought, halting her pace.

"You lied!" she exclaimed quietly. "No one saw us at all, did they?"

"I thought I saw someone. I guess I overreacted," Brandon replied casually, his eyes boring into hers. "At any rate, I figured it was better to be safe than sorry."

"Bull! You're interfering. For the life of me I can't fathom why Jeremy asked you for this favor, but you should've had the presence of mind to say no instead of toying with us."

Brandon averted his gaze, a look of mild shame crossed his chiseled face.

"Actually, I was the one who suggested the overlook for his romantic excursion," he confessed, meeting her eyes anew. "I thought it was a good idea; that is until I realized you were his date. By the time I did, it was too late to back out."

Speechless, Camile huffed in frustration as she made an about face to return to Jeremy.

"And just where do you think you're going?" he seized her arm.

"Where do you think?" Camile hissed, pulling away.

"Back to your quarters. That's where. Jeremy's on duty now, so he's in no position to socialize. Besides, it's coming up on your curfew. Not to mention, I want you nice and fresh tomorrow. Your defense skills have been getting a little sloppy as of late. Apparently there's a serious imbalance of business and pleasure on your part."

"Me? Imbalanced?" She chortled in disbelief. "Maybe you should reevaluate your actions for the past two hours. And for the record, my pleasure is none of your business."

"It's a shame, isn't it? Then again, that was your decision. Ask yourself something. Why do you think he's trying so hard to be so romantic? He's trying to mask the fact his feelings for you only run but so deep. Thing is, you're so blinded by what you think is love you fail to see it for yourself."

"I think that's your jealousy talking," she fumed.

"Possible, but you forgot about one thing, I love you and I'm willing to sacrifice everything to be with you. You see, when I love, I love fearlessly without restriction. I don't hold anything back. I wouldn't settle for having to restrain it for the sake of my career. Can you say the same about him?"

Camile was filled with a sudden sense of panic as a result of Brandon's amorous outpour. She hated the fact she couldn't come up with a rebuttal to his statement about Jeremy. Instead, she stood in stunned silence as he continued.

"Why do you think he split up with my sister?" His eyes narrowed. "Jeremy's trying to disassociate with conflict in every way imaginable. He can't be with anyone of warrior status and that includes you. Strong women may intimidate him, but they fascinate me. *You* fascinate me. You have a chance to end your mistake now before you get hurt."

"Brandon, the only one hurting me right now is you." Her voice quivered. "One of the things I've learned when I got to this world is how to persevere against all odds. What I have with Jeremy may not be perfect, but no relationship is. Even so, I'm determined to make it work."

"I see." Brandon's nostrils flared slightly as he pursed his lips. "Just so you know, it takes two to carry a successful relationship. I sure hope you're prepared to pick up his slack."

"You should be ashamed of yourself," she hissed. "Jeremy holds you in high regard as a friend. By badmouthing him behind his back, all you did was prove that you're not worthy of his praises."

Apparently, her words stung him as sharply as a slap to his face, which reflected his shock. Filled with a dizzying mixture of frustration, guilt and disgrace, Camile knew she had no choice but to follow Brandon to the compound. She did so without saying another word to him.

Chapter 58

Charmed

"I can't hold it anymore." Camile gritted her teeth as her body shook with resistance. The more she looked at the floor, the more she wanted to meet it.

"You can go a little longer. Don't be a lazy ass," Justine said dismissively.

"I'm not lazy. It hurts!" Camile groaned as her arms gave out. Falling flat on the floor, her lips nearly kissed the surface. Instead, she rested her forehead against it. She, and the rest of the class had been holding the start of a pushup, keeping their bodies as tight and as straight as possible. In the Coexistent World, the position is known as the *Plank Pose*. It was an exercise Camile dreaded since her upper body strength was, in her opinion, sub-par. One by one, Brandon and Justine had relieved several pupils from the pose until Camile was the last one holding the position, that is until her arms gave up.

This was one of the few sessions held in the larger gym facility, where many of the officers came to train for the physical rigors of their jobs, though it wasn't uncommon for civilians to use the indoor grounds as well. A large jogging track and several obstacle courses were just a few of the impressive amenities housed at the location.

"Camile, you're not excused. Get back into position," Justine sternly ordered.

She's never this ruthless! Did he tell her about me and Jeremy out of spite? Camile wondered.

"Her upper body seems inadequate for the task. Maybe her lower body will fare better," Brandon said as he approached, gesturing for Camile to stand. "Do you think your legs are strong enough to run eight laps?"

"I'm not sure," Camile answered, rotating her burning shoulders a few times to loosen the tight muscles.

Leaning in, he whispered into her ear. "What's the matter? You didn't wear them out, did you?"

Camile resented the question. Judging the tone of his voice she knew he meant it more as an insinuating insult than a genuine inquiry. Meeting her gaze anew, he added, "I guess I'll have to judge for myself."

He ordered Camile to begin running her laps on the track before commanding the students to resume their exercises. As she ran, she had plenty of time to process the anger she felt towards Brandon, who was obviously punishing her with fitness, and Justine, who seemed to enjoy watching her struggle. Camile knew it wasn't a coincidence that her physical training sessions were getting increasingly demanding, but she couldn't prove it was a direct result of Brandon's jealousy of her relationship with Jeremy. Therefore, filing a complaint was out of the question. However, Camile was sure to voice her displeasure once the session concluded. She lagged behind when the rest of the class dispersed, giving the three of them some privacy.

"I ought to report both of you for abusing your authority," she said, still catching her breath as she recovered from her lengthy jog.

"Excuse me?" Justine smirked in apparent amusement.

"Don't give me that look; like you don't know what I'm talking about. Just because neither of you agree with the fact I'm with Jeremy, doesn't give you free license to chastise me like you did today."

Justine looked as though she had gotten the wind knocked out of her as she turned to Brandon. It appeared Camile had unwittingly delivered her strongest blow to her occasional sparring opponent in the form of shocking news. Equally stunned was Camile, herself, as it became painfully clear that Brandon hadn't revealed the news to his sister after all.

"What—?" Justine toggled her gaze between Camile and Brandon a few times before settling on the latter. "You knew about this and didn't tell me?" she asked, her voice hushed as she returned her fiery stare to Camile. "I think I should leave before I do something that lands me in the EDC." Justine frowned, before exiting abruptly.

Brandon and Camile locked in a tense gaze until he closed his eyes. Shaking his head, he angled it downward.

"You didn't tell her, did you?" Camile intoned in more of a statement than a question, already knowing the answer.

"Of course I didn't." Brandon frowned. "I knew it would break what's left of her heart. In case you didn't notice, she still has a space left in it for Jeremy. I'd love to stay and chat, but I have to find my sister."

*　　*　.　*

That evening, Camile retreated to her quarters and immediately settled into bed. Her mind was preoccupied and she wasn't very good company for Jeremy, who had fallen asleep beside her. Theirs was a sweetly bizarre relationship in that although they sometimes slumbered in each other's arms, they never crossed the threshold of sexual intercourse. Though the temptation always lingered at the close of each make out session, Camile enjoyed the purity of their bond. She was forming a closeness with Jeremy that was lacking in her prior relationship, during which she gave her heart and body. It was a choice she regretted making too soon, which made it easier to go slower this time around. Yet, there were lonely nights when her flesh cried out for a soothing release that she knew Jeremy wasn't ready to supply. On occasion, her imagination pacified her craving as her mind envisioned her hands as his.

Camile watched as he slumbered peacefully for awhile before sinking against her pillows and attempting to read up on current events. Distraction came swiftly as she shifted her attention to her sore muscles.

Damn you, Brandon, she thought, wincing as she ran her hands over her exposed midsection. She paused, feeling the sensation of fabric that shouldn't have been there. Sitting up slightly to inspect the area, resulting in a mildly painful contraction in her overworked abs, she saw that it was bandaged beneath her midriff top. Puzzled, she pulled it gently to peek underneath. Not only were her scars fresh, but there were traces of blood inside the gauze. Turning her attention to her surroundings, she saw the open entrance to the room was heavily guarded. Though it wasn't her room, it contained a strong sense of familiarity.

Commander Wilder entered wearing a serious expression as he cast a quick glance her way. After surrendering his weapon to one of the guards at the entrance, he sent them into the corridor, ordering the door shut behind him.

"If you came here to gloat, you might as well leave now," Akalina drawled lazily as she stretched with caution so as not to reopen her wounds. "Bad enough I'm a prisoner in my own quarters."

"I just wanted to see how your recovery is going," he said as reached her bedside. "I wasn't going to bring it up, but since we're on the subject; why

420

didn't you just listen to me when I told you to get out of there? Why do you always have to insist on being so damn stubborn?" he scolded.

"I have my reasons. I don't expect you to understand any of them." Akalina shrugged.

"In the twenty-two years I've known you I think I've managed to pick up a few things. I also understand that Jezebel sent you on a mission she knew you might not return from. She needs to pay for what she put you through. She conveniently went into hiding after you got these injuries. Are you aware of that?"

Akalina grimaced, shaking her head.

"She's using you as her scapegoat and I want no part of it," Brandon continued, his voice shrouded in bitter disappointment. "As soon as I'm done with my shift I'll make sure her involvement in the raid will be well documented. Even better, I'll expose her hideout. Accept my wishes for a speedy recovery. I only hope you'll be willing to trust me a little more in the future." He turned to leave, but Akalina grabbed his arm as she climbed out of bed.

"No," she exclaimed before lowering her voice. "You can't do that. I need her in order to find Camile. My life depends on it. Besides, you'll only implicate yourself in the report if you reveal everything, not to mention Jezebel will take revenge by blabbing about your involvement. She'll take you down with her. You can be sure of that."

Nodding, Brandon pursed his plump pink lips. "I'm aware of the risk, but it'll be a small price to pay to see that Jezebel gets what's coming to her for what she's done to you."

"That's sweet of you, but what if I'm willing to pay a substantial price for your silence?" Akalina smiled.

She slid her hands up his chest and around his neck. It amused her to see his eyes close in enjoyment as a soft moan escaped his throat. By the time he reopened them, Akalina was pulling him into a kiss, stretching her body upward on her tip-toes so she could reach his lips. She liked how his body dwarfed hers. It presented her with a sense of security, though she knew she didn't require it since she was more than capable of handling herself. While one hand played in his dark, tousled hair, the other slowly lingered down his back and eventually grasped his firm backside. Brandon's brief resistance quickly faltered and he followed suit as he held her even tighter, fervently contributing to the kiss. As a result of his overzealous embrace, her wounds reminded her that she still had some healing to do. She whimpered in pain, pushing slightly against him to break his contact with that area.

"What's wrong?" Brandon asked as he loosened his hold.

"I'm still pretty sore. Sir Drayden Sebastard and that damn tiger really did a number on me." She gently massaged her bandaged oblique.

"I'm sorry. You're still recovering. Maybe this isn't the best time to do this. I should get back to my post." Brandon slowly pulled away, but Akalina seized his arms and reeled him back in.

"Please, don't stop. Suffering is all I've ever known all my life. If you want to save me from something, save me from that. Show me what it means to know pleasure for once. Prove to me that the *Leih'klav* isn't based on myth. If you succeed, I'm sure the endorphins will help speed my recovery and make me forget all about the pain. At least for awhile." Akalina punctuated random words with hungry kisses as she clumsily unfastened his uniform jacket. Brandon appeared to resist, but soon relented. Akalina had him, and she knew it.

Though she had reemerged from the sweltering recollection of Brandon and Akalina's salacious rendezvous, Camile couldn't shake the lingering stimulation remaining from the revisited experience. It clung to her like the sweat on her skin. Nor could she forget the vivid sensation of the strong hands caressing her body, exciting her with a sense of protection, yet allowing her intervals of dominance. His kisses seemed to remain on her flesh like steamy fingerprints on frosty glass. She could almost still taste them on her lips. It left Camile with the tainted reminder that her arousal had been brought on by a man other than the one lying next to her.

Whoa! She thought, relaxing her grip on the sheets she'd been clenching. Sitting up, she caught her breath as she wiped the perspiration from her forehead.

"Hey." Jeremy's voice sliced into her guilty thoughts as he touched her shoulder. His hand felt disturbingly foreign since she was still recovering from her dream.

"Oh! You're up." Camile placed her hand on her chest. "I hope I didn't wake you."

"You didn't, but I'm due for it." He yawned. "Anyway, you were moaning. Bad dream?"

"Something like that." Camile forced a smile, but couldn't bring herself to make prolonged eye contact. "Thank God it was just a dream."

However, she knew it wasn't really a dream at all. Camile was aware that it was a memory of an extended part of herself. A memory Brandon wanted to rekindle with her. Even so, that fact was shaping up to be the least of her worries. It was becoming apparent that Brandon was more deeply involved in Akalina's schemes than she thought. Furthermore, Akalina had already revealed Jezebel's involvement to at least one council member prior to Brandon's offer to do so. Yet, she had stopped him from coming forward. It wasn't an attempt to protect Jezebel or herself, but him. This fact made it abundantly obvious that although Akalina may or may not have loved Brandon, she certainly cared about him enough to stop him from exposing himself as a rogue. Then again, Camile considered the possibility that Akalina was simply using him.

The latter proved correct days later in a subsequent dream in which she witnessed her negative half conferring with Jezebel. The pair appeared to be in the middle of the *Forsaken Square* during the early evening.

"You're here." Jezebel sighed almost impatiently. "I was beginning to think you weren't as serious about this as I thought."

"I'm dead serious when it comes to my survival. I was just taking care of a little problem," Akalina said coolly.

"It wasn't Brandon, was it?" Her mentor's eyes widened.

"As a matter of fact, it was."

Jezebel's eyes darted back and forth as she palmed her forehead.

"You didn't kill him yet, did you?" she asked.

Akalina bit her lower lip, smirking at the memory of how she spent the last hour.

"If that's what they call it nowadays, I slaughtered him." Seeing her mentor's worried expression, she added, "Don't worry. Last I checked, Brandon was still alive...and very, *very* well."

Eyes closed, Jezebel sighed.

Akalina narrowed her orbs. "What? I thought you wanted him dead."

"I did, but something's come to my attention. It turns out he has the potential to become a valuable asset to the rebels."

"Hell, I could've told you that. He's very resourceful."

"Well, aren't you the smitten one." Jezebel crossed her arms in front of her petite frame.

"Pssh!" Akalina rolled her eyes. "Not in the least. He just happens to be the one I go to when I'm feeling a little lonely. That's all there is to it."

"Does he know you're taking such a casual approach towards the relationship?"

"No, but it's not like it matters; kinda like how he doesn't know about the fact you wanted him dead. And there *is* no relationship. Besides, it would've been stupid to get emotionally attached to the man I was about to kill," Akalina deadpanned.

Together, Jezebel and Akalina ventured through a rift and into the Coexistent World. New York was their city of choice since it housed Camile, their target.

Camile now contained the memories of the pair's recognizance stint. She experienced a belated invasion of her privacy as she recalled Jezebel's tedious spying on her during her most personal moments. There was something particularly chilling that she had been able to breach her home beyond physical means. Growing increasingly disgusted, Camile remembered how Akalina initially entered her life as an attractive, yet wounded woman in search of a friend. Of course, time had revealed the murderous motivation beneath Akalina's unassuming facade.

*   *   *

The afternoon sun retired behind the overcast that was predicted to dominate the heavens for the next two days. It gave the sky the deceptive appearance of an oncoming storm. As she waited for the shaman in the atrium, Camile watched people going about their routines. Her mind wandered back to the vivid memory of Akalina's coupling with Brandon and the discussion that preceded it. She found herself struggling with whether or not to broach the subject with her parents. After all, she had misinterpreted her flashbacks of Sir Drayden's situation with Akalina. Camile had no desire to repeat the same mistake.

"Commander Wilder sure does a body good, doesn't he?" Nancy remarked upon joining her at the table.

"Wh—what do you mean?" Camile grew flustered, wondering if Nancy somehow knew about the dream.

"Are you serious, woman? Haven't you looked in a mirror lately? You look great! I saw you at the pool this morning. Tried to get your attention, but I guess you didn't see me." Nancy laughed, "Don't get me wrong. I love my curves and all, but I think I could be a little more fit, you know? I think I should sign up for one of his classes," she quipped.

Camile smiled, exhaling a steady breath of relief as she relaxed.

"Thanks, Nancy. It's not all it's cracked up to be, but I guess it does have its advantages."

Their conversation was cut short upon the shaman's arrival. After exchanging greetings, Nancy retreated to a table, joining a few of her colleagues from the infirmary. Camile hadn't realized she had slipped into a daze until the shaman brought her out of it.

"Something on your mind?" she asked, gesturing that they walk along the scenic path overlooking the mountainside.

"Yeah. Lunch," Camile quipped after becoming aware of her grumbling stomach. However, there was much more than the prospect of food knocking around in her head. "But on a more serious note, there's always something on my mind these days." She forced a smile, hoping it would deter her counselor from prying. As insurance, she followed up with a question of her own, "How's it goin' with the devourer repellent?"

"Oh, it's goin'..." Tabitha sighed through a frown before reversing it to a slight smile. "But, this meeting isn't about me, or the repellent. How have you been coping?"

"Better than usual. Could be better. Everything in good time, I guess."

"I admire your honesty. Sounds to me like you've been improving quite a lot, my child. Even my superior has noticed significant growth in your performance, but apparently my boss isn't the only one you've made an impression on, lately." Tabitha raised an eyebrow, briefly shifting her glance to Jeremy, who was trailing several feet behind them.

"I'm not sure what you mean by that, Your Wisest," Camile replied, sincerely hoping the counselor wasn't aware of her relationship with her apprentice.

"Oh, I think you do." Tabitha laughed softly, halting her steps to face the foggy scenery outdoors. "My goodness…The visibility is terrible today. Ordinarily, it would be a good day to go hiking, but not under these circumstances. I hope no one was foolish enough to hit the trails unprepared. They'd be in a world of trouble if they did. Not to mention the risk they'd take in getting hurt," she sighed solemnly, before rejoining eye contact with Camile, who suspected the remark was a euphemism to describe her situation.

"Anyway, I digress. Back to the matter at hand," Tabitha continued. "Yes, there's always room for improvement, but you should take time to enjoy the progress you have made. I have the feeling you'll have an opportunity to do so soon enough. There's a special event coming up, isn't there?"

Camile grimaced. She knew of no notable occasions in the immediate pipeline. Tabitha laughed anew, apparently at her obliviousness.

"It'll come to you, my child." She smiled. "You might feel a little foolish when it does."

Chapter 59

A Cry for Help

Camile didn't have to wait long before her counselor's words were realized. Her parents informed her of a special celebration that was to take place that week. In addition, the event would fall on the same day as her birthday, an occasion she had completely forgotten about. Tabitha's premonition about her feeling silly about that fact proved true. Not wanting to be placed in an even brighter spotlight, Camile implored her parents not to make a big deal of it among the community. They agreed, understanding the awkward atmosphere it could potentially create.

The crowded ballroom reminded Camile of the first public gathering she had attended at Caldaq. However, the atmosphere was noticeably more relaxed this time around. The citizens were now accustomed to her presence and displayed signs that they were beginning to accept her as a member of their community. The room was filled with an explosion of vibrant color emanating from the food, decor and the guests' attire. Camile wore a long dress that accentuated the results of all her physical training. It had been left at her quarters in a gift box along with a matching floral hair clip, which she used to secure some of her flowing waves behind an ear. No note was left with the gift, so she assumed it was from Jeremy.

The soft tone of the peach-colored dress complimented her golden complexion. The combination of fine mesh and solid textures presented the illusion that her body was wrapped in a spiraling blossom of flowers.

Portions of her body were revealed in tasteful glimpses and pulled a trail of eyes behind her as she traveled through the room. Jeremy was among the first to approach her with a remark on the impressiveness of her appearance. She could tell he wanted to greet her with a kiss, but she knew it would have to wait since they were still concealing their relationship. In any case, it gave her something to look forward to later that evening, or whenever they would manage to steal a moment of privacy.

"I never would've guessed you had such a sharp taste for fashion. Thanks for the dress. I love it," she whispered to him.

"If this is your way of trying to figure out what I got you, it's not working. You'll have to wait until later." Jeremy laughed.

"What? So, you mean…you *didn't* get me this?" Camile furrowed her brow in confusion.

"No, but I'm curious to find out who did." Jeremy matched her expression.

When he stepped away to mingle with the rest of the crowd, Camile searched the space with her eyes and spotted Joval animatedly telling a story to Justine, who glared at her from across the room. Now instilled with a reminder of her impulsive error, Camile looked away, hoping to alleviate the tension. It didn't work. Her conscience quickly disproved the Coexistent idiom *'out of sight, out of mind'*. Luckily for her, distraction came in the form of a group dance.

The routine was unusual. The participants were divided into several sets of outer and inner circles—men and women, respectively, facing each other. Each circle of dancers would rotate at intervals in accordance to cues communicated via percussion. One cue prompted the dancers to pause the rotation, allowing them to dance with the partner they stopped in front of. Another signal prompted each set of dancers to merge into a single circle and face the center, where a single dancer would have a few moments to take the limelight and showcase their best steps. The random order was determined by a spotlight that highlighted the selected dancer. During this time, all instruments would cease playing except for the drums. The thumping bass added to the intensity of the dance. Adding to the percussion, were clapping hands and stomping feet punctuated by the excited cheers of the crowd.

Each group contained approximately twelve men that formed an outer ring around a circle of an equal number of women. The men and women in each group traveled in an opposite motion, giving each man and woman a chance to dance with one another. Each party laughed joyously as the men showed off their impressive dance steps. When Camile was paired with Joval, she could hardly contain her amusement. He was a skillful dancer and was sure to make everyone aware of the fact. His moves were rhythmic, soulful and even acrobatic at times. Though Camile kept up with the beat, she didn't want to miss one step of his performance. Eventually, she just stood in place laughing, clapping her hands in time to the rhythm.

"Man, Joval! I didn't know you had skills like that," she said. "Go on, you dancin' fool! Don't hurt nobody, now!"

Camile turned to see if anyone else was as amused and impressed as she was. In doing so, she saw Jeremy and Justine in deep conversation. She was puzzled and mildly disturbed to see that they were both laughing.

What are they talking about? she wondered before Joval pulled her from her thoughts.

"Come on, Cam! Don't go breaking the rhythm," he shouted jubilantly.

*   *   *

Even though the crowd had dispersed significantly Camile was unable to locate Jeremy. Knowing she had last seen him with Justine, it resulted in a slight queasiness in her stomach as she pondered the possibility they had gone someplace quieter to continue their conversation. Deciding to return to her quarters, Camile turned to exit, bumping into Brandon in the process. He was smartly clad in a white and gold dress uniform. Had he not held her, she probably would have done a face-plant into his chest and stained it with her makeup.

"Sheesh! You scared me." She laughed nervously.

"Thinking about something you're not supposed to?" Brandon smirked, eyeing her in an almost suspicious manner.

"No," Camile answered before redirecting their discussion. "You missed the party. I thought you of all people would be there showing off your moves."

"I had business to take care of." A roguish expression crossed his face as he stepped forward, closing the already narrow space between them. "Don't worry, I'd be more than willing to give you a private performance. Come to think of it, it'll be a good time for us to settle that bet you lost awhile back. Don't think I forgot about that."

Well, I walked right into that one, Camile thought, taking a step backward. She didn't need to see him on the dance floor to know that the man had some serious rhythm. She tried to fight the inconvenient revisiting of the memory of Akalina's scintillating episode with him. She tried to forget what a good kisser he was and how skillful his hands were.

"I don't think that's a good idea," she said before clearing her throat and regaining her poise. "Besides, Jeremy wouldn't appreciate that."

Brandon's playful smile faded.

"No, I don't suppose he would," he said, backing off. "But it begs the question; why would he leave you all alone, especially when you're wearing such an enticing dress? Speaking of which, you look absolutely radiant tonight."

Good question, she thought curiously before answering. "Two people know about our relationship. In my opinion, that's enough. No need to draw unwanted suspicion by joining at the hip in public." Camile was impressed by her own response, but continued to wonder where Jeremy had gone off to. "So, I take it you're not still angry with me for what happened with Justine. I really didn't mean for it to come out the way it did."

"Nah." Brandon shrugged. "I'm not upset about that anymore and I think she's getting over it, too. Besides, you've made stupider choices, but let's not get into that right now."

"Let's not." Camile frowned, resenting the remark. She knew to what choice he was referring.

"Consider that my *other* gift to you." He winked, taking her hand and kissing the back of it. "Happy Birthday," he said, meeting her eyes.

Camile lowered her gaze, rubbing a thumb over where his lips had been. Suddenly, she recalled the discussion he and Akalina had about Jezebel in one of her flashbacks. Determined to find out more about his part in the raid, Camile looked up to ask Brandon about it only to discover he was no longer there.

Be real. If he did participate in the attack on the compound, would he just come out and tell me about it? she chided herself, figuring it was best she didn't have the chance to bring her doubts about him to his attention. Then something he said struck her as odd.

What did he mean by 'other gift'?

Gasping quietly, she realized Brandon was the one who gave her the dress. It was a moment of clarity that almost made all the clues obvious in hindsight, the biggest one being the floral theme of the gift and how it matched his nickname for her.

*   *   *

Camile's breath quickened as the excitement continued to build. The electric sensations were building up slowly as she rocked gently, Jeremy's hands guiding her, caressing her body. They were one step closer to making the ultimate physical declaration of their unity. She wondered if it would happen tonight. She wondered if the time was right. They were still separated by layers of fabric, yet to be breached. Taking in a deep breath, her mouth opened, preparing to moan softly. A scream filled the air, but it wasn't one of passion. It was an outcry of extreme desperation; and it wasn't coming from her. Nor was it coming from Jeremy, who was perplexed as to why she had stopped her movements.

"You didn't hear that?" she asked, still catching her breath as she looked down to meet his eyes with her own. Until that moment they had been enclosed in the anticipation of ecstasy, which grew increasingly distant as the echoing words *'Give me a chance!'* lingered in her mind. It replaced her anxiety about the fact he and Justine seemed to be on amicable terms again. She didn't wish them to be enemies. Nor did she want them to have too close of a friendship. Jeremy tried to reassure Camile that she had no reason to feel threatened by his camaraderie with Justine. However, that didn't dispel Camile's need to remind Jeremy that although Justine was his past, *she* was his present and hopefully his future. It made the current interruption all the more inconvenient.

"Hear what?" Jeremy inquired after pausing a moment to listen.

"I heard someone screaming, a woman."

"I didn't hear anyone screaming." Jeremy frowned. "Are you okay?"

"Yeah, I'm fine. It was just really scary," Camile admitted.

The desperate voice still echoing in her mind, Camile was no longer in a romantic mood. Instead, she settled into Jeremy's arms and slept, praying the scream wouldn't follow her into slumber.

*   *   *

The following day Camile couldn't shake the thought of the screaming woman. It filled her with a haunting uneasiness. She was tempted to think she may have been delusional, but thought better of it. Camile decided to speak to her parents about the unusual occurrence.

"A scream? Are you sure you weren't dreaming?" Zephyr inquired.

"I was wide awake. What was so unusual about it was what the woman said."

"And what was that?" asked her mother.

"She said...*Give me a chance.*" Camile shuddered. "The way she said it still gives me chills. She sounded so...desperate."

Sir Drayden's eyes shifted downward, parting his lips as he ran his tongue over his molars.

"Where you alone when you heard the voice?" He regarded her with prying orbs.

Camile unconsciously swallowed, hoping nobody noticed.

"Of course," she lied, looking him square in the eye.

430

"The entire night?" he pressed.

"The only company I had after returning from the party were my notes, sir." Camile held fast.

Beneath her steady exterior lay apprehension as she wondered if he was onto her and Jeremy. If so, why didn't he expose them right then and there? What was he waiting for? She figured maybe it was due to the fact that Jeremy wasn't present to defend himself. After taking a deep breath, she convinced herself that her own guilt was triggering her overreaction.

"Do you think the voice you heard is linked to Akalina's past? Maybe it's part of a memory about one of her victims," Zephyr wondered aloud.

"Possibly, but I'm not sure." Camile answered. "Why would the person be asking her to give them a chance?"

"At the moment, your guess is as good as ours. Maybe it'll come to you soon. Was that all you heard?"

Camile thought of the recollection of Akalina convincing Brandon to keep quiet about Jezebel's involvement in the rebel's raid on the compound just years earlier. She opened her mouth to bring it up, but changed her mind at the last minute. She wanted to hear Brandon's side of the story first before revealing the information that could potentially change his life for the worst.

"Yes. That was all," she answered.

Chapter 60

Deceptive Appearance

The conference hall was so silent it contradicted the fact it contained the presence of several cadets in addition to the Arvainan Minister of Defense. Camile's father invited her to attend the briefing since she would be accompanying the team on an assignment. He looked valiant in his dark uniform, which was accented with sleek silver-toned fastenings. His glossy dark hair was neatly combed away from his face in a conservative style. Zephyr allowed the silence to stretch on for several moments as he regarded the small team with a serious expression intensified by his shimmering gray eyes.

"You have been selected to assist me with a mission. It will be the first of many which will test your cumulative skills and allow the council to determine which of you possess the strength and character to become fully-fledged officers of the Arvainan defense system," Zephyr explained. "I don't expect all of you to succeed, but I do expect you all to do nothing less than your very best. We've been receiving numerous reports about suspicious activity taking place in Tahblor, located in a rural region of the state of Quelzwan.

According to Zephyr, Quelzwan, located approximately two-hundred fifty two miles north of Deltine, had been experiencing a substantial decline in livestock population. Asphyxia was the common cause of death.

"No clear source for this mysterious phenomenon has been revealed and even worse, several residents have succumbed to the same condition," he continued. "Maybe we can find something the locals missed. Since many of you have limited field experience, I thought this would be the perfect opportunity for you to put your analytical skills into practice. Who knows, maybe one of you will impress me by teaching *me* a thing or two." His lips curled into a barely noticeable grin as he flashed a quick wink at his daughter.

Returning his attention to the rest of the group, he added, "Out of the several dozen candidates I had to choose from, I've selected the very best; the seven of you. I hope you will prove my decision was not made in error."

Once the meeting concluded, the team had roughly an hour to prepare for their departure. Camile spotted Justine in the corridor as she exited the meeting hall. She appeared as though she had been waiting there for awhile.

"I need to speak to you," Justine said plainly.

Would it kill you to be a little more polite? Camile thought. She didn't have time to deal with the drama surrounding Justine's disapproval of her union with Jeremy, so she continued walking as she responded.

"Sorry, but it'll have to wait until I get back. I have less than an hour to—"

"We can walk and talk at the same time. What I have to say won't take long."

"It's about Jeremy, isn't it?" Camile asked, not breaking her stride.

"Actually, it's about my brother."

Justine's answer stopped Camile in her tracks. She faced her head-on, her brows furrowed.

"What about him?"

"Akalina corrupted him. In case you haven't noticed, I'm doing all I can to make sure that doesn't happen again. It took time for him to get his life back on track after she nearly ruined him and—"

"Wait." Camile raised her hand. "How many times do I have to explain? I'm *not* Akalina."

"Maybe not, but there's no denying your affect on my brother. The only other time I've seen him like this was when he was in her clutches. He's lost so much already. Spare him the heartache of losing himself again." Justine turned to leave, but regarded Camile anew with a parting statement: "I can see the little triangle forming between you and two of the most important men in my life. Toying with a man's heart can be dangerous. It's one of the few things that can destroy the boundaries that restrain a person's temperament, especially in Transcendent humans. But I guess you've already seen a preview of that for yourself. In any case, I'll give you some advice; watch yourself."

"Justine, I don't intend to hurt either of them. I know you probably don't want to hear this, but I love Jeremy."

"But you're also attracted to my brother," Justine said with a prying look.

"Well, I'd be lying if I said no."

"At least you're honest about it. Truthfully, I can't blame you. When we were younger I used to wish he wasn't my brother." Justine chuckled before regarding Camile with a look that conveyed embarrassment.

"You had a crush on your own brother?" Camile's mouth went agape.

"Shh!" Justine hushed sharply, looking around to make sure their conversation wasn't overheard. Returning her attention to Camile, she whispered, "We're not blood-related. Not that it justifies things. Like I said, it was a very long time ago," she pointed a finger to Camile's chest, "You breathe a word of this to him, or anybody else, you're dead."

Been there, done that, Camile thought amusedly.

"My lips are sealed," she said. "But seriously, lady, there are some things you just shouldn't say out loud."

"Hey, shouldn't you be getting ready to head out?" a voice called from behind. It was Camile's father. She informed him that she was on her way to her quarters. With a subtle nod of his head, Zephyr retreated down the corridor with several officials.

"I really gotta get going," she said to Justine, who gently seized her arm as she attempted to walk away.

"One more thing." Justine frowned slightly, briefly lowering her gaze before meeting Camile's eyes anew. "I'm not gonna give you any grief about you and Jeremy." She expelled a deep breath. "I might not like the fact that you're together, but I've grown to accept things for what they are. Look, let's be straight, here. I'm not saying that I want to be your friend or anything, but I respect Jeremy enough to respect his choice…even though it's not me. Just make sure you treat him right."

Having said her piece, Justine reversed course and the two women went their separate ways.

*   *   *

Within less than an hour, the team arrived at the location via a high-capacity land vehicle called a *Nomad*. It contained amenities that provided a few homey comforts, which came in handy when traveling long distances.

Tahblor was a rural area mainly comprised of agricultural settlements. The team combed the questionable patch of land that had been pointed out to them by the groundskeepers, a young couple with two small children and another on the way. The lush green grass was still moist from the afternoon rain that had rolled out of the area a few hours prior to the team's arrival. The cloudy sky was beginning to give way to intervals of sunshine, projecting rainbows onto the moderate mist that remained. As Camile's father led the team on their surveillance quest it seemed as though they were chasing a series of false reports. Even so, she was still impressed with how effortlessly he led the group and delegated orders, always preparing a backup plan in case communication failed or if they were to become separated.

"Minister, I'm picking up something here. It's an opening," a female officer announced in a husky voice while scanning an area approximately four feet above the ground. "It's pretty small, but still large enough to accommodate intruders...or defectors. A tight squeeze, but nonetheless..."

"What stage is it in?" Zephyr asked.

"It's pretty fresh, sir. I estimate no older than a week. Maybe less. If it remains undisturbed, the rift should heal itself in about a month." The woman paused, regarding her commander with uneasy green eyes. "There's something else, sir."

"What is it, lieutenant?"

"Well, I know rifts are usually formed by an occurrence of some kind of earth-linked destruction or disaster brought about by the four elements, but this rift is unlike any I've ever studied personally. Take a look." Handing him the reading instrument, the officer continued, "Apparently, it was intentionally created by a cognitive being. Notice the patterns surrounding the entryway?"

Zephyr nodded, his expression heavy with concern. "They're specific, as if they were pre-plotted. Whoever did this worked damn hard to make it a challenge for anyone to find."

"Sir, we have activity here," one of the lanky male officers called from a short distance. "It's a bird; still alive, but appears to be suffocating."

Camile, her father and a few of the other team members approached, noticing the officer holding the struggling bird in his hands.

"It looks like something's lodged in its mouth," Camile said upon noticing a cottony object beyond its beak resembling a balled-up spider web. The group concurred and tried to figure out some way of removing it.

Feeling a faint pinch on her hand, Camile slapped it. Upon inspecting the area, she saw a spatter of blood surrounding a small crushed insect. Immediately identifying the species, Camile regarded her father to express her bewilderment.

"I thought you said there were no mosquitoes in this dimension," she remarked.

"There aren't. At least there shouldn't be." Camile's father immediately inspected her arm as alarmed expressions crossed the faces of all the other team members.

"What's wrong? Is something gonna happen to me?"

"You'll be fine, but others may not be so fortunate."

Zephyr ordered everyone to remain vigilant while examining the perimeter for the source of the insect. Before they could begin the inspection, the officer holding the bird cried out, dropping the creature to the ground. It was as stiff as a taxidermist's creation. Yet, the corpse rolled around haphazardly as though possessed. A stream of fluttering black and shimmering gray spewed out of the creature's mouth, forming a billowing cloud of mosquitoes. The swarm buzzed past the group in a frenzy before vanishing in the middle of the field. A few dozen stragglers remained behind to sample the blood of the team, all of whom quickly swatted them away.

"Damn! It went into the rift. We have to go after it, but stay alert...all of you." Zephyr said urgently before requesting a line of rope from one of the officers. "I'll be going in first."

"Dad. No," Camile whispered, touching her father's arm. She couldn't bear the thought of possibly losing him after they'd already been robbed of so much time. In that instance, she realize that lack of time together didn't equate to lack of love.

"I have to do this, sweetheart," Zephyr said as he tightly fastened the rope around his waist, creating a makeshift harness. "Don't worry."

The husky voiced female officer politely disagreed and volunteered to be the first to enter the rift.

"Should anything happen to you, the team would be without a leader and I would be without a mentor," she stated. "Besides, I have to earn my stars sometime." She cracked a smile, but it failed to hide the underlying uncertainty in her emerald gaze.

Zephyr met his daughter's pleading eyes, apparently considering the proposal. Nodding with apparent partial reluctance, he said, "Very well, lieutenant. Just make sure you stay vigilant and give the signal at the first sign of trouble. That's an order."

After the team hoisted the lieutenant up into the rift back-first, they lowered her slowly as she vanished. Receiving the all clear, half the team followed suit while the other half kept vigil on the other side. Camile was the last to descend. Immediately upon reaching the other side her ears were invaded by the competing sounds of rap, reggae, rock and house music amidst laughter and loud conversations. The smell of barbecue, grass and citrus filled the air. The bayside campsite was populated by several families taking advantage of the Indian Summer temperatures. One voice cut through the jubilation, catching the attention of the team, who saw a man furiously slapping his face and body.

"Damn it! This is the worst case of mosquitoes ever," he complained.

The more he and his family swatted at the nagging pests, the more of them would suddenly emerge from the bay.

"That's a wrap! This trip is officially over," his wife exclaimed, gathering the kids and running towards the parking lot.

"We came all this way to exterminate a bug problem?" Camile asked.

"Not quite." her father frowned.

As the team drew closer to the bay, he pulled a device from his utility belt that was about the size and shape of a stick of gum. Pressing a button, he activated it. A high-pitched sound filled the air and gradually increased until Camile could no longer hear it, but it had a clear effect on the mosquitoes, forcing them into a cluster. Camile watched in awe as the massive cloud of the blood-sucking insects emerged from the water's surface. Flying in formation, they took the shape of something she'd hoped never to encounter again. The astonishing occurrence drew a crowd of spectators, most of whom made remarks about how unusual the event was. However, it appeared they were unaware of Camile or the team.

"A devourer?" she asked.

"You got it. This is what happens when someone tries to kill a devourer and fails. When not slain properly, they somehow gain the ability to transform into any creature that feeds on human blood; mosquitoes, leeches, bed bugs, you name it. It makes it easier for them to breach the Coexistent World," Zephyr explained. On his mark, one of the team members fired a weapon, discharging an explosive grenade-like device that met its mark with devastating accuracy. As the devourer vaporized it presented a display reminiscent of fireworks.

*   *   *

During the return trip to Caldaq, Camile sat beside her father, who was busy reviewing the data that had been collected during the mission. The ride was mainly silent, aside from the subtle hum of the vehicle and the soft sound of snoring coming from one of the slumbering officers sitting several rows in front of them. The sound incited her to yawn as she fought the temptation to doze off, but eventually surrendered to the alluring pull of warm darkness as it enveloped her like a blanket. When it slowly pulled back, it revealed Brandon's face, which bore an unusually intense expression of determination.

"Why do you continue to defend Jezebel even after everything she's put you through?" he asked sharply, his voice saturated with impatience. "She obviously wants to control you,"

"If she hears you talking like this, she'll rip your tongue out." Akalina scowled, bringing herself to stand toe-to-toe with him, craning her head upward to meet his eyes. "Matter of fact, if you don't stop it, I'll do it myself. What you're saying is treasonous!"

"Call it what you will, but I'm telling the truth. I know you want to kill Camile more than anything, but there's a good reason why you shouldn't."

"Oh, and why not? You wanna bang her too, is that it?" Akalina folded her arms, not bothering to mask her doubt. "If so, you can dream on. I'm down for a lot of things, but three's a crowd, if you get my drift."

"She isn't your sister," he replied, ignoring her insinuation, though his face indicated his resentment.

"Okay, you clearly have your wires crossed. She's my twin for crying out loud. Being siblings is a prerequisite for that, don't you think?"

"Akalina, I know all of this is difficult to grasp, but please, trust me on this one. I lo—" He paused. "I care about you a lot. If you don't listen to what I'm saying, you could be lost forever. If you kill Camile, you'll become nothing more than a zombie for Jezebel to control."

"Oh, really...?" Akalina smirked, her brow arched. "And why's that?"

"Like I said, Camile's not your sister..." Brandon paused. "She's your other half."

"*What?* You must be out of your damn mind! Why are you saying these things?"

"Because they're true and I'll prove it to you." He stepped closer until they were just inches apart. "I'll open my memories to you. You'll be able to see and hear the conversation for yourself. Jezebel wants revenge on both, you and Camile for something that happened when you were only a child. When you're done looking into my memories, do the same with Jezebel. Have her show you her memories of anything pertaining to your life as a baby. Have her show you any memory of you and Camile together as infants. I bet she won't be able to. You and Camile never existed separately until you were six years old."

"You see, that's one of the reasons why I need to find Camile. Among other things, the bitch stole my telepathy. So, you have no way of proving your wild accusations. Do you expect me to take your word over the woman who has sworn to help me get back what's mine?"

"Yes, but you don't have to. The fact Jezebel left you in a lurch on the night of the raid should speak for itself. She's using you and you're allowing her to because you're so blinded by your need for revenge, Akalina. Wake up!" Brandon implored.

*   *   *

"Wake up. We're home," a voice announced as her body was gently jostled, but the intonation wasn't the same. The tone was more patient and relaxed.

Once Camile opened her eyes, she saw her father regarding her with an adoring expression. She had fallen asleep on his shoulder. The moisture at the corner of her agape mouth was an indication that she had been relaxed enough to nearly drool on him. Lucky for them both, she had awakened before it happened. Still, she was mildly embarrassed as she tried to discretely wipe her mouth on her sleeve. Zephyr briefly diverted his attention, possibly an attempt to lessen her abashment, but his deepening dimples and crinkled eyes revealed his amusement.

"You were under pretty deep. Dream of anything interesting?" he asked, meeting her eyes anew. Once again, Camile couldn't help but admire how vividly his gray eyes contrasted with his full brows and dark, mildly graying hair, still slightly tousled from that evening's expedition.

"I guess you can say that. It was actually a continuation of a dream I had earlier," she answered, not wanting to go into details about exactly how long she had been withholding her subconscious voyages.

After smoothing a few of her father's stray locks, Camile stared at him in silence for several moments. She found herself trying to figure out the best way to break the news. Realizing there was no easy way to report a betrayal, she decided to let the words flow naturally.

"I'm not sure how to tell you this, so I'll just say it. I think Akalina convinced Commander Wilder to play both sides. If the dreams and memories I've been having are correct, he's been working with the rebels for quite a while," Camile gingerly explained, noticing a sober expression crossing her father's features.

"I'm well aware of his involvement with them, but it wasn't Akalina's doing." He sighed. "It was my own. Remember the mysterious mission I mentioned awhile back?"

Camile's eyebrows all but merged with her hairline as she finally realized Brandon had been working as a double agent for the council. She found it both intriguing and unsettling since she was aware that such people lived their lives like a raging flame that is usually snuffed out all too soon. As a result, those closest to them were liable to get hurt—if not by the stark, sudden extinguishment of their blaze, then by the intensity of it.

"You mentioned it, but didn't go into detail," she pried.

"Because I couldn't...And I still can't," Zephyr said, to Camile's disappointment.

"But this means Akalina already knew that we were two parts of the same being. Why did she try to kill me that night if she knew she would either die too or become catatonic?" she asked before she was hit with a sudden epiphany. "It was all an act! It was a diversion for something else. *That's* why she made the arrangement with the devourers!" she acknowledged in almost a whisper.

"That's a disturbing conclusion, but unfortunately it makes a lot of sense. Question is, what was the diversion for?" Zephyr frowned.

Chapter 61

Persuasion

"You have managed to defy your intelligence and my trust by stooping to a level of stupidity far beyond comprehension," a voice hissed. "I don't care how you do it, but I expect you to fix this problem *immediately!*"

Camile froze outside the entrance to Jeremy's quarters. She didn't need to guess whose voice she was hearing. She knew of only one man who had such a vocal inflection and perfect articulation, even when upset. It was obvious that her date with Jeremy would be delayed, so she decided to return to her quarters and check back later. Before she could walk away, the door slid open. Sir Drayden exited, the displeasure on his face exceeded that which she had heard in his voice. He bypassed her without saying a word, filling her with a mild mixture of relief and discomfort.

"What was that all about?" Camile asked after Jeremy greeted her in the doorway.

"Just business. Don't worry about it," he answered, softening his bewildered expression with a faint smile.

"He doesn't know about us, does he?" Camile whispered, training her gaze down the corridor to make sure Sir Drayden was out of earshot.

"I said don't worry about it. I just have a few things I need to evaluate and sort out. You've been making incredible progress with your training; we can't have you ruining your emotional equilibrium with unnecessary anxiety. Relax."

Camile expelled a slow deep breath, closing her eyes in a brief meditative exercise.

"That's it," he encouraged, his smile broadening. "It's amazing how much a simple thing like proper breathing can rejuvenate one's body and mind. There's nothing quite like it."

"I can think of a few things that come close," Camile said flirtatiously.

"When you're right, you're right." Jeremy laughed softly.

"What now?"

"I'm sorry to say that due to circumstances beyond my control, I'll have other plans this evening."

"For some odd reason I figured as much," Camile replied with a note of playful sarcasm.

In the days that followed, Jeremy continually refused to reveal the details of his discussion with Sir Drayden. However, Camile could tell it still weighed heavily on his mind as he became increasingly preoccupied and somewhat withdrawn. It was frustrating, but she initially decided against pushing the matter since he had already endured Sir Drayden's wrath. She of all people knew what that was like. However, as their communication continued on a downward path, she could no longer endure the cold chill developing between them. Concerned about their regressing relationship, Camile decided to make an unannounced visit to his quarters.

"Shouldn't you be on your way to meditation with Sir Drayden?" he asked as he stepped aside, allowing her to enter.

"You know today's my break day. Or did you already forget since you barely speak to me nowadays? Hell, we barely see each other at all." Camile frowned. "They might have this anchor thing placed on me somehow, but I can still tell something's wrong. Something's changed with us, I can feel it."

"You're right. I didn't want to get into this, but everything in my life changed the day we began our relationship. We've complicated our lives to such a degree that neither of us can see straight. As a result, I think we should make an important decision in order to restore what we altered and regain sight of the work that needs to be done."

"What the—? We've been together for what seems like a minute and you're already dumping me? Everything was fine until a few days ago. Where's this all coming from?" Camile asked, her voice laden with disbelief.

"There's too much at stake. We can't continue our relationship. It's proven to be too much of a distraction," Jeremy softly responded.

"Don't do this, Jeremy. Whatever this is, we can work through it." Camile took his hands in hers. "You have to believe what we have is worth fighting for. Give it a chance."

"I don't dispute the value of what we had, but times change." He slowly pulled away from her grip. "Sacrifices have to be made for the sake of duty."

"So, what, you're throwing our relationship away like garbage for the sake of your professional ambitions?" Angry tears stung her eyes, but she refused to let them fall for the man who was currently breaking her heart—something she had vowed not to let happen again.

"I'm not throwing anything away, but we don't have any other choice but to end this, Camile. This is how it has to be."

"That's bullshit, Jeremy! Don't I get a say in this?" Camile waited for a response, but Jeremy remained quiet, much to her aggravation. The silence was crippling. The tension in her chest made breathing more laborious than she was used to. Her emotional distress was resonating through her body in the form of mild nausea. She couldn't bear the thought of having been used yet again. But Jeremy wasn't that kind of man—he couldn't be. Their relationship never crossed into the ultimate level of physical bonding, but to Camile, their souls were in the process of forming a deep connection. At least she thought they were. Jeremy's intentions were a complete mystery to her now.

Typical! Why can't men just say what's on their minds? If I did something wrong, just tell me. If there's something more personal you're struggling with, trust me enough to sort it out together. Do something, anything but make me have to deal with another shattered puzzle!

An epiphany broke through her stark confusion.

"You're doing this because of him, aren't you?" She cracked a bitter smile. "Sir Drayden doesn't want us to be together and you're listening to him! That's what that discussion was about the other day, wasn't it? Why didn't you just tell me when I brought it up?"

"Because, Camile, I know you would rush into unnecessary confrontation."

"Jeremy, sometimes confrontation is necessary when it comes to pursuing what you want. For goodness sake, man, grow a pair and stand up to the man for a change. Don't let him control your life like this. It's not right!"

"It's not that simple. There are things you don't understand."

"Then *make* me understand them. Are you and Sir Drayden on the down low or something?"

"*What?* No!" Jeremy spat. "Where'd you get a crazy idea like that?"

"Well, you're breaking up with me because of him. What other explanation could there possibly be?"

Jeremy opened his mouth as though to give an answer, but instead requested that she leave.

"Fine. If you want to be a spineless coward, be my guest. If you won't stand up to him, I will! Before I do, I need to know, how did he find out? Did Justine tell him? I find it awfully suspicious that just two days before he chewed you out, she comes to tell me she accepts our relationship."

"No, Camile. Justine didn't tell him. You did."

"Me? I didn't say a damn thing to him about us."

"Maybe not with your mouth, but in case you didn't notice, Sir Drayden is a master at reading things beyond the physical level of expression. He read your feelings for me like a book and you practically put it in his hands. I warned you about this in the past, keeping your emotions overly exposed on the surface. You're lucky it was Sir Drayden who found out and not anybody with mal-intent to use it against you. So, next time, before you blame somebody, take a good look at yourself," Jeremy lectured. It was the angriest Camile had ever seen him. Even so, it was eerily controlled.

As she exited Jeremy's quarters, she saw Sir Drayden walking towards the middle of the corridor, several officials on either side of him. She partially wished she had been granted the luxury of having more time before being in his presence. At least that would have provided her with an opportunity to calm herself to a level where she could communicate more efficiently.

"I need to speak to you," Camile announced rather sharply, but the elder continued his stride as she struggled to keep up.

"Whatever it is will have to wait," was his casual response.

"The hell it will! If you're gonna ruin my life, the least you can do is explain why," Camile hissed, prompting Sir Drayden to halt his steps and make an about face. The glare in his eyes nearly chilled her to the core, but her anger was more than enough to keep her warm. With a wave, he signaled the officials to proceed without him. After exchanging surprised glances, they obliged.

"This better be important," he said impatiently.

"What you did was completely uncalled for. How dare you interfere with my personal life? Are you doing it to get revenge for what Akalina did to Hya—?" Suddenly, Camile lost her ability to speak. At that moment, she knew she had gone too far.

"That's quite enough," he said, his voice jarringly calm as he advanced, forcing Camile to backpedal. "You got a problem with me, fine, but you leave her out of this. Your relationship with Jeremy has presented a clear issue of a conflict of interest—not to mention a breach of an agreement he made long before you knew he existed." Sir Drayden released her from his invisible clutches once she backed into the wall. She gasped, testing her voice.

"In the future," he continued, " I expect you to respectfully make an appointment to speak with me rather than pull me away from my official duties to discuss such trivial matters."

Before she could address him again, he was gone. She clearly hit a nerve by mentioning his dead wife—a woman her darker half, Akalina, had murdered in cold blood.

*　　*　　*

Not even two hours had elapsed since the exchange when Nancy invited Camile to play some games at the amusement park at Daebrayk Peak. The two settled on a pastime strikingly similar to the *Ski Ball* games Camile used to play during her childhood in the Coexistent World. Once they were well into their respective games, played on adjoining alleys, the dialogue between the two women took an unexpected turn.

"Did I hear correctly?" asked Nancy, who pumped her arm after rolling one of the orbs into the highest scoring slot. "You and Jeremy broke up? I wasn't even aware you were in a relationship."

"Thanks to Sir Drayden, it wasn't exactly long-term. I usually blame myself for my failed relationships, but this time it turns out I had some help." Camile threw her ball too hard, causing it to ricochet off the board. After catching it, she furrowed her brow as she contemplated the promptness of Nancy's inquiry. "How did you find out about it?"

"I overheard your conversation with Sir Drayden in the hall. It seemed pretty intense, so I didn't think it was a good time to bug either of you. I tried my best to wait before speaking to you about it, but you know me; I can't keep my mouth shut for long."

Camile chortled as Nancy continued.

"As your friend, I think I should tell you there's no way to *make* a man want to be with you. Sometimes I wish there was," she quipped. "Actually, there are some people in regions in both worlds who swear by certain methods of luring a person into a relationship even when they don't desire it, but it's extremely taboo, not to mention dangerous as hell." She shuddered. "Ugh! I shouldn't even talk about it. Anyway, what I guess I'm trying to say is that nothing good can come out of a forced relationship."

"It certainly didn't feel forced at the time. Jeremy doesn't strike me as the type who'd falsify his feelings or enter a one-sided relationship."

"That may be the case, but apparently something has changed."

"Can't argue with that." Camile shrugged. "Well, I've had disappointments in matters of love before. This, too, shall pass. Anyway, I have bigger fish to fry than to worry about why Jeremy decided to choose his professional ambitions over me. Then again, looking at it from his perspective, he's known his career a lot longer than he's known me. So, in some odd way he made the safest choice."

Camile couldn't help but find the irony in the likelihood Jeremy had made his decision based on the same logic she had used to avoid a relationship with Brandon.

"Yeah, well, a career can't keep you warm at night," Nancy added.

"Tell that to Jeremy." Camile chortled. "Who knows, maybe he invested in heavy blankets. The way he's going, he's gonna need them for a *very* long time."

Chapter 62

Taste of Treachery

The sharp stench wafting through the cold night air was overwhelming. Fighting the urge to vomit, Camile continued to follow the group into the dwelling. Immediately upon entering, they were met with an even stronger bitterness mingling with the scent of decay. Though their torch lights provided ample lighting, they created eerie shadows as they traveled through the rooms. Eventually, they came to an icy cold basement, where the smell intensified to such a level it stung the eyes of all whom entered. The source of the odor wasn't easily distinguishable since the room appeared empty. However, upon further inspection, a hidden room was found behind a false wall. Inside were dozens of wooden crates, none longer than four feet. Commander Wilder hoisted the heavy lid off one of them, placing it onto the floor with a slight, unavoidable bang. In doing so, the lower half of a body was revealed soaking in a pungent liquid solution.

"Not exactly my idea of a bath, but to each their own." He scrunched his face while fanning the sharp fumes that had risen to his nose.

Camile wondered why she had been selected to accompany the highly capable squad on their mission to exterminate the devourer nest. She surmised that it was to build experience and to gain courage by facing danger head-on. Her thoughts were interrupted when the commander instructed her to uncap one of the large vials of Quenching Powder located in her utility belt and sprinkle the contents on top of the mutilated body.

447

He explained that doing so would prevent the upper and lower portions of the devourer from being rejoined and would eventually result in its death. Camile poised herself to carry out the command when something pushed her from behind. The vial slipped from her hand, shattering on the dusty wooden floor. Her torchlight also fell and rocked on the ground, causing the shadows to shimmy on the walls.

She could hear the commotion of a fight going on behind her as she scrambled to her feet. Once she turned around she witnessed Brandon in a vicious clash with an androgynous looking devourer. It had slipped into the chamber beyond the detection of the squad members in the adjacent room. They immediately rushed in upon hearing the ruckus. The tussle between Brandon and the devourer was so tight, no one could get a clear shot at the creature. Two officers were knocked down when they tried to get close enough to assist their leader. Camile instinctively leapt onto the devourer's back in an attempt to slow it down. Unprepared for how freakishly strong it was, she was thrown to the ground hitting a vat of brine on the way down. Mildly disoriented, she pulled her mind away from the pain in her back as she regarded the scene before her.

"You'll pay for that." Brandon sneered as the battle continued.

"I know who she is," the devourer said in a surprisingly delicate voice. "I can turn her and bring back your beloved Akalina. As a bonus, I'll even get rid of the witnesses. No one will ever know you had any part in it. All you have to do is release me."

The struggle came to a standstill as Brandon met Camile's eyes.

He can't possibly be considering it!

"Yes...That's it." The devourer smiled as Brandon's grip loosened. "You'll have the woman of your dreams before you know it."

"I'm counting on it." Brandon smirked, keeping his eyes locked on Camile, who speechlessly shook her head in protest as he released the creature. Suddenly, his gaze shifted to indicate the broken vial lying beside her on the ground. "But I don't need your help to get her."

Activating his *Styngrae*, he rammed it in the devourer's side.

Scooping up some of the powder, now mixed with dust, Camile's wrist burned; evidence it had been scraped during her fall. She quickly flung the particles onto the creature, who immediately howled and staggered out the room, leaving a trail of smoldering residue and the stench of sulfur. The other squad members were promptly on its tail. Camile heard the sound of the devourer's demise shortly thereafter. Retrieving her torchlight, she noticed Brandon approaching with her utility belt, which had been ripped off during the struggle.

"Thanks for the quick thinking. You'll need to have this repaired when we get back to Caldaq." He draped the belt around her waist and secured it.

His hands lingered on her hips as their eyes locked in that frozen moment of tense silence. "Until then, be careful not to lose it again."

Pulling out his canteen, he poured water so Camile could wash the toxic residue from her numbing hands.

"For a moment there, I thought you were gonna give me up to that thing," she said through a tremulous breath as she shook away the excess water.

"Guess that goes to show how well you know me. I would never give you up...to anyone."

Brandon resumed his professional demeanor once Camile made a brief break in eye contact. "You have enough Quenching Powder for the devourers on this side of the room, but try not to get anymore on your skin," he said. "I'll take care of the rest. Apparently, one of their sentinels already spotted us, so we have to be quick if we want to avoid more company."

Once they were done, Camile and Brandon quickly left the dwelling to rejoin the group. That's when she noticed something she hadn't seen in the dark basement.

"You're hurt," she said, seeing several scratches across his cheek.

"I've had worse," he said after dabbing the wound to check how badly he was bleeding.

"You're not gonna turn into one of those things now, are you?" she asked, unable to suppress her concern.

"No." Brandon cracked a half smile. "It takes a larger transfusion of their fluids in order to infect a person."

Camile was struck with the chilling recollection of Makeda, the devourer who nearly managed to convert her.

"So, why don't we go for it?" Brandon cut into her thoughts.

"What?"

"You know...*us*. You can't tell me you didn't feel anything back there. I could practically hear your heart pounding."

"Yeah, it's called being in fear for my life, or getting turned into one of those things," Camile chuckled awkwardly.

"You sure it's not your fear of taking a chance with me? You're afraid I'll prove to you what we already know; that we're suited for each other in many ways." Brandon's eyes briefly traveled over her body. "Come on, it's not like you and Jeremy are still together. If you are, he's clearly not doing his job. I noticed how tense you've been lately."

Appalled at his arrogant bravado, Camile rolled her eyes.

"First of all, it was a mutual decision. We both decided it was for the best," she fibbed. "Second of all, I need to focus on my training and my upcoming missions. I don't have time for a relationship right now. It's a complication I don't need."

"Okay. Whatever gets you through the night, Wildflower." He clearly wasn't buying her story.

"Screw you, Brandon," she muttered under her breath, not intending for him to hear it.

"I wish you would. That's one way to test my theory." His plump rosy lips curled impishly. "By the way, do you know you get this ravenous look in your eyes when you're angry? It's very sexy."

"You're incorrigible." Camile shook her head, quickening her pace to walk ahead of him.

*   *   *

Their bodies clashed in an aggressive embrace. Brandon's lips met hers so forcefully it hurt at first. Still, there was something sweetly intoxicating about the passionate kiss and the subtle discomfort of its inception. There was a certain thrill, knowing she might be kissing him for the last time and she surmised it was the reason behind the aggressive lip lock. She let her uncertainties evaporate in the heat of the moment as she shoved him into a chair and straddled him. Brandon used his hands to guide the slow swivel of her hips before tugging her hair so he could raid her neck with his mouth.

"I know how bad you want it, but pull my hair out and it's your ass," Akalina warned breathily.

"Oh, it's my ass alright," Brandon murmured as he grasped her buttock, pressing her closer against him as his lips rejoined hers.

Breaching the seal of his shirt, she stripped it from his body while running her palms over his powerful shoulders and arms. She slid her hands over his pectorals, pushing him back slightly so she could look into his eyes. So electric and gluttonous, they were. Akalina got almost as much a thrill in enticing him as she did during the height of their passion. There was great control in reducing such a powerful man to a creature, driven wild with pure feral desire. Yet, she had met her match with Brandon, who returned her taunting fervor as his warm hands traveled up her torso, seizing her shirt along the way.

Raking his nails gently down her back, he chuckled throatily upon hearing her moan. They seemed to be in a competition to see who could drive the other the craziest by causing the most anticipation and pleasure. It was a stalemate until he seized the opportunity to tackle the sweet spot on her neck. She shuddered as he bit it tenderly, working it with his tongue as he suckled. She could even feel his hips taking charge as they dictated the slow, deep rotation of their joint movements.

450

Brandon had years on her, as far as *Leih'klav* experience went, but Akalina was a willing student. As they came up for air, Akalina saw that her kisses weren't enough to dispel the apparent concern in his eyes. Avoiding his penetrative gaze, she moved in for another round. He pulled his face away slightly, all the while maintaining his grip on her waist.

"Akalina, you know I don't want you to do this, right?" He searched her eyes with his own.

"A little late for that, don't you think? Looks like you're up for the occasion, if you know what I mean," she quipped, referring to the familiar sensation of his firmness pressing against her. He briefly lowered his gaze before meeting her eyes anew. The seductive smirk on his face faded slightly.

"That's not what I meant." He narrowed his eyes. "I don't want you to go on this crazy mission."

"It would be crazier for me to sit around here, waiting for her to replace me. Why do you have to bring this up now? You're killing the mood."

"I just hate to think this'll be our last night together," he replied softly, stroking her neck with his fingertips.

"Aw, I thought you were more positive than that, Brandon." Akalina chuckled softly as she shifted her body slightly. She then traced her fingers down his chest and fearlessly ventured to his belt. "Well, maybe there's some erotic benefit in pretending this'll be our last time," she purred, toying with his buckle. Caressing him anew, her touch lingered near, but avoided direct contact with the areas she knew his body was crying out for it most. Her goal was to tantalize him to an extent where she could manipulate his mind with the same ease with which she coaxed his flesh.

"You wicked woman," he moaned, his breathing quickened.

"What would you do if you knew this would be your last chance to have me this way?" she looked up into his eyes, keeping her face slightly downturned. "How will you make sure I'll never forget you?"

In the aftermath of the eruption of blinding passion, the two lay loosely in each other's arms. Their tremulous dewy bodies shimmered in the moonlight. Brandon's lips were like satiny pillows, planting soft kisses along her neck as he cupped her bare breast. Tempted to go yet another round, but knowing she was running out of time, she sat up to evade his. He joined her, asking if something was wrong. Akalina regarded her lover with a flirtatious smile, stating that she had changed her mind about going after Camile.

"Really?" Brandon raised his brow, tracing swirly patterns on her bent leg with his fingertips. "What made you change your mind?"

"You just did." Akalina moaned. The feathery sensation of his teasing touch was beginning to distract her. "There's no way I can turn my back on this. Just promise me you won't tell my parents or anyone else where I am. I ditched them for a reason and I'm not ready to go back yet. I'm not sure I ever will be."

Brandon frowned. "I'm not happy about keeping your location a secret from them, but I guess it's a fair trade since you're not going through with your original plan." The corners of his mouth turned upward. "I'm glad you came to your senses."

"I wouldn't say that. Thanks to you, I think I came out of my senses," Akalina winked, earning a chortle from her lover, who shook his head.

"Is that right?" A roguish expression crossed his features as he shoved her back against the pillows. He pressed a finger to her lip, as though to silence her, before dragging it down to her cleavage. It was soon followed by his warm lips, trailing kisses to her navel, in which he played with his tongue.

There's no time for this, Akalina thought, looking up at the wooden leaf ceiling fan.

She needed to meet Jezebel. Tonight was the night where she would finally be shown the exact location of her double. Of course she couldn't tell Brandon about it. Her original plan to wear him out and steal away as he slept had backfired. Now, she was in his clutches and he wasn't about to let her out of his sight. It seemed as though he wanted to make sure she wouldn't go back on her word.

"I'm gonna show you how happy I am to know that the woman I love will find an alternative solution to this situation rather than rush into destruction," Brandon murmured.

Akalina's heart skipped as she contemplated his statement. She suddenly felt the need to put distance between them, but could only bring herself to sit upright on the bed. Filled with the uncomfortable sensation of panic, Akalina's mind spun with confusion.

Damn it! Why did he have to say he loves me? Way to spoil things, she thought, trying to figure out what it all meant and where she would go from that point on.

"You have no idea how hard it is, not being able to communicate with you telepathically," Brandon hugged her from behind as he trailed kisses along her neck and shoulders. "What's going on in that pretty little head of yours?"

Finding it increasingly difficult to breathe, Akalina knew she needed to get away from the suffocating presence of his adoration.

"Nothing," she answered, turning to flash him a smile. "I wasn't lying when I said you cleared my senses."

She scooted to the edge of the bed when Brandon gently seized her arm.

"Not so fast. I'm not finished with you yet. You may have changed your mind about the mission, but I still want to make sure you never forget about me." He raised an eyebrow as he tried to reel her in.

"Easy, boy," Akalina forced a laugh before excusing herself to visit the bathroom.

"Alright, but don't keep me waiting."

As she crossed the bedroom, Brandon declared his love for her anew.

"I know," she uttered. Knowing he couldn't see her face, Akalina rolled her eyes on her way out.

Camile reflected on her most recent dream knowing Akalina had lied to Brandon's face. Despite her promise, she did, in fact, travel to the Coexistent World in order to claim the medallion and attempt killing her positive half. Brandon was so desperate for love that he failed to see through Akalina's deception and Camile pitied him for it.

Chapter 63

Weight of Command

Camile couldn't deny how good it felt to be on the receiving end of unconditional love, even if it was through Akalina's memories. It led her to wonder what it would be like to enter a relationship with Brandon. She shook the thought, knowing it was way too premature to even consider such a thing. She also knew moving on with him would mean admitting her relationship with Jeremy, something she hadn't given up on rekindling, had truly failed. Her difficulties in her personal life propelled her determination to throw herself into her remaining assignments. During this time she noticed a sudden, but slight boost in her intuitive abilities. It led her to wonder if her anchor had been removed and, if so, why? Since the matter hadn't been raised by her parents or any of the council members, Camile decided to keep the development to herself since she harbored mild anxiety that they would reinstate her restrictions.

One afternoon, just prior to her latest assignment, Camile was summoned to meet with her parents in their quarters. Following the usual small talk they got down to the purpose of the gathering. Camile thought it odd that although there was a general briefing scheduled in less than an hour, they insisted on speaking with her beforehand. The primary objective of the assignment, she was told, was not to merely observe, but to lead a tagging expedition of four prospective recruits and the collection of one recruit. Camile's breath caught in the back of her throat since she knew how serious the assignment was.

"We're not throwing you out there on your own," her father explained. "Commander Wilder and other team members will assist you, but ultimately this mission will be a test of all you've learned so far. Therefore, we urge you to be on your guard at all times. Each moment will hold the possibility of something going awry. It will be up to you to figure out what to do once that occurs."

"You sound certain of that," Camile remarked.

"Nothing's certain, sweetheart. That's what we're trying to tell you. When you lead a team, you have to be prepared for anything that might happen. It'll be up to you to figure out what to do when the unexpected occurs. You have to trust your intuition. It's one of your most powerful gifts." Her father paused, regarding her with a knowing gaze. "Your anchor has been slackened over the past few days. Do you feel the difference?"

Camile nodded, her face growing warm as she realized she'd been withholding information of which her parents were already aware.

"Use your senses wisely and keep your wits about you," her mother advised. "This will possibly be your most difficult task yet, but it's an important step that must be taken in order to ensure your ability to hold your own."

*   *   *

"Each mission is accompanied by the possibility you won't return," Zephyr stated at the briefing just moments after meeting with his daughter.

The assembly hall was packed with teams, designated for various assignments throughout the Coexistent World. Like in previous briefings, Camile noticed some officers dressed in heavy uniforms as though prepared for combat. The sight of them, accompanied with her father's next words, made her further understand the ominous magnitude of the situation.

"It has recently been brought to the council's attention that the rebels are preparing for the next phase of their attack on the Coexistent World. We've gathered limited intelligence on the matter since it's still in the preliminary stages of development, but we do know that they're referring to it as *The Awakening.* Our sources haven't been able to gather much else, but they're working on changing that," Camile's father explained. "The name of the operation, alone, doesn't give us much to go on but, I have a hunch it's the next step in their attempt to prevent the *Age of Ascension.* This, of course, makes your job all the more dangerous. There is always a chance you will be captured, tortured and/or killed," Zephyr said firmly.

"Certain freedoms come with a hefty price tag, as does the right to sustain the human race, be it Transcendent or Coexistent." He swept his arms outward, before resting them on the podium. "In the grand scheme of things, it's a worthy investment. As your strategic commander, I order you to keep this in mind when you feel you can no longer shoulder the weight of the situation. As your brother, I ask you to remember what your meditation has taught you, should you face your darkest hour; that pain and discomfort, though unpleasant, are temporary conditions. And as a man who has had personal dealings with death in the past." His eyes briefly shifted to Camile before roaming the crowd, "I tell you that it is not always your enemy. It must not be feared or loathed. However, do your best to avoid meeting it senselessly."

The teams were deployed shortly thereafter. Camile and Commander Wilder co-headed a team of five. She was nervous about her level of responsibility and apparently, Brandon saw it. He pulled her aside to have a word with her in private.

"Hey, don't be nervous," he said gently. "Ironically enough, the fear of making mistakes usually leads you to make them. Don't worry. I got your back, just make sure you watch your front." He winked. Camile responded by smiling.

Upon reviewing the mission plan, Camile noticed that she'd be visiting yet another place she'd never been—Downtown Detroit. She was grateful that all of their targets were located in the same building. For efficiency purposes, she designated two of the most experienced members to tag two of the targets while she, Brandon and the least experienced team member tagged the others. She decided that they would collect the recruit last. Prior to dividing the team, Camile designated a rendezvous site and time.

Everything went according to plan and Camile breathed a sigh of relief as the mission was finally drawing to a close. She and Brandon had successfully guided the team back to the rift and watched as they safely escorted the recruit to the other side. Prior to reentering the Transcendent World, Camile and Brandon visually inspected the area to ensure no one from the Coexistent World had become aware of the cross-world aperture. Evening was drawing near and the city lights were coming alive. As they made their way toward the rift, Brandon took the opportunity to commend her on a job well done. His kind sentiments were nearly drowned out by chanting crowds pouring down both sides of the street.

The cacophonic chants grew into hysterical screams set to the chaotic tune of blocked traffic and crashing of random vehicles being upturned. It didn't take long for the pair to notice that they were about to be sandwiched by two angry rival factions. They were forced further away from the rift as they dodged bottles and other objects being hurled between the two groups that were now clashing in a grand brawl. Brandon aggressively fought his way through the chaotic scene, making a path in the shifting crowd as he reached for Camile's hand. Following his lead, she, too, fought her way through. Breaking free, they ran toward their exit. Tightening his grip, Brandon urgently pulled Camile, prompting her to quicken her pace.

"Time's running out! It's closing," he shouted over his shoulder. His voice could barely compete with the roar of the rapidly dispersing crowd and blaring sirens. Suddenly, he halted. His eyes widened in alarm as he quickly reversed course. Camile had never seen them sparkle with such intensity. Then she realized the reaction was due to the abrupt change in lighting. Brandon pushed her so hard she flew a few feet backward, landing hard on the concrete. She grimaced in pain, giving her eyes a split second disadvantage, preventing her from witnessing the full scale of the events taking place. Once they reopened, she screamed as she attempted to leap to her feet to save Brandon. It was too late. One of several police cars that had sped onto the scene had already hit him, sending him flying through the air until he vanished. In that moment, Camile felt as though a part of herself had died inside. It seemed fitting that darkness was now claiming the sky.

As the riot continued to clear, she noticed the torchlight from her utility belt had fallen a short distance away. Her effort to retrieve it was interrupted when a man beat her to it. The streetlight above was busted, but Camile could vaguely see his face, pitted all over with beady eyes peeking at her from beneath his bushy brows.

"A lil' early to be dressin' up for Halloween, ain't it?" He smirked as he approached, looking her up and down before coming face-to-face with her. His breath reeked of cheap cigarettes and apple gum, which failed to mask the smell of the former. "But damn, you sure is fine. So, baby, you trickin' or treatin'? Either way works for me."

Camile saw the rift about to close and became impatient.

"I don't have time for this," she muttered, snatching the device and starting toward the rift, but he grabbed hold of her arm.

"Hey, it's rude of you to leave without givin' me my treat."

Feeling threatened and knowing he wouldn't release her otherwise, Camile kicked his shin and hit him across the face with the torchlight.

"There's your treat, jerk!"

She ran, leaping out for the rift. Landing painfully on her stomach she realized her leap had come just seconds too late. The rift was gone.

"I don't believe this shit!" She shook her head.

Scrambling to her feet, she saw the tacky man limping in her direction while massaging his jaw. As he stepped out of the shadows, she noticed something she couldn't see earlier—his badge. Much to her dismay, the man was a police officer.

Damn!

She turned to make a getaway, but her body stiffened like a board before meeting the ground, yet again. Her muscles tensed painfully with an electric fueled buzz, but scariest of all was her total loss of motor control. Once she felt the prongs being removed from her back, she knew she had been stunned. The sensation of the icy cuffs binding her wrists increased her awareness of the cold heat on the side of her face, bringing with it the knowledge that she had scraped it on the pavement. Looking up, she saw the sneering face of the disgruntled officer. She knew it was too late to make nice, so she spared herself the dishonor of such an attempt by remaining silent.

"There's *your* treat, bitch!" The officer punctuated the end of his statement with a hard kick to Camile's already sore stomach. She relented her silence involuntarily as the air was forced from her body.

During her trip to the station, Camile's thoughts circled around Brandon. The image of him getting hit by the car and being thrown like a ragdoll was etched in her mind and not even her current situation could erase it, or the intense worry she felt for him. She tried to hold onto the possibility he was still alive and had received treatment on the other side of the veil, but occasionally her hope was obscured by doubt as visions of his demise played in her mind.

Her interrogation was going terribly; there was no evidence of her existence. Camile knew the reason for this, but refused to tell since it would only worsen her situation. In the meantime, she desperately hoped someone would come and get her out of the sticky mess she had landed in. During the questioning, she saw one of the detectives playing around with the *Styngrae.*

"No! Don't touch that," she exclaimed, startling everyone in the room.

"What, you think they'll damage your little toy?" The interrogator laughed.

"It's not a toy. It's a highly sophisticated weapon. If your friend wants to kill himself with it, that's his business," Camile muttered.

"Not a toy, huh?" The interrogator signaled the detective to hand the weapon to Camile. "Go on, show us how it works."

"Okay, you asked for it," Camile sighed, rising from her seat. She activated the whip-like device and slung it around like a lion tamer.

"Satisfied?"

The detectives regarded each other with looks of astonishment.

"Well, uh…" The interrogator cleared his throat. "That's quite something. Where'd you say you got that thing?"

"I didn't. But you wouldn't believe me if I told you, so I won't bother."

"I'm curious as to what it feels like. Hit me with it."

This man must be into that S & M stuff, Camile thought before saying, "I've been on the receiving end of this thing. Trust me, you don't want a taste of this. It might kill you. If you must see a demonstration, why don't you let me test it on the cop that kicked me."

"I think you've done enough damage to Officer Anderson. He's out with a fractured fibula." The interrogator laughed. "I'm a tough guy. I've been shot twice, so I think I can handle it."

"Don't say I didn't warn you," Camile lashed to strike his extended arm and was amazed to see it pass through his body with no effect. Everyone in the room—except for her—broke out in hysterical laughter.

"You're killin' me! I surrender!" The interrogator choked through his amusement.

Camile came to the conclusion that they were unable to witness the weapon in action. To them, it was just a useless cylindrical piece of metal.

Chapter 64

Submergence

Just as she had expected—and feared—she was ordered to undergo a mental evaluation. Her best attempts to appear sane proved unsuccessful. Upon failing the assessment, she was eventually admitted to a mental institution. All the while she tried to remain hopeful that somewhere along her journey she would encounter a willing ear, but all those around her were deaf with skepticism. Nevertheless, she continued to protest until a staff member met her with an onslaught of debilitating drugs after confiscating her medallion. It seemed as though each time Camile would wake, they'd induce sleep by injecting her with more. Upon her fifth sedation, she came face-to-face with the shaman.

"Your Wisest! You've gotta get me out of here," Camile implored.

"We've been looking all over for you. Where are you?" The shaman asked.

"I'm stuck in some mental hospital in the Coexistent World. They think I'm crazy and they keep drugging me. If you don't get me out of here soon, I think I really might go nuts."

"Just try to hang in there, Camile. We're having trouble tracking you. Do you still have your medallion?"

"No. They took it as soon as I got here."

The shaman asked for the name of the facility, something Camile found herself straining to remember. She vaguely recalled seeing it embroidered on one of the nurses' uniforms, but it remained blurred in her mind.

"Don't worry, my child, we'll find you," the shaman reassured. "But, it's very important that you—"

She roused upon feeling someone jostling her shoulder. Training her eyes upward, she saw the face of a nurse. Knowing that the shaman's message had been interrupted, Camile's frustration escalated.

"Sounds like you were having a nightmare. Who were you talking to?" the nurse asked.

"Why'd you wake me up? I was about to find out something important!" Camile exclaimed.

I didn't even get to ask about Brandon, she thought.

"You were having a nightmare. I did you a favor."

"I wasn't having a nightmare, I was talking to—" Camile thought better of elaborating any further, but it was already too late.

"Someone named *Your Wisest*, who's from another world, right?" The nurse arched her brow. "Why did you say you were stuck in the Coexistent World, huh?"

"Like you said, it was just a nightmare." Camile sighed, her eyes roaming to the nurse's uniform on which the name Evy Crow was embroidered above *Sync Mental Health Services.*

"You don't sound too convinced of that."

"What do you care?" Camile asked.

At least she now knew the name of the facility in which she was being held, even though she was still unaware of its geographical location.

"Actually, I don't." Evy smiled. "You see, unlike you, I get to leave here in a few hours, go home to my wonderful family, eat a decent hot meal and do whatever the hell I please. In the meantime, you'll stay here, staring at these dreary walls with nothing but your nightmares and imaginary friends to keep you company. Such a pity, you, likely staying here for the rest of your miserable life."

Camile scrunched her face.

You wicked bitch! I bet you get off on seeing people suffer here.

"Oh, why the long face?" The nurse asked, batting her lashes. "The truth hurts, doesn't it?"

Camile had enough. Before she realized what she was doing, she leapt up and smacked the nurse across the face, giving her a nosebleed.

"Hurts, doesn't it?" she asked, mocking the nurse's previous question while shaking the sting out of her hand.

Inevitably, security was called to the scene after the nurse screamed that she had been attacked. Camile was immediately strapped to the bed and sedated yet again.

Oh, well, she thought. *At least I'll see Tabitha and we can figure out a way to get me the hell out of here.*

Unfortunately for Camile, she didn't see the shaman or anyone else from Caldaq that night, the next night or the night following that. Eventually, her isolation began eating away at her and she resorted to prayer, something she hadn't done in quite some time.

"Please…" she implored. "Please, send someone to come get me— *anyone*. I don't even care if it's Sir Drayden. I just wanna get out of here."

That's the way she fell asleep every evening. The sun and moon moved like chase lights across the sky and she eventually lost track of how much time had elapsed since she was taken in. Resentful at her ill-treatment, Camile grew rebellious. Her continued defiance resulted in forced injections and further abuse. Bound to the bed, Camile lost all sense of freedom and her continence was soon to follow. First was the warm flood of relief before the cold dampness of reality set in. It wasn't for the lack of trying to keep a firm grasp of control, but her requests to properly relieve herself went ignored. Clearly, Nurse Evy Crow was trying to teach her a lesson. If that lesson was to test how long she'd be able to withstand the sensation of lying in her own waste, she learned it very quickly.

Eventually, one of the other staff members believed Camile's grievances after witnessing the maltreatment. This led to an immediate reassignment, though Camile still saw her tormentor in passing, mainly while traveling to her therapy sessions. Realizing that her struggle was only further ensnaring her in captivity, she thought of Blake, the man the shaman had personally recruited months ago. She decided to follow his example and play along with the people now in charge. Perhaps doing so would increase her chances of freedom.

There was a danger to her plan and she soon encountered it head-on. Slowly, but surely she eased into her new way of life as though slipping into a roomy pair of pajamas. The drugs continued to corrupt her mind, tearing down her focus and mental defenses bit by bit. In time, the faces of her family, friends and colleagues became a blur, dissolving into distant memories that were steadily fading away. Soon, the boundary between truth and lies, reality and illusion seemed nothing more than a diminishing shadow as she drifted light-years away from everything coherent. Occasionally, she considered killing Nurse Crow to determine whether or not she—and the abuse she'd inflicted—was a figment of her imagination. Yet, Camile's newly adopted compliance prevented her from acting on her curiosity. Her mind was becoming as malleable as modeling clay and the doctors were attempting to mold it as they saw fit.

In time, Camile could remember nothing other than her life in the institution. She no longer experienced the emotional pain she felt during the process of detaching herself from her memories. In many ways she had become acclimated to her new environment. She spent most of her days sketching in a book she had received for her good behavior. In it were drawings of unusual spider-like creatures, strange animals, sharply dressed figures and unusual places. Camile and her doctors were convinced the sketches were renderings of things generated by her vivid creativity.

"See? You're finally putting that active imagination of yours to good use. If you keep this up, you could have a decent career in illustration when you get out of here. I'll tell you what, I'll see if I can get you some crayons so you can color your sketches," the doctor told her. Camile smiled and wondered if the doctor had read her mind. She had secretly been wishing for them.

The doctor ended the session as a large dark-skinned female nurse entered the room. She was aptly named Ebony Night. She preferred to be addressed casually since formality made her feel old and rigid. Ebony was among the most decent of all the employees Camile had seen, but she also had a no-nonsense attitude.

"Wanna see my drawings?" Camile asked eagerly.

"After you take your meds." Ebony droned, handing over the tiny plastic cup.

"I've been improving. Is it still necessary for me to take them? They make me feel so...disoriented."

"Girl, don't be givin' me no grief. You know the rules by now." Ebony straightened her shiny pink headband in her hair, which desperately needed trimming.

Camile frowned as she swallowed the pills. Opening her mouth, she lifted her tongue—an obligatory routine to prove she had indeed swallowed them. Just then, Nurse Crow entered the room and spoke with Ebony. During this time, Camile noticed something oddly familiar—the unusual necklace Nurse Crow was wearing.

"That's really pretty," Camile complimented, no longer recognizing the necklace as her own. "Where'd you get it?"

"It was a gift, if you must know." Nurse Crow rolled her eyes as though inconvenienced by her curiosity.

"It's beautiful," Camile said, her eyes fixed on the medallion, nearly entranced.

Apparently uncomfortable with Camile's transfixion, Nurse Crow tucked the necklace into the generous bosom filling her blouse.

"Damn! Didn't anybody ever tell you it's impolite to stare," she said rather abruptly. "I worked hard to get this, so you better not be thinkin' about stealin' it."

"I thought you said it was a gift," Camile wondered.

"It was a gift to myself, smart ass." Nurse Crow frowned.

Camile didn't want to upset her. She knew that doing so would ruin her chances of seeing the item again. She found it unusually soothing.

"I'm not trying to cause trouble," she said. "It probably sounds strange, but looking at the necklace makes me feel like I'm not all alone in the world, almost like I have a family somewhere out there looking for me. If you don't mind, I'd like to see it again."

"Hmph! And a lot of patients want out." Nurse Crow snorted. "It's just a stupid necklace, girl! Remember how they found you—all alone, no records, not a penny to your name. In all the time you've been here not *one* person has come looking for you. Nobody gives a shit about you, remember that."

Nurse Crow left without giving her the gratification of seeing the medallion once more. Camile refused to believe her caustic statements even though they did burn. She had to come from somewhere. There had to be some kind of purpose for her life other than being the mental punching bag for the disgruntled. The remaining nurse tried to alleviate the inflammatory words with some encouraging sentiments.

"Try not to let the witch get to you. I can't stand her either. Almost cheered when I heard that you belted her one." Ebony laughed heartily. "But seriously, girl, I know you been here awhile, but don't give up. You too good a person to be up in here. And nowadays, good people don't just come out of the blue. Someone put a lot of love into raising you and I got a feeling they out there looking for you. They gonna find you soon, that's real talk."

"Exactly how long have I been here?" Camile asked.

"'bout a month."

"Strange. Feels like it's been years."

"I ain't surprised. Time tends to stand still in a place like this." Ebony shook her head.

"What did you say?"

Ebony repeated her statement.

"I think I've heard that somewhere before."

"That don't surprise me either. You probably heard it from one of the other patients."

Camile disagreed with Ebony, but kept it to herself as she started drawing on a fresh page in her sketchbook. She decided to draw the unusual necklace.

*　　*　　*

Later that evening, Camile fell asleep clutching her completed sketch. Just as she submerged into slumber, something touched her arm. She saw no one in the room when she awoke. At first, she figured it was a muscle spasm, but panicked when she experienced the sensation a second time. She felt the warmth of a hand she couldn't see.

"There's a ghost in my room! Somebody help me," she yelled, jumping out of bed.

Someone immediately rushed to her aid. It wasn't a hospital worker, but a fellow patient named Monica, a woman she befriended shortly after her arrival at the institution. She had only seen her a few times. Even so, she had made Camile uncomfortable by saying that she now knew that she spent the past three years of her hellish life at the institution for the sole purpose of meeting her. Even so, Camile couldn't shake the strange air of familiarity surrounding her acquaintance. Physically, she thought Monica's mahogany skin, dark eyes and mousy brown hair seemed odd. Occasionally, she'd have flashes of the woman with a completely opposite appearance. Yet, the facial features remained nearly exactly the same. Camile wondered where she got the idea that Monica would look more appropriate with pale white skin, hair and pink eyes, but shrugged it off as a delusion.

"Shh! It's okay," Monica hushed, briefly covering Camile's mouth. "You have to be quiet. You don't want them to drug you again."

"But the medicine might make them go away. They're scaring me, Monica," Camile said tremulously, her voice calmer now that she wasn't alone.

"They're not ghosts and they're not here to hurt you. One of them gave me a message for you. They're taking you home tonight."

"No. Don't let them take me!" Camile clung to Monica's arm, much like how a child clings to a parent to seek protection against a monster.

"What?" Monica asked, turning to her left, but Camile saw no one there. "Okay, I'll tell her."

"Tell me what?" Camile wrinkled her nose. Concerned, she loosened her grip. "Monica, maybe you should go back on your meds. You're talking to an empty space."

"No, I'm not. Her Wisest told me to—"

"What in the hell? Why y'all makin' all this noise this time o' night?" Ebony asked as she entered the room.

There was an awkward moment of silence as Camile debated whether or not she should trust Monica or report her to the nurse. She decided on the former.

"Sorry. Just a silly nightmare." Camile smiled shakily. "Monica was just helping me to get over it."

Ebony raised her eyebrows.

"Very nice, Monica. About time you break away from your anti-social behavior." She grinned. "Okay. You got five minutes, but then you gotta go back to your own room. Bad enough I gotta do a double shift with Evil Crow, I don't need no mo' problems, ya hear?"

After Ebony left, Monica wasted no time in seizing Camile's sketchbook and flipping to the page with the drawing of the necklace.

"Look familiar, Camile?"

"It's Nurse Crow's necklace."

"No, Camile. It's *yours*. She stole it from you, but they couldn't steal your memory. Only you can do that and you don't have to. Take a good look at it. Remember where it came from, where *you* came from. Remember your parents and how much they love you. The memory of all those things aren't gone. They're still in your head, you just locked them away. You did such a good job protecting them that you hid them from yourself."

Camile shook her head, grimacing as she tried to wrap her head around the things being said. Monica placed her hand on Camile's chest.

"You feel something missing, don't you? The drugs may have affected your memory on a physical level, but it can't change your soul, who you really are."

As Monica continued to talk, displaying obvious signs of being coached, the heavy fog around Camile's mind began to thin out. Gradually, she saw several figures emerge beside her, all wearing long dark coats. She found their appearance frightening, like something she had seen in a movie about a sadistic cult that practiced human sacrifice. Though such movies weren't allowed at the facility, one of the nurses had disregarded the rule and played it anyway to indulge her own curiosity.

There was an older woman with salt and pepper hair. Standing beside her was a tall muscular man with lush dark russet hair and aquamarine eyes. Behind him was a middle-aged pair—a woman with caramel skin and a fair-skinned man. Next to them was an older, large-nosed man with immaculate silver hair and piercing blue eyes that seemed to emit a cat-like glow in the low light.

Camile gasped, backing in a corner.

"Good job, Monica." The older woman smiled.

"Wh—? You tricked me," Camile exclaimed.

She tried to escape, but someone grabbed her from behind. There was a brief tussle. The defense moves she used seemed to come naturally, though she couldn't remember how she had learned them. She landed several good hits before the aquamarine eyed man overpowered her, hoisting her over his shoulder. She kicked and screamed at the top of her lungs for help as she punched at her captor's back. It was useless. Nurse Crow and a couple of guards raced into the hall to investigate the ruckus. All three of their faces drained of color when they saw what was happening, their mouths agape as they stared at the unfolding scene with wide eyes. Camile's captor trailed the others down a corridor while the middle-aged man traveled in the opposite direction.

Camile cried out for help as she reached for the startled hospital staff, but no one budged. They appeared to be afraid to come anywhere near her.

"Calm down, Wildflower." Her captor gently tapped her bottom. "You're okay now. You'll be home soon."

"Oh, my God," the nurse exclaimed, her voice barely audible. "She's...*floating!*"

Camile watched helplessly as the hospital ward, guards and Nurse Crow, who fainted after the middle aged man snatched the necklace from her, faded away.

Chapter 65

Resurfacing

Camile demanded her release as she pounded on the heavy sealed door. There was no response. She had been placed in a small vacant room with no windows and only two chairs. Figuring resistance would prove unsuccessful and even more painful to her hands, Camile retreated to a chair, but then sat on the floor, as though to protest in any way she could. Seeing that her constant screaming was equally fruitless, she remained silent. She didn't want to end up on the menu for the massive white tiger that had followed her new captors to the entrance of the mountainous building as they carried her inside. After what she guessed to be a few hours, the door opened just long enough for the officers to send a little girl into the room. She said nothing to Camile as she sat in the chair across from her.

"Looks like they gave us both a time out, huh, kiddo?" Camile asked.

"Looks like," the child shrugged, smoothing back her long braided pigtails.

"Got a name?"

"Gia. What's yours?"

"Camile. At least I think it is. How old are you, Gia? You look a bit young to be in prison."

"Seven and a half, in physical years," Gia answered before pausing slightly, "You know, there's really no need to worry. The situation isn't as dire as it appears."

Camile frowned at the unusual response, but refused to ask any further questions. She had much on her mind as she tried to think of ways to escape her current captivity. Despite Gia's reassurance, the situation seemed futile. In addition to the tiger, Camile had noticed countless guards between the entrance and the room in which she now sat. She knew it would be impossible to make a clean getaway. Therefore, she began contemplating about how she would try to convince her captors to release her.

"Your hair's really pretty. Can I touch it?" Gia interrupted her thoughts.

Camile was taken aback by the compliment since her locks had been disheveled in her struggle with her captors. She initially considered denying the little girl's request, but changed her mind when she noticed how lonely she seemed.

"Sure. Go ahead," she said wearily.

Gia slowly approached Camile, who was now kneeling on the floor. Now standing face-to-face, the girl outstretched her small hands to either side of Camile's head and paused. She stared Camile in the eye cautiously as though seeking confirmation of her consent. Before Camile could give her reassurance, the girl grabbed her head tightly in a vice-like grip. Camile gasped in shock as her mind was flooded with rapid images and memories. The experience was overwhelming and it took her a moment to realize that her hands were tightly grasping the girl's wrists, desperately trying to pry Gia's hands from her head. It was useless. She fell onto her side, but the girl tumbled with her, never disconnecting until she was done. Camile lost consciousness shortly thereafter.

*   *   *

As parts of her memory was restored, Camile received a painful jolt of truth. In hindsight, she now understood how blissful she had been during her brief tour of ignorance. Now, she felt a renewed burden of reality bearing heavily on her mind. Setting this aside as best she could, Camile briefed the council on what had gone wrong during the mission; at least the parts she could recall. As the briefing drew to a close, Camile voiced the single question circling her mind:

"Why didn't the Styngrae work?"

The answer she received intrigued her. It was explained that since her captors had such a powerful belief her weapon wasn't real, it had no effect on them.

"It's an extremely rare phenomenon, mind you, but it's powerful," her father said. "Even so, just because he didn't immediately experience the effect of your lash, chances are that in time, his mind and body will no longer be able to resist the result. This has happened in the past. Belief and denial both hold significant power. People who are seemingly impervious to our weapons sometimes experience delayed reactions, some more severe than others. Everything from minor rashes to gangrene and death."

Camile grimaced upon hearing the explicit details of previous incidents.

"You see, both belief and denial require reaffirmation to continuously support or disprove a claim." Her mother added. "Once it falters, the mind and body become susceptible to outside influence."

*   *   *

Camile wanted to put her horrific imprisonment behind her, but found it virtually impossible. The wounds were far too fresh to ignore. Yet, she erected a facade to deflect the concerned inquiries from her parents. She also tried to convince them she was fit to continue her training as well as her remaining assignments. They, as well as Sir Drayden and the shaman, suggested that she take time off to process what had happened. They gave her a few weeks to do so and mentioned that it could be extended if necessary. The prospect seemed like further punishment. The last thing Camile felt she needed was inactive time to reflect and relive the inhumane treatment that had been inflicted on her. Determined for some form of distraction, she occupied her time with her studies and frequent workouts. All the while she wondered if Akalina had been right in thinking the Coexistents weren't worthy of the council's help. She wondered what was the point in assisting people who had the capability of such cruelty and spitefulness.

What makes them worth saving?

The answer used to come so easily to her, but now her mind found it difficult to grasp. Still, she clung to the knowledge that in the midst of her trouble she was graced with the compassionate aid of Ebony and Monica.

Camile was slightly apprehensive about entering Jeremy's quarters despite the fact he had summoned her there. He and Brandon had been noticeably absent at the briefing, but then again, their presence wasn't required. She paused in the doorway, wondering if Jeremy had finally realized what she had known all along, that life was too short to allow others to dictate how one should live it. She considered the possibility that in just a matter of moments, their relationship would be revived and strengthened to a point where not even Sir Drayden could breach it.

Figuring she had stalled long enough, she entered to find Jeremy reviewing a large map, located on a transparent film-like material that unfurled like a scroll from a black cylindrical base. After spreading it out on the table he raised his eyes upon noticing her presence. She continued to cross the room until she was standing before him.

Jeremy greeted her with a gentle hug, much to her delight. For the first time since her return, she felt like she could fully relax.

"Welcome home," he said. "You're late. I almost thought you weren't coming. Anyway, it's good to see you. If we lost you out there it would've been devastating. How are you holding up?"

"As well as I can. If you don't mind, I'd rather not get into it right now."

Overjoyed to be in his arms again, Camile loosened her end of the embrace and moved to kiss his lips.

"I think you misunderstood me." He held her shoulders, keeping her at nearly an arms distance. "What happened was unfortunate, but it doesn't change the status of our relationship."

"But you just said—"

"I would've been devastated if we lost you because you mean too much to our mission. Without you, it'll be damn near impossible to save the people we need to."

Camile narrowed her eyes. "Jeremy, I know we weren't together very long, but you can't honestly tell me it means nothing to you."

"What we had was good while it lasted, but you have to accept that it's over. I'm sorry, but this is the way it has to be." He furrowed his brow. "I thought I already made this clear."

"I see." Camile pulled away slowly, heating up with embarrassment. Despite her frustration, she managed a faint chortle. "And here I thought you called me here to reconcile. I guess I just made a complete ass of myself, huh?"

Her attempts to steady her shaky voice seemed to have the opposite effect. The cold grip of exhaustion grasped for her heart and mind. She tried to fend it off with a carefree smile, but found it impossible.

"I wanted to make sure you were okay, given the ordeal you just endured," Jeremy said. "I wanted to offer my support. Don't feel bad about the misunderstanding. I can see how you might've been confused." He cupped her shoulder. "Can we continue this discussion later? Something's come up and I have to prepare for a meeting with Vincent in a few minutes."

Camile nodded in quiet humiliation before turning to make her exit. Beneath her forced, poised demeanor lurked chaotic thoughts of frustration.

Don't feel bad? Is he serious? Is that honestly the best he could do? Never mind him. Just leave and move on with your crazy life.

Camile's internal pep talk proved for naught as she whipped around to face Jeremy anew. Her dignity wanted to abandon the scene as it stood, but her pride was not prepared to go quietly.

"Don't feel bad?" She laughed in disbelief. "I'm sorry, Jeremy, but I can't help but feel bad that after I was nearly lost you still don't have feelings for me at all. Was it a lie when you said you cared about me?"

He did say he cared about me, didn't he? My recovering memory didn't just invent that; it couldn't have.

"My feelings about the situation are irrelevant. What is, is the fact that you're safe and that we can get back to work. I hate to be blunt, but you need to stay focused on your responsibilities instead of what could've been with our relationship."

"Whoa! Okay, I see you're taking notes from Sir Drayden. Well, while we're on the subject of being blunt, let me tell you this; not everyone can disregard their feelings completely. You may be a Transcendent human, but you're still human and emotions are part of the package. Maybe it will someday, but so far your emotional impotence hasn't rubbed off on me."

"You should know; you come from a world full of emotionally imbalanced people. Maybe you just never realized it since they try to hide it with the occasional good deed," Jeremy retorted.

Before Camile could address the statement, they were interrupted.

"Careful, someone might take that as an anti-Coexistent remark." Vincent entered the room wearing his usual mysterious smirk. "Am I interrupting something?"

"No. I was just leaving." Camile glared at Jeremy before exiting the room.

She fought the fleeting impulse to go running to Brandon and give in to him to spite Jeremy. Actually, it wouldn't have been just out of spite, but her desperate need to escape the rampant thoughts burning through her head. However, she knew it wouldn't be fair to anyone involved. Camile also figured Jeremy probably wouldn't give a damn whether or not she pursued a rebound relationship. If anything, he'd probably use it as another reason to look down on her. Furthermore, she didn't want to sacrifice what was left of her dignity for the sake of revenge. Refusing to allow her emotions to get the better of her and dictate her decisions, she pressed forward.

Sitting in the garden, her focus shifted to the sound of the fountains and the sweet floral scent in the chilly air. Though her eyes were closed, she could still sense the soft light of the fading day as the songbirds completed their final melodies before nightfall. Without realizing it, she smiled in appreciation of what had alleviated her stress. Sensing she was no longer alone, she opened her eyes and saw the commander standing in front of her.

"I see my favorite wildflower's back in the garden," he greeted.

"How long have you been standing there?"

"Not long, but that smile was enough to make my afternoon a whole lot brighter."

Camile thought the sentiment was sweet, albeit a bit corny and a departure from his naughtier comments. Seeing that he was waiting for an invitation to sit with her, she gave him one after first giving him a hug.

"Thank God you're okay," she said. "I thought you were killed."

"Not a chance," Brandon said, pressing his cheek against her head before releasing her. "The only thing I lost that day were my shoes."

The two laughed as they sat.

"Looks like you're the one who lucked out." Camile scratched her head. "Things have been getting more familiar, but there's still quite a bit I can't remember."

"Like our marriage?" Brandon raised an eyebrow.

Camile grimaced a moment, then nudged the commander upon seeing his smile.

"Nice try." She smirked. "But seriously, no head games."

After speaking about her experience at the institution, the commander complicated things for Camile even further by doing something Jeremy didn't—show unrestricted compassion.

"I have to admit, when you didn't make it to the other side of the rift, I was worried. I mean, I'm confident in your skills and all, but the Coexistent World can be tough."

"I know. I lived there most of my life, remember?" Camile chortled, rubbing her hands to offset the chill in the air.

"Yeah, but you've changed since then and you've adapted to this world. Getting stuck the way you did can be really confusing, which makes it easy to forget where you belong. I'm just glad you made it back home. This might sound kind of silly since I know we're not together...*yet*," he smirked, "but I missed you a lot."

"You gave me quite a scare, yourself. When I saw you get hit by that car, I..." Not knowing what else to say, Camile let the sentence hang there as she broke eye contact. She didn't want to relive the moment she thought he had been permanently removed from her life. Nor did she want her heart to remember the hollow feeling it had endured in the instant of the frightening occurrence. She knew that doing so would only complicate matters further.

"Well, I guess we're even then," she joked in an attempt to offset the seriousness of the conversation.

"The car didn't kill me, but that smile might," Brandon amorously remarked.

"Maybe it's time for a checkup, Commander," a voice interrupted.

Camile shifted her attention behind Brandon and saw Sir Drayden emerging from around a corner. Jeremy was with him.

Well, if it isn't the dynamic duo! Camile thought bitterly.

Chapter 66

Age of Ascension

As the council continued to receive news of the worsening chaos in the Coexistent World, Camile's hope in humanity plummeted further. Her despondency was magnified by the fact her heart had recently been broken. She was also beginning to wonder if love was just a mutated form of affliction. Just as disturbingly, her mind had lapses where it superimposed the actions of unscrupulous individuals over the entire Coexistent race. She usually managed to refocus her distorted vision, but given the state of things, it wasn't easy to do this time around. Concerned, she sought guidance from the shaman, who she met in one of the botanical gardens.

"Hope and belief illuminates the pathway of change and possibility, but before the road is constructed, it must first be envisioned. Humans can't create anything, tangible or otherwise, without initial thought and belief. Contemplation, supported with conviction, provides the blueprint of creation." Tabitha looked deeply into Camile's eyes, as though searching the depths of her soul. Finally, she said, "My child, I think it's time for you to know what the Age of Ascension really is and what we're really fighting for."

Blinking, Camile cocked her head. "I was already told, the Age of Ascension will be the time when Coexistents truly learn to value life beyond the physical level."

"That's only part of it," the shaman replied as they resumed walking along the external corridor lining the Courtyard of Serenity.

"The Age of Ascension will be the time when Coexistents rise to possess the same abilities we do. It's one of the main reasons why the rebels are so determined to dominate them while they're still bound by their own limitations. The rebels will do everything they can to prevent them from gaining such power. They want the Coexistents to remain oppressed and ignorant to the fact of what they're really capable of."

"So, how are we gonna beat them, the rebels?"

"It's not entirely up to us. And the outcome is unknown since the most important part of the Invisible War depends solely on the Coexistents themselves. Our role is to teach them to defend themselves...and to remind them of who they truly are."

"What? Now we have to remind them that they're human too?" Camile chortled faintly.

"No, we have to remind them that they're more than human. Much more."

"But how can we do that and make sure they receive their powers through the Age of Ascension? How can we prevent the rebels from stealing them?"

"It's not up to us to make sure they get their powers, but I can assure you, the rebels can't steal them. You see, they can't take something the Coexistents already possess."

Camile narrowed her eyes, contemplating the shaman's statement.

"You mean...they already *have* the same abilities we do?"

Tabitha nodded. "Each and every one of them. They just don't know it yet. To phrase it more correctly, they simply forgot they have them."

Apparently amused by Camile's astonished expression, the shaman laughed.

"Oh, come on, my child. Don't tell me it surprises you. Take a look at Coexistent history. For many years people have been accused of—and executed for—witchcraft, heresy, simply for being able to do what others couldn't. You see, for centuries, *all* humans were capable of all sorts of remarkable achievements that didn't depend solely on the material world. By the same token, terrible things have been accomplished using similar methods. How else would you explain a single person being able to bend entire nations to their whim, convincing the masses to do unspeakable things, leading them into war, massacre and catastrophe? Do you think all those stories about miracles, extraordinary events and disasters are all coincidental?"

"I don't know. I just never knew that *everyone*..." Camile's voice trailed off.

"Thought you were the only one, did you?" Tabitha said with a warm chuckle. "Sure some people have more powerful abilities than others, but that's only due to the different levels of faith they have; in themselves, others and the world around them. Yes, it's inevitable, the Coexistents *will* regain the full extent of their abilities, whether they know it or not— whether we like it or not. You see, that's the dangerous part, the part the rebels refuse to understand. It will work one of two ways; either we help teach the Coexistents to use their abilities responsibly, or we sit back and watch them destroy themselves, and possibly us as well, by using those abilities unwittingly and irresponsibly."

The shaman took a moment to smell the aroma of a large white flower before continuing.

"Humans have been endowed with these abilities since the dawn of existence. At first they were proud of them and they embraced them. But eventually, so many of them became so wrapped up in the physical aspect of the world. There was something so tempting and irresistible about performing tasks with their physical bodies. They enjoyed the sensation of interacting with their environment and each other. They eventually became dependent on their bodies and the material world up to the point that they would do heinous, unspeakable things in order to preserve their material lives for as long as they could. The physical sensations became so addictive, that they preferred to suffer the burden of pain than to ascend to their former selves. They had eventually forsaken their higher abilities and The Supreme Origin from which they came. Seeking something to fill the void, they relied on the material comforts of currency, lavishness, baubles and so on. When these things are removed, they often feel hollow and lost. You see, nothing can substitute the fulfillment that only The Supreme Origin can provide."

Camile's eyes narrowed. "Are you talking about God?"

"If that what it means to you, then yes. The Supreme Origin is many things to many people. Therefore, there are so many different names for it. Some think The Supreme Origin is male, some believe it's female, others believe it's a combination of both or a genderless force of nature. As a result, everyone has their own theory about what we need to do to return to The Supreme Origin. Different theories and opinions on the subject have sparked wars for ages. Some say that if you follow one set of rules you're guaranteed to rejoin your creator."

"Thing is, The Supreme Origin is said to be a supreme power beyond limitation. So how can a single set of rules based on the limitations of the physical world lead to our reunification with The Supreme Origin? When it comes to describing it, all people come short of describing exactly what it is. You see, since we are limited in our physical forms within an equally physical world we can only truly understand what The Supreme Origin is when we finally let go of it all and travel beyond our limitations, both mental and physical."

"You mean...*death?*"

"If you mean the time when our physical bodies can no longer accommodate the power of our divine energy or core, then yes, I'm talking about death."

*   *   *

As Camile continued to recover from her recent emotional setback, she began to experience difficulties of a different sort. Her occasional clumsiness was growing more chronic and she would find herself knocking things over, accidentally striking or bumping into people. What made this even more unusual was the fact she appeared to do all these things without direct physical contact. She tried to rationalize these occurrences as freaky coincidences or a result of her paranoia. However, she knew she could no longer do so upon being summoned by her father, who described the phenomenon as Propulsion or Core Projection.

"Propulsion is a driving force, propagated by the core energy of sentient beings," he explained. "When a person establishes control of their propulsion, they are able to manipulate things in the physical world as though they are touching them directly."

Camile's father continued his elaboration, stating that in order for one to master their propulsive abilities, it required mapping themselves in relation to the object they wished to manipulate. The way he explained it made it seem as though one could use their spiritual core as a remote control to the world around them. At first it struck Camile as strange, but after each meeting with her father on the subject it began to make perfect sense. This was especially so when he demonstrated his own ability, effortlessly propelling an orb around the vacant gym as Kylie looked on. The object slowly came to a halt, hovering between Camile and her father as they faced one another.

Zephyr instructed Camile to keep her mind still and quiet, balancing her physical, mental and spiritual portions of her being. He said that only in peace could one gauge the levels of the energy to be displaced.

"You have to feel it and know it, simultaneously," he stated. "Focus on it and concentrate the intensity with your mind. Allow it to build inside your core, but keep it contained. Release it only when you are ready, but map the path in your mind first. This is important, you must control the direction of the release."

Camile followed his instructions to the letter and was rewarded with a slight vibrating sensation in her midsection. A chill spread outward across her body, but the warm buzzing sensation remained in her chest. Camile's father instructed her to extend her palm toward the suspended target, a handball-sized orb.

"Visualize the chain reaction taking place through the air, connecting you to the sphere. Feel it strengthen to the point the air around you becomes an extension of your own body. Use it to compensate for your inability to make physical contact with the object."

She had watched his demonstration just moments earlier and was impressed with how precisely he had shifted the floating orb to the end of the room and back. She felt the weight of the object increase and deduced that her father was gradually easing his control. Camile knew she was now holding it on her own. It was at once empowering and daunting. Her nerves kicked in and resonated in the shakiness of the orb.

"Relax. You have it. Don't let your mind wander. Steady your thoughts and you'll find it will be reflected in your dexterity."

Camile successfully applied her father's suggestion, much to his delight.

"You're doing great, sweetheart," he praised. "Now, for something a little tougher. Let's see if you can make it travel. Visualize the feeling in your chest slowly intensifying, traveling up past your heart. Feel it move gently to your shoulder, coursing its way down your arm until it stops at your elbow."

"It feels weird." Camile grimaced. "It tingles."

"That's normal. Now, open your eyes and unleash it on the target."

Until that point Camile wasn't aware she had shut her eyes to offset the unusual sensations building up in her arm. In fact, she was no longer aware of anything other than the overwhelming power within her, just screaming to be released. Unable to contain it any longer, she felt it pour out of her palm with an electric chill. The target was violently thrown from its suspended orbit. It ricocheted off a wall and careened towards her mother, who extended both hands in front of her. Much to Camile's relief and surprise, the sphere hovered in mid-air as her mother manipulated it without physical contact.

Amazed, Camile stood in silence.

"You mean to tell me all this time you could do that?" she finally managed to ask. "So, that day on the hill…it *was* you deflecting the knife!"

Her mother nodded with a somewhat reluctant smile.

"I guess the cat's out of the bag now," she murmured, tossing the orb to her daughter. "We thought it was best to wait until you knew the truth about the Coexistents' latent abilities before informing you of mine. Now that you know, I must ask you not to reveal this fact to anyone else."

"Why?"

"Because, if the rebels knew the Coexistents already had these abilities, things could get nastier than they already are. The rebels believe that Transcendents evolved from the Coexistents into the powerful people they are. They believe that the Coexistents' jealousy and hatred drove them out of their world, forcing them to start anew, here. At the moment, the rebels only seek to prevent the Coexistents from receiving their power. If they knew it was already within them, lying dormant, the rebels will seek to destroy them all."

"Or manipulate them for control," Zephyr added, his face reflecting the weight he was likely carrying in his heart.

Chapter 67

Promise & Payment

It was about to happen and they only had one chance to get it right and save their target. Their mission was to intercept a planned attack on the musician, currently set to take the stage. Camile felt her heart thudding in her chest almost synchronously with the bass as she and the team grew closer. Everyone in the crowd began to look increasingly suspicious to her. The rebel—or rebels—lurking in plain sight had the advantage of anonymity. The objective, as given by the council, was to retrieve both, the intended victim and the suspect and return them to the compound. The musician possessed the gift of song and music, his arsenals to combat the malignant violence and addiction plaguing the Coexistent World. Despite his noble cause, he was met with fierce opposition which would stop at nothing to claim his life.

The concert stadium was packed with revelers, screaming and dancing wildly to loud music. Camile could feel the pulsating bass vibrating beneath her feet as she and her group moved closer to the stage. Red, yellow and blue lights swept over the crowd as strobes flashed in near perfect unison to the music. Two thunderous explosions rocked the stage, inciting the crowd to a roaring cheer. The clearing smoke revealed the terrifying reality, the vibrant pyrotechnic display was actually the beginning of a ruthless attack. The music halted as injured performers joined the panicking audience in an attempt to flee.

"Well, damn! When they say *kill the DJ*, they really mean it," someone in the crowd remarked.

"It's a diversion!" Camile exclaimed upon seeing two people traveling against the chaotic tides of the fleeing crowd. Both were getting dangerously close to their target. When he attempted to escape, one of his pursuers extended their palm and hit him with an invisible energy wave, nearly knocking him out cold.

The exits proved too narrow to accommodate the mass exodus resulting in the unsightly trampling of bodies. Camile tried to shout over the clamoring swarm of people, but her voice merely blended into the audible collage of utter lunacy. Making an executive decision, Camile took it upon herself to pursue the offenders. Her *Styngrae* ready, she extended her tingling palm, repelling the crowd before her as she traveled. Now just a few feet away from the target and his captors, she immediately demanded his immediate release.

"Your wish is our command." The first captor smiled, drawing a baton, swinging it toward the musician with deadly force. Camile quickly activated her *Styngrae* and intercepted the blow, disarming her opponent. She immediately retrieved the weapon. The captor remarked that the move was impressive, yet unexpected and utterly inconvenient.

"I ruin your plans?" Camile mocked, beckoning the musician to get behind her.

"No. Not *our* plans." The frowned captor, glancing at her partner, who was still armed.

"Keep your eyes forward!" Camile commanded before requesting that the second rebel hand over his weapon, which he did with obvious reluctance.

Joval arrived and Camile instructed him to watch over the musician so she could restrain the two rebels. Stowing her *Styngrae*, Camile removed two flexible wrist restraints from a dispenser on her utility belt, all the while inquiring about their mission and who had sent them. Her questions went unanswered as she secured the male first, but as she approached the female, she spontaneously attacked, shoving Camile off-balance. Joval leapt between them and activated his *Dysarrae*, sending the female and several unintended targets to the ground. However, the woman was still lucid enough to crawl over to her partner and place something into his mouth, then her own. In a matter of moments, both fell silent and were as still as wax figures. Even before Camile checked their vitals she knew they were dead.

"Shit," she exclaimed, fighting the urge to resuscitate them since whatever they had ingested would likely get into her body.

Camile searched the bodies for identification, but found nothing useful. In that moment, she had nearly forgotten about the chaotic scene swirling around her. Her focus shifted to the unsettling loneliness surrounding Joval and realized the musician was nowhere to be seen. Hoping Joval had somehow taken him to the other team members, Camile inquired about his whereabouts.

"He's right h—" Joval's expression sank as he looked over his shoulder. "Wait. Where'd he go?" He palmed his head before laughing nervously. "Aw, man! Now, we're screwed. The council's gonna have our asses on a platter for this. I can't *believe* this! I get a chance to impress Sir Drayden and I screw up by losing our subject. That's it. We're dead. All that's left to do is wait 'til the rigor mortis sets in."

"Joval, keep it together, man!" Camile said sharply before softening her demeanor to reassure her friend. "We'll find him, but only if we stay focused. Got it"

He nodded, taking a deep breath.

Camile began to devise a plan to find the musician, but it soon became apparent that doing so wouldn't be necessary. Vincent and Sir Drayden approached with the target walking safely between them. The knight stared at Camile and her partner in a cautionary manner. Relief soon turned to mild anxiety as she pondered the inevitable reprimand she would face. What the elder said next indicated that her unease was justified.

"We'll discuss this later," he said knowingly before instructing the musician to play his instrument, a violin he'd been carrying on his back. The young man, visibly exhausted, initially declined, but was eventually swayed by Sir Drayden's persuasion.

The moment the musician's bow hit the strings it unleashed the sweetest melody. It seemed to repair the damage caused by the auditory assault that had preceded it. The panicked crowd simmered to a hush, entranced by the sound of the reluctant violinist. Camile noticed some of the spectators weeping silent tears as each note played seemed to erase the madness that had just transpired. The musician began to lose his focus and as he did, the crowd displayed signs of revisiting their panicked behavior.

Sir Drayden handed Vincent what appeared to be an old wooden musical pipe. Camile immediately recognized the hauntingly aged instrument as the one she'd seen during her first visit to the Caldaq Museum.

"I thought this was out of commission." Vincent smirked, twirling the apparatus almost teasingly.

"Just play it."

Vincent's smile deepened, but faded into a serious expression of concentration once he brought the device to his lips. With his eyes closed, he played a gentle melody. It barely rose above the bustle of the crowd, yet supported the weakening sound of the lone violin. Soon, he increased the tempo until his fingers seemed to move in a blur along the instrument. The crowd suddenly grew to an entranced hush as they marveled at the spectacular performance. The sly glare in Vincent's eyes conveyed the boastful pride he took in his work.

Once civility had been restored, the crowd dispersed in an organized fashion. Camile couldn't ignore her curiosity and inquired about the origin of Vincent's remarkable musical skill. In her mind, only an extraordinarily talented person could such an incredible sound out of the archaic wooden device.

"I haven't been asked that question in ages." He sighed through a broad smile, apparently eager to tell his story. "I was taught by a musical prodigy during my time in Germany. I had been traveling there on assignment when I met a fellow Transcendent from Bauldana. He was in the area for an unrelated mission. As I recall, he was an exceptionally snazzy dresser, so I assumed he was well off. I heard him play the most exquisite music I had ever heard from a woodwind instrument. Being a music lover, myself, I couldn't resist inquiring about both, the instrument and the composition. He wasn't much for company at first, but eventually took me on as his musical protégé. Nevertheless, he was guarded when it came to anything else. Never even revealed his real name. So, I ended up calling him Fernando."

Vincent chortled, shaking his head. "I don't know why I did it; the name just seemed to suit him. I think it grew on him after awhile. He was mainly an introverted fellow who usually kept to himself, but he was kind enough to help the area residents with a pesky rodent problem."

Camile furrowed her brow. The story was beginning to sound very familiar.

"And what a problem it was!" Vincent continued. "Still, Fernando made his kind gesture and the people promised to pay him in return. Here's the kicker; he didn't ask for anything. They *offered* to pay him. Sadly for them, the cheeky bastards didn't uphold their end of the bargain."

"Sadly for *them?*"

"Fernando was so disappointed that the townspeople had gone back on their word, he decided a little comeuppance was in order. You see, he didn't give a damn about the money. Their money was worthless to him. What ticked him off was their deceitfulness."

So, it really happened? Camile thought, remembering why the tale sounded so familiar.

"Shortly after they screwed him over, he returned to the town for an encore performance. Only this time it wasn't mice he lead away, but children; well over a hundred of them. It always seems to be the children who are left to pay the interest on the debt neglected by adults. More often than not, the interest far surpasses the debt itself. After Fernando made his message clear, the townspeople labeled him with a name that stuck."

"The Pied Piper," Camile said almost to herself.

"Precisely." Vincent smiled. "You'd be surprised how many so-called myths, legends and fairytales are actually exaggerated events, woven into society. People find harsh realities easier to accept when presented beneath the dazzling mask of fiction."

"What happened to the children?" Camile inquired, noticing Sir Drayden engaged in a discussion with Joval.

Based on the devastated expression on her friend's face, she knew he was getting chewed out by the oft-domineering elder. He appeared to plead his case, but the knight shook his head, leaving Joval standing alone in apparent shock.

"There have been many theories and variations to the story," the commissioner continued, "the most popular being that he led the children into a river to let them drown like the rats he exterminated. The entire town repeatedly searched for the children, but try as they might their efforts turned up nothing...except for this." Vincent proudly held up the musical instrument he'd been playing just moments earlier.

Camile grimaced. "Wait a minute. That story is centuries old. How old are you?"

"Old enough to fart dust, as the kids say, but I'll spare you the demonstration." He chortled.

Just as Vincent finished his statement, Sir Drayden approached, requesting the flute be returned. After a brief moment of tension, Vincent reluctantly handed it over.

"I see old habits die hard for thieves." He frowned.

"You can't steal what didn't belong to someone in the first place," the knight replied coolly.

"Perhaps not, but you sure as hell can, can't you?" Vincent sneered.

Sir Drayden said nothing further as he walked away.

What's that all about? Camile wondered.

*   *   *

During the next several days Camile had a tough time locating Joval, who was extremely busy. Camile figured he was upset at what had happened during their assignment. She decided to make an unannounced visit to his quarters and was puzzled to find it all but stripped bare, crates and baggage full of his belongings sitting at the entrance. He emerged from one of the recessed rooms and saw her standing there.

"Hey, Cam. What brings you here?" he greeted casually.

"You didn't answer any of my messages...so I figured I'd stop by," Camile said, still trying to make sense of what was happening. Finally, she asked, "You going on a trip or something?"

"Or something," Joval quipped with a grin so tight his lips nearly vanished, which was no easy feat. He busied himself with checking and rechecking the contents of the packed containers stacked throughout the room. Camile blocked his way to a section he had inspected at least twice.

"Hey, I haven't seen you in days and now you're ignoring me? What's up with that?" she asked.

Joval sighed, removing the band that had been holding his dreadlocks in a high, spiky ponytail. Shaking his head, he let them hang wildly.

"Hair too tight, is that it?" Camile joked, eliciting a smile from him as he sat on a large crate. She joined him.

"I'm sorry I've been avoiding you. I guess I just didn't know how to break the news," he explained. "I still have to tell my brother."

Camile looked at the barren room around them. "You didn't get banished or anything, did you?"

"That's my Cam. Ever so nosy—I mean curious." He smiled. "No, I'm not being banished. Actually, I've been promoted."

"Really? That's wonderful!" Camile hugged him, feeling the coarseness of his locks against her cheek. "See? And you were worried about the little mistakes you made here and there. Told you it would be fine."

When she ended the embrace she noticed Joval was no longer smiling.

"Why so glum?" she asked.

"I don't think I'm ready for this sort of thing. I'll miss everyone here, you know. Even you." He winked.

"We'll, I certainly won't miss your wise cracks," Camile quipped, elbowing him. "Come on. You'll be able to visit and contact us every once in awhile, won't you?"

"I'm not sure." He shrugged. "Depends on what assignment I happen to get."

"Maybe I can visit you. Where will you be going?"

"Not allowed to say. Security protocols and all that. You know how it is."

"All too well." Camile rolled her eyes.

"With everything changing as fast as it is—and with all that's happened recently—it's got me to thinking; do you ever think that maybe, just maybe, life is the ultimate test to see what we do with the powers we were given?" Joval tugged at the sleeve of his chunky sweater. "I mean, how do we know this ain't part of a grand selection process to weed out the weak in order to progress to a higher calling, to earn our way back to where we really belong? I try to look at life this way, sometimes. It makes it a lot easier to cope with all the shit that's been happening, but it don't seem like it's enough anymore. Something tells me we've all been failing terribly."

Camile pressed her lips together as she thought a moment.

"I'm not sure. I know what you mean about failing though. One thing's for sure, I'm starting to see life as the valley between heaven and hell; we get a taste of both before we die. But for those who keep their eyes open and pay attention, they'll end up in the right place. At least that's what I choose to believe." She forced a smile. "I try not to think about it too much. It might drive me nuts otherwise. After all, it scares the shit out of me to think I'll have to pay for the sins of the life that preceded me here."

Camile noticed Joval's eyes grew distant as he tapped his foot on the ground.

"Are you sure you're okay?" She frowned. "You seem unusually tense."

"I'm fine." The corners of his mouth upturned shakily. "I just need to get the rest of my stuff in order."

"If you're worried about something Sir Drayden said—"

"Cam, lay off it, please!" He huffed impatiently, rising from his seat.

It was the first time she heard him raise his voice, albeit only slightly.

"I'm sorry." He sighed. "Look, I really have to finish packing. Don't worry about me, alright? You have enough on your plate. I'll be fine."

Camile wanted to press further, but figured he just needed a little time to process things.

Stroking his back, she said, "If you need to talk or meditate, you know where to find me, okay?"

"Sure thing. See you later, Cam."

The uneasy feeling Joval had instilled in her lingered long after she departed. She feared he was beginning to crack under the pressure of a new position he hadn't even started.

*   *   *

Leaving the EDC, Camile headed back to Coronis Peak after a follow-up meeting with Lumera, who had been happily reunited with her sister, Monica. The memory of the reunion warmed Camile's heart as she recalled the goodwill inherent in both sisters. She found inspiration in their strength and endurance.

While traveling through the frosty Courtyard of Serenity, Camile spotted a violet-colored bubble floating in the air. She had never seen anything like it and couldn't resist following it with her eyes as it rose high into the sky. It dipped and danced between a few tree branches before meeting its end on one of them. It was replaced by a few other bubbles in shades of blue, pink and yellow. Before long, Camile realized they were forming a scattered trail with every shade of the rainbow. Unable to resist her curiosity, she took a detour to follow it. With each step, it seemed as though she was stepping back to a time of childhood carelessness and freedom. She indulged herself by leaping a few times to pop some of them with her leather-shrouded fingers.

When she reached the source of the jubilant display, her eyes were met with thousands of multi-colored bubbles of all sizes being blown by laughing children. She was filled with youthful contentment as she witnessed kids simply being kids. In the Coexistent World, she had all too often seen youngsters being forced to shoulder the burdensome consequences of the mistakes of negligent adults. All too often she had seen the tragic results of children growing up far too soon. Watching the cheerful scene before her defibrillated her heart with hope; hope that the world's innocence hadn't been completely snuffed out. It also reiterated the importance of its preservation.

One of the children bore a striking, yet distant familiarity to someone she hadn't seen in awhile. Focusing her attention on his laughing face, Camile dashed over to him, elated.

"Isaac!" she called. However, her enthusiasm produced an adverse reaction from the little boy as he ducked behind one of the caretakers.

"Excuse me. May I help you, Ms. Leon?" the woman asked sternly as she shielded the child.

"That's Isaac, the kidnapped scribe," Camile explained. "The council's been looking all over for him. I can't believe he's been right under their noses all along."

The woman grimaced, shaking her head.

"I'm sorry, but I think you're mistaken. This is Bartholomew."

Upon taking another look at the now startled child, Camile saw that he looked nothing like Isaac. She frowned to herself before apologizing for her embarrassing error.

That evening she followed up on the investigation only to be met with news of very little progress. However, there was also a slight note of optimism when it was revealed that the trail in Isaac's case appeared to be reemerging.

Chapter 68

Humanity

Camile had been to Caldaq's primary museum on several occasions. However, this was the first time she had been to this particular section of the structure. As she was led down the lengthy corridor leading to the observation room, she noticed dozens of legendary artifacts encased in the walls. Everyone who had been guiding her education was present in the octagonal room, with the exception of Commissioner Thornton, who had other business to attend to.

The meeting got underway shortly thereafter. Camile was informed that the Joint Transcendent Council had placed scientists, politicians and specialists within the Coexistent World. Their purpose was to control the rate of Coexistent advancement, in essence acting much like the anchor that had been placed upon her. Their most powerful tools were the physical, judicial and spiritual laws created to protect the Coexistent people by enforcing guidelines to prevent them from coming into awareness too soon.

She had heard of the league before. They were known as the SATHRI and worked with Coexistent recruits to organize and release certain scientific and archeological discoveries at times designated by the joint council. It was explained that the rebels recently proved that they had their own agents in place as an attempt to counter these provisions.

"I understand Tabitha has explained the depth of the *Age of Ascension*," Camile's father said, gesturing her to sit in the empty seat beside him. It's only fitting that you see how it all falls together."

A three-dimensional projection emerged in the center of the darkening room, presenting a simple illustration of the Transcendent universe. As Camile's parents explained the theory of how the Transcendent World and others are intertwined at specific intervals, described as fixed veils, the illustration grew increasingly complex as it expanded. Jeremy reduced the magnification of the map as Camile, her parents, Sir Drayden and Tabitha looked on. In doing so, it clarified the correlation between the Transcendent dimension and other universes. During this time it was explained that the scientific laws and rules known by most humans were put in place by the universe, itself, to prevent people from taking advantage of its construction.

"You're probably wondering how all this factors into the lives of the Transcendents and Coexistents," Zephyr continued. "For centuries, our people were persecuted and ridiculed for our abilities and our defiance. We refused to forsake our powers and beliefs. Over time, things worsened and the punishment for what they called witchcraft and heresy rose to the extreme. As our numbers dwindled, we were forced to practice our abilities in private, but even that wasn't enough for our adversaries. Some of our people were still caught, tortured, killed and put on horrific display as a message to others. In essence, our physical forms were used and manipulated in an attempt to break our spirit. As the situation escalated, the bloodshed worsened when a band of our people decided to fight back. As if that wasn't bad enough, there were wars brewing over land, resources and supremacy.

"One day, our people saw an opportunity, one that would allow us to practice our beliefs freely, without fear of being attacked or killed. There was an opening to this world. At the time, none of our ancestors knew what they would encounter once they reached the other side, but they figured it was worth the risk. They had hope and faith it would lead them to a better life. As it turned out, our ancestors weren't the first refugees to flee from the Coexistent World."

Camile immediately thought of the gigantic reptiles living in the Transcendent lands.

"The sauruses," she whispered.

"Exactly!" Zephyr held up his index finger.

He ordered Jeremy to switch to the Coexistent World map and zoom in on the Yucatan peninsula.

"When the meteor hit, creating the *Chicxulub* crater approximately 65 million years ago, a vast majority of them died as a result of the catastrophe that followed," Sir Drayden explained. His eyes glistened as he looked up into the projection. "As we explained earlier, the impact created a rift in the veil that separates our worlds. A small number of sauruses were able to make it through and eventually repopulated here."

"We've come to the conclusion that the rifts our ancestors traveled through over the centuries since then were caused by a series of catastrophic events taking place in the Coexistent World at the time," Jeremy added. "Like the sauruses, our ancestors were also able to repopulate here." He faded the map to reveal the *Vas Navelle* in the Transcendent World.

"But we never forgot about our Coexistent siblings," Camile's father added. "That's why we want to help them in spite of everything. Yes, they may have put our ancestors through a lot, but they're putting themselves through far more turmoil as time progresses. Our society has had to work diligently in order to preserve as much peace as humanly possible. It hasn't been an easy road to get where we are. Regrettably, our world has seen the destructive force perpetuated by war and chaos. For a time, our ancestors found themselves ensnared in the very webs of self-entitlement and greed from which they had escaped. They eventually discovered that the source of the problem was embedded within their way of thinking. It's the same mentality we're hoping to change in the Coexistents."

"Meanwhile, over the centuries, the Coexistents continued to slip away from their full spiritual awareness," the shaman added. "As a result, their confidence also deviated, leading them to commit desperate and terrible acts. Every now and then, brave and unique individuals emerge to guide and motivate those in the Coexistent World. These people are meant to counter the degradation in their behavior and to restore their faith. Such individuals are meant to serve as a physical example that although our energy is restricted within our bodies, we are all capable of achieving a greatness we never knew possible. Sadly, sometimes these people are not widely accepted until long after their deaths, some of which were unspeakably horrific. Even more tragic are those who die without recognition of their valiant efforts."

The shaman expelled a quick breath as she lowered her gaze. During her brief pause, a mask of sorrow fell over her face, but lifted before anyone had a chance to inquire about her emotional state. She continued:

"Jealousy and greed—by those who wanted to be supreme rulers—fueled the thirst for blood, execution, persecution and elimination of individuals who performed so-called *magic* and *witchcraft*. It's always the labels and titles that cause the biggest problems. One man's magic is another man's miracle. By the same token, one man's miracle can be another man's curse. After all, much of what once was considered sorcery and magic is now known as science. The difference between miracle and magic, good and bad, right and wrong, is often shaped by individual perception."

"Historical documents were tampered with in order to further the agendas of gluttonous rulers," Brandon added. "To supplement this deception, various laws were created to keep people ignorant and suppress them from reaching their full potential. Scores of people were separated and forced into a state of regression, but power this great can only be hidden for so long. Ironically, Transcendent governments would later uphold some of those laws for the Coexistent peoples' own protection."

Sir Drayden nodded. "Man has grown to fear the things that cannot be governed, controlled or understood. Since the power itself wasn't understood nearly as well as it is today, man sought to control the enlightened through systems of belief. Those who believed in anything other than what was deemed acceptable were often punished or eliminated altogether. Though their abilities were repressed throughout the centuries, they never completely disappeared. They only remained buried beneath obligation, fear and doubt. Their fearful oppressors failed to realize that they were comprised of the very thing they sought to repress. Our abilities are a huge part of who we are, whether we like it or not. Forgetting the fact that we possess them, or simply ignoring the fact that we do, won't make them go away."

"Instead of focusing on their common beliefs about their history, the Coexistents are focusing on their differences and using it as an excuse to divide," Camile's mother stated. "Many fail to realize that the clarity of events tend to blur; if not by the vast passage of time, then by the variance in human perception. It is impossible for any historical account to be one-hundred percent accurate. Past events are often exaggerated, played down or colored by those who try to alter the sequence of events for their own personal gain. However, it would be foolish to disregard historical records altogether since even the distorted accounts may have a foundation of fact."

"I don't understand…How come the people who maintained their powers didn't gather enough force to fight back and overpower their oppressors?" Camile asked.

"The same reason why countless individuals have been oppressed throughout history. Brainwashing and segregation have proven to be the most effective tools to suppress specific groups of people." Zephyr frowned.

It was an enlightening moment of clarity that realigned Camile's perspective. Mentally, she glanced at the roads she traversed to arrive at that moment, actually believing that all existence had been cut from the solitary fabric of the universe. Life, it seemed, was a spiraling cycle of repeating events, increasing with intensity throughout the passage of time. In that instant, it all seemed so simple to her, yet she knew how fleeting simplicity could be.

*   *   *

The crash came unexpectedly, resulting in a loudness that jolted Camile with an alarming acknowledgement of danger. Joval had gone into the building just moments before the collapse. Up until that moment, the mission had been going extremely well. It was to be Camile's last before the completion of her advanced studies. Looking forward to the upcoming break, the two had joked about who would eat the most at dinner that evening.

Their task seemed simple enough. All they needed to do was convince the Coexistent inhabitants of a mid-sized tenement building to vacate the premises. Apparently, there was a destabilization in the rift surrounding that area, threatening the collapse of the structure. Under the guise of building inspectors, they had achieved their goal with minutes to spare, or so Camile thought prior to Joval's report that he'd witnessed several tenants reenter the building to retrieve belongings.

She screamed for him as she ran toward the rubble, but someone grabbed her from behind. She demanded that they release her.

Brandon commanded her to stop, but Camile continued to struggle against him.

"Camile, don't be stupid! You'll die if you go in there," he yelled.

"Drayden can save him! Where is he?" she cried, calling for the knight, but deep down she knew he was too far away. This was a fact confirmed by Brandon.

Infuriated, she cursed him for stopping her.

"I could've made it! You should've let me go save him!" She half-heartedly punched his shoulder as he tried to hold her.

"There's nothing you could've done," Brandon replied softly, cradling her against his chest.

She wasn't sure if it was a result of her meditation or shock-induced numbness, but she found herself unable to cry as she accepted Brandon's embrace. Her common sense made its way back from the stratosphere, joining her grief.

"He was almost like a brother to me," she said in little more than a tremulous whisper.

"Yeah, me too," Brandon replied softly, nuzzling her hair.

Chapter 69

The Dearly Departed

Sitting in the front row at Joval's memorial, Camile experienced an eerie sense of déjà vu. She knew it was because of the flashback of Akalina attending Hyacinth's memorial service. This tribute, however, was significantly different. The setting was noticeably less floral, but the demeanor of the attendees was similar to what she had recalled in the flashback. Though slightly weighted, the mood wasn't that of great sadness, but appreciation and reminiscence. Camile tried her best not to contaminate the atmosphere with her sorrow, but didn't know how long she'd be able to hold up. Nonetheless, she focused on maintaining her strength from one moment to the next, rather than for the duration of the entire service. Somehow, this method made it easier for her to cope.

As Sir Drayden spoke the closing words of the ceremony, Camile couldn't help but wonder if he felt remorseful for upsetting Joval that night in the concert hall. She put the thought out of her mind in an effort to prevent herself from becoming upset.

"Joval, for a brief season we have been blessed with the fruit of your company, friendship and wisdom," Sir Drayden said. "However, we are not to be deluded into thinking we claim ownership over your spirit. Though your body remains to help sustain and fertilize the earth, it is with dignity and honor that we accept your return to whence you came. Until we are reunited by destiny, we will continue to live our lives fully to honor your memory."

Camile was struck with a sudden wave of realization as she recalled one of the last conversations she had with Joval.

He knew he was going to die! That night at the concert, Sir Drayden wasn't reprimanding him, he was preparing him.

The ceremony was closed with a parting tune, a heavenly pentatonic chant, sung by one of the female elders of the council. The sound of a flute and chiming music served as the perfect backdrop for her voice. The combined harmonies echoed with preternatural beauty and serenity. Camile felt as though she could sense Joval's very soul being liberated and elevated by it. She watched as his casket was quietly carried away by six pallbearers, two of whom were Brandon and Jeremy. Both looked prestigious in their formal uniforms.

Camile's eye lingered on Jeremy. Their current setting magnified her feeling that their breakup was a terrible mistake. If there was no place for love in the string of life, duty and death, then what was the purpose of it all? As her gaze met his, there seemed to be a momentary flicker of hope as that same question appeared to resonate in his eyes. With a flash of a comforting smile, he and his fellow pallbearers exited the structure. The attendees dispersed shortly thereafter.

"Aren't they gonna bury him?" Camile asked her parents.

"Yes, but not now," her father answered gently.

Camile inwardly shuddered as he explained that in most Transcendent burial procedures the body of the departed is taken to a chamber where it is freeze dried. Once the body has been reduced to a fraction of its original weight, xylophonic crystals are played, causing a vibration that gently causes the body—usually contained in a highly biodegradable coffin—to disintegrate. Once buried, the contents are eventually absorbed by the earth, which is why most loved ones choose to plant a tree or foliage in honor of the departed. During anniversaries, either birth or death, loved ones sometimes visit the memorial site to personally water the area, plant flowers, or both. Curious to see the memorial plot, Camile asked her parents to take her there.

Upon arrival, she immediately took notice of the tranquil vibe. It wasn't a place that emphasized death and sadness, but the beautiful presence of life. There were bountiful trees, plants and bushes, all neatly arranged and well groomed. Most were ablaze with shades of autumn, but there was one tree in particular that stood out from the rest. Its black branches were exploding with bright pink flowers and bronze leaves. Not knowing why, Camile asked her parents for a moment alone before approaching it for a closer look. She could smell the faint fruity scent of the flowers long before she was covered by the tree's lush canopy. Surrounded by a sparse shower of pink petals, Camile smiled as she was filled with the sensation of restfulness—that is until she noticed the white, translucent plaque on the ground.

Although the daylight was still broad, the shade of the canopy revealed the tablet was glowing. She imagined the haunting beauty of the memorial grounds at dusk, once the light of the plaques illuminated the trees. On this particular plaque was the name Hyacinth Sebastian, carved in black Arvainan lettering. Upon reading the rest of the inscription, Camile discovered it was the seventeenth anniversary of her death.

She stood in stunned silence for several moments, feeling as though she shouldn't be standing there. However, instead of walking away, she surprised herself by speaking, apologizing to Hyacinth for what Akalina had done. She was in the middle of her apology when she stopped short, feeling a shadow overlapping the shade in which she was standing. A combination of past events and common sense told her Sir Drayden was standing behind her. As she turned her head, her eyes confirmed what her gut already knew.

There he was, holding a single flower and a watering can. For the first time, Camile caught a glimpse of his softer side. In another place and time he could have easily been bringing Hyacinth flowers as a romantic gesture, not as a token of remembrance. Camile had the feeling that his late wife was the one person who was able to convince him to let down his guard and coax out his sensitivity. Now, it seemed, what little softness he had left was buried deep down, either at the base of his heart or in the grave along with Hyacinth. After a quick greeting, Camile left him in private so he could pay his tribute.

After walking just a few paces, her ears were met with the sound of the elder singing in an unfamiliar language. Camile found Sir Drayden's performance warm, soothing and almost angelic—a complete contrast to his reserved demeanor. His voice dipped and dived from subtle falsettos, invoking nostalgia with a beauty and despair far beyond what Camile believed he was capable of. Listening to the performance made her feel strangely at peace; so much so, she couldn't bring herself to leave. Sitting behind a tree to remain hidden, she closed her eyes as she enjoyed the rest of his haunting serenade.

It wasn't until she felt a hand touch her shoulder that she realized she had fallen asleep. Parting her lids, she saw the smiling face of her father.

"You looked so peaceful, I decided to wait awhile before waking you," he said, helping her to her feet. "Come, there's something I want to show you."

After walking for nearly a quarter mile, they came to a wall. Camile found its iridescent texture strikingly familiar. Just beyond it, she could see the massive tree she crossed on the night of her reintegration. However, it felt as though she was looking at it for the first time. The radiance of its white bark seemed more intense than when she had last laid eyes on it. As a result, the tree's shimmering ruby red leaves appeared even more vibrant. Unlike the last time she had seen the tree, its leaves were not falling and disintegrating into the mysterious golden dust she remembered so well.

The entire area was placid in contrast to the death trap it appeared to be during her last visit there. In fact, Camile figured the area had undergone a significant renovation. Her father led her around the tree and pointed to a plaque that was set into the ground at an angle. The inscription was dedicated to Camile's grandparents, Zephyr Leon I and Camelia Leon, marking the spot as their final resting place.

She found herself speechless as her father explained that the tree went through a semi-annual shedding process, during the anniversary of their death and that of Akalina's separation from Camile. As they approached the wall she noticed a closed gate. Beyond it, were a few plants.

"This is our family plot," Zephyr announced.

At that moment, Camile noticed several blank markers arranged in neat rows that would eventually be replaced with the names of her relatives after their departures to the beyond. She inquired about the location being so distant from her grandparent's burial site.

"It was their request," Zephyr answered. "Your grandparents treasured their family and always led and watched over us in life. They wanted their memorial to reflect that."

As he finished his explanation, the area in which they stood came to life with a glow as warm as a summer sunset. Camile and her father synchronously turned, facing her grandparent's memorial tree. Her sight was met with the sun shining through the translucent crimson leaves, gently swaying in the delicate breeze. She returned her attention to the tinted light stretching across the unoccupied graves. Despite the warmth of the sun's enhanced caress, Camile caught a chill as she gawked at one of the blank markers, knowing that she could very well be looking at her future grave.

*   *   *

Although Camile was able to comprehend the manner in which most Transcendents accepted death, she found herself struggling to come to terms with it in spite of all she had learned. There were just some things comprehension couldn't quench, mend or pacify. No matter how hard she tried to meditate, it did nothing to extinguish the flames of despair, licking at her heart. That was one of her first clues that something was wrong; she had to *try* to meditate. In all this confusion, there was one thing that was certain, her sadness wasn't for Joval, but for herself. However, in all this, she successfully prevented her melancholy from manifesting itself through her tears. Camile gave her best attempt to conceal her internal struggle from everyone, but she knew her sudden seclusion was countering her efforts. Therefore, she wasn't surprised when her mother showed up at her quarters unannounced. Still not feeling strong enough to face anyone, Camile tried to tell her she was busy.

"I know you're not too busy to spare a few minutes to talk to your own mother." Kylie entered the room, not waiting for an invitation.

Camile's mother wasted no time in expressing her concern about her daughter's recent reclusive behavior.

"I'm fine, Mom. No need to worry. I just need some time to refocus, that's all." Camile gave a half-hearted smile, hoping that would be enough to end the conversation. It wasn't.

Stroking her daughter's hair, Kylie gazed knowingly into her eyes.

"Camile, there's a big difference between balancing your emotions and keeping them bottled up," she said. "It's okay to let it out, baby."

Suddenly, all the emotions Camile had fought so hard to repress were rising at a rapid pace. The pressure was too much to contain so she erupted into tears, sobbing in her mother's embrace. Not fully realizing it, she slid down and dropped her head in her mother's lap, curling herself into a fetal position as though regressing into infancy. She took advantage of the opportunity to release the pent up sorrow that had accumulated throughout the time since she had arrived in the Transcendent World. This included Joval's death, her recent breakup with Jeremy, the devastation she witnessed during her missions, her insecurities and everything else she was too distraught to recollect.

Just as quickly as the storm had arrived it was beginning to pull away. Inhaling a tremulous breath, Camile felt the sweet rays of relief beginning to break through the clouds of her despair. Nevertheless, she could feel a distant shadow of guilt looming over her for having lost her emotional control.

"It's okay, sweetheart. Don't feel like this makes you weak," Camile heard her mother say shakily. As she sat up and looked at her mother's face, she realized that she was also crying.

"Happens to the best of us." Kylie forced a chuckle through her waning tears.

Chapter 70

Those Left Behind

"The prophecy must be wrong. I'm not sure if I'm strong enough to deal with this...tragedy up close," Camile said at the start of her next meeting with the shaman, who was preparing batches of medicine for a list of her clients.

"Oh, you're strong enough," the shaman deadpanned, setting the list aside as she met Camile with her eyes. "What you need to do is stop making excuses for yourself."

Tabitha proceeded to pack her completed orders and store them in a cabinet beside the window.

"We keep trying to save them and we can't. The Coexistents just won't listen. If they did, maybe those tenants would still be alive. So would Joval."

"If you think you'll be able to save everyone, you're sadly mistaken," the shaman said, her back still turned. "In reality, you'll probably wind up saving a small fraction of the people you're assigned to." Turning her attention to Camile anew, she smiled. "Then again, it's not always up to you to save them. Sometimes you have to convince them to save themselves."

"So, why even bother? What's the point if they're too hard-headed?"

Camile heard Jeremy cough outside of the shaman's quarters and wondered if it was coincidental.

"The point, my child, is to take a chance by trying," Tabitha answered. "By doing that, you're increasing their odds of survival, even if it's by a slim margin. Faith is hard to come by and even more challenging to hold onto. But, for those who succeed in keeping it, they discover its true rewards once the storms have been weathered. Look at a meteor shower and tell me there isn't magic. Look at a newborn child and tell me there isn't hope. Look at a sunrise and tell me there isn't a new day, the dawn of another chance to get it right."

"Most of the deaths I've witnessed were of people who didn't have an unpleasant bone in them, especially Joval. And the children…What I don't understand is why them?" Camile's eyes watered. "It wasn't their time."

Her despair was interrupted by a faint chuckle from the shaman.

"What's so funny?" Camile frowned.

"It's not for you to determine the time of their departure from the physical world, child."

"No. I guess it's not. That's for you, Sir Drayden and the almighty council to decide, isn't it?" Camile retorted bitterly.

Tabitha shook her head. "It's not up to us at all. We're not the ones in charge of making those decisions, we just carry them out as we're ordered to, whether we like it or not. Everything happens for a reason, whether or not we comprehend it."

"What kind of sick boss do you work for?"

"Sick? No. Misunderstood? Often."

"If everything happens for a reason, then why do some people die so much sooner and violently than others? Don't they have as much a right to a full, long life as everyone else?"

"That's a very difficult question that's been around since the beginning of our existence. It's right up there with *Why does evil exist?'* I'll try my best to answer both questions, but please excuse me if some of the words don't come out quite right. Verbal language is limited."

Tabitha shifted in her seat before giving her explanation.

"Some individuals can't bear to be separated from The Supreme Origin for very long. Others just don't want a lengthy stay in a 'restricted' existence in a harsh, unforgiving world. Yet, they still want to do their part in helping people stay connected. So they're designated to missions that are shorter, so they can return to The Supreme Origin as soon as possible. Regrettably, these short missions are usually very tragic and emotionally taxing, but sometimes they're the most important missions and have the most powerful impact. It takes a very brave and powerful individual to undertake such missions; some take them voluntarily, others do it because they're selected." She took a deep breath before continuing. "Someone once asked me why certain people die so young and why do innocent children die? The simplest way I could explain it was that certain individuals complete their life's mission sooner than others. Others become so drained from the world that they need to return to The Supreme Origin to recharge sooner than the rest of us. That requires leaving the physical body behind. Now, when it comes to victims of murder, that's a different case entirely. They don't necessarily choose to abandon their bodies, but are often ejected to protect their core since it can't operate in a non-functioning vessel. So, they return to The Supreme Origin to be restored and to await the next cycle.

"Unfortunately, sometimes the only way people are reminded of their connection is through devastation and misery. There's a natural cycle that takes place where humans face adversity as dictated by nature. As tragic as these events are, they unite people who wouldn't have otherwise acknowledged each other. On the other hand, murderers and other criminals have disturbed the balance of how the cycle functions. When I was young, a very long time ago, I used to think of life in terms of good and bad. Over time I've changed my perspective. I now look at it in terms of positive and negative. Think about it. There are many things in life that only work when you have two opposing forces. Night and day helps us to determine the passage of time in the physical world. Wind is created when you have differential pressure. Batteries work only when you have positive and negative charges—"

"But life's not a battery!" Camile chuckled softly with disbelief at the notion.

"You're right, but the premise of life is simpler than you think. It's humans that tend to overcomplicate things. Think about it. I mean *really* think about it. If there were never any challenges or opposing forces, do you think life would progress or improve? Do you think it would even exist? It would just remain stagnant. If it were up to us, time wouldn't progress at all. We'd constantly stall for time while getting that last errand done, that last e-mail out or that final report completed. Camile, it's the natural opposing occurrences that keep life going. Without them, what would you have? *Nothing.* And what do most people associate with nothingness? *Death*, the *opposite* of life. You can't have positive without the negative or good without evil. Throughout time there have been harrowing tales about fighting and defeating evil. But the most effective way to deal with it is to cancel it out with an even more powerful positive reaction. Each negative must be counteracted with a positive. Each thing that is destroyed must be replenished. People are often at their best in times of adversity. Those are the times when they are close to realizing their true potential and full power. Unfortunate events happen so that people can advance and grow closer to the discovery of what they truly are. Without challenges, complacency would plague humanity and there would never be any advancement or desire to improve."

Camile found Tabitha's explanation astonishing.

"I never thought about negativity in that way," she said.

"Most people don't. However, the negativity in the world has gotten to be extremely out of balance. So much of it is continually being created and absorbed, but there aren't enough positives to offset it. The problem can still be corrected though, but it will take a lot of work, trust and faith," Tabitha explained.

"And time…" Camile added wistfully.

"Unfortunately, time isn't something we have in abundance," Tabitha replied. A grim expression crossed her features, her eyes fixed on something across the room. Camile followed the direction of her counselor's gaze and locked eyes with Sir Drayden, standing in the doorway.

Chapter 71

Time

As they entered the central courtyard behind Coronis peak, Camile shuddered slightly in response to the early evening chill in the air. It was then that she realized she had neglected to fasten her coat. She corrected the oversight as Sir Drayden led her deeper into the unusually vacant square. The darkening sky was filled with thick, cottony clouds. They appeared motionless above the broad terrain of the mountainside and stretched over the city of Deltine. The clarity of the scene made Camile feel as though she had walked into a painting where time itself was absent.

"Have you ever thought about the concept of time?" Sir Drayden broke the tranquil silence. "What is it exactly? No one truly knows, but it holds the greatest value of anything we can quantify. Sure, we have been able to measure instances of time based on the physical elements of the universe like the earth, sun and the moon. However, that system of measurement has proven to be inaccurate on some level or another, which is why most Coexistent humans readjust it every year. Have you ever wondered why something inside you sometimes feels the time is wrong? Have you fallen asleep and awakened to see that hours have passed, but you felt like you've been asleep for a much longer or shorter period of time? Have you ever experienced déjà vu?"

Camile nodded, wondering where the conversation was headed as Sir Drayden continued.

"What most people often fail to realize is that time isn't bound by the physical tools by which man measures it. Time isn't as general as people think it is. It's wonderfully complex and multi-faceted. Our knowledge of this fact has played a large part in the reversal of your death."

Sir Drayden nodded to one of the guards standing at the courtyard entrance. As if on cue, the guard summoned a squad of approximately thirty officers, all wielding crossbows. They lined up in formation in two rows of fifteen, directly facing Camile and the aquatic-eyed, silver-haired knight.

The first row of officers knelt, giving their comrades behind them a clear shot. Camile knew the chill she felt hadn't come from the frosty air or the snowflakes that were just starting to fall, but the fact she and Sir Drayden were facing a firing squad. Unable to speak, Camile toggled her attention between the officers and the knight, who gave a subtle nod, signaling the men to fire. At the same time, he suddenly grasped her hand so firmly it nearly hurt. Feeling something round and hot break between her palm and his, Camile winced. Despite the sensation, she gripped his hand tightly, digging her nails into him as the arrows soared in their direction. Her pulse quickened like the beat of hummingbird wings as did her breathing. Dizziness soon followed and she nearly succumbed to it as her knees weakened for a moment.

When the sensation subsided, she noticed the arrows appeared to have frozen in place just a few feet away from her and the elder. She felt as though she had been encased in a bizarre snow globe as the flakes around her also seemed to hang suspended. It wasn't until Sir Drayden slackened his grip that Camile pulled her hand away slowly, as though afraid to let go of the magical enchantment he had somehow placed around them. Gathering her courage, she took a closer look at the arrows hovered in mid-air and realized they were still traveling, albeit at a snail's pace, though faster than the light snowfall. Whatever had effected the arrows was also apparently affecting the officers since they, too, were moving extremely slowly. Some appeared to be sleeping, but Camile knew that they were actually in the middle of blinking. As she cautiously navigated the area, analyzing the fascinating situation, Sir Drayden continued his lecture.

"Humans have monitored the Earth's position in relation to the sun and have developed tools such as clocks so we can synchronize with each other and the physical world," he explained while leisurely walking around Camile's orbit. "However, what many people don't realize is, time transcends the physical world and is individualized within each person. For example, everyone is born and will die at different times. Therefore, it's only natural for people to live at varying rates. But, humans—Coexistent humans in particular—have locked themselves into trying to live beyond their means in an attempt to keep up with others. There's a certain pressure to develop physically and socially at a competitive rate to their neighbors. They've begun to clock their lives to such an extreme that they're racing to do more in less time. They've even made a trend out of breeding far before they're mentally or spiritually equipped to accept the responsibility. As a result, their lives are filled with more quantity than quality. In their mad rush, many of them still fail to realize they're headed for destruction. Much of this you've already witnessed for yourself." He paused briefly before saying, "Now would be a good time to step aside. They're about to catch up with us."

"What?" Camile asked, dazed at the sudden shift in conversation.

She realized that she had come full circle, back into the fatal path of the arrows. Filled with a sense of urgency, she leapt like a gazelle, but felt something push her from behind, giving her a boost. She surmised Sir Drayden, who was now standing a safe distance away from the firing zone, had used his power to help her. As soon as her feet were reunited with the ground in front of him, her ears were met with the sound of a series of thumps. It sounded like a frantic beat of a drum, but Camile knew what she heard hadn't emanated from any type of musical instrument.

Looking over her shoulder, she saw the wall behind her was covered in arrows. Turning her head to regain eye contact with Sir Drayden, her cheek brushed against cold leather. Grimacing slightly, she froze in place, realizing her palms were experiencing the same sensation. Once she felt the side of his chin press slightly against the top of her head, Camile broke the pace of her breathing as she realized what was happening. She and Sir Drayden had somehow become locked in a loose embrace that tightened gently on both sides. Though confused, Camile let her head go heavy, resting it on his shoulder, feeling his large hand hold it in place.

With each second that elapsed, the more comfortable and natural it felt for her to be there. In fact, she felt as though she could sleep peacefully despite the fact she was standing upright. The howling of the sudden wind gust and the flapping of their leather coats wasn't enough to mask the tremulous sigh that escaped Sir Drayden's lips. Camile felt an intense hybrid of emotions that brought her close to weeping. Before she could do so, Sir Drayden suddenly ended their embrace by gently pushing her away. Turning his back to her, he took a few steps, increasing the distance between them. Apparently, the unusual sensation Camile felt was mutual. The two stood in awkward silence for a moment that seemed to stretch for hours. Finally, she voiced the dominant question in her mind.

"Wh—what just happened?" she stuttered.

"You just witnessed the power of time. Maybe I should have chosen a less dangerous way to demonstrate it. You almost got skewered," he answered, keeping his back to her. "Eventually, you'll learn how to read time and even foresee certain changes which will allow you to evade dangerous situations. But for now, you should rest up. The next few days will be very busy for you."

"I wasn't referring to the demonstration," Camile clarified as she attempted to walk to his front to face him. "I'm talking about—"

"That was an order, young lady," he said, his voice stern and steady as he walked away.

*   *   *

Camile returned to her quarters in almost a zombie-like state. Her mind was devoted to sorting out what had just occurred. Her thought process focused on one question:

Why did the hug happen in the first place and who initiated it?

She couldn't deny the feelings that stemmed from their embrace and it confused the hell out of her. As she entered her quarters, the emotional hybrid had been broken into segments that she easily identified. However, she was experiencing them all at once. She found herself wiping stray tears from her eyes—tears of longing, loneliness, guilt and regret. The startling part of this identification process was that she realized those emotions were not only her own, but Sir Drayden's as well. Yet, the context remained woefully unclear. Since Camile didn't feel liberated enough to bring her inquiries directly to the source, she wrote them in her journal in the form of a loose poem:

> *Eyes like the morning sky, a deceptive facade masking the dark weight of guilt. Does it resonate from the torment you unleashed upon the half I reluctantly carry? Is your conscience searing your mind like the flesh you destroyed, the flesh I now wear?*
>
> *Conscience is a word I never thought would apply to you, yet today I felt the evidence that there's a part of you that is still vulnerable. You mask it with the callous layers of ridicule beyond a fortress of loathing and distrust for others. For a brief moment, I caught a glimpse beyond those frigid walls and into the shadow of your emotions. It may have been as vague as your intent, but there is no denying that they still exist. It's rare that you hold your tongue in sacrifice for the feelings of others, so I wonder why you've decided to continue bearing the burden of whatever's oppressing your compassion.*

Chapter 72

Exposed

Camile enjoyed the praise she received for her hard work, but she knew there was much more to be done. For now, her current assignment was to rest and recover from her hectic year. To facilitate this, she was given the option of traveling throughout Arvaina, abroad, or remaining at Caldaq for the extent of her vacation. Camile figured she'd had enough excitement, but was tempted to try something new. She decided to poll some of her people to ascertain which destination would be best for her.

Entering Tabitha's quarters, Camile noticed all of her materials were neatly stowed away in cabinets and cases. There wasn't even a sheet of paper on the table. The unusual orderliness denoted a pending departure.

"You're leaving?" Camile asked.

"Sure am." Tabitha smiled, smoothing back the tendrils framing her French-braided hair. "You're not the only one who gets a break, you know. Besides, it's been too long since the last time I saw my relatives. I just hope I can make it out in time before the storm gets here." She shifted her gaze to the window. "It's gonna be a real doozy."

Camile looked through the glass pane and noticed the heavy clouds approaching.

She furrowed her brow. "I just realized, you never mentioned your family before."

"You never asked." The shaman laughed.

"Probably because I was too wrapped up in my own drama." Camile said, slumping her shoulders. "So, who are you visiting, your children?"

"This old body has never had the honor of child-bearing and I'm afraid that ship has sailed." Tabitha's chortle morphed a sigh. A distant look crossed her face.

Camile frowned. "Looks like I touched a sore spot. Sorry."

"Don't be. My life may not have turned out as I expected, but I've been blessed to experience the joy of parenthood through others."

"Your ride's here, Your Wisest," Jeremy announced upon entering the room. He paused once he locked eyes with Camile. Like she had done countless times before, she wondered what thoughts were circling behind his dark intense gaze. Remorse? Regret? Indifference?

"Oh, good. Bright and early. I'd better get going." Tabitha's cheerful voice burned into her thoughts like the sun through a cloud.

Smiling, the shaman wrapped Camile a warm hug as Jeremy gathered her bags.

"Enjoy your time off, my child. You don't know when's the next time you'll get a chance to relax."

"Are you leaving, too?" Camile asked Jeremy.

"Her Wisest prefers I stay here. She'll be safe where she's headed and she's traveling with a highly capable security convoy."

Following the shaman and her loyal apprentice into the corridor, Camile waved farewell as they descended the passageway.

*　　　*　　　*

Sitting in the conservatory lounge, Camile reviewed several destinations suggested by her parents. She was distracted by the sight of a petite woman, walking along one of the trails. For some reason, Camile felt compelled to tail her.

Was she oblivious to the fact she was being followed? Her confident pace through the thickening woods seemed to indicate so. The conservatory paths were rapidly swallowed by the Forsaken Forest.

As Akalina continued her silent pursuit, she watched the graceful sway of Jezebel's small body as she headed in the general direction of the rebel camp. Akalina broke her stride all the while keeping her eyes fixed on her target, moving deeper into the woods. There was a gradual shift in her course and Akalina wondered why. A nudge from behind prompted her to continue, reminding her of the fact she wasn't alone. She could see only one of her travel companions, but knew there were several others just a short distance behind them. This trip wasn't entirely voluntary, but it didn't take much coercion to convince her to come along. Part of her wanted to be there, to confront the deceptive woman, now just a dozen or so feet in front of her. Yet, she knew everything was about to change and there was an uncertainty that accompanied this knowledge. Akalina soon realized the woman wasn't as oblivious as she thought. Halting her steps, Jezebel voiced what Akalina had suspected, her presence had been felt.

"Is there a reason why you're following me, Akalina?" Jezebel inquired, her back still turned. When she finally faced her stalker, her puzzled expression morphed into utter disgust when she noticed Akalina wasn't alone.

"She has a very good reason," Zephyr answered for his daughter.

"You weak, filthy skank! I took you under my wing when your own parents abandoned you and this is how you repay me?" Jezebel spat, glaring at Akalina.

"Abandoned her?" Zephyr grimaced, stepping forward, "Is that the lie you planted in her head to get her to agree to your treachery?"

Jezebel said nothing as she seethed, her attention still focused on her former protégé.

"Like you told me once, Jezebel; *everyone has their own method of survival.*" Akalina smirked, sending Jezebel into a frenzy.

"You ungrateful little leech! I'll kill you!" She leapt to attack, but was intercepted by Zephyr.

Akalina laughed as she watched the brief tussle.

"You're under arrest for mutiny and treason. Surrender peacefully and no one will get hurt," Zephyr ordered, seizing both of Jezebel's arms.

"Someone's about to get hurt, alright, because I have no intention of going quietly." She sneered, turning her gaze skyward.

As though on cue, several rebels descended from the trees in order to defend their leader. Zephyr was knocked down instantly, but quickly used his *Styngrae* to disable his attackers. While his back was turned, Jezebel struck with full force, knocking the weapon from his hand. He attempted to subdue her, but was unsuccessful as she propelled him into a tree. Though stunned, he promptly staggered to his feet.

"If I'm going down, you're coming with me!" Her venomous declaration was directed at Akalina.

Jezebel didn't have a chance to fulfill her threat before her small body was thrown into a tree by an unseen force. When the source came into view, she widened her dark eyes in mild terror as she gasped for air. The impact had apparently knocked the wind out of her. Akalina had seen this expression on Jezebel's face once—the day she tried to prevent the silver-haired elder from accessing her thoughts. She seemed frozen in place with her back to the tree trunk until she slowly raised a quivering hand to open her jacket. In doing so she whimpered, realizing she had been impaled on a stumpy branch. Equally shocked, but not necessarily displeased, was Akalina, who took a moment to regard the approaching knight. Judging by the look on his face, Jezebel's injury was an unplanned result of his attempt to subdue her.

Jezebel's labored breathing intensified and she coughed into her hand. It soon became apparent to Akalina that the action was done to mask the true reason for Jezebel bringing her hand to her mouth.

"She's eating something," she revealed, rushing over and kneeling before her one-time mentor.

"Akalina, don't—!" Zephyr demanded, but it was too late. His daughter was already squeezing Jezebel's cheeks, trying to force her mouth open. A broken portion of a tablet dropped to the ground from Jezebel's lips.

"Open your mouth! You don't get to poison yourself. You don't get to escape him. It's your turn to face the same shit that was done to me because of you!" Akalina hissed, her teeth gritted with vengeful determination. "The best part about this whole thing is that I don't need you anymore. You already showed me where I can find Camile. The bitch actually thinks I'm her friend, but she means less to me than you do, but not by much."

Jezebel's frown deepened as her eyes bore into her former protégé. After swallowing the remainder of the pill, she parted her lips just enough to spit in Akalina's face. Incensed, Akalina was poised to backhand her, but the blow was intercepted by Sir Drayden, who instructed Zephyr to distance her.

"Now, I don't blame you...for what you did to that weasel," Jezebel wheezed, her demeanor becoming unusually relaxed, almost drunken, given the events which had just transpired. "By the way..." she added, "...you don't fight fair."

Sir Drayden glanced around at the fallen rebels who were being apprehended by the able-bodied guards who'd escaped the attack with minor injuries.

"Neither do you." His lips curled into a somber smirk as he crouched beside her. "And although you can't blame me for my unfortunate crossings with Akalina, I can certainly blame you. Because of you, I was forced to cross lines I had drawn, myself." By the time the knight finished his statement, his face bore a deep frown.

"Touché." Jezebel chortled. "Any chance of you...allowing me to move?" With her head, she indicated her body, now motionless from the neck down. "You don't have to restrain me like this. I'm not exactly in a position to run away." She sighed, briefly closing her eyes.

Sir Drayden dismissed her request with a simple shake of his head. "What did you take? Utopium?"

"Mmm-hmmm...It's...taking so damn long to work. Guess that's what happens...when you don't...take the full dose." She took a moment to cast a hateful look at Akalina before returning her eyes to Sir Drayden. "Yes, *Utopium*. Rolls off the tongue, doesn't it?" Jezebel mused before creating a stifled off-the-cuff melody of the poison's name. During this time, Zephyr, now standing at a safe distance with his daughter, inquired about possibly saving Jezebel's life. Sir Drayden revealed that she was already too far gone, both physically and mentally.

Briefly regaining lucidity, a smug grin crossed the fading woman's face. "I guess this…is goodbye. My legacy will live on and…the rebels…" She choked, a hint of blood gathering at the corner of her mouth. "…they will know I've led by example. Looks like you lose this round, Sir Drayden Sebastard."

"No, Jezebel. I'm afraid you're the one who loses." Sir Drayden's eyes seemed distant, his face bearing a grim expression. "I've seen your future beyond this world. You're about to go on a very unpleasant one-way trip. When you get there, you'll realize that your martyrdom came at a very high price. I doubt you'll believe it was worth it."

He fixed his icy gaze just a few feet from Jezebel's slumping body. A small patch of the ground smoldered, spewing fluid-like smoke up into the air. It seemed as though it was growing out of the earth as it took shape, forming an *Intermediary*. Its eyes were the color of fire and coal, set in ashen skin. The black cloaked figure stood beside Sir Drayden, making him appear angelic by comparison. Inspecting its prize, the *Intermediary* flashed a tarnished jagged-toothed smile. As she headed into the sunset of her physical existence, a horrified expression washed over Jezebel's face as she begged Sir Drayden for help. It had become obvious that she could see the visitor as she left her body.

"I'm sorry, Jezebel. I'm afraid it's a little too late for that. It's out of my hands," he answered, stepping back to allow the Intermediary to extract her soul. When it was done, the Intermediary reverted to the thick trail of smoke and swept through the area before seeping back into the ground. The phenomenon pulled Akalina's eyes to the base of a gargantuan tree in the distance and remained transfixed there. Its roots were like dozens of boney fingers, kneading the earth's soil—or concealing a valuable secret.

"It's a shame. I think she may have been our last hope in finding Isaac." Zephyr's voice broke the silence. It was laced with disappointment.

Camile found herself back in the conservatory staring at the path before her. It took her a moment to reacquaint herself with reality. Once she did, she gave in to her internal propulsion, her desire to go to the scene of Jezebel's death. She knew it held a certain significance that would hopefully lead her to Isaac. Using her instinct as a compass, Camile left the compound and traveled as fast as she could to the Forsaken Forest, knowing how dangerous it was. She could only hope that Vincent's eyes of the forest would watch over her without revealing her illegal detour to the council. At least not until she had gotten to the bottom of her latest flashback.

*   *   *

Upon arriving at the large tree she saw in the vision, her intuition told her that there was an entrance somewhere within the roots. This was confirmed when she heard the muffled sound of the young boy. Camile feverishly began clearing away the soil and mulch, breaking a couple of nails on some random rocks. After what seemed like hours she saw a portion of a cave entrance. She continued speaking to the boy, reassuring him that salvation was near. Working through her sore muscles, Camile cleared the last of the logs and quickly squeezed her way into the tunnel. With a faint thud she hit the soil-padded ground.

In the dim light streaming from the outside, she could see a ratty looking ladder leading out of the chamber back to where she had come from. This filled her with a moment of relief that heightened when she turned around. There in the center of the cold den was the shivering body of a young child curled in a fetal position. Camile removed her coat and quickly draped it over the child's shoulders before realizing there was nothing above it. Her screams echoed all around her as she stared wide-eyed at the headless corpse before her.

"Oh, God! I'm too late!" She sobbed, wanting to hug the child, but didn't have the heart to touch the body. Instead, she hugged her knees into her chest and wept. "Who did this to you?" she asked quietly, not expecting an answer, but was surprised when she received one.

"You already know. You're just too afraid to remember." The soft, comforting voice caressed her ears like a warm breeze. When she looked up, she saw Isaac perched upon a boulder across from her. "I can help you if you want."

"You want to *help* me?" Camile asked, her voiced laden with disbelief and self-disappointment. "I couldn't even help you in time. You're....dead because I was too late."

"My body's not alive anymore, but if I'm dead, would I be able to talk to you right now?"

The past year of Camile's education suddenly came flooding back to her, but it did little to numb her emotional pain.

"Anyway, there's not much you could've done from the beginning. My body's been gone for quite awhile now."

Reluctantly looking at the body once more Camile realized he was right. Based on the current stage of decomposition, Camile guessed that he'd been dead well over a year, if not more. Upon returning her gaze to Isaac, she was slightly startled to see him kneeling just inches in front of her.

"I don't understand." Camile struggled for words. "Why'd you ask me to come find you? What was the point?"

"That's what I'm here to show you...If you're ready," the boy responded, an inquisitive expression gracing his features.

Taking it more as a question than a statement, Camile nodded. Without warning, Isaac lunged forward so quickly, she barely had time to recoil. Before the apparition made contact with her body it expanded and thinned out into a fog-like substance that shrouded her like a mummy. His energy seemed to permeate every cell in her body, vibrating slightly as she grew numb. Her blurring vision slowly surrendered to darkness.

*   *   *

Camile momentarily debated if Isaac had possessed her, but eventually dismissed that theory as she felt the unsettling familiarity of something else. As the blackness faded, she watched the autumn leaves falling from the majestic trees. Strolling at a leisurely pace, she caught one in her left hand and crushed it. Her right hand held something far heavier.

Wielding the long blade, Akalina slowly approached the young scribe from behind as he sat cross-legged on a bed of amber leaves. She halted her steps and made a sudden about face, handing the weapon to one of the rebels.

"Hey, newbie. I've already proven my allegiance, now it's your turn," she whispered.

The reluctance was written on the rebel's face.

"But he's just a kid. My baby brother's not much older than he is," she protested as quietly as possible.

"Do it, or take his place. The choice is yours," Akalina whispered. After staring the rebel down for a moment, she walked in front of the child to face him.

He apparently hadn't heard the exchange as he played with the leaves on the ground. Akalina initiated a conversation with him, smiling gently as she did.

"Good news. We're letting you go," she said.

"Home?" he asked.

"Where else?" Akalina asked rhetorically. "I just wish you could've been more helpful to us. You see, the rebels aren't as bad as people make us out to be. You could've stayed with us, but it's clear where your loyalties lie."

"Did it not make you happy to know the one you hate most will promote you?"

At first, Akalina said nothing, only sighing in an almost amorous manner. Rising to her feet, she kissed the boy on the forehead before stepping back.

"Yes, Isaac. It makes me *very* happy." She chuckled softly. "That's why I decided not to prolong your release. So, I guess this is goodbye. You know, I think I might miss you."

"You will, but not for awhile," the boy smiled softly.

After a moment of hesitation, the rebel quietly approached from behind and with one swift motion, severed the young boy's head. Akalina felt a warm spray across her face. Upon wiping her cheek, she saw the bright red nectar of innocence.

"If this doesn't get the message across to the council to stay out of our way, I don't know what will. Let's see if they can put little Humpty together again." Akalina smirked before ordering the troubled rebel to clean up the mess.

Now knowing the reason for her repeated hallucinations of blood, Camile sat motionless, staring at her own hands in disbelief. More than anything, she wanted to be re-separated from her other half. She feared it was like a disease that was infecting her body, permeating every cell of it. The very thought of it repulsed her. She vomited as she struggled to remove the gruesome images of Isaac's abrupt death from her mind. Due to the inheritance of the darker part of herself, she was now responsible for the death of yet another person—and an innocent one at that. Her anguish made way for a moment of clarity. It suddenly dawned on her that the reason for the lack of action to investigate the boy's clues was not out of disinterest, but prior knowledge of his fate. A soft wail escaped her mouth as she dropped her head into her hands.

"Why didn't they tell me?" Her voice quivered in barely a whisper.

"I don't know," a voice answered calmly.

Raising her gaze, Camile saw Isaac standing before her. She immediately scrambled to her knees and begged for his forgiveness.

"I'm sorry, I can't do that," he answered, crushing her heart even further. "You're not the same person who did this to me. But since you carry the one who did, I accept the apology."

"Thank you!" Camile tearfully exclaimed.

"Don't. I'm not doing it for you, her or anyone else. I'm doing it for myself. It's the only way I can move on. Before I do, I have a confession…" Isaac momentarily broke eye contact, glancing at the ground as though ashamed. Meeting Camile's gaze anew, he said, "I stole something before I transferred, but I don't need to hold it anymore, now that you're here. I want you to have it. I think it'll help you."

After a moment's hesitation Camile extended her hand, all the while thinking she didn't deserve to take anything from him since Akalina had ordered his death. However, he faded as quickly as he had appeared, leaving Camile and his body behind. Suddenly, it hit her—the object he was referring to was somewhere on his corpse. Still shaky, Camile removed the cloak she had draped over it and saw one of the corpse's hands resting on its midsection. The fingers were tightly clenched.

Trying to be as gentle as possible, she tried to loosen their grip, but to no avail. Using a bit more force, she managed to open the fist just wide enough for an object to slide out, landing onto the ground. It was a yellow gem medallion set in a simple silver frame. It was suspended from a silver chain, slightly dull and dusty due to age. She somehow knew that Akalina had been carrying it in her pocket when she had kissed Isaac. Camile surmised that he had taken it at that time. The item looked familiar, but her despair wouldn't allow her mind to place it. Suddenly, the words Isaac told Akalina poured through Camile's mind like scalding water, *"...the one you hate most will promote you."*

Her heart sank when she realized that with Jezebel dead, Akalina now had control of the rebels. Out of all the thoughts racing through her mind at that moment, one was paramount—her instinct to return to Caldaq immediately. She knew she had to warn the others right away. Somehow, she also knew she had a limited time to do so.

*   *   *

Camile felt herself growing progressively weaker as she ran with all her might, stumbling in the grassy field. As though her body hadn't been tested enough, the darkening sky yielded a downpour of rain. Camile could feel the rumbling thunder beneath her feet after a lightning bolt struck somewhere in the distance. She felt as though the devil himself was at her back, trying to prevent her from exposing the devastating truth.

"Give me a break!" She panted.

Nearing the compound, she could see her parents standing beside Jeremy and Sir Drayden, gazing at the approaching storm. Camile waved furiously as she called out to them.

"Akalina's...the new rebel leader!" She shouted breathlessly, but knew they were too far to hear her.

Camile could sense their concern as the group came out to meet her. She tried her best to somehow open telepathic communication with her father, but failed and collapsed to the ground. The yellow medallion slipped from her fingers in the process. Rolling onto her back, Camile felt herself rapidly slipping into a state of paralysis. Her parents quickly arrived at her side, followed by Sir Drayden and Jeremy.

"Camile, what's wrong?" her father asked, his face losing color as he retrieved the fallen necklace. After exchanging an immensely concerned gaze with Kylie, Zephyr's voice grew more urgent as he tried to rouse his daughter. "Come on, baby! Speak to me. What happened? Where did you get this?"

Camile opened her mouth to answer, but was unable to speak. The most she could manage was a faint, throaty exhalation of air. She felt her warm tears mingle with the cold rain falling on her face as the world around her grew distant. She felt herself slipping away despite her strained attempt to cling on to her consciousness. Once again, she found herself staring up into Sir Drayden's gaze, only this time she knew it wasn't him she should fear. The sound of her own erratic breathing terrified her even further as she widened her eyes, as if doing so would prevent her from going under. Her very body was turning against her as it repeatedly slammed against the ground in a violent seizure before she was elevated a few feet off the ground. She surmised that Sir Drayden had levitated her body to prevent her from injuring herself.

"Hold on." She heard someone say as her vision failed, but the voice was so warped she couldn't tell to whom it belonged.

Though she knew her jolting body was suspended in the air, Camile felt as though she was falling backwards into a dark abyss as she lost consciousness. Before long, she found herself standing face-to-face with her nemesis.

"Well, you didn't forget about me, did you?" Akalina smirked.

Camile repeatedly tried to regain consciousness, but to no avail.

"Nice try, Camile, but this time I'm in the driver's seat and it's going to be a *very* bumpy ride."

Akalina began fading away. Somehow, Camile understood that if she vanished from her sight at that moment she'd establish dominance over her body.

"Nah-uh. I don't think so," Camile exclaimed, holding her palm in front of her. Suddenly, Akalina reappeared.

"Let me go or you'll be sorry," she warned. A confused yet irritated expression crossed her features.

"Funny, I was gonna tell you the same thing." Camile sneered. "I'll be *damned* if I let you kill another innocent person."

"You're right." Akalina smirked. "If you don't let me go, you *will* be damned."

The two of them remained locked together in each other's powerful grip, waiting for the other to falter. Camile could still hear her parents calling out to her from somewhere beyond the darkness. She could still sense their combined attempts to revive her. However, she was unable to respond. All of her strength was focused on avoiding falling into the fracture of her dark-mirrored existence during the fight to reestablish control over her mind, body and soul once and for all.

Stay tuned for the next installment of the CAMILEON saga!

ABOUT THE AUTHOR

Shykia Bell was born and raised in Brooklyn, New York. She developed a love for drawing and literature at a very young age and often wrote poetry and short stories throughout her school years. The latter passion, fostered by her mother and the television show *Reading Rainbow,* became her refuge from bullying and violence. Nonetheless, she considered it a hobby since her artistic ability shone in other ways. Thinking she'd have better luck pursuing a career in the design field, Shykia attended Maxwell Vocational High School where she studied fashion design.

During this time, she still dabbled in writing on occasion, but soon began drifting away from it as life, career and obligation eventually took hold. She also shifted gears just prior to attending New York City Technical College, where she decided to pursue a career in graphic design and advertising, figuring she'd have a better chance to have her work recognized in that field while combining both her loves.

Despite being told that she'd never attain her degree while holding a full-time job, Shykia earned her bachelor degree in 2002, not long after successfully completing an internship at MTA New York City Transit. Still, she struggled to find work in the post 9/11 job market. Though uncertain about the future, she was gripped with a sobering reminder that she quit her retail job in the World Trade Center Mall months before that fateful day due to college scheduling conflicts.

After much determination, she landed a job at an outdoor media company, then an international law firm before realizing that she had a need for self-expression that her occupation didn't allow. While on sabbatical, she rediscovered herself and her love for writing thanks to the tireless support of her husband, Max, in addition to inspiration she drew from *Star Trek: The Next Generation*. It was after she self-published *Camileon* that she came across an old journal from high school. Only a few pages were filled, but contained the premise she had just completed.

Shykia resides in Brooklyn with her husband, Max and their pet cat and cockatiel. At present, she is working on subsequent installments of the *Camileon* saga. In her spare time she enjoys trying new recipes, learning do-it-yourself projects and reading. Most recently, she has gotten back into sketching and painting.

www.ingramcontent.com/pod-product-compliance
Lightning Source LLC
Chambersburg PA
CBHW030751260626
47169CB00001B/5